The Seed

By J.W. Sebert

For Rox

From whispers on walks to this.

A story born of our play.

Thank you.

TABLE OF CONTENTS

Chapter 1: On Call

Time: 20:34

Date: Thursday, April 12th

Location: Apartment 104A, Southeast Portland

It was the same sleepless night, in the same boxy room, and dug into his bed, Rory Nash waited.

He rechecked his pager, half hoping, half dreading it would end the standoff, but found no *S.O.S.* He groaned and considered trying to sleep again but knew that was a lost cause. Rising, he stretched his back that the old mattress had taxed and stumbled through the dark over boxes and discarded clothes. The fridge's bulb was burned out, which suited him fine, and he served himself up a bowl of Lucky Charms. His stomach could never figure out what time it was.

The milk sloshed as he plopped on the couch and turned on the TV to get his mind off work. "George Zimmerman was taken into custody today," said the news anchor, his white smile blinding.

Ugh. "Too sad," Rory said, clicking his remote.

A blue-suited politician appeared on the screen behind a red, white, and blue lectern. "On the anniversary of the American Civil War, we find ourselves on the precipice of another conflict. We, as a nation, need to . . ."

"Any good news?" Rory sighed, punching the button again.

Another anchor—this time a woman with shiny blonde hair but a face carefully grim. "Another two bodies were found today, linked to the so-called Vacuum Seal Killer terrorizing the West Coast. A warning: the following image may be upsetting."

Rory leaned forward as he rubbed his beard. A blurry body filled the screen. He paused, unsure what to make of the ghoul thing. *No.* He squinted. "That's a mummy." Hearing it aloud made him more confident; it certainly looked like the ones in the Egyptian exhibit, except this one didn't have its bandages. It was leathery and ancient, and for a brief, stunned moment, he wondered if his long-dead corpse would be dug up for study, too. His stomach roiled. Something in him said *no,* and he shook away the thought. *Pass.*

The screen flickered to another cable news anchor. "The Sudan War took a turn for the worse today. News that a stray missile hit a children's hospital was confirmed."

Oh, no. Rory rocked back as though struck by an icy wind. He blinked and held his breath.

"At least fifty wounded, including several staff members killed trying to save—"

Rory hit mute and dropped the remote. He knew the rest. Maybe not the number, but the story. People killing people trying to help people. The stupidest story on earth.

He felt a wet, velvety nose press against his hand and looked down to see a fluffy orange tabby investigating the scene, her tail swishing expectantly.

"You too?" he said, stroking the cat as she investigated the bowl.

She was a far cry from the mangy, flea-ridden kitten who snuck into his apartment last summer. Without air-conditioning, he'd left his windows open, but the apartment sweltered anyway. When he finally gave up on sleep, he'd caught her munching on the chicken he'd left out. Surprisingly, she didn't bolt, but continued her meal with one eye on him. Rory was impressed, and a week later, after days of chicken bribes, she moved in and was now the resident cereal-bowl cleaner.

"You can have the rest, but," he said, holding back the bowl, "a roommate thing first. Don't puke in my shoes again, okay? That's really gross. And not cool."

Sneaks purred loudly, leaning into his fingers.

Rory smiled, never getting his guarantee, and set the bowl on the floor next to the others. Fetching the remote, he quickly changed the channel. "Let's skip the news."

He skipped a few more anchors until the screen shifted to a pair sitting on a raised stage. Oversized bowl chairs cradled both of them, and the caption along the bottom read: *Abigail Sage, Professor of Nursing at Jericho University.* Rory gaped. He hadn't seen her since graduation, yet nothing about his old teacher seemed to have changed. Rory set down the remote as she took a sip of water.

"Welcome back, everyone," the bespectacled man across from her said. "We are continuing our conversation with Professor Sage about her book, *Sponges of Society.* Professor, let me get this right for anyone joining us at the end of our show: sponges are individuals within a society. You say, and I quote, 'They care for the discarded, abused, and forgotten.' Furthermore, you claim that these individuals are key indicators for the overall health of a society. We'll start there. Can you elaborate?"

"Absolutely. Sponges are your civil servants, not the ones politicians claim to be, but the everyday people—in the trenches—throwing stitches into wounds and sopping up the blood and tears of our collective, complex world. Every society that has accomplished anything in human history has had these individuals empowered on their civilization's ascent and disempowered, typically by power-seeking interests, on their decline."

Rory nodded along. She'd told his class something similar years ago, but the context was everything now, and her words struck the iron core of what he'd experienced since those insulated lectures.

The interviewer nodded agreeably. "You discuss nurses in your book."

"Yes, because that's my experience, but there are many, many others out there. More than I can name, but you can guess many of them. Just look who's out in the streets. Paramedics, police, firefighters. Bus drivers. Teachers. Coaches. Volunteers at community centers. Bartenders, you get the idea. These people who work with and help people are the ones best positioned to critique and, as I've said many times, need a larger voice and representation in places of power."

Rory nodded, wondering how anyone could make policies on something they'd never experienced.

The moderator turned a page. "You use the canary in the coal mine analogy."

"Absolutely. It's very fitting."

"Yep," said Rory, grimly. He leaned back and sighed.

Beep-beep-beep!

Rory jerked, startled, knocking over the bowl. The cat scurried away.

"Damn it . . ." he muttered, blinking the television's glare away.

Beep-beep-beep!

Rory clicked the television off. The bright light vanished, leaving only streaks of lamplight cutting through the slats of his window. His eyes adjusted as he felt along the back of his couch and found a damp towel from an earlier shower. Trying to soak up the cereal milk, he leaned forward and grabbed the small black pager off his cardboard coffee table. The narrow digital screen read *999-999-9999.*

Rory sighed and rubbed his beard. *So much for a quiet night off,* he thought.

He rose and carefully picked his way around his unpacked boxes and dirty dishes. After working the night shift, he'd gotten skilled at navigating the small hospital rooms in the low light.

His apartment wasn't much bigger. Besides a couch and a bed, his unopened boxes of dishes and books made for makeshift furniture.

He flipped on the bathroom light and winced, squinting at himself in the mirror. Dark bags under both his eyes greeted him. For a twenty-three-year-old, he knew he wasn't sleeping well. Insomnia was supposed to be an elderly issue, wasn't it? Even mighty melatonin wasn't helping anymore, but he wasn't sure what else to try.

Washing his hands, Rory's eyes drifted to his growing midsection. All that fast food hadn't done him any favors. *Tomorrow*, he told himself. *I'll get a workout in tomorrow.*

Rory wet his hands, splashing water on his face to wake himself up. He ran his fingers through his red-brown hair, slowing at the base of his skull. His fingers gently found the puckered skin that ran three inches straight down his neck. The scar had long ago healed into a silvery pink, but touching it still conjured the memories of bitter-tasting medicine and weekly chemotherapy.

Pulling off his sweats, he felt his way back to the tiny slip of a kitchen, finding his phone on the narrow stretch of white-tiled counter. He searched his contacts and pulled up the Pediatric Intensive Care Unit, but stopped before hitting SEND. He took a deep breath.

"Please be something simple," he whispered. But he knew they didn't page for something simple, and if Rory remembered correctly, Bell was in charge tonight. The veteran nurse never paged for anything short of an emergency. She was always saying that nurses had to get a life before they could save them. Rory looked around his dim, dirty apartment and shook his head. No one told him finding one would be so hard.

Sneaks rubbed against his leg, and he reached down, scratching her back. She chattered back at him, probably demanding food.

"I'll get you a treat in a sec. I have to make a call." She meowed as he rose.

Standing in the dark, Rory peered into his glowing screen but hesitated to hit SEND. His hands shook, and he lowered the phone. "What am I doing?" He rubbed his face, and when he opened his eyes, he spotted a bright green unicorn hanging on the wall. His first present from a patient. Beneath it, at the counter's far end, were stacks of gifts, cards, and more drawings. A colorful beaded necklace from toddlers, and another of hemp from a teen reading *BFF*. Thank-you letters in crayon and funeral announcements in ink sat in a small pile or propped against the wall. A dried rose, broken but lovely. He hadn't had the heart to throw it out. It was from Virdy's family. A pile of different colored plastic bracelets, each with its own inspirational saying, each a rallying cry for hope. All tokens of past battles, some won, some lost. Rory dropped his hand, smiling but sad. The victories were second to none; a second chance was rare and uplifting, but recently, they barely covered the losses.

Still, it was worth it to save a life. Right?

"No one goes alone," he whispered and blew out a long breath. He rolled his neck to each side and set his shoulders back. Then, he hit SEND.

It rang once, then she picked up.

"Rory?" Bell's tenor voice came over the speaker. "I wouldn't be calling unless—"

"The unit needed it, I know." Rory finished for her, stifling a sigh. *It's bad.* "Don't worry, you aren't ruining any plans."

"Oh? I thought you had a date tonight. Number two."

Rory smiled, knowing Bell's tactics well after two years. Sad news could wait, she'd told him once—start with the fun because nurses need their patients' trust, and few things build trust faster than a little play.

14

"Wasn't much point after the first." Rory scanned the apartment for his laundry and found it still stuffed in a hamper. "She was more involved in texting updates to her friend sitting at the bar than talking with me. She wasn't that—"

"Don't you say interesting, Rory Nash." He could picture Bell shaking her head.

He chuckled, crossed the room, and began rummaging through the pile for clean scrubs. "I was going to say engaging but interesting works. She wanted me to pay for everything, too. Come on, it's like, who doesn't have student loans? And rent!"

Bell chuckled. "You're looking in the wrong places, that's all. Don't give up. You're young. What, twenty-four?"

"Twenty-three," Rory corrected. He still couldn't believe he was that old. He pulled out a wrinkled blue scrub top and shook it with one hand, which did nothing, before awkwardly pulling it on.

"Baby," Bell said. "Took me thirty years to find my Walt. Took me one date to know he was for me, and not a day goes by that I don't thank God for him. He's my rock when this place comes crashing down. You need a rock, Rory. You hear me?"

"I do, Bell, but it's hard to meet people anymore," Rory said, retrieving the matching blue bottoms. "I mean, milkshake joints are out of style these days."

"Milkshakes? I'm not that old! You—" She cut off, and Rory grinned as he pictured her eyebrow-raised scowl. "You're a terrible flirt, Rory, but you're wasting that charm on me. You need—"

Rory couldn't make out the voice that interrupted Bell in the background. There was a brief pause before Bell returned. "Sorry, Rory. Duty calls." Her tone shifted, losing the playfulness. "I'm calling because we have an inbound life flight."

Rory cringed. "How bad?"

"Not good. Peds versus auto. Messy."

Rory's stomach dropped. *Messy.* He knew the truth. Automobile traumas were long, grueling, and bloody. And after the sweat and tears, you had to relive everything as you explained to the family again and again and again, trying to soothe their grief-soaked incomprehension. How could their lives so suddenly and cruelly change? Or worse—how could their child be gone?

A mess. He wasn't sure he could clean up another one.

If not me, then who? Rory asked himself. After two years in the PICU, he still didn't have an answer.

"You there?" Bell's voice broke his train of thought.

"Yeah, sorry. Uh, do we have a full report yet?" Rory asked, walking over to his stack of thank-you cards and small gifts. He picked up a dark blue plastic bracelet—a leukemia patient still out there somewhere. Written in blocky white letters was *KYLIE'S KLUB.*

"We can wait until—"

"Tell me what you have," Rory said, turning the bracelet over. The opposite side read *FAMILY. HEALING. HOPE.* He ran his thumb over the words and slipped it over his wrist. It worked for Kylie. Maybe it would work tonight.

"Rory . . ." Bell's voice trailed off. *She doesn't want to tell me.*

"Bell, it's just been an . . . unlucky few months. I'm okay. Really." He paused but heard nothing. "Next patient up, right? And besides, it's better than me sitting here alone. These student loans have a killer interest rate."

Bell inhaled sharply, and Rory felt his stomach knot tighter. *It was bad.*

Finally, Bell's voice returned. "I wouldn't have called if the unit wasn't slammed tonight."

"I know."

"I'll be here to help as much as I can."

"I know, you always are." Rory grabbed his badge and marveled at the young man smiling innocently back at him. *Rory Nash, RN, BSN, CCRN, CPN,* and below that, *Pediatric Intensive Care Unit.* No beard, not even a whisker. A fresh baby nurse without a patient to his name. The picture felt like a lifetime ago.

Sneaks curled against his leg, purring madly.

"Rory, are you still there?" Bell asked gently.

"Yeah, sorry. Just getting ready." He didn't move.

Another pause and Rory cringed, not wanting Bell to know.

"Alright, but we'll do a report when you get here. We set you up in Room 4. Bike safe, okay?"

"I will," Rory said, feeling a familiar dread creep into him. He was plunging back in. "I'll see everyone soon."

Rory hopped on his bike, a yellow reflective vest and messenger bag slung loosely over his back, and took off for the hospital. He did not know he was being watched.

Across the street from his brick-faced Hawthorne Street apartment was a park with swings, a merry-go-round, and a big, blue jungle gym with a tall, twisting slide. Two strangers sat tucked in the gym's shadows. A street lamp loomed nearby, but its radiance did a strange thing as it approached them. The light bent toward the taller of the two, soaking into them, while the gleam repelled off the second hooded figure like dew dripping off waxy leaves.

"That's him," the hooded one said. She was shorter by a head, and her silhouette merged with the dark bushes behind her.

"Interesting. You say he's a nurse?" asked the taller of the two in a gentle whisper. Lithe and long, she wore a strip of clean white cloth over both eyes and a long green cloak. The light gave her skin a subtle, luminous glow.

The hooded one nodded. "Yep. Kids nurse."

They watched quietly as Rory pedaled down the street.

"Rare. His history?"

"His records aren't much help," the hooded one replied. "Medical foster kid since he was ten. Bounced around homes until high school. He stole some beer once, but other than that, he's a damn boy scout. Volunteers and all that crap."

The taller one turned, smiling. "Then he must have a significant Stain. Those left behind often do."

The hooded figure grunted consent, and they watched Rory turn the corner and disappear.

"Has his Stain infected others?"

"Doesn't seem t've. Nothing on record, at least," the shorter one said and glanced up and down the street. "Have you—"

The blindfolded woman shook her head. "I've seen no ill will. We are safe for now."

Despite the reassurance, the hooded figure's face screwed tighter, keeping her dark eyes where Rory had turned.

"Peace, love," the tall one said. "We have a choice before us."

"Not much of a choice."

"No, but it is ours," the taller one replied soothingly. "I say we test him in the morning. Nothing big. The Minor Assay of Aid should do."

"He's a nurse. I'm not worried about aid." The shorter woman shifted uncomfortably. A sliver of lamplight touched her, briefly illuminating the folded leather sleeve of her left arm, but the shadows wrapped themselves back around her, and she faded into the night. "We need a fighter. The Broken Star—"

"Haven't found us," the taller one cut in. "Yet. And do we need a fighter or a warrior? There is an important difference."

The shorter one grunted, and they stood together in silence, listening to the creak of the swings in the wind.

"What if the Seed is wrong again?"

The tall woman nodded thoughtfully. "Then it is, and we start over."

"We don't have that kind of time."

"Then let us hope that Rory Nash is what the Seed thinks him capable of." She turned and smiled at her companion. "Which is exactly why he must be tested. Tomorrow morning. Need I remind you? *You* found him."

"Running into him in a crosswalk isn't really a find." The hooded figure reached up and rubbed their chest. "Damn thing did somersaults when I touched him, but a bloodline doesn't mean crap if he has crooked virtues."

"Thus, the need for thorough testing." The taller one reached into the shadows and caressed their companion's shoulder. "Your caution is understandable, love. You're nervous."

"Of course I'm nervous. We can't screw this up." The shorter one reached into her pocket and drew out a pack of cigarettes and a matchbook. "*I* can't screw this up."

"I wish you wouldn't use those," the taller one said, gesturing to the pack.

"Why not?" The small woman held a cigarette between her chapped lips, fumbling with the matches. "If'm dead anyway, might as well do some damage on the wa'out." She took a long draw, coughing and sputtering as she tried to hold in the smoke.

The taller one frowned but said nothing as a thick cloud of smoke surrounded her.

"Ahhh." The shorter one coughed. "Smooth."

The taller one shook her head and waved away the smoke. "Let us focus. Which ploy should we use? And don't say kidnapping. That blew up in our faces last time."

"You're no fun." She sighed, inhaled—sputtering less than before—and nodded. "Lost-old-lady routine? You pull it off, and it gets you close enough to feel his Stain."

The taller one nodded. "Excellent idea. Should he fail, we'll be only a strange story for him to tell his friends."

The shorter one nodded once and took another drag. Her nose wrinkled. "Ugh." She dropped the cigarette and stomped it out. "These things are gross. They even taste like death."

The companion smiled, shook her head, and held out her arm. "Come, love. There is much to prepare. If the Seed is right about Rory Nash, then we have a great deal to do. And quickly."

The shorter one looped her arm through her companion's and

leaned her head against her arm. "Poor sucker. He's in for a hell of a ride."

Chapter 3: A Healer's War

Time: 21:21

Location: Oates Children's Hospital, Portland, Oregon

The PICU wasn't large, only twenty rooms spread around the perimeter of the rectangular unit. Each small room had its own patient bed, monitors, infusion tower, futon in the back, bathroom, and, to enter, a wall-length sliding glass door. Only a thin beige and green checkered curtain provided any privacy from the pair of nurses' stations flanking the medication and supply room at the unit's center. While the unit wasn't as large as the ones in some bigger cities, it punched above its weight with high patient acuity and expertly orchestrated chaos.

Rory arrived, sweaty and nervous. Room 4 was already a flurry of activity. The stinging scent of cleaners carried in the dry, filtered air. Staff flowed in and out, bringing stacks of sterile gauze and catheter supplies. People packed the room, their shoes squeaking as they crammed around the bulky bed and blinking machines, reaching over one another to prepare the space. No one spoke. There was no need yet. They all knew what to do. Preparing was the simple part.

Above the bed, silent monitors were ready to scream, and beside them, a respiratory therapist dialed in a boxy ventilator. In the back of the room, someone had already prepared the built-in futon with crisp, tucked sheets, pillows, an extra blanket, a new toothbrush, a towel if the family needed to shower, and lots of tissues.

The people and machines that couldn't fit in the room lined the hall outside. Resident physicians, still fresh from medical school, huddled close to their attendings, going over resuscitation scenarios. A nurse drew up medications from a red code cart, while another pair primed the lines for a tower of syringe and infusion pumps. Beside them, a stack of white

Styrofoam boxes sat with enough ice inside to keep the donor blood cold until inevitably needed.

By the time Rory said hello to the team and situated himself, the attending physician, the one who'd run the code, gathered the team for a verbal report. It wasn't good.

"Welcome, everyone, and thank you for being here. The patient is an eight-year-old female named Octavia, Peds versus Auto. She's twenty-seven kilograms. Unresponsive with sluggish pupils. Pulses x4, but thready. 64/25 after two boluses of crystalloid. Intubated at the scene and is being bagged on 8L at 50%. Suspected liver and kidney lacerations based on some bruising and blood in her urine." She adjusted her glasses on her nose, glanced up at the team, then returned to her notes.

We'll need more blood.

"Spine uncleared, C collared and back braced. Face, arm, and lower extremities lacerations. Suspected bilateral comminuted fractures of femurs, tibias, and fibulas. Probable shattered pelvis is believed to be where the bumper struck first, according to eyewitnesses at the scene."

This is really bad. The attending took a deep breath and clenched her jaw.

"The driver of the car that struck the patient was drunk, blowing a 0.25 blood alcohol content after being caught trying to run with a suspended license." She pulled down her glasses and looked up.

Rory bristled. *For fuck's sake . . .* Angry murmurs and gasps rippled through the room. There were plenty of crazy stories in pediatrics. Most ended well, but the ones that didn't hurt. And the most painful were the genuine tragedies—those that were preventable. Like this one.

Society's sponge, Rory thought bitterly. The tension thickened as the staff talked in sharp whispers. A hot flush rushed up Rory's throat, but he quickly swallowed the heartache. It wouldn't do him, or his patient, any good right now.

Crossing the room to grab a pair of gloves and a face mask, Rory spotted two residents, a young man and woman in fresh white coats, huddled together, reviewing the code cards—flow chart directions on how to save a life—with pale expressions. Bell had taught him to recognize the face, what it meant, and how to help.

"Spiritus boni, everyone," Rory said, exhaling.

The two residents looked up and stared while the nurses and older doctors smiled. "Spiritus boni," they repeated.

"What does that mean?" the young woman asked, her dark blue eyes fixed on Rory.

He was momentarily speechless.

A soft chuckle ran through the veteran staff.

Rory blinked, inhaled, and smiled at her. "It means breathing is good."

The man slowly frowned, but she nodded back and drew in a long breath, her color returning.

"They've landed," the attending announced. "Three minutes."

Conversations sparked about priorities and roles. Who would rotate on compressions? Who would record? Who would draw medications? Rory volunteered for compressions, and slowly, the tension drained from the room as everyone settled into their roles and their training took hold, providing a mental reprieve from anger in a comfortable autopilot.

They were ready. The patient was in the elevator.

Seconds later, a shrill alarm echoed down the hall, growing louder with each heartbeat.

Rory closed his eyes and filled his lungs with the dry hospital air. It made his mouth tacky, and he regretted not grabbing that last drink of water—a rookie mistake. He wouldn't get a break for hours.

When he opened his eyes, the blue-uniformed paramedics raced into the room, pushing a gurney between them. Rory met the medic's eye and glanced at the girl—Octavia. His chest tightened as his mind processed the grisly scene. *Oh god.*

"Who's the nurse taking over?" the medic asked.

Rory stepped forward, steady, as they prepared to move her off the gurney and onto a hospital bed.

The medic gave him a sympathetic nod. Rory understood. He felt the same way. They both knew they'd need a miracle to beat death today.

Focus, he told himself. *Fear won't help her.*

"My name is Rory," he told the medic. "I'll be her nurse."

It is nearly impossible to say precisely when a Stain forms because its birth occurs in secret. This has mostly to do with the cocktail of hormones the body releases in traumatic moments. One of these hormones, adrenaline, is the body's fight, flight, or freeze response, responsible for ensuring we survive an unpredictable world. Combined with the other hormones, this slurry drives us to forget in favor of survival, letting us temporarily ignore pain, and imprints the searing moment deep into our hearts, influencing the patterns of our behavior, ensuring we never feel this way again. During Octavia's code, that was what happened inside Rory.

After the time of death was called, he sat on a stool in the hallway. His heart still raced, beating as it cemented the moment into his tissue. Because of the hormones, he could only remember bits and pieces of the fight for Octavia's life. He remembered the alarms and the now deafening silence. He remembered shaking as he rotated off chest compressions, another nurse taking his place, and watched Octavia's heartbeat limp across the monitor's screen. He remembered rotating back in and choking back the bile as her ribs cracked beneath his bloody, gloved hands. Octavia said nothing. Purpling and swollen, she was eerily silent in the surrounding chaos, like the grisly eye of a hurricane. Rory pushed down again and again and again, each time keeping the girl's blood pumping one moment longer.

If he had the presence of mind, he might have thanked adrenaline, as there were long stretches he didn't remember. It was like something shielded him. He didn't remember how many rounds of compressions he did. Ten? Twenty? He knew at the end he was soaked in sweat. At some point, Bell put her hand on his arm mid-compression and gently told him that the attending had already called it. But he wasn't done fighting yet.

We can do more! He wanted to keep going—had to keep going. They couldn't leave her alone. *No, not yet.* Octavia deserved a second chance, too.

He didn't remember being walked to a stool in the hall outside and sat down as a wary line of practitioners exited the room. If Rory had the presence of mind, he might have seen the fresh wound they, too, carried in their downcast eyes. But he didn't—couldn't. Heartache and anger froze him solid.

They had failed . . . No, *he'd* failed. He could have done more. It didn't matter the odds were stacked against them. It didn't matter they'd tried to move a mountain with shovels. It didn't matter why she was there in the first place or who had put her there. They'd lost, which meant they could have done more . . . *He* could have done more. He doubled over and heaved as something gave way inside him. Unknown to him, right there on that stool, a new Stain took root.

Most Stains are small and can heal quickly if addressed. Others are larger and take longer. Rory's broadest Stain had been festering since he was ten—old enough to comprehend but not wise enough yet to understand. And while the mind often tries to forget, the body always keeps the tab.

Rory looked down at his shaking hands. *Eight . . . in eight weeks. How can so many be forgotten?*

While death was familiar in healthcare, those eight deaths were all the result of other people's choices. Every one of them was a tragedy. In his bones, Rory knew that they could have prevented those deaths. *Should* have been prevented. There were laws designed to prevent them even. Making each one feel like a hammer blow into his well-crafted suit of armor. The first blow just leaves a dent, and the second drives it deeper—but the armor holds. By the eighth, the armor cracks, gashing the flesh beneath.

Left to fester, a Stain can destroy a person. Its use of shame is a potent deterrent. In time, whether seconds or years, the mind will be so thoroughly soaked with shame and its chronic friend resentment that the entire body will seethe with wrath. Eventually, that wrath boils out, and the Stain spreads violently to others.

But all is not lost. With Stains, Frost had it right: the best way out is always through. And through hurts. But from that pain comes growth—a slow, cramping expansion that generates power. It's that power—no matter how insignificant or silly we tell ourselves it is—that generates hope and carries us through. Unfortunately, not all who suffer make the journey.

Sitting on that stool, gloved fists clenched, Rory's hope splintered as pieces of him struggled desperately to keep from shattering. He clung to himself, holding on to a thread of hope that perhaps somehow, in some way, help would come before he fell apart.

Chapter 5: Aftermath

Friday, April 13th, 02:35

How could this happen?

Rory stared down at his trembling fists. The gray plastic stretched tightly across his knuckles. Blood speckled the back of his hands—he dared not look at the palms. They smelled of iron. He breathed shallowly as the sweat dripped off his nose.

This shouldn't have happened.

A pressure rose in his chest and up his neck. He pictured the drunk driver, nameless, faceless. Rory seized the silhouette and drove his fist into their blurry features again and again, his fist keeping beat with his thundering heart. He squeezed his eyes shut.

A weighty hand touched Rory's shoulder like a gentle request.

His fantasy vanished, the pounding in his ears quieted, and he looked up blankly.

Bell's crinkled smile shone somberly back down at him. "Hey."

In two years, little had changed about Bell. A few more wrinkles framed her sharp brown eyes. The same pink scrunchie still held her white curls. She'd added a few fresh stories about Walt's antics, but they all still ended sweetly. The only thing that regularly changed was her scrub top, each with a different cat theme. Tonight's featured a skateboarding tabby that looked just like Sneaks.

She held out a plastic cup of water. "Drink."

Rory stirred, feeling the stool beneath him now, and found his body slumped forward with an aching back. "What time is it?" he asked, his tongue thick and dry. His eyes darted to the offered cup, and he took it in both hands, downing it in one gulp.

"Half-past two," Bell said.

Rory blinked, surprised. *How long were we fighting?* He straightened his back with a groan and uncurled his fists. He heard the blood on his palms peeling apart and smelled a fresh burst of iron. Slowly, Rory raised his eyes to Octavia's room.

Diluted blood streaked the tile floor, soaked up by the haphazardly discarded wrappers that littered the ground. On the bed, with a clean white blanket draped over her husk, was Octavia.

Dr. Abigail Deedee stood between two residents at the bedside, whispering, attempting to make the most of a teaching opportunity for the young, downtrodden doctors. Rory's stomach roiled, and he looked away.

Bell brushed a white curl from her damp brow and nodded at his hands. "Might want to take those off."

"What?" Rory looked down at his gloves. "Oh. I was just—"

"Go shower, then head home."

"The family will be here soon," Rory said. "I'm the nurse. I should talk to them. Tell them . . ."

Tell them what?

He looked up at Bell, who raised an eyebrow, unleashing *the look*. The rest of Rory's protest fizzled. She was right.

Seeing Rory relent, her expression softened. "I'll see everything gets set for the family."

He glanced around the unit. Empty hallways and full rooms—the unit was packed tonight. "You're slammed. Let me take one of Megan's kids."

"Megan's caught up, and everyone's getting tucked in." Bell reached over and knocked on the wooden desk. Rory absently did the same. Superstition was part of the profession.

"I can restock," he offered, giving Bell his best reassuring smile. "Let me decompress before I go home. Please, Bell, I'm here, and I can help. Next patient up, right? As you always say."

Bell folded her arms, appraising him. "That doesn't mean wonderful nurses don't crack after terrible nights, Rory. Sad is still sad."

Rory swallowed. She wouldn't let him stay unless . . .

"I really need the hours, Bell. Rent keeps going up, and my loans . . ." he trailed off, giving Bell his most pathetic look. "Please."

Bell rolled her eyes and studied him a moment before she sighed, shaking her head. "You're young. And so talented, Rory. Your time management skills are excellent, you know your pharmacology, and the families love you. You're a wonderful nurse, maybe even skilled enough to earn one of these one day." She tapped one of four golden pins decorating her badge, each the shape of a hand: the Healing Hand Award, annually given to the unit's most outstanding nurse.

Rory felt his throat tighten. "Wow, Bell, that . . . that means a lot."

"*If*," she continued over him, "you last long enough. You've seen what this place can do to good nurses."

He had. Many times. Patricia, Joanne, Libs, and Mark—all transferred. Sam left the profession altogether and said it was too much. He was the last one of his hire group.

Bell's tone softened. "Do you remember the first thing I told you when you started?"

"Dr. Magus is an asshole?"

Bell swatted Rory's shoulder with her rolled-up bed report, a charge nurse's baton.

"Hey!" Rory chuckled. It felt good to laugh.

Bell smiled. "The other thing."

This again. "Use your vacation time," Rory deadpanned.

"Which a paycheck would help me afford. So you can—"

Bell nodded. "What else?"

"Get a hobby."

"Have you done either?"

"I . . . play, uh, games . . . sometimes . . ."

Bell swatted him again.

"Hey! What'd I do?" Rory shielded himself.

"You don't fool me, Rory Nash. I know you get more than a paycheck out of this place. I've seen you with your patients. You care. And that care takes something from you, something that's got to be replenished." She jabbed her charge baton at him, scowling. "Hobbies and vacations. Neither are suggestions."

"I'll go on a hike tomorrow, okay?"

"That's a start," Bell said. "But you know Band-Aids aren't cures. Cures take time."

Too much time, Rory thought. *And there are no cures for the dead.*

He winced and reddened, choking back his unprofessional tears. A part of him needed to leave, wanted to run, cry, and yet he couldn't. *HOPE. FAMILY. HEALING.* stared up at him from his blue bracelet. He couldn't leave. Not yet.

A joke slipped into his mind, something about nightclubs and illicit drugs to lighten the conversation. It was what Bell would do, but when he opened his mouth, he found her staring into Room 4.

"It's not right," Bell whispered. "This one . . . It ain't right."

Rory's joke fizzled. He'd never seen Bell like this.

She turned back to him with a sad smile. "We could have done everything perfectly, and that little girl still would have died, bless her. We can't save them all, Rory, no matter how badly we

32

want to." She drew in a shuddering breath. "God . . . has a plan."

Hearing the defeat in Bell's voice dusted off an old memory from his second foster family—a home with a crucified Christ in every room. He remembered sitting on a hard pew, his foster mother shushing him while a red-faced priest preached of damnation from the pulpit. The elegantly robed man told them to pray and pray hard, for only then would God deliver their salvation. So young Rory tried it. Every night for years, he asked for the same thing, and every night for years, it never worked— only mum silence and the occasional new home. So, he stopped praying and decided for himself that, God or not, his parents were never coming back.

Rory swallowed down the memory. "We had to try, though, right?"

Bell nodded but remained silent, alarming Rory. Bell never got shaken.

"Maybe we should have prayed more." He shrugged. "I hear God makes miracles. Maybe they can spare one for us."

Bell stared into Room 4, no humor in her face. "What would you give, Rory?" The silence lingered, and his eyes followed Bell's, resting on Octavia. She was so still. How could someone so young be so still?

I'd give anything. He felt nauseous. "Is it supposed to be this hard?"

Bell nodded. "It's the job. And it's just us." She drew in a deep breath and exhaled. "Moments like this, though, they make it hard to remember it is a privilege."

A dreadful pressure welled in his chest, twisting as it reached up and pressed against the back of his eyes. He nodded, afraid to speak.

Inhaling sharply, she straightened. "Besides, if there were miracles, we'd be out of a job." Her jaw set. "Take a quick break, then do what needs to be done to take care of yourself."

"Thanks, Bell."

Dr. Deedee emerged from Room 4, gently guiding the two pale residents out. She eschewed the usual doctor's coat for a warm blanket draped around her and wore her light brown hair back in a ponytail. Her oversized glasses made her eyes seem twice as large, which felt fitting given Deedee saw twice as much as most. She gestured toward the call room, and the residents walked by with empty expressions.

Deedee was newer to the unit, but had decades of experience. She'd come north from Bay Area Children's and quickly become a favorite of the nursing staff with snacks and soundtracks during nightly rounds. As she got to know everyone, Deedee even made custom playlists, a song for each nurse. Rory had felt very seen when she played his "Smells Like Teen Spirit" by Nirvana, an astute guess about a Northwest kid growing up in the 90s. Rory had been a big fan of Deedee ever since.

She stopped next to Rory and watched the residents head down the hall. "That was their first code that didn't go according to plan."

"They took it well," Bell said over her shoulder. "No one passed out."

Deedee nodded. "It'll stick with them. They'll learn from this. We all will." Her eyes lingered on Octavia, and she pulled her blankets around her before turning to Rory. "You did well tonight, Rory. That was a good catch on the epinephrine dilution."

"Oh?" he said. *I did?* He couldn't remember, but quickly tried to play it off with a shrug. "I've dropped a zero before, too. It's easy to do with all the monitors screaming at you." He gave a half-hearted smile. *It changed nothing.*

"Regardless, nice work," Deedee said.

Rory's chest ached. "Thanks."

Deedee turned to Bell. "I think we might want to add a mock code to our education day. We weren't as tight as we could have been. I think everyone could use the practice."

"Already on the schedule." Bell nodded.

"Good." Deedee stretched and twisted out her back. "My feet are screaming, and I need to go chart this mess for the police report. At least I get to sit."

"Don't get too comfy, Deedee," Bell said and nodded down the hall. "I think Room 9 is misbehaving."

Rory turned and saw Megan closing quickly, carrying a nebulizer and an extended length of clear plastic tubing.

"Deedee." Megan waved, her face nearly matching the red of her scrubs. She wore her customary long black sleeves beneath her top, and Rory always wondered how she didn't roast. Her third-trimester belly—her fourth—pulled the fabric around her abdomen taut.

"Nine is being a pain in my ass," Megan hissed. "I already suctioned him twice. Thick, ropey stuff, but he's still struggling to move air." She held up the tubing. "Can we give another breathing treatment a try before we tweak the ventilator?"

"No rest for the weary, eh?" Deedee sighed and rolled her neck out. "Good idea. I'd rather not go up on his vent settings again tonight, either. I better come look."

"I'll come help," Bell said.

"Thanks, I could use the extra hands," Megan said, then glanced behind Rory into Room 4. She cringed and shot him a sympathetic smile. "You okay?"

All three women turned and looked at him.

"Um, yeah. Fine," Rory said, not liking all this attention. He nodded at her belly, changing the topic. "How's Parasite?"

Megan rubbed her swollen abdomen. "Tap dancing on my bladder again. I always need to pee, but at least we are on the home stretch." She looked up and peered closer at his face. "Rory, you look horrible. I thought you were off tonight."

Rory shrugged. "And miss the party?" He hoped he'd kept the bitterness out of his tone.

Megan didn't appear entirely convinced. "Sure you're okay?"

He wanted to say no, to scream it. The words were practically bursting out of him, but what good would that do? Make everyone else sad? Or worse, make them feel sorry for him?

"I'm good." The words burned in his chest.

Deedee nodded at him. "Keep your chin up, Rory. You did well." She turned to Megan. "Shall we?"

"Be right there," Bell called after them. "Oh, and Abigail, the fresh blankets in the warmer should be toasty by now."

Deedee waved over her shoulder. "You're an angel, Bell."

"Go wash up," Bell said to Rory. "Then think about what I said while you're stocking, alright? Make sure you get yourself—"

"Ready for the next patient." Rory finished for her. "I will."

Bell grunted an acknowledgment and walked into Room 4, turning off the monitor before stopping beside Octavia's body.

Rory stood and hurried off the unit, each step building the growing pressure behind his eyes. He stepped through the double doors and found the back hall empty. Free, he felt something inside him crack. Dazed and panting, he ran to the locker room. He turned up the shower's heat, but the water couldn't get hot enough to stop his trembling. He stood underneath the spray, staring blankly at the wall when it hit him. His sobs came violently, wracking his body as he gulped down air. He leaned his forehead against the wall and slid to the ground. Curling into his knees, he asked himself the same question again and again as he cried, the sound echoing off the tiles.

How could this happen?

Chapter 6: Sales Calls

Best America Insurance - Training Database

Customer Service Agent - Raven Lee

Outgoing Audio Log - Friday, 13th of April, 6:45 AM

Ring. Ring. Click.

-

"Hello, Mr. Smith? My name is Ja-er, Raven Lee. How are you today?"

-

"Well, I'm glad to hear that, sir. I'm calling today on behalf of Fatsack's Whoopsies Coverage."

-

"No, sir, that's not the actual name of the company. It's something more official, but the same general idea. I was wondering, sir, if you have health insurance?"

-

"Well, I think it's a racket too, sir. Criminal, even. You should see the scripts they give us. Woof. Talk about fear-mongering. I'm supposed to ask you about your family and then make up a scenario where one of them dies. Isn't that terrible? But I'll admit, the improv is fun."

-

"Well, yes—a straight shooter, sir. I'm a big fan of the truth. Speaking of shooting straight, according to your profile here, you are sixty-two. And male. So, how's your aim these days, sir? Health insurance will help with that prostate." *muffled laughter*

-

muffled laughter "Now, there is no need to swear, sir. I'm just lightening the mood. Death and disease . . . it's all pretty heavy, wouldn't you say? My therapist says I use humor to cope, which I think she's actually right about for once. Anyway, I meant nothing by it. Especially since your file says you're a gun collector."

-

"Alright, easy does it. You sound mad, sir, but let's practice saying 'muff' instead of those other four-letter words."

-

"Yes, like earmuffs."

-

"Yup. You nailed it."

-

"Am I high? Yes, sir, but don't tell my boss. For obvious reasons. It's against company policy."

-

"Wait! You can, of course, hang up, but my data-mined records show that you don't have health insurance, and while the fiscal and political entities of Fatsacks are questionable at best, I think it's important to have a contingency plan that doesn't involve losing the farm."

-

"Phoenix, Arizona?! Oh, well, I'm sorry to hear that. I hear you are running out of water down there. Looks like we need to update your file. Oh hey, one sec, my boss is headed over, and it looks like he is going to pee himself. Can I give you one piece of free advice, Mr. Smith? It's not sexy, and it's not to help my sales quota: get the insurance. Not for you, not for the company, but for your fellow taxpayers, the ones who will foot your bill if you don't. I know it's a stupid system, but don't be that guy, Mr. Smith. And if that doesn't sway you, think of your family, so the massive bill you get if you trip and break your ankle on a sprinkler head doesn't totally muff them over, too. And I hear you have lots of them down there."

-

"Yes, your wife. Talk it over with her. If you don't hang up when I come back, I promise I'll get you a screaming deal."

-

"Wonderful! Okay. I'm going to put you on hold now."

-

HOLD

———

Raven removed her headset and smoothed her short, bright pink hair against her neck. Her balding manager, Seth, was coming— she followed his crinkled forehead as it bounced over the top of the thin-walled gray cubicles. She popped the top of her citrus oils to mask the stench of stale coffee, took a deep breath, and listened.

The click of dial pads, followed by company-mandated greetings, was constant around her little oasis. Just down the aisle, Debbie shared her story about swimming with sharks for the umpteenth time while fluorescent lights buzzed over her. Someone mumbled a curse, probably at the copy machine, which rhythmically wasted paper.

Seth's forced chortle burst into her sanctuary. Raven cringed. He made that particularly grating sound when buttering up the N.A.I.C.'s regulators—but they came on their scheduled visit three weeks ago. That laugh was supposed to go away, but when Seth over-laughed again, adding a throaty gasp, her curiosity piqued.

It must be new.

The thought sent a hungry jolt through her, like smelling hot food after a long fast. After letting her mind briefly flirt with implications, Raven's gaze swept her cluttered desk. If Seth saw all the contraband, there would be nothing new—only the same old policy recited in that dreadful monotone. *Not today.*

She downed the thick dregs of her coffee, quickly called with two pair, and minimized her online poker game, pulling up Mr. Smith's forms. She tucked her stool beneath the desk and spun her chair, her scuffed dress shoes dangling over the edge as she spritzed her orange oils into the air, hoping to cover the smell. As she came back around, she snatched her thin wooden pipe and souvenir San Francisco ashtray and tossed them in her purse. Next, she collected her well-thumbed copy of *Arabian Nights* and shoved it—along with her rubber band gun—in the top drawer.

Desktop cleared, Raven nodded at her record setting pace, but she wasn't done yet. If Seth was nervous, she might need her biggest deterrent. Kneeling on her chair, she peeked above the wall of her cubicle and strained to reach the top flip-up cabinet. Inside, she found three identical plaques and took them out. She smiled mockingly at her achievements, each from a recent quarter and each with "Top Salesperson" etched into the brass above her assumed name, *Raven Lee*. Her therapist would have told her to keep them out, but then again, her therapist didn't know about her masquerade as Raven, either. Even though the plaques were ridiculous, they seemed to prevent Seth's policy sermons, so she kept them around.

Plopping back down, Raven surveyed her desk for anything else and landed on the picture of her twin sister, Grace. She pulled the photo closer to her screen, recalling the warm spring day at the tulip farm. Grace hugged her two towering children, also twins, with a rainbow field of flowers behind them. The two gremlins smiled innocently in the picture, but Raven knew the truth. They all had the Kim family mischief, love of games, and bright brown eyes, though it seemed by their exposed socks and wrists that Grace's kids avoided inheriting the Kim family stature.

Seth's voice grew louder, and she questioned one last decoration: the framed taekwondo belts. White, yellow, orange, green, blue, blue/black, and brown filled the case. It was almost full. The gift was from her sister to commemorate last year's rapid advancement. "Something to be proud of," she called it. What started as an activity to get to know her niece and nephew and explore her heritage turned into a full-on obsession between the three. They converted the garage into a dojang and sparred whenever Grace had to work on lesson plans.

Raven advanced so quickly that her coach said she was a *jaeneung-issneun gaein*—a gifted individual. It was flattering, but exaggerated. She had an unfair advantage over the other students: hundreds of investigations and interrogations, and chiefly, years of combat training. All of which, if the Director hadn't erased them, were enshrined in the Academy's record books. But that was Jane Kim, she told herself. Raven Lee is learning taekwondo with her family.

"You have a visitor," Seth said, sliding into her cubicle. He wore his checkered tie and striped shirt pairing. Raven thought they were through this phase, but at least he'd stopped wearing the top and bottom khaki combos.

"That's what they say in prison, Seth."

He dropped his voice. "Hilarious, Raven, really, but please, it's federal. They asked for you." He sniffed the air. "Have you been smoking again?"

"Neither of us wants that answer, Seth." She nodded behind him. "Regulators?"

"Not sure. Wouldn't say. A special unit," he mumbled, glancing around nervously. There was only one unit that would come looking for her, regardless of her name. *Muff me.*

"Doesn't matter. Just stick to the approved script!" Seth jumped and smiled too widely as someone stepped up behind him. "Hello, sir. This is Raven."

The young man was jarringly handsome—a kind of beautiful that made you pause and look around, wondering if you'd wandered into a movie set. Tall, olive-skinned, and filling out his tailored black suit. Raven scanned his face, stunned. There was confidence in his eyes mixed with a tentative hitch of inexperience as he fidgeted with his buttons. She smelled bait and bad news. Folding her arms, she waited.

Seth gestured to her, apparently unsure if he should speak. He was the only person she'd ever seen who smiled with his teeth not touching, his mouth wide open. It was creepy.

"Raven Lee?" the young man asked.

"The same," she replied sweetly.

"Agent Emmett Torin," he said. His hands hung at his sides, and his gray eyes scanned her cubicle, lingering on the plaques and belts. She watched him squint at their titles. "May we speak in private?" His eyes flicked up to her hair.

"Too pink?" Raven asked, fluffing her bright pink locks.

"It certainly . . . catches the eye," he said. "I would have gone brighter, though."

"Really? I know a guy. Agent Torin, was it? You'd look good in pink."

"It'd be hard to work undercover with hair like that."

"Undercover? Gorgeous types like you don't really blend in." She gestured to her face. "Too many angles."

A touch of red came to his cheeks, and he covered it with a laugh. "I was told you'd be . . . eccentric. Raven."

Raven grinned. He knew who she really was, which meant the

43

jig was up—the Director had found her. A shame. Jane liked Raven. "Ms. Lee, please."

Seth cleared his throat, looking between them. Jane rolled her eyes, nodding at him. "My boss here is worried you're investigating us for fraud. Again."

Seth's eyes widened, and he stammered. "I, uh . . . no, I . . ."

Jane put her hands up. "Tell him you're not before he has another stroke."

"How do you know I'm not?" Emmett asked.

"Because you're looking for me."

Emmett considered her for a moment before he nodded once. "I'm just here to ask some questions."

Jane turned to Seth. "See? You're good."

Seth cleared his throat again and folded his arms.

Jane sighed. She hated the stupid slogan, but there was no better way to get Seth out of her cubicle. She turned to face Emmett and deadpanned. "We at Best America Insurance believe our customers are number one. And number one deserves excellent customer service, fair prices, and unmatched quality. Best America Insurance, because America deserves the best."

Seth nodded approvingly, smiled at Agent Torin, and drifted down the aisle. Jane noted he didn't drift far.

"Company man?" Agent Torin nodded at Seth a few rows down.

"Middle management, through and through." Jane shrugged. "Poor guy is jammed between us drones and the higher powers. It's enough to squeeze the humanity out of anyone. I guess I can respect that he picked a side, at least. He makes us repeat that motto to anyone with a badge. I once watched him make Brenda in accounting say it to a meter maid in the parking lot. Seems to be a bit of paranoia coming down from on high."

Agent Torin's gaze swept over the cubicles. "What are you even

44

doing here? You left the Bureau for telemarketing?"

A bitter taste crawled into her mouth, and she squared up to him. "The Bureau left me." She inhaled slowly, resetting. "If you're here, then the Director knows."

He nodded.

"Bummer. I thought I had him this time. But damn, when that man blacklists you, he doesn't mess around."

"But why . . . here?" He vaguely gestured to the sea of headsets.

She double-checked to make sure Seth hadn't crawled back and shrugged. "I want to say revenge, to sound cool, but it's helping pay my sister's mortgage. I mean, hypothetically, yes, since the Director owns a majority of this company, I could work my way up and subvert this piggy bank and get him on fraud or something. Could be fun. Unlikely, but fun." She gestured to her plaques. "To do that, though, I'd have to grind out a paycheck for a couple of years, during which I'm actually making *him* money. A fact that escapes neither of us. Gotta love the irony."

"So leave."

Jane rolled her eyes and held up five fingers. "Last two years, I've been fired five times under five different aliases. Five! One, sure. Two, maybe, but not all of them. The Director is pulling the strings. I'm not that big of a pain."

He chuckled, intriguing her. There was something in his eyes— fixed on hers. "He said you'd be honest."

"Really? Because *he* taught me how to lie, how to weaponize it. Did he tell you about the big game?"

"Uh-huh. I'm afraid to ask, but—" He grinned. "What's the big game?"

"So, he didn't tell you?"

Agent Torin flattened his lips as he shook his head. Jane noted the whiff of annoyance. She leaned forward, lowering her voice. "I don't think it really has an official name, but I call it Tyrant's Chess. Defined boundaries, unique pieces with unique abilities, and this fog of war that shrouds the number of players and their secrets." She looked at him eagerly. "It's why our ancestors invented spies."

"Tyrant's. Chess." He nodded slowly. "Right. Well, I figured out a new career for you. There are some websites that might pay for theories like that. Or, better yet, just write it on a sandwich board and stand on the corner with a cowbell."

"Ha-ha." Jane deadpanned. "I've tried that. It doesn't work, but the joke's on you, *Emmett*." She wagged her finger at him. "You're in his game right now. And if you're not a player, you're definitely a pawn. And since only players have enough power to change the rules, you're *stuck* as a pawn. It is not a very fun game for most of us."

He rocked on his heels, studying her as the din of the call center droned on. Jane sighed, waiting for the inevitable news coming. Impatiently, she shook her hands. "Okay, let's get this over with. I doubt you're here to promote me, so you're here to either give me the boot or just muff with me."

"None of the above, actually," Emmett said and grinned, obviously enjoying the suspense. Jane prickled. Not knowing made her uncomfortable, but the implication had already captivated her. If not to fire her, then what? What did *he* want with her?

"What's 'muff,' by the way? Company policy against cussing?"

"Muff? Ugh, no." Jane stuck out her tongue. "It's a more palatable cuss word. According to both my therapist and sister, I need to *express* myself better."

"So, you don't cuss?"

"Nope. Linguistically celibate."

"Any other little quirks?"

"Muff off."

Emmett laughed and scanned her office again. Jane wondered what her cubicle told him about her. Did it mesh with the Director's story? How much had he even shared? She noticed his eyes linger on her belts. His posture changed—a subtle shift, standing slightly taller. The new insight surprised her. *He's nervous. And either a brilliant actor or . . .*

"You're a new agent," Jane said, spotting a file box in the corner, one that looked big enough to carry her belongings. She'd figured she would save time and just pack up. She hopped down from her chair, noting how still Emmett had become.

"Why do you say that?" he asked.

"Call it a hunch. The Director told you about me?"

"The Director told me enough."

Jane sniffed, doubting the Director had told him much of anything, and started loading her books and toys inside.

The young man lifted his chin. "He said I was perfect for the assignment, actually."

"Oh? So there is a case," Jane said, the pieces quickly snapping into place. "I see. You're not just new. You're fresh from the Academy. Your first lead, then, is it?"

Emmett's mouth opened to speak, then closed again. She'd hit a nerve. "How—"

"My therapist calls it hyper-vigilance. But don't change the subject. I get this now," she said, finger bouncing between them. "It's like the movies. You're my bait, so I'll come help you with something—one last job or whatever. Something the Director really wants. But I hate the Director. It's all very cute and complicated. Maybe we could even have a buddy-cop relationship by the end. Ooo! I bet he promised you something.

What? Money? Prestige? So cliche. Please correct me if I'm wrong. But I'm not."

Emmett's eyes narrowed. "I'm not bait."

"Sounds like something bait would say." Jane emptied her snack drawer into the box. "The Director didn't mention my stints lecturing at the Academy? He knows I loved teaching, and here comes a fresh baby agent with a magnificent bone structure, asking for help. I bet you got big dreams, too, right?" She lifted one of her plaques, wondering if she should even bring it home.

"I have a few ideas, yeah . . ."

"BAAAIT," Jane crowed, tucking the plaque inside—she'd earned them, after all. "You're bait, Emmett. Face it. It's okay! Hey, we're all bait at some point. And you're modest too, how delicious, but"—she turned and patted him on the arm—"I'm done being the Director's pawn. I'm freelance now." She opened the top drawer, pulled out the rubber band gun, and offered it to Emmett. "Do you want this? Something to remember me by."

He looked down at Jane and set his jaw. "I'm not bait," he said flatly, but without raising his voice. Jane noted his control. The kid wasn't without some talent. She had a way of getting under people's skin. "It took quite a bit of convincing to get him to agree to this, you know. This is my case."

Jane paused a moment. "You talked *him* into recruiting *me*?"

"I did."

Something has changed, then. The Director was far from foolish, and the man did nothing by accident. Which meant this could be an opportunity to . . . *No! Don't do it.* This was just another play in the same old game. Shaking her head, she set the rubber band gun in the box and continued packing up.

Emmett took a step closer. "He also called you the best hunter he's ever had. You've tracked down what? Over a hundred fugitives all over the world?"

"A hundred and three," Jane muttered. "But who's counting?"

"Exactly!" Emmett said. "They etched your name into half the entries in the record hall. You're a legend."

"He said that? That I was the best?" Jane said, her head swimming with the compliment. But she shook her head. "No. Cheap tricks. Bad, Bait, bad."

He folded his hands together. "Look, you're right. This is my first case. I need your help. Please."

Emmett's tone tugged at Jane's heart. Being new often meant being overwhelmed, and no one deserved to flounder alone. She sighed, setting down her box on the desk, and turned to face him. He extended a manila folder. She eyed it warily, curiosity bubbling, but from the corner of her eye, she spotted the blinking red dot on her headset. The call was still on hold, maybe her last call.

"Well, I'm in the middle of a call," Jane said casually, enjoying being chased. She leaned toward Emmett and the folder, then stopped. This was a trap with a huge red sign above it flashing DANGER. "I'm sorry, but . . ."

Emmett stepped closer and kneeled, resting the folder on his knee.

"What are you— Don't beg." Jane sighed. "Stand up."

Emmett didn't move. In a low voice, he said, "The Director told me to tell you that if you helped, he'd tell you what a . . . what the seed is. That you'd know what he meant."

Jane froze. "*The* Seed? He said *the* Seed?" Her heart raced.

It doesn't matter now, her fugitive had said all those years ago, as blood pooled from their chest. *The Seed is safe. I've done my job* . . . Not a day went by that Jane didn't think of that face and those words. Whatever the Seed was, Jane had shot and killed a woman for protecting it, and the Director had blacklisted her for demanding to know why. Whatever it was, she knew the

Director couldn't have it.

Emmett nodded.

Jane shook her head and took a step back. "Did the Director tell you why I left?"

"You quit after a long manhunt. He didn't go into detail."

She blinked dizzily, lost in thought, wondering if this answer was worth risking her life.

"This is muffed." She plopped down hard in her chair, spun around, popped her headset on, and hit the HOLD button.

"Mr. Smith, just one more second. I'm getting you a discount." She hit HOLD again and swiveled around, aiming a finger at Emmett. "I get my badge back?"

He shook his head. "No badge, no gun. But he said that afterward, you could keep your job here."

"Oh wow, how magnanimous."

"So, you'll help me?" he asked tentatively. On his knees, he looked pitiful, like a wide-eyed begging boy—except for the suit, the gold watch, and, of course, the leather holster peeking out from his jacket. Jane rethought her analogy: *less beggar, more . . . Men in Black?*

"I . . ." Jane drummed her fingers on the desk, feeling an irritating pang of responsibility accompany her intrigue. The kid was desperate. She groaned as she weighed her options. Stay or go. Grind it out here, or take the bait. Neither option sounded appealing, but at least if she took the bait, she wouldn't have to deal with Seth anymore and maybe, just maybe, get some answers. And this could be her last chance to get them. She sighed, sidestepping the choice. "Tell me what's weird about the bodies."

"I can't."

"Then the answer is no."

Emmett frowned, setting his jaw. *A stubborn one.*

Jane glanced at her phone. "Come on, Agent Bait. You wouldn't have dug me up for a normal assignment." She wiggled her fingers at the folder, coaxing it closer.

"So that's a yes?"

"It's not a no. Gimme gimme."

Emmett considered a moment, then grinned, handing it to her. Jane tapped it once on the desk to settle the papers inside and opened it up.

It was empty.

She turned and scowled at Emmett, who raised both hands defensively. "A guy can't be careful?"

She closed the empty folder and tossed it aside. "Highlights. Now." Emmett looked uncomfortably around, and she pointed up. "Do you hear all that? All those headsets and chatter? No one is listening. No one cares." She tapped her right temple twice. "Plus, I need the info up front so I can load it into my noggin. Let it percolate." She pointed at the blinking red light. "You have one minute. Go."

Emmett blinked. "This is confidential. If you—"

"Yes, yes. Imprisonment. Treason. Blah-blah. Details!"

"There is a killer on the loose."

"Obviously."

"On the run for five years."

"Strong run. They're good. Stayed out of the news?"

"Mostly, but they're catching up quickly."

"Impressive."

"The victims are all . . . mummified. We think."

Jane's eyebrow shot up. "Like, Egyptian-style?"

Emmett checked over his shoulder and rocked forward, close enough to smell his minty breath. "Not exactly. The killer is burning their hearts from the inside out."

"Gross. How many victims?"

"We have thirty-eight victims over five years."

Jane coughed. "Three? Eight? Thirty-eight?!"

Emmett nodded. "All across the country, but the most recent have been in Northern California and Oregon. We think they are moving up the West Coast."

"Mother muffing muff . . ." This would be the biggest case of her career, and combined with a chance to learn about the Seed, Jane's stomach dropped. "The perfect bait," she muttered.

"What was that?"

"I said—" She stopped, feeling the familiar sense of excitement rising in her she always got before a hunt. The same one that had a tendency to get her in trouble. "I said . . ." She hated what she was about to say. "Fine . . . I'm in."

Emmett's face lit up. "Thank you!" He grabbed the armrests of her chair and shook her gently. "I know we can do this!"

"Ya-ya, rah-rah." A thought came to her, and she cringed. *Grace. How am I going to tell her?*

Seth emerged around the corner and stopped, eyeing them both. "Everything . . . okay?"

Emmett quickly stood. "Very good, sir. Jane here—"

She kicked him.

"Raven, sorry. She was just . . ."

Jane didn't have time for niceties. "Yes, Seth. Thank you for checking on us." Once again, he smiled widely, completely missing her sarcasm. Rolling her eyes, Jane pointed at her headset as excitement simmered in her belly. Despite enjoying parts of Raven's life, she dreamed about this day. No sale ever matched the thrill of the hunt. "Uh, Seth. I'd like to finish this call, but then I quit."

"Q . . . quit?" Seth sputtered.

"It's just one case, Raven," Emmett said quickly. "Maybe you shouldn't—"

Seth sputtered, his face growing red. "You can't . . . HR will—"

Jane ignored the rambling, keeping her focus on Emmett. "Gotta do it, Agent Bait. You're not sharp if you're not desperate."

Emmett closed his eyes, and Jane enjoyed watching him convince himself to stay the course. She slid off her chair and reached up to Emmett's shoulder, patting it reassuringly. "This is good for us, I promise. Grace calls it growth. Give me a day to pack?"

Emmett nodded, resigned, and handed her his card. "Call me when you're ready."

Jane slipped the card into her pocket. Emmett shook his head, then strolled back down the aisle.

"Wait, sir!" Seth pleaded. He glared at Jane. "What did you say, Raven?"

"I need a 50% discount on this policy," Jane said, pointing at her headset.

"What?!" Seth hissed. The vein in his forehead bulged. "Of course not!"

"Then I'll tell the VP all about you and Brenda at the Christmas party. Company policy states—"

Seth blanched. "No, no. No. We don't need that. Fifty percent off is fine. My code is—"

"Oh, I got it," Jane said, chipper. She pointed down the hall. "He's getting away. There is no telling what damning secrets I spilled."

Seth pursed his chapped lips together and turned, running after Emmett. "Wait! I want to assure you that, on behalf of Best America Insur—" His voice trailed off, blending into the blur of phones and voices.

———

BEEP

"Mr. Smith! I'm sorry that took so long. I—"

-

"Wonderful! And I secured approval for that discount for being so patient. How's 50% off sound?"

-

"Well, you are very welcome. Let's get started on the right forms here. Say, while I'm pulling these up, mind if I ask you a question? How much sunscreen do you all go through down there?"

Chapter 7: Good Samaritan

Friday, April 13th, 07:07

In a haze, Rory dried and dressed, and the rest of his shift passed quietly. The breathing treatment in Room 9 was effective, and everyone settled in until morning blood draws by *0400*. Rory restocked mechanically, focusing on something Bell had said—something he wasn't sure how to do this time. He couldn't shake the image of Octavia.

"Get ready for the next patient," Bell's voice repeated in his head.

Rory winced. There was always a "next patient," but this time felt different. And it bothered him he couldn't put his finger on it. *Later*, he told himself. *I'll figure it out later.*

At 07:00 and without a patient assignment, Rory skipped the morning report and went back to the locker room. Seeing the shower, his face flushed with embarrassment; he really hoped no one had heard him. He changed into bright green leggings and cycling shoes and removed his helmet from his backpack before balling up his scrubs and stuffing them inside, along with his badge and keys. Last, he pulled on his yellow raincoat. Only transplants and tourists trusted a sunny Northwest forecast in April.

Rory walked past the unit out of habit—one last look to make sure he didn't forget to chart some vitals or sign a note. He saw Dr. Deedee and Bell walking two sobbing parents into a consultation room. Bell held the door for them and glanced up to see Rory, giving him a small wave before stepping into the room. He knew who they were: Octavia's parents. They were about to have the worst conversation of their lives.

Some parents wept quietly when they heard the news, others wailed or threw chairs, a few blamed the staff, but most just sat and asked the same question again and again. Some version of,

"Are you sure?" Those were the hardest, only because you had to rehash the details over and over until their new reality finally sank in.

Rory's pocket vibrated as he hurried downstairs toward the employee exit, grateful to be leaving. He pulled out his phone and found a blinking notification from his dating app. Hovering his finger over it, a voice in his head asked, *What are you going to talk about?* He pictured Octavia and could script the typical conversation.

It would start with, "So what do you do?" and normally ended quickly when Rory replied, "Pediatric intensive care nurse." For the small percent that clarified, some version of "That's the really sick kids?" came next. When Rory nodded, the conversation inevitably swerved to more universal topics, like celebrities, the weather, or, God-forbid, family.

"Not tonight," he said, wanting to avoid another time-sucking dead-end. He swiped the notification aside before typing out a quick message to Patrick.

Oliver's at 7 PM? I need a drink.

———

07:15

"Excuse me, sir, can I help you?" A man in a blue hospital-security uniform and cap blocked Rory's path. He wore a granite scowl on his clean-shaven face, and Rory wondered if he'd been in the military.

Rory glanced into the security office—called the Fish Bowl by the staff because of its glass walls. A bank of monitors showed the hospital waking as physicians and families joined the nurses and patients. During the day shift, the hospital was a flurry of activity: consults and treatments, visitors, and guest lectures. Then, when night came again and the cycle reset, only then did the hospital breathe and settle down in hopes of true rest.

"I'll need to see your badge, sir," the burly guard said.

They'd spoken before, but Rory couldn't remember his name. *Cameron . . . no, Carl . . . no. Kyle?*

"Kyle, right?" Rory asked.

"Yes, sir." He pointed at his name badge. A mirrored, stoic expression stared back.

Rory cringed. *Smooth.* "My name is Rory. I work up in the PICU. And I want to go home now." He heard the edge in his voice and regretted his tone. "Sorry. Long shift." He pointed past Kyle toward the fogged, sliding glass doors marked EMPLOYEES ONLY in large red letters at the end of the hall. "I parked my bike that way."

Kyle's eyes narrowed for a moment before he offered his hand. A little surprised, Rory took it and felt the power in Kyle's grip. "I remember you. You gave the presentation at orientation about the importance of hand hygiene. I follow your guidance daily." He reached over to a wall-mounted container of hand sanitizer, squirted a healthy dollop, and rubbed his hands. "Proper hygiene saves lives."

Rory swallowed. "Cool, nice work. I'll just—"

"Do you have your badge, sir?"

"But you know me, and I'm . . . leaving . . ."

Kyle folded his arms. "No badge, no access."

"Alright." Rory swung his backpack around and rummaged through the side pouch. "Okay. I get it. Just doing your job," he mumbled.

He found his badge and held it out to Kyle. "There you go. And I promise I'm not a doppelgänger either." He smiled, hoping Kyle might relax a little, but the guard took the badge without a sound and scrutinized it, even teasing the corners of his picture with his fingernail.

Oh, come on now. "Is there a problem?"

Kyle handed the badge back. "Proper identification should be worn at the collar or chest level at all times, sir. Next time, I'll have to cite you and record the encounter."

Rory gritted his teeth. *He's just doing his stupid job.*

"Will do. Thanks, Kyle," Rory said, trying to sound genuine.

"Where are you parked, sir?"

"I bike." He gestured to his helmet again. "Chained up by the east staff lot."

"I've had a report of someone rummaging through trash cans and harassing employees. Would you like an escort?" He snapped his walkie-talkie off his hip. "I can have another unit here in five minutes."

"No!" Rory blurted. The last thing he wanted was someone else talking to him. "That's really unnecessary. Uh, thank you, though."

Kyle frowned as he tucked the radio away.

"Excuse me?" A soft voice came from down the hall.

Rory and Kyle both turned as an elderly woman in a tan buttoned-up trench coat stepped through the sliding glass doors. She tapped the tiles in front of her with a long, candy-striped cane as she steadied herself against the white walls with her other hand. Long strands of wispy white hair hung down from beneath a rainbow Rasta cap. She smiled at them from beneath a pair of dark glasses. She was blind, Rory judged, and apparently lost.

"Do you know where the bus stop is?" she asked.

"Ma'am, this is an employee-only area," Kyle said. "The bus stop is back outside and to the left."

"Oh," the woman sighed. "I missed it then. Oh dear, it's my first time up here. Could one of you show me? I think my bus comes soon, and I'd hate to miss it." She tapped the tiles with her cane as she turned back toward the door. "Is it this way?" Rory watched her for a moment, knowing that if she missed her bus, the next one might not come for an hour.

Kyle reached for his walkie-talkie.

"I'll take her," Rory said, readying himself for more small talk. "It's on my way."

"You're sure, sir?"

"Yeah." He gave Kyle a little salute. "Have a good morning, Kyle."

Kyle nodded back. "You too. And please, remember—"

"My badge. Got it." Rory tapped his temple twice and hustled to catch up with the old woman.

Rory marveled at how much taller the woman seemed up close, and a heavy cloud of lavender and rosemary hung over her. "Hello, hi. Uh, my name is Rory. Did you need help to catch your bus?" Part of him hoped she'd say no.

"Oh yes, thank you, Rory." She groped the air in his direction with long fingers, each adorned with a silver ring. Rory stepped forward, offering his arm, but when her finger touched him, a jolt shocked them both. Rory yelped and jumped back. Static electricity was a common consequence of the dry hospital air, but this shock hurt. His left hand tingled, and he could feel where her fingers had touched him. A wave of heartburn crawled up his chest but receded as quickly as it had come. *That was weird.*

"Oh my, I'm sorry," the woman said. "Look at me, being a bother."

"It's okay," Rory said, rubbing his chest. "Happens more than you think around here. And it's no bother at all. A little extra fresh air sounds nice, actually." He blinked, remembering his manners. "I'm sorry, I didn't get your name."

The woman grinned. "It's Caroline."

"Well, Caroline." Rory offered his arm again. "Shall we?"

Caroline touched his arm again, and to his relief, without the shock this time. She leaned on him, and he absorbed her light frame easily. The two turned and walked toward the exit, exchanging polite conversation about the changing season.

———

07:30

The cool morning wind rolled over the small bus shelter. Red and green graffiti covered the glass window behind the shelter bench, with a bright blue sky highlighting the dark edges of the surrounding pine trees. Nestled among the evergreens, Rory spotted a cherry tree with its pink blossoms nearly ready to burst open and blanket the city and its long river-walk with lush pink petals. The blossoms were late this year, damaged after January's cyclone layered the entire city in thick sheets of ice.

Rory leaned his head against the signpost—Route 99, it read—and drew in a deep breath. He tasted the damp air before he shrugged.

"Sometimes the schedules are wrong. I know there's another bus stop on the other side of campus, and, well, Hill Hospital is a bit of a maze. If this one doesn't come in the next couple of minutes, you can catch that one, but you'll need a guide."

"These joints don't do distance well these days."

"Well, then, I'll wait with you," Rory said. "No problem. Really."

"That's very sweet of you," she replied. "I hope I don't sound rude, but you sound like you need to rest, dear."

Rory chuckled. She wasn't wrong. "It's that obvious?"

"You sound half asleep already."

"I'll survive for a few extra minutes." Rory stretched, dreading the bike ride home on weary legs.

"Are you a doctor?" Caroline asked.

He sniffed. If he had a dollar for every time a patient called him a doctor, he could afford a plane ticket somewhere nice. "I'm a nurse. Pediatrics." He left his unit out.

"Working with kids," Caroline said, nodding. "That must be hard."

Rory winced and was glad she couldn't see him. "Some nights."

"I know that sound. The resignation. I was a nurse too for many years."

Rory perked up. "Oh yeah? What unit?"

"We didn't really have units when I worked, just plenty of patients. And my sisters and I never seemed to have enough hands to treat them all."

Sisters? The only medical order of sisters that Rory knew of ran the Christian hospital out west. Those nurses wore black and white uniforms, wore beads, and raved about a dead guy.

"Are you a nun?"

Caroline tipped her head to the side, considering. "Well, I suppose I am, though not the nuns you're thinking of. My remedies are more . . . natural."

"A naturopath nurse?" *How old school is she?* "Haven't heard of that specialty before, but being short-staffed transcends the profession, I think. Your eyes then, they . . ." he trailed off, realizing he might sound insensitive.

"My eyes? No, that happened later." Caroline waved off his concern. "Don't worry, dear. No offense taken. It's been a long time since then."

Rory sighed, relieved, and checked the road for any sign of the bus.

"Tough shift?" Caroline said, pulling back Rory's attention. He glanced back at the hospital and sighed. He thought about lying, avoiding Octavia altogether, but something about Caroline's manner put him at ease. Maybe it was because she'd been a nurse or her cool-grandmother vibe. Or maybe he just needed to talk—either way, he heard himself speak before he knew what he was saying. "I lost a patient tonight."

"Oh, Rory. I am so sorry," said Caroline, turning to face him. "Loss can leave such a lasting wound. I remember."

He nodded again, uncertain why he had said it, though it felt good. "It was stupid, too. A drunk. Speeding through some neighborhood. They just . . . ran her over. I mean, what were they thinking?"

"They probably weren't," Caroline said.

"What do you mean?"

"I make no excuses for them, Rory, but that driver, I imagine, was very sick and didn't know it." She inhaled and looked up at the sky. "Haste and vice are two symptoms of a much broader, deeper affliction than just one drunk."

"And what affliction is that?"

She turned toward him. "Despair. It's hard not to absorb it."

Rory swallowed down the lump rising in his throat. "Like a sponge." He shrugged, trying to lessen the tightness in his chest. "We did what we could, but . . ."

"There are some fights we can't win."

"Ya."

Caroline rocked back on the bench, nodding thoughtfully. "Sounds like you needed a miracle."

Rory raised an eyebrow. "Something like that."

She shifted her hands on her cane. "Miracles are scarce. Especially these days."

"An understatement."

Caroline considered him a moment, then asked, "What if you had such a power? What would you do with it?"

Rory distractedly looked down the road again, hoping for the bus. This conversation had veered into bizarre territory. "I don't know. Save it for the next kid, I guess. It's only a matter of time before we'd need it again. I hear there is this nasty affliction going around."

"Interesting."

"What?"

"You wouldn't use it for yourself?" Caroline pressed.

Rory considered, picturing a crowd of people around him clamoring for his attention. The warm thought faded quickly, though, and he felt the stifling press of their faces and hands close around him. *A fantasy*, he told himself. *Miracles don't exist. And even if they did, they don't for people like me. Not a second time.*

"I'd like to think not," he said. "But . . . I don't know. It's a tough question at, what, eight in the morning."

Caroline chuckled, shifting on the bench. She moved slowly, groaning as she settled into a new position. Rory checked his phone again and blew out a long breath. *Where is this bus?*

"Rory, might I ask you another question?"

He shrugged. "Why not? We have time."

Caroline raised an eyebrow. "Indeed. What would you say . . . if I told you there was a way to save your patients?"

Rory laughed, looking at the strange woman and expecting to see her in on the joke, but her expression was clear and pensive. *She's kidding, right?.* "I'd say some people make up fantastic stories."

"There are few greater inventions than the story," Caroline said, waving her hand at the world around her. "Everything we have built is based upon them."

Rory stared at her, waiting again for the gotcha, but it never came. "You're not kidding."

"No," Caroline said flatly.

Crazy old lady. Rory sniffed, shaking his head. *This is ridiculous.*

"Perhaps, Mr. Nash." Caroline's rings clinked together as she folded her hands. "But crazy is a matter of perception. Perhaps you need a little more in your life."

Rory leaned back. *How did she do that?*

Caroline shook her head. "I am offering you a chance, Rory Nash. The chance at true healing."

"If this is a joke, then it's a pretty shitty one," Rory said, looking around for cameras, but saw none.

"You'd walk away from such an offer?"

Rory ran a hand over his face. *I'm too tired for this.* "From a stranger I just met, yes. Now, if you'll—" A sharp point probed his side. "What the—"

"Shut your mouth and drop the bag. Now," someone said behind him. The voice was low and raspy.

Am I being robbed? Of course this would happen today.

"What's going on?" Caroline demanded from the bench.

"You shut up," said the voice. "Unload those rings, lady. Now!"

Caroline clasped her hands against her chest. "Rory? What's going on?"

"Let's just calm down, okay?" Rory turned around, but the point dug in deeper. He winced and stopped.

"Eyes forward, hero," the mugger said.

Rory reluctantly complied. A backpack and a couple of rings weren't worth losing a kidney over. "Alright. Alright."

"Slowly," the mugger said, "or I swear you'll bleed."

Rory slipped one arm out and turned enough to let the backpack slide down his arm. "There, take it." He wondered if they would inspect its contents to find it was only full of dirty scrubs.

"Drop it!" the mugger said.

He did.

"The rings, too. Hurry the hell up. I'm not asking again."

"My rings?" Caroline whimpered. "Please, no, they are from my sisters."

"I don't give a shit about your sisters. Rings. Now, or your friend here gets stuck."

Caroline's mouth fell from disbelief to sorrow as she removed her rings.

"Hey, leave her alone," Rory said. "She's just confused and lost. Just take my bag and go, alright?"

"You shut it, or you'll be pissing blood," the voice snapped. "Rings! Now!"

A fire flared in Rory. He tensed and waited, deciding.

Caroline sniffed, sliding off her rings and holding them out in a trembling hand, though only in the vague direction of the voice. The mugger leaned toward her, and the sharp pressure on Rory's back suddenly let up.

Now.

Rory spun, swung a hand low, grabbed the mugger's wrist, and jerked their arm back. Or he would have if their arm hadn't felt like solid stone. When the arm didn't budge, Rory's stomach dropped as he met a pair of dangerous green eyes.

Pale-skinned and wearing an over-sized orange and brown

beanie down over their eyebrows, the mugger glared at Rory. She wore loose gray sweatpants and a threadbare black hoodie. Rory had several inches and at least forty pounds on her, yet when he pushed against her arm again, she didn't even grimace.

Holy crap, she's strong.

In her hand, her only hand, he saw not a knife but a sharpened number two pencil. Three safety pins held the opposite sleeve up, folded against her shoulder.

Rory wrapped his other hand around hers, and he pushed down with his entire body, using his full weight to leverage the weapon away. Her arm gave, though her expression didn't betray any sense of struggle, only resignation. He jerked the pencil free of her hand and tossed it aside.

"What's going on?" Caroline's cane tapped against the pavement.

"She's robbing us with a pencil." Rory spotted his backpack on the ground and lunged for it. The mugger grabbed a strap.

"Give me the bag, hero!" She pulled hard, jerking Rory forward, nearly breaking his grip. He set his feet, yanked, and heard the threads pop.

"There's nothing in it!"

"Then let it go, damn it!"

He wouldn't. He couldn't.

"Help!" Rory yelled. "We're being robbed!"

"Shut your mouth," the mugger said and pulled again, but Rory clung on.

Rrriiippp.

The mugger's strap tore, and the tension on the bag suddenly gave.

"Security!" Rory shouted, stumbling.

"Be quiet!" the mugger hissed.

"Security!"

"I warned you!" the mugger snarled, and Rory looked over in time to see her winding up a thick-knuckled fist.

Crack!

Stars flashed through his vision, and the world tipped below him. He landed hard. After a moment, his thoughts stopped spinning, giving way to the pain in his burning cheek. He opened his mouth, and his jaw clicked uncomfortably. *At least it works.*

Caroline squatted gracefully beside him. Heels flat and knees wide, she was a far cry from a hobbling old woman from a moment ago. *How?* Then his cheek throbbed, and he winced. *Ow.*

She set her cane down and folded her arms, setting each elbow on the tips of her knees. Then, most alien of all, she set her chin on her arms, black lenses staring at him. "Are you hurt?"

Rory turned, propping up on an elbow on the pavement, as his mind bounced between her sudden change and her question. "Uh, ya." His face and head throbbed. "Ohh. No."

"My apologies, but pain is a necessary component."

"Component of . . ."

Her hand lashed out, too fast for her age, and clamped an iron grip over his mouth. Rory's eyes went wide. He tried to rise, to push her away, but his legs wouldn't work, and she wouldn't move.

"*Geg oph!*"

She swept his elbow aside with her free hand and drove him against the cement. The stars returned with a fresh wave of pain.

"This will be uncomfortable," Caroline said as the stars danced away. Her grip tightened, squeezing his face until his lips puckered out like a fish. She pulled suddenly close. Rory froze, too shocked to move. Her nose brushed his, bringing a strong scent of rosemary. "Fear not, healer. This memory won't burden you long."

Alarms screamed in his head. Instincts won out. He balled his right fist, his strong arm, and swung with everything he could muster. A home-run hit, but from the corner of his eye, he watched his elbow flop uselessly, wagging a balled fist like a little white flag. A cold drop of dread spread from his belly. *What is happening?!* He swung with his left, but it didn't even move.

Caroline followed his thought down to his balled fist, and he felt a flash of embarrassment, no deeper—humiliation.

But she turned back with a smile. "I have such high hopes for you."

Hopes for . . .

Then she kissed him, snuffing out the sun as he burst apart.

—

Light returned first. He recollected into himself but felt airy and light, as though filled with mist instead of marrow.

Breathe, he told himself, a hot flush clawing up his neck; his heart sprinted, his fear talked. Bell's voice came to him, as it did more often these days. A mantra she had when a co-worker called for help and she entered the room. *Calm and assess. Calm. And assess.* He breathed again and focused on the details of his environment but saw only white and light and gray horizon around him. *Okay.* It wasn't much, but it did ease his fear. He seemed to be alive, at least.

Then he fell, or felt like it, at least. There was no wind or stomach to tell him, just a faint tingle in his ear. He landed on his feet, stumbling on wobbly legs a moment before his balance returned. Despite the fall, he didn't feel heavy. His surroundings had changed; he stood in the center of a small room. A mural of dancing purple hippos against a sky covered three walls, the perfect shade of a calming blue for giving bad news. A brown couch lay opposite the door with two matching chairs and end tables to the side. *It's not the PICU. No patient bed. Or computer. Is it a consult room?* Hill Hospital had dozens of those.

His gaze swept the space again, and a burst of color caught his attention. It hadn't been there before. The couch sprouted a rainbow patch.

Rory's jaw dropped. *I know that patch.* He'd spent many infusions beside it.

"I know this place . . ." he whispered, but his voice sounded thick and distant.

The edges of the room rippled. A pudgy, red-haired boy, perhaps nine or ten years old, sat alone reading a creased and yellowing paperback book with an IV pole standing beside him. He held the book in one hand, keeping his other arm extended with an intravenous catheter inserted into the bend. Pumps clicked away on the pole beside him, infusing a trio of fluids—each the same size, color, and neatly labeled. Pale to the point of glowing, mixed with a sickly shade of green, the boy fought to keep his eyes open as he set the book down to turn the page. He looked not just sick, but dying.

Rory choked on his breath as the memory played before him. *That's me.* The boy shifted on the couch, and the full realization slammed into him. "Wait," he said, turning and taking in the room. "No . . ." *Not this day.*

Muffled shouts seeped through the walls, and the boy wilted, giving the wall a dutiful glance. He sighed and returned to his book, but Rory felt the cramped, chronic frustration in the simple gesture. The "*Why are they fighting again?*" look. It never seemed to get a suitable answer.

The boy picked up his book again, and Rory knew which one it was without looking. *Fellowship of the Ring* by J. R. R. Tolkien. The cover pictured a short, furry-footed fellow staring out over hillside hollows and the forest far beyond. He'd read that book until it had nearly fallen apart. He smiled sadly, seeing it again, remembering when a thick-browed bully at his third foster home had burned it with a blowtorch.

Rory knew how this day ended—the day everything changed. He was about to get news that he had an aggressive brain tumor requiring three grueling surgeries, years of treatment, and hundreds of procedures. But that wasn't the worst news. Any second now, his parents would abandon him—making him and his tumor someone else's problem.

Another ripple distorted the scene, and when it settled, the shouting ceased. Rory turned and saw the boy curled up on the couch, soundly sleeping with the book drooping in his hand. The door opened, and nurse Susie Fellow stepped into the room. A boyish swoon passed through Rory, and he blushed. Way back when he'd had a crush on her, and those old nerves woke up seeing her again. Even years later, he found her as beautiful as ever. Young with dark skin and wavy hair that seemed to glow in the hospital's blue fluorescence. She always squinted but never wore glasses and often smirked, seeming on the verge of unleashing her big, toothy grin. Always the storyteller, she got him through the worst of his radiation treatments, his relapse, and remission. In many ways, Susie was the reason he became a nurse. No one made him feel safe like Susie.

As she approached the sleeping boy, Rory swallowed, and the bubbles of adolescent infatuation popped. As a nurse now, he saw the scene differently. *What must she have felt that day?* Delivering bad news to parents was difficult, but delivering bad news to children was terrible. You know you're dashing a piece of their innocence.

"Rory." Susie kneeled beside the couch and gently touched the boy's arm. "Time to wake up."

He stirred, peeking one eye at the nurse, then the other. "Where are my mom and dad?"

Susie swallowed. "They left, Rory."

The words echoed painfully as he watched the boy frown, unable to understand. How could he? How could anyone?

He sat up. "They left . . . without me?"

Susie nodded. "I know you have lots of questions, and my friend here will answer them. She's very nice and will help you get settled." She gestured to the door where a tall woman with jet-black hair and a tan pantsuit stood. Rory's first social worker—though he couldn't recall her name. She hadn't lasted long enough for him to remember; few of his caseworkers did.

"You're going to go with her right now, but don't you worry. You and me, we'll get to see each other almost every day for a while. I'll introduce you to the other nurses and we'll play games and read stories and have a good time of it, alright? Do you like your book?"

Rory nodded. "I like Frodo."

"He's my favorite too," Susie said, showing her dazzling smile. "Did you know there are two more books after this one?"

"Two?" The boy's face split into a smile, though it didn't last long as he cast a suspicious glance at the social worker. "So, we find out if Frodo keeps the ring? I think he should, to keep it safe."

"Is that so?" Susie said. "Well, you'll need to read to find out. I'll tell you what, though. After you finish them, you can keep them so if you're ever feeling lonely, you can find some friends. Deal?"

The boy glanced between the book and the social worker.

"Don't do it," Rory said, but no one in the room noticed him.

The boy looked back at Susie. "But . . . my mom and dad are coming back, right?"

Rory winced, knowing the answer Susie danced around. He

didn't want to hear anymore, but he couldn't seem to look away either. *They aren't ever coming back, kid.*

The social worker cut in. "You're going to a new home for a little while. You'll make new friends and see new places. Doesn't that sound fun?"

The boy didn't look convinced, looking between the adults for a better explanation that would never come. Rory pitied his confused younger self. As an adult, he had long ago figured out the answer himself. It was simple, actually. His cancer had been the last straw of an already splintering family. It was his fault they'd left him, really. Ever since his first seizure, he'd become a burden. Could he really blame them? The way Rory saw it, if he'd shown anything worthwhile, worth loving, then his parents would have stayed.

"Hey," Susie said, taking both his hands. "No one goes it alone. I'll be with you. And others will too. You just might not have met them yet. Okay?"

The boy nodded.

Susie rose. "Come on, Rory." She beckoned him. "You need more medicine. After that, we'll answer all your questions. And for being so brave tonight, I think you earned a cookie."

The boy smiled at Susie and then cast another suspicious look at the social worker before reaching for Susie's hand.

As their fingers touched, he burst again, dissolving into darkness.

—-

Rory's eyes popped open, and the sun peered at him over the trees. The cool morning air filled his nose.

I'm alive?

He lifted his hand, and it moved. All of it.

I'm alive!

The burning pain in his cheek followed a moment later as a shadow passed over his face. In front of the bright morning sun, he squinted at Caroline's silhouette.

"Conjoined Stains," Caroline said, rising to her feet. "How very interesting."

"Care!" a gruff voice called, and Rory turned to see the one-armed mugger dashing for the tree line. "Let's go."

"Yes. Coming." Caroline cupped both hands in front of her and gave Rory a slight bow. "It was a pleasure to meet you, Rory Nash." Rory blinked. In one smooth motion, Caroline snatched up her cane and bounded off as graceful as a deer. The shuffling blind woman had been an act. *But why? What the hell just happened?*

Rory reached for the unraveling memory of Susie and the rainbow patch, but could only hold glimpses, as though waking from a dream. He sat on the pavement as a bus approached, staring into the trees. The shame and guilt consumed him, remembering that the boy would soon learn his parents had left him in the state's custody. His various caseworkers, foster parents, and occasionally a well-meaning teacher would all offer theories about why they left: money, time, and several doubted they were fit to parent.

"Perhaps this was a good thing," they said. "You got out of there."

The memory thinned and vanished, along with Caroline saying it would; both submerged beneath the confusion and pain and returned to the vault nestled in his heart. Rory pushed himself up to his feet and brushed the loose pebbles off his knees. He looked around blankly and reached up to test his clicking jaw.

At the edge of the parking lot, he spotted the two women disappearing into the thick row of pines. A sense of injustice flooded Rory, boiling up hot in his ears.

They robbed me! I walked her over, and . . . she set me up!

73

His torn backpack sat on the ground beside him with one broken strap, unopened. He lifted the bag, feeling the lumps of his scrubs inside, then checked his pockets and found his wallet, keys, and phone. They took nothing.

Friday, 19:15

"What did security do?" Patrick asked, scratching his bushy brown beard as Rory finished telling him about his harrowing morning. Patrick's wide frame filled half the booth. The light caught his crooked nose, a by-product of their brief obsession with Jackie Chan as kids, and gave Rory's big friend the look of a brawler, though he was a teddy bear.

Rory skimmed over the previous night's code and its aftermath, but spared no detail about his encounter with Caroline and the mugger—as much as he could recall, at least; the end was a little fuzzy. The more Rory thought about it, the more he realized getting not-mugged was the strangest event in his brief life. He tried to recount every detail he could remember.

"Nothing." Rory shook his head, his glass nearly empty, though they'd only been there a few minutes. "They got away."

Patrick frowned. "Weird that they didn't even take anything . . ."

"I thought the offer about saving my patients was stranger, personally."

Patrick snorted. "You obviously don't ride the bus enough. Crazy folks out there."

Rory nodded and finished his beer while looking around for a server. The Crooked Rooster was quiet tonight, at least for now. The owner, Oliver, worked the bar, wearing his customary bowler cap and rosy-cheeked smile. Dozens of license plates from different states and countries hung behind the bar and glistened like fish scales in the pub's low light. Rory did not know if Oliver even knew how many he had now, though the stout Brit claimed to have every continent and proudly displayed his "Antarctica Devron Six" naval plate right beside the liquor license.

Rory stifled a yawn, still sluggish from flipping his sleep schedule again. Days to nights, nights to days. Four hours of sleep was manageable, but it left little energy to do anything interesting, and with the Rooster so much closer than the mountains, Rory skipped laundry and his hike and ordered an early round.

"Gotta be careful these days, though," Patrick said. "Did you hear about the killer?"

Rory nodded, vaguely remembering something about it on the news. "The Vac-Seal Killer?"

"Mhm." Patrick glanced around and leaned forward. "I read last night there's a manhunt underway. Very hush-hush. And chasing a trail of bodies up from Nevada. They made it to Oregon even."

"It's not very hush-hush if it's on the internet," Rory whispered. "This sounds like a theory cooked up in a basement."

"That's what I said on the message board," Patrick said.

"Ah, Pat, don't engage with those conspiracy theorists." Some things never changed: gravity, the tides, and Patrick's unending appetite for anything alien, abominable, or the Illuminati. In middle school, for social studies class, he did a report defending Sasquatch and somehow still earned a respectable B+.

"Another round?" a sweet voice said.

Rory turned and found their cute tattooed waitress standing with an empty tray resting against her hip.

"Make it two pitchers," Patrick said.

"I have an education day in the morning."

"Just one pitcher then. I have to help install the new coil tomorrow, too."

"The new MRI suite?" Rory said. "An 8T?"

"You're not supposed to know about that."

"You know nurses hear everything."

"One more glass?" the waitress asked.

"Ya—" Rory started.

"Two, please," Patrick cut in.

Oh. Rory raised an eyebrow, feeling a pang of sadness. "Ana's coming?"

"Soon. She got caught up with a brief, but she really wants to see you."

Rory loved Ana like a sister, and ever since she and Patrick met during sophomore year, it had often been the three of them, plus whomever Rory was dating. Still, it had been a while since it was just him and Patrick. He felt bad for it, but sometimes he just missed playing games and shooting the breeze like when they were teens.

"That's sweet." The waitress grinned, revealing two dimples that Rory guessed earned her extra tips. Her eyes fell on Rory, then focused on his cheek. "Ouch. Nice shiner."

"What?" Rory touched his tender cheek and winced. "Yeah, a souvenir."

"Tell her how you got it," Patrick said from across the table.

"Oh, I don't think—"

The waitress raised an eyebrow and waited.

Rory sighed. "There isn't much to the story. I—"

"This short, buck-ten woman decked him." Patrick snickered. "Laid him out. Bam." He punched his fist for effect.

Their waitress bit down on her lips, stifling her smile, but her eyes laughed.

"It's more complicated." Rory paused. "We were being mugged, and then it was just me being mugged, but I wasn't actually robbed in the end . . ."

"He was protecting a stranger," Patrick said. "An old, blind lady."

The waitress's eyebrows shot up as her smile slipped away. "How chivalrous of you."

"And he's single," Patrick rattled off. "And a kid's nurse. And—"

Rory had heard enough. "I think she's got the picture." He shot him a glare, but Patrick grinned, pleased with himself.

A touch of red shaded the waitress's cheeks. "No way. You don't hear about many guy nurses. I'm actually starting nursing school in the fall. I'm nervous, I'm embarrassed to admit." She gave him a shy look. "Maybe . . . I can pick your brain about it? Over a drink?"

Oh. Rory's mouth flopped open, then closed. "I, uh . . ."

"He'd love to," Patrick said.

The waitress beamed, showing off neat rows of teeth. "Well, I think Oliver would comp a round for a local hero."

Hero. The word burned in Rory's chest.

"I'm no hero." Rory's face flushed hot. *A hero actually saves people.* "I'll pay for the drinks."

"Dude," said Patrick. "Let the pretty lady buy us drinks." He turned to her. "What my modest friend meant to say is thank you, right, Rory?"

Rory nodded, trying to laugh it off. "Of course. Sorry. And thank you."

"Anytime, hero." She smiled and walked back to the bar. Rory turned and saw three other tables watching her go.

"That was shameless," Rory said.

"What? How?" said Patrick. "She's hot and into you. Hey, five bucks says she leaves her number on the receipt. And for the record, what you did today was pretty cool, even if it ended up . . . weird."

"Weird . . ." Rory muttered, and the still image of Octavia flashed through his thoughts.

"What was that?"

"Nothing, I just—" Rory paused, wondering how to explain the constant tightness in his chest. He gave up and settled for a more familiar argument. "Kid's nurse thing—people don't want to hear about it. For a moment, I thought you were going to tell her about my cancer. Always very sexy." Rory rolled his eyes.

Patrick shrugged. "I would have if the kid's nurse thing didn't work."

"See? Shameless."

Patrick chuckled, hiding his response in a quick gulp of beer.

The front door opened, and a large group of twenty-somethings entered, half heading straight to the bar and the other half staking claim to the dartboard at the far end of the pub. Despite the laughter, Rory felt a gloom settle on him like a heavy blanket. *What's wrong with me?*

"Hey," Patrick said, crashing into Rory's thoughts. "Are you still looking to buy a car?"

"Half-looking," Rory said. "I don't have much extra cash right now. I'm trying to burn through my loans."

"A friend's neighbor is selling a camper van. I haven't seen it, but my buddy said it's barely used. I know we've talked about seeing Yellowstone, finally. Our last road trip ended a bit abruptly."

Rory cringed, remembering the searing pain in his right side and finishing up their road trip in the hospital. "Stupid appendix."

"I thought you might be interested. And if you go, maybe I could meet up with you for a week or two. I know I could use the vacation, too."

Rory considered a moment, remembering the long, lazy summer days on the road, seeing the far corners of the country before college started. Some days were nothing but pavement and flat fields, others spent twisting through the mountains, but nearly all of them ended in something majestic. After last night, a long, lazy day sounded nice. "What was the guy asking for the camper?"

"Six grand. Could get him down to five, I bet."

Rory sucked in a breath through clenched teeth. He'd have to drain his paltry emergency funds to afford that. Rent and loans alone were enough to bury him, not to mention food. His first foster mom always told him if he'd worked hard he could climb any mountain, but how does one climb a mountain that charges interest and grows taller by the day?

"Should I tell him you're interested?" Patrick asked, shifting in his seat.

"Can he give me until the end of the week to think it over? I just need—"

Rory's phone vibrated in his pocket, and he fished it out reflexively. He thought it would be the unit, but when he saw the screen, he frowned and held it up. On the screen, it read *Pat*.

"Again? Dude, you really need to change your login."

Patrick's cheeks flushed, and he reached into his back pocket. "I thought I fixed it."

"Obviously not." Rory hung up. "Last week, I had the privilege of overhearing a riveting trip down the produce aisle.

Iceberg or Romaine. It was a big choice."

"Very funny."

"Funny would have been my favorite butt-dial of all time when you and Ana were discussing which vibrator to—"

"Dude. Shush," Patrick hissed. "Point taken, alright? I'll change my password."

Rory grinned, feeling a little better.

"Change your password for what?"

Rory turned and saw Ana standing table-side. She wore a black suit and red lipstick and the thick tail of her dark hair pulled back into what she called her business pony. She set her leather purse on the table and slid in beside Patrick, planting a quick kiss on his bushy, round cheek before smiling at Rory. "Did he butt-dial you again?"

"From three feet away," Rory said. "A new all-time low."

"Hey!" Patrick said, wounded. "No double teams."

Ana smiled wickedly while rubbing Patrick's back. "You deserve it, babe."

Patrick sighed, though he leaned into her touch.

Ana's bright green eyes turned to Rory, and her smile slipped away. She gestured to her cheek. "Please tell me you didn't do something stupid like join a fight club."

No. That was middle school, Rory thought.

"He got mugged," Patrick said, dispersing Rory's memory.

"Mugged? Oh my God, Rory!" Ana's mouth dropped. "If you need a lawyer, I can help . . . I mean, once I pass the bar."

Rory knew the offer was a good one. In college, while Patrick and Rory often worked hard to find new kinds of trouble, like the proper Mentos to Coke ratio, Ana would be in the library working for extra credit. She claimed she had to maintain her

GPA for her scholarships, but Rory knew Ana preferred her books. Rory sighed, not wanting to tell the story again, but he knew Ana wouldn't let it drop until she'd heard it herself. As he began, their pitcher arrived, and Patrick poured them all a pint while Rory talked.

"So," Rory finished. "I doubt there will be a trial."

Ana's mouth twisted into a frown. "Well, if you want to press charges, the offer stands, okay? I know some people."

"You sound like a hitman."

"Hitwoman," Ana said. "Oh! Good news from the realtor. Everything went through, so we can pick up the keys tomorrow."

Realtor? Keys?

"No way!" Patrick said, pumping his fist. Then he paused and glanced at Rory. "Sorry, man. We were keeping it quiet."

"You bought a . . . house?" Rory asked, stunned. The distance over the table seemed to open. Rory wondered what a down payment would look like in his bank account. "Wow. You never mentioned that, Pat. That's . . . big news."

"Didn't want to get my hopes up, I guess." Patrick shrugged. "It's a sweet place. Big basement. I'm going to get a new gaming table and throw some shelves up. I already got the kegerator picked out, so we'll, like, never have to leave."

Leave?

"What about the Rooster?" Rory tried to joke, but it came across as whining. He tried to recover. "I mean, it'll kill Oliver's business."

Patrick's smile faded, and he glanced at Ana, who nodded. Rory suddenly got the feeling he'd been the topic of conversation recently.

"Um, the realtor called me on the way over. I better call her back," Ana said and pushed herself out of the seat.

As she walked away, Rory's chest tightened. *What's going on?*

Patrick looked down at his glass before he sighed and met Rory's eyes. There was a somberness there Rory hadn't expected. "Rory, you're my best friend. You've always been there for me, and I've tried—"

"Pat. You don't—"

"Let me finish," Patrick said, putting his big hand up. Rory fell quiet.

Patrick started again. "I've always tried to be there for you, too. Like when we were kids. But things are changing now." He glanced in the direction Ana left before he reached down and pulled out a black velvet box.

Rory knew what was inside. It surprised him more that this hadn't come sooner. "You're going to propose?"

Patrick nodded. "She knows I have it. We picked our rings out together. I want you to be my best man."

"Really?" Rory said, unsure of what else to say. "I mean. Of course."

The thought warmed Rory, and he nodded, which fueled Patrick's enthusiasm. "We're talking about kids and all that. I'm excited, Rory. About all of it. I'm ready to be a dad. A better one than mine, at least."

A dad? This all felt too fast. Sure, Patrick and Ana would be great parents, but a lingering question cut in.

"What about Yellowstone?" *What about us?*

Patrick smiled. "We'll make Yellowstone happen. It'll just take more planning, is all."

Rory heard the hopefulness in his friend's voice, the yearning to be okay, to understand. This was big news, joyful even, and yet Rory couldn't help but feel distant and even more alone. He shook his head, forcing his thoughts into order.

"I'm sorry, Pat," he said. "This is such great news. All of it. I'm happy for you. And Ana."

"Yeah?" Patrick looked relieved. "I knew you would be. Uncle Rory has a nice ring to it, right?" He held up his glass, and Rory mirrored him, clinking their pints and each taking a long gulp.

Ana returned, her eyes searching them both with apprehension.

"What's wrong?" Rory asked.

"We need to leave. Sorry."

"You just got here," Patrick said.

"The realtor wants to meet to go over the last few things. Something's wrong with escrow."

What's escrow? "It can't wait until tomorrow?"

Patrick clicked his teeth quietly, looking between Ana and Rory.

This is how it starts, Rory thought bitterly, but he forced a smile instead. "Sorry. What am I saying? This is a big deal, go. I get it. Really. Life stuff."

"I'm really sorry, Rory," Ana said. "Let us make it up to you. We'll cook dinner for you. Anytime you want. You could bring a date."

"The waitress was flirting with him," Patrick said, waggling his eyebrows. Ana found her at the bar and nodded approvingly as they both slid out of the booth.

"I'll take you up on that," Rory said, wondering if he would.

They apologized again and, ignoring Rory's protests about who would buy the pitcher, set more than enough cash on the

84

table to cover, leaving Rory at the table alone with half a pitcher and three empty glasses.

Chapter 9: Final Offer

Friday, 21:10

Apartment 104A

Rory shut his door against the wind. *What a day . . .*

On his ride home, another spring storm rolled in from the west and chased him back to his apartment. Luckily, the wind was behind him, so he made great time. He leaned his muddy bike and helmet against the entryway wall, flipped on the lights, and blew out a long breath through his nose. The clutter and pile of laundry was a problem for future Rory, and he flopped onto the couch, telling himself he'd clean up after the education day tomorrow.

Settled, Rory pulled out his wallet and found the receipt from Oliver's. Written in looping numbers was their waitress's phone number. He gazed at the beautiful numbers, thought about telling the cute woman about his life, and crumpled up the paper, tossing it onto the floor.

Rory owed Patrick five bucks and an apology. *What kind of asshole gets mad when his best friend says he's buying a house?* He should have hugged them both and bought the round. The bike ride helped sort his thoughts into identifiable categories, and he decided he would take Ana up on her dinner offer. He looked down at the crumpled paper. Maybe he'd call.

Thud.

The sound came from the other side of the couch.

"Sneaks?"

He walked around the couch and saw his backpack on the floor, half an orange tabby tail poking out from the gash the mugger tore. Sneaks loved rolling in his dirty scrubs.

"Come on, gross. Get out of there." He reached into the bag and fetched Sneaks out, who meowed indignantly. In his arms, she settled into a steady stream of purrs as Rory scratched her neck. "You don't want another bath, do you?"

She curled into his finger and closed her eyes. She was a far cry from the mangy, flea-ridden kitten that snuck into his apartment last summer. Without air-conditioning, he'd left his windows open, but the apartment sweltered anyway. When he finally gave up on sleep, he caught her munching on the dinner he'd left out. A stray, like him, and she'd stuck around ever since.

"That's what I thought."

Sneaks nipped at his fingers, struggled from his arms, and scampered away.

Cats, Rory thought, shaking his head and watching her stop and groom just out of arm's reach. He reached down for his backpack but stopped when he saw a faint purple glow emanating through the opening.

What the—

He picked up the bag, and as the clothes within shifted, the violet light poured out brighter. Rory didn't remember packing a flashlight or anything purple. He unzipped the bag, pulled out his balled-up blue scrubs, and tossed them into the laundry pile. Underneath was a small canvas pouch with leather ties, no larger than a handful. The light radiated from inside.

Where did this come from?

Rory hesitated, but then recalled Sneaks had touched it and lived. He reached inside, keeping the bag at arm's length, in case it . . . he didn't know. Exploded? Carefully, he pulled the pouch out. It was soft, old, and worn and clinked as he examined it. He dropped his backpack and squinted closer, unlacing the loosely cinched ties, and looked within. The light burst out, and he marveled in wonder, pulling out a warm, corked vial filled with radiant purple fluid. A creamy color swirled, mixing with the deep hues, and Rory remembered breaking glow sticks and dumping them in water for a similar effect. But as the fluid shifted shades again, dark to light, he couldn't remember any of their homemade concoctions doing that.

"Maybe it's a new . . . solution?" Hearing himself, he knew he was wrong. He tried again. "It's, uh . . . it's . . ." *A prank? Why? Who?*

Sneaks approached behind him, purring as she rubbed against his leg and sniffed the air.

"What did you find, Sneaks?"

She meowed, but offered no theories and moved back toward his bag. Something else was still inside. He stooped down and wrenched it open to find another object—a smooth, round stone wrapped in a piece of thin, tan paper. Holding the objects in his hands, Rory stared and tried to make sense of it all. He took them over the counter and laid them out one by one: a stone, a vial, and what appeared to be a note.

Written on the front in a thin, elegant script was: *To Rory Nash.*

His stomach leaped into his chest.

"How did this get in?"

He'd answered his own question before he'd finished asking it.

"That woman. Caroline."

Just throw it away! he told himself, but his name called to him. He unfolded the thin paper.

Dear Rory,

I apologize for the suddenness of my departure and for Jacklyn's behavior. I assure you there was a good reason for it, though I cannot say why just yet. You have a generous soul, and I enjoyed our conversation, but I can't help but feel we left it unfinished.

I am sorry about your patient. I understand both your practitioner's pain, desire to stay, and the hope that it can all change. But that isn't how change works. Passivity is impossible; your pain will only build until you change the fray. Tragedy is a harrowing experience made worse in isolation. But, Rory Nash, you are not alone anymore.

I know you feel lost and angry. I do, too. Anger is all-consuming, and feeling lost is but a cousin to fear. The human response to fear is simple. Run, run far, but running won't soothe our anger. It wouldn't convert our fears into power. Only justice quenches both. And so, I offer you that chance.

If you're angry enough and tired of waiting, please drink the vial and follow your wisp. Don't forget the keystone.

If you're convinced I'm insane, please throw these away and never think of us again.

We are here to help you fight,

Caroline

Rory read it over again before he set the note down, his thoughts racing.

This all seemed like a grim joke.

What was in the vial? Poison?

Tired of waiting for what?

What is a wisp?

You're not alone.

The words swam in his head, and he swung from indignant to hopeful. He felt a deep longing for it all to be true building inside him. *Just drink this purple liquid, and all your problems will disappear. Riiight.* The more he thought it over, the more absurd the offer sounded, like some fairy tale, and those had dark endings.

"I'm not playing your game," he said, picking up the smooth stone—the "keystone," he guessed. A key to what? Etched into it was a deep groove flowing in a single smooth arch that wrapped around, nearly completing the circle. *Anyone could do*

89

that, given enough time with a chisel. But as he ran his thumb over it, he doubted his assessment. It looked flawless, beautiful. No rough edges, no cracks. It was as though someone scooped the stone out.

He set it back down and picked up the vial again, watching the fluid shift shades. Sneaks meowed, pawing at his leg to get at the shimmering light.

"Sorry, Sneaks. This, whatever it is, is going into the dumpster. I'm not ending up in the hospital tonight."

Chapter 10: Education Day

Saturday, April 14th, 08:30

Hill Hospital Auditorium

Rory arrived early, and the auditorium stood nearly empty. Head down, he climbed the stairs to the empty back row. He waved at a few nurses getting settled in the first few rows. Behind the raised stage and podium were the words *Welcome PICU RNs* projected on a white screen. Sitting uncomfortably in the tiny chair, he shifted and stretched. He'd slept badly, with Caroline's weird letter playing over and over in his head. *Let's get this over with.*

As more voices filled the hall, Rory pulled out his phone and skimmed the headlines.

Wild Goat Named Voldemort Chases Boy Up Tree.

Hotel Replaces Bible with Fifty Shades of Grey.

Tupac's Hologram Gets Twitter Account.

Shakira Attacked by Sea Lion.

Rory stopped at the next one. *Oregon Senator Gretta Grady Declares Nurses "Only Play Cards" at Work.* The article's picture showed a grandstanding mid-fifties woman in a red suit speaking outside a courthouse with a mask of outrage.

"You gotta be kidding me," Rory muttered.

"Drink." A cup of coffee appeared between his face and his phone. He looked up and saw Megan. "We got eight hours of this." She stopped and peered at his bruised cheek. "Jeez, Rambo. What happened?"

"There really isn't—"

"Speak," she said, thrusting the cup at him again.

He accepted the cup and breathed in the beautiful smell.

"Thanks. I needed this."

Megan groaned as she lowered herself into the chair beside him, supporting her pregnant belly with a hand. "Cruel and unusual punishment, these chairs." She dropped the last couple of inches, sighing in relief as she sat. "There we go. Now, let's hear it."

To her credit, Megan didn't laugh when Rory described the events of the previous day, adding in the occasional "ohs" or "mhm" where appropriate and wincing sympathetically when he described getting punched by the small woman. He left out the part about the note and glowing vial, though. The story was strange enough.

"Ugh, and after that awful night, too." She grimaced. "You doing okay? You've had record-breaking bad luck recently."

Rory swallowed down the pressure in his chest. "Yeah, just . . . you know . . . processing."

"It's a lot to process. It's so much, Rory," Megan said. She reached over and rubbed his shoulder, and Rory was thankful to have her there. In two quick years, Megan had become what Rory imagined a sister was like: caring, funny, and unafraid to tell him how he'd messed up. "I've been there. It's rough. And I'm here if—"

"I'm alright, Meg," Rory cut in, sounding curter than he wished. She drew back her hand and gave him an appraising look. Rory took a breath and soothed his tone. "Just . . . getting ready for the next patient. You know me. I'll be good."

Megan looked worried. "You sound like Bell."

"Well, yeah," he said. "She knows what she's doing. Hey, speaking of which." Rory happily transitioned topics by grabbing his phone, hoping Megan would take the bait. "Did you see this?" He held up the "lazy nurses" article.

Megan regarded him sadly, but instead of pushing, she squinted at the screen, mumbling the headline as she read. Rory felt his shoulders loosen, relieved not to talk about Octavia.

"CARDS AT WORK!" Megan scoffed. "Oh, so apparently, the patients save themselves. Amazing! It's a freaking miracle."

"This lady does not know what she's talking about."

"Nope," Megan said, stewing. "Sitting around, please. I'd like to see her work six straight night shifts and still get everyone, with lunches, to school on time. Pshh, I wouldn't wish it on any parent to see how *little* we sit around."

Megan pointed to the front row where Katherine sat front and center, notebook out, chatting with Antoni, a dayshift nurse. She'd already filled a full page of notes despite the presentation not having started. This didn't surprise Rory; no one knew policies and procedures like her. Katherine was a living safety manual.

"And then you look at what Katherine's going through right now," Megan said. "That woman could chew lead and spit out nails."

"What's going on?"

"Rodger got deployed," Megan whispered.

Her husband? Oh.

"Katherine is working full-time nights and then goes home to wrangle three boys during the day. She's a damn saint. And must be exhausted."

"Geez. I didn't know," Rory said.

"Don't tell her I told you, okay? You know. She's private."

Rory nodded, unsure of what to say. He wondered how he might get Katherine an extra break or two when they worked together next.

As more nurses trickled into the auditorium, Rory glanced at the clock again—*08:37. Starting late again.*

"Hey," Megan said. He turned and found her studying him. "You're only supposed to look this worn down after a newborn. What's going on?"

"Neighbors started partying early this morning," Rory lied. Or rather, it was a half-truth. The music had been loud, but he was long since awake—the nightmares had returned. The newest iterations featured Octavia as a vengeful zombie shrieking, "Aren't you angry enough?" from Caroline's letter over and over. But Bell was right. It was time to move on. He wouldn't do anyone any good moping around. *On to the next patient.* The thought made Rory sink into his tiny chair.

"You know, the house down the street from us is going on the market soon." Megan wagged her eyebrows. "We could be neighbors."

"That would be amazing, but I don't have that kind of money. Plus, I know you're just angling for free babysitting."

"Yeah." She laughed. "And, you know, friendship. It'd be good to have you around more. Skyla loves you. Oh, by the way, ever since you babysat the other week, she's been talking non-stop about black holes. She even asked Owen how the universe started. The poor guy wasn't ready for that one. What did you watch with her?"

"Cosmos, with our good friend Carl Sagan," Rory said. "She asked if stars had babies, so I thought we should just jump right in."

"She's six," Megan said.

"She loved it! You might have an astronaut on your hands."

"Fair point." Megan considered. "I'll pick up supplies, and we can try to build a rocket with her tomorrow. Could be fun."

"That right there is why you and Owen are wonderful parents. You try. You—" Rory fumbled with what to add. *I wish I had parents like that,* felt like too much, too exposed, so he went with, "Your kids . . . they are lucky to have you."

Megan's cheeks reddened, and she dabbed her eyes with her sleeve. "Don't make me cry, you jerk. I'm very hormonal right now."

Rory grinned. He meant every word.

"You'd think they'd know to start on time with a bunch of nurses." Megan clicked her tongue and reached into her bag, pulling out a *People* magazine. "At least it lets me catch up on my reading."

Rory pointed to the headline: *Hot and Not! Summer Beach Bodies.* "I don't think this counts as reading."

Megan flipped through the pages. "So what? I love it. Now leave me alone." She smiled.

Rory chuckled and let his mind wander. In the quiet din of the auditorium, he daydreamed about Yellowstone and traveling with Patrick. But he remembered yesterday's conversation and frowned, chewing his cheek. His mood soured, and images of zombie Octavia reappeared, saying, "I know you feel lost and angry."

Rory shook his head to clear his thoughts and took a sip of his coffee. *On to the next . . .*

Distracting himself, he peered over Megan's shoulder and saw a full-page picture of a regal man in a striped suit waving from the stairs of a private jet. He commanded the cameras with his smile. A politician? Behind him, an awkward, red-haired girl wearing a hoodie and big sunglasses covered her face with her hand. A daughter, perhaps? Rory peered a little closer. Maybe it was the print, but her skin was pale and blotchy. And she couldn't have been over fifty kilos soaking wet, way underweight for her height. *Sick, I'd bet. And trying to hide it?*

"Who are they?" Rory asked.

"Seriously?" Megan gaped at him.

"Uhm." Rory's face flushed. "Should I know?"

"Dr. Kenneth Connell? *The* Dr. Connell?"

Rory shook his head.

"You live under a rock," Megan said, shifting to face him. "He's only the single most attractive widower on the planet. Super-eligible."

A snort escaped him. "Sad, hot, rich guy. I know this one . . . Is he Batman?"

Megan shot him a flat look, then pointed at the picture. "Kenneth Connell is the crown prince of bio-tech." Her fingers moved to the logo on the side of the jet: two italicized, orange letters—an interlocking D and C.

Rory knew the symbol well. "Wait. Doran Corp Pharma?"

"Yep. One of his company's many divisions."

"They supply, like, half our medications."

"Exactly," Megan said. "And you had to have heard of the Evergreen Society?"

Rory nodded. "The think tank, yeah." It was hard not to know about the Evergreen Society with all their commercials. Smiling, multiethnic friends shaking hands, with voiceovers talking about a bright future for all. The ads showed everything from electric semi-trucks to synthetic chlorophyll to cybernetic limbs. It looked like science fiction. Rory doubted he'd ever see their world come true—not with shareholders to appease.

"Well, he started that, too." Megan shrugged. "And I heard from a flight attendant friend he's seen Dr. Connell's private jet all over the country. I think he flies around recruiting." She grinned. "Mmm. What I won't give for a personal invitation from him." She wagged her eyebrows.

Rory studied the picture. Ken looked comfortable, polished. It made him uneasy.

"Anyway." Megan waved her hand. "He got his start working somewhere top secret, which he never talks about. I think it was genetics and modifying fetus genomes, but Addy, you know her—over in Adult T.I.C.U.—she showed me this interview once where someone caught him on tape talking about his facility blowing up. It almost kills him, but he survives and has one of those near-death epiphanies. So he starts his own pharmaceutical research company, but bad luck comes again when his wife dies a few months later from a mysterious heart defect."

"Yikes," Rory said, shaking his head.

Megan continued, "Yeah, I know. A bunch of the blogs I read think his entire company, all of it, is just him trying to figure out what happened to her. I, for one, think it's pretty romantic."

"Who's the girl with him?"

Megan looked at the picture. "His daughter. I heard from a friend over at Boston Children's that they see the Connell limousine outside the clinics every Monday morning, early, before shift change, I guess."

"Telling me this violates HIPAA."

"That's why I didn't say who my friend was."

Rory chuckled. "So she's pretty sick then, needing that many appointments." He studied the picture again. *Something doesn't fit here.* "This guy employs an army of doctors and researchers, and he still needs to take his daughter in for check-ups? That's interesting, right?"

Megan considered, then nodded. "I suppose. Boston's got a great cardiac team." She began flipping through her magazine again. "I went to school with a couple of them."

"Cardiac? Huh." Rory felt something there, but couldn't place it.

Rory heard some throat-clearing from on stage, and they looked up. Bell had taken the podium and was frowning, rarely a good sign. She wore a simple pink blouse with pants instead of scrubs and her aura of command. "Listen up now." The auditorium went quiet. "Management isn't making it in."

A collective groan came from the audience and a few chuckles.

"I know, I know." Bell held up her hands, but even she couldn't control the murmurs that followed.

"Of course they aren't!" Megan shouted. "This is only for the grunts."

A ripple of laughter washed through the audience, and even Bell smiled.

"Now, now." Bell said. "Today will be challenging, but we embrace challenges daily. Today, we get better, so tomorrow we do better. Let's keep our groans to a minimum and keep our patients first." She scanned the audience, watching for any dissent. None came.

With a nod, Bell continued, "Thank you all for being here. I promise to make sure management understands our . . . disappointment."

Rory shook his head. *Ridiculous.*

"Now," Bell continued, "the consolation is they are feeding us. Coffee and donuts are outside now, and lunch comes later."

Murmurs of approval followed.

"Hearts and minds," Rory whispered to Megan.

Megan shrugged. "If it's dry-ass turkey sandwiches again, I'll riot. I'll do it. You'll see my pregnant ass flipping tables."

Rory chuckled as Bell went on. "We have several presenters this morning. Dr. Magus will be in later to talk about a new trial he's launching and how it will affect our unit flow. Occupational Health is here to go over some safety data, and we'll have a couple of announcements before our first break. We have stations set up in the unit downstairs for the breakout sessions afterward. Please, everyone, make sure you go to every station and get checked off. It's the only way you'll get credit for today." She swept a challenging eye over the audience. "I don't want to take anyone off the schedule because they skipped a signature, understood?"

The crowd nodded, and Bell seemed satisfied. "Alright. Please welcome Samuel from Occupational Health."

A fit young man in a purple dress shirt bounded onto the stage to scattered applause.

"Good morning!" Samuel's voice boomed over the speakers.

Rory winced and took a deep gulp of coffee.

"Uh oh," Megan said. "He's perky."

"I'm glad to see so many smiles out so early!" Samuel said, showing off a wide grin. "My name is Sam, and I'm an analyst from O.H. I have a fantastic presentation for you all today. I hope you'll all leave here today with at least three actionable takeaways." He picked up a remote, and a slide appeared on the screen. *Occupational Health: Q1 Injury Reports.*

"Shoot me now," Megan said.

"Quiet, here comes the pie chart!" Rory feigned excitement.

The screen flashed, and a pie chart appeared with over twenty colored slices and an unintelligible legend. Rory squinted, trying to read the tiny type, and saw many in the crowd leaning forward, too.

"Tough to read, I know," Sam said, "but don't you worry. I'll break down each section."

The audience slumped back in their chairs.

Sam didn't seem to notice. "Can anyone tell me the leading cause of health-care-related injuries for nurses?"

Katherine's eager hand shot up.

Sam pointed at her. "Yes!"

Katherine straightened. "Needle sticks."

"Absolutely right!" Sam used a laser pointer to circle the largest blue slice of the pie. Then his pointer dropped to the next largest. "Followed by back injuries. Other injuries. And patient-related incidents."

"That's a nice way of saying getting bitten," Megan whispered.

Rory raised a hand.

"Yes, at the back," Sam said.

"What about when a patient attacks the nurse with a needle?" Rory said.

Megan snorted next to him.

"Oh . . . well, that could be, uh . . ." Sam started.

Katherine raised her hand, and Sam pointed at her. "Or when your patient's family brings in their heroin needles secretly and leaves them in the patient's bed? And the nurse gets stuck?"

Sam studied his graph. "Umm, that's a new . . . well—"

Sitting next to Katherine, Antoni raised his hand. The well-muscled man had a tower of candy wrappers stacked on his desk. Rory couldn't fathom how someone could eat so much candy and be so fit. It wasn't fair.

Sam waved halfheartedly at him. "Go ahead."

"What about when a dad brings his new wife in without telling his ex-wife, who's already there, and the nurse gets hit with a laptop because the ex-wife can't aim?" Laughter rippled through the audience as they all leaned forward.

"Seriously?" Sam looked stunned.

"I have the scar to prove it." Antoni started lifting his shirt, but a blushing Katherine stopped him. Megan booed, causing whoops of laughter as Antoni mocked outrage with a mischievous grin. Only after Bell rose to give "the look" did the audience settle back down. But as the silence returned, Rory felt a question burning. He raised his hand again.

"We need to move on," Sam said.

"Can you tell us where those all fit in your graph?"

Sam swallowed, and the microphone amplified the gulp. "Uh." He turned and studied the chart. "Well . . . perhaps in other injuries?"

Rory scowled, feeling a heat rise in him. *Other injuries?* He wanted better than that. He raised his hand again, but Megan tugged on his sleeve, whispering. "Easy. Don't scare the poor guy."

"Someone should know what the data means—for us," Rory grumbled, lowering his hand. "Sane people puke seeing what we've normalized."

Megan sighed. "You're not wrong, okay?" She sagged back in her chair and spread her legs, giving her swollen belly more room. "But don't take your frustration out on poor Sam, yeah? He's just a messenger."

Sam blinked at the room. "Questions?" When no hands went up, he rushed forward. "Awesome! Let's move on to data processing."

Rory tuned him out, annoyed. He wondered if he should say something, write something to counter the senator, and began crafting a snarky opening sentence in his mind, though he didn't get far. *Why bother? Even if I do, no one outside this room is going to care.*

Sam had moved on to intervention strategies when a door behind them at the back of the auditorium opened, and a blonde woman rushed in, finding a seat in the back row, six chairs from Rory. With a flushed face, she searched the audience. A pair of thin-rimmed glasses perched on her nose as a collared red blouse peeked out from beneath her wrinkled white physician's coat. *The resident from Octavia's code.*

She must have felt him staring and turned to give Rory a small smile of recognition before checking her watch and unzipping her planner. Rory gazed at several glittering silver bands on her fingers and thumbs as she took notes.

"Quit gawking," Megan nudged him.

Rory's eyes snapped back toward Sam, who circled a two-tone bar graph on the screen.

Megan rolled her eyes. "Men." She leaned forward, looked at the newcomer, and sat back with a satisfied grunt. "She is cute, though."

No, she is beautiful.

Rory spent the next half hour paying little attention to proper needle-handling techniques. He kept stealing side glances at the woman. *A new resident?* He couldn't make out the name or credentials on her jacket. *Which service?*

She looked over at him again, and he glanced.

Megan jammed him with her elbow.

Rory blinked and focused on the projection, pretending to take notes. The slide changed to a picture of a sad-looking nurse sitting on a stool staring out a window. Several monitors and an empty patient room surrounded her. Rory suddenly felt hot.

"I'll finish up today talking about a new epidemic among healthcare workers," Sam said somberly. "Can you guess what it is?" Before anyone could raise their hands, he brought his palms together. "Burnout. Burnout is the leading mental health issue in front-line staff. Its symptoms are no laughing matter." Sam held up four fingers, counting them down. "Lateness, anger, distraction, and maybe worst of all, medication errors. Research shows you are twice as likely to make a medication error when you are displaying even one of these symptoms and further concludes that chronic exposure to stressful medical situations and inadequate staffing has seen a spike in burnout-related departures nationwide and is contributing to a looming nursing shortage."

"This is nothing new," Rory whispered to Megan. "This is—"

Megan pressed a finger to her lips, and it was only then that Rory saw how still the audience was.

Sam continued, "Newer studies are continuing to research burnout. There isn't enough data to create formal intervention strategies. Yet. With that said, we at Occupational Health want to remind everyone to take care of themselves outside of work. Sunshine, exercise, yoga—who here does yoga?" A few nurses near the front raised their hands.

Rory rolled his eyes.

"Me too! That's great! And please, take advantage of some offered health programs. Counseling is available."

What a waste of time. Rory bit his lip, knowing if he had said that aloud, Megan would have started in on him again. He felt her watching him and kept his expression pensive, adding a somber nod for effect.

"Well, that's my presentation," Sam concluded. "But on a personal note, I just want you all to know that I think what you all do here is incredible. Thank you." The nurses applauded as he left the stage.

Rory took another sip of his now cold coffee and glanced over at Megan, who was still watching him with narrowed eyes. "What?" he said.

"I'm just looking to see if any of that sank in."

He had to give her something. "The job is hard, but it has to be done." Rory shrugged. "He said himself there isn't enough data."

She jabbed him with her finger. "Doesn't mean it isn't true."

"Ow." Rory rubbed his shoulder.

"Excuse me."

Rory turned to see the mystery resident leaning toward him. "I didn't catch the first part. Anything pressing?"

"Don't worry," he whispered back. "You can catch everything again in three months. They add a couple of graphs and change the colors, but it's the same thing: *This job is hard. Keep going. Do yoga.*"

She looked at him for a beat, and then, to his great surprise, her face blossomed into a dazzling smile. Rory forgot to breathe.

Beep-beep! The woman sighed, fumbled for her jacket pocket, and produced a pager, reading and silencing it as several nurses turned and looked. She cringed and gave a small wave. "Sorry."

"Hey, would you mind silencing that, please?" Rory pointed at the empty stage. "Some of us are trying to learn."

She rolled her eyes, but she was still smiling. "Well then, you'd better pay attention." She zipped up her planner and made her way down the steps toward the stage.

"Could you be more obvious?" Megan whispered.

Rory scowled playfully and watched the resident go.

On stage, Bell took the microphone. "Next, we have Dr. Magus and—"

The resident waved at Bell and tapped her chest.

Bell stopped. "Oh. Well, Dr. Magus isn't . . . here yet." The audience laughed, and many shook their heads. "In the meantime, we'll have—"

"Khloe Seeker," the woman whispered off the microphone.

"Dr. Khloe Seeker." Bell shrugged.

Rory leaned forward in his seat as Khloe took the podium.

"Hello, hi. I'm Khloe Seeker. Doctor Seeker . . . Khloe . . ." she trailed off, fidgeting with the button on her coat. She looked up, steadying herself. "I'm a new resident here at Hill. Dr. Magus would like me to convey his apologies for being late and that he'll be here . . . uh, soon."

Rory knew this tune; they all did. Many of Magus's white-coated flock had sung it before. One joy of working the night shift was seeing the surgical attending and their residents come in early for rounds. The attending was always in front, talking loudly as the residents hurried behind, scribbling notes as they tried to keep up. Among the nurses, it earned the residents the collective nickname of ducklings.

"Where are you from?" Megan called out. She winked at Rory afterward.

"Me? Oh, across the country," Khloe said. "I went to med school at—"

The doors at the front of the room burst open, and Dr. Sigmund Magus strolled into the room with his phone to his ear. The top button on his crisp blue shirt was undone—a tuft of white hair billowed out, and Rory wondered if his silver suit was worth more than he had in savings.

Patients and researchers traveled from all over the world to see him, and he had the burgeoning ego to prove it. Rory had witnessed more than one resident brought to tears during one of his self-aggrandizing interrogations. Once, a resident made an honest error when he mislabeled a medication order. Luckily for the patient, Saint Katherine caught the mistake before it caused harm. But Magus screamed at the poor guy for thirty minutes. Rory heard the resident had transferred the following day.

The older staff always warned the new nurses about the Napoleon of Cancer. It was unofficially part of unit orientation now, and Rory once heard from a surgical staffer that Magus needed a custom stool to get him high enough in the OR. And that he would refuse to operate if Mozart wasn't blasting in his theater. But there was a reason everyone put up with him. Magus was the best.

". . . presentation. Yes. No. I'll call you back." Dr. Magus pocketed his phone and walked over to the podium. "Ah, Khloe, thank you for introducing me." He moved in front of her. She awkwardly stepped aside, tripping a bit, and retreated to an empty seat in the front row. He hit the audience with a manicured white smile, and Rory saw several nurses straighten.

"Ladies," Magus said, gesturing to the room. "Thank you for having me today."

Rory shook his head and spotted Antoni doing the same. Being called a lady didn't annoy him. Compared to some titles patients and their parents had called him, "lady" was respectful. What annoyed him was the chronic obliviousness.

Magus took a moment to bathe in the attention, then began. "Soon, we will open the Oates Family Cancer Center. I personally designed this facility to be the best pediatric cancer research center in the world. At long last, we will have the resources and tools to pioneer a new era of therapies and techniques that will push cancer treatments forward. To do so, Oates Children's Hospital will need to be prepared to take on additional patients, all with poor prognoses but not yet on palliative care. That will fall primarily on our incredible pediatric ICU and its talented nurses to continue to give such excellent care to our patients."

The room came alive again, shifting, groaning.

"You gotta be kidding me . . ." Rory hissed. "We're short-staffed already. More patients? We'll have to triple up assignments."

"Nope, no way." Megan crossed her arms over her belly. "If they ask me to admit while I'm running ECMO . . ."

"To accommodate this," Magus's voice rose, "we have two generous donors who'd like to remain anonymous for now, who've agreed to fund the expansion of our pediatric ICU from twenty to thirty beds. This will mean some construction in the coming months and some logistical challenges, but with some additional training, combined with your talents, we will provide the best-in-class care for children and families. I can't stress enough how incredible this opportunity is for us and thank you in advance for your assistance."

Magus stepped off the podium and waved for Khloe to follow him. She glanced up over her shoulder at the stunned audience and looked like she wanted to apologize. Magus swept by, muttering something to her, and she gave the scowling crowd another sympathetic look before standing and following out the door.

"Uh . . . what just happened?" Rory turned to Megan.

"They're asking us to do more with less. *Again*." Megan raised her voice, calling to the stage. "Are we adding staff, then? Because we can't double up the kids he's talking about, they are one-to-ones!"

The audience murmured their agreement.

Bell hustled to the podium and took the microphone. "This is the first I've heard of it, too. If management were here—"

"The senior administration approved this?" Katherine called out.

"I'm certain we'll get more information soon," Bell said, her hands raised, though that didn't seem to calm the crowd as more voices rose. Bell let them boil over for a moment, taking a deep breath.

"Listen up!" The speakers thundered. She waited a moment before she relaxed. "Spiritus boni, everyone."

The audience inhaled.

"I don't like it either," Bell said. "Once again, we're being asked, with no notice, to step in and step up for patients who need us. Scary as it is, we get the opportunity to help a lot more families find hope. That's a gift, ladies *and* gentlemen. Now, the charge nurses have a meeting coming up. We'll talk to management about staffing concerns. Good enough for now?"

For now, Rory thought.

Bell paused, leaving room for comments, but no one spoke up. "Thank you. Now, we have a scheduled break here, but before we go, I have three quick announcements. First, get your votes in for the Healing Hand Award. This is a great way to recognize superb teamwork and outstanding nursing for someone in our unit. Please vote. It closes today."

Rory nudged Megan. "It's totally you."

"That's what you said last year."

"Yeah, because you deserved it then, too."

Megan beamed and nudged Rory with her shoulder.

"Second," Bell said, gathering attention again. "Get your unconscious bias module done. No one should lose shifts over this. It takes twenty minutes—get it done. And last, while on break, please avoid Bay 1. Dr. Magus is having some sort of video shoot with a donor for the new cancer center. They don't need anyone photo-jumping. I'm looking at you, Antoni."

Antoni gasped and pouted playfully. The audience chuckled.

Photo jumping?

"You mean photo *bombing*, Bell?"

Bell peered up at Rory over her glasses. "It's jumping into someone else's photo, isn't it?" She smirked up at him. "Be back at a quarter to eleven."

Chapter 11: Acts of Courage

Saturday, April 14th, 10:35

With a little time to kill, Rory wandered down to the unit to say hi to the day-shifters. He snatched a tray of muffins and a coffee box and dropped them off in the break room, knowing how much his weary colleagues would appreciate the treats. During a busy shift, which they all were recently, snacks were all you had time for; lunch was a luxury.

He made his rounds, starting at Room 20 and working his way in a loop. He waved through the glass sliding doors at the nurses in their rooms and gave updates about the lectures to those who asked. Most folks were busy and, after a few pleasant exchanges, hurried back to their work.

Rory moved along, counting down the numbered rooms. When he reached Room 4, he skipped it, walking by quickly. There wasn't any need to go back there. Up ahead, he noticed a small crowd of well-dressed people outside Room 1, not a scrub in sight. No photo jumping. He chuckled to himself.

Rory checked the wall clock. Ten minutes still.

He was heading for the exit, thinking about more coffee, when a young girl's voice cried out from Room 1. "No! I don't want to!"

He stopped and turned back. He recognized that sound—fear.

"I said NO!" the girl shrieked.

The group of suits fidgeted and stepped back from the room.

Sounds like it's going well in there.

He replayed Bell's warning in his head, but his instincts got the better of him. Slowly, he approached, not wanting to appear too eager. One suit gave him a quizzical look as he got close, but said nothing. Rory took that as approval and stepped beside them to peer inside.

A little girl with tangled brown hair sat upright in a hospital bed, her face screwed into a deep scowl, both arms crossed tightly over her chest. He'd seen less compliance in a patient, but not by much—at least she wasn't taking swings at anyone. Eight years old, maybe nine? She wore a mint-green hospital gown and stared at the side table, covered by what appeared to be a random grab bag from the supply room.

Rory scanned the adults in the room, all standing back from the bed, wide-eyed. It was clear who was running this show. A portly man whose red face nearly matched his sweater stood at the end of the bed, holding a camera with tight-pressed lips. Everyone else stood behind him, at the back of the room, except the girl and a striking actor in blue scrubs beside her. Stiff with both eyes closed, the actor white-knuckled his stethoscope with both hands. He turned away, fuming, and pulled out his cell phone. Even mad, he was magazine-handsome.

"No. No," the director said, waving his camera. He spoke with a slight accent. French? Italian? Rory couldn't quite place it, and he suddenly felt unwelcome. "Don't call your manager. I will fix this."

"This is silly," the actor said, holding his phone up to his ear. "It's one line, Jerry! One. We could have the dog do it, voice it over. Or a puppet. I don't care because it's one line that they'll probably cut because it's a local commercial." He scowled at the little girl. She stuck out her tongue. He gasped, outraged, and stormed out, pushing between two suits on his way out. The girl tried to hide her smile.

"Tracy," a stern voice came from the audience. A hunched, graying man rose from a chair, grabbed his gold-tipped cane, and eased himself over to the bed. "That's not very respectful."

Tracy's tucked her chin, appearing cute and cowed. "Sorry, Grandpa."

"Go get him, please," the director said, waving a hand after the actor. One of the camera team broke off and dipped into the crowd. "We just need to say, for the fifteenth time, that there are no pokes. No stabs, no sharps. Okay. Okay? Good. Tracy"—he pointed at the girl on the bed, staring intently at her now like he was charming a snake—"remember, you are tired. You are healing, yes? Your nurse comes over, and you say—"

"No!" Tracy shouted. "I want to go home."

Home. The scar on the back of Rory's neck tingled—a side effect of a severed nerve, they told him. Dusty, bittersweet memories came, flashing moments of his time as a patient. Susie's books, wheelchair parades, asking to go home, his old home. He did that a lot back then. Home was supposed to be safe.

The director's head dropped. "Can someone please . . ." He waved a hand at her.

The grandfather sat on the side of the bed. "No pokes, Tracy. We're all done with those, remember? And if you smile for the camera, how about we go to the stables afterward? I think you'll have earned it."

Tracy watched him for a moment; then her entire face scrunched up. "I don't want to do this anymore."

"You don't want to be on TV?" the old man asked.

Tracy's expression softened, and she peered at the supplies piled on the table. "I don't want a shot."

"Sweetheart." The old man sighed. "It's okay. There aren't any needles. This is all pretend. For the commercial."

"I don't want to anymore, Grandpa!" Tears welled in her eyes.

"Please, Tracy," the director pleaded. "No needles, you see?" The director walked over and shuffled the supplies on the side table. "There aren't even any in the room."

That wasn't true. Rory spotted two different gauge IV catheters from where he was standing. And how was no one seeing Tracy was past her breaking point? She needed a reset before any more negotiations. Who was in charge of this farce? He inched forward just enough to see the rest of the room. Dr. Magus stood in the corner, finger stuffed in his ear as he whispered earnestly on the phone. Two other white-haired men whispered just inside the door, neither paying attention to the terrified little girl in front of them. Rory massaged the bridge of his nose, trying to relieve his growing headache.

You're off duty, Rory told himself. Just head on back. He glanced down the hallway. They'll be starting again soon.

"You've done this all before, sweetie," the grandfather said. "Just smile, say the line, and we go."

"NO!" Tracy shrieked, forcing the suits to cover their phones.

"Can you be a big girl?"

Tracy's chin quivered as fat tears rolled down her cheeks.

Here comes the meltdown.

The girl then turned and sobbed into her pillow. And so they'd lost her. Watching her turn over, Rory suddenly spotted an unmistakable pale line running down the back of her neck—a surgical scar, just like his.

A chill ran down his arms and legs. He acutely understood Tracy's resistance now. This wasn't about today. She'd passed her breaking point a long, long time ago. If her chemo journey was anything like his, her treatments never waited for her to be ready. Tracy's tears weren't about this needle; they were about all the needles she screamed "NO" to, but they happened anyway. Saying no was the only piece she could control. But the adults weren't seeing that. If they did, they'd be respecting her hard-earned fear, giving her space. She and they needed help, and Rory was the only one here who spoke Tracy's dialect. I guess the lecture will wait.

"Excuse me," Rory whispered and worked his way through the huddle.

The grandfather continued negotiations, but the conversation ended when Tracy ripped the blankets up over her head. His shoulders slumped, and he looked around the room for help. Rory thought that was as good a cue as any.

"Maybe she needs a break," Rory said, his voice booming in the small room.

Everyone turned, and he felt their collective eyes bear down on him.

The director rolled his eyes. "This is a closed set."

Rory took a breath. He knew pushing Tracy now could cause harm. And besides, this was his turf. "I know, and I'm sorry, but in my professional opinion, if you keep pushing, you'll never get anything done. She needs a moment."

The director clicked his tongue and threw up his arms, looking around for support. Luckily, Magus was still on the phone. Rory approached the grandfather.

"Hello, sir. My name is Rory Nash. I'm a nurse here."

"Sir!" The director stepped forward. "We are on a schedule here. We can't—"

"Hold on, now," the grandfather said, the older man's bright eyes sizing him up. "I don't know if a break will help. Tracy is so stubborn—like her mother. God rest her."

Rory took a moment to review what he'd seen. "Has Tracy been having nightmares leading up to the shoot?"

The grandfather's eyebrows shot up. "Now, how could you know that?"

"I'm a survivor too, sir. This place"—he waved a hand at the room—"it can be triggering."

The old man frowned a moment, then nodded. "Ah, I see." He

sighed, and Rory heard the fatigue.

"Can I talk with her, sir?" Rory pressed. "Alone, if possible. I think I know how to help. I had my fair share of hospitals growing up, too." Rory realized everyone was staring at him. He cleared his throat and looked around. "There are, uh . . . muffins and coffee upstairs."

The suits all looked to the grandfather, and Rory wondered whom he'd been talking to.

Suddenly, Khloe stepped into the light from the shadowy corner near Magus. She looked even lovelier up close, sharp-eyed, on the verge of a retort. Rory's confidence wavered. Calm. He straightened and met her eyes, quickly regaining composure. He was on the job now.

"I can show everyone the way upstairs," she said, casting a sideways glance at Rory. "Let's give our brave girl a moment." He gave her a nod of thanks.

A red flush crept up the director's neck. "This is ridiculous. He won't—"

"Very well," the grandfather said, addressing the director. "A break now." He reached out and touched Tracy's foot over the blanket, but she jerked it away. He turned to Rory. "A cup of tea sounds good."

"How about a tour of the new MRI suite with your tea?" Khloe said, smiling warmly.

"Ah, yes. I've been curious to see this wonderful machine."

Khloe nodded. "Dr. Magus will be delighted."

"Hm?" Dr. Magus lowered his phone and saw the man looking at him. "Oh, yes, my new MRI. State-of-the-art. Eight Tesla, experimental no more. It is the strongest ever made. It will act as my theater with built-in diagnostics and imaging. Absolutely beautiful." Dr. Magus continued to talk as he led the procession down the hall.

The director muttered something about "my valuable time" to Rory on his way out.

At the door, the grandfather looked at Rory, then over at Tracy. "I thought this would help show her how far she's come by coming back here. It had been so long, but . . ." he shook his head. "She said she wanted to be on TV."

Rory felt for the guy. He had good intent.

"My name is Sidney," the man said, extending his hand to Rory.

Rory took it with a firm grip. "Rory Nash. It's nice to meet you, sir. Enjoy your tea."

"I will." Sidney leaned in close. "But I'd prefer a good scotch." He turned back toward the bed. "Tracy, I'm stepping out for a minute. Mr. Nash here is a nurse, and my friend. He's going to sit with you."

"Go away!" Tracy shouted back from under her blanket, followed by a fresh, snotty sob.

Sidney raised an eyebrow at Rory as though to ask him if he was ready for this. When Rory didn't back down, he patted him on the arm and left with Khloe behind him. They locked eyes as she passed, and she whispered, "Good luck." He watched her white coat swish out the door.

Focus. He had a job to do.

With the room finally quiet, Rory stepped forward and sat at the end of the bed. He didn't reach out, didn't say anything; he just waited patiently as Tracy's sobs slowly faded. Outside, the clouds drifted by—lazy white puffs set against the vast blue sky, crowning the Portland cityscape. When he heard a pair of wet sniffs, he took his cue.

"I used to dread the hospital, too." Rory picked through the pile of supplies, nudging aside caps and spikes and wondering why someone grabbed a urinary catheter.

Another sniff came before Tracy peered out from beneath her blanket at the empty room. "Where's Grandpa?"

"He went to get some tea. I told him I would wait with you." Rory picked up a pre-filled syringe full of saline. It was an amazing tool. Irrigation, flush, and squirt gun all in one. "You know what I hated the most when I was getting my chemo? How the saline tastes. Even through my chest port, I could still taste the saltiness."

Tracy lowered the blanket. Her brown eyes were puffy and suspicious. "It's gross."

"Did you use to get scared of back pokes, too?"

"The lumbar punctures?" she said, sitting up a bit more.

Rory nodded. "Yeah, that's the name."

Tracy wiped her eyes. "They were okay. I got to push my own sleepy medicine and see how long I could count."

The door slid open, and Khloe reappeared, holding two cups of coffee. She said nothing and stepped off to the side. Rory smiled at her, and to his surprise, she smiled back creating questions out of thin air.

Focus.

Rory turned back. "Pushing your own medicine. That's pretty brave." He slid a little closer to Tracy and leaned in. "What number did you count to?"

She dropped the blanket into her lap. "Twelve. And I didn't even cheat by counting fast."

"Twelve?" Rory put both hands on his head, feigning amazement. Though, to Tracy's credit, twelve was impressive. "I only ever made it to ten!"

Tracy giggled, and Rory offered her a tissue.

Turning his head, he pointed to the pale line on the back of his head. "I have a scar, too. I called my tumor 'Freeloader.' Does

116

yours have a name?"

"Mr. Lame," Tracy said.

Rory tossed his head back and belly laughed. Tracy beamed, pulling down the front of her gown to point at the scar on her chest. "I had my button here, but they took that out after Mr. Lame went away. I came in every week for my infusion, then Grandpa took me out for ice cream."

"Every week! You might be the bravest kid I know. Seriously. Mr. Lame sounds tough."

"He was, but I was tougher."

"That's right!" Rory offered a high-five, which Tracy readily slapped.

Tracy's eyes went over to Khloe, and she squeezed her blanket. "I don't want to do the commercial."

"Hey," Rory said, gathering Tracy's attention. "I need someone super brave to help me with something."

"That's me!" Tracy said, throwing a hand in the air. "I'm super brave."

She's as ready as she'll ever be. Rory switched gears. "Can you show me?" He slowly reached over to the side table, but as he did, Tracy's eyes narrowed, and she shrank away.

"Is it this one?" Rory grabbed the IV catheter packages, and Tracy drew her blanket up protectively. He opened the package quickly, pressing the small button on the catheter's side. Click. The spring fired, and the needle retracted back safely into the plastic sheath, and he held out the remaining plastic straw connected with its yellow winged hub.

"See? No more needle." Rory touched the plastic to his skin, and it bent painlessly.

Tracy didn't look convinced, but neither did she withdraw. Progress.

117

"Can you be super-duper brave by letting me tape this to your arm? No needles, just tape. After that, you get to be a star."

Tracy's eyes danced back and forth between the catheter and her arm, and Rory watched her wrestle with her fear. He stayed calm and tore off a small piece of tape, then idly bounced the plastic catheter against his arm.

Tracy watched the catheter. "It won't hurt?"

"Nope, I promise. I'd tell you if it would," Rory said.

Tracy swallowed and then cautiously offered her arm. Rory taped the catheter in place in one smooth motion. "There, done. Thank you for being so brave!"

Tracy leaned back and inspected the tape. "It didn't hurt."

"See? I promised," Rory said. "Now, anyone brave enough to beat Mr. Lame can definitely say one line, right? You've already done the hardest part."

Tracy thought for a moment, then nodded. "I can try."

"Do you remember your line?"

"Ya. I say, 'Good morning.' I'm feeling much better."

Rory paused, waiting for her to say the rest. When she didn't, he glanced over at Khloe, who cringed and nodded her head.

Ok . . . ay. "Sounds to me like you're ready."

"Ya! Ready! Then I get to go see my horse, Phoebe." Tracy said then her eyes flashed to something behind him.

Rory turned to see Sidney standing with a steaming cup in hand. Behind him stood the director and nurse-model.

"The tour was rather droll, so I thought we might try with a smaller crowd." He gestured to Tracy, "Things are going well, I see."

"I think Tracy is ready for her close-up." He turned back to her and winked. Tracy giggled.

118

"Where is Dr. Magus?" Khloe asked.

"Off puffing his feathers for the rest of the board, I imagine," Sidney said.

Khloe laughed, but quickly covered her mouth. "Sorry, Mr. Oates."

Sidney chuckled. "No need, Dr. Seeker. It's the truth."

Mister Oates? Rory's chest seized, and he turned back to the mysterious elderly man. The Oates family was the wealthiest in the state, maybe in the region, and had their name plastered all over the hospital. *Easy, Rory,* he told himself. *They're the same as any other family . . . sorta.*

The actor stormed back in, the director on his heels, both still in a huff.

"Before she changes her mind, please," the actor said, taking his place beside the bed.

Rory rose, taking his cue to leave, and headed for the exit. Sidney put up his hand as he made for the door.

"Thank you. That was sweet of you to help her."

"Tracy did all the work, sir," Rory said.

"Modest, too. Very good." Sidney clapped Rory on the arm again and turned back to the production.

"Okay, Tracy," the director said, aiming the camera at her. "You are in recovery. But a fighter! But tired—"

Rory slipped out of the room, down the hall, and spotted the clock: 10:46. He was late.

"Hey!"

Rory stopped and turned.

Khloe caught up with the two cups still in hand. "If Samuel was any indication, you'll need this." She offered him a cup.

"That's not for your boss?" Rory asked.

"Magus doesn't drink coffee. His ego fuels him."

He laughed and accepted the drink. "Thanks."

"I've seen you in the ICU," Khloe said.

"Yeah, they haven't fired me yet."

She smiled, then glanced back at Room 1. "I have to go, but I wanted to ask . . . That was pretty gutsy. Why'd you help?"

"When no one speaks your language, it's . . . isolating." Rory shrugged, nodding at the room. "I spoke hers, and . . . well, I don't think anyone should go it alone."

"Well, you saved the day. That was getting ugly." She considered him a moment, then added, "You're very good at *that*."

Rory grinned. "Thanks. I've had outstanding teachers." He glanced down at her white jacket. Stitched in red thread above her chest pocket, it read: Khloe Seeker, M.D. Pediatric Hemato-Oncology. *Seeker*, Rory thought. *What a beautiful name.*

"Hey, uh . . ." Khloe checked over her shoulder. "Would you want to go get something to eat sometime? I'd love to hear your story. You don't see many guys doing what you do, and I need a break from cafeteria food."

Is she asking me out? The thought tripped him. *Look at her. She's gorgeous. And me? I'm not . . . I can't . . .*

"You okay?" Khloe said. "Looks like I lost you there for a second."

Rory blinked. "Uh, I'm pretty busy right now. Not that I don't want to. I just . . . timing, you know? I'm trying to figure some stuff out," he finished lamely.

Khloe sighed with a slow nod. "You and me both. Well, no worries. Just thought it might be fun." She shrugged and her deep blue eyes found his and sent a bolt of electricity through him.

Khloe tried to rouse him. "You okay?"

"Yeah, good." He quickly took a gulp of coffee.

"Right . . . looks like you need to get out more than I do." Khloe's eyes sparkled as she clicked her rings together thoughtfully. Then she stuck out her hand. "Phone, please."

"What?"

"You have a phone, right?"

Rory hesitated, but drew his phone out, unlocked it, and handed it over. Khloe tapped the screen several times before she started typing. "Don't stress, Rory. This is strictly professional. In case you have inquiries about recent literature or research."

"Of course. Professional inquiries only."

"Yep," Khloe said and handed back his phone and turned to walk back toward Room 1. Over her shoulder, she added, "Unless, of course, you get hungry."

Chapter 12: Leaving Home

Saturday, April 14th, 19:41

"Come on! Just zip!" Jane grunted, kneeling on top of her stuffed gray travel case. The zipper stuck. Again. "Stupid muffing case!" Jane wiggled, pulled, and pleaded until the clog gave, and the zipper shot down its track with a satisfying *ZIP*. Panting and sweaty, Jane slid off the bed, feeling the cold concrete beneath the grainy throw rug. Bag packed, she stopped and took in her makeshift bedroom one last time.

Grace had made this space for her when she'd arrived two years ago. In the basement, she'd strung a line and a curtain to make a wall and door, propped up a wire wardrobe that held the few suits Jane had left, and hung pictures of their childhood together beside Jane's small bed. Trips to the lake, that old rickety rollercoaster on the pier, and summer campfires. Since Jane moved in, though, she'd added pictures Grace had snapped at taekwondo class, the mountainous view from their road trip to the East Coast, and the massive ice-cream cones the four of them discovered after a lazy day at a river-side park. Every picture was a memory shared. Every picture, a vision of a life worth living.

She'd found happiness here with her sister, which made it all the harder to walk away. Since leaving with Emmett's empty dossier, she'd questioned her decision again and again, knowing Grace's reaction. She had to laugh—the Director knew her too well. The promise of the Seed, of getting back in the game, would be too much for her to refuse.

"Time to go to work," Jane said, feeling a pang of reluctance.

With both hands on the suitcase handle, Jane heaved, dragging it off the bed. It thumped down beside her, and she double-checked she had everything. She was looking under the bed when the curtain pulled open. She pressed her eyes closed. Grace wasn't supposed to be home for another couple of hours, long after Jane had left. She'd even written a lovely note to leave on her pillow.

"So," Grace said in her motherly tone, "were you planning on saying goodbye or just sneaking out again?"

"I wouldn't call it sneaking . . . exactly." On her hands and knees, Jane turned to face her twin. "More like strategic avoidance."

Grace's round cheeks stretched as she smiled sadly. Her thick black hair sat twirled on top of her head, held in place by a modest clip. Smears of reds, blues, yellows, and greens covered her face and denim overalls.

"What happened to you?" Jane laughed, standing and smoothing out her navy suit jacket. It still smelled musty.

Grace looked her up and down. "I ran the art booth at the school fair."

"They missed a spot, but . . . not many." Jane laughed.

Grace walked over to the bed and plopped down, her eyes searching the suitcase on the floor. "You promised you'd tell me before you left again. That was the only rule."

"To be clear, it was *your* rule. I signed nothing," Jane said, hoping Grace might smile. No luck. "Fine, I was . . . sneaking. But the rule was only in place so you could talk me out of leaving."

"To keep you safe, dodo. Someone has to talk some sense into you." Grace folded her arms. "You've been avoiding me." She put her hands up. "No, don't deny it. I know your weird brain. And we're going to skip the banter. Just tell me what happened."

Jane drummed her fingers against her suitcase, looking her sister over again. Grace came ready to fight. As though to confirm her hunch, she met Jane's eye and looked exactly like their mother as both her brows arched, ready.

123

Still, Jane had to try. "I don't know what you're talking about."

Grace sighed and pointed to the corner of the room. "Then what's all that?" There, on the floor, was everything from Jane's cubicle they'd let her walk out with and a stapler they hadn't. Grace stood, walked over, and lifted out Jane's belt case as though presenting a jury with irrefutable evidence.

"Oh, yeah," Jane scolded herself for not hiding it. "Well . . . I am—"

Grace sighed and pressed the tips of her index fingers into her temples. "Jane. I'm tired. I'm sticky, and my right sock is wet with what I *hope* is paint. Right now, I don't have the energy for games, or rules, or players, or any other conspiracies. I'm sorry, I don't. So, can you just tell me what happened, please?"

Jane heard it then—the end of Grace's patience. It tugged at her chest. "I quit."

Grace looked crestfallen. "No. Jane." She set the belts back in the box. "What happened?"

"I . . . got another job offer."

Grace frowned. "You mean a promotion?"

"No, it wasn't internal. It's a . . . consulting job."

"Uh, huh," Grace said, taking a step forward. "Consulting for whom?"

Jane bit her lip. "An organization."

A series of emotions flickered over Grace's face. Surprise, followed by confusion, which evolved into a tight-lipped scowl. "No. You're not going back."

"Grace!" Jane threw up her hands. "This is my chance! I—"

"No! I don't want to hear it. You almost died last time, remember? You go see Dr. Garcia twice a week because of them."

Jane had been ready for this. "Dr. Garcia told me I had to—"

"I don't care!" Grace shouted, trembling.

Jane's well-crafted point vanished before Grace's fury. Her twin never yelled.

"Don't do this to yourself again," Grace said, her eyes glistening. "You don't owe anyone anything. You did your time and brought a lot of bad people to justice. Mom and Dad are proud. I'm proud, but Jane . . . it won't bring Simon back."

Hearing their brother's name made Jane's face hot. That day had been normal—then the phone rang. Someone shot their older brother in a random case of mistaken identity. Jane was just ten years old and cried for a week. No one played like Simon. No one fought off closet monsters like him, either.

When the police fumbled their leads, young Jane took it upon herself. As others continued to weep and do nothing, she snuck out and conducted interviews. While others grieved, she found the pistol on the riverbank. And that night, while others watched Simon lowered into the ground, she'd watched the man who shot her brother escorted away in handcuffs, crying. Jane savored his tears. She'd gotten him. Just a girl and her imagination piecing together the puzzle. It was as though Lady Justice extended her hand and welcomed Jane to her team.

"This isn't about Simon, Grace," Jane said, but it wasn't entirely true. Simon was the reason she'd ended up at the Bureau and eventually on the Director's radar. "Okay, it is in a roundabout way, but this is also new. And huge! Like, as big as it gets. And I—"

Grace stopped her again, the limit of her patience reached. "You tried to kill yourself, Jane. Remember that? And if you go back, I'm afraid this time you'll succeed." Her words rang in the silence, and Jane could see the creases of worry her sister tried so hard to hide.

Grace's expression softened, and she wiped her face. "And what

125

about the kids? They love having you around. They are doing better in school, too. Please . . . just—"

A tight lump rose in Jane's throat. Without a word, she stepped forward and wrapped both her arms around her sister, squeezing her close. Grace leaned into her, and Jane absorbed her weight.

"Please," Grace whispered into her neck. "I need you here . . . You might never do the dishes, but at least you're here to cook."

Jane chuckled. "You call that cooking? You're way too nice to me."

They both laughed, holding each other close. Jane hated hurting Grace, but this time, she knew she had no choice.

"I have to know, Grace," Jane said slowly. "The Seed . . . what the Director is up to. I have to know. So I can stop it."

"But why you?" Grace whispered.

"I don't know. Maybe it's my bubbly personality."

Grace snorted and pressed her face deep into Jane's shoulder, squeezing. The simple gesture threatened to take the fight out of Jane. She heard Dr. Garcia's voice in her head. "Being vulnerable is taking our power back," and where Jane was going, she'd need all the power she could muster. So, Jane gave it a try.

"I know I haven't shared much from . . . those days. But when I left the Bureau, they took something from me I didn't know I had. My sense of . . . me. Of justice. And power and purpose. And ya, Simon too. For a while there, I knew I was one of the good guys doing good things. The money didn't hurt; the thrill was the best. And it was gone. Poof. Because of some stupid game with some big stupid secrets that little ole me wasn't allowed to know. I found out I was just a worker bee, easily replaced when I asked about touchy subjects. Turns out, it's a habit."

Grace chuckled. "I'm aware."

Jane missed Grace's laugh. "Ever since they tossed me out, I have felt this . . . this hollowness in my heart. Shame, maybe, but it feels like they ripped something out. I don't know if I can get back what they took, but I have to try."

Grace sighed, released her grip, and took a big step back. "Is the answer worth your life, though?"

Jane talked to her therapist often about that precise question, but never thought she'd ever get an answer until Emmett Torin walked into her cubicle. Sure, it could be a lie and was certainly a trap, but it was the only way Jane could even attempt to be whole again.

"I wouldn't be me if I didn't try, Grace. I love it here, I do, but there is more to this world. Some of it we can understand, some we can't. There is a line between them I want to find, and I have a hunch this *Seed* is a good place to start. I know you don't want me to go, and I wouldn't if I could help it, but this is something I have to do. That I know I can do. For me."

"That's your pride speaking."

"Probably." Jane grinned. "Call it a Kim family trait."

Grace shook her head, but Jane was relieved to see a smile shading the edge of her lips. "It's from Dad."

"I don't know. Mom hates being wrong."

"Yeah, but at least she admits it," Grace said. "Dad still denies his farts smell."

They laughed together, and for a moment, Jane felt young again. "Can we still be sisters?"

Grace wiped her eyes, streaking the red paint on her cheek. "Of course, dodo. We're twins. I'll always support you. Just . . . come back, okay?"

"I plan to," Jane said. "And you can help with that."

Grace blinked, not following.

Jane walked to the cardboard wardrobe and slid it to the side, revealing a small panel in the wall.

Grace's eyes narrowed. "When did you install that?"

"A couple of weeks after I moved in," Jane said, opening the panel to reveal a small wall safe. She spun the dial with practiced precision, and it opened with a satisfying click. The door was heavy for something so small, and inside was a single silver key. Taking it, Jane turned and presented it to Grace.

"What's it for?" Grace said, not reaching for the key.

"A lockbox," Jane said, producing a slip of paper from her pocket. "The address is on here. In the lockbox is a data reel with a bunch of encrypted files that the Director is pretty keen to keep quiet. Did you know yetis are actually real? Blew my mind."

Grace blinked, then looked at the key, then back to Jane. "This was in my house?"

"I had to. I'm sorry. It was the only way to keep us safe." Jane had pictured a better way of telling her, but every time she thought she might, she put it off. If Grace had been wrong about one thing, it was that Jane was walking into danger when, in truth, it never left.

"You've been holding a hostage in my house?"

Jane cringed and nodded.

"Jane! Jesus, you should have told me. The kids—"

"I know! I know, I never found a good time, which sounds extra dumb when I say it now. Be mad; I get it. Just know I did it to keep us all safe. And please don't be too mad."

"Oh, Jane." Grace stared at the key for a long moment, long enough that Jane wondered if a lecture was coming, but her sister sighed instead and took the key and paper from Jane's hand. "What do I do?"

"You're the best, you know that?"

"I'm aware of that too," Grace said as she read the note.

"If you don't hear from me in two weeks"—Jane pointed at the note—"go to this address, use the key, and take the data reel to the press. There's a journal with it, my notes about how it's encrypted. Give them that, too."

Grace nodded without saying a word.

Jane didn't like the idea of leaving on this sour note. "Hey, I'm sorry I didn't tell you sooner."

Grace tucked the paper in her pocket and nodded. She looked sick.

"We . . . good?" Jane asked tentatively.

Grace drew in a shuddering breath and nodded. "Yeah, Jane, we're good. I honestly should have expected that you'd blackmail a government agency." Jane's heart relaxed, but before she could say anything, Grace continued, "You have to say goodbye to the kids. They would be crushed if you didn't."

"I'll do story time before I go. Plus, you look like you need a shower and a glass of wine."

"Two," Grace amended as tears welled in her eyes.

Jane chuckled, "Two. You've earned it." She held her arms open, coaxing her in. Grace sniffed and they embraced, squeezing each other like they had thousands of times before. There, perhaps for the last time, Jane wondered what she'd done to deserve her life with Grace.

Chapter 13: Recurring Themes

Sunday, April 15th

The next day at work, Rory didn't see Khloe. Initially, he felt relieved. The pressure of being clever and cute felt draining, but by the time he got his patient assignment, a surprising pang of disappointment nested in him, and he was so anxious that for the rest of the night, he kept hoping she'd walk by.

"Rory, you've got Jenny again. Mom—Danielle—will be with her today. Let us know if you need any help."

He beamed. Jenny was a frequent flier, a name lovingly dubbed for repeat patients in the PICU. Rory had cared for her several times before and had bonded with the family. Danielle was fun and easy to talk to, and he sighed, relaxing. No exhausting small talk needed today.

With a smooth shift on the horizon, Rory hurried to the unit to get a report from the outgoing day-shift nurse—and kept an eye out for Khloe.

19:50

"*Lion King* at ten?" Rory asked, fluffing a lumpy pillow.

Sweat ran down his back. He could feel his scrubs sticking to him now. Small, stuffy rooms and multiple layers made it mandatory for a nurse to invest in strong antiperspirants, especially when the patient was under isolation precautions. Clever marketers advertised the paper-like yellow isolation gowns as lightweight, which they were, and breathable, which they weren't.

"Same time every day, isn't that right, bubs?" Danielle sat beside the bed, tucking her long platinum-blonde hair behind her ear. "We love those sing-alongs."

The former bodybuilder had made a name for herself on the unit with her sugar cookies, but she became a celebrity when Katherine discovered her international weight-lifting records. Rory loved her stories, and they'd spent long hours talking about everything from doping tests, seventy-hour weeks of work and lifting, and then setting it all aside for her special needs daughter. That, and Danielle was just kind. You always felt a little better after talking to her.

"Ooh, I just can't wait . . ." she sang to Jenny.

In the bed, the eleven-year-old flailed her hands, cooing happily as she played with her painted blocks. Drool ran down her chin onto the cloth straps holding her tracheotomy tube in place. Danielle reached over and wiped the drool away and smoothed Jenny's sweaty hair off her face. Jenny wriggled in protest, grinding her teeth and feebly attempting to bat her mother's hands away.

"Are you going to behave for Rory and me tonight?"

Jenny puffed out her cheeks and glared at her mother, who laughed. "We want to be nice to Rory. He does a great job helping us, doesn't he?"

Jenny clicked her teeth together and returned to playing with her blocks.

"That's very sweet of you," Rory said.

"It's true," Danielle said. "I'm always so grateful when we get you."

Rory felt his cheeks warm, but he wasn't sure if that was from the isolation gown or the compliment. He rounded the bed and slid a pillow beneath Jenny's legs to relieve her lower back. Danielle shifted the monitoring cables and tugged at the corners of her covers, tucking them into the sides of the guard rails.

"So, ten works with your assignment?" Danielle asked, curling her legs up beneath her in the chair. "Jenny loves it when you

131

sing."

"Should, but I'll need to warm up this time," Rory said, with a wink at Jenny.

"Did you hear that, Jenny? Yay." Danielle clapped her hands, and Jenny knocked together two blocks. *Clack-clack.* "Another couple of days, and we'll be back in our own beds."

"Anything we can do to help you be more comfortable?" Rory went over and collected a few empty vials for Jenny's evening lab draw.

"It's okay. It's just that pull-out is rough." Danielle chuckled. "A night's sleep with no alarms and interruptions? Oh, a woman can dream." Her voice trailed off as she looked at the slatted window at the back of the room. Rory gave space for the silence, knowing how rare it was in the ICU. Instead of talking, he made faces at Jenny, bringing a lopsided smile to her round face. As he finished filling the last vial from the IV, Danielle turned back.

"Speaking of home, how's Sneaks doing?"

"Temperamental and aloof, so still a cat."

"Consistent." Then she added in a soft voice, "Have you gone dancing again recently?"

Rory shook his head and gathered up the vials of Jenny's blood, giving them a gentle shake to prevent clotting. "I haven't gone for a few months."

Danielle sighed. "I remember dancing. It started out as balance training, but I fell in love with it. Wish I had time . . ." Her voice trailed off. Jenny blew a loud raspberry and kicked her legs, untucking the sheets.

"Oh, will you look at what you've done?" Danielle stood and kissed each of Jenny's palms before readjusting the blankets.

Rory saw the fatigue and exasperation and felt a swell of admiration for Danielle. Caring for Jenny was a full-time job.

With all of her medications, nebulizer treatments, and suctioning, Danielle would be lucky to have an hour to herself each day.

He checked the clock. "I'll drop off the labs and get the eight o'clocks ready." He slid open the glass door and stepped into the small antechamber, but stopped and poked his head back in. "Normal break time tonight?"

"If you don't mind. I know I should quit, but it's my one little vice while we are here."

Rory understood. This place was punishing. "As soon as *The Lion King* gets going."

Danielle nodded. "Thanks, Rory. You're the best."

Jenny babbled and clapped her hands as Rory closed the door behind him. The sound dulled when he shut the glass slider.

Alone in the tiny antechamber, with only the whine of the ceiling vents, Rory took a quick breath, enjoying the relative peace. He removed his sweaty gown and gloves and washed his hands, humming "Row, Row, Row Your Boat" for the required twenty seconds. Bell always said nursing had one golden rule: keep the patient safe. The simplest way to do that was to wash your hands.

A knock came on the antechamber door, and Bell ducked her head in. "Rory, we've got something cooking, and I need you to take it."

Rory stifled a sigh. "Is anyone else available?"

She shook her head, her white curls bouncing against her glasses. "I already called the entire on-call list in for the other admissions. I'm sorry. Room 16 is crashing on ECMO, so I had to shift assignments around. I tried to keep yours calm, but . . . God's asking for our help again."

Rory forced a smile, feeling his hands shake. "Yep, no worries, I can take it."

"Thank you, Rory. I'm proud of you."

That makes one of us.

He followed Bell out into the hall, pulling out a folded sheet of paper from his pocket. On it, in his tiny handwriting, was everything he needed to know for his shift: Jenny's schedule, medications, respiratory treatments, lights-out time, and even her wake-up for morning vitals, all neatly laid out in twelve rows. Nurses called this piece of paper their "brains," because misplacing the paper mid-shift was akin to losing one's mind.

Rory flipped it over to the blank side and readied his pen. "Give it to me."

Bell stopped and leaned in, keeping her voice low. "Another tough one. I'm so sorry. Tommy Winfield, a ten-month-old boy, who has bilateral subdural hemorrhages. I put you in Room 4. I know. But it was the only one available."

Rory's stomach dropped as he struggled to keep his writing steady. "What happened?"

"Little guy somehow threw his head against the wall."

Rory clenched his jaw. *No. Goddamnit.* "Another N.A.T.?"

N.A.T. stood for Non-Accidental Trauma. Simply put, someone purposefully hurt the patient. "Bell," he breathed, not looking at her, "this is the ninth one in four months."

She nodded. "I know. So ugly. And I'm so grateful you're here to help these kids." She checked over her shoulder. No one was within earshot, so Bell added, "We need your presence in the room. There's a boyfriend involved."

"Why is it always a damn boyfriend?"

"Hey. Look at me," Bell commanded softly. Rory blinked and turned. "There are detectives trying to figure out what happened—that's their job." She shook her head. "But between you and me, I don't see how this boy hit the wall this hard any other way. There's a mid-line shift, and . . . well, the ED down in Eugene thinks he might be posturing. DHS is involved already, and we'll work them up once they get here. For now, both mom and boyfriend are inbound with the kid. The boyfriend was watching at the time of injury while mom was out. He called it in."

"So he's lying."

"Maybe, but that's not our job," Bell said, looking into his eyes. "We take care of the patient. We watch, and we take detailed notes."

Notes?! Rory thought a baseball bat would be more appropriate.

He folded his "brains" carefully and put them in his pocket, willing his anger to cool. "I can't picture how someone 'accidentally' throws a child," he hissed.

Bell watched him for a long moment before she nodded and unrolled her patient list. "Listen, I can switch some assignments around if you can't take this one. After Friday, I understand if—"

"No," Rory said, surprising himself. He wanted this case—he needed this case. If nothing else, he wanted to look the guy in the eye and see for himself. "I'm good, Bell. I got it."

Bell raised an eyebrow.

"Really. It's best for the unit if I take him, anyway."

She nodded. "I'll be checking in on you, understand?" She glanced up at the wall clock: *20:01.* "They'll be here in about ten minutes. Best get your room ready."

———

Monday, April 16th, 02:02

Rory missed the sing-along with Danielle and Jenny.

"It's like a crazy dream, you know?" The boyfriend fidgeted. His name was Chuck, and he wore a faded black hoodie that reeked of sour smoke. Standing at the edge of the bed, the young man clung to the crib's railing like prison bars.

As Rory untangled the nest of infusion lines, he felt Chuck's eyes watching him, but each time Rory glanced up, forcing himself not to glare, Chuck looked away.

Detailed notes, Bell had said. He was standing four feet from an abuser, and all he could do was take detailed notes . . . if he wanted to keep his job.

Luckily for Tommy, but unfortunately for Rory, Chuck got chatty when he got nervous. "This is crazy, huh? But you see stuff like this all the time, right?"

Rory swallowed down a shout. "Part of the job."

"Yeah, y'know." Chuck laughed nervously. "I didn't see what happened, y'know? But he just, like, *BAM!* Fell and knocked his head on the bookshelf, y'know? I hardly saw it."

Tommy, the unconscious and badly bruised little brunette boy in the crib, was worse than reported. Rory expected facial swelling, but this boy's eyes had swollen shut. *Jesus, how hard did he throw him?* It looked like a car had hit him. He looked like Octavia.

Rory blinked and clenched his jaw. Another one. His eyes burned.

After four long hours, the surgeons relieved the pressure and cauterized Tommy's bleeding brain while the machines continued to breathe for him. They placed a metal bolt on the top of his head to measure his intra-cranial pressure, which read as a steady orange line below his other vitals. With the drain and bolt in place, the short-term danger had passed, and the brain and lungs could rest. It was a waiting game.

The door slid open, and Tommy's mother, Deborah, entered, holding several small bags of chips. "I found some snacks." She dropped the bags on the chair and stood next to Chuck, who looped his arm around her. To Rory's disgust, she leaned down and snapped a quick selfie of her and Tommy. "He'll like that one when he wakes up."

Wakes up? The anger roiled in Rory. *This kid isn't waking up.*

Deborah looked up at Rory with an oblivious grin. "Tommy is always getting bruises. He's wild. This one time, when he was little, he was crawling on the television and almost pulled it down on himself. He doesn't know his own strength."

Rory wasn't sure if it was shock, or ignorance, or denial, but the mother did not grasp what was going on. He pressed his lips together. "Tommy's on medications to help him sleep while we watch his brain swelling for the next seventy-two hours."

"Where can I get some of those meds, right?" the boyfriend almost shouted, adding an uncomfortable chuckle. "He's never slept this hard at home."

"Totally," Deborah said as she plopped down in the bedside chair, grabbed a bag of chips, and pulled out her phone.

"Gimme one," Chuck demanded.

Deborah kept scrolling.

"Hey!" Chuck said, kicking her chair.

Deborah tossed him a bag without looking up.

Chuck snatched it and tore in. Though he was young, his teeth were yellowing, and his face was gaunt. Junkies in pediatrics were rare, occasionally a teen or a parent, but you didn't forget their pall after you'd seen it.

Just . . . put it in the notes.

Rory straightened Tommy's lines and moved on to the reflex test. He expected little, poking a dull needle into the arch of Tommy's right foot. A responsive brain should pull the foot back, should twitch, or do anything to protect the body. Instead, Tommy just lay there, his chest rising and falling with the ventilator.

"He'll be up soon," Chuck said. "He's a wild little kid, man. Total wacko, right, babe?"

Rory imagined what his fist would feel like against the man's nose. *Act professional*, he reminded himself and drew in a long breath. He grabbed a temperature probe and slid it into Tommy's mouth. They needed to be vigilant for infection, too.

"Totally," Deborah said again. The glow of her phone illuminated her sunken eyes.

"I'm not surprised the dog tripped him. He went flying into the, uh, fireplace."

The dog tripped him?

Rory stopped and turned to face Chuck. "I thought you said he fell into a bookshelf." The details had been changing all night, and Rory was constantly updating his mental notes for the detective.

The boyfriend froze. "Uh. Um, yeah, what'd I say? Bookshelf. Like, they're right next to each other. He was going so fast. Like I said."

"So you did see what happened?"

"Uh, well, kind of. I . . . was . . . on my phone."

Rory set the probe down and felt his entire body trembling. "Your phone?" He stared hard at Chuck's dark eyes, and the man's thin smile disappeared.

"Isn't that right, babe?" He nudged the mother's chair with his boot.

"Huh? Ya," she said without looking up. "Always checking the news."

"There you go," Chuck said, as though it absolved him of something.

There were so many things Rory wanted to say and many more things he wanted to do. *I'm a nurse,* Rory reminded himself. *Take care of the patient.* Biting back his fury, he spoke as evenly as possible. "I need to chart at the station outside. Tommy is comfortable right now. His vitals are stable. We are going to let him rest."

The boyfriend sagged. "Thanks, man. It's been a crazy night. I'm really tired."

Rory forced himself to say nothing and left the room. His hands shook as he slid the door shut. Two steps later, he stopped, staring at the ground. He felt plastic sticking to his palm and saw he'd forgotten to take his gloves off again. Seething, Rory ripped them off and threw them into the trash.

This is fucked up.

Chuck was guilty, of that Rory was certain, and while he could hand notes of their conversation to the police, that was the extent of his power.

And I can't do shit!

Rory, the team, could do everything perfectly tonight and tomorrow, and for the next month, Tommy could receive the best possible care. But nothing could bring him back from this. His chest rose and fell, throat tight.

His breath caught, and something cracked, like a dam breached by a flooded river.

I can't do this anymore. The thought filled his belly with lead and sent his heart racing. *I can't.* He wanted to cry; he wanted to run. *What will Bell say? I'm a failure? I'm weak?* His eyes swam, but the thought of smiling at another Chuck down the road made him sick. *There will always be more.*

The sliding door opened behind him.

Chuck poked his head out. "Hey, I need another blanket and more pillows."

Rory folded his hands together to settle their shaking. "I'll be right back in with those."

Chuck closed the door behind him without another word.

Rory glanced back through the glass at Tommy's swollen face. He drew out his phone and typed out a message to Patrick: *Tell your guy I want to buy the van.* Without hesitation, Rory hit send.

Chapter 14: Beggar's Choice

Monday, April 16th, 08:38

Rory made record time on his misty bike ride home, replaying his conversation with Chuck again and again, pumping his pedals with stinging eyes.

By the time he plopped down on his couch, physically and emotionally exhausted, the questions buzzed in his mind like biting flies. What does he say when he quits? Should he keep it brief or explain? Did it matter? Would anyone care? Those who remained barely remembered the nurses who had left. They could replace anyone. He looked down into his lap, at his hands, but caught the blue plastic band around his wrist.

Family. Healing. Hope.

Those three commandments felt hollow. He pulled the bracelet off and tossed it on the cardboard coffee table. *What's the point?* No matter what he did, no matter how long or hard he fought, it wouldn't differ. As things were, tragedies like Tommy would never stop. The sickness was too deep, the sponge too full. He thought about Chuck's weak story and Deborah's ridiculous hope. *And what can a single person possibly do about that?*

A sharp silence replied, long and lingering, and Rory knew the answer. *Nothing.*

THUP.

Rory looked down at his feet, surprised at not seeing an orange fluff ball demanding pets. "Sneaks?"

Thup-thup.

The sound came from beneath the sofa. He stood, his body heavy. "Did you find the catnip again?" he mumbled.

Rory grabbed the flashlight off the fridge and hoped it had

batteries. It needed a good shake first, but the flashlight turned on, and Rory crouched down, peering under the couch. Sneaks's eyes shimmered green in the light as she batted something small and solid.

"What'd you get?" Rory lay on his side and reached for the object. It felt small and smooth.

The stone from the pouch. Caroline.

"Where did you get this?" Rory pushed himself up. Sneaks, not done with her game, emerged from under the couch and rubbed against Rory's leg, purring. He turned it over, running his thumb over the grooved arch etched into the surface.

If you're angry enough and tired of waiting, Caroline's note read. *Drink the vial, follow the wisps, and . . .* There was another part, but Rory couldn't remember.

And tired of waiting . . . He paused, shaking his head as a fire built in him. *What am I waiting for?*

For the last two years, Rory had absorbed blow after blow. He could feel his heart breaking. He could hear that senator's voice. "This is what we pay you to do. You're just lazy. Deal with it. Or get a new job." He felt dizzy.

Turning the river stone over his palm, Rory pictured Tommy lying in his crib, helpless and dying. In such a complex world, it was often difficult to tell right from wrong, but . . . that was wrong. Chuck had to be stopped.

If you're angry enough . . .

Caroline's note was crazy—any rational person could see that. The sick didn't just get better. Magic didn't exist, and drinking glowing vials of mystery liquid from a stranger was a terrible idea. But as he stared at his choices, he shook his head, dismayed. It was all bad. *How the hell did it come to this?*

Curling his fingers around the smooth river stone, Rory squeezed it, feeling something inside his heart give way.

"Maybe we need a little crazy, Sneaks."

Sneaks nudged his fist, purring.

"No more waiting," he whispered.

The cat rose on her back legs and nipped gently at his hand. Rory envied her simple existence. He was tired of being human.

Beep-beep-beep! CHUNK.

Trash day—

A jolt of panic raced through Rory. "The vial!" He jumped to his feet, sending Sneaks racing back under the sofa. Dropping the stone on the counter, Rory sprinted for the door and burst into the misty spring morning.

"Wait!" he shouted, running down the steps and over to the lumbering garbage truck. "Hold on!" he panted. "I accidentally threw something away."

The sleepy-looking older man in a green jumpsuit shrugged and waved back at the driver. "Hold up." The big truck rumbled as it idled.

Rory pushed himself up and lifted the lid. A swarm of flies billowed out, and he leaned back, swatting. The lid dropped with a heavy *CLUNG.*

The garbage man chuckled. "What did you toss?"

"Uh, my . . . glow stick."

The man raised an eyebrow.

He spotted a faint purple light between two black trash bags. He eyed the rest of the pile and saw the trip wouldn't be clean. "I'm, uh, really into . . . raves," Rory said and jumped inside.

The smell of old fish and diapers overwhelmed him. Something squished against his calf as he took another step, and he forced himself not to look. Finally, he leaned as far as he could forward, snatched up the canvas bag, and crawled back out.

"Thanks, man," Rory coughed. The garbage man looked at Rory's hands, and then shook his head and shrugged.

"Kids and their drugs," Rory heard him mumble as he walked back to the cab. Nearly shouting he was twenty-three, he held off, wondering if the guy was right. He'd never felt like an adult.

Back in his apartment, he set the vial down on the kitchen counter and stared at the swirling, purple-white fluid. Sneaks had reemerged, and her tail twitched curiously, circling Rory's feet.

"I guess I just drink it?"

The hue of the potion shifted a shade brighter, and he ran a hand through his hair, his fingers finding his scar. He turned, looking for another answer, another option, but found only cardboard and shadows until he spotted the cards and pictures from his patients. Rory dropped his arms and looked down at his naked wrist.

Family. Healing. Hope.

His stomach knotted. Hope. And the way he saw it, there were only three real scenarios: get the camper van and quit nursing, stay and suffer the Chucks of the world again and again, or drink the mystery vial and see what happens. The options didn't seem fair, each a worse choice than the last—like picking a direction in the middle of a midnight thunderstorm without a compass. But that wasn't right. He had a compass: Tommy. And the only option that *might* give that boy a chance also felt like the most asinine. He had to drink the vial.

"Fuck me." Rory picked up the vial and uncorked it. "To Tommy."

He closed his eyes, threw back his head, and chugged the contents as fast as possible. His mouth puckered at the bitter taste. Coughing, he forced himself to finish, choking down the last mouthful. Rory slammed the vial back on the counter, feeling his guts twist. A sudden wave of nausea rolled over him, and he dropped to his knees and heaved. A searing pain seized him as every muscle in his body contracted, locking him with his mouth open, staring at the stained carpet.

He heaved again, but this time, he felt something move up his throat. Not bile. It didn't burn, but it was warm and full. He heaved again, and it slid further up, stopping at the back of his throat. Rory braced himself with both hands, trembling and terrified. His muscles spasmed again, and warmth erupted from his mouth, not in a crimson spray or vomit, but a floating ball of twinkling white light.

Rory's body unclenched, and he sagged forward, panting. He wiped the drool off his beard as he watched with open-mouthed awe as the ball of light bobbed around his apartment. "That's not possible . . ." And yet, there it was in front of him—Caroline's wisp.

Now . . . what? All the note said was to follow it. But where? It just bobbed around in a circle.

"Uh, hello?"

The wisp continued on, with Sneaks stalking it from the ground.

"This woman, Caroline, said that—"

The wisp quivered midair and darted over to Rory, stopping inches from his face. He screamed and staggered back.

Rory waited, but the wisp waited, too. "Can you, uh, take me to her?"

The wisp welled with light and shot over to the door, slipping beneath it and vanishing.

"Wait!" Without another thought, Rory grabbed his bike helmet and sprinted after.

Chapter 15: Flight by Wisplight

Monday, April 16th

The wisp darted through the morning rush hour. Sleepy-eyed drivers rolled on with their daily pilgrimage without a care for the floating ball of light zipping between fenders. By the way they drove, it seemed no one could see Rory's guide, though several honked at him as he chased after it.

"Watch it!" someone yelled after him.

"Sorry!"

Rory's heart raced, and his legs burned as he weaved his bicycle between idling cars, sucking down lungfuls of exhaust. He sputtered a cough as he gathered his bearings. They were near the river now. The wisp pulled him west. *But where?*

The wisp cut hard to the left, directing him across two lanes of traffic. Rory jabbed out a quick signal and turned. A horn blared behind him, and he heard brakes squeal, but all he could manage was an apologetic wave over his shoulder as he pedaled onward.

He gained ground, but the wisp whipped right, ignored the red light, and shot through a group of pedestrians strolling across the street.

"Look out!" Rory shouted.

People jumped out of his way as he zipped through the crowd.

"Excuse me! Sorry!"

Rory sped on, standing on his pedals now. Up ahead, the wisp darted down an alley.

Skidding around the corner, Rory prayed for no nails or glass, not wanting to ride on rims. He shot out from the alley, narrowly avoiding a black cat with its hackles up, and spotted the wisp gliding down a familiar stretch of road with a green bike lane. He'd just biked in the other direction on his way home.

Downhill, past the science museum, over the footbridge, and to the sky tram at the base of the Hill. *Is it taking me back to work?*

Rory pointed his front wheel after the wisp, hopped the curb into the bike lane, and leaned into his pedals. His legs screamed. He made it another block, skirting along a row of parked cars, when a raised blue pickup truck with a fluttering flag of stars and stripes threw open its door.

Rory cranked his handlebars and tried to brake, but he had too much momentum.

WHAM!

A flash of pain lit him up. His body stopped, slamming into the leather interior of the truck's door. His bicycle disappeared from beneath him, sparking as it careened forward. Rory landed on the wet asphalt and skidded before coming to a rest. After a moment, Rory patched together his surroundings. Slowly, he picked himself up, trembling from shock. His shoulder and ribs throbbed. He reached a hand up and felt the side of his forehead. A long crack snaked down the center of the helmet, and he was thankful the helmet split and not his skull.

Onlookers gathered on the surrounding sidewalk, watching him with concerned faces, though no one approached. He looked down at his legs and saw his green leggings shredded below his right knee, bleeding from a long strip of road rash. He hoped his bike was in better shape.

"What did you do to my truck?!" a deep voice bellowed.

He turned and found a broad-chested man glaring down at him. In his thick arms, he held an oversized, fluffy pink unicorn that seemed at odds with his denim overalls and tufts of brown hair poking out beneath a red baseball cap.

"I . . . I . . ." Rory stammered, and a flash of light caught his attention.

The wisp orbited the man's head, illuminating his sunbaked face.

147

"You're going to pay for this." The big man shook the unicorn at a sizable dent in the door's panel. "Look at that! You better have insurance." He paid the little light no mind as it passed in front of his eyes. *How is he not seeing that?*

The wisp circled again, twinkling lazily, as if waiting for Rory. "Sir—" Rory managed, trying to organize his thoughts, but before he could, the wisp swelled with light and shot back into the bike lane, fading fast.

"I gotta go!"

"What?!" the big man said, stepping closer. "You're not going any—"

"Sorry!" Rory darted for his bike. His knees and rib balked but eased into an ache.

"Stop!"

Rory ducked around the door and mounted his bike. The handlebars were a mess but functional, and aside from some chipped paint, the bike was rideable.

"Get back here!"

Rory couldn't go back now. He had to move forward.

Chapter 16: Warm and Sunny

Monday, April 16th

A morning downpour arrived as Rory reached the bottom of the Hill, bringing with it, and rare for the Northwest, rumbles of thunder. A great black cloud squatted on the valley, blotting out the sun. Snakes of silver lightning lashed across the storm bank, and the city below shivered and sheltered everyone but Rory and his wisp.

He squinted through the rain and followed the bobbing wisp up the hillside. From shoulder to shin, his body ached with each rapid heartbeat, but he focused on steady, quick breaths and his pedals to ignore his pain. At first, they stuck to paved roads, but as the hospital came into view through the trees, his path turned into a muddy gravel trail Rory had never noticed on his commute before. He groaned and gritted his teeth as his front tire slipped in the muck.

Another bolt of lightning flashed overhead, illuminating the roots and rocks of the forest floor. Rory hadn't seen another soul since he turned off the paved road, and he whispered a quick prayer to anyone listening. *Please don't let me crash and die alone out here.*

The wisp turned again, this time down a path so narrow Rory hadn't seen it through the trees. He skidded past the turn and backed up a few feet, his toes squishing inside his shoes. The wisp disappeared when another bolt cut through the sky, illuminating the low-hanging branches of thick, gnarled oaks. In their shadows, he thought he saw faces in the trunks and long, knotted hands coated in leaves.

He wiped rain and mud from his eyes, and the wisp floated back into view ahead of him. With an uneasy glance at the trees, Rory continued ahead carefully. The path twisted downward, and he picked up more speed than he intended. Narrowly avoiding a large rock, he banked around a sharp corner, his mangled handlebars bucking as he clung on. The path ended, emptying onto the narrow shoulder of a gravel service road. To both his left and right, the road curled around the hillside. Across the road lay a wall of blackberry bramble eight feet high and brimming with thorns. At its center, Rory found the wisp dancing lazily over a slight indentation—a deer path.

Rory spat out rainwater and squinted. "Through there?"

The wisp twinkled. Rory took that as a yes.

I've come this far. He shivered, checking the road. He was alone.

"This is mental."

―――

Rory walked his bike, following the wisp through the bramble and deeper into the forest. His legs trembled, but he told himself that was just from his frantic ride. The farther he went, the denser the canopy grew. Thick and wild, it obscured his view of the dark sky. Long thorny vines grew over the path, forcing Rory to pick his footing carefully. The wisp bobbed about just overhead, as if excited to be in this strange and ominous place. Rory didn't share its enthusiasm.

"How much further?" he asked the wisp, but the light just swayed back and forth.

Rory eyed the old trees, one hand raised, half expecting someone or something to jump out. He couldn't say why, but he knew he was being watched.

Soon, the thorns gave way to a small clearing filled with trash. A collapsed tent pooled water lying next to a dugout fire pit. Piles of wet cardboard, rusty grocery carts, and fast-food wrappers littered the space. A blue tarp hung at the center, suspended between two bushes. Someone lived here once, he judged, but had moved on.

Rory moved into the clearing, straining to listen over his own breaths. It was quiet. Eerily quiet. Only then did he notice the lack of wind. None of the trees moved despite a distant howl, yet the edges of the tarp billowed in an unfelt breeze. The hairs on Rory's neck rose; there was something wrong with this place.

The wisp drifted over to the tarp, but as it drew near, its light extinguished, finally spent at the end of its journey.

"Wait!" Rory said, lunging after, but the wisp was gone.

Rory turned around, alone in the dark. *Now what?*

"Uh, Caroline? Hello?" he called out, but hearing his voice made him feel stupid. *What am I doing here? This is . . .*

The tarp billowed toward him. Rory's eyes narrowed. *What the—* Reaching out his hand, he felt the tarp flutter again. From the other side of it, he swore he heard the call of gulls and the crash of waves.

SCREECH!

Rory yelped, spinning toward the source of the sound behind him. "C . . . Caroline?" He scanned the silent forest. He swallowed down the hard lump in his throat. "I'm here?"

The pile of empty bottles and plastic bags twitched beside him with a dull, scraping sound. Rory jumped back, nearly tripping over the collapsed tent.

"Hello?" he said, taking another step back. "Caroline told me to drink that solution, then follow the wisp, and, uh, I did. And I—" Then the third line of Caroline's directions burst from his memory. *The keystone!*

He reached into his pocket. "I brought the—" But it wasn't there. He checked his jacket's other pockets, but no stone. *Don't forget the keystone.* Caroline's directions had been specific enough. "Where did . . . Sneaks." The cat must have knocked it off the counter while he was dumpster diving. Or, in his rush, he'd just forgotten it. *Crap.*

151

In the side of his vision, the trash pile shifted and rose to face him: two blue, glowing eyes peering from the heap. Something under his foot shifted, and the pile beneath him moved. He whipped his head around to see a long-fingered hand of mud, food, and rusty metal crawling from the pile. The limb didn't look complete, like a skeleton with patchy flesh made from garbage and earth.

He scrambled back, putting distance between him and the rising creatures, but now more piles were twitching to life.

"Caroline invited me!" he pleaded. His eyes darted to the tarp, where the wisp had vanished.

Follow the wisp.

Rory dropped his bike and ran to the tarp. He pulled it aside, and his breath caught in his chest. *That's not possible . . .*

Behind the tarp and down a narrow, overgrown path lay a white sand cove with distant black cliffs and lapping blue waves. He reached out his hand and felt a warm breeze. *What the hell?* Paralyzed by the shock, he blinked at the unexpected, bright light. But a loud grind of metal exploded behind him, and he plunged forward into the new world.

———

Rory's ears plugged and popped as though he had ascended a mountain in a few bounds. He threw his hand over his face to shield the sudden bright sunlight. Dripping wet, he shivered and squinted across the pristine white-sand beach. Gulls called from overhead. Red crabs scurried toward the tide.

"Caroline?" he called out, wobbling. "It's Rory!"

Click-click-click.

He spun around and saw one of the trash creatures emerging through the bushes and into the sunlight. It was human-shaped, the size of a child, but it was not human. Fat mushroom caps, each a rich, radiant turquoise, dotted the shoulders and head of the little stooped body and emanated a faint blue light. What looked like veins—strands of mycelium—snaked through the creature's body like sprawling roots, twisting around its feet and over the tip of its oversized, rusty claws. All over its body, bits of orange-red metal peeked through the gaps of mud, exposing its skeleton. Garbage, empty cans, plastic bags, and half-rotted cardboard made up its mismatched skin. Most disturbing, though, were its eyes. Two fist-sized, blue sockets formed the only features of its face, and both their dark pinpoint pupils scanned him intently.

Rory backed away, stumbling in the sand. "I'm trying to find Caroline!"

The creature stopped a moment, its head dipping to the side in an eerie display of understanding, but just as Rory hoped he got through, it raised a creaky claw and lunged at him. He sprang back, falling, and the claw thumped into the sand, only an inch from his leg. Pulling back its arm, it advanced as more of the creatures emerged from the bushes.

Rory kicked sand at the creature and retreated, scanning the open expanse of the beach. "Help!"

The things clicked closer behind him. He scrambled up and sprinted for the black cliffs, hoping that these creatures couldn't climb. "Anyone!"

The sun's glare faded, and as he ran, he made out a tall green pavilion nestled against the cliffs. Next to it was a row of overflowing grocery carts, each wrapped in orange bungee cords and beach towels. Outside the large tent was a small fire and a cloaked figure stooping over the flames.

"Help!" Rory waved his arms, praying it was her. He glanced over his shoulder and saw the creatures swinging on their enormous claws like crutches as they closed on him. "Caro—"

The figure rose and pulled back their hood. Caroline's long white hair caught the breeze, fluttering with the strip of pink cloth covering her eyes. Her white teeth flashed a moment, until she saw the scene. The crashing waves swallowed what she yelled, but then she was moving fast toward him. Her cloak opened as she ran, revealing a string of three colored lights hanging around her neck and a long purple and white tie-dye dress.

She yelled again, but all he heard was "—out!"

The sand in front of Rory shifted, and he spotted a glint of rusty metal. His mind screamed for him to stop, but his body reacted a moment too late as he collided with the rising creature and toppled into the sand. Scrambling, he spat out the salty grains and turned in time to see one of the rusty skeletons draw back a terrible claw. He kicked his legs, trying to turn, but he just thrashed in the sand. The creature plunged its metal fingers into Rory's stomach.

The pain consumed him, fire in every nerve. Rory's world went red, then white, and threatened to go black.

"Ahhh!"

The creature drew out its bloody claw, bringing a fresh surge of agony.

Rory clenched his teeth together, blinking rapidly to keep himself conscious, a trick he learned from an epileptic teenager. He pressed both hands against the wound and felt hot blood pulse between his fingers. *My blood.*

The creature advanced on him again, its red claw poised. Rory held out a trembling hand.

"*Sa-sha-delune!*" Caroline shouted. The creature twitched, its bright eyes flickering with the glow of the mushrooms. Then they went dark. Lightless, the creature swayed and fell face-first into the sand.

Rory blinked at the still creature, but the agony kept him present as he pushed harder against his wound.

Caroline fell to her knees at his side. Up close, he saw the lights around her neck were different gemstones: a blue sapphire, a green emerald, and a yellow topaz, each with its own mysterious internal light that fluttered as it swam within the gem. Rory had seen nothing like them, and for a moment, awe masked the pain. The reprieve didn't last. He felt more hot blood pass between his fingers, gritting his teeth.

Caroline grabbed his hand, and he started, but regretted the reflex as the pain spiked. All he could do was whimper. She squeezed his hand gently, and he felt a warm surge pass through her hand, lingering around his wound. He managed a deep breath and peeked down at his stomach. Bright blood soaked his jacket. *This is bad.*

"It struck an artery," Caroline whispered.

Dozens of questions flooded his mind, but he could only mumble one word. "Hospital."

"You are within and apart now, Rory. A hospital won't save you." She turned over her shoulder and whistled a lilting bird call.

"I'm coming," a gruff voice came over the breeze. Stomping up from the pavilion was the mugger, still wearing an orange and black beanie but now sporting a loose flower-print shirt and khaki shorts. She looked like a grumpy tourist.

His guts spasmed again, and he inhaled, fighting to stay conscious. "Please . . . hospital."

The woman arrived and peered over Caroline's shoulder, then back at Rory. "Where's the keystone, hero?"

"I—" Rory started, but Caroline cut him off.

"Now is not the time, Jacklyn."

She crossed her arms. "The golems wouldn't have attacked if he'd followed directions."

Golems?

Caroline frowned. "And were you flawless in your trials?"

Jacklyn grunted, muttering something to herself before taking aim at Rory. He could practically feel her balancing the scales.

"Why bother?" Jacklyn said at last. "He obviously doesn't have it."

"You don't know that," Caroline shot back. "No one can. Except him."

Jacklyn sighed and lifted her head, studying the bushes where he'd entered. "Was he followed?"

"Hospital," Rory said again, "please." Talking hurt, which meant the wound was deep. He needed surgery and fast. He tried to move again, but the pain lanced down to his toes.

Caroline looked down at him and smiled behind her blindfold. "He came alone. And risked much to follow his wisp."

"That's not good enough," Jacklyn said.

"Hur—" Rory started, but Caroline squeezed his hand gently, and he forgot what he was going to say.

"He heals children with games and riddles," Caroline said.

How does she know that?

Jacklyn didn't budge. "That doesn't mean—"

"Jacklyn!" Caroline snapped, and even the sun seemed to dim against her anger. "We are not having this conversation again. This was your choice, so now this is your duty. Help him."

Jacklyn sank back a step, her face twisting between outrage and sadness, as if Caroline had just slapped her. Rory wasn't sure what was going on, but knew he was losing the fight. *I need a surgeon.* He wanted to say such, but his voice wasn't working. Caroline's grip tightened. *What is she doing to me?*

The anger slid from Caroline's face into a pensive frown. "I'm sorry, my love, but we must."

"Fine." Jacklyn threw her arm up and stormed over, taking her time as Rory's eyelids grew heavy. He couldn't struggle when she reached into his pocket and drew out his wallet.

"Take anything," Rory groaned. "Please . . . hospital."

"I'm not going to rob you," Jacklyn scoffed, pulled out Rory's driver's license, and tossed the rest in the sand.

"Rory Nash, 3130 SE Hawthorne Boulevard, Unit # 104A. I know where to find you. One sniff of this gets out to anyone, even your diary, and we'll be paying you a swift visit, understand?"

He blinked, his head lolling to the side. His vision narrowed. Jacklyn reached forward with her stumped arm, but Rory flinched back. Moving was a major mistake. Pain crashed into him, pulling him down. He was drowning.

"Do you want to live?" Jacklyn said.

He did. More than anything, he wanted to live.

"It's your turn to be healed, Rory," Caroline said.

He swore he could feel her eyes on him from behind the blindfold. He submitted, tumbling backward away from the warm sun. As he fell, he heard Jacklyn's voice echo into nothingness.

"This'll hurt, hero."

Chapter 17: Negotiations

Monday, April 16th, 17:50

A small, wet nose pressed against Rory's cheek.

"Sneaks?" Rory mumbled. He cracked open a dry eye to see the orange tabby an inch away from his face. The boxes, the couch, the old TV—he was back in his apartment. "What the—" He winced as he tried to rise, finding his body protesting each little movement. It felt like he'd been hit by a truck.

Sneaks jumped away as he rose, but a gentle hand touched his shoulder.

"Slowly," he heard Caroline say. "Your wounds are mended but need time to seal."

Rory lay back, looking down. He was shirtless and wearing sweatpants instead of his torn leggings. They had changed him. He touched his stomach, remembering the creature's claw. She called them golems. A silver, puckered scar ran down his belly. No stitches. No blood. No staples. The wound looked healed, as though he'd had it for years.

Rory inhaled. "That's not possible."

"Possibility is relative," Caroline said. "It's just been unknown to you until this moment." The hand released his shoulder, and he propped himself up. He ran his fingers down his fresh scar again and looked up to where Caroline sat on the couch's arm, watching him. Her olive green cloak wrapped around her, framing the string of three glowing crystals against her tan skin.

His mind flooded with questions. "What went . . . how did this—"

"That's need to know only, hero," Jacklyn said from near the window. Her leather jacket hung loose, with the collar popped up, covering her mouth and nose, while she'd pulled her orange beanie down over her ears and eyebrows, leaving only a sliver for her dark eyes. She peered through the drawn slats, scanning the parking lot.

Rory sat up carefully, his fresh scar pulling taut as he took in his apartment. Confused at first, it took him a moment to realize he could see the floor. The pile of laundry had disappeared, folded into a stack. Cereal bowls, gone. The place looked great.

"I can't believe you live like this." Jacklyn shook her head. "Bare walls and an empty fridge? It's . . . grim."

"Peace, love," Caroline said. She shifted, pulling an old leather satchel into her lap that clinked softly. Patches covered the bag: purple peace signs, "Peace and Music 1969," different national flags, and a yellow smiley face. "Let Rory recover."

Jacklyn grunted and returned to her surveillance. "We can't stay, Care. It's not safe here."

"Safe?" Rory turned to Caroline, and his skin prickled. "From who?"

"You ask a lot of questions." Jacklyn shot him a look. "But you don't want to know the answers. Trust me."

"We can stay a moment longer," Caroline said. "It's nice to be out."

Jacklyn looked about to protest when Sneaks curled around her leg. Her scowl broke into the first smile Rory had seen from her, and she reached down and scooped up the cat with her one hand. "Who's a pretty kitty?" Jacklyn cooed. "Fine, a couple more minutes." Sneaks batted at her hand.

Rory tried again. "What happened?"

"Jacklyn healed you," Caroline said matter-of-factly. "You're going to need to accept that, Rory, because we don't have the time to repeat ourselves."

Rory's jaw dropped. *That's . . . that's . . .* his brain sputtered. The words didn't come. *Healed? So fast? That's . . . what? Magic?* Everything life had taught Rory said that magic wasn't real, and yet he felt a thrill pass through him. Magic . . . He touched the perfect scar on his abdomen again, gawking.

"Um, I don't—" Rory tried. "Magic can't be . . . uh." The words felt insane to say.

"Real?" Caroline offered for him. She pointed at his bare stomach. "You wear the evidence."

"Magic." Jacklyn scoffed. "It's always 'magic' this or 'miracle' that when something novel happens."

"Its proper name is casting," Caroline offered, shooting Jacklyn a scowl before she continued. "And casting, like all natural things, has rules."

"And consequences for breaking them," Jacklyn added, shifting the slats.

"Indeed," Caroline said, then shook her head. "We don't have time now. For our purposes, you need only know that Jacklyn did an excellent job mending you and that you'll be fine."

"Pretty proud of that patch job," Jacklyn said, sticking her tongue out at Sneaks. "Arteries are easy enough, but nerves are tricky."

Rory fell back, running both hands over his head. He remembered the wisp and the truck. The tarp and those mushroom things coming after him. He remembered his blood. Lots of blood. This happened.

"We brought you and your bicycle back here to recover," Caroline said, glancing around the apartment. "And picked up a little. Your home is in disarray."

"You saved my life . . . then cleaned my apartment?" Rory looked around again, stunned. "Wha . . . Thank you?" His eyes fell to his stomach.

"Why did it . . . Golems—" Rory aimed the word at Caroline, who nodded. "Why did the golem attack me?"

"Because someone couldn't follow directions," Jacklyn said.

Caroline sighed and reached into her satchel, drawing out the smooth keystone. "There was a miscommunication, and, as often happens, someone got hurt because of it. I'm sorry, Rory, but I hope this reinforces the importance of observing our rules."

Rory nodded, his mind reeling. He'd already messed up and felt a hot wash of shame. He supposed it was like nursing. Sloppy nurses meant hurt patients.

Patients. The word buzzed to the front of Rory's mind. *Something about my patients.* His thoughts felt thick. *What was it?*

"Did you have something to ask us?" Caroline said.

"I think so, but . . . I can't remember."

"The healing can do that—muddle memories, but they should return in time."

Jacklyn set Sneaks down and peeked through the shades again. "Time to go, Care. While he's still innocent."

Innocent . . . Tommy!

Rory pointed at his stomach. "Can you do this again?"

Both Jacklyn and Caroline stopped, looking at him.

"Not for me, but one of my patients? He's going to . . ." Rory choked on the word. "He's going to die without help. Without . . . a miracle. You asked if I was tired of waiting, and I am. Please, can you help him?"

Jacklyn and Caroline exchanged a long look, and Rory's heart drummed in his chest.

"Please," Rory said again. "I'm begging. This little kid, his name is Tommy." He paused. "He's why I drank the vial."

Jacklyn gestured to the counter and the stack of cards and drawings. "Those are from your patients?"

Rory nodded.

"Why do you keep them?" Caroline asked.

Rory swallowed hard. "They, uh . . . help me . . . keep going."

Jacklyn raised an eyebrow but said nothing. Finally, her eyes moved to Caroline, who gave a single, sharp nod. Rory's heart leaped. *Is that a yes?* He tamped down his enthusiasm, seeing Jacklyn's frown twist deeper.

"You're sure, Care?" said Jacklyn.

Caroline nodded again. "I believe he can. He has the Stains, but your question is for you to answer, not me."

Rory felt a wave of frustration. Again, he was on the outside. "I have the what? Stain?"

Neither of them seemed to notice.

"If we are wrong—" Jacklyn started.

Caroline cut in. "If we are right."

Rory looked back and forth between them. *Right about what? Right about who? Me? You came to me!*

"Wait," Rory said more strongly than he intended, pointing at Jacklyn. "You attacked me, remember?" His finger snapped to Caroline. "And you needed someone to show . . ." He stopped. "You didn't need me to walk you to the bus stop, did you?"

Caroline shook her head.

"Why the charade?"

Caroline looked at Jacklyn, who rolled her eyes. "Fine. Tell him."

"It was a test."

"Test?"

162

Caroline rose, her long frame stretching until she loomed over Rory. "Of your character, your resolve. We needed to see if you were ready. It is no small mental feat to witness casting and keep one's sanity. It can crack the mind if not prepared."

"Okay . . ." Rory shook his head, wondering what was crazier: her answer or him? "If it helps Tommy, fine, but no more tests."

Jacklyn snickered, shaking her head.

"What?" Rory turned to face her, annoyed.

"Life, hero. Life is one big test. Deal with it."

"You don't know the first thing about me." Jacklyn met his eyes, and he swallowed. "Look . . . I want to be a partner in this. Equals."

Caroline dipped her head. "As do we."

"We. Ha," Jacklyn muttered. "I'll be doing all the work."

Caroline ignored her. "What are you proposing, Rory?"

"Just one. Tonight. Tommy. He—"

Jacklyn waved off his next comment. "Yeah, yeah. It's a heartbreaking story, I'm sure. How are we getting me to him? Hospitals these days are like prisons. Cameras, security, restricted entry—"

"I'll sneak you in," Rory said. "I should have the same assignment as last night, and we can pass you off as a visiting family member easily enough. No one would think twice about a distant relative coming to pay final respects."

Jacklyn didn't look convinced. "Sounds flimsy . . ."

"It sounds reasonable," Caroline said. "We accept."

"You do?" Rory could barely believe his ears.

"We do?" Jacklyn said, but a quick look from Caroline kept her from protesting further.

Rory saw his advantage and continued, "You'll need to, uh, dress the part, though."

Jacklyn picked at her jacket. "What's wrong with my clothes?"

"Nothing. If you're at a motorcycle rally."

Caroline chuckled, earning a dirty look from Jacklyn.

"And shower," Rory added. "Get something clean and meet me in the smoking area, around the corner from the staff entrance at midnight. There are bushes and trees, plenty of cover. We'll have a small window where I can get you in and out without too many people seeing."

Jacklyn shook her head, making the puff ball on her beanie bounce. "One is too many."

"Trust me, we both want to keep this quiet. I could get fired. And you obviously have a lot of secrets—that's fine, keep them. But we're going into my world, so you'll need to listen to me inside. We're both there to help Tommy."

"Sounds like the kid is a goner already," Jacklyn said. "Why should we help him?"

"Because if we don't, no one will." Rory snapped, hotter than he wanted. "Not his parents, not the state, not anyone. We can't just abandon him, not when we can save his life . . . right?"

Caroline smiled and turned to Jacklyn. "There's your fighter."

Rory wasn't sure what she meant, but he felt a surge of pride.

"Might taste sweet to do some good."

"Exactly." Rory extended a hand. "Partners?"

Jacklyn didn't budge. "Sure, hero. Partners, so long as you remember that out here, we're in our world, and in our world, there are rules."

Rory sighed. "So you've said. Such as?"

Jacklyn held up a finger. "First, no questions. All you need to know is there are bad people who will kill you and who have killed others to get their hands on us and our"—she pumped her fingers in air quotes—"magic. The less you know, the safer for everyone. Got it?"

He nodded. The news wasn't comforting, but he'd expected it. Why else would they go to such lengths to stay hidden?

"Anything else?" he said.

"I need food. Casting isn't free. It takes a huge amount of energy, so I get real hungry."

"What kind of food?"

"Whatever. Just no tomatoes. Disgusting . . . nasty, slimy . . . Just keep the food coming, okay?"

"That won't be cheap," Rory said.

"Not my problem."

How much could she really eat?

"Okay, fast food it is. Anything else?"

"Yeah." Jacklyn came around and squatted down in front of him. She leaned closer until her nose was only a few inches from his. A chilling quiet filled the apartment. "If you tell anyone, I will kill you."

Rory waited for the smile, the joke, but Jacklyn's expression was deadly serious. It sent an icy shiver down his spine. "Yes, ma'am," he whispered.

"I'm glad we settled that early." She rose and stuck out her lone hand. "Do we have a deal?"

Rory swallowed again. Silence and money, but if that was all it cost to undo what Chuck had done, then the deal felt like a bargain. Rory couldn't let that monster win.

For Tommy.

Rory shook Jacklyn's hand.

"Excellent," Caroline said. Glass clinked inside her satchel as she reached inside and drew out a tarnished gold hilt of what appeared to be a bladeless sword. Etched down the pommel were three organic, flowing symbols that Rory had never seen before. They reminded him of a cross between the Sumerian cuneiform script and the Celtic runes he'd studied in history classes. Embedded at the center of the cross guard was a chunk of cloudy, crudely cut crystal.

Caroline held it out to Rory. "Hold this, please."

"What is it?"

Jacklyn scowled. "We just covered this. No questions."

"I just want to know if I'm getting cursed or if it'll suck my blood."

Jacklyn raised an eyebrow. "You have an active imagination, hero. Do you want to help the kid?"

Rory nodded, but frowned as he eyed the hilt. With a sigh, he braced and grasped it. He felt a tingle in his palm and a rush of heat in his chest, but that was it. He waited, watching the hilt, but nothing happened.

"Is it . . . supposed to do something?" Rory asked, wondering if it needed batteries.

"Not yet," Caroline said, taking the hilt back and sliding it into her satchel. "Perhaps in time." The cryptic comments were getting annoying, and he doubted they'd stop anytime soon.

Both Jacklyn and Caroline moved together toward the front door. Rory watched them go, a hundred questions still on his tongue, but he didn't want to test his new alliance by breaking the rules already.

"Midnight," Jacklyn said. "Don't be late, hero."

"I'll be there," Rory said.

Caroline opened the door for Jacklyn, who wandered into the morning sunlight without another word. Caroline paused halfway through the door, "I'm pleased you came to us, Rory. It was a very brave thing to do."

"Tommy's dead otherwise. I had to."

Caroline nodded. "All great deeds begin in despair. Farewell, Rory Nash. I'll see you again soon."

Rory gave a feeble wave as she shut the door behind them.

Alone in the dark, Rory sat for a long while. His stomach knotted as he thought about what could happen, but the longer he thought, the more his nerves mingled with an excited fluttering. He was ready for a change, even if that meant breaking the rules.

Chapter 18: Visitor, Room 4

Monday, April 16th, 23:50

"Rory?" Megan set down her crossword. They sat in rolling chairs in the hall outside their patients' rooms—neighbors for the night. "Do you mind if I take an early lunch before my admit arrives?" Her stomach grumbled loudly, and she rubbed her pregnant belly.

Rory chuckled. "Parasite demands food." He checked the clock. Megan was right on schedule. His plan needed luck, and given the timing, he'd somehow found it. He gently rapped his knuckles on the table, knowing it was silly, but every nurse he knew was a little superstitious on a quiet night.

"My admit is still an hour out." She shrugged.

"That's the oxy siblings?" asked Rory.

Megan nodded. "Found unresponsive with auntie's empty pill bottle next to them. So sad, but paramedics said they are responding to Narcan."

"Lucky kids," said Rory.

"Lucky aunt."

"Mind if I pee before you go?"

"Go for it," she said, returning to her crossword. It's what she always did before a fight—word games. She said it focused her, "steeled her," as she called it, and let her block out everything else. Rory envied her that.

"Anything I need to know about Tommy?" She raised her eyes to him as he stood.

The question was innocent enough, common between nurses covering assignments, but it made Rory feel suddenly hot.

"No, we're still in wait-and-see mode," he replied casually.

"Poor kid." Megan shook her head and squinted at her crossword. "Hey, you're a nerd. What's the name of *a werewolf's affliction*? Eleven letters, begins with an L, maybe ends with a Y."

"Wolf disease with an L? Lycan . . . thropy?"

"L . . . y . . . c . . ." She scribbled down the letters as she said them out loud. "Fits. Boom! Twenty-five down, done. Go pee, nerd." She waved him off with a smirk.

Rory hurried through the double doors and down the back hallway. The only person he passed was a housekeeper bobbing her head to music while dancing with a mop. He turned the corner, took the five flights of stairs two at a time, speed-walked down the staff hallway, passed the locker rooms, and reached the soft blue glow of the security office. Just beyond were the pair of sliding glass doors to the employee lot.

Rory approached quietly, hoping to slip by unnoticed. He crept past the windows and saw Officer Kyle sitting upright, basking in the security monitors' glow, his back to him. He slid past, proud of his stealth, but managed only one more step before the overhead lights flashed on. Rory looked up. Nestled in the ceiling's corner, a red light blinked. He'd forgotten about the motion-sensing camera.

Officer Kyle spun around. "Badge, please."

Rory sighed and held up his badge sheepishly. After a thorough inspection, Officer Kyle waved him through with a nod.

The sliding doors glided apart automatically, and rain drizzled through the opening. His skin goose-fleshed. Grabbing his arms, his thin scrubs dotting with rain, Rory stepped out into the lamp-lit night. The doors slid closed behind him, and he rounded the corner to the smoking area. Thick rhododendron bushes, with their waxy green leaves and spheres of wild-pink flowers, surrounded the small dirt yard.

Rory walked to the center. "Jacklyn?"

No reply. *Am I early?*

He checked his phone: *0001.*

She should be here.

Rory peered into the bushes hesitantly. "Jacklyn?"

Still nothing. *Did she set me up? This better not be another stupid test.*

"Jacklyn!" he called louder.

A police car slowly drove by, and Rory felt their eyes on him. The car slowed, and Rory's heart picked up. Thinking quickly, he turned his back to the wind—and the cop—cupping his hands over his mouth and miming lighting a cigarette. *Be cool.* He threw a relaxed wave at the officer, who waved back and drove on. As the patrol car passed, a nervous laugh bubbled up from Rory's stomach. *What am I doing here?*

The bushes rustled behind him. Rory spun, ready to run, but breathed in relief when Jacklyn's silhouette emerged from the darkness. Strangely, though, and to Rory's growing unease, the light didn't seem to touch her. Even the aggressive fluorescent lamps couldn't, which, as Rory's eyes tried to focus on her but kept failing, distorted her features into a dark blur. Then, stepping fully into the light, she focused, and the cloak of shadows slipped off her shoulders and retreated into the bushes. The hairs on Rory's neck snapped to attention. *Light shouldn't do that . . .*

"What are you doing waving?" Jacklyn hissed. "And yelling my name?" She eyed his fake cigarette pose.

"I don't know." Rory threw up his hands. "This whole situation is a little out of my comfort zone." He stopped and looked at her. "What are you wearing?" Instead of sweatpants and a hoodie, she wore faded jeans and a pink T-shirt with gold letters reading "Party Girl," topped by her usual leather jacket and ever-present orange beanie. It wasn't the wardrobe change Rory had in mind.

"What? You said new clothes."

"Yeah, I meant more . . ." Rory was at a loss. "Grown up?"

"I like this shirt," Jacklyn protested.

He shook his head. "Doesn't matter now. Are you ready?"

Jacklyn scowled at him before peering around the bush toward the employee entrance. "In there?"

"Wear this. Don't take it off." Rory handed over the visitor sticker with the number four written in blocky black ink. "If anyone stops you, you're lost. Say something about the hospital being a maze. Whoever stopped you will help you. There is also a chance I won't be able to walk you out, so again, just pretend to be lost and—"

"That wasn't part of the deal," Jacklyn said flatly.

"If you do what you're supposed to do, I'm going to get very busy, very quickly, with Tommy. That means you're going to have to get yourself home."

Jacklyn knitted her brow and shook her head. Finally, she sighed. "Okay, hero. Don't get us caught."

———

"Badges, please," Officer Kyle said.

Jacklyn stiffened as Rory showed his badge.

Officer Kyle inspected it thoroughly before nodding at Jacklyn. "And yours, ma'am?"

"Um." Jacklyn pointed at the visitor sticker on her chest. "It's a maze."

Rory cringed. "She's a visitor, and I gave her bad directions to the smoking area. Totally my fault."

Officer Kyle was unreadable. "After-hours entrance, for all family, is through the front of the main hospital."

"I know," Rory said, "but that's all the way on the other side of

171

the Hill, and we are right here. I can vouch for her."

"Sorry, the rules state—"

"Please," Jacklyn said in a sticky, sweet voice. "My nephew is ill, and I'm not comfortable walking around a dark campus at night. Could you spare an exception, just this once?"

Rory stared at her, masking his surprise poorly.

Officer Kyle checked up and down the empty hallway and sighed. "I'll need to log it, so consider this a warning. Name?"

Jacklyn didn't miss a beat. "My name is Jackie Seed." She stepped forward and flashed an eager smile. "But everyone calls me Aunt Jackie."

"Seed . . ." Kyle scribbled, his eyes narrowing. Rory forced himself to focus on breathing when Kyle set his pen down. "Welcome to Hill Hospital, Aunt Jackie. I hope your nephew gets better."

"Oh, thank you, sir. Thank you."

"I owe you a coffee," Rory said, stepping past the burly officer.

"Just use the correct entrance next time," he said and stepped back into his office.

Rory led Jacklyn to the first stairwell and opened the door for her. "Easy on the treacle."

"Sweet is what they want. Submissive. Everyone loves the nice old lady." She patted Rory's shoulder. "Especially the heroes." She winked at him and pointed up the stairs. "This way?"

Rory bristled. "Will you stop calling me that?"

She started up the steps. "Isn't that how you wanna be seen, right? A do-gooder?" She paused and looked down at him. "Isn't that what we're doing here?"

Rory opened his mouth, but nothing came out. She wasn't wrong.

"Here's some advice, hero. You can't save everyone." He suddenly felt dizzy—and oddly seen. "But what the hell, right?" She continued climbing, her footfalls ringing through the concrete stairwell. He blinked, regaining his balance, and hurried to keep up.

Three flights up, Jacklyn breathed heavily, leaning on the rails. He searched his thoughts for a question, something to distract himself from her supposed "advice."

"Hey," Rory said. "Why did you give him your real name back there?"

She chuckled. "Who says that's my real name?"

"Oh . . . I—"

Jacklyn waved him off. "I've tried hiding behind different names before, hero. It makes no difference; you'll be found just the same." She stopped and inhaled a pair of deep breaths. "Geez, how many steps?"

"Best not to think about it," Rory said, passing her. "Just take them one at a time, Aunt Jackie."

———

The janitor had moved on, leaving the hall clear. Another bit of luck.

Rory waved for Jacklyn to follow, but they had made it only three steps before a bleary-eyed resident burst through the double doors. Rory jumped, but the resident just raised an enormous coffee cup in salute as they passed and didn't look twice at Jacklyn. Rory exhaled through his teeth and led her to the double doors of the unit. Peering through the narrow window, he spotted Megan with her hands on her hips, stretching her back outside their neighboring rooms.

"Stay behind these doors. No one uses them this time of night."

Jacklyn pointed behind them. "Someone just did."

"Relax. That resident is finishing a forty-eight-hour shift. He won't remember anything." He pointed through the window. "After Megan leaves, I'll wave you over. Walk calmly. You have a sticker, so they'll only question you if you seem nervous."

"But I am nervous," Jacklyn interrupted, leaning in. "Hospitals make my skin crawl. What if . . . I can't do this?"

"Hey, you healed me, didn't you?"

"You were easy. Puncture, simple in and out. Brains, though? Damn. I'm basically resurrecting this kid from death, and, well . . . I haven't done that before."

"What?" Rory froze. "You could have mentioned that sooner!"

"I got caught up in the moment. You made a good pitch."

"If you're not sure though, you should—"

"Would it have changed anything?"

Rory blinked, not liking how easy his answer came. Tommy wouldn't get a better chance than this. He groaned, unable to refute, and through the door's glass, saw Megan pace with both hands supporting her belly. She checked the clock. *Crap.* He'd been gone too long.

"Hey, look at me." They faced each other. "I sometimes precept—"

Jacklyn popped a questioning eyebrow.

"It's like teaching," he quickly continued. "Students from the nursing school shadow me during some shifts. They are super nervous, but I always tell them that there will be plenty of first-times: first procedures, first codes, first crazy families, but that even if it's the first time, they gotta make sure everyone in that room thinks it's your hundredth."

"That sounds like lying."

"It's . . . projecting confidence," Rory corrected, fumbling. "Look, I'm butchering the analogy, but my point is that doing

174

anything new involves a first time, which is scary. But you can calm that fear with the right . . . mindset." He shrugged, hoping that made any sort of sense.

Jacklyn's eyebrows lifted, and Rory felt her jibe coming. He quickly added, "Can you heal Tommy? Yes or no?"

"Theoretically, yes," Jacklyn said.

It wasn't the answer Rory wanted, but it was better than no. "It's what we got. Okay, just wait here for my signal."

Rory's mind raced. *Confidence.* He sucked in a deep breath, blew it out, squared his shoulders, and pushed open the door.

———

"Jeez, how bad did you have to pee?" Megan said.

"Well, uh . . ."

"Gross. Don't want to know."

Megan collected her jacket and thermos. "I wrote my patient report." She gestured to a piece of paper on the desk. "Nothing new that can't wait thirty minutes." She stopped, eyeing him. "You're all . . . sweaty."

"The closer bathroom was locked, so I went to the locker rooms. I'm good. Go eat."

Megan shrugged and waddled off toward the break room.

Rory waited until she stepped out of view and quickly scanned for her phone or anything else she might have left. He found nothing.

The clock read *00:16*. They had thirty minutes before Megan would be back. Rory turned to the doors and waved Jacklyn over.

———

"This is him?" Jacklyn walked up to Tommy's bedside. "Damn, he's just a toddler."

175

Rory slid the door closed behind them and checked once more that no one was coming. Bell's patrols were well known, but Rory hoped the two pending admits would keep her occupied elsewhere. He drew the curtain and flipped off the lights, making it look like he'd tucked Tommy in for the night.

The room plunged into darkness, illuminated only by the faint glow and steady beeps of the machines. Tommy's heartbeat still registered as a thin pink line, but it had slowed since yesterday.

Jacklyn shook her head. "Someone—"

"Against a wall, we think. The details change in every telling."

"Damn . . ." She stared down at Tommy. Outrage, pain, and sorrow flickered across her face, and she opened her mouth to say more but couldn't seem to settle on the words. She closed her eyes and exhaled. "Should we expect any family?"

Rory shook his head. "They left this morning. We aren't sure where."

"Poor kid."

"Maybe he's better off," Rory reflexively said, but felt a hot flush of shame when he caught Jacklyn studying him. He cleared his throat and checked the clock: *00:20*. "Okay. What happens next?"

Jacklyn's gaze lingered a moment longer before returning to the boy. "I'll need to touch his skin, but when I tell you, close your eyes."

"Why?"

"Because rules, hero!" Jacklyn snapped. "And don't peek. I'll know if you peek. Don't do that to yourself."

Rory couldn't help but feel that was another threat, but he just nodded.

Jacklyn pulled out a pair of aviator sunglasses and put them on. She looked silly wearing them in the dark room. "I didn't bring extras."

Rory looked skeptical. "What do I need sunglasses—" He stopped himself. *No questions.* "Close my eyes. Got it."

Jacklyn stepped closer to the bed and extended her arm stump. Rory stifled another blossoming question.

"Are you ready?" she said.

"How fast does it work?"

"Should be instant."

Should?! Rory nodded.

"Close 'em!"

Rory squeezed his eyes shut. A cold slap struck him across the front of his body. His jaw chattered once before a white explosion erupted behind his eyelids. Shielding his face, his palms stung in the intense and sudden chill. The light disappeared as quickly as it had come, and Rory shivered, slowly dropping his hands and opening his eyes.

"Is it done?" he asked, blinking away the splotches in his vision.

No reply.

"Jack—" Rory blinked again and stepped around the bed, bumping into the guardrails.

Jacklyn lay on the floor, eyes closed, with smoke rising off her stump with a faint sizzle. A hurricane of emotions ripped through Rory, but seeing a person down triggered hundreds of hours of training. *Calm down and assess.* He dropped to examine her. The hurricane quieted, blowing the fear and questions aside so he could focus. *Is she breathing?* Her chest rose steadily, and he exhaled. *Good. Heartbeat?*

"Jacklyn?" he whispered. "I'm going to touch you." No reply. Rory pressed his fingers against the notch to the side of Jacklyn's throat and felt the strong *lub-dub* of her heart. *We have a heartbeat.*

"Jacklyn, can you hear me?" Rory asked loudly, tapping her cheek. Her skin was hot and blotchy, and only then did he see the steady trickle of blood running from both nostrils.

"Hey! Wake up!"

Nothing. He glanced up at the bed. Tommy remained still, with no change to the slowly beeping monitors.

It didn't work.

"This was so stupid," Rory whispered, fumbling with what to do next. He had to get Jacklyn out of there. "Wake up!" He grabbed her finger and pressed down hard on her nail bed—a trick to see if someone was really asleep.

Jacklyn groaned and pulled her hand away. Rory pumped his fist in the air with relief. Her eyes fluttered open, and she hacked, her entire body convulsing. He grabbed a white washcloth from a stack on the counter and handed it to her. She retched into it.

Rory cringed as he watched her hack, and when the fit passed, Jacklyn drew in a shaky breath, lowering the red-stained cloth. *Her lungs are bleeding.*

"Are you okay?" Rory asked, eyeing the blood.

"That was a trip." Jacklyn shivered violently. "Got a blanket? I'm freezing."

Rory sprang across the room and pulled a blanket from the cabinet. He wrapped it around her and kneeled back down. "You're bleeding."

Jacklyn checked the washcloth. "Oh damn. Didn't expect to need that much energy. Get me up, hero, but watch your shoes. I might throw up."

Rory hooked her arm and helped her to her feet. "Did it work?"

Jacklyn looked over at Tommy. "I dunno."

"You don't know? You can't, like, feel it or something?"

"After I throw up"—Jacklyn wheezed—"I'm going to need, like, ten burritos." She burped and clutched at her stomach. "Where's the trash?"

Rory slid it over just in time to catch the first retch. There wasn't much to it, but it was the color of strawberry tea.

A knock came at the door. Jacklyn looked at Rory wide-eyed, but before he could answer, it slid open. Bell stood silhouetted by the white light behind her. "Rory? Is everything okay?"

"Yeah. I'm . . . we're good. Aunt Jackie here got a little overwhelmed seeing Tommy." Rory nodded sympathetically.

"Poor dear must have been a fright," Bell said, looking concerned. "What was that bright light, then?"

"Camera flash."

Bell cocked a hip. "Now, you know, no pictures. It's policy."

"Sorry, Bell. I thought this could be an exception."

Bell clicked her tongue. "Well, let me get some crackers to settle her stomach and—"

Jacklyn wiped her mouth. "I could use some air."

"Good idea," Rory said quickly. "Bell, could you watch Tommy and next door for five minutes while I see Jack—"

Jacklyn coughed loudly.

"—Aunt Jackie out?" Rory finished.

Bell's mouth pressed into a flat line as she checked her watch. "I could use a few minutes off my feet. Go on."

"Thanks so much," Rory said as they passed. Bell gently reached for his shoulder.

"You need to remind Aunt Jackie that visitors' hours stop at ten." Bell's tone was hard. "Rules are in place for a reason. We can't be making too many exceptions, or the rules stop applying."

"I'm sorry," Jacklyn said. She sounded genuine. "I didn't mean

179

to cause a fuss."

Bell's serene smile returned. "Don't you worry, dear. You didn't know. It's good to see Tommy with visitors. Lord knows the boy could use family."

"He's got the angels he needs."

"Oh well, you come on back anytime. Just make sure it's between 8:00 AM and 10:00 PM."

Rory hooked Jacklyn's arm. "I'll walk you out." He nodded at Bell. "I'll be right back."

———

Jacklyn regained her color by the time they reached the front entrance. Rory didn't want to risk passing Officer Kyle again, so he took her the long way, past the physicians' sleeping rooms. At the end of the hall, he swore he heard a door close behind him, but when he turned, he didn't see anyone. Rory sighed, deciding he was imagining things or was just a sleepy resident. Either way, they were short on time. Everything now was damage control.

Color-coded pipes ran the long walls of the maintenance tunnels, with the only sound coming from their footsteps echoing off the concrete. Each pipe had a label: *Hot. Cold. Air. Waste.* All with matching-colored arrows. They followed the gray waste line, which Rory thought fitting given their spectacular failure. He wondered how he could be so naïve. *Magic . . . Come on, Rory.* But the thin scar on his stomach still said otherwise. *What did I do wrong?*

Finally, standing at the edge of campus and away from the hospital's lights, Rory risked asking the question.

"What happened?" he tried. "Why didn't it work?"

"Might have been too big a cast."

"*Might have?* You said you could do this!"

180

"Theoretically," Jacklyn amended.

"Gah!" Rory threw his arms up. She had warned him, but he wasn't about to admit that. He gestured to her stump. "And what was up with the smoke off your arm? That could have set off the alarms."

"The 'smoke' isn't your concern." Jacklyn rounded on him. "Have you ever tried rebuilding a dying brain? We tried. We failed. Get over it." Another coughing fit overcame her, and she clutched at her chest with her hand. Rory grabbed her shoulder, and she leaned against him. Feeling her hack, his frustration faded. He knew that sound—the deep rattle of a hospice cough. He glanced around and saw no one. Jacklyn kept her head toward her knees and drew in a pair of wheezing breaths before the fit finally subsided.

"You're right. Sorry," Rory said, embarrassed he'd lost his temper. "That was just . . . so close."

Jacklyn breathed slowly.

"I mean it," Rory pressed. "Thank you."

Jacklyn wiped her mouth and nodded toward the front doors. "Will Bell talk?"

Rory shook his head. "I don't think so, but she will know you if she sees you again. She remembers everyone."

"The wannabe cop?"

"Kyle? He's a good guy. Intense, but means well. His report shouldn't be an issue. No one actually reads them, anyway. They just get boxed up."

"How long?"

Rory shrugged. "If it's anything like our records . . . couple weeks?"

"Two weeks is a long time."

"Don't worry. This is my part, remember? In and out." Rory

glanced at his phone. "I have to get back. Can you—"

"I'm fine, hero." Jacklyn cleared her throat and added, "And, uh . . . sorry, it didn't work. I guess I don't have the same juice I once did." She looked down at her feet and nudged a stone with her toe. "A win would've been nice."

"Yeah." Rory assessed her with a glance. She looked stable again. "That wasn't an insignificant amount of blood. Do you smoke?"

"Once. Nasty things."

"Okay. And everything else feels normal?"

"You're as bad as Caroline." Jacklyn shook her head. "But I appreciate the concern, but we both have people waiting for us. Best get back to where we belong."

Rory reached into his pocket and pulled out his wallet, plucking out the few bills he had and handing them over. "For some burritos. A deal's a deal."

Jacklyn took the money, grinning. "Maybe she was right." She slipped the money into her pocket without elaborating and walked gingerly toward the trees, muttering something about being stiff tomorrow.

Rory looked up at the patchy night sky. *We were so close . . .*

Chapter 19: Game Changer

Tuesday, April 17th, 00:33

On the stairs back to the unit, Rory's adrenaline finally faded, and his professionally pent-up emotions broke free. His knees gave out, and the frustration and fear boiled out of him, hot and stifling, choking his air. He clutched his chest, feeling as though his heart had cracked. Perhaps it had.

Some piece of him tried to talk himself out of the feeling—that he'd tried, that he should be proud of that at least, but it did little to soothe the growing pressure behind his eyes. Tears broke free and splashed onto the cold steps. He clutched his fists next to his temples, leaned against the wall, and trembled. He wept for Tommy and Octavia and all the others he couldn't save. It wasn't the first time he'd cried in this stairwell. These steps had soaked up many nurses' tears over the years.

Between sobs, a voice reminded him he still had a patient to care for and people waiting on him. He managed a few ragged breaths to settle himself and wiped the dripping snot from his nose.

No more. I'm done. For real, this time.

The thought warmed him, calmed him, and the pressure in his chest lifted. A single path became clear. A simple path. An easy path. One without the need to cry secretly in the stairwell. He sniffed and wiped his eyes, hoping his sleeve dried before he returned to the unit. He didn't want to explain anything more to Bell.

His pocket vibrated, and on his phone, he found a text message from Patrick: *Van guy wants to meet Saturday and even knocked down the price when I told him about you. 5K!*

Rory cleared his throat, typing out a quick message: *Saturday it is.* He hit send and continued up the stairs. He'd need to give his notice and finish out the schedule, but then . . . he'd be free.

Maybe he'd try photography, or maybe he'd pick up the guitar again and see where that might take him. Maybe he should try something totally new, like scuba diving or bullfighting.

As Rory climbed, old memories crept in—memories from his treatments, of coloring outside the lines with his nurse Florence, and how Susie snuck him extra sorbet during those long infusion hours. He remembered being taught how to make a squirt gun out of a syringe, tubing, and wall air. He remembered his nurses building him forts of blankets and pillows just so the monsters couldn't find him.

Rory had reached the eighth-floor landing when a thought stopped him. *If I'm not a nurse, then what am I?*

He didn't have an answer. He never thought he'd need it. It made him nauseous. At least here, he made a difference, little by little, person by person. Even on the worst nights, he could claim that. That's where he wanted to be, in the trenches with the people, fighting for the fractions. He wouldn't find that in an office, banging out memos, no matter how good the mission was. That just wasn't him.

Maybe I'll try adults? A smaller shake-up to start. He still had bills, after all. Maybe after a stop in Yellowstone, he'd find work at a rural clinic and learn to be a jack-of-all-trades? Then, slowly, sadly, more reality dripped back in.

What about Patrick and Anna? And Khloe? Who knows where that was going to go, if anywhere? Was it even worth trying? Starting over would be lonely at first, but Rory was used to the darkness. He survived it plenty of times before, and at least this time, it would be his choice. The idea of leaving felt so enticing, so pure.

Rory stepped into the back hall, dabbing his eyes and trying to come back to the present moment. He braced himself for a lecture from Bell regarding hospital policies. He deserved it.

As he approached the double doors' windows, he saw a frenzy

of activity outside Room 4. Tommy's room.

Oh shit. He's coding.

If one ever runs, actually runs, in a hospital, it's life and death. Rory sprinted.

Both residents stood outside Room 4 talking on their cell phones, and nurses buzzed in and out like bees. The respiratory therapist rolled a ventilator *out* of the room. Rory slowed; his heart raced as he listened. Laughter flowed down the hallway, and he saw a resident's face. Smiling. Crying.

Dr. Deedee stepped out of the room, wiping her eyes. She spoke with a resident who nodded, her hair in chaos, matted down on one side, and red lines streaked her face from a pillow. She spotted Rory and waved him over with a wide grin.

"He's AWAKE!" Dr. Deedee croaked.

"Awake?" Rory couldn't make the thought stick. He didn't understand. It hadn't worked. "You mean he's . . . alive?"

Deedee nodded through laughter. "See for yourself."

Slowly, Rory stepped over the threshold and into Room 4.

Round, red, and smiling, Tommy reached up and cupped Bell's wet cheeks. She cradled him, cooing. Tears streamed down her face. Rory's legs wobbled, and he braced himself against the doorway. The boy had come back from the dead.

He's alive?! Rory felt more tears building, but this time, he didn't care if anyone saw him.

Taking his eyes off Bell, Tommy watched the nurses flow around him with confusion. Two orchestrated the collection of vitals and labs, while a third distracted him with a stuffed lion. Bell tapped Tommy's nose with hers, refocusing his attention. The boy giggled and grabbed her snowy curls.

"I've been doing this a long time, Rory," Dr. Deedee said from next to him, blotting her eyes with a tissue. "And I've seen some spectacular recoveries, but I have never even heard of anything like this. It tempts you to believe in miracles."

Rory nodded, dumbfounded. *It's called casting . . .* The word *miracle* now felt too small to describe everything he'd seen over the last day.

Deedee nudged Rory with her elbow and nodded back toward the unit. Parents from other rooms poked their heads out and watched the commotion. "The unit needed this. Morale is low. And this . . . is a big win."

Pride swelled in Rory's chest. *A win.* Thoughts of travel slipped away as Rory drafted a pitch to Jacklyn in his head. *We can do this again.*

One resident held up their phone and called for Deedee. As she stepped away, Tommy turned his head and met Rory's eyes briefly. The boy blinked once, then unleashed a toothy smile. It stunned him. *The dead don't smile.*

For the first time in months, Rory felt the tightness in his chest release. He breathed lighter. *We did it.* He barely believed the thought. The relief and joy of the revelation cracked him open, shattering his professional mask. Happy tears followed. He sniffed and discreetly aimed his phone and pressed "record." Aunt Jackie needed to see this.

Chapter 20: Dirty Job

Tuesday, April 17th, 06:30

Seven miles east of Springfield, Oregon

In a damp wood near a city, by a river, two bodies lay half-buried at the bottom of a deep, muddy pit. Based on the sheer volume of empty beer cans and crushed red cups, this was a popular spot for parties. Yards of yellow *Caution* tape and little numbered flags poked up everywhere. Surveying the scene, Jane guessed Emmett's forensics team had already been through. They marked every food wrapper, every bottle cap, and what looked like footprints at the lip of the pit. With its ragged muck, upturned red soil, and the ring of gray mushrooms around its edge, it reminded Jane of an open wound.

"Must have been a hell of a shock," Jane said, brushing a pink strand from her face.

"Huh?" Emmett said next to her, still glued to his phone. He hadn't really set it down since they arrived, coordinating an entire manhunt through that tiny screen.

"The kid who found the bodies. Must have been a shock."

Emmett finished his message and slipped his phone away. "We're getting the last testimony now." He pointed through the trees, about a hundred feet off, where a group of college students, most wearing Greek letters on their sweatshirts, stood in a loose group with a pair of agents watching over them. Their eyes were downcast and somber—fearful, Jane noted. "Apparently, one guy went to pee and fell in. Came face to face with our mummies."

"That'll sober you up real quick."

Emmett nodded, chuckling, and pointed at a smear of dirt and orange-red clay from the fall. "About three hours ago."

Jane raised an eyebrow. "Three hours? Nice response time."

"We got lucky being so close," Emmett said. "Unfortunately, the bodies aren't much good. Forensics tells me they are too decomposed to pull much evidence. Been here a couple weeks, exposed." He sighed. "Still, this is the freshest scene to date. We're normally months behind."

"Or the killer is just months further ahead," Jane muttered, squinting down at the bodies. "Well . . . shall we go look?" She meant to wait for a reply, but already took a step.

Emmett grabbed her shoulder and guided her back. "Hold on. Forensics went to get a piece of special equipment. They think they might salvage something from the bodies, but told me to keep everyone from contaminating the site before they get back."

"But isn't this your investigation?" Jane said, not understanding Emmett's passivity. "This is your call."

"Exactly, Jane. I work *with* my team," Emmett countered. "And I listen to orders. The Director wants this place analyzed first. Then we can go poke around. Just be patient."

"Patience." Jane rolled her eyes. She glanced up through the trees and saw an ominous cloud filling the horizon. "When that storm hits, your pit will turn into a pond in a hurry, and you can kiss whatever shreds of evidence goodbye."

"Anything down there can survive a little rain," Emmett said.

Jane pointed at the clouds. "That one looks angry, and a hard rain could flush something we want to see." It felt flimsy, even to her, but it's what she had with Emmett sticking to the Director's guns. She had some work to do.

"My call, Jane. My orders."

Orders. Jane turned up her nose. What he really meant was obedience. "You are playing as a pawn, Emmett." She scoffed. "Standing still like this makes you predictable—an easy mark for any half-decent con."

Emmett looked at her, and for a fleeting moment, she thought she might have gotten through to him.

Instead, he said, "Spoken like a true thief. Stay out of the pit."

Thief, was that what the Director was calling her these days? She sighed, disappointed but unsurprised to see the Director's orders coming out of this rookie's mouth. The man poured honey into your ear. So sweet that he'd persuaded Jane to look the other way on all the little moral dilemmas that had come up for years, with drips of promotions, plausible lies, and delicious compliments. She couldn't see then that it was actually poison to keep her loyal and following orders. That didn't absolve her of the choices, though. Those were hers. She pulled the trigger. Emmett hadn't yet. Maybe there was time to stop him.

Emmett turned back to his phone, leaving Jane alone with the two ghosts in the pit. After a moment, she decided her own ghosts were plenty and wandered over to a tree stump.

The wood was damp, with a string of ants marching by its base. She dusted the spot with her hand, trying to avoid any sap on her pants, and sat, wondering when she'd get her hands on these bodies. Not that she expected much. The weather around here likely washed out everything, but she had that irritating buzz, the kind that only came with unturned leads. She didn't know for sure; there could be something down there. The only way to know was to go look.

Not seeing any budge from Emmett, Jane carefully picked through her memory, pulling up the mental pictures she had taken while sifting through the stacks of case folders. She spent the last two days poring over the autopsy reports and officer notes, finding Emmett's early descriptions accurate. The bodies always came in pairs, stashed somewhere remote, and carried chest burns, though all the photos were too maggot-eaten to know what had caused the burn.

The only piece Emmett exaggerated was about the mummification. According to the reports, the organs hadn't been removed surgically, like a true mummification. The coroners had found the bodies filled with "organ dust"—a small difference, but important. Jane had to do a little research, but she learned there are two types of mummification: by people or by nature. By people takes seventeen days—a period of ritual and mourning. Spontaneous mummification arose from forces of nature like volcanoes or mudslides, both swift blitzes of immense, entombing power. Jane bet that whatever happened to these people happened in seconds, but the thought made her shiver. If her hunch was right, it meant their killer used a force of nature on those two people. Who wielded that kind of power? And why?

Another key difference came from their posture. The bodies she'd seen in the pictures all looked peaceful, relaxed even, like they'd been asleep when their end came. The bodies in the pit were different. Even from the rim, she could see the half-submerged screams both victims wore on their leathery faces, their limbs curled painfully inward like the legs of a dead spider. The killer either hadn't had time or changed their strategy for some unknown reason, but there just wasn't enough evidence to know which yet. At a dead-end, Jane logged both possibilities in her memory for later retrieval.

A wet drop struck her cheek, and she looked up to see the dark clouds looming overhead. The storm was nearly here. Emmett paced near the edge of the pit, typing away on his phone.

Jane sighed and crossed back over to Emmett as the volley of soft *pit-pats* intensified against the dirt. She stuffed her hands in her pockets.

"So . . . this is what passes as an investigation now? Staring at your phone while the evidence gets washed out? As your consultant, I feel obligated to tell you when you're being an idiot."

Emmett shot her a side-eye glare but kept typing. "Well, maybe you should do your thing. That's why you're here, isn't it?"

"My thing?"

"Yeah," Emmett said, waving an arm over the pit. "The Director said you have a thing, the master detective thing. Like Sherlock Holmes."

Jane smiled but hated herself for it. "He called me Sherlock Holmes?"

"Uh-huh. He said you could find a shoe print in the mud that tells you the killer's favorite dinner, or a hair on a shirt that points to the killer's cat, or semen on—"

"Ok . . . ay," Jane cut him off. "Easy tiger. I don't have a *thing*. I just pay attention, study, and then see where my hunches take me."

Emmett's fingers idled over his screen, and he looked up. "You said that the other day, too. What's a hunch?"

Jane considered. "Hm. Well . . . think of it like an itch. Right here." She tapped the crown of her pink hair. "Or here." She waved a hand over her stomach. "But deep inside. Subconscious even, until you scratch it with the answer."

"Uh-huh," Emmett said, not impressed. "Well, what does your hunch say now?"

"That I should be in the pit," Jane deadpanned.

Emmett sighed. "No pit, Jane." He resumed typing.

She felt her frustration rise, ready to grab the damn phone and chuck it at their mummies just to see how fast Emmett would break his own rule. She judged she was fast enough to pull it off. Emmett looked athletic, but she was whip quick. The issue was the consequences. They'd only just arrived, and until they got an actual clue, she might as well kiss learning anything about the killer or the Seed goodbye. She needed a new strategy, one to

191

catch Emmett's attention.

Bzzz, bzzz.

"Hold on." Emmett peered at his phone. "Forensics found the tool apparently and are on their way back."

Jane looked up at the sky as the rain steadily increased. They would be too late.

She turned away and drew out a small wooden pipe from her pocket. In her other pocket, she found a small bag with mossy green buds and a lighter. She caught Emmett watching her with unease.

"Come on, Jane, really?"

Jane feigned shame. "I know, but all the best creative minds seem to smoke, don't they? Sherlock had his hat, his address, and most importantly, his pipe. Gandalf. Miles Davis. Churchill! Einstein. They all seemed to do something right." She winked and removed a pinch from the baggie.

Emmett didn't appear convinced. "That's tobacco, right?"

Jane dramatically placed a hand over her heart. "Why, Emmett, this is a federal investigation." She carefully stuffed the pipe's chamber.

Emmett frowned at her and tucked his phone back into his pocket. His gaze drifted down to the bodies. "What do you think? More model citizens?"

Jane snorted. "I'll give it to our killer. At least they're consistent. Every victim has carried a nasty record. Can't say I'm mad about any of them being dead."

"It's not our job to judge."

"Not your job, maybe, but it's my specialty." Jane stashed the baggie back in her pocket and brought out a lighter. "Killer could be a vigilante. Revenge is a powerful payoff and obscures consequences."

"Speaking from experience?" Emmett said.

Jane frowned, then touched fire to the chamber and inhaled deeply. Her throat burned slightly, and she felt her inflexible thoughts soften into wisps of smoke.

Emmett eyed the pipe a moment, then returned to the bodies. "I agree, though. This feels like a textbook vigilante. They go city to city, picking off a few loners before they move on. Probably have some personal code they use to justify their actions." Jane sputtered out a cough, and Emmett rolled his eyes. "It doesn't explain the burns, though."

"A brand," Jane said, and a puff of smoke escaped.

"Like a calling card?" Emmett's nose wrinkled.

Jane exhaled a thick cloud of skunky smoke. "Something like that. I once caught a guy who left totems of his victims, branding them with all sorts of weird symbols. Each part of a ritual to open hell's gate." She shuddered at the grisly memory. Emmett cringed, turning a little green, so Jane pivoted. "Our killer? Well, it's hard to tell from the reports alone. None of them have clear photos. Bodies are too decomposed. If we figure out what the brand looks like, well . . . that clue will tell us a lot more about who we're playing with. Which, I'd like to remind you, might be *in* the pit."

Emmett's face flushed when a deep rumble from the woods pulled both their attention to the narrow path leading back to the main gravel road. A hulking black Humvee with thick armored plates rumbled up to a crunching stop by the black SUVs. Jane eyed the vehicle, finding it odd that a manhunt required military-grade hardware. Who did the Director expect them to find?

"Good," Emmett sighed, stepping toward the truck. "Agent Dawson is here."

Jane whipped around. "Dawson? *Donald* Dawson?"

Emmett suddenly looked guilty. "Yes."

"You knew and didn't tell me?!"

"I was told not to, sorry. The Director said you two were partners once before you left. And something about him taking your promotion afterward."

"That dirty mother muffer . . ." Jane muttered. "He swooped my job! Not that I wanted it, mind you, but it's the principle!"

The Humvee's passenger door opened, and Jane barely recognized the giant of a man who stepped out. Dawson wore long-sleeved, khaki fatigues with his pants tucked neatly into combat boots. The outfit was the same as she remembered, but the scrawny parasite had packed on slabs of muscle, stretching the uniform tight.

"*That's* Dawson?" Jane said, dumbfounded.

Emmett nodded and squinted at the sky as the rain picked up, pattering on the dense forest carpet.

Dawson took off his knit cap, and steam rose from his bald scalp as he surveyed the scene. Jane spotted perhaps the only thing that hadn't changed on her ex-partner: a long, thick braid of red hair still hung from his chin. *Why did he keep the furry chin dildo?*

He stalked over to the group of witnesses, beard flopping, and they shuffled back as he approached. While she couldn't hear what her former partner said, the fear on the students' faces, as they stared up at him, told Jane all she needed to know. He hadn't changed. He was still the Director's favorite attack dog.

"Wow," Emmett said. "I never thought I'd see you so quiet."

"I never thought I'd see my old partner look like Hitler's Übermensch. What the hell happened to him?"

"Not sure. Gym membership? He's my logistics coordinator," Emmett said. "Takes care of the public side of the investigation. You know how adamant the Director is about discretion. He doesn't want to spook the public, and Dawson is the best. We already have journalists on our trail and this case would be irresistible to the media, not to mention the public would devour it. The Director said that if the full story gets out, our killer might go to ground or worse, gain publicity."

Full story? "What got out?"

"A couple of photos leaked. Enough for the regional news to make a nickname—the Vacuum-Seal Killer, but not much else. Dawson bottled it up quickly and has kept everything mostly quiet. If we're careful and attention cool, the public will move on, and we'll have more freedom to operate." Jane didn't like it, but it made sense. When she glanced around, she noted the lack of news vans or reporters.

"After the leak, I got the job," Emmett said. "The Director said I had excellent organization skills."

"Hm. Honeyed words," Jane said. "He likes those."

"Cute, Jane, but it's out of my hands," Emmett said, irritated. "You're going to have to play nice if you want to stick around. We're all on the same team now."

Same team. The words made Jane's skin crawl. "I'll play nice only if he does."

A sudden thought struck her. If Dawson was here, an experienced agent, then Emmett probably had even less control of the investigation than he thought. Jane had to give it to the Director—baiting her with the rookie but having the devil as his second. A clever move. Making her only way forward . . . *through.*

The voice in her head shouted at her to get into the pit and cramped her gut to make sure she got the point. She looked down the muddy slopes, plotting. *Permission or forgiveness?* Forgiveness was always easier.

As soon as Emmett turned his back, Jane saw her opportunity. She stuffed the pipe into her pocket and jumped into the pit.

Slipping on muddy leaves and branches, she bounded down, keeping her arms spread wide to keep her balance.

"Hey! Stop!" Emmett shouted behind her.

Too late. As though the sky had been waiting for a signal, the clouds opened up, dumping sheets of pummeling rain. Jane was thankful; the stinging scent of the murky, stagnant water was overwhelming. She stuffed her nose into the crook of her elbow, shoes crunching down on cans and plastic cups and splashing brown water onto the nearest corpse.

"Jane, stop!"

Jane ignored him, squatting down to examine the body. White grubs squirmed between the holes in the victim's faded shirt. The leathery skin was taut, stretched thin against the bone, just like the others. Rats must have chewed away the ears along with several toes from a bare foot. Using her sleeve to cover her hand, Jane shoved the corpse. It was light, almost hollow. She looked into the shrieking face, then back to the chest where the mangled arms twisted in, obscuring the burns. Through the victim's gnarled, bony fingers, Jane saw a chunk of charred green flesh still intact. There was something there, but getting it would certainly break orders.

Jane shrugged—she'd come this far already. She reached out, seized both skeletal arms, and pulled.

"Hey! What are you—" Emmett shouted, and she vaguely heard him splashing in the pit behind her. Bracing her feet, Jane heaved.

The bones quivered beneath the strain, followed by two audible snaps. Jane stumbled back, holding two broken forearms in either hand as Emmett seized her shoulders from behind, spinning her around. She gave her most innocent smile. "Emmett! You came down."

"What the hell are you—" His voice cut off as he saw the corpse. "Is . . . is that a handprint?"

At the center of the corpse's chest, branded into the sickly, ragged skin, was the shape of a human hand. The water lapped against the skin's edge, pulling pieces away while the pit slowly filled. Jane's hunch was right again.

"Not just any handprint," Jane said, examining closer. "A left hand. Our killer's a southpaw."

It wasn't much, just a little detail, but it sent a thrill of excitement through Jane. She hadn't felt it in many years and couldn't help but grin. She nodded at the second body. "I bet our other friend has the same brand."

"We shouldn't be down here," Emmett said firmly.

"Yet here we are," Jane shot back. "Don't ruin my high, Emmett. Hey, do you know what we really need now?"

"A rope." Emmett eyed the muddy slopes back up.

"No, a fresh body!"

"You want them to kill again?"

"Well, yeah, how else do we get new clues? This place is as cold as these corpses. We got lucky finding the burn intact."

Emmett's nostrils flared as he closed his eyes, seething. Jane wondered if she'd pushed him too far.

The rain continued, and Emmett wiped the water from his eyes, glancing back and forth between Jane, still holding the forearms and the bodies. Enough water had collected in the pit that the empty cans floated. Jane took a step back, examining the body, but her foot plunged into the oily rainwater, and the cold soaked into her sock. Cringing, Jane wondered if her shoes needed to be burned now.

"This was a bad idea," Emmett finally said. Not what Jane was hoping to hear, but at least the shock seemed to wear off. "The Director wouldn't want—"

"Stop!" Jane snapped, and Emmett looked down at her blankly.

She stepped toward him. "Free advice, Emmett. The Director always gets what he wants. He never missteps. Let me guess: he told you not to worry about receipts or expense reports, right? He used to tell me the same thing. Sounded convenient for me— a favor—but it's because he didn't want a paper trail."

Emmett went still. "I thought it was an odd request, too, but I—"

Jane finished for him, "Didn't want to rock the boat on your first case? See. The man knows subversion."

Emmett nodded, and his gaze focused through her on something Jane couldn't see.

"Need a smoke? It helps me with these big *wow* moments."

"No!" Emmett looked around. "We have to get out of here. Dawson will—"

"Be very disappointed," a deep voice boomed above them. Jane turned and saw Dawson at the pit's edge, wearing a sour look.

"Hello, Donald," Jane said, waving a broken forearm.

"Jane." Dawson's eyes narrowed at her. "I heard you died."

"You didn't send flowers."

"I should have sent a thank you." Dawson grinned, displaying unnaturally white teeth.

"Agent Dawson," Emmett said nervously. "She went down. I had to get her out."

"Oh, you know you wanted to come in, Emmett," Jane said.

Emmett's mouth dropped. "No. You! Sir, Agent Dawson, I didn't . . . I—"

"I don't care," Dawson growled. "Get out. Now."

Jane gestured to the mud-slick slope. "Mind giving us a hand up?"

Dawson grunted and disappeared.

Emmett sighed. "The Director is going to give me hell about this."

Jane lowered her voice, watching for Dawson's return. "Donald is a bully. And this is *your* muffing investigation, Emmett. Not theirs. When Donald gets grumpy, remember this: you're the head pawn. Act like it."

The rain continued relentlessly, and it seemed the pep-talk had the desired effect. Emmett stiffened and scowled at her, but withheld any comments. For the better, she supposed, it meant he was thinking it over instead of getting defensive. Unfortunately, she felt she might have over-sold Emmett's control of the situation, given Dawson's presence. If she was going to unplug him from the Director, she needed him to be confident and curious, not meek. But teaching had taught her that when you aim to motivate and oversell, you run the risk of delusion. Jane really hoped her pep-talk didn't come back to bite her.

Dawson reappeared a moment later and tossed down a rope.

"After you, Agent Bait." Jane gestured to the rope with her forearm.

Emmett frowned, his eyes flicking back and forth between Dawson and Jane. Taking the rope, he climbed, slipping and sliding the whole way up. Jane dropped her arms and followed, picking her footing carefully. Reaching the top, she felt her wet clothes sticking to her with smudges of mud and who knows what else covering her pants and jacket.

"Gross. Hey Emmett, what's the budget for dry-cleaning—"

A shadow suddenly loomed over her, and she looked up at the imposing figure. Jane was certain Dawson had grown another six inches since last she saw him, and despite both being in their forties, Dawson didn't look like he'd aged. Rationally, she knew that was impossible, but the evidence stood before her with a self-satisfied sneer.

"How're we looking?" Emmett asked.

Dawson peeled his eyes off Jane and turned to face Emmett. "The situation is under control. Our witnesses have been . . . asked to keep silent."

Jane spotted the group of college students now being escorted away from the campsite, looking terrified. "Good luck. As soon as they are out of here, they'll post the whole thing."

Dawson chuckled. "Not this time. The Director has given me full jurisdiction. I told those little shits if they said anything, I'd see all their student loans tripled and implied they might find trouble ever securing a job." He shrugged. "After that, they didn't seem eager to talk."

"Sounds familiar," Jane deadpanned.

"You can't do that," Emmett said quietly. "They're citizens."

Dawson sniffed and crossed his thick arms over his chest. "For now. *Sir.*" Her former partner pointed back toward the parked SUVs scattered among the trees. "The forensics team is five minutes out."

Jane looked down into the rapidly filling pit. "Good luck to them."

Bzzz, bzzz.

Emmett pulled out his phone, and his face paled. "It's the Director."

"Keeping you on a short leash, isn't he?" Jane said.

Emmett trudged off toward the SUVs with his phone pressed to his ear. Thunder rumbled in the distance, and Jane suddenly realized she was freezing. A shiver started in her toes and ran up the length of her body, but when she glanced over at Dawson, the big man didn't seem to notice the rain. Instead, he narrowed his eyes and grinned like a canny wolf.

"I know your scheme, Jane," Dawson said. "But the kid is more loyal than you ever were."

"I'm sorry, can you start over? I was distracted by your stupid beard."

"You won't turn him."

"Won't I?" Jane considered. "Well, I think it's too early to tell. Plus, he still has something you gave away."

Dawson raised an eyebrow. "Oh yes? What's that?"

"A soul."

"Ha!" Dawson laughed. "Overrated. Maybe I did miss you, Jane. You're always good for a laugh." Chuckling, he shadowed Emmett back to the vehicles.

A chill that had nothing to do with the cold ran down Jane's back as she peered down at the sinking bodies. Dawson's presence and apparent transformation complicated things, but she had plenty of time to worm her way in. She'd already found an important clue. *A left-handed brand.* Jane was puzzled by its meaning. Everything was speculation without more evidence. *We need a fresh scene.*

Dripping, she ducked her head against the storm and ran for the vehicles.

Chapter 21: Mushroom Hunt

Wednesday, April 18th

When his shift ended, Rory couldn't leave—he found himself stuck, retelling Tommy's incredible story again and again to the stunned day shift crew. Not the whole story—he had a promise to keep—but by retelling it, he kept the spark of wonder alive in himself and passed it on for others to experience. It wasn't until around ten in the morning before he slowly biked home, collapsed on his couch, and spent the rest of his day dozing as he watched the news coverage with Sneaks curled on his lap. The news continued all night long with the same two or three details expounded upon endlessly, and anything new, important or not, labeled "BREAKING!"

Rory watched, delighted, knowing none of the talking heads knew what really happened. How could they? He barely did, and he was there, but that didn't stop the growing sense of pride at seeing Tommy's smiling face on the screen again and again. Strange though, there was no mention of the mother or boyfriend—only that "an accident" landed Tommy in the hospital. The public didn't want their hope tainted by tragedy.

Wednesday morning, Rory nearly spit out his cereal when Dr. Deedee appeared on his TV screen. The media by then had dubbed the event "The Rose City Wonder" and seemed to enjoy playing up the more fantastical theories regarding Tommy's recovery. Divine intervention, top-secret serums, and even aliens were all considered.

To Deedee's credit, she deftly dodged the words *miracle* and *magic* the interviewer kept using as bait. Still, the interviewer persisted and asked for three different ways in which Tommy could have woken up, but Deedee, sticking to her story, admitted she didn't know, but that they were looking into it. She wrapped up with a pensive frown, obviously flustering the reporter, who missed his sound bite, and Rory saw the flicker of the man's frown as he passed the coverage back to the studio.

Rory's spoon scraped the bottom of the bowl, so he rose and got ready to go. Jacklyn had to see the video of Tommy waking up and hugging the nurses. If she had a heart, after seeing it, she'd have to agree to heal others. But just in case, Rory picked up a few burgers on the way up the hill. Jacklyn seemed ravenous after last night. *And sick.* Rory could feel it. The blood. It worried him—especially the amount she coughed up. And the fainting. One bad angle and she could have struck her head, maybe even died. Rory couldn't let that happen; he needed her.

Next time, he'd be prepared. Maybe stand behind her? Some pillows might help.

Why did she pass out? How does this "casting" work?

Rory sighed, knowing there wouldn't be answers anytime soon, not with Jacklyn's strict rules. But they presented a puzzle he was keen to crack: how do you get an answer without a question?

———

Same day, 10:16

Rory biked back and forth across the hill, using the hospital as a landmark. After an hour of searching and several thorny off-roading attempts, he found the turnoff and followed it through the bramble. The barbed wall didn't appear as imposing in the daylight, though he wasn't about to test it. Ducking around a thick, mean-looking vine, he jumped.

"Oh, hello, Rory!"

Caroline reclined in a yellow folding chair. Eyes closed, it was the most of her face he'd ever seen, with her white blindfold lying across her lap. She was lovely, maternally, like Bell or Megan. The sunlight peeked over the tree line, soaking into her tanned skin with a warm glow as a soft breeze plucked at her loose-fitting floral dress. Beside her chair rested a pile of cardboard and wrappers, but Rory doubted that was all it was. He dismounted and approached carefully, squeezing both handlebars and eyeing the pile. Two turquoise eyes snapped open and leveled on him.

"It's alright, dear." Caroline rose, keeping her eyes closed as she lifted her blindfold and tied it around her head. The three gemstones hanging around her neck clattered together as she stepped barefoot across the jagged gravel. "I am so happy to see you."

Behind her, the trash slid forward, just a step behind the tall, wispy woman, its bright eyes fixed on Rory. He tensed, turning his front tire in case the golem charged.

Caroline stopped, and the pile also stopped, its eyes shifting up to her innocently. "Oh, yes," she said. "I spoke with them, but to be safe, it's best you wear a keystone." She reached down into her pocket and drew out the etched river stone, now hanging from a silver chain. "I made an improvement, so your Sneaks can't be blamed."

Rory heard the accusation and blushed. "I didn't mean . . . She's always . . ."

Caroline's smile blossomed, and the skin above her blindfold crinkled. It took a moment, but Rory caught the wry joke.

"You're kidding."

"I am. It's healthy to laugh, soothing." Caroline held the keystone out to Rory. "You've seen its medical properties, yes?"

Rory had, countless times from Bell, and chuckled as he reached for the stone. "Bell, my charge nurse, tries to get us to laugh at the beginning of each shift. Especially the tough nights. It helps. Cuts the tension, you know? Brings us together." The moment his fingers touched the stone, the golem's eyes closed, and it slid back toward the bramble. He exhaled and slipped the necklace on.

Caroline nodded. "A wise woman."

Rory wondered what Caroline and Bell might talk about if they ever went for drinks.

Caroline cleared her throat. "Perhaps we should leave the road before we continue our discussion?"

Rory shook his head and checked the road in both directions. "Yeah. Of course. But, uh, why were you out here?"

Were you waiting for me? A part of him hoped she was.

Caroline turned to face the sunbeams cutting over the trees. "I worship the sunlight." Silly as it was, he felt the bite of disappointment. She inhaled the crisp air, slow and deep, and as she did, the bright light illuminated her lined face, and her white hair glittered. For a beat, her tan skin reflected a golden glow. She was radiant and beautiful. *An angel.*

Rory realized he was staring and glanced down at his handlebars. "Don't you get sun at your beach?"

"It's a cove," Caroline corrected, stretching out her arms wide. "And that was technically a question. I'll let it slide, but Jacklyn won't. They're in a gray mood today."

That wasn't the start Rory was hoping for. *Maybe I should come back later.*

The sun slid behind a cloud, and the light faded. Caroline sighed longingly and lowered her arms. "I did hope you'd come, though." She turned and nodded at his bike. "Did you bring food? I assume you have another proposal." She stepped closer, leaning toward him. "You appear lighter than last I saw you, so I suspect so. Optimism bubbles within you."

Rory felt revealed, naked. "How did you—" He knew he wouldn't get an answer, so he dropped it. "I came to—"

Caroline held up one lithe finger and Rory fell silent. "Whatever your reasons, save it for Jacklyn and know food is key to her attention."

Rory nodded, patting the saddlebag over his back wheel. "Burgers okay?"

"Unsustainable, but they will do." She stepped aside and gestured down the path. "Shall we?"

Rory hesitated. At the edge of the bramble, a golem reached out its claw from the pile and pushed against the ground. The heap unfolded, sliding smoothly into a stooped, two-legged creature with fat mushroom caps. The golem used its large, spindly claws like a chimpanzee might, swinging its short legs forward. It made three long strides before it jerked to a stop, as one claw tangled in the bramble. It struggled, pulling and twisting, only getting further snared. Slashing at the thorns with its free hand, the creature cleaved off a thick branch but snagged its claw on a thicker stalk. After a few more feeble thrashes, the golem went limp, turning its enormous eyes on Caroline and clicking its long claws meekly.

Caroline sighed. "It's hard to give a mushroom a body and expect them to be graceful. The poor things have never quite figured out how limbs work."

Rory checked the roadway and hurried to keep up. "Wait. Golems are mushrooms?"

Caroline arched an eyebrow, folding her yellow chair. "You can't help yourself, can you?"

Rory frowned. *No questions.* He tried again, slowly. "Golems have mushrooms . . . that . . . control them."

"You listen well, Rory. We call the mushrooms Psybelles."

Psybelles?

"Never heard of them."

"That, my dear, is by design." She waved for him to follow. "Come, we better help before it hurts itself."

Rory didn't move, unsure what she meant. *Designed by whom? Jacklyn? Or those hunting her?* A hollowness dropped into his gut, realizing there was an entire world he knew nothing about. Just the way Jacklyn wanted. The hollowness quickly turned to dread. *What if Jacklyn finds out I know about Psybelles?*

Caroline stopped short of the golem and turned, tipping her head to the side. "Don't worry, Rory. I won't tell her. Yet."

There again, Rory felt exposed, seen. *Can she see what I think?*

Caroline smiled as if in reply. "Jacklyn defends her secrets jealously, yes, but I know which demons she truly fears. I won't violate those, for now, but if we are working together, we must trust one another—despite her stubbornness. To do so, knowledge must be shared." She gave a crisp nod, punctuating the end of that conversation, then added, "Aren't you coming?"

Behind her, the golem clicked again, rustling the bramble.

Rory blinked and, despite his hoard of questions, felt a sense of assurance and security in Caroline, like a floundering ship spotting the lighthouse in a storm. He couldn't place why or what, just the powerful impulse to let himself move into the unknown, knowing she'd guide the way. Swiping his reticence aside, he pushed his bike and followed.

Caroline resumed her walk, though hardly in a rush. "Now, where was I? Ah yes. Psybelles are nearly extinct. We cultivate them in the cave you have seen. They like the moisture but not the wind. The fungus thrives in waste and compost and can even break down some inorganics."

"Like rusty metal. Its, uh . . . bones." Rory glanced back at the road. *Clear.*

Caroline nodded. "Very good. We spent a great deal of time in scrap yards, finding the right aged rust the Psybelles prefer. They are rather picky." She paused a moment, considering. "I tell you this next piece because it's mine to protect, not Jacklyn's. For ten thousand years, my people cultivated the Psybelles to build the golems. They are clever and make diligent, albeit clumsy, helpers and once formed the cornerstone of my people's vast empire."

Once? Empire? Rory thought back to the old empires from his history classes. Egyptians, Babylonians, and even Mesopotamians—the oldest of all—didn't stretch past 4000 B.C. Ten thousand years, though, what was around that long ago? Rory felt insignificant in the vastness of time he tried to contemplate. *How big is this? How . . .* He frowned, trying to grasp all the implications.

Caroline cleared her throat, and Rory looked up. She'd stopped over the golem, and both of them were studying him quietly. "You must have a mountain of questions."

"That's an understatement," he said, picking his next words carefully. "I would like to know . . . more."

Subtle, Rory.

"Another time, I'm afraid."

Rory inhaled, frustrated, but left it at that. He had little leverage to push.

"Patience, Rory," Caroline said. She set her chair down and hiked up her dress before kneeling and inspecting the tangle with her hands. Rory expected her to yelp when she snagged a thorn, but the shout never came as she probed the snare. "There is a great deal to learn through experience. Time. Exposure. For now, we will teach you, but only that which maintains our safety." She tugged on a vine, testing it, before shaking her head. "You've gone and caught yourself, little one."

Rory stood with Caroline between him and the golem. "You speak to them?"

Caroline reached into the thicket to her bare shoulder, trying to untangle the golem's claw. "It's a subtle language." She tugged on another vine. "Simple. The mushrooms have limited sentience."

She said it all so casually that Rory expected Jacklyn to jump out and yell, "Gotcha, hero!" Rory felt the now-familiar wave of dizziness wash over him again. Sentient mushrooms. A figment of his imagination? A psychotic break? He blinked, steadying himself again.

You are seeing this. This is a mushroom-guided golem trapped in a bramble patch. It's just another Wednesday.

Caroline gave a satisfied grunt and jerked a long green vine bristling with thorns from the patch. Before she reached back in, she raised an eyebrow. "Are you unwell?"

"No, I'm just . . ." Rory searched for the right word, but nothing fit. "Uh, processing?" *Good enough.* "They . . . think?" Rory paused, trying it another way. "You have thinking mushrooms." Both sounded nuts. He shook his head.

Caroline nodded. "Is it so hard to believe? They were here and evolving long before we were." She tugged on another branch. "The Psybelles have an array of basic commands and clicks, similar to a well-trained canine. Personally, I believe they listen more to the music and tenor of the word than its meaning."

"Like a dog."

She considered, then nodded. "An apt comparison."

"I heard you say something earlier. Something I'd never heard before."

Caroline nodded. "*Sa-sha-delune.*"

Rory touched his new scar. "It is soothing. *Sa-sha-delune.*" He felt the word roll gently through his thoughts.

"Very good. It means sleep. A helpful command for mischievous golems." Caroline patted the ground beside her. "Now, I need your help to liberate our little friend here. They will not attack. Your keystone has live Psybelle spores within. As long as you

209

wear it, the golems see you as one of them. You have nothing to worry about. Grab its arm. We pull on three."

The golem looked over at him and started clicking again; it looked so innocent. Rory blew out a breath and leaned his bike against a wall of bushes. "I'm here to help," he told the golem as he kneeled, but the creature only stared at him with luminous eyes. He swallowed and reached forward, the golem watching his every move. He grasped an oddly warm arm and felt mud squelch between his fingers.

"Ready?" Caroline asked.

Rory nodded. "Okay."

"One, two, pull!"

He heaved. Branches cracked. A sudden shift in weight sent him sprawling backward. The golem toppled out, free, and landed beside him, looking up. Rory froze, feeling the cool keystone sitting against his chest. The golem lifted a claw, and Rory scrambled back, but the creature stopped, tapping the tips of its rusty claws together in a rapid set of clicks. Finished, it pushed itself up and swung down the path.

"It said thank you," Caroline said.

"Right . . ." Rory said, watching the creature stop at the edge of the trees. There, it folded to the ground and went still, camouflaged as little more than a damp pile of cardboard and trash.

What have I gotten myself into?

"Um, hello?" said a voice behind them.

Rory jumped and turned around to see a young man, around sixteen, with matted brown hair and an oil-stained puffy red vest. The boy looked as though he hadn't seen a shower in months. Behind him, he pulled a dented wagon carrying a sleeping bag, tarps, and a worn guitar. Rory knew the look of impermanence. Bouncing between foster homes led to a childhood designed to be mobile and carry few possessions. A spark of pity welled in Rory's chest; he recognized loneliness too.

The kid looked ready to bolt as his eyes darted back and forth between Rory and Caroline. By that startled look, Rory judged this must have been his first visit. He glanced back at the trash pile, expecting to see the golem crawling forward, but found the creature still, its two turquoise eyes peering out from the heap.

"Karl sent me," the boy began hesitantly. "I drank the nasty purple . . . stuff a . . . and I have the stone?" He held out an identical keystone to the one Rory wore.

Who's Karl, and how did he get a keystone? Apparently, he wasn't alone in seeking Jacklyn, and the idea simultaneously relieved and disappointed him. Caroline and Jacklyn had invited others to the Cove. How many had come before Rory? *Where were they now?*

The teen's eyes flicked up and traced a lazy path through the air. Rory looked up and saw nothing, but he suspected he knew what the teen was watching—*a wisp.*

"You did well," Caroline said.

The teen's shoulders slumped forward with relief. "So you can help me? With the voices, I mean." He edged forward, his wagon creaking behind him.

Caroline squared up to him. "What is your name?"

"Maxwell, ma'am."

"And did you tell anyone you were coming here?"

Maxwell shook his head quickly. "No, ma'am. I just followed . . . uh, that." He pointed into the empty sky above them.

"Good," Caroline said. "Follow us and don't stray." She waved for them both and started down the path. "You too, Rory. You're both in for a treat."

Chapter 22: The Hidden Cove

Wednesday, April 18th

Translated from:

Disc - Shepherd's Stone

Sub-ring - *Accounts*

Script - *The Hidden Cove*

Link unknown, the Seed connects to the space which its Host cannot find. The Cove reflects a where, but no perceivable when. Here, all needs are met. Storms brew in anger, the sun beams in high spirits, and its entrance is little more than a wrinkle in time.

In this place, rest is found.

In this place, the Seed is safe.

Amendment(s):

(224 AA) - Safety is not guaranteed.

—

Caroline had been right about Jacklyn's gray mood.

From the edge of the surf, Rory watched a thick fog roll in from the sea, blanketing everything in a damp cold. Through it, he caught glimpses of the crashing waves and heard the gulls call out from the encroaching mist. Somewhere out there, he imagined a sun, bright, warm, and beautiful, ready to peek out and bask them all. But as the clouds continued their endless crawl past him, he shivered and grew doubts about the light. Wishing he'd worn a thicker jacket, Rory found the Cove was little like the tropical paradise he'd seen before.

Jacklyn, still wearing a floral shirt and baggy shorts, barely spoke to him after stomping over from their camp. It was more a grunt and a scowl than a hello. She whispered heatedly to Caroline, and they moved further down the surf line before they continued their argument. Rory tried to eavesdrop, but the wind and his chattering teeth made it impossible. So, instead, he waited, enjoying the crash of the tide and relieved he wasn't Maxwell.

The teen stood up to his waist in the surf, about twenty feet away, arms wrapped around himself and shivering. Caroline insisted he "cool his mind" before talking with Jacklyn, but Rory didn't see how a bath and hypothermia would help. He also knew he was out of his depth with magic, but got nervous a minute ago when Maxwell's lips turned blue. Standing alone in the sea, the teen looked so young and reminded Rory that only six years ago, he'd had his own brief stint without a home. Help was rare back then, but when it came, it kept you fueled.

Rory's reverie broke when the bubbling surf encroached on his shoes. He stepped back, wondering how much longer before he needed to intervene for Maxwell's safety. Trying to be discreet, he glanced over at Caroline and Jacklyn standing several car lengths away. Neither of them seemed to notice as the water washed over their bare feet.

Mid-argument, Jacklyn's pale face flushed bright red, and she pointed forcefully at Rory. Over the wind, he heard something about bad habits but didn't have any context to place the meaning. Rory studied Caroline, impressed that her composure never wavered as she absorbed Jacklyn's temper. The tall, whip-thin woman spoke briefly during pauses and then allowed Jacklyn to vent again. The longer it went, the more Rory glimpsed that the fog bank thickened, darkening the Cove. Rory looked between Jacklyn and the fog. *Is she . . . doing that?* Shaking his head, Rory dismissed the idea. But when Jacklyn stomped her foot, thunder rolled in the distance. *Wow . . .*

Finally, Jacklyn's anger seemed spent, and she muttered to herself, kicking at the water as she marched shin-deep in the surf. Caroline folded her hands and watched her patiently.

"Come here, Maxwell," Jacklyn said with no apparent effort, but even from twenty feet down the beach, it sounded to Rory like she stood beside him—like surround sound at a theater. He turned, expecting to see a speaker, but found only little brown sandpipers scurrying in and out of the waves. The wind carried her words.

Maxwell turned, blue-lipped and visibly shaking. He approached Jacklyn cautiously.

Caroline appeared at Rory's side and slipped her arm through his, guiding him into the water. Her skin was hot, like holding a cup of steaming tea, which was a thankful ballast when the frigid sea splashed against his knees, soaking his shoes and socks. Despite the unwelcome chill, he kept his mouth shut; this wasn't a moment to complain.

"Maxwell," Jacklyn said through the fog. "Why did you follow the wisp?"

"Karl, h . . . he said you could help me." The fog muffled his voice, but closer now, Rory could pick out each word. The teen's panicked eyes darted to his and back. "Karl said you helped him with his . . . voices."

"We did," Jacklyn murmured, but her face remained locked in a scowl.

They've helped others? Rory leaned forward, earning a gentle tug back from Caroline.

"Have you done anything the voices have said?" Jacklyn asked. "Not the soft ones, but the angry ones? Those that tell you to hurt others."

Maxwell shook his head.

"Do not lie, Maxwell." Jacklyn's tone hardened. "I can help you, but you will die here if you lie."

Rory's stomach clenched. He turned to Caroline, but she shook her head and nodded back toward Maxwell. Rory swallowed his

215

unease. *She wouldn't actually kill him . . . right?* He didn't know, and that reality struck him like a tidal wave.

"I never did. Never," Maxwell pleaded. "Not even when they screamed."

"Are they screaming at you now?"

Maxwell's jaw trembled.

"What are they saying?"

"That . . . that you're going to kill me. Please, I'm not lying, I swear." He choked back a sob and steadied himself. Tears ran wet tracts down his cheeks.

Watching Maxwell, Rory's heart cracked. He knew that cry well; he'd heard it from himself many times before, normally after lights out in the bunks. Hearing *that* cry again, Rory knew his instincts were right. *Maxwell has no one but himself.*

"Why are you afraid?" Jacklyn asked tenderly. The switch in her voice surprised Rory, but her eyes were genuine.

"Because Karl said to believe what you said."

And he came anyway. The thought stunned him.

Beside him, Caroline leaned over and whispered. "Maxwell possesses a rare strain of courage, does he not?"

Rory nodded slowly. "He didn't know if he'd survive coming here."

"Sounds like another recent visitor."

Rory's cheeks flushed, and he didn't know how to respond. He'd needed to come for Tommy, not himself. It wasn't a choice.

"Do you want the voices to go away?" Jacklyn asked.

Maxwell nodded.

"Close your eyes and step forward."

He sloshed through the waves toward her, eyes shut tightly, arms out to steady himself against the retreating surf. Caroline slipped off Rory's arm and waded out to Jacklyn.

"You too, hero."

Rory jumped, being addressed so suddenly, and saw Maxwell open his eyes and peek at him. Their eyes met, and for a moment, Rory saw his awe and confusion reflected.

"Hey!" Jacklyn snapped, putting on her sunglasses. "Shut'm. Last warning."

Maxwell squeezed his eyes shut, and Rory joined him.

For a sweet beat, he heard only the waves and bird calls until Jacklyn said, "Stay still. This will sting."

Like before, with Tommy, the cold came first, then the light and heat followed, though not as intensely. Maxwell yelped. The damp air hissed, singeing Rory's arms and face. When the heat subsided, he cautiously opened his eyes, finding Caroline pressed to Jacklyn's side with an arm around her. Jacklyn sagged, still conscious, with a smoking left arm stump. For the second time in as many days, Rory marveled at the sight of smoke rising off unburnt flesh.

Maxwell swayed in place as thin ribbons of steam spiraled from beneath his smudged vest. Rory splashed out into the surf, ready to catch him. The frigid water soaked his shorts.

The teen nearly toppled over but regained his balance as Rory arrived within arm's reach. "I'm okay," he said, shaking his head, his greasy hair in his eyes. "I just . . ." He paused, listening. Slowly, a smile spread across his face. "It's . . . quiet," he whispered, pausing again. "It's quiet!"

"Look at me," Caroline said, with Jacklyn draped over her shoulder. Maxwell looked at her, eyes wide, mouth open. "We have a favor to ask you."

Maxwell nodded, excited. "Anything."

What kind of favor? Rory nearly asked for the teen, but forced himself to remain mute.

"Here." Caroline slid a hand into her dress and drew out a vial of blazing orange liquid. "Not that one," she said and returned the container before shuffling through another pocket. *How many potions does she have?* She fished out a shimmering purple-white vial and held it out. "You may only share this gift with one other."

Maxwell reached out and took the vial. "How will I know?"

"She'll find you," Jacklyn said, regaining her footing. *She?* Who else should they be expecting?

"Yeah. Okay. I promise," Maxwell said. "I'll be careful."

Jacklyn nodded, satisfied. "Go see your family. Your sister misses you, and yes, your father is mad, but he can love you again."

Rory's throat tightened as he watched Maxwell's grin melt into regret. "What should I say?" he asked quietly.

"Your truth," Jacklyn said. "Or make something up. Say you found Jesus. You kicked the dope. Whatever it is. They are your family, and it might hurt, but they'll listen, eventually, or you'll go find a new one."

She makes it sound so easy, Rory thought bitterly, but quickly dismissed it.

Maxwell nodded. "I will. Thank you. Thank you for this." He looked over at his wagon, stuck in the sand beside Rory's bicycle, near the gateway bushes. "I don't have any money . . ."

"You can leave whatever you don't need as payment," Caroline said. "We'll put it to use here, but leave nothing you treasure. You won't be coming back."

Maxwell nodded and hurried up the beach toward his loaded wagon. Rory watched him rummage through his belongings, pulling out a backpack, a bedroll, and a pair of books.

"Thank you!" Maxwell yelled, waving at them.

"Safe journey." Caroline waved back, and Rory couldn't help but marvel at the teen's infectious grin—a powerful thing knowing someone cared.

A moment later, Maxwell walked through the bushes and back into the real world. As soon as he was gone, Jacklyn turned to Rory, the thick fog closing in.

"What are you doing here?" she demanded.

Rory remembered his phone and the entire reason he'd come. "I, uh, came to show you this. Tommy. He's . . . he's alive."

"What?" Jacklyn said, and the fog shuddered as the entire Cove crawled to a halt. The waves rolled, then froze mid-break, the birds mid-flight. The deafening roar of the sea and breeze ceased. Rory gaped at the still.

"Are you sure?" Caroline said.

"Yeah. See for yourself." Rory's hands shook as he pulled up the video. Jacklyn and Caroline pressed close, the smell of lavender mixing with leather and salt. On the small screen, they watched Tommy smiling in Bell's lap. Crying and loud sniffs came from behind the camera. When the video ended, it stopped on just Tommy's face—a bright, smiling, alive little boy.

"We did it . . ." Jacklyn said, stunned. Slowly, the sound returned. The waves crashed, resuming their churn to the chorus of gulls as the wind reversed, sucking the fog back to sea. Rory couldn't believe his senses. *What is this place?*

Rory shook his head. *Stay focused.* "You did it," he corrected.

"May I?" Jacklyn gestured at the phone.

Rory handed it to her. "Of course, you just push—"

"I know how to play a video," Jacklyn groused.

A warm wind rolled over the Cove, brushing away the last of the fog. The sun returned, and its warmth took the edge off the bone-deep chill. Rory marveled at the now blue sky.

Caroline kissed Jacklyn on the cheek. "Congratulations, my love."

Jacklyn blushed but covered up her embarrassment by hitting play on the video again. Rory had already watched it dozens of times himself. Motion at the top of the beach drew Rory's gaze, and he spotted a trio of golems creeping closer to Maxwell's wagon and his bike. Caroline and Jacklyn continued to watch the video as the three pounced and sifted through the abandoned belongings.

"Umm . . ." Rory started.

"Nothing in there can hurt them," Jacklyn said as the video ended. She turned and faced Rory. "This is incredible. A brain."

Rory's chest swelled. "I have more good news."

"Oh?" Caroline said.

"I know you're big on privacy, so you'll be happy to hear that while there's been some news coverage, it's all speculation. No one's contacted me either, so I think we're in the clear."

Both Caroline and Jacklyn looked relieved.

Up at the wagon, the golems tossed aside a blue tarp and worn blankets. One pulled out a toy mask and peeked through the eyeholes, while another picked up the guitar with its long, awkward claws and turned it over slowly, obviously uncertain what the thing was.

"That was amazing," Rory said. "With Maxwell, I mean. The look on his face . . . you changed his life."

Jacklyn's cheeks reddened. "Don't go blowing it out of proportion now."

"You're too modest, love," Caroline whispered. "Rory is correct.

You did good today."

Rory swallowed, his carefully planned pitch forgotten while watching Maxwell, but he felt the opportunity open with an excited jitter. "We can do good again," he said. "I know how. I can get a volunteer badge for the next one. That'll give you access through the employee area. After that, I'll think of something else more permanent and—"

"Jacklyn needs her rest," Caroline cut him off.

"I can speak for myself, Care," Jacklyn said.

Caroline tipped her chin up without a word as the tails of her blindfold flowed in the breeze. *FLANG.* An off-key chord reverberated from farther up the beach. The golem dropped the instrument and fled into the nearby dune grass. The instrument sat motionless in the sand until, slowly, a bold golem cautiously approached and carefully strummed the strings again. *Flang.* It clicked its claws excitedly, drawing other curious golems from hiding.

"We best get that away from them," Caroline said, all the good humor gone from her voice. "Or they'll be playing it all night."

"Care . . ." Jacklyn said and reached for her hand, but Caroline ignored her and hurried up the beach.

Jacklyn sighed. "Care, I didn't mean to—" But Caroline was already gone. Jacklyn shook her head, regret plain on her face, until she turned to Rory and scowled. "What? You have that look where you want to speak."

"I have so many questions," Rory began. Before Jacklyn could retort, he added, "And I know you have rules, but I hope, since I'm a medical professional, you won't mind me asking how you're feeling today. Your healing, uh, powers obviously take a toll on you."

Jacklyn studied him a moment, then shrugged nonchalantly. "Believe it or not, I've been in worse shape."

"At this point"—Rory gestured at the Cove—"I'm willing to believe almost anything. This place responds to you."

Jacklyn grinned. "You're an observant one, hero. Good, it will save time."

Flang. The brave golem held the guitar triumphantly over its head. The surrounding golems clamored for their chance, but the brave golem took off toward camp with the crowd in tow. Caroline called after them to stop as she gave chase, like a parent after a herd of mischievous toddlers.

Jacklyn chuckled. "They are going to be in big trouble when she catches them."

Then Rory remembered the other thing he brought. "Oh, I brought burgers!"

"Bribing me now?"

"It was the deal, right?" Rory said. "I just want to keep it going. We can do so much good together." He paused. "Please?"

Jacklyn considered for a moment. "Hmm. It's risky."

"We'll be careful."

"You pick the kids?"

Rory nodded. "Just the no-hopers. I'll be discreet."

Jacklyn nodded. "I don't want to wear a uniform."

Rory raised an eyebrow. He expected more . . . resistance. "Really? That easy?"

"Do you want me to say no?" Jacklyn replied.

"No! Not at all. I just—I just thought I'd have to convince you."

Jacklyn held up the phone. "Seeing Tommy alive did the work for you. And don't think I don't know who was crying behind the camera. This meant a lot to you, too, hero. We both did good. Give yourself credit. Just give me a few days. Care's right, I need to rest. Leave town for a couple of days."

"Where are—" He stopped himself. "Sorry. Habit. Um, that's good. I need time to scout our options."

"It's settled then." She sighed again and started toward camp. "Come on, enough business. Grab the burgers and come warm up by the fire. That video is too short. I want to hear all the details."

Rory took a step, but a nagging question stopped him, and he couldn't help but ask, especially after seeing Maxwell with a keystone. "I don't want to sound ungrateful and don't want you to get mad at me for asking, but I just . . ." He stopped, not sure where he was going. "I gotta know. With all the people in the world, why *me*?"

Jacklyn turned slowly, and Rory feared she was angry. Instead, she wore a thoughtful expression. "Hmm. The answer's pretty simple. Won't hurt for you to know . . ." She shrugged. "The reason is two-fold: most people who find the Cove are trying to find hope for themselves. Like Maxwell. A good kid with a kind heart, but troubled. They want my power for themselves. You were different. You came here for others. Call me curious."

Rory straightened. He felt competent, seen, feelings only nursing had provided before. And if he wasn't mistaken, Jacklyn seemed to soften *toward* him, little by little. Tommy had bonded them, he realized.

She cleared her throat. "But uh, that was the last question, understand? We have a deal."

"Wait. What is the second reason?"

Jacklyn grinned. "That's need to know only, hero." She beckoned him toward camp. "Hurry up. I'm starving."

Rory sighed. Maybe not softened as much as he'd like. "Right behind you."

———

Sometime later, after telling Tommy's story to Jacklyn's

223

satisfaction, Rory sat near a fire, drying out as he drifted in and out of sleep. The steady roll of the waves, the cool night air, the popping embers, and even Jacklyn's low, slow snoring all played their part in lulling him in his chair. Rory enjoyed napping. It helped flip his sleep schedule and was a valuable skill working the night shift. Even done well, though, it sometimes created a time warp where entire days zipped past in a foggy blur, and others seemed to stretch for an eternity. Naps helped minimize the whiplash.

In his dream, a little marching band of golems, each with a rusty horn or drum, played jazz. One was tapping out a spirited solo when Caroline's voice burst in.

"Rory. It's late."

His eyes opened to see her standing over him. The firelight reflected off her face, and he noted the small, almond-shaped leaves stuck in her hair and bits of twigs and dirt on her tie-dye dress. The golems had given her a chase, but she held Maxwell's guitar.

"Sorry, I dozed off."

Caroline grinned, nodding to the darkness beyond the fire. "This place was designed for rest. You have nothing to apologize for."

He nodded at the guitar. "Tough fight?"

"The golems are opportunists," Caroline said. "One is manageable, but when they outnumber you, they grow bold."

Rory nodded as if he understood and inhaled deeply. He held his breath and looked up at the panorama of constellations and the thousands of stars dotting the blue-purple swath of the Milky Way galaxy. He exhaled. "Now that's a view."

Caroline nodded but said nothing as they both watched the twinkling heavens as the tide rolled in and out. It had been a while since Rory was so still.

The fire popped, and Jacklyn snorted, breaking the spell. She thrashed in her chair, mumbling in her sleep. Caroline set the guitar against the lone empty chair and hurried over. She slid Jacklyn's beanie off, and strands of silver hair tumbled from beneath the hat. Rory had never seen hair shimmer like that before, and it reminded him of Christmas tinsel. Caroline stroked Jacklyn's sweat-soaked hair, revealing a clean-shaven scalp on one side that her silver hair hid. Without the beanie, Jacklyn looked smaller, almost frail, but also tougher in a way— like a cancer survivor. Caroline hummed a sweet tune, and slowly, Jacklyn calmed, settling back into steady breaths of sleep.

Caroline pulled her blanket up. "She'll be alright. She just gets nightmares from time to time. Did I miss Tommy's story?"

"I'll tell it again," Rory whispered, trying not to disturb Jacklyn.

"Perhaps another time. It is late." Caroline slid into the empty chair. "I wanted to thank you for coming and showing Jacklyn that video. I haven't seen her smile like that in a long, long time. You gave her a magnificent gift."

Rory's cheek's flushed hot. "It was teamwork."

"It was generous," Caroline corrected. "And generosity needs to be encouraged. So, let me repay yours with mine. I request your presence at a performance I give every year. It's an important holiday for my people. Please say you'll come. I'd love to know your thoughts."

"Me?"

She nodded. "It's this Monday. A bit late, but I thought that might work with your nocturnal schedule."

Though he wasn't scheduled to work Monday, he tried to think up a reason to decline, not sure if knowing more would mean more trouble down the road, but when he looked up, he found Caroline watching him with earnest hope. He couldn't refuse her. "Well, okay, yeah, but—" He glanced over at Jacklyn. "You sure Jacklyn would be okay with this?"

"This invitation is not Jacklyn's to deny," Caroline said flatly. "Your knowing more about my people's story will not endanger us, and it is my tradition, not hers. It is the day we remember those who came before. Our foundation." A sly grin crossed Caroline's face. "Besides, Jacklyn will be out of town running errands. She needn't know."

He looked back up at the stars, feeling his doubts roll off him to the sound of the sea. Only a fool would refuse such an offer. "I'm in."

Chapter 23: Fresh Momentum

Friday, April 20th

"Hello?" Rory croaked into his phone. The fog of sleep still muddled his thoughts.

"Hi, Rory, it's Ana."

"Huh? Oh hey, what's up?" Rory opened his eyes and wiped drool from his mouth. He sat up in bed, groggy and annoyed he'd slept through his alarm.

"Sorry, did I wake you up? Patrick forgot his dinner. Again."

"Classic Pat. Want me to bring it to him?"

"That would be so helpful. I would, but I have a case to prepare and—"

"Don't worry about it. I'll swing by"—Rory glanced at the clock on his phone: *17:43*; it was nearly time for work—"soon."

"Thank you!"

Rory showered quickly, not having time to trim his beard or comb his hair. Glancing at himself in the bathroom mirror, he saw the deepening rings under his eyes. Staying out late at the Cove had its price to pay in the real world. Still, despite looking terrible, he felt amazing. Invincible. He grinned at himself in the mirror before hurrying to throw on his scrubs.

Jacklyn said yes.

\#

Ana prepared two dinners and wouldn't let Rory leave without taking both. They didn't chat long, but before he left, she shared the news: they'd bought the house. Rory's head swam. He remembered saying congratulations and smiling, though both felt hollow.

Back on his bike, he vaguely remembered agreeing to come over for dinner to celebrate the new place, though his mind mostly hovered over whether he'd ever pay off his loans and scrape together enough money for a down payment. Maybe in his thirties? Maybe never.

Deep in the hospital's drafty basement, Rory spotted Patrick by the gleam of his scalp in the old MRI suite. With ten minutes before he needed to head to report, Rory stayed to chat, glad to have a little time. He missed Patrick and wanted so badly to tell him what he'd seen, what was really happening. But Jacklyn would never forgive him, so instead, he listened to the latest gossip. While he'd never admit it to Megan, hospital gossip was a guilty pleasure—a product, he guessed, of rarely seeing beyond the same four walls.

Patrick complained about not being able to play with Magus's fancy new 8T MRI scanner. Apparently, it was one of a kind—a cutting-edge research project in collaboration with the local university and, to Rory's surprise, operational. All it needed was a ribbon-cutting ceremony before it saw its first patient. Patrick threw out some physics terms Rory loosely remembered from his labs and lectures and nodded along. According to Patrick, the new scanner's imaging was so sharp that it would pick out individual cerebral micro-vessels if the patient remained completely still. A nearby technician laughed, saying half their job was babysitting an expensive machine and the other half was the anxious people inside it.

"Oh hey, by the way, any word on what happened to that kid?" Patrick raised both thick eyebrows expectantly. The thought of telling the truth passed through him again, but left just as quickly. It was strange not telling Patrick, like stepping back, creating distance where there had been none before.

Rory's chest tightened. "We, uh . . ."

It was only then that he noticed the other technicians gathered around, listening. "We still don't know," Rory lied, keeping his face straight. He threw in a shrug as Patrick frowned, disappointed. "It was unbelievable being there, though."

The techs all nodded, but Patrick pushed. "Nothing at all? Not even a theory?"

"Nothing for the message boards, Pat."

Patrick opened his mouth to defend himself, but closed it as the other technicians laughed.

"Honestly," Rory continued, his confidence growing. "I think it's pretty simple." All the techs went quiet, looking at him. "We work with the best."

That seemed to do it. Everyone was smiling now, even Patrick. The techs all began talking at once.

"Amazing that they got the swelling down in time."

"No way, that's not even possible. Did you see that CT?!"

"Hey, pull up his images. I want to see them again."

"Someone needs to do a paper on this!"

Rory's stomach clenched—he hadn't considered that someone might want to follow up with research. A study meant more questions. And interviews. He forced himself not to react, reminding himself that no one knew, and even if somebody found out he'd snuck someone in that night, the recovery was too miraculous to prove.

Just stick to the story. It was a miracle.

————

Friday, 21:45

The automatic door to the PICU's central medication room slid open, and Rory found Megan at the white counter, an array of orange syringes and three different-sized bags of clear medications spread on the table. Despite electronic records, she had her pen and paper out, checking off boxes on her paper brains and carefully labeling each syringe. And . . . she was alone. *Perfect.* Rory hadn't yet had time to scout candidates, but if anyone knew the story of every kid on the unit, it was Megan. She'd help him find the next case.

"Back for more Versed?" she asked casually, without looking up. She shifted her stance wider and paused, drawing in a deep breath as she pressed down on her belly.

He knew the look. "Parasite kicking your ribs again?"

She nodded and took another deep breath. "Only when they're not doing somersaults." She exhaled and resumed inspecting the syringes. "Room 9 must be a fighter."

Rory nodded. "Another four milligrams IV. His last one, hopefully. The kid's running out of steam. Deedee just wants a sedative on hand in case he comes out swinging again." He slid over to the medication dispenser, punched in his credentials, and selected Versed.

Megan pulled up her long sleeves and shot him a raised eyebrow. "You're smiling a lot for getting screamed at for the last hour."

"Am I? Well, I'm having a good day, and a white powder prince in Room 9 won't ruin that."

"There are many kinds of crazy. Seen most of them working here, but of all of them, there is nothing like cocaine crazy. It's entertaining."

"Until your heart explodes."

Megan sniffed and set aside another labeled syringe. "That's three overdose teens in the last month? Geez . . . I remember partying when it was just wearing cute cut-offs and taking shots from plastic cups in the woods. Ted's uncle would bring the keg, and we blasted the radio all night." She paused. "Huh, I haven't thought about Ted's uncle in a while. That guy was creepy. He always wanted to play truth-or-dare." She shrugged and picked up the next syringe.

"We grew up very differently." The dispenser's drawer popped open. Rory fished out a vial, punched in the count, and shut the drawer. "My wildest high school parties included Mountain Dew, Nintendo, and as much pizza as we could stomach."

Megan snorted. "Such a nerd."

Rory drew up the entire vial, flicked the syringe to settle the bubbles at the top, and pushed out one milligram into the sink. He screwed on the red cap and held out the syringe and empty vial for Megan. "Can you double-check me? Four milligrams IV Versed for the cocaine kid in nine."

Megan squinted at both before nodding. "Looks good." Mimicking Bell's voice, she repeated, "Five rights, safe night."

Rory chuckled. "You do Bell pretty well."

She rolled her eyes. "Five years here. I've heard her say it enough."

He eyed the steadily growing pile of syringes in front of her. "Is this for your kid in six?"

"For Katherine's. She's swamped in ten with that life flight from the coast."

"Oh?" Rory spun around. "What's ten's story?"

"Drowning. Or near-drowning, I guess. Undertow, but they fished her out. The patient improved en route. We're just watching her, really. Probably transfer to the ward in the morning. It's the bickering family's got Katherine stuck in there. I thought we were going to have to call a Dr. Strong and get security up here."

"Hmph." *Not a candidate.* Rory's disappointment surprised him. Was he rooting for sick kids now? *Not rooting, just ready.* He told himself to be patient—that he needed the *right* candidate.

"Is Jenny discharging home?" Megan asked.

"Last dose of antibiotics tonight. Then she's free and clear."

"Good news. Danielle is great, isn't she?" Before Rory could say yes, she blurted, "Oh! Did you hear about Tommy?"

He felt momentarily stunned. He'd completely forgotten to ask about Tommy.

"They moved him to the ward, and he's getting discharged."

"Discharged? To whom? The mother?" Rory remembered the woman with sunken eyes taking selfies. She'd been more interested in selfies and chips than her abused son. He pictured the boyfriend, his nervous twitching, his shifting story. He clenched his fist and prayed the police had enough evidence to put that asshole away.

To his relief, Megan shook her head. "I heard his grandparents are taking him. I guess no one can contact the mother. It's like she disappeared."

That doesn't sound good. Whatever misgivings Rory had about the woman as a mother, no one deserved to be abused or manipulated. "I hope she's okay. And . . . maybe this is best for Tommy."

"Maybe." Megan shook her head. "Still seems wrong, though, doesn't it? A kid should have their parents."

Rory winced and felt a familiar hollowness expand around his heart. Megan was too busy labeling to notice the stiff silence in the medication room, broken only by the muffled beeps and soft voices of the unit. As usual, she was right: kids should have their parents, but not every kid was that lucky. He'd never told Megan about his life before he started at Hill. It was his life, after all. *Why should she care?* Rory had thought about telling her before, but it never seemed the right time to tell someone their parents abandoned them after they got diagnosed with brain cancer. In his experience, it was a conversation ender.

Not that he hadn't tried before. He had, several times. A coach, a teacher, a guidance counselor, but they all seemed to treat him differently after he told them, like he was fragile and about to break. Now, whenever the past came up, Rory deployed one of his curated childhood stories—not too sad, not too long—then shifted the topic to brighter themes with a thoughtful question aimed at the asker. He'd learned early that people loved talking about themselves.

"I'll bet you get the Healing Hand Award for Tommy," Megan said, breaking the still. "It's big on the news, so they practically have to give it to you now. Be careful, though; that's the unofficial first step in becoming a charge nurse."

Rory snorted out a laugh and felt the hollowness recede. "No, thank you. I'll leave it for Bell. Besides, it's your year."

"No, it—" Megan started, but Rory cut her off.

"You *deserve* it. I know I'm voting for you. If nothing else, so you have to go to the awards dinner and give a speech."

Megan wrinkled her nose. "You ass. You can't do that to me. All those grown-ups . . . Ugh. The small talk." She wagged a finger at him. "I'm dragging you to the damn ceremony. If I win."

"When you win."

Megan reddened and hurriedly gathered her pile of medications and tubes.

"You know it's true, Meg."

"Stop," Megan said. "I know it'll be you."

"We'll see."

————

The overdose in Room 9 finally hit his wall, and he slept while Rory tiptoed around the room, quietly organizing the mess before the family came back. When the relieved parents saw their son breathing, he stayed to answer their questions, then took his cue to leave, exiting with a quiet "You're welcome" and "Of course." He patrolled the unit, gently inquiring about everyone's patients, but none of them seemed to meet the qualifier of a no-hoper. *Which is a good thing*, he reminded himself.

When he went to open the door of Jenny's room, he nearly ran into Megan stepping out. She bit her lip to suppress a grin.

Rory sighed. "What?"

"I changed out your flush."

"Thank you." Rory's eyes narrowed. There was more. Megan didn't wear that smirk for nothing. "And?"

Megan stepped out into the hall, closed the door behind her, and leaned in. "Danielle has a question for you. One she said *I* couldn't answer. She's asking for *you*." She snorted as she walked to the charge station. Rory chased after her.

"Stop."

"I'm just saying she is definitely wearing fresh makeup."

"She's married!"

Megan scoffed. "That does not mean a woman can't flirt. Or that she can't feel herself." She wagged her eyebrows.

Rory felt his cheeks grow warm, but he couldn't help but laugh. "Thank you for your help. Very professional."

"I bet you . . ." Megan's gaze drifted down the hall behind Rory. "Oh, no," she groaned. "Shouldn't he be at his cigar retreat?"

From down the bright hall, Dr. Magus stalked toward them, followed by a cluster of white-coated residents. He wore a blue striped polo, tan slacks, and heeled Italian leather shoes, which gave him the illusion of height. Rory took a deep breath. With everything happening, he'd forgotten about Khloe. *Crap.* He scanned Magus's ducklings and didn't see her. Some carried notepads, others laptops. But none of them were Khloe, and he sighed with mixed relief.

No sooner did the relief exhale from his body than the double doors opened at the opposite end of the hall. Through them marched Khloe Seeker. She had one sleeve of her white jacket pulled on hastily and cradled her laptop with the same arm. In the other, she carried a lidless, steaming cup of coffee. She wore flats and jeans, the light catching on her ringed fingers. A pair of dark circles sagged beneath her eyes, and a loose blonde braid swished behind her. She was sweaty and flushed, and Rory couldn't take his eyes off her.

"Hey," Megan whispered. "Close your mouth."

Rory tried to look casual as Magus turned and stopped outside Room 18, just across the unit. Megan's room.

"Let's go see what he wants." Rory followed Megan past the station toward eighteen.

Khloe struggled into her second sleeve, carefully managing the hot coffee, and looked more official by the time she reached them. She took a gulp and handed the cup over to another resident he recognized from Octavia's code—the man who hadn't been impressed with Rory's pep talk. Rory noticed he was staring at Khloe and frowned.

"Thanks, Trent," Khloe said.

Trent . . . Rory's eyes narrowed.

"Nice of you to join us, Dr. Seeker," Magus said flatly.

"Sorry, sir," Khloe stammered. "I was in the reading room. I didn't see your page."

"Perhaps you need to pay closer attention." He rounded on her. "For practice, you'll carry the on-call pager first this weekend."

She cringed while the other residents looked relieved.

"Is that an issue?" It wasn't a question.

"No, sir."

"Good. Now, I'm leaving in the morning and will be gone all weekend. Here." He handed Khloe a sheet of paper with tiny print on it. "These are my orders and contingencies for this

235

patient"—he gestured to eighteen—"and my others on the ward. If something comes up, read first, then do. I should only be called if you've made a mistake."

The residents all nodded, though Rory noted Khloe was busy scouring Magus's orders.

"Very good." Magus said. "I will see everyone on—"

"Sir?" Khloe said, raising her hand.

Magus sighed. "Yes, Dr. Seeker."

"I don't see a patient on here."

"Oh? And who did I miss?"

"Tommy, the boy who—"

"I know who he is." Magus talked over her. "He's going home, Dr. Seeker. I signed off on the discharge orders this morning."

"I'm aware, sir," Khloe continued. Rory could hear the strain in her voice. "But I think we missed something. I'm concerned about his heart."

Rory slid a step closer, dread seeping into him. *What did she find?*

"Oh?" Magus folded his arms. "I read his labs. They were unremarkable."

"But his X-ray, sir." Khloe clicked something on her laptop and turned the screen around. "I was reviewing it in the reading room." The screen showed a bright abdominal X-ray with a white stomach and kidneys partially obscured by dark pockets of bowel gas. Both kidneys looked normal to Rory. Near the image's top, the black ribs enclosed a pair of opaque white lungs which flanked a gray cardiac silhouette.

Magus leaned in close and examined the shot. "I'm not sure what I'm looking for, Dr. Seeker. This image is normal."

Khloe tapped the top of the screen, right over the heart. "I think *this* is a mesothelioma or an inflamed nerve cluster on the SA node. It wasn't there before he woke up!"

It wasn't? Was she sure? Rory's dread crawled into his throat and pulsed. He didn't think Jacklyn knew about this possibility—she seemed genuinely surprised to see Tommy alive. Rory squinted at the picture again. While he wasn't a radiologist, he'd read enough films to know what he was looking for. He squinted. *Looks normal to me, too.*

Dr. Magus took the computer and studied the screen. As his eyes scoured the image, the creases of his scowl deepened. "I don't see the issue."

"I . . . well, sir, I respectfully disagree," Khloe said, drawing concerned looks from the other residents. No one openly defied Magus except Bell. "We should consult cardiology and use the new 8 Tesla MRI to—"

Magus looked up and sighed loudly. "An MRI, Dr. Seeker? MRIs cost a great deal of time and resources."

Khloe seemed prepared and quickly countered, "Another X-ray, then. We shouldn't discharge until—"

"Do you think exploring a hunch is a good use of hospital resources? He's had no symptoms, correct?"

Uh oh. Rory watched Khloe's momentum falter.

"No, sir, but—" she started, and Magus moved in for the kill.

"So, we have no symptoms and no other supporting diagnostics." He handed back her computer and turned away.

"Sir, I just think—"

Magus spun back around and raised his voice. "Are you a radiologist, Dr. Seeker?" The nearby families and staff slowed to watch. Most cast concerned looks, but the unit veterans rolled their eyes.

"No, but I did study for the cert—"

"Ah, you have *studied*," he hissed, cutting her off.

Khloe straightened and took a small step back, holding his gaze. A few of the other residents dared a smile, though most looked too scared to react.

Magus rose to his full height, filling the stage he'd set for himself, but he could never fully reach Khloe's eyes. "And how many years of experience do you have?" He didn't wait for an answer. "That's right. So, is there anything indicating an issue with the heart except your *studied* hunch?"

She frowned and slowly shook her head. His tone dropped back to conversational. "Cardiology has already seen the patient and cleared them to discharge. You'll find their note in the chart if you look. And cardiologists specialize in what part of the body?"

Khloe's knuckles went white, squeezing her laptop. "The heart."

Rory wanted to say something but feebly looked at Megan instead, who watched with a naked grimace. *This is brutal.*

"Very good," Magus said, looking every part the victorious general. "I'm glad we agree on something." With a nod, he turned to leave but came face to face with Bell.

"What are you *doing*?" Bell demanded. "I can hear you from the back of the unit."

"We've just finished," Magus said dismissively, stepping around her. The residents scattered for the exits, obviously excited about their open weekend since Khloe was now on call. Only Trent stayed. He stepped close to her, handing back her coffee.

"Gutsy," he whispered.

"Ha, yeah. Thanks. You go ahead, I'll catch up."

Trent drifted over to a nearby workstation, busying himself with notes.

"What happened?" Bell asked, watching Magus strut off the unit.

"Just Magus being Magus," Rory said.

Bell nodded and slid over to Khloe. "It's alright, dear."

"There is something wrong with this patient's heart," Khloe mumbled, gesturing to her laptop. "I know it. We could do the scan tonight. I could do it myself. And even cut the sequences down to three to trim cost. I could do it."

Bell rubbed Khloe's back and nodded. "Don't let him shake you. Dr. Magus is always grumpy around the weekends."

"No," Khloe said, just loud enough for her voice to carry. "He's grumpy because he's an asshole. Friday has nothing to do with it." She looked over at Megan and then straight at Rory.

He froze. *Should I say something?* She didn't look away. *Say something!*

Luckily, Megan rescued him. She started laughing so hard her eyes filled with tears. Bell, more practiced than either Rory or Megan, suppressed hers into a bubbling giggle. Rory exhaled, feeling the spotlight slide off him.

"Friday has nothing to do with it . . ." Megan said, wiping her eyes. "Oh, I wish he'd heard you."

Khloe went white. "Oh, please don't. I shouldn't have said that. He's my boss."

Bell patted her shoulder. "Someone needed to say it."

"Yeah, over the intercom," Megan hooted.

Khloe seemed to relax. Her blue eyes lifted back to Rory. "Hey."

"Hi," Rory said back. "Uh, I'm interested in what you found. I want to know what happened with Tommy, too."

"Exactly!" Khloe said. "Thank you! Someone else who thinks this is all a little crazy. For some reason, everyone else, Magus, the administrators, hell, even the other residents, none of them are digging. Something really amazing and *weird* happened to that kid."

More than you know, than I know . . . "If you need someone, uh, else to help, I'm here."

Khloe regarded him, and a small smile curled at the edge of her mouth.

"Bell," Megan said quickly. "Can you help me over here with a, uh . . . chart?"

"Oh, yes," Bell said, and the two busied themselves with something by the computer, but within obvious earshot.

Khloe stepped closer. "I'd love your perspective. Maybe we could grab some coffee or food this weekend?"

He bit his cheek and fidgeted. "Well, yeah, sure, but I work Saturday night. Sunday?"

"I'll have passed the pager off by then."

"I know some spots," Rory offered.

"Great. I haven't gotten to see much of the city yet." She held up the pager. "Busy."

"Sunday then."

Down by the nurses' station, Trent waved at Khloe and pointed at his watch.

Rory hid his irritation. "Looks like you already have a— "

"Study group," Khloe cut in. "Wait. Sunday . . . I have kickboxing class until six."

Rory's eyebrows shot up. "Kickboxing?"

"It's for beginners. Basically, dance class with pads."

"So, you're a dancer?"

Khloe shrugged. "On my good days."

Rory chuckled. "Well, how does seven—"

Khloe jerked up with a thumb.

"—thirty sound?" he finished. "Meet me on the west esplanade, first bench north of the Hawthorne Bridge."

"First bench," Khloe repeated. "I'll see you then."

Rory's stomach fluttered. "Ya. See you then."

Khloe walked past Bell and Megan, nodding to them both. Rory watched her go and immediately second-guessed everything he'd just said: *So, you're a dancer? Ugh! I sounded like an idiot!*

Khloe reached the nurses' station and threw a little wave at him before she disappeared around the corner. Rory waved back, watching Trent fall into step behind Khloe. *Trent.*

When he turned back, both Bell and Megan were grinning at him.

"What?"

"Oh, I *love* her," Megan said.

"Mhm." Bell nodded. "She's good for you."

"We've talked three times."

Megan cleared her throat. "Sorry, Rory. Bell's right."

Rory stared at the empty space Khloe left.

Bell chuckled. "You've got it bad already. Look at you!"

Rory felt his cheeks pink. "I don't know. We're pretty different." The words sounded thin, rehearsed.

"You can't know that yet," Bell said, then considered. "Sure, she's pretty country, but give it a few dates. Different can be good for you. Look at my Walt and me."

"Wait, how do you know that? That she's country?"

"Because . . . hmm. Because we country women carry a certain . . . strength you can only find out there. It keeps you grounded."

Megan nodded. "Look at Katherine. She's rural, too."

Ah. "Good point."

"Now"—Bell pointed at his collar—"wear something with buttons and, for heaven's sake, please trim that beard. No one wants to kiss a briar patch. Maybe take it off and see what you think of yourself."

"Not the beard," Rory whined, scrunching up his nose. "I'll look like a baby."

"You look like Bigfoot right now."

Rory reached for his face. "It's that long?"

They both nodded.

"Come on, Rory." Megan laughed, shaking her head. "Try it. You might like it. And beards grow back."

He sighed. *Perhaps it's time for a change.*

Chapter 24: Death's Touch

Saturday, April 21st*, 9:54*

McMinnville, Oregon (thirty-seven miles southwest of Portland)

"Deb!" Chuck roared. "Damn it. I told you to clean this shit up!"

Deborah's head throbbed before she even opened her eyes. Her joints ached, her skin itched everywhere, and the cramps and nausea wouldn't be far behind. She felt sticky—she was already sweating. The comedown was always the worst part of the high.

"Hey!" *Thump.* The couch shook, and she clutched her head. She peeked open an eye and saw Chuck standing over her in a black and yellow football jersey, his dark hair slicked back. A gold watch glittered on his wrist as he gestured to the floor covered in toys. Tommy's toys.

"I said clean it up," Chuck growled. "You know I have a meeting today!" He turned around and mumbled to himself. "Old man would shit himself if he knew how many zeros I'm going to see." His old man again. Chuck could never please the ghost.

Deborah fell to her knees and started gathering up the toys. Her hands found a small stuffed monkey. "Tommy," she sobbed quietly, closing her eyes again. She needed another dose. She wasn't there when Tommy got hurt, but the guilt was constant, anyway. An accident, he'd said.

"My baby." Her vision blurred. "You didn't let me say goodbye."

Chuck's expression softened, and he sat down on the couch beside her. "No, no, babe. They kicked us out. They did this to us. I tried to get back to see him, but they locked the doors. They didn't want people like us there. I didn't want to leave either, but . . . hey, don't worry though, I got my lawyers on it. We won't let that hospital get away with killing Tommy, I promise."

Fat tears welled in Deborah's eyes. She wasn't a mother

anymore. They'd taken her baby away from her and hid what happened. They were monsters. That was what Chuck had told her, and he'd always looked out for her and Tommy. He'd taken her in, hadn't he? Why would he lie?

"Now come on," Chuck continued, gently wiping the tears off her cheek. "Trust me."

Deborah sniffed. "Can I have my phone back, at least? I have videos of him."

"Not yet, babe. I'm still having my guys check it for bugs. They could have got it while we were sleeping."

Deborah nodded. Even in her fog, she remembered the warning. Chuck said they had to be extra careful right now. He was always checking his rear-view mirror, certain that another raid was coming. Since moving in, Deborah had gotten used to only shopping at night and dodging phone calls from her family. Chuck often reminded her that her family was working with the police, trying to tear them apart and shut down the business they were growing together. If she slipped up, then the cops would get them, and she'd be alone again.

Chuck rubbed her back. "I miss Tommy, too."

"You do?"

Chuck hadn't seemed one way or the other about it after they'd gone to the safe house. He spent most of his day in the basement, cooking.

"But you said he was bad for business."

"I . . ." Chuck sighed. "Hey. The next batch is done, and it's a good one. Come help me, and you can have some."

A deep craving rose in Deborah, pushing aside her hollow longing. She licked her lips. "Really?"

He nodded.

Muffled barks came from the front yard. Chuck hurried to the door, grabbed the shotgun leaning against the wall, and pulled the blinds aside. "Damn that fucking dog." He banged on the window, and the barking stopped. "Shut up!" He set the shotgun down and stormed across the stained and cigarette-burnt green carpet. "Come on, we gotta finish."

Deborah pushed herself up, and her head pulsed. She closed her eyes and let herself sag until the spell passed. The hatch over the basement steps creaked as Chuck pulled it open and Deborah opened her eyes. Looking down at herself, she saw the same pink sweatpants as yesterday. She blew out a breath and stood on shaky legs, making her way gingerly to the hatch.

Chuck pressed a goggled gas mask into her hands, and she pulled it over her face. It was stifling and hot. Descending the old stairs, she was careful to pull the hatch closed to keep the smell contained. She'd left it open before, and it took weeks to get the stench of burnt sulfur and ammonia out of the house.

The basement was a mix of cliché mad scientist with old cloudy beakers over hissing propane burners and a fancy-looking research lab with stainless steel vacuum hoods, sleek metal tabletops, and boxy silver refrigerators. Chuck never passed a garage sale without looking for a new piece or upgrade. Recently, he'd bought an old computer—something to replace all the random papers and notes that used to cover the tables, stained and burned. Whenever he lost something—a recipe or even a pen—he'd yell at her and call her ugly names. She'd spend hours helping him look and apologizing. Though it was rarely her fault.

"Alright," he said. The respirator muffled his voice. "Now, when I say you need ..." He paused, looking at the ceiling and listening. Over the hum of the kitchen, Deborah heard the dog barking again. Even through the mask, she saw Chuck's face redden.

"I'll take care of it!" Deborah said through her mask. She was eager to get out of her mask. "Probably just the neighbors again."

245

Chuck nodded. "Grab the gun, though, 'case it's not."

Deborah hurried up the stairs and crossed over to the front window. She spotted the dog, Chuck's chocolate-brown mutt, Cane. Instead of running the fence line, harassing the neighbors, Cane was halfway up the front steps, barking furiously at the front door, but not daring to come up the last step.

Cops? When she heard a footstep behind her, her heart leaped. She grabbed the shotgun and spun around, trembling at the shadow. "Hey!" she'd meant to shout, but managed only a whisper.

A woman stepped into view from the kitchen. She wore a leather jacket and had one arm raised because she only had one. A safety pin held her other sleeve up at the shoulder. Silver hair flowed over one shoulder, exposing the shaved and pale skin on one side of her head.

"Don't shoot," she said with a smoker's rasp. "I'm here to help you."

Deborah held the gun up. Her withdrawal made her thoughts sticky. She swayed. Outside, Cane barked.

The woman took a step forward, and Deborah jabbed the barrel at her. "Stay . . . stay there!" She drew in a breath, ready to call out to Chuck.

"Wait, wait." The woman held up her hand. "Tommy. Your son. He's alive."

The words splashed Deborah like cold water. "That . . . No, he's . . . he died." She could barely get the words out.

The woman shook her head. "No. I've seen him. He's alive. Beautiful kid. Anyone telling you otherwise is lying."

Deborah listed, her knees wobbling. *A trick?* Chuck had told her about the tricks cops used to get you to trust them. "Who are you?"

"My name is Jackie," she said. "And Tommy, he's at the hospital waiting for you." She lowered her hand, asking Deborah to lower the shotgun. "Go to him. Get clean. He needs his mother."

From the basement, Chuck's voice suddenly boomed. "Are you going to shut the dog up?!"

Deborah's eyes flicked to the hatch and back to Jackie. "Chuck . . . would have told me."

"Would he?" Jackie's tone made Deborah's throat tighten. "Let's ask him."

Without a reply, Jackie pulled off her jacket, and Deborah thought her thin body didn't match her gruff, raspy tone. She wore a white tank top that hung loose from her gaunt collarbones. A wide starburst scar splayed out across her narrow chest.

From the basement, footfalls stomped up the stairs.

Jackie lifted her left arm stump and nodded to Deborah, who hesitated but lowered the gun. If Tommy was alive, she had to know the truth.

Jackie turned and stepped to the side of the hatch. As Chuck reached the top of the stairs, a thick pool of black mist poured from her stump, condensing into an ashy forearm.

Deborah froze. Every instinct screamed to get away from this woman, but she stayed. Staring, watching. For Tommy.

The hatch door lifted, and Chuck came roaring out with his mask halfway off. "What did I fu—" He spotted Deborah holding the shotgun at her side, and his eyes narrowed, but Jackie was too fast. She seized his arm and wrenched it behind his back. Chuck screamed in pain as something popped. With a grunt, Jackie forced him to his knees as the shadow and ash coming off her stump thickened. Wispy fingers and a palm solidified. Deborah felt sick and dropped the gun.

"Ask him, Deborah," Jackie said.

247

Chuck swayed on his knees, whimpering and puffing out short, painful breaths. Deborah fought the instinct to check on him, to soothe his anger. Chuck sputtered, saliva dripping off his lips. "You b . . . broke my arm!"

Jackie wrenched his arm, and Chuck cried out again.

"Ask him!" Jackie commanded.

"What the hell is this?" Chuck grunted. "I know people, and they—"

Jackie applied more pressure, and Chuck's threat ended in a whimper. "Shut up. The adults are talking."

Deborah shook her head. This was happening. "Is . . ." her voice wavered, and she stopped, straightening herself. She had the power here, not him. "Is Tommy alive? Did the hospital try to call me?"

Chuck panted but remained quiet until Jackie applied pressure again. He bared his teeth as he groaned. Jackie unclamped, and Chuck exhaled, gasping for air.

"Answer her, Chuck, or I pick a new bone. Tell her the truth."

Chuck raised his chin, briefly meeting Deborah's eyes before scowling at the floor.

"Yes, fine. Okay! They called. The kid is alive."

Deborah closed her eyes, the vomit rising. When she opened them again, she spit out some stomach acid onto the floor and looked at Chuck. Small, weak, and pleading.

"How . . . could you?" She steadied herself against the wall. Her entire world splintered. "Why?"

"Good question." Jackie nodded. "Why did Tommy end up in the hospital in the first place?"

Chuck breathed heavily and looked at the ceiling.

Jackie leaned down so her lips were only an inch from his ear.

"You're at the pearly gates, Chuck." She swung her billowing black hand around in front of his face. "Time to come clean."

Chuck's eyes widened, and he made a sound like a child. "Me!" he blurted. "The kid was fucking everything up . . . he, he wouldn't stop crying. It was driving me crazy. Please!" he whimpered pitifully. "I'm sorry, please. Don't kill me."

Deborah's head spun, sick with rage: her phone, the business, his lies.

"You hurt him?" Deborah snatched the shotgun off the floor and aimed it at Chuck. She stepped forward, barrel trembling with her finger on the trigger.

"Deborah, stop!" Jackie yelled. Deborah shook as she stared down the barrel at a cowering Chuck. The man who'd kept her high and empty now blubbered and whined, snot and tears streaking down his face. "P . . . please," he moaned.

"Kill him, and you'll never see Tommy again," Jackie said, soothing her. Deborah looked up at Jackie. "You're not this person."

"He . . ." Deborah seethed, the rage tumbling out of her.

"I know," said Jackie. "Don't worry, he'll get his due." Her words set off another wail from Chuck. Watching his display, the fight bled from Deborah. The shotgun was heavy in her hands, and she lowered it to the ground.

"What are you going to do?"

Jackie considered a moment, blowing a strand of silver hair from her face. "Put him to use for a greater good. Don't worry. He won't be hurting anyone else."

"No . . . no . . . no . . ." Chuck blubbered.

Deborah swallowed, staring at the smoke spinning off her demonic hand. "Are y . . . you," she stuttered, taking a step back, "death?"

"Sometimes." She nodded at the front door. "Go find Tommy and get far away from here. Disappear for a little while. This life is over. Go start something new, something better. And—this is very important—you never saw me. Understand? Never."

Deborah nodded, too stunned to talk.

"Go."

"No! You can't leave me!" Chuck yelled after her. "I'm sor . . . ARGH!"

Deborah didn't look back. She wiped away tears and ran out the front door. Shivering, maybe from the cold or the withdrawal, she threw up on the porch. A shriek pierced the air. Deborah didn't turn around. Instead, she wiped her mouth, unchained the dog, and ran away.

Saturday, April 21st, 21:07

Room 20, PICU

The mask felt hot and rough against Rory's naked cheek. Until shaving, he'd never noticed how much his beard had cushioned him from the rough fabric. The wind was colder, the sun warmer. As he walked, the air over his face made him feel faster, like the superheroes from the comics he read as a kid. He liked it, but it took some getting used to.

"Two, three, four . . ." Katherine froze and brushed back her black hair with the sleeve of her yellow gown. Over her blue facemask, her thin eyebrows knit together over a beak-like nose. "Oh, fudge," she whispered. "Rory, a leech is missing."

Rory drifted back from his musings, meeting Katherine's eyes. "Are you sure?"

She raised an eyebrow as though reminding him who she was. *Dumb question.* Katherine currently held the hospital-wide record for most consecutive days with no errors. And if the rumors were true, they had asked her to speak at the nursing school regarding her planning and preparation. If Katherine said a leech was missing, then a leech was missing.

"Right," he said and studied his patient's face. The sedated five-year-old lay on their back, covered in a pile of white blankets. The dog's bite had taken off most of the girl's upper lip and part of the bottom, leaving teeth and tissue exposed. Luckily, the dog dropped the lip when an older cousin hit it with a rake. The cousin then called for help, recovered the lip, and got the tissue on ice. Smart kid.

Rory studied the girl's mauled face and counted the dark-ridged leeches feeding on her upper lip. Modern medicine had its weaknesses, capillary regeneration being one of them, so the doctors turned to an ancient Greek treatment. What modern medicine couldn't provide, nature often already had a solution: leeching. The blood suckers' saliva promoted capillary recruitment. Plastics had reattached the lip, and the surgical notes gave it a coin toss if the graft would take. It all came down to returning blood flow. If the critters did their job, their patient might have a chance of smiling again.

Three . . . Four . . . One is missing.

"Another runner."

Katherine stooped down and searched the floor. "How are they so fast?"

"Leeches are natural sprinters." Rory squatted down. "Very dangerous over short distances." He expected her to laugh—she loved the nerdy references as much as he—but something was off tonight. She didn't even look up.

"Just look, okay?" she said. "The mom will be back soon."

"It's a leech, Katherine. We'll find it. I mean, imagine this from the leech's perspective. It just gorged itself, and now it just wants to take a nap. Off to find a soft bed—"

"Can you be serious?" Katherine snapped.

Rory closed his mouth. It wasn't like Katherine to snap. "Of course. Yeah," he said, unsure what he did. "Hey, I'm sorry. I'm—"

"No." Katherine exhaled slowly. "I'm sorry. I shouldn't yell at you. It's . . . it's just been a lot recently, with Rodger being gone . . . and the boys."

"Did he—" Rory didn't want to finish the sentence.

Katherine's head dipped, and she let out a shuddering breath. She nodded, but Rory wasn't sure what that meant, so he assumed the worst.

Oh, God . . . did Rodger get killed?

"Katherine, I'm so sorry. If you need—"

"No, no," Katherine sniffed, wiping her eyes with each shoulder. "Ugh. I told myself I would not do this tonight." She tipped back her head and blinked back her tears. "They activated Rodger's unit today. He's deploying."

"Oh. Where?"

"Near Baghdad, I think. That's where he's been stationed recently. We always finish our calls with him saying when he will call again, but he didn't last night. That only ever means one thing." She resumed her search as her tone steadied. "I could tell he was nervous, too. He keeps saying he'll be fine. That means the mission is dangerous." She sniffed again and looked at Rory. "I just worry about him. And my boys. The uncertainty is especially hard on them."

"I'm sorry, Katherine. I can't even imagine how hard that is. If you need a babysitter, I know an overqualified one, but he demands an arts and crafts budget."

Katherine laughed, and the tension in the room eased. "When Rodger gets back this summer, I'll take you up on that." Her eyes crinkled as she grinned behind her mask. "Thanks, Rory."

"You're not alone, yeah?" Rory waved a hand at the rest of the unit. "We're all here for you."

Katherine nodded, inhaled fully, and breathed out as she stood, turning her search to the patient's bed. Rory followed her, not finding any faint mucous trails on the floor. Together, they carefully tipped the little girl over to check beneath. No leech.

"Hey," he said. "How about we find this little sucker, and you can take a break? Go call your boys and gross them out."

Katherine laughed softly. "They would probably think leeches are cool." They tipped the girl in the other direction so Katherine could check under her. Still nothing.

The sliding glass door opened, and the girl's mother stepped into the room—a rotund woman with deep dimples, wavy brown hair, and puffy eyes. "Sorry about that."

"No, Momma," Katherine said, re-donning her professional demeanor. "You take all the time you need. It's hard to see your baby like this."

The mother looked down at her daughter and winced. "My brother will be up shortly. I had to . . . prepare him to see her. He acts tough, but his little Peanut turns him into putty." She smoothed her daughter's hair. "You have tissues?"

"I grabbed an extra box," Rory said. "Your brother sounds like a sweet guy."

She nodded. "He's a big teddy bear."

Straightening the sheets, Rory looked down and spotted a wet line disappearing over the edge. He bent down and found a bloated leech clinging to the underside of the bed, tucked safely in the shadows. "Found it," he said triumphantly to Katherine. "Napping."

She sniffed. "Well, you were right."

Rory picked it up gently with tweezers, dropped it into a specimen cup, and looked up at the girl's face. With one touch, Jacklyn could heal her, but she didn't meet the criteria. No one in the unit qualified as a "no-hoper" tonight, and with no admissions on the horizon, it was turning out to be a disappointing search. *But a good night for the patients*, Rory reminded himself. Still, there was nothing like the thrill of seeing Tommy alive.

"Another one got away?" The mom eyed the specimen cup tentatively.

"Yes, but don't worry." Rory stood and his calf cramped. He flexed his leg to work out the knot. "That's why there are two of us tonight. One person plays goalie and the other person nurses."

Katherine grinned. "I'm your nurse. He's the goalie."

"Because," Rory added, "I have the sharper eye."

"No," Katherine chided back, "it's because you have young knees."

Rory's big laugh caught him off guard, and he lost his rebuttal. It felt good. Hearing the nurses' banter, the mom relaxed and slid into the bedside chair.

Another leech detached and landed on the blanket. Rory traced it back to its spot near the corner of the girl's lip and saw a spot of pink among the grayed flesh. "There's some welcome news. It's pinked up a bit."

Katherine came around the bed and leaned in close. She nodded. "We have recruitment!"

The mom's face lit up. "Really? That's the thing the surgeons wanted to see, right?"

"It's encouraging, yes." Katherine plucked up the second leech and dropped it in the cup. "Did the surgeons teach you about angiogenesis at all?"

"Umm, maybe?" The girl's mom leaned back.

"Not to worry. There's a lot of jargon," Katherine said. "Here." She handed Rory the specimen cup. "Do you mind letting the attending know our blood-out estimates and see if Plastics can come look?"

"Did you need a break?" Rory replied.

Katherine considered and spied the mom smoothing her daughter's dark hair, eyeing the leeches warily.

"I'll be okay. My break can wait until after you get back."

Rory admired Katherine's grit. She was a superhero. "I'll take the long way."

"Not too long," Katherine warned, but her eyes beamed playfully. She produced a sheet of paper from her scrubs, sat down next to the girl's mom, and began drawing as Rory slid the door closed. "The first stage of angiogenesis is called sprouting . . ."

———

After peeling off his sweaty gown and washing his hands, Rory stepped out into a quiet hall, thinking about Katherine. She was a different kind of tough. His reverie didn't last long. A deep voice boomed from down the hall. "Which way?"

I know that voice . . .

At the end of the hall, a respiratory therapist stood a head shorter than a big man wearing flannel, jeans, and a bright red baseball cap. It took Rory a second, but a memory clicked into place. *The truck guy?* In the man's thick-knuckled hands, he clutched a balloon and a giant pink unicorn. *Him? That's the brother?!*

The respiratory therapist pointed toward Rory and then quickly went about their business. The brother turned, spotted Rory, and squinted. *Uh, oh.* The question never left his face as he stormed down the hall and Rory swore he saw his expression darken with each step.

"I know you," the brother said.

Rory sighed. There was no sense in denying it. "We, uh . . . had an . . . encounter the other day."

The brother frowned, and then a realization struck, and his eyebrows shot up. "You! You ran." He closed the distance in one long stride, so close Rory could smell the grass on the man's overalls. "I've been looking for—"

"Please keep your voice down," Rory said as calmly as he could manage, despite his speeding heart. He gestured to the neighboring room with its curtain drawn and lights off. "Patients are sleeping."

The man's face turned scarlet, but his eyes shifted over to the darkened room, and he held his tongue. Rory spotted Bell coming down the hall with her paper baton drawn, but he waved

256

her off. He could handle this.

Bell must have agreed. She stopped but monitored them.

The man jabbed the pink unicorn at Rory and forced a whisper. "You dented my truck."

"I know you're mad. I get it, we had an accident. And I'm sorry I had to take off, but—" *Should I do it?* It would be a lie, but a plausible one. *What's best for Peanut?* An obvious answer: family. Her uncle.

Rory needed to defuse this guy before he got escorted out by security. "I . . . I was biking in for an emergency." It was mostly true—the wisp wouldn't wait. "We didn't see each other, and I'm sorry about your truck. And I'm okay, by the way. A bit of road rash is all."

The red slowly drained from the man's face, and he lowered the unicorn. "*You* ran into *me*."

"And I doubt you looked before opening your door," Rory snapped, immediately regretting the impulse.

"If you think—" the man started again, his tone rising.

"Listen," Rory said, straightening. To his surprise, the man did. "What's your name?"

"Ben."

"Ben. My name is Rory, and I'm your niece's nurse tonight. Well, one of them. That's why I'm here—to help her and to help you process seeing her. Because you've never seen her like this and take it from a nurse, she's in rough shape. You're going to feel helpless in there, maybe even sick. Or angry. And that's normal. But Peanut needs her uncle right now." Rory waited a moment before adding gently, "Do you understand?"

Ben's mouth twisted thoughtfully, and he nodded.

"We don't need to agree on what happened before or who was wrong, but we both have important jobs to do right now for her."

Ben glanced toward the room and lowered the unicorn, sighing. "Promise me you'll do your best for her."

"Everything I can." Rory held out his hand.

Ben eyed him, considering, then took his outstretched hand. His fingers were thick and callused and crooked. *Rancher.* His foster mom's brother ran a ranch in eastern Oregon. He had the same hands.

Rory stepped to the side and gestured to the glass door. "She responded well to treatment. You can go in if you're ready."

Ben tucked the pink unicorn under one arm and tentatively slid open the door. From behind, Rory saw Ben see her. It was as though someone had punched him; he sagged back a step and exhaled sharply. He looked back at Rory. "Oh my God," he whispered.

"Katherine, this is Uncle Ben." Rory kept a hand behind Ben as they walked inside just in case he was a fainter. He wouldn't be able to catch the big man, but he could at least soften the fall. "He may need to sit for a minute. I'll grab crackers and juice and get those pages sent."

After getting Ben into a chair, Rory slipped back into the hallway and sagged against the wall, blowing out a long sigh of relief. He willed his heart and the adrenaline jitters to calm.

"Everything okay?" Bell approached from down the hall. "Do you need Dr. Strong?"

"No, I think we worked it out. Just a family situation."

Back in the room, the mother fanned her brother with a laminated hospital menu. Katherine kept a steady hand on his shoulder as she kneeled down beside him, speaking slowly and gesturing to his niece.

"Mhm, I see that," Bell chuckled, glancing into the room. "Back in the seventies, right out of school, I worked in Louisville, Kentucky, on what we called the Casualty Unit back then. An

ER now. We'd get all sorts out there, rural and urban. One time, I had this white gentleman take a shotgun shell to the chest— some nonsense between him and his neighbor. He was a bloody mess when he came in, but God somehow kept him alive long enough that he ended up in my care. My first time cleaning his wounds, I have my hands in his abdomen, picking out steel, and he spits in my face and calls me all kinds of vile names."

"They didn't sedate him?"

"Sedation wasn't what it is today." Bell shook her head at the memory. "Not even close. This gentleman kicked me out. Didn't trust me, he said. It hurt. I thought he was being so unreasonable, so needlessly vile. Next day, I hear he's kicked out every nurse in the unit. Shame, really. I sometimes wonder if he died because of it. Every nurse on our unit was Black."

"Damn, Bell." Rory turned toward her. "I'm . . ." He searched for the right word. Stunned? Angry? Ashamed? "I'm so sorry."

Bell shrugged. "That's the way it was. Some lessons hurt more than others. I cried, sure, but only once and never since. I had another patient to care for. After I picked myself up, I found a passage that still rings with me. John tells us, 'He came to that which was his own, but his own did not receive him.'" Bell shrugged. "Some folks don't even know what help looks like, bless them." She fell silent for a moment before adding, "My point is we don't always agree with our patients or their families, but it's our job to help them, anyway. Even in the face of hate."

Rory nodded, his mind crunching on the implication of the world Bell grew up in. It wasn't fair.

Bell stood, stretching her arms up with a yawn. "Sorry. I didn't sleep well."

Me neither. "Wait. Isn't this your night off?"

"I picked up Megan's shift so she could attend her birthing class."

"Weren't you telling me to work less?" he said, stretching his back. Chasing after leeches took its toll.

"And you should, but my shifts are winding down."

He blinked. *Winding down?* Then it hit him. "You're really retiring?"

She nodded. "August first. And it's about dang time. Should have been four years ago, but the economy didn't let me."

"Three months? Bell, you can't go. What will the unit do without you? Who's going to be Charge on nights?"

Bell cocked an eyebrow at him. "Who would you put?"

Rory considered. "Katherine would be great; she's got all the manuals memorized. Or Megan. The unit could burn down, and she'd calmly get everyone to the exit."

"They'd both be good. No doubt. Katherine might learn how to delegate, and Megan would have to put away her magazines, but they aren't the ones I recommended."

"Who else?" Rory thought through the roster, but no other names jumped to mind.

"How about you?" Bell said.

"Me?" *I'm not Charge material.* "No, someone else would . . . I've only been here a couple of years."

Bell waved that off. "I already talked to the other charge nurses and management. We all think you're ready to start orientation. You have a knack for people, Rory. You can't teach that. Don't worry, I'll train you up on the other parts before I go. It'll make me happy knowing I'm leaving this place in capable, young hands. And before you start with every which way this is wrong"—she put her hand up, shushing him—"you've come a long way from that baby nurse who walked on my unit. We'll start with orientation. Think of it as a trial run for everyone. You've earned the chance."

"I . . ." Words failed him. What was he supposed to say? He was still considering leaving. *Do I want this?* A thrill coursed through him, despite his doubts. *So, yes?* "Well, I'm not sure—"

Bell frowned, but before she could speak, another idea struck: being Charge would make getting Jacklyn in even easier. He could offer breaks and set the nursing assignments. *This is perfect.* "What took so long?"

Bell wagged a finger at him. "Don't make me regret it. Listen to you. Took so long."

"Thanks, Bell, really. I'm flattered."

"You keep that humor. It'll keep you, and everyone else, sane." She turned and nodded into his room. "Need me to come have a chat with this family about conduct?"

Back in the room, Ben and his sister sat huddled together, hands clasped, heads bent in prayer. Ben reached out and held his niece's tiny hand in his. Rory felt a lump grow in his throat.

"No, I think we came to an understanding."

"You remember what I taught you," she said. "You share, they share. Build that bond with your patient. Allies come in many shapes."

Rory nodded, dreading what needed to come next. Bell's technique was effective, but uncomfortable.

A resident waved at Bell from across the unit, and she patted Rory's shoulder. As she walked away, Rory tried to imagine the unit without her. There would be no replacing Bell with any single nurse. She did too much, knew too much, probably more than he realized. But he had one thing she didn't. He had Jacklyn.

———

Rory paged Plastics and left a note at the doctor's station about the blood output. He picked up an extra box of tissues and put on another yellow gown, gloves, and face mask before re-entering the room. While the family watched, Katherine showed him another spot that looked to be recruiting well. Only after Rory assured them it was good news did Ben and his sister relax, and Katherine finally got an extended break.

Plastics confirmed the graft had taken and they could start discussing weaning sedation medications if the skin continued to progress. The girl's mother teared up, celebrating the good news with her brother. She thanked Rory dozens of times. Ben even seemed to loosen up, giving a few hearty laughs. The conversation drifted to going home, and soon the mother was sharing the finer points of how to make a proper cheese curd. Rory listened mostly but asked questions when he felt a lull in the conversation coming. More leeches made a break for it, but Rory caught each one.

When midnight rolled around, Mom was asleep in the back, Katherine was charting outside, and Ben sat in a chair beside his niece, reading aloud. Rory listened as he primed the next infusion, impressed at Ben's constitution and enjoying the different voices he used for the big race between a rabbit and a turtle.

Finally, it came time to change the sheets. Between the leeches and the girl's sweat, the current set had had enough. Rory brought in fresh linens and asked Ben if he'd like to help. It was a trick Bell taught him long ago; always try to give the family something to do. They want to help, but more importantly, they need to have something to control. It was hard to mess up sheets, and they were also a visible reminder of the care given. Even if it took a few extra minutes, it was time well spent for both the patient and the family.

Ben grumbled at the idea at first, but then relented. And while he predictably proved inexperienced in the ways of changing a bed with someone in it, he only needed to be shown twice before he got the hang of it; tenderly turning his niece and stuffing pillows beneath her knees. By the end, Ben even smiled, wiping the sweat from his forehead and plopping back down in the bedside chair. *You share.*

"I've had easier times sinking new posts," Ben said. *They share.*

"Yeah?" Rory gathered the old linens off the floor. "At home?" *The follow-up.*

"East, near Sandy," Ben answered. Rory heard the moment open. *Be honest. Demonstrate you listened.*

"I've always loved that area. A nice reprieve from the city with the mountain right there. Beautiful," Rory said, picturing snow-capped Hood rising above the tree line. "How many head does your family own?"

The question surprised Ben. "Uh . . . fifty-one and half as many cattle. How'd you know?"

"Your hands." Rory gestured to him and let his guard down a little more. "You don't get hands like that without using them around big animals. My uncle—well, foster uncle—he raised hogs. I pieced the dairy bit together when your sister talked about cheese curds for thirty minutes."

Ben chuckled. "Yep, she loves her curds." He paused, considering Rory, who looked back pleasantly, waiting for him to continue. The big man drummed the book cover with three fingers and cleared his throat, and Rory felt the moment pass as though someone had closed the window. "Time for a smoke break, I . . ."

"What about the story?" Rory nodded at the book, trying to salvage the moment. "She's going to want to hear how it ends."

Ben looked uncomfortable now, and Rory knew it was time to let go. With a tinge of regret, he gathered the last of the dirty linens. "I'll go toss these in the chute. Give you two a little time."

Ben shifted in his chair but settled and reopened the book. "The

263

hare stopped. The tortoise was nowhere in sight . . ."

Rory sighed to himself. *Almost.* He excused himself and slipped out into the hallway, shutting the slider gently behind him. Despite the miss, Rory felt good. It had been a good shift. Reflexively, he rapped the wall gently, not wanting to invite bad luck. Some called it superstition, but Rory knew how quickly things could change.

Chapter 26: First Dates

Sunday, April 22nd, 19:29

The last rays of sunlight glittered off the Willamette River, flowing steadily past the wide, green lawns of Waterfront Park. A spring snow of pink blossoms swirled across the walkway, throwing tornadoes of petals through the legs of tight-walking pairs. Rory reclined against the first bench on the north side of the Hawthorne Bridge, hugging his repaired backpack beneath one arm, enjoying the race between a pair of dragon boats gliding upstream. He wore his best jeans, his cleanest pair of non-hospital shoes, and a collared green and red flannel he found beneath his bed, filling out the quintessential in Portland fashion: outdoor formal. He debated buying slacks, but thought better of it. *Why spend money on a onetime use?*

His knee started bouncing as he kept watch for Khloe. Each time he thought he spotted her, his breath caught in his chest and jitters filled his belly. After seeing it wasn't her, he felt queasy. *Calm down*, he told himself again and again, but deep down, something about Khloe felt different. She had a contagious intensity he'd never felt before. Talking to her was easy. Fun. Watching her stand up to Magus, despite falling short of her goal, both inspired and intimidated. He liked that combo.

Of course, it could all go south in a hurry. Khloe was asking questions about Tommy's recovery and could, though unlikely, discover his involvement and Jacklyn's power. Undeterred, she might find something he missed. A loose end? *The security tapes?* He doubted she would get access to those without more concrete evidence and clearance. Who knows how many Jacklyn could save before then? Still, he admired Khloe's instincts. She wasn't wrong: something magical had happened to Tommy, and of all the great minds that worked on the Hill, she appeared to be the only one not just asking but digging. Which brought about an interesting question, one he hoped to ask tonight. *Why?* Why didn't she sign off on Tommy's discharge like everyone else?

The wind kicked up from the south, and another flurry of cherry blossoms cascaded across the water. Despite his worries, Rory smiled. He couldn't have asked for better weather. Sunset was soon, and between the blossoms and the river, it was a stunning Northwest evening.

He checked up and down the river walk again, and seeing no sign of Khloe, unzipped his backpack to double-check his provisions: a sweater and jacket, two tall thermoses of discreet red wine, a couple of cheeses and a small tub of hummus, crackers, and olives to go with salami the guy at the counter recommended. It wasn't a gourmet meal, but it would fit Rory's purposes. They needed to be mobile to catch everything he had planned. Picnic, conversation, live music, and, if they had the energy, dancing. He briefly wondered if it was too much but reminded himself it was Khloe, and the little he knew about her told him she, too, would hate to waste a night like this inside. But doubt drove him to triple-check the cheese. *I hope she likes it.*

Rory quickly zipped up the backpack when another couple walked by, hand in hand. They both nodded politely at him and continued their conversation. Something about plankton and whales. Rory's mind drifted off to high school biology class.

Suddenly, he heard a wailing sob. To his left, a round-cheeked dad scooped up his exhausted toddler and peppered him with kisses while the boy launched into an exhausted meltdown. *Exhausted but healthy.* The man hurried west toward the towers of downtown Portland, passing a woman with long blonde hair.

Khloe emerged from the city and crossed the green lawn, eyes gathering in the picturesque scene. Her long-sleeved blue and yellow spring dress billowed in the breeze. Rory gaped. She looked stunning, like a fey of the forest come to life. Two steps later, the wind gusted again and sent her hair dancing in the fading sunlight. *I should have bought the slacks.*

Then, as though the wind were watching, it changed directions, throwing Khloe's hair up into her face and she sputtered, coughing. Rory suppressed a laugh as he stood.

"Stupid wind . . ." Khloe muttered, picking strands of hair from her mouth.

"Technical problems?" Rory joked.

"Environmental." Khloe smoothed out a tangle. "For the record, I brushed my hair for this. Ugh, this is why I normally wear it up."

"Well, you look . . . so nice." *Smooth.*

Khloe tossed her hair over her shoulder with a dramatic flourish. "Oh this, thank you. It's fun to have an excuse to dress up." She looked him over in a glance, and Rory tried to play it cool. "You look good, too," she said. "I like the shave." Rory beamed.

A glint of red from around her neck caught his eye. A silver necklace with a cloudy, rough-cut red stone hung delicately on a thin silver chain.

"Hey, eyes up here."

Rory's eyes flicked up, and his face flooded with heat. "I was . . . your necklace."

Khloe raised her eyebrows.

"I wasn't, well, then I was." Rory sighed, seeing no way to talk himself out of this. "A friend of mine . . ." He regained his composure. "She has a necklace like that. It's lovely but different."

Khloe clicked her thumb and pinkie rings together, and for a moment, Rory wondered if he'd messed up everything already. Seeing him squirm a little, she reached down for the stone against her freckled collarbone.

"It's my grandma's," she said. "*Was* my grandma's."

267

"Oh, I'm sorry," Rory said, inclining his head to find her eyes.

"No, no. She's still alive. She just, uh, went missing, I guess? Recently."

"Missing?"

Khloe nodded. "No one knows where she went. I woke up one day, during my last year of med school, and found the necklace and rings on my nightstand." She held up her hand, letting the light dance off the rings. "That afternoon, Mom calls and gives me the news."

Rory waited for the "gotcha," but it never came. "So, wait, your grandma broke into your apartment to give you a present?"

"Then disappeared. Yup. And that's not the craziest thing she's done." Khloe rubbed the stone between her ringed fingers. Before Rory could ask, she added, "I wish she'd left a note. Something to let us know where she went." He heard the longing in her voice, the sadness. It was hard to be left behind.

"Your grandma sounds mysterious," Rory said, stifling the ache in his chest. He told himself he was just nervous.

"She was. Is. Ugh," Khloe said to the ruby, then dropped the stone back against her chest. "Well, it's always nice to talk about family issues on a first date, isn't it? A great impression, I'm sure. Sorry. I didn't mean to unload."

"Oh, no," Rory said, trying to save the moment. "You're a great impression. Person." He heard himself say it before he could take it back. "Uh, well. That's out there now, for you . . . to not un-hear."

Khloe grinned, and Rory felt himself relax.

"For real, though," he said. "I know how hard it is to lose someone. Especially family."

"It sucks."

Rory nodded. "Yeah. For a long, long time." He felt the ache return, and he swallowed it down. *What the hell is going on?* He rubbed his chest, and Khloe looked at him questioningly.

"Heartburn. Or maybe I'm just nervous."

"I'll try to be nice." She grinned, nodding down the riverwalk. "Shall we?"

———

They walked for a while, talking about the city and work. Rory wanted to ask more about her grandmother, but hesitated. He kept glancing at the stone around her neck. Instead, he shifted into a well-honed nursing skill: the interview.

Bell gave him a valuable tip during his orientation that expounded upon the "you share, they share" dynamic: "People clam up around politics, religion, and money, and a nurse can't help someone who's silent. You want them to communicate? Ask about their interests." Rory actively avoided conversations about family, so he often chose pets. People loved their pets. It worked every time.

But it seemed Khloe had her own priorities. "Do you have any siblings?" she asked, adding quickly. "I have three older brothers. They're all knuckleheads."

Rory dodged, keeping the focus on her. "Ahh . . . That makes sense."

"What's that supposed to mean?" Khloe jabbed playfully.

"You can tell when a patient has an older sibling. They might be scared, but there is this . . . this resilience." Rory shrugged, not sure if he was making sense. "I guess siblings know they aren't alone in the world."

Khloe nodded slowly, looking at him sideways. "So I'm your patient now?" Rory stammered, but she cut in with a chuckle. "Yeah, I guess so. They always have my back. Sounds like you speak from experience?"

She brought it back around to him. *She listened.*

"I have a sister, yeah. Younger. She's off exploring the world, I think. We don't talk much. Aside from her, I've had lots of, um, foster siblings over the years, though I don't know where most of them are," he finished quickly.

The ache returned worse than before. From the corner of his eye, he saw Khloe watching him thoughtfully. He hated that look. The "*You're broken*" look. It always meant that something had changed for the worse. He quickly cleared his throat and changed the topic. "Are you hungry? There is a picnic on this tour."

"Starving," she said, without taking her eyes off him. "I didn't eat after class."

"I also brought"—he pulled out two thermoses—"wine."

"Rory," Khloe said, "we don't have to talk about anything you don't want to. I get it. And I'm sorry about your parents, whatever happened to them."

Rory lowered the thermoses, watching his perfect date crumble. *Why did I open my mouth?*

In one swift move, Khloe grabbed a thermos, popped the top, and inhaled. "Oh, this is perfect. I was dreading sitting inside on a night like this."

Rory blinked. *She's staying? She didn't balk.* "Me too."

She held her thermos up in toast. "To long walks at sunset."

"And good company," Rory added, meeting her eyes.

He scrambled for something to say in the sudden silence. *Something funny. No! Vulnerable! No . . .* But Khloe saved him.

"So, why pediatric nursing?" she said, then took a drink.

He fidgeted with the bottom button on his shirt and looked out at the water. "I think it picked me. I know that sounds weird, but

I practically grew up on the Hill." He turned his head and pointed at the scar running down his neck. "I had these really amazing nurses during my chemo treatments. So, yeah." He hoped he'd made sense, but Khloe didn't miss a beat.

"Do you remember them?"

"Flo, Mary, Susie. Oh, and Clara and Mags. They would play games with me and always knew what I needed. They're the reason I'm alive. I guess I'm trying to . . . pay it forward. It sounds so corny out loud."

"No. It's beautiful," Khloe said, stepping closer to his side.

"Thanks." Rory chewed his cheek. "I guess . . . life is hard enough, you know? And the extra hard stuff, it can't be done alone."

"How did that feel to say?"

"It made sense. For me."

Gam-Gam would say that's all that matters."

"You? Why pediatrics?"

Khloe took another sip of her wine and considered. "I was the oldest cousin growing up, so I was always around kids. I don't know. It just . . . felt right. They're more fun than adults, too."

He nodded. "And pretty resilient. I've seen some survive long odds."

"Like Tommy," Khloe said, turning and watching him closely. "He's an incredible case, isn't he? You were his nurse that night, right?"

Rory inhaled. *Does she know? She can't know. Can she? She's looking at you, say something!* "I was. Pretty unbelievable."

"Miraculous, more like it." Khloe's tone dropped as though she worried someone might overhear. "I saw you that night at the hospital. You were with a woman near the on-call rooms."

The door behind me. Rory fought to keep his expression casual and shrugged off her observation. "I was walking a family member out. I'm bummed I missed Tommy's wake-up."

"Bell said it was Tommy's aunt?"

She talked to Bell. Rory's heart sped. "Yeah. I wish she would have stuck around longer. She could have been there when he woke up."

Khloe took a deep breath, and he suppressed the urge to gulp. "She didn't . . . do anything strange in there?" She leaned in, eyes narrowed. "Bell said she saw a light flash."

Rory fought to keep his voice steady as his heart drummed in his chest. "She took a picture. I know it's against the rules, but we all thought it was the last time she'd see him."

"So nothing weird?"

Rory shook his head, trying to keep his composure casual.

Khloe sighed and looked out over the river. "Huh." She drifted over to the railing and leaned against it. "I was hoping she *did* something. Anything, really. Tommy's recovery doesn't make any *sense!*" she repeated, shaking her head. "Sorry, I ambushed you there. I guess part of me was hoping I was on to . . . something."

"I wish." Rory let himself relax a little.

"My research paper on Tommy is going nowhere. Magus has me on a tight leash and won't even let me draw labs. Can you believe that? I'm a doctor who isn't allowed to help patients. It's bullshit." She clicked her rings together again, irritated.

Rory stayed quiet, nodding, wanting her to continue. He needed to get an idea of how much she knew.

"Magus is so shortsighted," she continued. "Something truly amazing happened right underneath our noses. It's publishing gold! And maybe even a ticket into the Evergreen Society if I can figure it out . . ." she drifted off.

"The Evergreen Society?" Rory remembered Megan's magazine. The man on the cover. Ken, something. "The think tank?" A motorboat sped by, kicking up sprays of dark water. "You think they would be interested?"

"It's a research institute," she corrected. "Ever since Tommy, the medical research world has been quietly in a frenzy. People all over the world are trying to figure out what happened so they can replicate it. Big money is being thrown around, and I just *know* it has something to do with the anomalies I found in his chest." Khloe clenched the railing and shook herself. "I'm close to something huge. I know it!"

Rory looked down and kicked a loose stone into the water. It landed with a satisfying *plop*. "Sounds like you should be a researcher." He hoped to shift the conversation away from Tommy, Jacklyn, and just how far the Evergreen Society might go to learn the truth.

"Huh," Khloe said, blinking once at Rory as though she'd just landed back in her body. "Oh, uh. I guess, yeah. The Society is where all the innovative research is happening. Cutting-edge stuff." She reached up and touched her ruby, idly running her fingers over it. Rory let the silence linger between them, listening to the gently lapping waves while the clouds shifted colors on the horizon.

Khloe idly clicked her rings against the railing. "My Gam-Gam had this way of talking that rang true with me. I mean, everyone in my family knew she was a little nuts. My dad always threatened to send her to a home." She chuckled at the thought, shaking her head. "But she'd say these things that made me wonder how much bigger her world was than mine. Like, each spring, she'd go mushroom hunting but always complained she could never find the right type. Other times she'd go on about the stars inside each of us, full of energy and power, like a battery we just don't know how to tap into. It was hard to know what

273

was real for her and what was psychosis, but it always made you think beyond what you could sense."

Rory considered Khloe. She was an idealist, a dreamer. He slid closer to her on the railing. "Who knows? Maybe she's right. There is still so much we don't know about the body and mind. Where do emotions come from? How does memory work? What's a subconscious?"

Khloe's face lit up. "Exactly! There are so many unanswered questions!" She clicked her rings as she talked faster. "And Tommy couldn't have just healed out of nothing. That's not how the universe works. A huge amount of energy was needed to mend him. Energy that came from where?"

Rory wondered the same thing. *How does Jacklyn . . . work?* Khloe was onto something; he just didn't know what. *For all I know, there could be a nuclear reactor inside her.* The thought made him feel slightly dizzy.

He shook his head and changed the topic. "So, peds, but why surgery?"

Khloe considered. "I've always loved seeing how things work. Cars, computers, bodies—they are all machines. One day, when I was ten, my dad and I butchered a hog together. He told me about each organ's job as he took them out and plopped them into my hands. They were sticky and steaming and hot, and I couldn't believe how much fit inside one body. When I got older and learned I could save lives doing that with people, and that was that."

Rory laughed as she finished.

"What, is that gross?"

"No, no. That's just . . . a hell of an education. Did your family raise pigs?"

"No, not our pig. We would trade with our neighbors. Peaches for pork."

"A peach farm. In Oregon?" He shook his head, dismissing the thought. "No, you said you haven't been here long. Umm . . . California?"

Khloe shook her head. "Other coast."

"South Carolina?"

"Think more . . . obvious."

"Oh. Georgia?"

Khloe nodded.

"Really?" Rory said in disbelief. "No way, you don't have an accent at all. Hold on. Does that make you a southern—"

Khloe shot him a warning look. "I swear if you say belle, I'll throw you in the river."

Rory chuckled. "How often are you able to travel home?"

"Well." Khloe's eyes darkened. "My family . . . It's been hard since Gam-Gam left. And my accent, well, I got some bad advice, and things really haven't been the same since."

Rory couldn't make sense of it, but heard the pain in her voice. "I'm sorry. That sounds—"

Bzzz, bzzz.

They both stopped walking and reached for their pockets. "Sorry," Rory said, checking the screen. "Oh, Pat."

"A friend?"

"Yeah. MRI tech, actually. He butt-dials me all the time. Do you mind? I'm curious."

Khloe shrugged.

Rory hit the speaker button and picked up as they started walking again. A wave of sounds and voices came through the speaker. Something beeped, but Rory couldn't place it until he heard a muffled, "Paper or plastic?"

Rory hung up and stuffed his phone in his pocket. "Grocery shopping."

"Wait. Patrick? From MRI? Tall guy? Bald? I like him."

He nodded. "We've known each other a long time."

A group of cyclists rode by in a tight pack wearing brightly colored tights. Khloe and Rory stepped aside and let them fly past. He turned to find her watching him, puzzled.

"Can I ask a personal question?"

"More personal than family drama and career choices?"

Khloe nodded.

"Shoot."

"Last week, at the code, the one where . . . the girl died."

"Octavia," Rory said quietly before he could think. "Her name was Octavia." His tone was harder than he wanted. "Sorry, it was a hard one for me."

"Me too," Khloe said. "My question is, well, how do you deal with dying kids? The stuff they taught us in med school, and even during my internship—how to cope with death and everything—it's not working. That was just so tragic. They keep telling me to just do yoga and focus on the next patient, but I've been . . ." she sighed, searching for the words. "Just really struggling. This'll sound weird, but it's like I'm carrying a piece of her around."

Rory nodded, peering down at his hands. "Little things remind you of them."

"Yeah," Khloe said. "Exactly."

"Well, I, uh," Rory fumbled for what to say. His heartburn surged. Jacklyn would kill him if he told the truth, but he didn't think Khloe deserved a lie. *What do I tell her?*

"Mr. Nash!" a man called behind them. Rory said a silent prayer of thanks.

They both turned to see Mr. Oates approaching, wearing a black suit with an open jacket. He carried a phone to his ear, waving. Tracy burst from his side and came running up.

"Hi!" Tracy cried.

"Tracy!" Rory kneeled down, level with her. "What are you doing out so late?"

She stopped in front of him and pointed back at her grandfather. "We're seeing the cherry blossoms! They're my favorite."

Rory glanced up at Mr. Oates, who mimed a snarling face and a claw, and then pointed at Tracy. *Nightmares*, Rory guessed.

Mr. Oates held up a finger. "I have to go, Kenneth. I actually just ran into Tracy's nurse I was talking to you about. Very good. I'll call you right back." He tucked his phone away. "It's great to see you! I barely recognized you without your beard. You're all Tracy talks about."

"I've been brave, but . . ." Tracy looked over her shoulder at her grandpa before she leaned in and whispered, "There are needle monsters under my bed."

Rory feigned horror. "Do they have needly fingers?"

Tracy nodded, wide-eyed. "Long ones."

"Those mean monsters!" Rory stroked his stubbled chin. "Hmm, that's a tough one . . . needle hands." He turned to Khloe, who took the cue and kneeled down, too.

"Ooh, do you know what needle monsters are afraid of?" Khloe said.

Tracy shook her head.

"Toilet paper."

"Toilet paper?"

Rory slapped his forehead. "Of course! Khloe solved our puzzle.

Needle monsters are, in fact, scientifically *proven* to be afraid of toilet paper. She's a doctor. She knows." He barely kept a straight face.

Tracy didn't look convinced. "Are you sure?"

"When they try to poke, you block it with a roll, and their fingers get stuck. And then they look silly with toilet paper fingers." Khloe wiggled her ringed fingers for effect, and Tracy giggled. "And when you laugh at monsters, they lose all their power and run away."

"That sounds scary," Tracy said.

"Remember last time?" Rory leaned in. "What did we talk about?"

"Being brave."

"That's right, and you were brave then, remember, even though it was scary."

Tracy slowly grinned and turned to Mr. Oates, tugging on his sleeve. "We need toilet paper, Grandpa."

"And you shall have it," Mr. Oates announced. "We shall arm ourselves!" He winked at Rory before extending a hand to Khloe. "Dr. Seeker, correct? You work with Magus. Thank you for your expert advice."

Khloe shook his hand. "It's my pleasure, sir. Enjoy your evening."

"That I will, my dear. Come on, Tracy, let's leave them to enjoy the sunset." He gestured for her to follow.

"Ahh, why?" Tracy whined. "I want to stay with Mr. Nash."

"Because they need some grown-up time right now."

Rory and Khloe exchanged embarrassed looks.

"Can I have grown-up time?" Tracy asked.

"How about some cocoa instead?" Mr. Oates took her hand.

"I want marshmallows!"

"Say goodbye first." Mr. Oates gave Rory and Khloe a grateful smile and fished out his phone. As they walked away, Rory overheard, "Kenneth, right, yes. How's Sheen feeling?"

"Bye!" Tracy waved enthusiastically. Beyond them, over the skyscrapers and western hills, a seam of orange and purple highlighted the darkening sky.

Rory watched them go. "Seeing a family outside the hospital is always weird."

Khloe nodded. "That was my first time. It's nice. Like you get an update. A bit of closure."

"Hm, yeah, true."

They fell back into step and walked in silence for a time as Rory chewed on Khloe's unresolved question about Octavia. His chest ached.

Deep down, a piece of him wanted to tell her he wasn't just dealing with death but defying it with Jacklyn. He wanted to tell her why her research project into Tommy couldn't happen, but that she shouldn't stop trying. He wondered if she would figure it out and what Jacklyn would say. Maybe Khloe could help, and she seemed genuine. He couldn't reward her honesty with his lies.

"You asked how I dealt with Octavia, and I didn't give you a good answer."

"It's not a good first date question," Khloe said, waving it away in midair. "You don't—"

"No, no. It's okay. I want to try. And you were there, you saw. I've been thinking about her a lot recently. It's been hard, really hard, but I found . . . hmm, I found an alternative way to fight back."

"Alternative?" Khloe repeated, not understanding. Rory tried to find the words. The truth of Jacklyn, of her magic, hung on his lips, but the warning followed directly after, and Rory's impulse shriveled.

"By not forgetting her or the others like her. It's all we can do until someone discovers something better. A way to fix the bigger problems that brought her to us." He shrugged. "Until then, we look out for each other and keep helping the best way we can. And yoga, I guess. I keep hearing it's supposed to help."

Khloe laughed and glanced down at her hands. "Not a silver bullet, but still wise advice. I'll keep it in mind." She met his eyes and beamed back at him, but quickly took another sip from her thermos. "Enough with work. I want to just be right here for a little while. So, what's next?"

"The Sapphire Lounge for some live music?"

"Sounds fun," Khloe said and tilted her head. "Also, if you want to hold hands, I'd like that."

Rory grinned and intertwined his fingers with hers, feeling the heat of her skin and the cool metal of her rings. She leaned her head against his shoulder as they strolled through the swirls of pink petals.

Chapter 27: Gambler's Instincts

Monday, April 23rd, 13:00

McMinnville, OR

Jane loved McMinnville, which genuinely surprised her. Out this far, she expected more livestock than people, but instead of cattle, she found grapes. Row after row, acre after acre of trellised vines, rolled over lush green hills.

The cute main street, with its cafes and couples strolling between shops, lined the two-lane street. An elderly man held the door for a woman and her child. People waved to each other. It was a slower, steady pace, and Jane felt herself imagining a life owning a vineyard with her sister and the kids. They'd drink wine on the sunbaked terrace, wearing fabulous jewelry and designer clothes. What a life it could be! She caught her reflection in the sheriff's window.

"Bring the car 'round, Charles," she mumbled to herself.

The baby-faced sheriff glanced at her, confused, and pointed toward a rundown home at odds with its tidy neighborhood. The green exterior of the rundown home was weathered and peeling. Chips and loose siding exposed dark red paint beneath. The house looked sick.

"We found him just this morning," the sheriff said. Boxy with sharp eyes, he took the front steps carefully. "Neighbors started complaining about the smell. We didn't touch the body."

"Body," Jane said to his back. "As in, one?"

The sheriff nodded, not turning around.

"In-ter-est-ing," Jane said, hitting each syllable. The bodies usually came in pairs, which meant a change in pattern and, thus, the killer's behavior. Serial killers, like all humans, were creatures of habit, so any shift was significant. How significant,

Jane couldn't say, but she suspected today would be revealing.

The steps creaked beneath the sheriff's weight. "I figured you would want to look for yourselves, but we had to vent the place and turn off the cookers downstairs before the whole place caught. They had a huge operation going. Biggest I've ever seen."

Jane skimmed the surrounding houses as she sniffed the air. Sulfur, which grew more potent with each step. Something felt off, though. She turned back to the street and saw the two police cruisers parked outside. There were no lights. No media. No onlookers, even. The street was empty aside from Emmett's agents, who redirected a dog walker.

"Watch your step on the deck," the sheriff pointed. "It's rotted through."

If Emmett was nervous, he didn't show it as he followed the sheriff. Jane looked for lighter-colored patches of wood and carefully placed each foot, bending her knees and spreading out her weight.

"Will you walk normally?" Emmett whispered.

"You heard him. It's rrrotted," she trilled.

Emmett rolled his eyes. "Worst case is you fall through and get a bad splinter."

"No, Emmett, the worst that could happen is I fall through and land in a raccoon nest. Then I get mauled by raccoons who'll shred my clothes and give me rabies. Then, in manic panic, I run naked through the streets. It gets all over the evening news and the Director gets super pissed at you."

Emmett sighed. "There aren't raccoons under here."

"That you know of."

As the sheriff reached for the doorknob, it swung open. Head to toe in fatigues, Dawson filled the doorframe. A pungent cloud of rotten egg and formaldehyde slammed into Jane. Her eyes watered, and she pulled her collared shirt up over her nose, waving her hand in front of her face. "Wooo weee, Donald. Gross."

The sheriff flinched back and made room for Dawson as he ducked to step out of the house.

"Secure," Dawson announced, ignoring Jane. His braided beard bounced as he spoke. "One body, male, early thirties." He stared at the sheriff, who looked away.

"What happened when you arrived, sheriff?" Emmett said.

"We thought it was just another meth house fire. They light candles and pass out all the time. Burns a few houses down each year. We had one last month up north, but when I saw the body here—" He paused, fidgeting, and coughed. "Gave me the creeps. Do y'all know who . . . or what could have happened?" He lowered his voice. "This is some freaky stuff. My guys are scared."

"Sir, we—"

Dawson interrupted. "This investigation is classified. Who else went inside?"

"Just me and the three deputies here."

"Round them up," Dawson said. "We need to define silence."

The sheriff nodded. "Not to worry. My team is—"

"It wasn't a request."

The sheriff found a piece of his backbone and squared up. "Now, sir, that's not how we do things around here. I respect your jurisdiction, but I'm—"

Dawson stepped forward, the deck creaking under his weight. The sheriff fell silent, retreating. Dawson tilted his head and spoke. "Gather. Your. Troopers."

The sheriff looked to Emmett for support.

"It's standard procedure," Emmett said. "But I'm certain we can avoid any trouble here, right, Agent Dawson? The sheriff and his entire department have done an excellent job."

"Exemplary work." Dawson grinned without taking his eyes off the sheriff.

"Uh, thank you, sir." The sheriff nodded.

"Dawson will debrief you while Jane and I scout the scene."

The sheriff tipped his hat and retreated to his car.

Emmett watched the sheriff pass before he spoke. "Let's skip the threats, Dawson."

"With due respect," Dawson said, "I don't speak in threats. I speak in consequences."

"Just take it easy, okay? They're on our team."

Dawson grunted, and Emmett stepped into the house.

"The kid doesn't like your tactics, Donald." Jane reached up to pat Dawson's chest. "They haven't aged well."

"Like your whining about the Director."

Jane chuckled. "Touché. Hey, between us: for old time's sake, what are you going to threaten this time? Taking their guns? Seizing land?" She lowered her voice in mock horror. "Not the coffee and doughnuts!"

Dawson's eyes dropped to Jane. "They need only understand how hard their families' lives get should their pensions dry up."

"That's sinister, Donald."

"And efficient." Dawson departed without another word, and the deck groaned. Jane silently willed the boards to break. She imagined angry raccoons scurrying all over Dawson's bare ass and laughed.

———

The inside of the house was no better off than the outside, and it

284

smelled considerably worse. To her immediate left, on the yellowed sofa, Jane saw the mummified body. After the initial creeps, she swept past it, wanting first to get a lay of the land, a sense of who the victim was, how they lived, and the larger story. Her search revealed little. There was no blood or signs of forced entry, though occasionally, she heard the scratching of rodents in the ceiling above her. She found boxed-up toys tucked into the closet of a pink bedroom, and when she picked the lock of another room, she found a new sound system, a mattress covered in clothes, a mounted television with a gaming console, and an overturned ashtray. A bachelor pad, no doubt. She raised her hands, then gave the room two thumbs-up.

Inspecting the cigarette butts on the floor, she righted the ashtray to find the television remote next to it. Curious what the victim last watched, she pressed the POWER button. A thunderous heavy metal beat blasted out of the speakers, accompanied by growling vocals and a pealing guitar riff.

She shrieked and frantically mashed buttons.

SKIP.

AUX.

POWER.

The music ceased.

Jane dropped the remote and leaned against the wall, her heart pounding.

Emmett appeared at the doorway. "What was that?"

"Our victim's musical taste." Jane took deep, slow breaths. "Geez, it's like sonic cocaine."

Emmett shook his head, chuckling. He jerked a thumb over his shoulder. "Do you want to come look at the body or hang here and play DJ?"

"No, yeah. Coming." Jane reached into her pocket with a jittery hand and felt for her pipe, but caught Emmett watching her with a raised eyebrow. "Ugh. Fine."

Emmett led her back to the low-ceilinged living room with a built-in bookshelf, a fireplace, and the stained couch with the mummified body. Colorful wrappers and trash littered the ground and boxes, cables, and drink cups filled the corners of the room. Strange, she noted, that there were no flies.

Just like the other victims, the mummy was dried out, hollowed, lying face down. Unlike the other victims, one gaunt arm curled under them while the other stretched overhead with a single, ghastly finger raised, pointing.

"You're number one," Jane said.

Something else unique about this one was the location of the burn. Even from across the room, Jane could make out all five fingers burned into the center of the back, right between the shoulder blades.

"Bingo," Jane said, a little louder. "Yep, this is definitely our killer. But . . ." She paused, walking closer. "Why the change?" She stooped down beside the couch and craned her neck to get a look at the face buried in the cushions. She lifted the shoulder to see that a man's face was still frozen in his dying scream. The eyes were little more than shriveled sacs in each socket, and his leathery cheeks sucked in so deep she could see the ridges of each bone. Jane stood quickly, shaking off the shock, and spotted the shotgun by the front door. Looking around revealed no spent shells.

After a moment of silent consideration, she sighed. "Looks like he went down without a fight."

She turned and found Emmett staring at the body. Then Jane remembered: despite Emmett's excellent performance outside, he was still a rookie. Reading about the dead and studying photos differed from standing beside the deceased. She knew his look. He'd remember today for as long as he lived.

"Emmett?"

He said nothing.

"Are you going to puke?" she asked. No response.

She inhaled and walked over to him. "You never get used to it."

He slowly shook his head, but didn't take his eyes off the corpse. "I don't know if that makes me feel better or worse."

"That's a good thing," Jane said. "It means you're human."

She gave him another moment to absorb, then clapped her hands. Emmett jumped. "So! Who was our victim? Another clever criminal?"

Emmett shook off his stupor. "Charles Cook. Thirty-six. Lots of run-ins with the law, mostly drug-related. I'm guessing the lab downstairs was his. Multiple counts of domestic abuse with various women. Off the record, it looks like they were looking into him for the death of his father and a more recent case of child abuse, though it sounded like that was going nowhere. He fits our killer's MO."

"He does . . ." They were onto something. Jane could feel it in her gut. "Do we know if anyone else lived here?"

"No one registered."

Jane pointed over her shoulder. "I found kid toys in a closet. Maybe a girlfriend? With a kid? Recent child abuse, old accounts of domestic abuse . . . Muff. The killer may have done us all a favor."

"Our job is just to collect evidence," Emmett said, drawing out his phone. "I'll see if I can find anything about a girlfriend."

"No," Jane said, waving away his phone. "Focus on the kid. If there is a child abuse case, he was probably at a hospital. They'll have records. I'd start there."

Emmett nodded. "Good idea."

Jane let her mind release that thread and focus back on the body. She unfocused her eyes, trying to take in the entire scene, trying to find what she felt was missing. Someone positioned his body on the couch. No one would choose to lie like this. What happened?

"So, same victim profile as the others, but just one body?" Emmett asked, breaking her concentration. Jane felt a pang of agitation as her mind rebounded back to the present. "I don't know, Jane. This is feeling like another dead end—"

She cut him off. "There is something *weird* about his posture."

"Yeah, I guess it looks odd," Emmett said. "It's almost . . . staged."

Jane nodded, her mind racing. Why was the finger raised? She studied it closer, noting how the tight skin enhanced each knobby knuckle. She blinked.

"Or a clue," Jane whispered, following the finger to the bookshelf tucked in the corner.

"What's that?" Emmett said.

Jane held her breath, looking from the finger to its location on the shelf. "Our killer is trying to send us a message," she muttered, walking closer.

Emmett rolled his eyes. "Seriously? Don't go crazy on me, Jane. Let's just stick to procedure, yeah? Gather the evidence, and we'll get out of here. This scene is cold."

"Cold, eh?" Jane spun around and saw the Director talking through Emmett. She switched tactics. "Care to make a wager on that?"

"Come on. Not a chance," Emmett said.

"Whaddaya got to lose?"

"The case, Jane!" Emmett snapped. "The Director called me this morning, and he wasn't happy with my progress. He thinks bringing you on board was a bad idea until I assured him I had everything under control. We're on thin ice. So, we need some results. This, this is another dead end."

Jane raised an eyebrow. "Results? It's been what, a week since we started?"

"Nine days," he corrected.

"Doesn't that seem quick to demand results? Especially since this case has been open for, what, years? The Director—"

Then Jane understood. "He's been turning up the heat, hasn't he? Oh, he likes that strategy."

Emmett clenched his jaw, and Jane shifted. It wasn't time yet. "Okay, okay, how about this? If I'm wrong, I'll cooperate fully with where you take the investigation next. I'll do my thing, no questions asked, with minimal"—she took a deep breath— "interference."

Emmett watched her, considering. Jane saw her opening.

"But if my crazy hunch is right, and the killer left us something, I get to make the next call, and you have to back me, even if it makes the Director grumpy, frumpy sad face." She pouted.

"Threatening to withhold information from a federal investigation is a felony, Jane."

"Yeah, but arresting me won't get you any closer to the killer."

Emmett didn't budge.

"Come on, Emmett!" Jane threw her hands up. "You gotta go with me on this one. We're a lot alike. We both want to crack this one wide open. Look, if you can't trust me, fine. Trust yourself. What does your gut say?"

Emmett sighed and studied her a moment before shaking his head. "My gut says . . . yeah. This is weird." He groaned. "Fine, Jane, one chance. But I want your word that you'll back me for the rest of the case after we strike out."

Jane saluted. "Yes, sir!"

"And," Emmett added pointedly, "you'll play nice with Dawson. I'm tired of listening to you two."

Jane sucked in her lips, cringed but nodded.

"Then okay. Go for it," Emmett said, looking around. "Now, where is this non-existent message?"

"It's right in front of us." Jane gestured to the body. "Chuck here is pointing the way."

Emmett blinked and shook his head. "That's just how the rigor mortis set in."

"Is it?" Jane gestured back to the bookcase. "Subject one. Not very imaginative, but practical. Note the dust and the overall lack of books."

Emmett drew out a pair of gloves and joined her. He stooped down and inspected each shelf, one at a time.

Jane waited. "Your assessment?"

Emmett rocked back on his heels. "There isn't anything here. And it hasn't been touched in a long time. Look at this." He ran a gloved finger over the shelf and held up a thick layer of gray fuzz.

"Exactly." Jane turned back around to the shelf and eyeballed the level of the finger. "With all this dust, this shelf wouldn't likely gather much attention either. It could have been days before someone thought to inspect it. Brilliant, really." She drew an imaginary line in the air and pointed at the third tier of the shelf, right at Jane's eye level. Three books sat alone on the shelf, caked in so much dust that Jane couldn't make out the titles on their spines. Yet tucked between, a strip of clean brown paper protruded between two books.

"What's that?" Emmett said over her shoulder.

Jane pinched the paper and drew out an envelope. The paper was gritty, recycled pulp perhaps. She held it out to Emmett. "Would you like to do the honors?"

He looked unsure, but took it and turned it over, breaking the seal with a gloved finger. Pulling it open, Jane saw something shimmering inside and yelped. Carefully, she drew out several fine silver threads. Jane rubbed them between her gloved fingers.

"Hair?" Emmett asked.

Jane nodded. "But whose? Maybe our killer's." She lifted the strands in her fingers. "What else is in there?"

Emmett tipped it over, and a shower of white sand poured out, along with two pieces of paper.

"Interesting," Jane said, watching the last few grains fall out.

Emmett opened the first, frowning as he read. He lifted the paper too high for Jane to see what he was reading.

"What does it say?" she demanded.

"It's, uh . . . it's a translation?"

"Translation? Let me see."

Emmett handed the paper over. On it was a chalk impression, like the kind used to lift hieroglyphics off old Egyptian stone without damaging the original, but these weren't hieroglyphs. Those were angular and individual, these were stranger, curved pictographs arced as though they had come off a circle. The characters themselves baffled her, flowing into one another with grace she hadn't seen before from a man-made language. Oddest of all, below each row of elegance, were neat words. English words. Someone spoke this language enough to parse out a phrase.

"And his name was Death," Jane read in a hushed voice. "And shadow followed with him. And power was given unto them over the four parts of the earth—"

"Is that ..." Emmett's voice broke into Jane's awe. "Revelation?"

"It's similar," she said, reading the words again. "A different translation, but these symbols look a lot older than the Bible, so I don't know who was translating off whom." She ran a finger over the strange looping symbols. "Don't quote me on this. It's been a while since Sunday school, but that chapter was always a little vague on details. Mostly doom and gloom and feeling a bit tacked on, borrowed even. Like a piece of something else before. Something older. Something someone was trying to warn us about?"

"You're serious?"

"I think so," Jane said, still feeling the edge of doubt. "It makes sense. It is a time-honored tradition of humans to adapt old truths and tales to modern audiences. And besides, a little fear at the end of your book will make the reader pay attention, maybe even get them to convert." Her mind raced, trying to find confidence in meaning but coming up grasping. She needed more. *What was their killer trying to say? Were they Death? Do they know Death? Is Death coming?*

"What's on the other paper?" Emmett said, skepticism heavy in his voice.

Jane had forgotten about it, forcing herself to fold the symbols back up. Her body tingled as she unfolded the final piece, and her heart stopped when she read the first line: *Dear Jane Kim.*

"Muff me," Jane said, her smile growing as she read.

Let's get the easy part done with—I killed all those people. Me. And I did it using a weapon known as the Seed.

You've heard of it by now, I'm certain, and while time's razor has trimmed away most of what we know, we have enough to understand that the Seed destroyed the World That Was over ten thousand years ago. As Host, I bind it within me, protecting and containing its power. The murders are an unfortunate necessity

292

given my charge, but know I never took a life without first considering the consequences, and I selected my victims carefully. Each was a monster—like me.

So, why this letter? Why now? Because my time is running out and there is work we both must do before it ends. This letter and the translation are breadcrumbs for a task that only you can do and proof of a broader history that generations have worked so hard to keep hidden. Together, we must ensure the Seed continues to be carried by a capable, worthy Host. When you find me, if that work is done, I won't fight you. I'm ready to rest.

This letter is also an enormous risk, so I can't tell you everything. Maybe in time, but for now, you need to know three things:

First, what you might consider "magic" is real. Accept this quickly. It will make everything you're going to learn far easier and much faster.

Second, the Director can never, under any circumstances, possess the Seed. He and his ilk seek to wield it for their own, and while humanity might survive, it would only do so in a state of servitude and fear. Should they capture me before our work is done, you must set me free.

Finally, your next breadcrumb: find the young Maxwell. He lives near where you are—his sister should know where he's at. Pay attention to what he tells you and take what he gives you, especially if it seems strange. He will guide you to the next Host. Counsel them; they have need of wisdom I cannot by Law share. But you can. You have touched death and survived, so you must teach the next Host the secrets you learned in the dark.

You can't fuck this up. Now, read this again and burn everything.

Your Cooperative Fugitive,

Jacklyn

Jane lowered the page, blinking, her mind struggling to find a place to land, something concrete to absorb. All she found was

"Jacklyn." They had a name.

Emmett took the letter and read it.

"Secrets from touching death? Time's razor?" Emmett said. He snorted, shaking his head. "This is a joke, Jane. The killer is messing with us."

Jane inhaled, fidgeting with the pipe in her pocket. Maybe it was something in Jacklyn's voice, maybe it was finally getting some information on the Seed, but the tingle of excitement in her belly told her not to dismiss it. This was big, and it felt real. She didn't know what Laws Jacklyn was talking about or what being the *Host* meant. Her brush with death hadn't given her secrets— it had made the world feel raw and pulsing, like an open wound. Until Grace came.

"I don't know," Jane said, taking the note back. The second read-through magnified the flutters until she had to squeeze the paper to keep from shaking. "I think this is . . . something we should pay attention to."

"What? No. No, no, no, no." He pointed at the note. "That is a crazy person. The letter is a decoy. We're getting close. They're getting scared and trying to lead us off their trail with apocalyptic babble. They probably made those symbols up."

"Maybe," Jane said, drawing a little red lighter from her pocket. "But if an apocalypse is on the line, can we take the risk of ignorance?" She produced a flame.

"Wait!" Emmett shouted, but Jane had already touched the flame to the paper. He took a swipe, but Jane danced back across the sticky carpet and out of range. The fire licked up the dry papers.

"That's evidence!"

"Well. I won the bet," she said after a moment of stunned silence. "Which means I get to make the next call. That was the deal."

Emmett lowered his hands, staring at the ash. Jane checked for Dawson out the front window and, not seeing him, stomped them into the musky carpet.

"I was expecting something small," Emmett said. "Not a whole fake confession and made-up language." He pointed at the ground. "Which you just burned."

"Don't worry," Jane said, tapping the side of her head. "I got it up here. New Host. Death secrets. Real magic. See? Locked up tight."

Emmett closed his eyes and rubbed his temple. Jane needed to calm him down, or she'd lose him. Her mind wanted to chew through the contents of the letter, but she couldn't let it. She needed Emmett. He had the resources. Without him, she was back in her cubicle, back in her sister's basement, back where she started.

"Okay, look. I agree, this letter could be nothing. Or! It could be the only way to solve this muffing case. Right now, we can't know. We don't have the information. Which, Agent Torin, means —"

"We have to go find it."

Jane nodded eagerly.

Emmett sighed, staring down at the gray smudge on the carpet. "There has to be something else. Another way."

Jane looked around the empty home and shook her head. "I doubt it. Our killer is good. I barely noticed it. The letter is the only lead we have."

Emmett looked sick.

"Look, I'm nervous too, and I'm not interested in dying, but this is why you brought me here. Don't fall apart on me now, Emmett. Not when things are getting good!"

Emmett stayed quiet, clearly hating his options. Somewhere down the street, a dog barked, and she wondered if Dawson would silence the dog too. Emmett sighed, drawing her back.

"One day."

"Two, at least," Jane countered.

"*One*. I mean it. We'll go down this rabbit hole for one day."

Jane nearly fought for more, but saw Emmett was barely holding on. "Fine, one, but this stays out of your report."

"I can't lie to the Director."

"I agree. He'd see through it, anyway. Stick to the truth, just . . . leave this part out."

"Jane, I can't—"

"Yes. We. Can," Jane said.

Emmett's lip pressed into a scowl as he thought. His head bobbed back and forth, and Jane saw the battle between duty and curiosity. Jane bobbed on her heels and waited. She wondered if he'd say no right up until he nodded.

"I'll tell Dawson we're following up with locals who might have known the victim. It's reasonable enough."

"That's the spirit." Jane punched his arm. "Now . . . let's go find Maxwell."

Chapter 28: Keeping It Simple

Monday, April 23rd, 18:16

Rory's head buzzed from his evening with Khloe. Their mobile picnic, the folk trio at the Sapphire Lounge, and they'd even made it to open dance night at the Ballroom. Walking home, arm in arm beneath the street lamps, they swapped stories. Of school. Of joys and dreams. Rory learned about Khloe's ambition to work with the best and that the Evergreen Society was the best. She was a dreamer and an optimist, and for that, she completely enchanted him.

He even shared a few stories of growing up in foster care, like the time someone had locked him on the roof and he missed morning roll-call or the time he mooned a McDonald's drive-through because they skimped on the fries. Best of all, Khloe laughed at them. No pity like all the others, just an easy flow between them, back and forth, like the tides.

Halfway home, drunk on Khloe's smile and a thermos of wine, Rory learned her grandmother was a bit of an arsonist, apparently burning down the family barn not once but twice, and had set the mayor's mailbox on fire protesting a parking ticket. There was mischief in her eye as she told the stories and awe. The love there was palpable.

Suddenly, they were outside Khloe's apartment, tucked neatly between two towering office buildings downtown. Rory didn't want her to go inside. On the bottom step, he thought about asking to kiss her, then leaned in, giving himself away.

She leaned back. "Oh, I try not to kiss on first dates."

"Yeah." He hastily coughed, stepping back. "Me neither."

She laughed, taking the heat out of his cheeks. *That laugh.*

The front door swung open as one of Khloe's elderly neighbors barged past, muttering an apology. Feeling the moment vanish,

Rory offered a hug, which Khloe accepted. He felt dizzy as she pressed against him—how naturally she slid into the nook of his neck—taking in the grassy scent of her hair and the slight stickiness of her skin from a night of walking and dancing. But it had to end. Rory pulled away, letting her go. With a reluctant "goodnight," he forced his feet to walk down the stairs. As soon as the door closed behind her, he stopped, looking back. The next date couldn't come fast enough.

The next morning, he immediately reached for his phone, hoping she'd texted. Blinking in the light, he saw a notification, but instead of a text from Khloe, it was from Patrick.

Hey. What happened to you on Saturday? I waited and called. Not cool, dude. I'll be at the Rooster tomorrow until seven, if you want to talk.

Rory's stomach knotted, and he checked his phone log. He had a missed call.

The meeting! The campervan! I'm such a shit.

Rory felt the hot wave of shame overtake him. Then a counter of hope. He checked his watch—he had time.

———

Bodies packed the Rooster. Suits stood alongside skinny jeans and colorful abayas. What surprised Rory most was the number of people wearing shorts and tank tops. He laughed to himself, grateful, like the rest of the Portlanders, that the sun had shone again after a long winter. Which meant, once again, that seasonal optimists filled the streets.

Rory slipped off his raincoat and found Patrick sitting in a booth in the corner, two beers in front of him.

"Sorry, Pat." Rory slid into the booth, setting his helmet on the table. He reached for an untouched beer, but Patrick slid them both out of reach. Rory looked up.

"Okay, I deserve that. One of those for me?" Rory said

hopefully.

"Maybe," Patrick grumbled, picking up one beer and taking a long drink.

"I forgot. It was a . . . busy weekend. I'm sorry."

Patrick eyed him and set down his glass. "Where were you?"

"I . . ." *Something plausible.* "I worked the night before and just . . . overslept." *Nice, very plausible.*

"Overslept?" Patrick scowled. "Like how you overslept through my birthday hangout last month? Or how you overslept when my folks were here the other week? Mom says hi."

Shit . . . "Did I?" The shame returned. Rory shrank. "I guess I've been a bit flaky recently."

"A bit?"

"A lot." Rory nodded. "Did I mention I'm really sorry?"

Patrick raised an eyebrow and scratched idly at the table. Then he shook his head, sliding the untouched beer in front of him.

"Thanks, man." Rory picked up the beer, and they sat in silence for a moment, staring at their drinks.

"You shaved," Patrick said and took another drink. It felt almost normal.

Rory touched his stubbled chin. "Oh, yeah. I wanted to try something new."

"Looks good. Watch for ingrown hairs, though, as it comes back in."

Rory smiled. "Thanks, Pat."

"Ya, ya." Patrick cleared his throat. "I'm annoyed, but don't worry about the campervan guy too much. He left happy."

Rory frowned. "You . . ."

Patrick rubbed his fingers together.

"Bought it?"

He grinned. "It was a great deal, barely any miles on it. Just needs an oil change, really. You can pay me back for your half later, but I get dibs on the bigger bed."

Rory mentally stumbled, caught flatfooted by an old idea. He didn't want to leave. Jacklyn was here. And he didn't have that kind of money, half or not. Rory felt the words forming and dreaded seeing Patrick's disappointment, but an idea occurred to him. A mobile house might be useful in a pinch, especially if Jacklyn's "bad people" came looking. Or if too many questions started popping up around the hospital, they could start over again in a new city, with a new hospital and new patients. A backup plan.

"Deal." Rory raised his glass. "Here's to the next adventure."

"To getting out of town." They clinked glasses.

"I called you Saturday," Patrick said after another long pause.

Rory cringed. "I saw. I probably thought it was another butt dial . . . honestly, I don't know. Saturday is kind of a blur."

"Butt dial? But I changed my login." Patrick pulled out his phone. "Oh, no." He quickly put the device up to his ear. "Mom?"

Mom? Rory bit down on his lips to prevent himself from laughing.

"Hey, how long have you been listening?"

Patrick's face flushed, and he cupped the receiver. "Ugh, really? Maybe you should have hung up?"

"Hi, Mrs. Rockell!" Rory shouted at the phone.

"Dude." Patrick winced and plugged his ear. "What'd you say, Mom?" He looked at Rory and held the phone away. "She says hi and, uh, that she's proud of us."

"Thank you! How are you?"

Patrick jerked the phone back and covered the receiver. "Don't use my mom as your sympathy ammo."

Rory held up his hands.

"I gotta go, Mom. Yeah, I'll call this weekend. With Ana. No, we're just getting a beer." He waited. "No video games." Another pause. "Yeah, it has been a long time." Patrick glanced up at Rory. "Okay, love you too. Bye." He hung up and shook his head. He looked up at Rory and sighed. "To be clear, I'm still annoyed with you."

"I know. And I'm still sorry. I'll do better, trust me."

Patrick snorted and took another gulp of his beer. "I remember when you told me to trust you before the meteor shower our junior year. Sneaking beers on top of the music building."

Rory remembered the chilly night. The shower dazzled the dark sky with streaks of yellow-white light. Feeling so small, knowing how far those meteors must have traveled to give them a show.

"It was great," Patrick said. "Right until security arrived."

"The fence!" Laughter bubbled out of Rory. "Oh . . . the fence when you got stuck halfway over. I peed myself!"

"Those were new pants, too," Patrick said.

"Your legs were so white, I thought for sure the cops would see us. I wonder if they still have your pants in an evidence locker somewhere. A cold case."

"They'll never catch me," Patrick whispered, dramatically taking a drink. "Plus, it was worth it. I met Ana."

"She sprayed us with the hose."

"We were hiding in her yard. She thought we were bike thieves."

Rory shivered, remembering the icy water. "Well, you certainly made an impression."

"I'm lucky she has a sense of humor."

The Rooster's front door flew open, and a gust of wind whipped through the bar, tossing menus and napkins everywhere. People in varying degrees of dress, some wearing swimsuits, stumbled in as fat drops of rain hammered the sidewalk. Rory shook his head.

"That's why you don't trust a blue sky in April," Patrick said, watching Oliver hurry over to the newcomers. "Hey, remember that time we—"

"Yeah," Rory said, smiling, remembering a blustery day with torrential rain. "That was a good day."

Patrick nodded, then sighed and checked his phone. *He can't leave yet.* Rory felt a pang of frustration. "I went on a date!" he blurted, surprising himself.

Patrick looked startled. "Oh, yeah? With the waitress?"

Rory shook his head. "You know Khloe? The new resident?"

"Whoa yeah, I know her!" Patrick boomed. A few people at the nearby table glanced over, and he lowered his voice, but not his enthusiasm. "She's a whiz, man! Coil three went down again last week while she was down there. We'd had technicians out almost every month to check it out, but it kept shutting down mid-scan. She figured it out in like fifteen minutes. Turns out it was the chiller and the inlet, not the scanner." Patrick chuckled, shaking his head. "She's cute, too. Nice one! You going out again?"

Rory shrugged. "I was hoping my relationship guru had an idea for a second date."

Patrick shook his head. "Dude, I'm just a lucky thief." He checked his phone again. "Sorry, I got to go. I have, uh . . . therapy tonight."

"Therapy?" *Why does Patrick need therapy?*

"Yeah, something Ana recommended. Help with my dad stuff."

Rory nodded, remembering those late-night visits. In high school, Patrick would occasionally appear, always after last call, asking if he could sleep over. His dad would come home from the bars looking for a fight, and if Patrick wasn't there, he was safe.

"It's been helpful talking about it. And I thought, maybe, you could, uh, talk to my therapist too? If you wanted."

"About what?" Rory leaned back. He thought of Octavia and the others: *on to the next patient.*

"About your biological parents," Patrick said. "Cancer. Foster care. Work—maybe talk about your patients. That shit is heavy. You don't need to carry it alone."

Rory slumped, feeling the weight return. "There isn't much to talk about. Cancer happened twice. I survived. Done. My parents? Well, they liked their heroin or freedom or . . . whatever more than me. It's pretty simple. Done. And my patients . . . I'm working on that one. So, don't worry about me. I'm good." His tongue felt sticky, so he took another drink.

"I know, man," Patrick mumbled. "I know. Me too. But . . . but I don't know, talking . . . gives me context. Lets me tell my story, so I can hear it. It's helping me figure some things out. Here." He pulled out a card and slid it across the table before downing the rest of his beer. Rory left the card, eying it as though Patrick had passed him a dead animal.

Patrick rose out of the booth. "It's just a thought." He shurgged "And only the second date, just keep it simple. Take her out to dinner. Listen. Be you."

"We're both working most of the time."

Patrick shrugged. "Then do it at work."

Rory chewed his cheek.

Patrick took a step toward the door but stopped. "Hey, I'm on Wednesday for a stretch. Meet up for a break?"

"I'd like that. Thanks for the advice, Pat." Rory watched him go, feeling that something had changed between them, but he couldn't say what. He glanced at the therapist's card on the table.

I don't need therapy. I have Jacklyn.

Chapter 29: Remembrance Day

Monday, April 23rd, 23:56

Translated from:

Disc - Shepherd's Stone

Sub-ring - *Accounts*

Script - *Remembrance Day*

When the fourth shadow moon reaches its zenith, let the Festival of Remembrance begin. We of the Wyth usher two generations—one in, the other out, and continue the Great Cycle as the All-Mother taught. Eight lessons, eight plays (see Sub-ring Ritual) will stretch from sunset to sunrise, and all shall hold this night apart lest any who come after forget.

The First - The Shepherd's Discovery

The Second - Foundation of the Wyth

The Third - ***Translation Ends***

———

Passing the brambles, Rory clutched the keystone to his chest. *Where are the golems?*

The hairs on the back of his neck stood up. With each step down the path, the nervous ringing in his ears grew louder, muffled only by his breaths and the drum of his quickening heartbeat. When he reached the clearing, he saw the piles of trash, mud, and rust had disappeared. At the center, the blue tarp gently rippled in an unfelt breeze. *Who's guarding the Cove?*

Dread sank into his gut as he approached the tarp, eyes scanning the deep shadows of the tree line.

"Hello? It's Rory. I have my stone!"

The forest remained silent, spiking his dread. Then, faint as a whisper but growing stronger by the second, came a deep beat that shook the clearing.

Boom. Boom-boom. Boom. Boom-boom.

Rory spun, trying to locate the sound, and found it came from behind the tarp.

Boom. Boom-boom. Boom. Boom-boom.

Drums? There was no telling in Jacklyn's crazy world.

Fearing the worst, Rory plunged in, praying Jacklyn's hunters weren't there.

After the pressure came and went, a brilliant, starlit darkness consumed him. Against a moonless night, a massive bonfire blazed down on the beach, and the long stretch of white sand glittered in its orange light. Long shadows twitched and danced against the cliffs. Rory squinted. Tiny figures moved rhythmically around the flames.

BOOM. Boom-boom. BOOM. Boom-boom.

As Rory's eyes adjusted, he saw dozens of turquoise glowing golems in a kind of trance, their claws stretched skyward as they moved around the flames. Pairs sat around the circle's perimeter, each with a mallet, taking turns striking their drum in a synchronized call and response that reverberated deep in his chest.

BOOM. Boom-boom. BOOM. Boom-boom.

Like a moth to the flame, Rory stepped toward the fire, his fear morphing into yet more questions. His foot struck something solid in the sand. He looked down and, in the dim starlight, saw a non-glowing, un-mushroomed golem. It looked to be little more than a lump of mud and metal in the sand. *Dead?* In each of its hands, atop its chest, was a bouquet of pink, gold, and red flowers. *Buried?* Rory glanced over at the fire and the dancing golems, then back to the lump. Looking up, he saw dozens more mounds in the sand. He felt a pang of sadness. *What is going on?*

As Rory neared the circle, the drums abruptly stopped. "Our guest has arrived!" Caroline's voice cut through the quiet. The golems all turned in Rory's direction, where he stood quietly, brushing off his hands, trying to look like he belonged.

"Uh. Hi." He gave a little wave.

The golems shambled aside, making way for Caroline. She wore a hooded brown cloak, a plain red ribbon tied around her eyes, and carried a tall, hooked staff.

"I'm so happy you came." Caroline beckoned Rory forward.

"I wouldn't miss it."

She looped her arm through his and led him into the drum circle. Her grip was gentle yet firm, and while Rory's footsteps sank into the sand, she seemed to glide over it. All the golems and their glistening eyes followed him. Perhaps it was the bonfire, but heat rose in Rory's cheeks.

Caroline gestured to a red woven rug within the ring of drums. "You will sit here for the performance."

"I'm not . . . I really don't need—"

"Nonsense." Caroline waved away his protest. "You have come so far and seen so much. You are my honored guest."

He managed a smile and a nod, uncomfortable with the attention but glad to be wanted. She pressed closer to him, covering his hand with hers. "Come. We're about to begin." She led him away from the fire and up the gentle slope toward the black cliffs. When they reached the mouth of the yawning cave, Rory noticed a soft blue light welling from within.

"It is time!" Caroline called out, and Rory jumped. She raised the hooked staff and spun it in broad circles overhead. "Form a line, please." Holding the staff aloft, she pointed the hook back toward the fire.

Behind them, the golems tossed down their mallets and

scrambled over the sand, loping along on long claws, clicking excitedly.

"Welcome to Remembrance Day, Rory," Caroline said softly, facing the oncoming golems.

Rory took a step back, remembering his first encounter, feeling the stab of a long metal claw. His heart picked up again. "Uh . . . Caroline?"

She didn't seem to notice, gesturing into the sky with her free hand. "At the coming of the Fourth Shadow Moon, we celebrate the story of my people and pass it on to the next generation."

He glanced up, then quickly back down as the golems' clicks grew louder. *Next generation?* He pointed at the golems. "Uh, hey, are they going to stop?"

She patted his arm. "Watch. Listen."

The golems were only feet away when Caroline held out her palm. The golems skidded in the sand and clustered together, every blue-green eye locked onto her.

"Orderly, now," Caroline said. "I know you are all excited, but we must have order." She dipped the staff, touching the hook in the sand. "Line up. *Yoo-dai.*"

The golems quickly organized themselves into a long line, a few pushing and shoving to get closer to the front. Once they'd settled, Caroline nodded and turned back toward the cave, leading the procession.

Fat blue-purple fungal caps grew off the walls and ceiling, reminding Rory of a patient a few months back who had inhaled a jar of glitter. The fungi glowed and pulsed, each to their own rhythm, linked by luminous veins.

"Whoa," Rory said, taking in the dazzling sight. "This is . . . incredible."

Caroline only nodded as the line of golems shuffled forward.

Order held until the first golem reached the lip of the cave and broke into a clumsy run. Beneath the mushrooms, the rules deteriorated quickly, with golems jostling for position. Bouts of noisy clicks broke out as they filled the cave floor, with the biggest golems pushing in deepest.

As the last golems quieted, a reverent silence settled. They waited.

Rory glanced at Caroline. "What—"

Caroline shushed him and pointed at a bright cluster of fungus. The golem who'd started the shoving match to be in front clicked its long fingers excitedly. Suddenly, the tops of the caps swelled until they'd stretched taut like an inflated balloon. Rory watched in stunned silence, bracing for a loud pop. Instead, the caps split in soft *riiips*. A fog of glowing indigo spores wafted down from the deflating caps and washed over the golem in front. Most of the bright spores collected on its head, shoulders, and claws like luminescent snow. The coated golem held its claws over its head and backed up, carefully picking its way through the crowd and back toward the beach. More caps throughout the cave inflated, and soon a chorus of happy clicks echoed within the cave.

"Here." Caroline held out a strip of yellow fabric. "You don't want to breathe in the spores. Bad for the lungs."

Rory took the cloth and covered his mouth and nose as the first few spores drifted by him. The golems couldn't capture every spore; there weren't enough of them, so as more and more caps burst open, a thick layer of glowing snow covered the cave floor. He looked over and found that Caroline hadn't covered her face.

But before he could ask, she said, "Oh, I have been exposed dozens of times. Consider me inoculated."

Rory nodded slowly, not sure if he actually asked a question, but unable to peel his eyes off the spectacle. More glowing caps swelled and burst, thickening the glittering snowstorm.

Caroline leaned over. "This is a day of both mourning and

celebration among the Wyth. The psybelles both begin and end their life cycle. And we renew our commitment to another year of mutual service. The Wyth provide shelter, education, and legacy to the short-lived psybelles, and the psybelles provide—"

"Security and labor," Rory said, growing more impressed.

"Very good, Rory."

"So the golems are alive. Kind of. They're, like, machines, but . . . alive." Rory's mind flooded with potential applications for sentient semi-organic robots. "They could be really useful out in the world!"

"Mankind's greatest talent is the exploitation of resources." She eyed Rory knowingly. "Which is why the psybelles are kept safely here. Humanity, in its current state, could not respect the golems and their service. There would be domestic benefit, but how long would it be? Years? Months? Days? Before someone turned them to war?"

Rory knew the answer and sighed. *Not long enough.*

"Perhaps someday," Caroline said to herself. "But not this day." She pointed over at the first golem, which had finally broken through the crowd. It hurried over to the nearest darkened scrap lying in the sand. "Watch there."

"What's it doing?"

"When the psybelles bloom, the elder golems collect the spores and deliver them to each husk. I'm certain you saw them coming in."

The golem stood over the muddy lump of rust and shook its body like a wet dog. Most of the spores detached, drifting down. The golem didn't wait to watch. It ran back toward the cave again, passing other spore-covered golems coming out.

"We pack nutrients into the husk's soil so that psybelles grow quickly. In short order, Rory, this beach will be alive with

310

curious sporelings."

"Baby golems? How soon?"

Caroline nodded at the inoculated husk, and Rory turned. He held his breath and watched as thin threads crawled out from each spore, connecting with other strands to form a gleaming network of blue mycelium. A moment later, small fungal stalks rose from its head, and turquoise light welled in its eyes.

"Nothing grows that fast."

Caroline patted Rory's arm again.

"What happens to the older golems?"

"Their cycle ends."

"You mean they die?" Rory's jaw tightened as he watched more golems shake their spore-covered bodies.

Caroline turned to him. "The lucky ones get an entire year, but most get less than that. That is the meaning of Remembrance Day. To celebrate both the beginning and the end."

"I . . ." Rory had thought a great deal about death, especially during his second bout with cancer, but had never discussed it out loud—not even with Patrick. Speaking about it made it feel real, present. From his experience, he had a general understanding that there were really two ways to die. Alone or . . .

"I guess, if I got to choose, a party sounds pretty good." It sounded corny to hear it out loud, but Caroline's gentle presence soothed him.

"That is my dream, too." She looked back to the golems. "At sunrise. In Jacklyn's arms." A sad smile touched her thin lips. "Like how we started."

Rory swallowed, unnerved by the eerie specificity. He looked at Caroline, wondering just how much and how far she could see through that blindfold.

The inoculated husk twitched as the mycelium continued to spread. She pointed and grasped his hand, watching it rise on unsteady legs. "Look, there! Our first sporeling. This begins the second phase."

A pair of golems at the back of the line spotted the unsteady sporeling and hurried over. Rory didn't recognize the golems as the ones who inoculated it, but then again, it was hard to tell them apart. An elder golem helped the sporeling stand, gesturing at its feet with its claws. The small sporeling wobbled and clicked back, surprising itself with its sound.

Rory wiggled his fingers, watching the sporeling test out its claws. "Is that sign language?"

"Of sorts." Caroline considered for a moment, then added, "Think of it more as Morse code. Clicks and pauses."

Rory watched curiously as the cycle of golems flowed in and out of the cave. More sporelings rose, with more golems coming out of line to help them. Soon, the line had shrunk, and the number of golems chasing after curious sporelings exploring the waves would equal those waiting for more spores. Soon, the children would surpass their elders.

"It looks like we will get a good yield this year!" Caroline clapped her hands. "We were fortunate to find so much scrap metal in dump yards, and the eastern wind kept the cave damp all season. If we can stay healthy and hidden, we might finally grow our numbers next year."

The last few golems shuttled the spores to the last remaining husks. "So, what's phase three?"

"Phase three is my part." She turned to face him. "Help the elder golems gather the sporelings around the fire. I must go prepare." She slipped away, gliding toward the camp a short way up the beach.

"For what?" he called after her.

Caroline stopped and flicked the tail of her red blindfold dramatically over her shoulder. "The story! We cannot forget." She threw an arm out at the star-dotted sea. "Welcome home, Rory."

Rory raised his chin, feeling a rare pride well in him. Caroline wanted him here, she wanted him to see this. *Me.* The thought brought a broad smile. Surrounded by curious sporelings and their worried caretakers, he stretched out his arms to the stars and took a deep breath in. *Home.*

———

Corralling sporelings, Rory quickly discovered, was a lot like clipping Sneak's claws. He spent most of his time chasing and pleading, and when he'd finally catch her, he'd get one nail done before she'd wiggle free. Slowly, though, he helped the elders nudge the sporelings toward the fire and away from the waves. Rory walked with two sporelings, holding their claws warily while both clicked away at him. As the golems came together, the elders took their places around the perimeter, half to resume drumming and the other half to prevent bored sporelings from wandering off.

They gathered in a wide semi-circle around the fire, leaving a sandy stage. Rory's red blanket lay at the inside edge, front and center. As he took his place, the drums rumbled to life.

BOOM. Boom-boom. Boom. Boom-boom.

Caroline stepped into the circle, still dressed in her brown robe. She leaned against her hooked staff, holding a leather strap over her shoulder with the other hand. From Rory's seat, he couldn't make out what she carried on her back, though it looked to be a stack of pale-orange, manhole cover-sized discs. She walked forward and stooped slightly, perhaps theatrically or from the weight of her pack. The drums picked up speed.

Boom-da-da-boom. Boom-da-da-boom-boom.

Rory watched, waiting. It suddenly occurred to him he was

313

sitting on a hidden, magical beach, surrounded by thinking mushrooms, and watching a show put on by a witch. *How had this become my life?* A few trembling sporelings pressed closer to him. They smelled of musty earth, salt, and metal, and the fire was warm. He held his arms up, and a pair of golems pressed against his sides like nervous toddlers. He checked his keystone was still around his neck.

When Caroline reached center stage, the drums changed. The golems slapped their mallets against the side of the drum, driving the beat into a frenzy.

Boom-CLAK. Boom-CLAK. Boom-CLAK.

She carefully lowered her pack onto the sand, undoing the straps and reverently placing all three of the discs in the sand before her. Rory leaned closer and spotted the curved, chiseled characters like the rings of a tree. He squinted, trying to make out the symbols, but the flickering shadow mired them. Their pale-orange skin looked familiar though, reminding him of his middle school pottery class. *Clay.*

Caroline slowly raised her hooked staff, drawing out the anticipation. The drums beat faster, wilder.

Boom-CLAK. Boom-CLAK. Boom-CLAK.

Rory's heart tried to keep pace as the two sporelings squeezed against his sides.

Like lightning, she brought the staff down, driving its tip into the sand. The drums ceased, leaving their last note echoing off the cliffs.

"I am the Shepherd," she called out, surveying the crowd. "I founded the Wyth, I blazed the first Path, and I befriended the Titans. I have walked the world, built an empire, and seen it dashed into the sea. I am the Shepherd. But before I was, I first had to tame a lycin."

Rory leaned forward.

Caroline reached beneath her cloak and drew out her gemstone necklace: emerald, sapphire, and topaz—each cloudy stone glittering in the firelight.

"We start near the beginning, with a humble tribe in a world of titans." She tapped her emerald and spun, kicking up the surrounding sand. She leaped to the side as the sand bubbled and settled, creating what looked like a small village with squat, round huts.

"Wow," Rory whispered, the sporelings clicking quietly.

"It was a simple life, a happy life, but one destined to change." Caroline tapped the emerald again, and more huts popped out of the ground, spreading out. "As my tribe grew, so did its need for lumber and water and wheat. That appetite drew the attention of the jealous Titans, who did not want to share those lands and their bounty. They came as floods." The sapphire glowed, and water permeated the sand, washing away two huts.

"Quakes." A glint of green, and the sand shook and opened, dropping two more huts.

"And storms." She held a hand to the sky, but nothing happened. The Wyth frowned and held the topaz to her lips, whispering something as the fire popped behind her. Then she threw her hand into the air again. "And storms!"

The topaz glowed, and high overhead, the stars disappeared. Ominous clouds smashed together, and purple lightning flicked through the heavens as they wrestled. Thunder shook the beach, and Rory jumped, clutching the sporelings beside him. Elder golems moved among the crowd, clicking reassurances.

He felt a tickle on his arm and looked down to see his hair rising. The sky flashed, and a bolt of light tore through another pair of huts, leaving a jagged black line in the sand. As Caroline lowered her arm, the storm broke, and the thunder tumbled off into the distance. Rory barely breathed.

"Nothing appeased the Titans. Not tribute, not sacrifice,"

315

Caroline said, pacing her stage as she spoke. "We were a doomed people if *we* did not change. But." She paused, thumping the butt of her staff into the sand. "What if we could reason with them? Yes! If we could talk to the Titans, then we could know them and, through knowing, bond." Caroline turned slowly, smiling at the audience, letting the roaring bonfire fill the silence. "A bond of survival."

Caroline hurried toward the remaining sand huts, but she faltered as she neared, placing a lithe hand over her heart. "The chiefs of the tribes wouldn't listen!" She halted and stepped back. "They wished to hunt and enslave the Titans. They would not hear reason! But I knew the Titans' secret: they did not seek to destroy but to grow. As a troublesome youth, I'd snuck from my village and witnessed them transform bare black rock into a forest. Empty ocean into a reef. Even fire-swept forests regrew beneath their care. They are guardians of the lands, not tyrants, and I began to wonder if we might be the invaders."

Caroline waved her hand, and a wall rose around the remaining huts.

"As my people prepared for their futile war, I was ignored and exiled to the fields. Guardian of the flock, they said, but I knew I had angered the chiefs. As I wandered, I fought despair." The sand swirled and rose to form three life-sized sheep. The sand sheep moved, bopping their heads in mock grazing as Caroline strolled between them, glancing wistfully back at the village and its new wall. Slowly, the village slid into the sand and disappeared.

"One day, a pack of vicious lycin attacked my flock." Caroline gestured to the bonfire, and two wolves of sand and ember stepped forward. Standing on two grainy legs, Rory shivered as the beasts eyed the sheep with glowing red eyes. They snarled and lunged, biting one and dragging a second into the flames. Caroline walked over to the wounded sheep and petted the trembling sand. "I was days away from help, with no time." The sporelings pressed in closer. "You see," Caroline addressed the audience, "lycin carry in their teeth a terrible venom."

Caroline held up five fingers. "There are five symptoms. First is sleep, which lasts long past the night. Left alone, the lambs wither and die unless they are cared for and brought food and water."

She dropped a finger. "The second comes as a forgetful mind. The poor lambs can't remember what has happened, yet become panicked, ever watchful for an unseen attacker."

"The third is madness, as the lamb's mind breaks. They run and kick and lose all connection to the flock." Caroline dropped another finger. "The fourth is a mercy and avoids the fifth, for the lamb dies instead of dying within. The flock does not mourn but celebrates the sorrow, for the passing prevents a terrible tomorrow."

She lowered her arm, still with one finger extended, and pointed at the wounded sheep. "The fifth and final is what any shepherd fears most. The venom takes hold in the lamb. Its gentle nature shrivels and triggers a bone-breaking lycanthropy." Rory grimaced as the lamb's body contorted, mouth open in a soundless cry as its snout extended, revealing enormous fangs.

"For my people, there was only one recourse." Caroline raised her staff and brought it down on the new lycin's head, severing it, its entire body exploding into a sand pile. Then she darted this way and that as she prowled through an unseen jungle. "In anger, I pursued the lycin with a vengeance in my heart. I chased them through the woods and fields, hearing my poor sheep calling for me. When I finally caught up to them, though, I found something I never expected."

Caroline walked forward, and the sand rose behind her, growing a dune as tall as the flames. From the dune, a three-fingered hand emerged, reaching out toward the audience. Rory's eyes widened, and he yelped, sliding backward. The hand stopped above them, sprinkling sand on the terrified audience before it drew back slowly into the dune. Two brilliant emerald eyes opened near the top of the mound, and Rory froze, not daring to breathe until they closed.

"I discovered the lycin's den beside a slumbering titan of mud and stone—the same evil who shook my village only a season before. What a discovery! Lycin and Titan were living in communion! A vision of what I hoped for my people to achieve. It was there I discovered the key. I often visited, concealed, watched, and learned for years. Many times, I saw lycin and Titan touch and cooperate in hunt or mutual shelter, though they never spoke in my ear. It became clear. We could communicate with the Titans and maybe live in peace, but first, I needed a translator. I needed to tame a lycin. To do that, I'd need my people's help."

Caroline spun her staff around her body, and the dune melted into a swirling sandstorm before the grains settled into scattered doors. She moved between them, knocking on each, the disappointment on her face growing deeper and deeper until she walked back toward the audience, crestfallen. The bonfire dimmed, and the doors sank back into the beach, leaving Caroline alone on stage.

"Still, my village would not listen. And I was . . . banished." She turned and walked in place, the sand beneath her body moving her steps. "I left to learn how to soothe a beast and, in doing so, discovered the foundation of a new empire."

The sand stilled beneath Caroline's feet, and the bonfire swelled. Rory waited for more, but then Caroline threw back her hood and gave a deep bow.

Wait. That's it? Rory looked around; the golems were all frozen. Unsure of what to do, Rory did what came naturally when someone bowed at the end of a performance. He clapped. The golems all turned and looked at him, many tipping their heads questioningly. Then, one by one, they clicked their long claws

318

together until the entire cove was filled with a tinny ovation. Caroline beamed, bowing again, before walking straight to Rory. Quickly, the sporelings scattered, heading off with worried elders trailing behind them.

Sweat covered her face, soaking the top strip of her red blindfold. "What did you think?" she asked, panting.

"It was . . . amazing. Enchanting," Rory said. Caroline nodded knowingly. "The lycin and those huts. I mean, wow. That sand-hand thing was terrifying. How did you do all that?"

"A performer never reveals their secrets, Rory."

He sighed, expecting to hear as much.

"What else did you notice?"

"Uh, well. I don't mean to sound rude, but it ended, uh, weirdly. I felt like there was more story there. What happens to the Shepherd?"

"We don't know." She pointed back at the three clay discs still bound in the sand. "The rest of the story hides in there, on the Shepherd's Stones, waiting to be translated. I have to improvise most sections of the story because we only have partial translations, especially near the end. The symbols are . . . tricky to comprehend. Most have multiple meanings."

He nodded, pretending like any of this made sense. "Right." A pair of curious sporelings approached the bonfire, only to be shooed away by two elders. A sudden sadness overtook him as he watched them give chase. "When do the old golems—"

"At sunrise, they walk to the cave. Their mature psybelles release one last spore cloud, inoculating the cave. After, we clean the bodies and prepare them for next year. Thus, the cycle begins again."

Rory nodded, not because he understood, but because his brain was so stuffed it was numb. Titans and lycin and shepherds. The sand and the sporelings. He wondered how much of the story was true. His mind swerved to Khloe. He pictured her sitting beside him, eagerly watching Caroline's show. He bet she would have loved it.

"You are smiling," Caroline said. "From your heart."

"What? No. I—"

"Who were you thinking about?"

Am I that obvious? "I . . . met someone. Someone special."

"Wonderful news, though I hope you kept our agreement." She looked at him meaningfully.

"I didn't tell her anything, if that's what you mean."

"But you wanted to."

"I mean, sure. It's hard to keep magic and all this"—he made a wide, sweeping gesture to the golems and the beach—"bottled up. It's too, well, unbelievable!"

"I understand and appreciate your honesty. What is the name of this person?"

"Her name's Khloe. Khloe Seeker."

Caroline's face went slack. "Seeker?" she repeated softly.

Rory nodded, unsure. "Know her?"

Caroline remained still a moment longer, then briskly shook her head. Her surprise vanished. "No, just admiring the name. When do you see her again?"

"Hopefully tomorrow." He looked at her, feeling lost. "Is, uh . . . is everything okay?"

"Of course! A piece of advice from a veteran of love?" He nodded for her to continue. "There is no more powerful bond than one created by being vulnerable. Risk the hurt."

Before Rory could respond, a few clicks came from a pair of golems nearby.

"I'm needed. We have a great deal to teach the sporelings about our world before sunrise." She reached out and squeezed his shoulders firmly with both her hands. "Thank you for coming, Rory. Your presence meant a great deal to me." She dipped her head to the side, and Rory followed her cue, spotting a pack of sporelings staring at him with their massive blue-green eyes.

He blinked, unsure of what came next when a yawn overtook him. Unable to stifle it, he suddenly felt spent. *What time is it?* He could never tell here.

"Haven't been sleeping well?"

Rory shook his head. "Not at all." He sighed, scanning the beach teeming with active sporelings. "I should go, actually. Training tomorrow. This was . . . truly amazing, Caroline. Thank you for inviting me." Another thought stalled him, and he risked it. "I'm, I don't . . ." He paused, organizing his thoughts. "Maybe you could teach me more about the Wyth and . . . everything else? If Jacklyn . . ." He let the question hang.

Caroline considered for a moment, then smiled. "I'm certain we can come to an arrangement."

Chapter 30: Eagle Scout

Tuesday, April 24th, 07:30

Every two years, nurses make their journey to the old Office Block at the back of the Hill. To subbasement E2, classroom 13, for the required Pediatric Advanced Life Support training, a biennial, eight-hour certification class. There, each nurse spent the day saving countless plastic dummies from catastrophes: choking, heart attacks, poisoning, lightning strikes, and anything else the instructor thought sounded fun.

Biking in, all Rory could think about was Remembrance Day. He played Caroline's performance over and over in his head. *How did Jacklyn heal Tommy and Maxwell? Could anyone use magic? Why have I never heard of this?* He wondered what other stories might be on those clay discs and felt as though he'd tumbled down the rabbit hole. It was enormous and ancient and important and on the cutting edge of . . . something. But the memory he returned to the most, the one that warmed him even now, was how Caroline had taken his arm and walked him to the cave beneath the stars. *"Welcome home,"* she'd said.

Stay focused, he thought, while chaining his bike. *Pass the training. Find a candidate. Save a life.*

Nearing the staff entrance, he discovered a crowd of people in suits and dresses, some holding microphones and others hefting shoulder-mounted cameras with national and local TV logos. They jostled for position to get a good angle of the doors.

He said a silent prayer that all this attention was for a patient on the adult side—maybe a different miraculous turnaround? More likely, a wealthy hospital donor. Rory often felt bad for the adult-side nurses who had to deal with the magnifying glass that came with high-profile patients. With any patient, one slip could land you in trouble, but a slip about the wrong person, or God forbid a green banner donor, might mean your job. Nurses had to learn code phrases to thwart prying journalists or "family friends" calling for juicy information.

He picked his way through the crowd, avoiding elbows and camera operators. At the entrance, he saw Officer Kyle standing guard.

"Excuse me, sir, but this is the staff entrance." He held his hand to Rory's chest.

"Good morning, Kyle." Rory handed over his badge.

Kyle's dark-rimmed eyes darted back and forth between the badge and his face.

"Test, test!" a voice shouted over the commotion behind him.

Rory turned. A middle-aged woman in a smart maroon suit smoothed her hair and brushed something off her shoulder. "Let's try one. Test, test! Here we go. I'm here at Oates Children's with breaking news. Conner Grady, son of Senator Gretta Grady, is in critical condition following a tragic drowning during a Boy Scout camping trip." She lowered her mic. "That felt good. How did it sound?" The cameraman gave her a thumbs-up.

A senator's kid? He recognized the name. *From where, though . . .* Somewhere in his brain, he found the answer: that article in Megan's magazine. Senator Grady, who thought nurses did nothing on their shifts but play cards. *THAT senator's kid.* Rory scoffed, sadly enjoying the irony.

"Your badge, sir," Kyle said, handing back his badge. He gestured to his beard. "You shaved."

Rory rubbed his stubbly chin. "I'm trying a new look."

Kyle sniffed, and Rory checked his watch. "Hey, question. This isn't my normal shift, which means it is not yours either."

"Sick call. I volunteered."

Rory nodded. "Short-staffed?"

"Unfortunately, sir."

"That's rough." Rory shook his head. "Hey, can I get you a coffee at least?"

"Sir?"

"I have to come back through here anyway, and I'm grabbing one for myself." Rory's stomach knotted, and he fought to keep his expression pleasant.

Kyle didn't seem to notice. "Thank you. Cream, please, if you don't mind. But really, you don't—"

"No worries, Kyle!" Rory said, already walking away. "I'll be back."

The automatic double doors opened, and he picked up his pace down the hallway, making sure the door closed behind him. If Kyle was outside, the security office might be empty. Nabbing a volunteer badge would give Jacklyn better access.

He tip-toed toward the fishbowl of the security office, checking the entrance again to make sure no one was coming up behind him. Quietly, he peered inside, spotting a sleepy-looking guard sitting in front of several monitors. He ducked back around the corner, bracing for someone to yell or question him. Instead, he heard a soft snore. It seemed Kyle wasn't the only one picking up an extra shift. Pinned to a corkboard on the wall behind the guard were rows of volunteer badges. It was a tight squeeze into the small office, but Rory saw a way through.

When he stepped inside, he noticed a similar motion on one of the small screens. He stopped, spotting himself on the monitor. He looked up and stared into a ceiling-mounted security camera. *Well, shit . . .* Chewing his cheek, he checked the monitor again. *No one ever watches these things, anyway.* Awkwardly crouched, he weighed his options. He doubted he would see this opportunity again.

Screw it.

_____

Rory tucked the volunteer badge into his pocket and tried to pretend like he hadn't just broken the law. After exchanging an overly friendly wave with a passing day shifter, he tried to calm himself. *It's your hundredth time. It's your hundredth time.*

Waiting in line for coffee, he spotted facilities putting up the newest marketing poster behind the bar: a floor-to-ceiling picture of Bell and Tommy's smiling faces. Below it read: *Oates Children's Hospital: Where Miracles Happen.* He blew out a long breath. *They don't know the half of it.*

With a coffee in each hand and an impulse-buy cookie in his pocket, Rory arrived at the PICU. He saw which room was the senator's. Two tall men with sunglasses and navy suits flanked the door to the biggest room on the unit at the quietest end of the hall. Rory found them a bit cliché, but their effect on the staff was impressive. The nurses still went about their duties, but many glanced uneasily at Room 10.

An aide, pushing a resupply cart, stepped too close as she passed, and a guard swiftly intercepted her. Rory watched, fingering the volunteer badge in his pocket. *Would it be enough?*

"Rory!"

He jumped and saw Antoni approaching. The handsome unit-educator wore tight-fitting, dark gray scrubs, revealing toned arms. A utility belt with pink, white, and red tape, extra flushes, assorted chocolates, and three differently shaped scissors hung around his waist, like a medical Batman.

Antoni shifted the basin and soap he carried to his other arm and closed in for a one-armed hug. Rory opened his arms, careful not to spill any coffee. After a quick squeeze, Antoni stepped back and looked crestfallen. "What happened to your gorgeous beard? Look how young you look."

"I'm just trying it out."

"Uh huh," Antoni said. "Trying to impress a lady?"

"Well, maybe."

Antoni raised his eyebrows. "Oh, ho! Yes, Baby Rory!"

His naked cheeks grew warm. Antoni always had a knack for making him laugh and could disarm even the most stressed-out nurses. In the past two years, he had learned so much from Antoni. From quick games to play with patients to inserting emergency access—the educator was second to none as a calming presence. And Rory wasn't the only one who felt it. The pair of golden hands pinned to Antoni's badge declared that.

Peering from behind Antoni was a skinny teenager wearing a blue volunteer's polo and carrying an armful of blankets and sheets. Her chipper smile revealed braces and told Rory she was new and orienting. Rory gestured toward Room 10, careful to keep a casual tone. This could be his no-hoper. "Looks exciting in here."

"That?" Antoni sighed. "That is one hot mess."

"Whose assignment?"

"Mine." Antoni rolled his eyes and pulled out a red candy from his utility belt, unwrapped it, and popped it into his mouth.

Rory grimaced. "Sorry."

Antoni shrugged. "Well, I'm not bored, that's for sure. Anyway, what are you doing here? It's your day off."

"I got P.A.L.S. in a bit but saw all the cameras outside." Rory nodded toward the bodyguards. "What's the kid's story?"

"I . . . can't really talk about it." Antoni sighed. "You know how it goes."

"Yeah, I mean, I know it's the senator's kid," Rory pressed.

Antoni pursed his lips and frowned thoughtfully.

326

"How about this?" Rory said. "Put a note in for tomorrow. I'll take Room 10. We can think of this as giving report early."

Antoni's eyes narrowed, questioning. Rory pulled out the cookie from his pocket. "Oh hey, you can have this. Dark chocolate, caramel . . ."

Antoni's expression softened, and he looked longingly at the cookie. How Antoni was in such good shape with his sweet tooth was a source of endless speculation between Megan and Rory. The going theory was he was secretly a robot powered by sugar and push-ups.

"That's a dirty trick, Rory Nash." Antoni shook his head, grinning.

Rory waited, turning the cookie over. Antoni turned to the volunteer. "Can you drop those off in the room, please? You can let"—he glanced up at Rory—"Mom know I'll be in shortly, and we'll do a bed check."

The volunteer nodded and marched down the hall. When she was out of earshot, Rory handed the cookie over, and Antoni took it and slipped it into his utility belt. He led Rory to the side and dropped his voice. "You didn't hear this from me, okay?"

Rory nodded, leaning closer.

Antoni pulled out his paper brains. "It's sad. Sixteen-year-old male. Boy Scout—nice kid, and otherwise healthy. He was leading a group of Cub Scouts out on the McKenzie River, near Eugene. A raft flipped on a rapid and spilled the entire boat. One kid got struck by a downed tree, and I guess those trees act like underwater strainers—like, really dangerous—with the current forcing everything through, pinning the bigger debris. Conner was in a kayak and got the kid out, but when he tried to get off the tree, he flipped, and the current pulled him under and pinned him there."

Antoni checked over his shoulder and dropped his voice. "They got Conner out four minutes later. I heard a fisherperson saw it

327

happen and helped pull him out. He was unresponsive, but he caught a minor break because the snowmelt did him some good. Neuro thinks the cold water preserved at least part of his brain. Not sure how much yet, but his lungs and kidneys are wrecked. The family is still in shock."

"Damn, that's really sad," Rory said, his mind racing. *This sounds perfect!*

"It gets a little worse. He had a scholarship to play baseball at Stanford all lined up, too." Antoni shook his head. "Another depressing case of what might have been."

Rory chose his next words carefully. "That's terrible . . . well, maybe he turns it around?"

Antoni frowned. "His EEG says otherwise." He shifted his candy to his other cheek. "But that's why I like you, Rory. Always the optimist."

I am?

Down the hall, the guards stopped the volunteer outside Room 10. Antoni followed Rory's eyes and sighed. "She's just dropping off blankets, boys."

The volunteer pointed back at Antoni, and the guards turned. Rory spied the edge of a leather holster against the man's white dress shirt and swallowed. The guard shook his head and slid to block the volunteer's path forward.

"Those two are chapping my hide," Antoni said. "They won't let anyone in but assigned staff and family-approved consults."

"Oh, crap," Rory whispered, regretting speaking as Antoni looked back at him. He shrugged it off, and Rory watched his plan crumble.

"I have to go deal with this." Antoni sighed. "Don't know why you'd want to deal with this one, but I'll put you down for Room 10. High profile—it's gonna be a long week."

"Same place, different time." Rory nodded.

Damn it. As Antoni walked away, a flurry of ideas ran through his head, most of which he tossed away. He could distract them? Or maybe try to overpower them? Not a chance; those men were armed and trained. He was neither. Drug their coffee? He grimaced and laughed. Each crazy scenario likely ended with him punched, shot, or fired. *Come on, Rory. Think!*

He glanced at the clock: 07:49. Rory turned on his heel to head for the stairs and ran into Dr. Magus. Both men balanced their coffees without spilling.

"Watch where you're walking, please," Magus said, brushing by.

A trail of residents followed close behind, and from among them, Khloe stepped out of line and slid over beside him. "Oh, Rory, thank god—is that coffee for me?"

Nope. "I . . . I thought I . . . would surprise you."

Khloe beamed at him and accepted the cup. "You're a lifesaver. What are you doing here? You didn't come just to bring me coffee, did you?"

Rory paused a beat, knowing there was a good answer. "Yes?"

"Liar." She laughed.

Rory snapped his fingers. "Not quick enough. I have a certification class in ten minutes. I thought I'd come say hi to whoever is working today. And of course"—he shook his shoulders playfully—"to bring you coffee. Because"—he pointed to his chest—"gentleman."

Khloe smiled. "The other night was fun."

"So fun. Maybe we could do it again sometime?"

"What are you doing after your training?" she asked.

"No plans."

Khloe dug into her pocket and held up her on-call pager. "I hand off at five. But to be honest, the idea of doing anything after that makes me a little nauseous. I am. So. Tired." She sagged and took a long drink from the coffee cup.

Rory understood. "Me too." He'd gotten home after four and collapsed into bed. His alarm cruelly sounded only a couple of hours later. "We can keep it simple. Cafeteria when I'm done?"

She nodded. "That's perfect. Oh, and it's taco Tuesday!"

As he laughed, an angry shout from down the hall told him that Dr. Magus had reached the guards, who towered over him. He wagged his finger in their faces and tapped his badge. For a moment, Rory thought they weren't letting him through until they stepped aside and waved him in.

"Security looks tight," Rory said. "Shouldn't you . . ."

"He won't notice. He's all about his spotlight patients." Khloe mimed air quotes.

"Spotlight?"

"Patients that get enough press to give TV interviews," Khloe said. "They build his brand. Free publicity."

"That's . . . umm . . ." *Sleazy? Exploitative?*

"Unethical," Khloe said firmly.

"That's the word."

Magus's head poked back out of the room, and he waved Khloe over.

"Sorry, gotta go," Khloe said. "Meet you at three?"

A piece of Rory said no, that he needed to focus on Conner, but a louder voice rising in his chest said *YES ABSOLUTELY.*

"Three," Rory said. "Can't wait."

She brushed the strands of long hair from her face. "Okay, great." She gave a little wave. "Bye."

"Bye!" Rory said, waving with his free hand. He watched her

hustle down the hall and disappear into Conner's room with a second look from the guards. Rory made a note of that as he walked across campus. Nearing the security station, he remembered that he held only one coffee. He sighed and pressed the lid tight, knowing an un-caffeinated training was going to be rough. With a quick "Here ya go," he gave the cup to Kyle, who thanked him half a dozen times and ran to make his class.

Instead of listening to the lecture, he jotted down and scratched out idea after idea for how to get Jacklyn to see Conner. His mind buzzed with images and words: *agents, coffee, Khloe, clay discs, sporelings, Jacklyn's sunglasses, Tommy smiling in Bell's arms.* He had to make this work. Conner's life was in his hands.

Chapter 31: The One and Only

Tuesday, April 24th, 17:03

North Yamhill River Bridge, three miles northeast of McMinnville, OR

"Oh, oh, right here!" Jane, driving slowly along the shoulder of the road, pointed to the old bridge. "There should be a porta-potty . . . there!" A green, graffiti-covered port-a-potty looked ready to fall down an embankment above a riverbed. By how steep the drop was, she wondered how often the river flooded and carved away the hillside. Rolling down the window, the burble of the river caught her ear, coming from somewhere behind the ferns and anemic pines. Jane inhaled, drinking in the smell of wet earth and moving water.

"Right where Maxwell's sister said," Jane said, relieved. Their search for the young Maxwell neared the twenty-four-hour mark when his sister opened the door. He didn't live there anymore, Jane learned, but his sister knew where to find him and said he was acting strange. Not in trouble, but almost happier . . . lighter. He told her he'd been healed. Jane found that interesting and logged it away. Jane left, promising she'd look in on him.

In the car beside her, Emmett shook his head and said nothing. He was practically pouting.

"Real professional," Jane deadpanned.

"Let's just get this over with." He checked his watch. "Thirty minutes left, and we're done with that letter."

"Plenty of time." Jane pulled over and bounded out of the car while Emmett dragged himself behind. They had made it two precarious steps down the embankment when his phone rang again.

Jane fingered her pipe in her pocket. The Director seemed to have sniffed out something was wrong, calling frequently for updates. Although she reasoned, Dawson hadn't arrived, so perhaps the Director hadn't sussed out what. Yet. Emmett was evading the truth well enough. *Not bad for a rookie.*

Emmett excused himself back to the car to grab a pen, leaving Jane alone with only the bird songs and the rushing river below. She pulled out her pipe, looking back to see Emmett reaching through the car's window for something with the phone to his ear. She glanced between him and the port-a-potty, found her lighter, and ducked inside.

———

"Jane?" Emmett sounded far away. His footsteps crunched on the gravel.

She sputtered with a lungful of smoke and jumped down from the closed toilet seat. A thick cloud of smoke filled the air above her, blurring the red and blue graffiti covering every square inch of the interior. She saw something twitch in the urinal and jumped back, knocking her elbow against the side and spilling the red coals in her pipe onto the sticky floor.

"Muff!" Jane said and stomped on the smoldering embers. *Thump. Thump-thump.*

She waved the smoke toward the vents and away from Emmett.

"You okay in there?"

"Yeah, I'm good. Just, uh . . . wiping."

Emmett sighed. "Too much info, Jane . . . again."

"Who was on the phone? Dawson?"

"No. A buddy of mine from the Academy," Emmett said. "He finished looking into that abuse case against our last victim. You had a good hunch."

Jane perked up. "Yeah?" She tucked everything back into her pocket and rattled the toilet paper tube for effect.

"There was a kid there and a girlfriend, according to a postal worker. Looks like a nasty child abuse case was coming together against our victim, but it fell apart. Missing evidence. He probably would have walked."

"Poor kid . . ." Jane muttered.

"Don't feel too bad." Emmett's tone was weirdly chipper. "It turns out the kid is a celebrity now."

Rubbing her bloodshot eyes, Jane inspected herself in a semi-reflective mirror, half covered in blue spray paint. "Now?"

"Yeah! The kid was a goner. But then, poof. He wakes up, completely healed. How have you not heard of this? It's been all over the news."

Jane opened the door, and a haze billowed out. "Because I don't like the news, Emmett." She ignored Emmett's scowl as his nose wrinkled. "It's all fear-mongering and flashy headlines."

Emmett coughed, waving a hand in front of his face. "Really, Jane?"

"Which hospital?"

He folded his arms. "North."

Jane waved her hand, coaxing the answer from him. "Canada is north, Emmett. Be specific."

"Portland. At the big one . . . Hill Hospital. It's being called the—" He snapped his fingers. "Rose City Wonder." He waved away the cloud of skunky smoke. "And I'm beginning to see why the Director fired you."

"Hey," Jane snapped. "I quit."

"Right, and you don't have a drug problem either."

She winced. Emmett sounded just like her sister. She rolled her eyes to hide the ache and pushed past him, pacing down the narrow switch-back embankment. There was something about this miracle, something connected, that pinged her curiosity.

"Magic. Miracles. Weird, don't you think? Boyfriend of a mother of a miracle toddler gets murdered after skirting justice by someone who says magic is real," she said, ducking below crossing vines.

"I'm telling you, this killer is a vigilante," Emmett said, and Jane couldn't help but laugh. She had to hand it to him. When he latched onto an idea, he never let go, like a bulldog. *Like me.* She raised an eyebrow. "You're still so certain? Huh. It's not even in the realm of possibility the killer could tell the truth?"

"Magic, Jane?" Emmett said. "Please."

"I'm not totally convinced either, but I am keeping an open mind. Tell me, then. How do you explain the mummies?"

"New technology, maybe? A weapon we don't know about."

"You sound convinced."

He scowled at her. "It's a vigilante. There is no magic. We are wasting our time."

Jane threw up her arms. He was willingly being thick now. "You love that storyline, don't you? Big fan of comics growing up?" She couldn't keep the edge out of her voice.

"Yes. WOAH!" He stepped and slid a step down the embankment. He flailed but caught his balance, muttering something to himself before he turned. "A vigilante is the most plausible explanation, given the evidence. Everything else is fluff." He checked his watch. "We have seventeen more minutes."

Jane's frustration gnawed at her as she watched him start back down the path. She recognized this wall of his now. It was the one where he sounded like the Director. Emmett wouldn't budge, and so far, she hadn't been able to knock the barrier down. If anything, trying only seemed to undermine his mood and cooperation. She needed to pivot or risk smashing into it yet again. An idea came, and she went with it.

"You might be right about the vigilante, Agent Torin," she said casually. "I admit, the list of victims supports it."

"Thank you," he said, stepping over a fallen log.

"And you might be right about this whole magic thing, too. It is almost too good to be true."

"It is."

"The internet was too good to be true once. Phones, too."

"Here we go," Emmett said.

She ignored him. "In the 1800s, what you have in your pocket would be considered magic. And computers too. Now it's all magic we've named and that we understand. Binary language and circuits. Think about it, what would a text message be in antiquity? A holy whisper of angels? A hiss from the devil? They wouldn't know because they don't understand the rules."

Emmett shook his head. "I wish you wouldn't smoke . . ."

"It's not . . . uh," Jane said, knowing him at least partially right. She was being chatty. "I'm talking about the case. The killer's letter mentions 'Laws,' ones they couldn't break. Laws are rules, ones we don't understand. Just like we don't understand what's happening to our victims. How it is happening. What happened to that toddler in Portland, we don't understand that either and there is growing evidence they might be related. My whole point is to keep an open mind. If you're too locked in, you'll miss important details."

Emmett stopped, turning around with a pitying look. "You want magic to be real."

Jane felt oddly seen. Maybe she did. "Could be interesting."

"There is no magical world we get to discover, Jane." He scoffed. "This isn't a movie."

It was the patronizing tone that set her teeth grinding. She hit the wall, and this time, it stung.

"Heard, Agent Bait," she said, keeping her tone silk smooth. It was petty, but Emmett was acting too sure for someone so young.

His nostrils flared, somehow still handsome as he scowled, but she knew she'd hit her mark. He stormed down the trail. Jane bit her lip, staving off her grin as she followed.

———

The stomped-out trail switched back twice before emptying underneath the old bridge. A trio of tents—red, blue, and yellow—huddled together in the bridge's shadow. In the center, three people sat around a small fire.

All three heads turned at the sound of crunching rocks, and a dark, shaggy-haired boy rose. He wore an oil-smudged red vest, too baggy on his tall, skinny frame. He stepped backward, tripping over his seat, watching them with wide eyes.

"Maxwell," Jane whispered.

Emmett launched past her toward the camp, but Jane caught his arm, watching their mark.

"He'll bolt. Look at him."

The boy clutched his chest, and Jane could see a faint purple light coming from something in his hand. She squinted, but Emmett's voice drew her back.

"We've never been here."

Jane looked up and met Emmett's eyes. "Prey doesn't care which predator is trying to eat it; it cares about not getting eaten. The same goes for runaways."

Jane released his arm, and Emmett grabbed his badge and held it up.

"My name is Agent Emmett Torin!" he announced. "I'm looking for Maxwell. We just need—"

The boy turned and ran.

"Shit!" Emmett broke into a sprint, kicking stones up behind him. "Freeze!"

The boy bounded over the rocks.

"Mothermuffing muffer!" Jane sprang forward, but Emmett's longer legs bounded past her quickly. She slipped on the rocks, barely keeping her footing. The other two men stood, mouths open, watching them run past.

"Official! Business!" she shouted. Her lungs burned already, and her knees ached. She didn't remember them doing this before, and some part of her wondered when she had gotten older.

Emmett's youthful athleticism closed the gap, but the boy had a significant head start and was nearing the end of the gully and the blackberry bushes beyond. Jane did not want to chase him through brambles and put on as much speed as her short legs could summon. If he got to the bushes, he could disappear or force them into the thicket.

"Freeze!" Emmett shouted again.

Mid-sprint, Jane rolled her eyes. Then, shockingly, it worked.

The boy glanced back and made a crucial mistake—he triangulated instead of just running, and as he turned, he misplaced his second step, slipping on the wet rocks. He landed hard with a sickening *THUD*. Rocks sprayed everywhere as he slid. Jane grimaced. That had to hurt.

He scrambled to his feet and slipped again, wincing in pain. But by then, it was too late. Emmett tackled him from behind, and they tumbled across the riverbank, jostling and grunting.

Emmett ended up on top and wrenched one of the boy's arms behind his back. Dropping his head into the stones, the boy went limp, moaning. A thick purple goo covered his hands and put off a faint, fading light. On the bank beside them, more purple goo covered the rocks, intermingled with broken shards of glass. Jane wondered if it was a glow stick or whatever else kids were drinking these days to get high.

"You broke it, you asshole!" the boy shouted with his cheek pressed against stones. "You fucking asshole!"

Emmett cranked on his arm.

"Ow. Ow. Okay! Okay!" His voice was deeper than Jane expected.

"Not stopping when I yell to." Emmett panted, wiping his sweaty face with his torn jacket sleeve. A long strip of dirty white fabric, from cuff to elbow, hung tattered. He bled from a trio of cuts running the length of his forearm. "Ah, man, come on. This was new." He tapped the boy on the back of the head with two fingers. "Did you not hear me say to stop?"

"You said freeze, actually." Jane puffed. "Like a movie."

Emmett's lips pressed into a flat line as he glared at her.

Jane sat down cross-legged on the cool stones and fanned herself. "Phew, wow. That'll wake you up." She blew out a long breath. "Maxwell, right? My guy, what were you thinking?" She shifted her position to face him. The boy groaned, turning away and into the rocks. "You ran from federal authorities. That is a big no-no. We should take you straight to jail, right Agent Torin?" She winked at him, and he shook his head, confused. She rolled her eyes and nodded once at the boy. Emmett looked lost. Then, thankfully, his light clicked on.

Emmett puffed up, catching the act. "Ya. That's going to be a couple of years, at least. Plus, I think I heard him admit to theft—"

Maxwell lifted his head, and pebbles clung to his cheek. "I'm sorry. Dude, come on, please. Don't take me in."

Over at camp, Maxwell's neighbors watched, and Jane gave them a big wave. "We're just asking a few questions, and we'll let him go."

"You can't harass people like this!" one of them yelled.

"I'm aware, sir, but we wouldn't be here unless it was important."

Jane softened her voice. "We spoke with your sister. She said you got healed by someone. Is that right?"

"What are you doing?" Emmett whispered.

Jane shooed him off. "We're here to learn more about the people who healed you, and we were told you could be our guide."

Maxwell turned to face her, a river rock dropping off his cheek. "They told you to find me?"

Jane nodded, keeping her expression calm, the anticipation growing in her gut.

"I . . . I can't," he breathed.

"Can't or won't?" Emmett said, putting a little pressure on Maxwell's arm.

"Ow! Dude, get off me!"

Jane reached out and held Emmett's hand, giving him a reassuring nod. "Let him up. He's not going anywhere."

Emmett blinked at her. "What? He'll just run."

"He won't. Trust me."

Emmett looked down, shook his head, and released his grip. Gingerly, Maxwell pushed himself into a sitting position. Red indentations covered his face as he brushed the moss and dirt from his face.

"Why can't you tell us?" Jane said. "Is someone threatening you? Hurting you?"

Maxwell shook his head. "I just . . . They said I can only share it with one person, and I don't want to screw it up. They didn't just help me—they saved my life."

"Saved?" Jane said. She was dying to know who *they* were, but it wasn't time for that yet. She needed to follow the emotion first; she needed him to share. All these stories of healing and miracles that had cropped up recently felt interconnected. Even as a thrill spread through Jane, she kept calm. "How? And I'll be real honest with you. We're stuck in a dead end unless you point the way."

"Jane," Emmett hissed. She knew she was off script and violating many procedures, but her hunch prodded her to continue. Maxwell was honest. Why else would the killer have chosen him? Time to roll the dice.

"We're searching for someone named Jacklyn. She told us to find you. And that you'd have something for us." He looked at Jane, surprised. "We can keep these people safe while we figure out what's going on. But right now, you need to help us. Help them. You're the only one who can."

The boy stared at Jane, and she held his gaze, willing him to believe her. She'd meant every word. Maxwell broke eye contact and watched the river flow by as Jane's nerves knotted in her belly. Jane waved Emmett back, and thankfully, he took the cue and gave them space. Forcing the story wouldn't work.

When Maxwell sighed, Jane didn't let herself relax. She still had to play this carefully.

"Promise you'll help them?"

"We'll do our best."

"Can I stand?" Maxwell said, eyeing Emmett.

"Will you run?" Emmett said, halfway between a question and a threat.

"Mm-mm," he mumbled.

Emmett stepped closer as the boy rose, poised to pounce should Maxwell bolt, but the boy stayed put, brushing the last few stones from his pants. "That hurt, man."

"Yeah," Jane added. "Nice tackle."

"I played," Emmett replied curtly before his tone softened. He held up his tattered sleeve and inspected the damage with a frown. Maxwell sniffed—a small laugh.

For a second, Jane thought that was it. Maxwell wouldn't talk, but when he opened his mouth, a story came pouring out.

"It sounds crazy, okay, but I drank this purple drink, and I followed some lights to this beach in the woods. A woman was there. She wore a leather jacket and an orange beanie. Only one arm. This other lady, really skinny. And tall. She had a blindfold and a tie-dye dress. She was nice. Oh, and a fancy necklace, but they didn't look rich to me. The one-armed lady asked me some questions about my voice; then I shut my eyes. I don't know what they did, but there was a bright light, and it was hot for a second. I thought I was going to barf at first, but then suddenly . . . my head . . . it went quiet." Maxwell smiled. "It was just me."

"Was there anything else?" Jane said. "Any other people?"

"You're going to think I'm crazy, but there were these creepy little metal people. All rusted up with dirt and glowing eyes."

Jane blinked. "Come again? Metal people?"

Maxwell nodded. "Yeah, they moved. Big claws. They swung around on them like crutches. Oh, and another guy. Shorter than the hippie lady. He had a reddish beard. He didn't say much, but the one-armed lady called him a hero."

Jane stared, trying to piece it all together. Normally, she'd think this kid was delusional. Bad mushrooms, maybe, but that was before Jacklyn's letter, and so far, the breadcrumbs Jacklyn had left were lining up too well for coincidence.

"Did she call him a Host, by chance?" It was a shot in the dark, but maybe she'd get lucky.

Maxwell shook his head. No luck.

"You said there was a beach near some woods," Jane said. "Where at? Astoria? Seaside?"

"Not near. In," Maxwell corrected.

"In?" Jane said, not following.

"I don't know how else to describe it, and I don't know how to get back." Maxwell pointed at the purple goo on the stones. "That's what that was for. A potion or something. It was for you, but he broke it." The boy glared at Emmett, who scoffed and crossed his arms.

Potions? Jane's mind sifted through the additional details, ordering them by connections. *Miracles and potions and little metal men.*

Bzzz. Bzzz.

Emmett grabbed at his pocket, pulling out his phone.

Bzzz. Bzzzz.

He gave Maxwell a pointed look. "Stay . . . there."

Maxwell nodded.

"This is Agent Torin," he said, pressing the phone to his ear. He walked a few steps away, just out of earshot, with the river swallowing his voice.

Jane fished out her wallet and drew out five one-hundred-dollar bills, her stipend from the week. She handed it to Maxwell, who eyed her warily.

"No strings," Jane said. "Get some food, a shower, a room for the night, and some fresh clothes. Go see your sister. Something tells me she's willing to listen. And tell her she'd look great in pink hair."

Maxwell took the money with a nod and held the bills loose, as though they might turn to dust if he breathed too hard. "Thank . . . thank you."

"Don't tell my partner, yeah? He likes to stay inside his box." She winked.

Maxwell glanced over at Emmett, then reached into his vest and drew out what at first appeared to just be another river rock threaded on a necklace, but then Jane saw an intricate carving, a nearly complete circle. Maxwell cupped the smooth stone, rubbed its etching, and then handed it over. It was heavy and cold in her palm.

"I'm supposed to give this to whoever I tell. With the potion, but . . . I hope I didn't fuck it up too bad. I don't know how you're supposed to find them now."

"Luckily, I'm very good at finding people."

Emmett whistled and waved Jane over, continuing to talk on his phone.

"Be right back," she told Maxwell, and her sneakers crunched in the gravel over to where Emmett stood.

He covered the receiver. "It's Dawson. There was another set of murders."

"Another *pair*?"

Emmett's mouth twisted into a frown. "No, three this time. The sheriff found a banker, a priest, and a retired cop together in an abandoned industrial park."

"Three?" Jane muttered. Another pattern change.

"No, we're done here," Emmett said into the phone. "No leads. We'll meet you in Portland." He hung up and tucked his phone into his pocket. "Dawson is working on containment."

"Shouldn't we at least pull on this new thread? You heard the kid. There are three people involved: two women and this bearded 'hero' guy. We need faces and names, and I think we should contact the hospital. Get that miraculous kid's patient records. See if they have security footage available. Start with the night of the recovery and work our way out. I'm sure there's a link. It's too close to be coincidence."

"No." Emmett shook his head again. "Plus, patient records need senior approval. For now, we need to go check out the new bodies. Dawson will expect us."

"Well, we can't tell them!" She gritted her teeth. Emmett was choosing a poor time to cling to protocol.

"Yeah, I'm aware, Jane. I'm all for not telling the Director that a schizophrenic teen said to find a mysterious beach in a forest with little metal men." He tossed his arms up. "And hearing it out loud makes it worse. I can't believe I let it go this far . . . They killed again while we were chasing magic pixies!"

Jane sighed. The stretching hadn't worked. "Do you believe Maxwell?"

"I believe he believes himself." Emmett checked his watch. "Time is up, Jane. We're headed to Portland."

"If it's just about HIPAA and hospital regulations, I can get around that!" Jane tried to dance around him. "I forged the Director's signature plenty back in the day. Let's go get the forms." She tried to step in front of him.

"Listen to you! We are not forging the Director's signature! That's a federal offense."

Jane shrugged. "Yeah, but it bypasses most of the yelling."

"Absolutely not."

"So, we just, what? Sit back, ignore a lead, and see how it goes?"

"We are not forging his signature."

"You're just going to ignore what we just heard?" She waved her arms. She could practically feel his defenses rising.

He took a deep breath. "I'm not saying this isn't interesting. But we are getting way outside our mission parameters here. And this isn't a negotiation, Jane. I'm in charge. You can go back to

345

your cubicle whenever you want."

Jane stepped back, hurt by the low blow. She couldn't go back, and he knew it.

Seeing her, Emmett squared his shoulders. "I'll submit a request to the Director for the medical records with what we've learned. If there is something worth pursuing, then he'll approve. If not, well, then it's better he learns about this side trip early from me rather than later from Dawson."

Emmett's naïve defiance irked Jane. Her neck burned. "You submit that request, and the Director will put the clamps down! After that, you can kiss solving this case goodbye." She fumbled for the right words. "Look, hey." She took a step toward him. "Look, if there's a pile of treasure with a big, angry dragon sitting on top of it, you don't ask the dragon's permission to steal from it, right? You grab as much treasure as you can while it's snoring and then run like hell because there is zero percent chance the dragon won't burn the muff out of you. Just let me forge the signature, Emmett."

"No!" Emmett snapped. "I'm in command, and I say no." He stared down at her, daring her to push.

Jane closed her eyes, focusing instead on slowing the war drum in her chest. She heard the river and found a calmer tone, but couldn't get rid of the edge in her voice. "Alright, Agent Bait, we'll do it your way. And I swear, after this blows up, I won't say I told you so."

"Uh, hey," Maxwell said from behind them. "I can hear you both pretty well. Like most everything. Uh, the forest I saw was in Portland. Where those three, uh, people died. Right below a big hospital."

"Hill Hospital?" Jane asked.

"I think so. Yeah. I mean, it was on a hill."

Jane's heart quickened. Unfortunately, by Emmett's scowl, there

346

would be no selling a different course of action. He stepped back toward Maxwell, drawing out his wallet. "I'm sorry about tackling you. Here. Just don't run next time."

Maxwell protested, but caught Jane waggling her eyebrows and shut his mouth. Emmett handed over everything in his wallet—his stipend. "Take it. It's not a bribe. It is for food or . . . whatever. Just . . . don't buy drugs, okay? And one more thing, let's keep . . . all of this quiet, shall we?"

"I don't know what you're talking about," Maxwell said, tucking the money in his pocket.

Before Jane could speak, he pointed at her. "No. Whatever it is, no. Car." He walked back toward the trailhead without another word.

Jane watched him for a moment, then turned back to Maxwell. "You've been a tremendous help. I'll do everything I can to find and help your friend."

Maxwell nodded, and his eyes followed Emmett. "What about him?"

Jane sighed. "We'll find out."

Chapter 32: Second Date

Tuesday, April 24th, 16:52

"My grandma was not an *arsonist*," Khloe hissed, aiming a fork loaded with lettuce, onion, and beef.

"You told me she lit the barn on fire," Rory said, ripping off a piece of a tortilla and popping it in his mouth.

Khloe didn't look up from her food. "It was an accident."

"Twice? I mean, you do something like that twice, and it becomes your thing."

She snorted, covering her mouth as she laughed and looked at him. Rory thought it was the most beautiful sound in the world. He caught a pair in scrubs glancing their way from a nearby table. Taco Salad Tuesday drew a crowd—most tables in the sprawling cafeteria were full, but they'd found a small table near the back wall with some semblance of privacy.

Khloe aimed her fork at him again. "Be nice to my grandma."

He raised both hands in surrender. "From what I hear, she's an amazing woman who loved her brilliant granddaughter . . . and had a sensual passion for fire."

She rolled her eyes, pretending to flick a fork full of taco filling. Perhaps it was reflexes honed by working with children every day, or perhaps he was just relaxed for the first time in a long while, but he mimed being struck in the face and wiping off a sticky glob, earning another snort from Khloe. A crowd of white jackets at the next table glanced over. Rory recognized one from Magus's flock.

"I'm changing the topic. How was your class?"

"I saved some rubber dummies from choking, cardiac arrest, and, new this year, a swarm of bees. Thank goodness for Epi— made it pretty easy." Rory tried to sound casual, but the

348

combination of passing his training and trying to figure out how to sneak Jacklyn past the Secret Service exhausted him.

"Bees? I once—"

Bzzzz. Bzzzz.

Khloe reached down and grabbed the pager off her hip. She sighed. "Sorry, it's from . . . an outside number? Huh. I should go check on this."

Rory leaned forward. *About Conner? No, not from an outside number . . . right?*

"One sec," she said, hurrying for the phone bank on the far wall of the cafeteria. Rory took another bite and scanned the cafeteria. Most of the blue tables were full. A few families had pulled two or three together. A grandma sat beside her grandchild with a parent on the other side. Three generations, sitting together at a hospital. *Who are they here for?* He hoped they were okay.

He wiped his hands on his napkin and glanced back toward the phones. Khloe was shaking her head with a receiver to her ear. She turned, facing away from him, so he couldn't read her expression.

Outside, he could see the Willamette River sparkling as it flowed through the city below. One of the pleasant parts of working on the Hill was any view east would be a panorama of the city skyline. On the right day, at sunrise, a fog bank filled the river valley, and only the tallest towers of the city rose through the mist. Behind that, three mountains bathed in a blue-purple sky.

"It's a beautiful view," a woman said behind him.

Rory nearly choked. He knew the voice. Coughing, he cranked around in his chair. "Caroline?"

Rory almost didn't recognize her. She wore a navy pantsuit, a cream blouse, and aviator sunglasses. A candy-striped cane tapped the table leg, and she smoothly slid a chair from another table and sat beside him.

Before Rory could say anything, she gestured to his tray. "May I?"

"S . . . sure," Rory stuttered.

Caroline felt for the fork and stabbed away happily, forking up lettuce and tomatoes. The Wyth hummed quietly as she chewed.

"Uh, I can pick up some pizza or something and bring it by. Later." He punctuated the last word.

Caroline shook her head, not seeming to get his meaning. *Did Jacklyn know she was here?*

"No, dear, I'm just keeping my energy up. Sleep has been difficult." She quickly nodded over to Khloe, who was still on her call. "Is that the woman you spoke of?"

"Um, yeah. Why are you here?"

"Fascinating," Caroline said. "A Seeker."

What does Khloe's family have to do with this?

The group next to them got up and cleared their table, and Rory realized just how public they were. "Caroline, I think what this is can wait until—"

"It can't actually," Caroline said. "Not enough time for patience." Her fingertips bounced together until she adjusted her jacket, sitting up straighter. Rory hadn't seen her do this before. *She's . . . nervous?*

Caroline turned to him. "A little, yes, but I'm mostly excited."

Rory's stomach dropped. It was her seeing *thing* again. He resisted the urge to tug his scrub top up. *That's really annoying*, he thought, hoping she "saw" that too.

Caroline turned away without another word. "She's coming back."

Across the room, Khloe had hung up the phone and was jotting something down on a notepad.

"Please, Caroline. Please leave," Rory said.

"I don't think so."

"What? This isn't part of the deal. We're in the hospital. *My* place."

"Your deal with Jacklyn," Caroline corrected. "You remember I am Caroline, yes? Plus, this is a family matter. Shh." Caroline waved her hand, shushing him. "Don't spoil it, Rory."

Khloe neared the table, sliding her notepad back in her pocket with a sigh. She slowed a step when she saw Caroline raising an eyebrow at Rory. All he could do was shrug.

"Everything okay?" Rory said, filling the long pause.

"Uh, yeah," Khloe said, still watching Caroline curiously. "It was Trent." She slid into her seat. "He left his jacket and badge in the on-call room. I found them this morning."

Badge and jacket? Something pricked his memory, a problem he had but couldn't grasp.

Caroline gave a slight bow. "It is a pleasure to meet you, Dr. Seeker."

Khloe blinked. "Um . . . I'm sorry. Have we met?"

"Not yet," Caroline said. "I wish to change that."

Khloe's eyebrows shot up, and she looked at Rory, demanding information. *Take control of this.*

"Caroline is an old co-worker. She wanted—"

Caroline barreled through Rory's lie. "Rory told me about your grandmother."

"Did he?"

"I . . ." Rory started. "I mentioned her . . . once. Briefly."

"Was she always a Seeker?" Caroline asked. "I mean, did she take the name in union?"

351

Khloe shook her head slowly.

"I see. Did she wear a gemstone?" Caroline said, reaching into her suit jacket and drawing out her necklace of three cloudy gemstones. "Like one of these?"

Khloe stared, her surprise knitting together into concern. Rory swallowed. *What is Caroline doing?*

Khloe cocked her head, staring at the necklace, and reached into her pant pocket. She pulled out a cloudy, rough-cut ruby dangling on a silver chain. Rory leaned forward.

"She never took it off."

"Magnificent," Caroline whispered, tucking her gemstones away as she stared at the cloudy ruby. "Absolutely beautiful." She pointed at Khloe's hands, both with silver rings on the thumb and pinkie. "Those were your grandmother's as well?"

Khloe nodded.

"Mhm, then she was an adept on her Path. Knew the Core teachings but lacked control. I can imagine she had some difficulties controlling her casts. Was she prone to accidents or uncommon behavior? Ones involving fire?"

Khloe blinked, and she looked at Rory, shocked.

"I didn't tell her that," he said.

Khloe frowned, trying to piece something together. "She burned down our family barn. Twice."

"Fire is notoriously difficult to control. So willful. May I show you something, Dr. Seeker?" Caroline held out her hand on the table. "I'll need your grandmother's stone for it."

Rory looked around at everyone hunched over their food trays. *Here?!*

"Wait." Rory grabbed Caroline's arm. "This isn't a good place for a show. And I don't think . . . you-know-who would like this."

"Who?" Khloe asked.

"Just a . . . friend," Rory said pleadingly. A man in a dark blue-green maintenance uniform sat down at the empty table a couple of feet away.

Caroline looked down at Rory's hand holding her wrist. He knew she could break his grasp if she wanted. "Trust me, Rory."

This is a bad idea.

"Are you both being serious?" Khloe asked, watching them.

"Emphatically."

Khloe looked at Rory, ready for an answer. He sighed. "Uh . . . I believe her."

Caroline touched his arm. "Thank you."

"It doesn't always mean I agree with your timing."

"Ok . . . ay," Khloe said. "I'm curious. And a little freaked out. What are you going to do?"

"It's easier to demonstrate than explain." Caroline used her hand to gesture closer. "I'll give it back."

Khloe hesitated, then straightened in her chair and held out the ruby. "You won't break it?"

"I wouldn't dream of it." Caroline took the stone in one hand and ripped off a small piece of Rory's napkin. She held out the bit of napkin for Khloe to inspect. "Confirm this is just a bit of paper. It is not soaked in anything nor treated."

Khloe picked it up, nodded, and returned it to Caroline's palm. "Okay."

"And my hand. No wax or oils to prevent a burn." Khloe touched Caroline's finger, then jerked her hand back. "Ow."

"So sorry," Caroline said. "The air is so dry here. I get static-y."

Rory frowned. He'd heard that line before, but from a different disguise. *What is she up to?*

353

Khloe sucked on her burnt finger before cautiously touching Caroline again. Nothing seemed to happen, so she rubbed the pad of her thumb before she nodded. "Feels like skin."

Caroline produced a lighter from her pocket and handed it to Rory. "Sustain the fire."

Rory glanced around and didn't see anyone paying attention to them. A minor miracle. He flicked the lighter and cupped it. "Just hurry."

Caroline lifted the ruby to her lips. "Hello, my new friend. Show us you're awake." In her other hand, she held a small bit of napkin. Both Rory and Khloe leaned forward as Caroline lowered the stone and extended one lithe finger toward the fire. Rory cringed as the tip of her finger entered the orange flame. Or rather, the fire condensed and curled around her finger. He watched, stunned, as a tiny serpent formed from the fire and coiled around Caroline's finger.

Khloe's hands came up to her mouth. The fire reflected off her wide eyes. Behind her, a subtle shadow cast on the wall, setting alarm bells off in Rory's head. *Someone is bound to see the light.* He slid to the edge of his seat, touching shoulders with Caroline to block the bulk of the light. *Come on, come on.*

"Nice to meet you too," Caroline whispered. "May I borrow your heat?"

The tiny serpent flared, and its body unraveled back into a teardrop flame. A curl of smoke rose from the paper in Caroline's opposite palm. With a flash of heat and a puff of smoke, the napkin ignited. It burned for no longer than a second before turning to ash. Without a sound, Caroline pulled her finger from the fire and held it up for inspection. The skin was sooty but unburnt.

Shaking, Rory let the flame end. He checked over his shoulder and didn't see any worried expressions or closing security. He let out a sigh of relief, though still uncertain what he'd just seen.

The fire was alive . . . just like the sand on the beach.

"How did—" Khloe said from behind her hands. "What was that?"

"An Aspect," Caroline said.

"A what?" Rory and Khloe said in unison.

"Listen carefully, Khloe," Caroline said. "Your grandmother was a Wyth. That word means little to you now, but if you are willing to take a risk, I can teach you why it meant everything to her. The fact that she entrusted this little one"—she held out the ruby for Khloe to take—"to you is the highest praise one can give."

Khloe took the stone back, cupping it in her hands. Her expression danced between disbelief and outrage, and Rory prayed she landed on an open mind. Her eyes drifted over to him, but he felt as lost as she must have. All he managed was a smile and another shrug. "It's mostly new to me, too."

"I understand you feeling skeptical and overwhelmed," Caroline continued. "That makes complete sense, yet I'm asking you to suspend it and take a walk with me. If you do, I will share what secrets I can of your grandmother's world and more besides. I know there is one question in particular that has vexed you lately. One you wish you could unlock but can't find the door." She leaned across the table, dropping her voice to hush. "How was Tommy healed?"

WHAT?! Rory's mouth dropped. *Oh, no, no . . . Jacklyn will not like this.* "Shouldn't we—"

Caroline held up her hand but never took her eyes off Khloe. Rory stopped, irritation now crawling up his throat, but he kept it from forming into words. They wouldn't make any difference. Caroline had decided already. He ran his hands over his gritty cheeks, not believing what he was hearing. Jacklyn was going to freak out. Probably on him, even though this clearly wasn't his fault. Rory picked up his fork, jabbing at his last taco. *This is going to get ugly.*

355

Caroline lifted her chin. "So, Dr. Seeker. What will it be?"

Khloe went quiet for a long moment, rolling the ruby between her fingers as she studied Caroline, then Rory. He waited, the tense silence mounting. He wanted to break it, make it stop, but couldn't think what to say.

"Tommy is connected to"—Khloe waved the ruby—"this?"

"He is."

Rory frowned, not making the connection. *What does Tommy have to do with these Aspects?*

Khloe looked at him for confirmation.

"If Caroline says so, then . . . I guess he is."

Then, to Rory's great surprise, Khloe slapped the table. "I knew it!" She half jumped from her chair, thumping it against the wall. Eyes turned from every table. "I knew it."

"Keep it down," Rory said, coaxing her back into her chair. "It's a secret."

She blushed and sat back down, but didn't stop beaming. "I knew something was weird with Tommy."

"Rory is right," Caroline said. "Discretion is vital."

"Now discretion is important?" Rory said, his frustration finally breaking through. "Where was that before your little show? And Tommy? I thought that was a team decision."

"Circumstances change, so tactics need to adapt. Khloe is a sister's daughter. This becomes a choice no one can deny me." She looked at him meaningfully, and Rory felt a little taken aback. He wasn't completely sure what that meant. Caroline rose, and his irritation flared anew. *More freaking secrets.*

"Shall we?"

Khloe was out of her chair again in a flash, gathering her jacket.

Rory blew out a long breath. *This is going to be a disaster.*

"Rory?" Caroline said.

He didn't see any real alternatives. "Ya, I'm coming too." He took one more bite of his taco, finding it not as savory as before, and followed them out.

Tuesday, April 24th, 18:19

From the cafeteria to the trailhead, Rory told his story. From the caboose of their little procession, he answered numerous questions. Some of his answers made sense now, but not all. The bus stop, the staged mugging, the purple potion, the wisp, and the harrowing bike ride. Khloe examined the scar on his stomach as he recounted sneaking Jacklyn in to see Tommy and the chaotic aftermath that followed.

"How did you feel?" she'd asked. He couldn't answer that one.

She'd jotted down a few lines in her notepad when he told her about Remembrance Day. That felt like a good sign. Khloe hadn't laughed or scoffed while he talked, just listened—clinical. Rory was dying to know what was going on in her head.

His story done, Khloe shifted her questions to Caroline. To Rory's surprise and envy, Caroline didn't display any of the caution she'd shown before—back when it was just him. An irritating fact, though he wasn't sure why. He told himself he should be happy to have company, to get some direct answers for once, yet he couldn't help but feel like Caroline had already picked her favorite.

"So, how many types are there?" Khloe said, eyeing the bramble wall as they slipped down the deer trail. "Of Aspects, I mean."

"There are four," Caroline said from the lead. "One for each element. Fire, earth—"

"Wind and water, ya," Khloe said, jotting down something in her notepad. "Gam-Gam talked about those sometimes. And how do they get inside the . . . rock?"

"It happens when they die, we think. They are beings of energy, so the leading theory is they collapse into themselves, creating a new state."

A question came to him, and he tried his luck at an answer. "What were they before they were rocks?"

"The *rocks* are called mythstone. There is a classification system. A ruby mythstone is a Redstone. An emerald, a Greenstone. Sapphires and topaz, blue and yellow respectively."

Redstone? Rory snorted, and both women glanced back at him. "Sorry. It just seems really, uh, simple. I guess I expected something more . . . imaginative."

Caroline didn't seem upset. "Well, they did not design this for you, Rory," she said. "You are too old and skeptical. They are designed for more malleable minds. For children. A simple system, easily taught and built upon."

Rory opened and closed his mouth, feeling sure he had just been insulted. Brushing it aside, he squinted past Caroline at the path ahead. Thin pines steadily gave way to gnarled old growth and moss carpet. The forest seemed to grow wilder by the step. He felt the cool keystone against his chest. *Where are the golems?* He pictured the sporelings running across the beach. *Probably off playing.*

"To answer your question, though, Rory," Caroline said, "I don't know. I've never encountered one in the wild. Legend says they used to be massive, like the Titans in the stories, roaming forces of nature spread to each corner of the world, but . . . something happened, and they disappeared. All we have left is their essence trapped in bones."

"That's sad," Khloe said.

Rory nodded, wondering what they looked like.

"It is."

"Do they have names?"

Caroline lifted a low-hanging vine brimming with thorns and slipped beneath. "They do." She grabbed the sapphire hanging around her neck, which flared in blue-white light. Her foot landed in a puddle, and as it pulled out, the water clung together in the shape of a small koi fish. "This is Pond Skipper, my dearest and longest friend."

The little koi jumped to the next puddle and the next, flicking its tail playfully as it chased after Caroline.

Rory watched the little fish in awe, his sour mood evaporating at the incredible sight. *I don't know if I'll ever get used to this . . .*

"Wow," Khloe said. "Hi, Pond Skipper."

The little koi splashed into a puddle off to the side of the trail and bobbed there as Khloe stooped down and stuck her hand in the water. The little koi swam around her fingers.

"It tickles," Khloe said.

"Thank you, Skipper," Caroline said and took her fingers off the stone. The koi pouted. "We'll play later, I promise." That seemed to placate the elemental, and the koi disappeared into the dirty water.

Caroline tapped the emerald next. "Rory, you've already met Slumber Beneath Warm Silt. They had a starring role during my performance on the beach." The dirt beside his feet twitched, and a mound rose, stretching up and out until it formed a yawning house cat. Swirls of dark and light sand replaced its fur. The cat looked up sleepily, and it struck Rory how much the Aspect reminded him of Sneaks.

"The sand hand, ya. Hello."

Silt stretched again, blinking droopy eyes up at him.

"Sorry to wake you, Silt. You can go back to sleep," Caroline said. The earthen cat curled on a mossy patch, and its body tumbled apart. "Your grandmother's friend is named Hunter Among Weeds. They are small but potent. Excellent to learn with."

"Hunter." Khloe said and warmed the ruby in her palm. "Nice to meet you."

"What about your yellow, uh, mythstone?" Rory felt silly saying it aloud.

"They are called Splits the Night By Light, a naughty air Aspect, both grumpy and uncooperative."

"Why?" Khloe said.

"Because they are keen on their freedom, though I won't yet grant it."

"You mean . . . it's your prisoner?" Rory said.

Caroline stopped, bringing the procession to a sudden halt. "Prisoner is extreme . . . Entombed, maybe? No. Enlisted, perhaps? I plan to grant its request in time, but for now, their services are needed."

"How does it, uh, get free?" Khloe asked.

"When a mythstone breaks, the Aspect within dissipates. Forever. And no, I don't know where they go." The Wyth cleared her throat, seeming uncomfortable. "I think that's enough questions for now." She turned and started off again. "Our destination is just ahead."

They walked past another thick knot of blackberry vines where Rory was certain a golem would hide, but nothing appeared. "Up ahead is the clearing. We might see some golems," he said. "Those mushroomy metal things I was talking about."

"The thing that stabbed you?"

Rory ducked under a low branch. "It was a misunderstanding." He drew out the keystone from around his neck. "As long as I have this, they think we are friends." He aimed a question at Caroline. "Both of us?"

Caroline nodded, and Rory felt relieved.

"Caroline," Khloe said. "Your people have a thing for rocks, don't they?"

"Our people," Caroline corrected. "And yes. We do."

Khloe grinned, clutching her notebook and ruby tight.

They rounded the last bend to the clearing where the blue tarp hung, flapping gently between the two holly bushes. Shafts of sunlight broke through as it waved, filling the glade with the smell of warm salt. Rory pointed at the tarp. "Just through there. It covers a . . . portal or something like that. To a beach. Sorry, a Cove."

Khloe looked at him, mouth slightly open, but didn't speak.

"You two stay here," Caroline said without breaking stride. "I'll go talk to Jacklyn. Alone. I think it is best she hears the news from me. After I'm done, I'll come fetch you." She slipped behind the tarp without waiting for a response and vanished.

Khloe drifted over and lifted the flap, holding her palm to the wind. "It's warm," she said, inspecting the edge of the tarp and the rope holding it in place. It was only then that he noticed the golden thread woven into ropes. He'd never stopped to look before. A tree somewhere in the gloom creaked, causing Rory to turn. He was expecting to finally see a golem, but caught a flutter of motion above him instead. He jumped back but relaxed when he saw it was only a moth drifting down from the branches. Not realizing how tense he was, Rory laughed at himself and watched it pump its wings once and float toward him. As it came closer, his eyes widened. It was huge.

He held his hand out. "Khloe, hey. Look at this."

"Hm?" She turned, the rope between her fingers.

The downy moth landed on his index finger, its legs tickling his skin. It looked even bigger up close, the size of an apple. It turned around slowly, pumping its black and red-patterned wings as it investigated its landing pad.

Khloe walked over slowly and leaned in close. Her nose quickly wrinkled, and she backed away. "Ugh, it stinks! What is that?"

Rory frowned and brought the moth closer. The smell burned his nostrils, putrid, like a body late to the morgue. "It was on something dead."

"Um, maybe you shouldn't touch it?" The alarm in Khloe's voice put Rory on edge, and he wiggled his finger, but the moth clung tight. "Get off—" A hot flash of pain shot from his finger. "Ow!"

Rory whipped his hand back and forth, flinging off the moth. "It bit me!" He found a bead of blood welling on his finger. The tall ferns behind them rustled, and Rory stepped back, bumping into Khloe. A golem emerged from the ferns covered in lazily flapping moths perched atop each mushroom cap. The psybelle's normally tranquil turquoise glow had turned red as crimson streaks ran down the mycelium cables to its arms and legs. The infected golem stepped forward in an uncharacteristically smooth motion. Something was very wrong.

"Stay back," Rory whispered.

"Uh, Rory?" Khloe said, looking up.

Rory followed her eyes. A dense, red blanket of flapping moths loomed in the canopy above. He inched toward the tarp, keeping himself between Khloe and the golems. "We need Caroline." A second and third golem emerged, covered in moths, and blocked the path back to the road.

"I thought you said you were friends!"

Suddenly the golems charged. From above, the moths plummeted down like a smothering red rain.

"Run!"

———

The beach rippled beneath the baking sun, so hot the air stung Rory's throat. They stumbled into the sand, ears popping painfully. He looked over at Khloe. She rubbed at her ears with a wide mouth, eyes glued to the sparkling blue sea stretched out before them. He understood, but now wasn't the time to marvel.

"Keep moving!" he yelled, pulling her toward the tall green tent tucked into the cliff face.

"Where are we?"

"There!" His lungs ached from the heat, and he had a disorienting flash of déjà vu. "Caroline! Help!"

Across the beach, Caroline emerged from the tent. Her baggy yellow pants and white blindfold rippled in the wind. Something long and metallic shimmered from her arm. In a smooth motion, she bent, scooped a handful of sand, and sprinted toward them.

"They're coming!" Khloe screamed.

Over his shoulder, he saw three golems in pursuit, each using their oversized claws to throw themselves forward, like a pack of hunting apes. Rory tried to sprint, but his legs felt thick, running through the sand.

A flash of emerald light came from in front of them. A beat later, the ground rumbled, and Rory saw a three-foot mound of sand speeding across the beach straight toward them. He braced as the mound approached, but it dipped down and slid beneath them. A step later, the sand erupted behind them. A massive sandy hand rose high into the air. With a savage blow, the hand flattened a golem, dragging it thrashing beneath the beach.

Rory stumbled, barely keeping his footing, willing his legs to keep going. A shadow passed overhead, and he slowed, glimpsing a fluttering white ribbon. The sand burst as Caroline landed behind them, wearing an ornate white and gold gauntlet on her right forearm—a pair of three-foot parallel blades extending from the knuckles. The golems redirected, slashing at the Wyth with their enormous claws.

Without a word, Caroline began a terrifying dance.

She wasted no motion, each step precise, deadly. She ducked beneath a swipe, and her head dipped just in time to dodge a jab from behind. Her weapon flashed, and a golem fell, one of its legs removed at the hip. The wounded golem toppled over, still swinging wildly at her legs. Caroline squared with the remaining golem, retreating two quick steps as the creature's claws passed within an inch of her cheek. Rory could barely muster a "watch out!" before Caroline swung upward, catching the claw between her two blades, and twisted her arm.

Crack.

The golem's arm broke free of its body. It stumbled back, dazed. Caroline swept downward, her blades sparking as she sliced through the creature's rusty torso, dropping it. Sickeningly, both maimed golems wriggled, trying feebly to claw at Caroline. She smashed one of the red moths beneath her foot, and a section of the golem's body stopped moving. With a few quick cuts, she severed other moths and the infected mushroom caps, and both golems finally stilled.

She stood panting and staring sadly at the carnage. She took a deep breath and exhaled. "My poor friends . . ."

Rory remembered the mischievous sporelings and how they crowded around him during Caroline's performance. They had been so childlike, so innocent. And now, they'd been infected, driven mad, and killed. A grief coiled in Rory's chest. It wasn't fair.

Caroline turned to Rory and Khloe, sweat soaking into her blindfold. "Get to camp. There will be more—"

The ground beside her shifted, and another red-veined claw reached out of the sand. Caroline spun in time as a golem launched itself at her, red moths clinging tight to its infected caps. She caught its claw before it punctured her chest and pushed the attack aside. Around them, more rusty limbs emerged.

"Come on!" Khloe shouted, pulling Rory. "We can't help!" They stumbled backward toward the tent.

In front of them, the sand bubbled, and Rory reached for Khloe's hand, but not in time. A golem's claws shot out and pierced the bottom of Khloe's foot. She screamed in pain and crumpled, clutching her bleeding foot. An infected golem pulled itself up out of the sand, staring at her.

It's going to kill her.

Rage seized Rory, turning everything red. He heard himself scream as he charged the golem. He pounded the moth on its shoulder, hitting center mass. It was enough to break its grip, and the golem's entire arm sagged limply against its side, but that didn't stop it. Another moth controlling its opposite side and its savage counterblow drew a fiery line across Rory's side. Bleeding, he retreated, trying to keep out of range, but the creature kept advancing, dragging its useless arm. Behind it, on the ground, the separated moth recovered and spread its wings. Khloe reached over with her leg and stomped it into the sand, whimpering in pain.

Rory pressed a hand to his burning side and searched for Caroline. The Wyth had killed several golems, but long gashes and blood speckled her dress. She spun beneath a clawed swipe, dropping to a knee in the sand. Another green flash. A moment later, another massive hand of sand pulled another under.

"Rory!" Khloe cried out, pointing behind him. He spun around to see another pair of golems pulling themselves from the sand only a few feet away. *How many of these things are there?* He pictured the beach covered in waiting husks, and a chilling thought followed. *Were all the golems corrupted?* They'd be swarmed.

The two newcomers swiftly rounded on Rory. Empty-handed, he spotted a long length of driftwood toward the surf. He dashed several steps, scooped it up, and gripped it like a baseball bat.

The wood was far lighter than he wished.

The first golem rushed forward, and Rory swung with everything he had. His wounded side screamed in pain as he connected high on its chest. The driftwood bat ruptured. Splinters flew everywhere, leaving only half its length in his hand. The creature lashed back, and Rory retreated, dropping the broken wood. Warm blood trickled down his side.

"It's me!" Rory pleaded, holding out the keystone. "We're friends!"

The golem slashed, and he jumped back.

Not again . . . not like this.

"Khloe, run!" Rory said over his shoulder.

"My foot!" Khloe grunted, trying to rise.

He sized up the golems. Maybe he could buy her enough time to get to camp and . . . He did not know what to do after that. It was just them.

"I'm so sorry," he said.

"Shut up," she groaned. "We're not dead yet."

The lead golem surged forward, claw gleaming in the sunlight, and Rory raised his arms, hoping to block the worst of the swing. A blur flashed by, and the golem spasmed and froze mid-swing. Slowly, it rose in the air, convulsing. Rory squinted. A dark figure with silver hair and pallid white skin lifted the creature up.

"Jacklyn!" Rory breathed, lowering his arms.

The golem jerked violently, and Jacklyn tore a long length of mycelium cable from its back, severing several infected caps. A moth tumbled off, and she used the cord to swat it into the sand before stepping on it.

"I!" She brought her foot down again. "Hate!" She spun, driving her fist through the second golem's face. "Fucking!" She pulled and ripped another cord of red-spotted mycelium out and set about dispatching the remaining insects. "Moths!" She threw the cord into the sand and spat.

"Caroline!" Rory shouted.

Jacklyn looked at him wildly, then at Khloe behind him. Her eyes narrowed, but Rory pointed down the beach to Caroline, who splashed in the surf with two golems in pursuit. Another pair of husks lay in pieces.

Rory expected Jacklyn to race after her, but she seemed to relax. "No, hero. She's got this. The ocean will protect her."

Before Rory could ask, a gleam of sapphire light shot from Caroline's neck, and the surf swelled, rising ten feet in the air. The massive wave crashed into the creatures, throwing them back, tumbling, breaking apart, and disappearing.

Just as quickly as it started, the beach was quiet. Caroline listed in the water, sagging and tattered, but kept her feet.

"She's gonna feel that," Jacklyn said.

The Wyth shook her head, straightened with a roll of her neck, and marched up the beach toward them.

"What the hell happened? What were those?" Rory said, looking down at a smashed moth.

Jacklyn turned around. "Bloodmoths. Nasty little predators."

"What?" *Something hunts psybelles?*

"We're all their prey, hero."

"But . . ." Rory stared at the mangled sporelings. "They're just sporelings . . . How? How'd the moths get in?"

"Well, it wasn't an accident, I can tell you that," she said coldly, glancing back toward the yawning cave tucked into the cliff face. "They're a first-wave assault, sent to weaken us. Very effective." Her eyes shot over to Khloe, who uttered a small cry, clutching her foot.

Whoever was hunting, Jacklyn and Caroline also knew about the Wyth and their golems. Which begged the terrifying question: *Did they have magic, too?*

Caroline walked past Khloe and directly up to Rory. "Are you injured?" She didn't wait for him to answer before she slipped a finger through the tear in his shirt and poked his cut flank. He winced and pulled back. "Ow!"

She held up her finger, and the thickness of his blood surprised Rory.

"I'm fine." Rory brushed away. "Khloe needs help. It stabbed her foot."

"And why is *she* here?" Jacklyn demanded.

"She is my guest," Caroline said.

Rory opened his mouth, but a raised eyebrow from Caroline told him to shut it.

"Your what?!" Jacklyn roared. "You didn't think to swing this by me?"

Caroline turned and kneeled in the sand in front of Khloe. "May I see your foot?"

Khloe was pale and dazed, her eyes bouncing back and forth between Caroline and Jacklyn. "Wha . . . what . . ."

"The moth's bite injects eggs into the mushroom," Caroline explained as she examined her foot. "The eggs quickly hatch, and the larvae reprogram the psybelle, making them hyper-aggressive. After that, they hunt for hosts for their final stage of gestation. Humans. Don't worry; you'll both be fine with treatment, but I'll need to manually remove the larvae. I have an excellent tonic for the pain." She turned to Jacklyn. "If the moths are still here, the attack must have been recent. We must check the cave and ensure they didn't reach the growing chamber."

"I'm not going anywhere," Jacklyn said, crossing her arms.

"What's the, um, final stage?" Khloe asked, though not like she wanted the answer.

"They pupate within human flesh and devour the host from the inside out," Caroline said casually.

"Oh . . ." Khloe said, growing quiet.

"They eat people too?!" Rory said, picturing squirmy little worms crawling beneath his skin. It made him shiver.

"Enough, Care!" Jacklyn said, outraged.

Caroline coolly met Jacklyn's scowl. "They need treatment."

"They need to leave!"

"Wait. Someone attacked us?" Rory said, trying to piece everything together. "They could come again."

"Not someone. *Them*," Jacklyn said.

"They're getting close again, Jacklyn," Caroline said in the same well-worn way Rory introduced himself at work. "I think we should consider a new—"

Jacklyn cut her off, throwing up her hands. "We aren't having this discussion again."

"Circumstances have changed. We adapt."

"It's the law, Care!" Jacklyn said, exasperated. Rory guessed this was not the first or third time they'd had this talk. "I didn't make them up, but I'm sure as hell not going to be the first to break them. They're around for a reason."

Laws? Jacklyn's rules?

"You follow them blindly," Caroline snapped back, then stopped and held up a finger to Jacklyn's retort. "You are upset I invited a guest without consulting you. Fine. I apologize for not including you in that choice." Caroline gestured to Khloe. "But a sister's granddaughter appears and wishes to learn the ways of our people. I cannot turn her away."

Khloe looked up at Caroline, almost cross-eyed with confusion and pain. She looked to Rory for something, anything, to ground her. He had little to give.

Jacklyn's face flushed red. "Look at our home, Care! They wiped us out!" Jacklyn wheeled around and kicked one of the dead golems. It flopped over with a metal crunch.

"We don't know that," Caroline said, her voice strained. "Which is why we need to go check the cave."

"There are more pressing matters." Jacklyn's eyes locked onto Khloe, and the sun dimmed. "*She* shows up, and this all happens. Might be coincidence, or maybe she's no Wyth granddaughter. Maybe she's one of *their* spies." Somewhere in the distance, thunder rumbled.

Khloe pointed at her chest. "M . . . me?"

Caroline shook her head. "You're being paranoid, love."

Jacklyn looked deadly serious. She took a step toward Khloe as the sky grew another shade darker, stealing the heat. "She could be one of them, Care."

Khloe's eyes grew wide. "No, no. I just wanted answers about Tommy."

Jacklyn did not blink, rounding on Rory. "You told her?!"

"What? No!" He pointed at Caroline. "She—"

"Oh, hero," Jacklyn said. The wind and waves ceased as everything drew still. "You've messed up now."

Rory swallowed. "Let's just . . . stay calm. Talk this over."

"Jacklyn, you're being ridiculous," Caroline said dismissively.

"Am I?" Jacklyn tensed, looking ready to attack. The image of her tearing the golems apart jumped into Rory's mind. But this time, it would be Khloe. He stepped into Jacklyn's path.

"Get out of my way, Rory."

Not a hero anymore. His hands shook, but he held his ground. "I don't want to fight you."

She stepped up to him. "And what if you had to?" Her face was inches from his. "What if you had to kill to save a life? Your life. Could you?" Her eyes narrowed. "I'm not sure you've got it in you."

Rory's defiance faltered. He thought about Tommy, about how he had wanted to punch that boyfriend but couldn't bring himself to do it. As much as he wanted to, he wasn't sure he could either.

"That's what I thought," Jacklyn sneered.

"Jacklyn Seed!" Caroline's voice rang out like a bell. All three gemstones hanging around her neck illuminated, crackling with energy, as the strands of wispy white hair frizzed up off her shoulders.

To Rory's relief, Jacklyn sagged back, glaring at him as the wind and waves surged back, booming off the cliffs.

"In the cave! Now!" Caroline took a deep breath, her hair settled, and the gems dimmed. When she spoke again, she resumed her soft tone. "You're being a beast."

Jacklyn's entire body flinched. She eyed Khloe a moment longer before shooting a withering look at Rory. Without another word, she stormed off toward the cave, waving her hand and lecturing the sand as each step brightened the sky.

Rory's trembling legs told him to sit, and he crumbled to the sand beside Khloe.

"Thanks," she said.

"Uh, ya," Rory said, still shaking.

"My apologies for Jacklyn's behavior," Caroline said, kneeling before them. She set a warm hand on each of their shoulders. "Dr. Seeker, you are my guest, despite the poor welcome. I'll see your foot cared for."

"What about Jacklyn?" Rory said.

"Leave Jacklyn to me," Caroline said and squeezed before standing. "Rory, please help Khloe to camp. Get her comfortable with her foot elevated."

Rory nodded, glad to have a task.

"Where are you going?" Khloe asked.

Caroline's expression grew serious. "To have a heart-to-heart."

Chapter 34: Law of Hosts

Translated from:

Disc - Shepherd's Stone

Sub-ring - *Codex*

Script - *Law of Hosts*:

First Law: Assays must commence in stealth. Let each candidate show their motivation before teaching them.

Second Law: Minor Assays before Major Assays. Let each candidate show their values before their virtues.

Third Law: Quality of each Assay's completion is supreme. Let each candidate show their character by actions, not words.

Fourth Law: Failure of one Assay is a failure of all Assays. The Seed tolerates no exceptions.

—

Twenty-fourth of Apru, X643 AA

The Hidden Cove

The slow, roaring inhale of the waves, followed by the hushed exhale of the retreating water, reminded Caroline of a slumbering giant. She stopped just inside the cave's wide mouth, where the sound was loudest, and listened, syncing her lungs in time with the tide. All else emptied from her mind as she filled and released. Filled and released. Six breaths later, a thought spoiled her tranquility. *Jacklyn.* A spark of anger burst in her quiet mind, and she pressed inside.

The sound of waves quieted, replaced by irregular drips from the craggy ceiling. A trickle of water told her she was in the psybelles' growing chamber even before she saw the white-purple mushrooms coating the invisible walls against the slate gray background of her mind's eye. To her old eyes, the mushrooms would look turquoise as Jacklyn often described them, and she remembered them being magnificent when she saw them once at a long-ago Remembrance Day. She could still picture those glowing caverns and their clumsy golems. Maybe as a child, she wouldn't have given up such a sight, but these days, she wouldn't trade her vision for any other.

Occasionally, a neon cloud puffed from a cap like a dandelion's seeds in the wind. Her old eyes wouldn't have seen it. Across the cave, another cap responded with a matching cloud. Then another. Until a chain reaction crisscrossed across the cave, dissipating, but not before creating dense pockets of color where the psybelles' brilliant conversation intersected. On and on, with subtle changes in hue until all at once, a single belle would transform color. Sometimes, there was no response; sometimes, it stayed contained in small pockets, but every so often, the entire chamber exploded in a new color.

Caroline often wondered what it meant. Perhaps a new idea? A disagreement? Or something else entirely. In her many years, she'd found nothing that replicated human emotion like the psybelles, save the Aspects trapped in their stones. She often sat alone in the chamber, watching the conversations unfold.

Watching a fresh burst of red enter a green conversation, Caroline felt one worry slide away, though not without a heavy heart. Whatever casualties the sporelings had taken, at least the bloodmoths had not found the cave. She sighed. The Broken Star was in the city, and their use of bloodmoths meant one of the Merged was among them. It wouldn't be long before the Cove was under a more dire siege.

She shook her head, refocusing on the tasks at hand. She picked her footing carefully on the slippery stones, grazing her fingertips against the cold stone wall. Searching for sporelings was the priority. Afterward, she'd talk with Jacklyn, and they could decide whether to evacuate. That was easier said than done, though. A battle felt imminent now, and she doubted they could win this time. She shivered, uncertain if it was the cave, her battle-high, or the poor omens. A deep itch came over her. She needed to touch her artifacts. They offered hope.

"You had no right, Care," Jacklyn's voice erupted from the darkness, sharp with restraint.

Caroline started and took a moment to let her temper settle—she hated it when Jacklyn surprised her. She didn't turn. There was no point. She couldn't see Jacklyn anyway, not directly. The Seed made sure of that. "I wish you would announce yourself."

"Bringing that woman here was reckless and desperate." Jacklyn wanted a fight, Caroline could hear it, but it wouldn't help. Fights caused wounds, and wounds took time to heal. Time they didn't have.

Caroline considered her response as she navigated to a pair of grocery carts tucked inside in case of rain. She found the edge of the beach towel covering one, pulled it aside, and rummaged through. She pushed past the pillows and sleeping bag, searching for her treasures. "My love, we are not so rich in time as before."

"Don't talk to me like him. I'm not your student, Care." Jacklyn's voice shook with anger.

Caroline bristled, but kept it from her face. "If that's what it takes to do our duties, mine *and* yours, then so be it. You weren't here. I decided. Yes, Khloe has her flaws, but also the making of a powerful witch." She took another breath, feeling fatigue numb her legs. Calling on the Aspects was getting harder by the day. "And we should welcome the help. We are not young anymore."

"Don't change the subject!" Jacklyn snapped.

The psybelle's reds shifted pink as Caroline's hand struck something metallic wrapped in wool. She chose her next words carefully, removing the package. "You are angry. I understand that."

"Of course I'm angry!"

Caroline stopped and lifted her chin, keeping her expression neutral. "Would you like to discuss this later when you've calmed?" A long pause followed, and she stood patiently, ready for either answer.

"I'm under control," Jacklyn muttered. "Sorry for yelling."

"I'm glad. How are you feeling?"

"I'm fine."

Caroline heard the lie in her voice as she unfolded the wool. While she couldn't see them, she felt the Dozer's heavy hilt. Next to it, the sharp spines of a rigid metal feather pricked her skin as her fingers passed over it. The Iron Quill. She held them, admiring their weight and wishing she could also admire the intricate runes etched into them. As far as Caroline knew, these two artifacts were the last pieces of runetech in the world. Like mythstone, they were relics of the World That Was. She held them to her heart and took a deep breath. If battle came, they could tip the scale.

"'Fine' is a mask," she said calmly. Knowing what she had to say, her heart ached, but the truth needed to be made clear. "You are dying. Faster than either of us wants to admit. That is our situation." She turned, hoping to get some clue of Jacklyn's response, but could only make out a black smudge in the corner against the mushrooms' crimson gossip. Jacklyn created no surge of colorful emotion, not even a distinct silhouette. To Caroline, Jacklyn was a shifting black void against the gray of her mind's eye. Only against the psybelles' prismatic discussion could she track her beautiful blind spot.

"Someone will come." The scrape of shoes against stone followed, and Caroline pictured Jacklyn kicking at a rock.

Squeezing the runetech weapons close, Caroline wanted that to be true. "Our allies are lost. We are alone, but for those we now trust." She let those words hang in the air. She softened. "I have good news, though. Rory has taken strides in converting his

Stain. Khloe is helping."

"It's not fast enough."

"I know."

The cave took a breath, then another, and Jacklyn remained silent. Caroline understood, leaving the silence be—it wasn't a pleasant reality to address. She wrapped the artifacts in the strip of wool and tucked them back into the cart, knowing deep down she'd need them soon. She pulled the towel down and smoothed out the wrinkled edges.

"Battle is coming, Care," Jacklyn said, breaking the silence. "We can't avoid it."

"I feel it, too." Caroline turned back to the chamber, fluctuating pink and purple now. Heat soaked her skin, but thankfully, the damp air cooled her bare arms, whisking the burn away. There were alternatives to fighting, desperate ones. Ones she knew Jacklyn wouldn't stand, but here they were, shedding valuable time. "What if we tell Rory about the Seed? Tell him of his role as the next Host? The Laws weren't written for—"

"Absolutely not," Jacklyn said with an edge of finality. "We do it the right way. The safe way."

"Love, I know you're—"

"The Laws aren't negotiable!" Jacklyn shouted. The psybelles' conversation ceased abruptly, plunging the cave into darkness. Caroline brought her hands together, willing patience. Jacklyn wasn't seeing her point. This wasn't about the Laws of Hosts, which were outdated, or about duty or honor. It was a simple equation of physics and energy. If Jacklyn's body broke before the Seed passed . . .

"The timing will be tight," Jacklyn said. "But with his conjoined Stains, there is no way the Seed would reject him once they're converted."

"*If* he converts. He has days, not years like you did, and the Laws and their Assays were written to be completed over decades." She dropped her voice and took a small step forward. "We don't have the time."

Another long pause, and the darkness persisted. The psybelles were intrigued.

To Caroline's surprise, Jacklyn blew out a long, reluctant breath, sounding like a little white flag. Something was off. In their over one hundred years together, Jacklyn had never given up a fight this easily. She'd argue a point until she was cornered. It reminded her of Rory.

"I feel stuck, Care. Damned if I do, damned if I don't." She sighed. "The Seed's getting restless. It can sense I'm getting weaker." Her voice faltered, barely audible over the trickling stream. "And if I mess the handoff up, I'll be the last Host. I mean, I knew the end would come . . . someday. I just never thought it would be so hard."

"Me too, love, and you are not alone in this." She weighed her next words. "Do you want your Counselor's advice?"

A bubble of laughter came, but it trailed off quickly, leaving only the sound of the waves echoing through the cave. "Always. Even when I don't."

"We are closer than we can see. Rory is closer. He needs to forgive himself for something he didn't do, and then it's a matter of confidence. We must help him believe he is worthy. The Laws, the Assays, all of it will all fall into place if he can do those. And I believe in him. He will convert."

"Or he dies."

"Yes, or he dies."

"And how does Khloe help?"

A curious orange cloud emerged from a nearby psybelle as though repeating Jacklyn's question.

"I believe, on some level, Khloe understands that a Stain's most potent defense against conversion is shame and shadow. They are like two safety protocols locking down our crude consciousness after something unknown and terrible strikes. She feels shame intensely from the fallout of her grandmother's disappearance, blaming herself at one point, but now she is starting to give herself the grace to build that context, which is dragging her Stain into the light. She can teach Rory that. Or, at worst, demonstrate what it looks like so he can find his own foothold."

"So, you gauged her Stain?"

"I did."

"And?"

"It is potent. I think she'd be a good Counselor."

"What about Jane? I thought that was the whole point of arranging for Rory and her to meet."

"Perhaps Rory needs two."

"That's never been done."

"And the world has never been so confounding," Caroline countered. "Take it from the acting Counselor: it is difficult to offer guidance these days."

More psybelles picked up the orange question, and soon, the cave filled with color again. Caroline spotted Jacklyn moving against the mushrooms' hue. She stepped to her, reaching out a hand. Jacklyn's calloused fingers folded around hers. Caroline might not see Jacklyn's emotions, but she could feel them just fine. A thick layer of frustration pressed against her senses, but she felt it laced with deep dread and fear of loss. Jacklyn lifted Caroline's hand to her lips and kissed it.

"You're right about me too, Care. I'm fading fast. I can feel it."

The thought cut Caroline anew. "You're not sleeping well. I hear your terrors. The voices . . . maybe you've been reaving too much?"

"I have to keep my energy up somehow," Jacklyn said.

That reminded Caroline of Jacklyn's errand. "Your trip?"

"Ya. Sent the mom after the boy. I think she'll get there."

"You've done wonderful work, my love."

"That's what I tell myself, too."

Caroline heard the weight in Jacklyn's voice. She stepped back, keeping Jacklyn's hand in hers. "I promise, I broke no Laws."

Jacklyn snorted. "Hard to tell sometimes. You take plenty of liberties with their interpretations. But," she added, cutting off Caroline's protest, "they are pretty old. And vague. And we need to adapt." She squeezed Caroline's hand. "A beautiful young witch taught me that."

A pang of guilt lanced through her. Jacklyn had given her a beautiful olive branch. Caroline cupped Jacklyn's cheeks and lifted her face up. Gently, she pressed her forehead against Jacklyn's and closed her eyes. Jacklyn's hands rose and found hers, and there, skin-to-skin, they breathed together in rhythm with the tide. If time could stop, Caroline would have willed it then. She knew there weren't many hours left together, and she wanted to savor every second, but . . . they didn't have enough time for such luxuries.

"Care?"

"Yes?"

"Rory is going to ask me to heal again, isn't he?"

"I believe so." She paused before adding. "Can you?"

"Tommy took a lot out of me, but—"

Caroline pressed Jacklyn's cheeks into her hands. "You have to. We've already got Rory's focus."

Jane cleared her throat. "I won't do it for him. I'll do it for me. Everything I've done as Host, the people I've killed . . . it's nice, in the end, to do some good, you know? I can manage one more."

One more. The thought cracked Caroline's heart.

"Hey," Jacklyn said, "we'll have our sunset, Care. You hear me? That one is happening."

Caroline wiped away a tear. "Now who's reading emotions?"

Jacklyn laughed and released first. She kissed each of Caroline's cheeks, leaving a warm memory on both before stepping back. "We need to prepare to surrender the Cove. Jane is good. She found my letter and should have located Maxwell by now. The wolves will be close behind her. The Director was clever to keep tabs on her."

Caroline hated for their moment to end, but duty called. "I'll start preparations. We'll make the Merged pay dearly for their siege.

Across the room, a burst of blue filled half the cavern, mingling at the edge with the orange light. Was it fear? A cheer? Or something unrelated? Caroline stopped, marveling at the sight. She wished she could share it with Jacklyn.

Jacklyn's silhouette shifted toward the back of the cave. "I'll go check for sporelings," her voice echoed. "Maybe some actually listened."

"And I should extract the larvae before they migrate."

Jacklyn's blur stopped. "What are you going to tell them?"

The question caught her off guard. "What can I tell them?"

"At this point, so long as we don't break the Laws, I don't care. But that's a hard line for me. Nothing about Rory's candidacy and definitely nothing about the Seed. Not until he converts. He's got to earn it, or the Seed will chew him up."

Caroline inhaled, her irritation flaring. She hated the Laws sometimes, but understood their purpose. Telling Rory of his role in the wider world would be the simplest way forward, but the Seed was too powerful to end up in unworthy hands. Proper vetting had to be done. "And their Stains? They've seen me cast now, and they're bound to be curious about how it's powered. And converted or not, Stains impact us. It's vital knowledge for anyone to have."

"Fine. Stains too, but only if they ask first. We can't risk one of them experimenting alone and killing themselves."

"Very well, but I insist that everything else is fair game. Even the Broken Star . . ." She let her voice trail off meaningfully, and when Jacklyn groaned again, she knew it had the intended effect. "The moths announced them to us. I guarantee I'll go out there, and Rory and Khloe will have pieced enough together. We'll need to ensure they have it correct, or they'll fill in gaps with dangerous assumptions."

"You're pushing it," Jacklyn groused. "But . . . you're right, as usual. There is no hiding it anymore. Still, I don't like it. It feels too close to the Seed."

"We're bending the Laws, not breaking them."

"Please don't remind me," Jacklyn said. Then, after another pause, she continued, "I'll see you out there?"

"Of course, my love."

Wet footfalls receded deeper into the cave, leaving Caroline alone in her gray world of colorful mushrooms. She waited, watching the psybelles all go blue now with a little pocket of white and pink in different corners. It felt good to align with Jacklyn again, though her admission did little to sway the worry in Caroline's heart. It was all ending soon, and there was nothing she could do to stop it. Caroline savored the cool air and exhaled over four heartbeats, letting her lungs empty the worry and tension in her body. Feeling her body settle, her mind focused, and she set her feet toward the beach. There was work to do.

Chapter 35: The Broken Star

Tuesday, April 24th, 19:57

The Hidden Cove

The yellowy tonic tasted terrible. Caroline mentioned something about pain and phase-slug mucus, which not only sounded disgusting, but left the flavor of burnt hair and acid stuck to the roof of Rory's mouth.

Despite the tonic's unpleasant flavor, he was glad to have it on board. His head swam in a warm cloud of contentment as he thought about all the patients he'd sedated. "Not so bad . . ." he mumbled to himself.

Caroline rooted around his ribs for the blood moth larvae using hook-nose tweezers. He felt no pain, only the occasional pressure spike as he reclined beside the fire, toasting his feet with his legs kicked up on a rock. Above them, the starry sky stretched horizon to horizon. Watching the stars, he discovered he'd started humming.

Khloe sat beside him in a blue camp chair with her wounded foot atop a piece of driftwood. The adrenaline had worn off, leaving them both spent. While Rory hummed, Khloe stared at the fire, blinking at the coals. He understood. He'd taken the mind-blowing plunge into the Cove and knew how the many questions clogged up his thoughts. Or maybe it was the shock or the tonic. She'd been silent since they'd sat down.

When Caroline returned from the cave, announcing everything was in order, he felt relieved that Jacklyn wouldn't kill them. "Oh . . . good."

Khloe barely nodded.

There was more good news. The psybelles were safe, and Jacklyn searched the cave for hiding sporelings. Caroline seemed upbeat, dipping her finger several times into the steaming iron cauldron hanging over the fire. Presumably at the right temperature, she tossed in an assortment of odd ingredients from the leather satchel she collected from the tent. Fat green scales, a handful of spotted yellow leaves, and what Rory was certain was a leathery bat wing. He chuckled. "Witches brrrew," he'd whispered to Khloe in a high voice. His drunken attempt to get her to laugh failed; she just stared. Caroline mixed the solution and tasted it before adding another scale from her patch-covered satchel, then ladled it into a pair of mugs. Rory took his and wrinkled his nose at the smell. Caroline urged him, and he drank, gagging. Khloe accepted hers without a word but didn't drink. Caroline whispered something. Khloe nodded and sipped without a grimace.

A few minutes later, Rory's head swam lazily among the stars.

"Ah, found it," Caroline said, drawing his attention back. He felt the pressure against his rib increase. Then a pinch and he looked down in time to see a long, bright orange tapeworm extracted from his side. "It was heading for your lung."

"Whoa." It was all Rory could muster. He might have felt scared, but the tonic washed away his worry too. Caroline whipped the worm into the fire, where it hissed and popped.

"I didn't feel a thing," he slurred. "This stuff is . . . something." He thought for a moment. "Will I remember this?"

Caroline chuckled as she packed his wound with white gauze. "You'll both remember, but you might be stiff in the morning. I haven't been able to work out that side effect. More bat leather, perhaps?"

Ah ha, it was a bat . . . Rory looked over at the steaming cauldron. "Wing. Cool."

Caroline leaned back. "Congratulations, Rory. I believe you'll live."

She rose and walked over to Khloe, who didn't look up. Caroline touched her shoulder, and Khloe's eyes drifted from the fire. The older woman whispered something and pointed to her foot. Even stunned, Khloe nodded, and her eyes seemed to refocus as she watched Caroline pull back a flap of sandy skin hanging from the bottom of her foot. She didn't flinch, which meant the tonic was working, but her brow furrowed.

"What are you thinking, dear?" Caroline asked, rinsing the sand off with a canteen.

"I . . . uh. I guess I keep asking myself why?"

"Why what?" Rory asked.

"Why didn't she tell me?" She pulled out the cloudy ruby from her pocket. "Why didn't she trust me?" She turned the stone over in her hands.

It took Rory a moment to catch up. The tonic thickened his thoughts. Her grandmother . . . He found Caroline staring at him behind her white blindfold. Umm, what? She tipped her head toward Khloe. Oh. Oh!

"What, uh. Happened?" Rory said. Caroline raised an eyebrow, then returned to work, rinsing Khloe's wound.

Khloe clicked the stone against her thumb ring. "Depends on who you ask. Gam-Gam was always searching for things. Mushrooms, or places that don't exist, or having long conversations with her jewelry. I think she found what she was looking for and went." She shifted in her chair, admiring the sky. "Seeing this place, I think I understand why she had to go."

She shifted in her chair and sighed. "My family, though, well, my dad, blames me for her disappearing—says it's because I didn't come home enough, so she got sad and lost her mind. Which, you know, maybe he's right. I was the only one she talked to before I left. But I figured that also means she would have told me something about"—she looked up for the first time, a smile playing at the corner of her mouth—"this."

"Why didn't you go home?" Rory said.

Khloe's head lolled over. "I mentioned I got some terrible advice before?"

He nodded, vaguely remembering their walk under the cherry blossoms back when everything seemed simple.

"My advisor," Khloe said. "That asshole convinced little freshman me that my accent—he called it too rural—would prevent me from ever being taken seriously by medical schools. I wanted to be a doctor so bad, the first in my family, so I believed him. I took speech lessons and practiced in the mirror every day until I spoke without an accent. But when I went home, it all came right back. Undid some of the work. It was like living a double life. So, I made excuses and stopped going home. Told myself it was for the best. That the sacrifice was for my dream. I found out later, during my medical school interviews, that they don't care what I sound like as long as I can think. It crushed me." She scowled. "I gave up all that time with her. For what? Trying to be someone I'm not?"

"Damn . . ." Rory said. He felt a distant frustration, but the medicine snuffed it out. "Sorry, Khloe. That sucks."

Khloe shrugged. "The stuff my dad says, I know it's not true— most days, at least. He made up the story because he's scared and doesn't know why. None of us did."

"Doesn't make it hurt any less," Rory said, feeling an ache grow in his chest.

Khloe shook her head but stayed quiet.

"You did nothing wrong, dear," Caroline said, setting down the canteen. "People reach for any story with meaning when they hurt."

"But why didn't she tell Khloe?" Rory said.

Caroline's brow creased as she adjusted her tweezers. "I doubt it was mistrust. My guess is she was trying to protect you."

Khloe didn't look convinced. "I hope that's true."

Caroline paused, lifting her gaze to meet Khloe's. "It is."

That drew a sliver of a grin from Khloe as Caroline resumed her work.

"Protect from who, though?" Rory pressed.

"Before I answer that, Rory, you need context." Caroline submerged her tweezers in a cup of a clear solution that smelled like the tonic. She flicked off the excess liquid and went to work on Khloe's foot. "Understand, there are large gaps in our knowledge, but from what we've gathered, we know that many thousands of years before the Sumerians started tabulating on clay, there was a terrible and devastating event that wiped out most of the world. Our ancestors who survived worked tirelessly to erase themselves, and the event, from history."

"Pre-Sumerian?" Khloe mumbled. "That's . . . four thousand years ago."

"Try ten," Caroline said.

"Ten thousand?" Rory whistled. "But why?"

Caroline wrinkled her nose and then jerked the tweezers back. "Ah! Got it." She drew out a long worm from Khloe's foot and threw it into the flames. Rory shifted in his seat as the larva sizzled.

Khloe paled, watching the worm burn. "How?" she asked slowly. "There is nowhere to hide anymore. The world has filled in. The internet . . ." she trailed off.

"Our maps are more detailed, yes, but they aren't filled in. Hidden places exist. I know, I was raised in one among a village of Wyth."

Rory looked away from the fire and out at the miraculous beach, mulling Caroline's words. He blinked. Something didn't quite add up. "So, the Wyth hid for thousands of years?"

"And we didn't hide, per se," Caroline said, then returned to

Khloe's foot as she spoke. "We lived on the fringes, trying to influence society where we could, keeping humanity away from the disasters of the past. Over time, that interaction with civilization earned us many names. The Chinese named us *gui po*. The Romans called us druids. The Protestants burned us as witches. And in the 1960s, the American government dubbed us hippies and malcontents after we tried our hand at modern politics. For a couple of years, I'd thought we'd broken through."

"Did you have a favorite name?" Khloe said. Rory perked up for the answer.

"Hmm. I've never been asked that . . ." Caroline drifted off. "Of all our titles, I suppose my favorite has always been from Arabia. They called us djinn. It's nice to think people search for us, even if it's for three wishes. The bit about lamps is amusing." She slid another worm out of Khloe's foot. "There we are." The worm burned while Caroline gathered her gauze. "I just need to pack your foot now, Dr. Seeker."

"Thank you. Um, so . . ." Khloe tried to work it out through her stupor.

"But someone is hunting you," Rory said. "So that means others survived, right? Not just the Wyth?" A terrifying thought followed. "Do they have Aspects too?"

Caroline nodded. "Our earliest records call them the Broken Star, but we call them the Merged."

Who? Rory loved reading about the Illuminati, Stonemasons, and Templars growing up. He and Patrick would make their own secret handshakes and send each other hidden messages with cryptic icons, the kinds of things kids love.

Caroline wrapped Khloe's foot in white gauze, moving with the steady grace of practiced hands. "Like the origins of the Wyth, theirs too is veiled by time, but to answer your question, Rory. Yes, they have Aspects."

"Why didn't they just use the Aspects to take over?" Khloe said.

"Both sides are careful to keep any conflict in the shadows. If the Aspects and casting become public knowledge, we assume it would only be a matter of time before whatever destroyed the world would do it again. Another apocalypse benefits no one." She put down her gauze and inspected her wrapping job.

Merged. What a weird name. Rory shook his head, swimming and foggy. He caught Khloe looking at him, mouth open in questioning. Rory shrugged. He felt like his chair was floating and spinning. A log popped, and the stack of wood collapsed a little, sending up a swirling cloud of glowing embers. They looked like fireflies against the dark sky.

"All done, Dr. Seeker," Caroline said proudly, returning her supplies to her satchel.

Khloe leaned forward and inspected the dressed wound. "How did you do that with a blindfold on?"

"Jacklyn has provided me ample opportunity to practice," Caroline said, setting up a third camp chair between Rory and Khloe. She lowered herself down with a relieved sigh and held her hands out to the fire. "But you meant my vision. It . . . isn't the easiest to explain. I suppose, simply put, I see emotion instead of light. Or rather, I see the world and its people as they really are, not how they want to be seen."

Khloe muttered something and inhaled while Rory tried to picture it. He wondered how he could use such sight as a nurse, able to know what a patient or a family member felt. Seeing sadness and knowing how to intervene or seeing hesitancy at the bedside gives a parent more opportunities to help. No more guessing. What a gift.

An intrusive thought butted in and pressed a word against his mind: *Merged.*

"Why're they called the Merged?" Rory said, slurring a little.

Caroline gestured to her necklace. "There is another way a mythstone can be used to cast. It is possible, through terrible means, to fuse oneself with an Aspect and share its power."

"That sounds cool . . ." Rory said, uncertain if it was.

"But a body should only hold one soul, Rory." Caroline snatched up a long stick and jabbed it into the fire. "The Merged are abominations and violate everything the Wyth teach. Their group, the Broken Star, corrupts the Aspects to gain and retain power."

"Oh, uh, uncool," Rory corrected.

"Uncool," Khloe echoed, her eyelids half drawn.

"Despicable," Caroline hissed, rolling over a glowing log. The fire flared anew, adding a layer of heat over him as he looked up at the stars. Part of him wanted to ask more questions, but the rest didn't care. This tonic was potent stuff.

"Look what I found!" Jacklyn called out. Rory jerked, half asleep. His vision lagged, making his head spin. He closed his eyes momentarily, feeling the heavy blanket of fatigue. When he opened them, he spotted Jacklyn walking up, holding a sporeling's claw in one hand and leading a small troop of them down from the cave.

"They live!" Caroline leaped from her chair and ran toward them.

Jacklyn and Caroline embraced. They talked briefly before Caroline called over the golems, and Jacklyn marched straight at him. Rory tried to sit up, but he felt too heavy, the sand too warm.

"Hero!" Jacklyn said, startling him. She stood over him. "You have something you want to ask me."

"I do?" His thoughts felt like sludge.

"Yes. Another kid?"

Rory blinked, and something ignited a thought. "Conner?"

"Conner?" Jacklyn said. "Who's Conner?"

"Roo . . . oom 10?" Khloe slurred.

Rory stuck out his thick tongue, willing it to form words. "Thhh. Boy scout. Drowning." He hurried, feeling himself sink. "Like Tommy." He pointed at the white jacket lying in the sand beside Khloe. "Badge." He pointed at Jacklyn. "Consult."

"What?" Jacklyn said.

Khloe's eyes closed, but thankfully, she nodded, seeming to understand. "T'morrow?"

"Zacly."

"Anyone wanna tell me?" Jacklyn said.

Khloe's head drooped into her chest, and she snored.

Rory fought it, wanting to make sure he was clear. "Help. To-morr-ow. Eight. Dress nice." He paused, and his eyes slid closed. "Nicer."

"Another no-hoper?"

Rory grunted yes and let his head rest for just a second.

"Alright, hero," Jacklyn's voice echoed in the distance, sludge-y and warped. "Eight . . ." He was vaguely aware of someone moving around him, and as sleep took hold, the last sounds of the crackling fire faded. Overwhelmed, he let his thoughts go.

Conner. Broken Star. Aspects. Hidden. Hidden . . .

Wednesday, April 25th, 20:03

Oates Children's Hospital – Physicians' On-Call Room

On-Call Hall reminded Rory of a train car: a narrow corridor with doors at either end and four private rooms labeled A through D, all to one side. On-Call Hall was where the residents and attending physicians working twenty-four-hour shifts went to sleep when they had breaks while the nurses safeguarded the patients. As Rory passed room B, he heard a gasp and a giggle from inside—a couple was taking advantage of the quiet halls during shift change. He stepped quietly to Room C and knocked softly.

"It's me," he whispered, trying to catch his breath.

"Rory?" The door opened a crack, and he saw Khloe's blue eyes peer at him. "What took you so long?" Before he could answer, she grabbed the front of his scrubs and yanked him inside.

A bunk bed occupied half the tiny room, and the computer desk took up another quarter. As Jacklyn paced, a small desk lamp cast long shadows on the far wall. She looked strange, wearing a leather buckskin beneath a white physician's coat, one sleeve dangling. Stitched in red on the coat's left breast, *T. Wingscythe, MD Ph.D. Pediatric Surgery.* Clipped to her chest was a badge with a carefully taped photo of Jacklyn covering Trent's face. It was the best idea Rory could come up with, and seeing it now, he wondered how on earth they could pull this off. Then again, he'd worked with stranger doctors.

"I had to fake indigestion," Rory said, winded. He'd jogged the back hall from the PICU. "That's harder than it sounds. I'm duping professionals."

Khloe pointed at Jacklyn with a sigh. "She won't take off the leather jacket. It will be a dead giveaway."

"Two jackets will be fine," Rory said, waving away her concern. "Deedee wears a blanket all the time."

"But not leather," Khloe countered.

"Trust me. It'll work out," Rory said. Khloe chuffed but didn't propose an alternative. Rory pointed at Jacklyn's long, silver hair shimmering in the desk lamplight. "That will get noticed, though. You couldn't change it?"

Jacklyn gave him a deep scowl, and Rory held up his hands in surrender. *She's nervous, too.*

"Can you do without the leather?" Rory asked hopefully.

She picked up her dangling left sleeve. "You see how flimsy this is? I need layers. It's freezing in here. I'm not sure how doctors think with only this napkin covering them. Barely feel my damn fingers," she muttered, then pointed at the red script stitched into the left breast of her jacket. "And who is T. Wingscythe?"

"He's a coworker," Rory said.

"He's my friend," Khloe corrected. "Another doctor in my department."

"Uh, huh. What kind of friend?" Jacklyn raised an eyebrow. "How friendly we talkin' about?"

To his surprise, Khloe blushed. Rory suddenly felt like punching someone. *Trent . . .*

"That's private," Khloe said. "For today, you are Trent. Leave the medical jargon to us. How much time do we have, Rory?"

"Fifteen minutes, maybe. Katherine is covering for me. If I play up my upset stomach, more, but regardless, we gotta go. There are two admits inbound from Ashland, so the night is going to get busy fast. With everyone doing their first checks, this is our best window, and Conner's parents just stepped out to talk to the hospice team, so there are just the two agents and . . ."

"Agents?" Jacklyn's eyes narrowed.

"Uh, like guards. Two. Outside the door," Rory said.

"But you said *agents*," Jacklyn said, stepping back.

"What's the difference?" Khloe asked.

"*Agents* mean government, and government means no deal," Jacklyn said, starting to take off the white coat. "We played that game in the 1970s, and they turned Care and me into lab rats."

Lab rats? "The government. *Our* government knows about you?" Rory said, stunned. "I thought you said it was this other group . . . the Broken Star?"

"The Star has their tentacles in anything they can leverage for power. Finance, military, and especially the government."

Khloe kept her voice calm, but the strain carried through. "You could have told us that a little sooner."

"I thought it was implied!" Jacklyn snapped.

Stay focused. He tried to ignore the alarms in his head. *We're here to save a kid's life.* "So what?" Rory said, shrugging. "Conner's mother is a senator. She could be a president or a pauper; it makes no difference to our care." That line was one of Rory's favorite Bell-isms.

Jacklyn scoffed. "A pauper can't get you locked up for the rest of your damn life or rip your memories right out of your head. You ever have anyone steal your memories, hero? It hurts."

Rory swallowed the hard lump in his throat. "I didn't know."

Khloe plopped down on the bottom bunk and massaged her temples.

Jacklyn trembled. Rory had never seen her so mad. "They . . . hurt Care. They hurt her bad. I won't let that happen again."

"Is that how—" Rory pointed at his eyes.

Jacklyn shook her head. "No, but they did take something from her. She doesn't laugh the same anymore."

A long silence swallowed the room, leaving only a quiet snore coming through the shared wall.

Jacklyn slipped her arm from under the white coat and tossed it on the bed.

"What are you doing?"

"Going back to the cove. I think we rushed this one." She tossed the coat on the bed next to Khloe.

"I agree," Khloe said. "We need to evaluate this and—"

"No!" he barked, surprising himself. Both women faced him, and he stammered. He searched for a plausible lie, but found the truth instead. "I know everyone is scared. And for good reason—this is scary shit. But who Conner's mom is isn't his fault. Honestly, I don't particularly like her. I didn't vote for her, but that doesn't matter. Conner needs help. Jacklyn." He faced her, but she wouldn't meet his eyes. He turned. "Khloe. You know this better than either of us. Without us, he's dead." He took a breath in. "*Spiritus boni*, right?"

Khloe inhaled, then shook her head. "But we're so screwed if we get caught."

Rory stepped closer to her, trying to find her eyes. "You wanted to know. Well, this is the price."

"I . . . I don't know."

Give her time to think. Rory shifted to Jacklyn, who instantly scowled at him.

"I'm not going back there, hero."

"Remember Tommy?" he pleaded. Jacklyn's scowl cracked. "You gave him back his life. Someone hurt him, and *you* saved him. Leave if you want, that's your choice, but if you stay, *you* can reverse a tragedy no one else can. That's amazing. That's . . . the closest thing I can think of to pure good."

Jacklyn looked down at the white coat.

Come on, come on. Rory spotted the clock hanging above the doorway and winced. He picked up Trent's coat. "Can we give it a shot?"

She closed her eyes, and Rory waited. Suddenly, she snatched it out of his hand. "For the kid."

YES!

"Those are feds out there," Jacklyn said, pushing her arm through the sleeve again. "Not your bubble-gum security downstairs."

"They're still people," Rory said.

"Highly trained and armed people." Jacklyn tugged the jacket over her stump and looked down at the dangling sleeve. "Who will not believe I'm a doctor?"

"It's all about looking the part." Rory pulled open the desk drawer and pulled out several safety pins. "This is our secret stash, in case we rip our scrubs."

"That happens?"

Rory nodded. "All the time." He gestured to her sleeve. "Raise your arm."

He folded the sleeve, threaded the pin through, and clipped it in place. He smoothed the fabric and stepped back. "There, now you look like you've worn that jacket before. For the next ten minutes, Jacklyn, you are Dr. Wingscythe. You've done patient consults hundreds of times, and you'll do it hundreds more. This is routine. Boring."

Jacklyn inspected the sleeve and tested her range of motion. "That's pretty good."

Rory turned to Khloe. "What do you say? Give it a chance?"

Khloe sniffed, shaking her head. "If I don't, I'll regret it." She rose. "Okay, yeah. Let's go save a life."

They walked together through the unit, Rory carrying a bag of saline and a fresh line. Khloe walked beside him, her strides even and confident on the familiar turf, but he spotted white knuckles where she clutched the chart. Jacklyn kept close on their heels, doing her best to look bored. Her face betrayed nothing. They drew casual glances from nurses and respiratory therapists going about their nightly tasks, but no one stopped them or asked questions; they were all too busy in their charts and triple checks, tucking families in for the night.

Anticipation swallowed Rory. *Just one foot in front of the other.* They rounded the corner and approached Room 10. Only one tall, suit-wearing agent stood outside. *We've got luck on our side tonight.*

"Let me do the talking," he whispered as they neared.

"Identification, please," the man said. Rory guessed he was in his late twenties, though his square jaw and earpiece made him appear older. Deep rings hung beneath his eyes, and the overnight shift was only just beginning. Not that he didn't look like he could manage it.

They all presented their badges.

"Is the transplant team still talking with the parents?" Rory said.

The guard nodded, scrutinizing each badge. He lingered on T. Wingscythe.

Jacklyn held her breath, but Rory wouldn't let himself turn around. *The hundredth time.* The guard squinted at the badge, rubbing his finger over the picture.

"Is there an issue?" Rory asked. It was suddenly too hot, too stifling.

"Smudged." The guard stifled a yawn and handed back their

badges and addressed Khloe and Jacklyn. "Your team already came through today. The parents want to explore other options."

Khloe opened her mouth, but Jacklyn beat her to it. "We have another idea, an experimental treatment."

Rory froze, but kept his face neutral. *What is she doing?!*

Khloe didn't miss a beat, adding, "We just need a quick assessment to see if he's a candidate for plasma tau protein therapy. It could help Conner's brain function."

A what? Rory had never heard of the treatment.

"Well, you need to wait," the guard said. "I can't let anyone in until his family returns—"

"Sir," Khloe cut him off. "I won't tell you how to do your job, but we're just trying to do ours. Time isn't on Conner's side."

Nicely done, Khloe.

The man frowned and glanced down the hall toward the patient council room. This wasn't going according to plan. Rory was pretty sure he could tackle the guy, stun him long enough for Jacklyn to get in and out before they were all arrested. After that, though . . . the hospital locks down like a prison. He noticed the bulge beneath the man's jacket, a gun, most likely. *Bad idea.*

The guard's gaze dropped on Rory. "And you?"

"Me?" Rory held up a saline bag. "I'm Conner's nurse tonight. We met already, about thirty minutes ago."

The guard squinted at Rory, and recognition crossed his face. "Oh, right. The guy nurse. Hey, sorry. My relief got reassigned, and . . . well, I guess you get it."

"Oh ya," Rory said. "They keep us burning at both ends."

The guard chuckled. "You got that right." He sighed and leveled on Rory. "If something . . . else happens to Conner, and his parents aren't here—they've just been through enough."

Something slid into place. "You've been with the family for a while?"

The agent nodded. "Couple years. Since his mom took office."

"You must spend a lot of time with Conner, then."

"Ya. Parents are busy."

"We only need a couple of minutes." Khloe unleashed her warmest smile, and Rory almost felt bad for the guy. "Grab some coffee and stretch your legs. You can even see the room from the coffee machine. When you get back, we'll be done. No one has to know, and maybe we can find Conner a solution."

The agent looked back down the hall. "Just a couple minutes?"

"Three tops," Jacklyn said.

The guard took a small step to the side. "Yeah, a break sounds good." He turned to Jacklyn. "Hey. Uh, I know it doesn't look good, but if you can, please help him. He's a great kid. Smart. He wants to be a biologist if he doesn't go pro. To teach. He's . . . he's kind, you know?"

Jacklyn nodded, "I'll do my best."

"Thanks," the agent said. "All of you." He hurried toward the community kitchen at the heart of the unit.

Rory felt a rush of relief mingled with excitement, and he couldn't decide if he needed to throw up as he opened the sliding door. Khloe and Jacklyn slipped inside. He checked to make sure no one was watching before he followed them into the darkened room and closed the curtain.

———

20:14

Bell once told Rory he'd know a tough assignment by the sound of the room. Silent rooms meant quiet nights and stable patients. Loud rooms, like Conner's, were a completely different story. An army of machines beeped, puffed, and ticked away, all to

400

their own rhythm. On the bed, a wiry sixteen-year-old with round cheeks and fading acne lay motionless, but for the rise and fall of his chest to the sound of the ventilator's hiss. Layers of blankets covered him to the neck, and every manner of cord and cable snaked beneath the sheets. Rory glanced at his heart rate—the steady bounce indicating a still living, but fragile, boy.

"His pressure's dropped," Khloe said quietly. "We might need to up his Epi and—"

"That's why we are here," Rory said, keeping focus. "Jacklyn. Jacklyn?"

She was at the bedside, staring at Conner.

"Is she okay?" Khloe asked.

He shrugged. "She didn't do this last time. Hey . . ."

"He drowned?"

Rory nodded. "Yeah, saving another kid."

Jacklyn nodded. "He's . . . big."

"That okay?"

"I hope so," she said.

The beeps filled the ensuing silence.

"Time check," Khloe said, eyeing the door.

"You're on," Rory said.

"I heard her," Jacklyn growled and removed her sunglasses from her pocket.

Khloe quirked an eyebrow, and Rory scolded himself for not remembering. Since Tommy and again with Maxwell, Rory couldn't stop wondering what casting looked like. He imagined energy bolts and purple lightning. Or maybe it was simple and elegant, like a hand sliding fluidly through the skin. *But I forgot my damn glasses.* They were on the kitchen counter next to his lunch.

Rory positioned himself behind Jacklyn, just in case she collapsed again.

"Close your eyes," Jacklyn said. "I'll know if you look." She slipped her stump out of her pinned sleeve. "Close 'em."

Khloe inhaled sharply and glanced at Rory, who nodded. Curious as he was, he didn't want to test Jacklyn again so soon after last night. Khloe squeezed her eyes shut, and Rory followed suit.

He heard the rustling of blankets, and the wave of cold washed over him. He violently shivered as the world went white. Sudden heat singed his face and hands before fading as fast as it had come. Then she sagged against him, her inexplicable weight driving the air out of him. He blinked, trying to clear the white blobs in his vision. Something in his back twinged, and he dropped to a knee. Carefully, he lowered Jacklyn to the ground, thankful his back didn't seize.

"Did she do it?" Khloe asked nearby. "Did it work?"

Conner lay still on the bed, his vital signs unchanged. Only time would tell.

"Jacklyn?" Rory asked. No response. Jacklyn's skin was hot to the touch as he searched for her pulse. "Hey, wake up."

He couldn't feel one on her wrist. He felt her neck. Nothing.

"She . . . she doesn't have a pulse." Rory heard the alarm in his voice and forced himself to hold his nerve.

Khloe dropped and grabbed Jacklyn's arm. In the faint light, she watched her pale.

"Oh, shit," she said. "We need to start chest compressions."

"Jacklyn, I'm going to touch you now," Rory said. Still no response.

Rory yanked open the front of her white coat, sending a button flying across the room. "Watch the door," he said. "The light drew attention last time." *It's okay. She'll be okay.*

Khloe stood up and peeked around the curtain.

Rory fumbled with the zipper on Jacklyn's leather coat. "I'm touching your chest." He pulled open the jacket and found a pale blue button-up shirt beneath. *She actually dressed up. She listened.*

He laced his fingers and pressed his palm against her sternum. "One, two, three," he said as he pushed. After the third, he felt one of her ribs pop. Images of Octavia flooded his mind—the blood and bodies flowing around him. He forced the memories aside and swallowed down the bile in his throat. "Four, five, six . . ."

"He's coming back!" Khloe hissed and hurried over, pressing her fingers against Jacklyn's neck. Rory continued to pump, looking at her hopefully, but Khloe shook her head.

"Ten, eleven, twelve . . ." Rory pushed hard, but this time felt something slide against his palm. "What the—" He jerked his hand back as Khloe yelped and jumped to her feet.

"What *is* that?" she hissed, pointing at Jacklyn's chest.

Beneath Jacklyn's pale skin, something long and slithering bulged out, pulling the skin taut as it slipped between her ribs and disappeared. Rory couldn't move. An intense crimson glow welled up from within Jacklyn's chest. As the light grew, it stung his eyes and outlined her ribs and sternum like a red-tinted X-ray. But the still of the image broke when a trio of dark barbed tentacles coiled around her bones.

"Oh my god!" Khloe covered her mouth with both hands.

Slowly, Rory leaned down, unable to take his eyes off that . . . *thing.* It shifted again, but the glow faded and disappeared. Rory blinked, still too stunned to move, until a knock came on the glass door.

Rory shook his head. *Focus.* He closed Jacklyn's clothing before the door slid open.

The agent's head poked in. "All done?" He spotted Jacklyn on the ground. "What happened?" He stopped and sniffed at the air. "Is something burning?" The alarm rose in his voice, and Rory pictured the situation getting out of hand quickly.

Keep it calm. "A bulb blew," Rory said, pointing at the ceiling. "It startled Dr. Wingscythe. She let her blood sugar get too low. It happens all the time."

As though on cue, Jacklyn sucked in a breath, and her chest rose and fell. *Thank goodness.*

"Oh, I'll, uh," the man stammered, "I'll go get a nurse."

Already here. "No, no," Rory said. "We're okay. Could you grab a wheelchair from down the hall for us? Really, she's doing just fine now." Rory patted Jacklyn's cheek. She sluggishly swiped at him. "See? She just needs some crackers and juice."

The agent didn't appear convinced, but had few options. Everyone was in the wrong, so it was best for everyone to wrap it up quickly and forget about it. The agent nodded and ducked out of view, and Rory was glad they arrived at a similar conclusion.

"Jacklyn, open your eyes!" Rory said.

She didn't, but she continued to breathe.

Khloe kneeled down and felt for a pulse. She paled. "It's really weak."

Shit, shit, shit. We need to move her.

"Rory," Khloe said with a note of concern. She looked down at his hands. He found them both shaking. *Not again. Not now.* "It's nothing." He squeezed his hands into fists, willing them to stop. *Come on. Focus.* In his roiling confusion, one thing was clear: Jacklyn was in worse shape than she let on.

"She almost died," Rory said.

"She still might."

Rory didn't want to think about that. "Help me sit her up."

"And take her where?"

"I don't know, but we can't leave her on the floor." Rory got his hands under Jacklyn's arms.

Khloe's eyes dropped to Jacklyn. "Rory, what was that *thing*?"

"I don't know!" Rory said, irritated. He wished he knew. Then this might not be as terrifying. "I'm winging it too, so don't hold back any ideas. Now come on, help me."

Khloe frowned a moment, then pushed herself up. She grabbed the front of Jacklyn's jacket. Blood speckled the white.

"One, two, three." They both heaved and got Jacklyn sitting against the bed. Her chin slumped down onto her rising and falling chest.

"Why is she so heavy?" Khloe said, panting, then put up her hands. "Sorry, I know you . . ." She stopped and smiled. "No way."

"What?"

"I think I know what to do."

"Please, share."

"When you don't know, you need data," Khloe recited.

"Data?"

"Magus actually taught me this. He yells it every time someone can't figure out a diagnosis. We need information to make a better choice. We need tests, assessments, anything that provides a fresh perspective."

Rory wiped his forehead and nodded at Jacklyn. "She has a monster in her chest." It was strange how casual it sounded out loud.

"That's my point," Khloe said. "We don't know what is in her

405

chest, so we call it a monster. Could it be the thing healing? If it is, is it still monstrous?"

Khloe's question rang with one of his own, fizzling his rebuttal. That question, *what* was healing, was still a vast hole in Jacklyn's story, and he'd made lots of theories to try to fill it. Returning deities, alien technology, and the devil all felt childish after feeling that *thing* move. *Khloe is right. We need to know now.* He pictured Jacklyn again, moments before, smoke curling off her white jacket—still as stone. The image stole his breath. *She can't die.*

"Okay, ya. Data then. Something fast. An X-ray?"

Jacklyn groaned, and he wasn't sure if it was a protest.

"The techs will be in and out all night. The Emergency Department is packed."

"Damn," Rory said. *Bad luck.*

"Blood work?"

"Too slow. MRI?" Hearing it out loud, he shook his head. "No. Too long."

"Wait. MRI, yes," Khloe said. "The new MRI suite, the 8T. No one is over there yet. Most stuff is still in plastic. And I can cut the sequence down to only a couple of images—"

"A couple?"

"One image. Five, maybe ten minutes of scan time."

"Ten minutes . . ." That felt like an eternity they didn't have. "Who's going to run it?"

"I can. I have a log-in and everything." She looked at him expectantly. "This is the best shot to figure out what is going on and hopefully help Jacklyn."

Rory sighed, knowing his answer even as he tried to talk himself out of it. He wanted to know too and if the cost was ten minutes, and a little more risk, then that seemed worth the price. He brandished his finger. "One sequence."

The door slid open, and the agent rolled in a wide wheelchair with an IV pole attached. "This one?"

"Wheels and a chair. Perfect," Rory said enthusiastically. "We're going to take Dr. Wingscythe to get checked out, just to be safe. She'll probably be fine with some fluids. Oh, and don't worry about the bulb; I'll put a maintenance report in but fudge the time a little. We'll keep this minor incident off the record."

The agent looked relieved, though still watching Jacklyn warily. He glanced back out into the hall. Rory and Khloe each took an arm and lifted again. Rory stumbled a step but kept his balance as they lowered Jacklyn into the wheelchair, leaning her head gently against the IV pole.

The agent frowned. "You're sure she's okay?"

"Oh, ya. Happens all the time."

Chapter 37: Brotherly Love

Wednesday, April 25th, 20:33

The MRI's vault door hissed, and Rory pressed it closed, dampening the steady clicks and chirps of the giant magnet within.

"She's asleep," he said. "I got the SAT probe on her finger."

"Did you pat her down?"

Rory nodded. "No metal." He glanced at the clock above the row of white cabinets. "I've been gone too long. The unit—"

"The unit is fine," Khloe said, lifting a bulging white plastic bag off the U-shaped computer desk. "So is Conner. I need you here. You sold the stomachache, right?" She set the bag on the ground, revealing a remote monitor behind it, and pressed the power button. *Ding.* The monitor flickered to life. "What did you blame it on?"

"Bad chicken."

"Then we're good." Khloe pointed down the narrow hall where dozens of clear supply bags held boxes of gloves, flushes, and sanitizer. There were so many in such a small space that mounds of plastic bags ran the length of the unwrapped suite. "Go make sure we're alone if you're worried." But her expression told him something else. *Calm down.*

"How are you not freaking out?"

"I am," Khloe breathed, plugging a series of cables into the back of a computer monitor. "*Spiritus boni*, right?"

Rory breathed, and the alarm in his head receded into the background. Through the window and into the MRI suite. Through the great machine's donut hole, he watched the pile of blankets atop Jacklyn rise and fall steadily. *She's still breathing, too.*

408

Over Khloe's shoulder, Rory checked the black computer screens.

"I think I got it . . ." Khloe said, jiggling the mouse. The monitor turned blue, and a panel popped up, asking for a password. "There she goes! We're in business." She quickly typed in her credentials and a long, complicated password and punched ENTER.

An error message appeared: *Your username and/or password do not exist in this system.*

"What?" Khloe hissed, and Rory's stomach cramped. "Let me try . . ." She typed everything in again, but the same message appeared. She shook her head, stunned. "That should have worked."

Should have? Rory kept his breathing steady. "You don't have the password?"

Jacklyn's monitor began beeping in a steady cadence. *Ding ding ding.* Her heart rate increased, but held a rhythm. Rory silenced the alarm.

"I did, unless they . . . shit!" She tried again, and this time the error message told her she only had one more attempt before it locked her out. "They reset the system for the opening."

"Let's get her out."

Squeak, squeak.

Rory froze, listening. The sound grew louder. The unmistakable sound of sneakers on tile echoed down the hall. *Squeak, squeak.*

Khloe pulled open the nearest drawer. "Where do they keep the lab supplies—"

"Shhh!" Rory instinctively ducked and turned toward the suite's entrance. "Someone is coming. Hide."

"Where?" Khloe said and pointed down the hall toward the door. "There is only one way in here, and Jacklyn's on the table."

"Just . . . turn off the lights and get under the bags. It's probably the janitor."

Khloe quickly clicked off the monitor, and after a couple of attempts on the wall switches, she got all but the emergency lighting to turn off. Rory lifted two bags, and they slid beneath. He pulled another bag over their legs, and they tried to breathe quietly.

Squeak, squeak. Click. The door handle turned, and Rory sank deeper into their hideout.

An off-key tenor poured into the room as the door swung open. ". . . halfway there. Whoa-oh! Livin' on a prayer! Take my hand . . ."

Rory knew that song. And he knew that voice. He'd listened to this performance many times in his dorm room.

"Patrick?" Rory squinted into the low light and, through the gap in the bags, saw light blue scrubs dancing around the mounds of supplies with a pair of headphone cables dangling from each ear. He must have hit the song's bridge because he suddenly stopped singing and started swiveling his hips.

Khloe shifted to get a look. "You two are friends, right?"

"Stop moving," Rory hissed. "Shit. He's probably getting this place cleaned up for the grand opening. He could be here for hours."

Patrick pulled open one of the white bags, head bobbing, and started unloading boxes of gloves into an empty cabinet.

"He's got to have a log-in."

"What? No," Rory said. "We can't drag him into this, too."

The overhead lights came on, and Rory blinked in the bright light. Patrick danced toward them, spinning with both arms in the air. He brought his foot down on one bag with a crunch, stooped down, pulled the bag open, and removed a caved-in box of medium-sized gloves. Patrick popped out one of his earbuds and examined the crumpled box. "You'll be going in the back," he told the box.

"We need his help," Khloe whispered.

"No, we could get him fired."

Patrick lifted his head and pulled out an earbud. "Hello?" he said tentatively.

Craaap. Rory tried to shrink as footsteps approached.

"It's alright," Patrick said. "I know this is your home, Mr. Ghost. I acknowledge you, and I set you free . . ."

Rory and Khloe exchanged curious looks, and the footsteps stopped. Rory leaned his head to the side, watching Patrick survey the area between a pair of bags. Patrick looked into the suite, and his mouth fell open. Rory's stomach fell. *He saw Jacklyn.* Patrick scrambled for the phone.

"Pat! Don't!" Rory shouted, bursting from beneath the bags.

Patrick shrieked and jumped back into the desk, sending the monitors rocking precariously. He ripped his earbuds out of his ears as Rory stumbled on a bag of syringes. "What the . . . Rory? Jeez, you scared me . . ." He put a hand over his chest. "Oh, man. Wait, shouldn't you be upstairs?"

"Yes, but let me explain," Rory said slowly, his hands outstretched. His mind generated a feeble lie, something simple. They also found Jacklyn in the scanner, but that would still mean security and investigations and probably getting everyone fired. There was no room for an escape. The other options involved fighting his best friend, which felt impossible. He had to tell the truth, or at least a near truth. "We need the new coil to scan this patient's chest."

"This one isn't even—" Patrick stopped and listened. Then he spun around. "How did you get the machine on?"

"I bypassed the—" Khloe stood.

"Don't worry about it," Rory said. "We just need the password for the scanner. Can you help us?"

Patrick looked quickly between the two of them, confused. "Ya, I've been doing its diagnostics." He pointed into the scanner. "Who's in there? That doesn't look like a kid."

"I . . . uh, can't tell you, Pat," Rory said. "Not because I don't want to. I just . . . You can't get involved. It is for your safety."

"Rory . . . what the hell is going on?"

Witches, golems, killer moths. Rory shook his head. *That would make things worse.* "We just need an image, and we can all forget this happened. No one will ever know."

"I don't know, man."

Rory knew he had to give a little more. "It's life and death, Pat. And I don't say that lightly." He checked his watch: *20:40.* "I have to get back to the unit. Please, Pat. Help me out here, brother. It's important to me."

Despite eyes full of worry, Patrick smiled. "Yeah, okay. Fine. I'll take one image, delete it, and then you leave."

Rory threw his arms around his old friend. "Thank you!"

"Ya, ya. Just don't get me fired." Patrick blew out a long breath and spun a chair around for himself. When the password panel appeared, he punched in a long string of numbers and letters and hit ENTER. The screen switched to a desktop display with colored icons in the corner. "We're in. What are we scanning?"

Khloe slipped into the chair beside him. "The chest. Can we get a coronal view?"

"Mhm." Patrick opened the program. "I'll need . . . seven minutes to finish booting up."

"You got seven minutes, Rory," Khloe said. "Go get sent home. I'll keep an eye on our friend while Patrick gets the scanner going." She turned the remote monitor, and he watched Jacklyn's green heartbeat bounce across the screen, slow and steady. "She is doing fine. Go. You don't want to miss this."

Chapter 38: The Seed

Wednesday, April 25th, 20:47

Rory hated leaving the unit short, but by the time he reached the PICU, he was sweaty, nervous, and without another option. If he wanted to keep his job *and* help Jacklyn, it left him with only a lie. He just prayed he was a skilled enough performer.

Fortunately, the run up the stairs helped. All he had to do was play up the cramps and look appropriately pathetic. He formed a plausible lie about throwing up in the locker room. While his performance felt a little melodramatic to him, it went well enough to earn him sympathy, crackers, a half dozen tea recommendations, and a ticket home.

But he wasn't going home. He hobbled through the double doors, waited until they closed behind him, and ran. Jumping the last steps on each of the nine flights down, he reached the MRI suites, panting, but with a minute to spare. He opened the plastic-wrapped door and heard the MRI's massive pulse, accompanying itself with a sharp snap on the downbeat.

Khloe and Patrick looked up from the computer screen and quickly back.

"Still asleep." Khloe waved him over. "We have thirty seconds left on the coronal. You good?"

"Yeah, I'm off."

Khloe sighed, relieved. "That's one less thing to worry about. Patrick figured out how to delete the images and the log history."

"The sooner, the better," Patrick muttered. "Twenty seconds."

Rory craned his neck and spotted Jacklyn in the middle of the MRI's donut tube, still and breathing. On the monitor, her heart rate steadily increased.

"It's been going up since we started," Khloe said, following his gaze.

"Something is irritating her. Has she moved?"

Patrick shook his head. "You're sure she had no metal?"

Rory nodded. *Come on, come on. Stay still a little longer.*

"Must be the noise," Khloe said, but didn't sound convinced.

"Fifteen seconds. So . . . what are we looking for?"

"We don't know," Khloe said. "That's part of the problem."

Patrick glanced over at her with a frown and then up to Rory, who nodded glumly. "Okay," he said. "Ten seconds."

Rory tapped his finger on the table, humming in anticipation. He vibrated with excitement. There was no turning back now.

"Five seconds."

Rory and Khloe both leaned in.

"Here's the first image," Patrick said.

A black and white coronal cut, from shoulder to shoulder, of Jacklyn's chest appeared on the screen. It took Rory a second to orient himself, but he recognized the unmistakable white chain of blocks, the spine stacked down the image's center. A pair of oblong plates flanked the spine, Jacklyn's scapulae, and twelve sets of ribs crowned at the neck by her clavicles. Cloudy opacities filled each lung like a dense fog. *Pneumonia.* He remembered the blood.

"Her lungs are a wreck," he said.

Khloe tipped her head to the side. "Where was that *thing*? Did the scanner detect it?"

"It was around the ribs before." Rory squinted closer.

"It?" Patrick said warily.

Khloe pointed between the two lungs. "Can you cut to the cardiac notch?"

Patrick spun the scroll wheel on the mouse slowly. The spine shrank away as the coronal cuts glided anteriorly. Rory watched the space between Jacklyn's lungs, expecting to see the four chambers of her heart slide into view, but the space between her lungs instead filled with a bright white mass, like a nova burst in Jacklyn's chest.

"So . . . what are we—" Patrick squinted at the image. "What the . . . hell are these?" He scrolled again and traced long, slender strips of white curling down each rib. As the nova shrank, Rory's chest tightened. *That's it.*

Patrick scrolled back out and began tracing another, snaking around the lungs. He stopped and paled as he leaned back in his chair. "Where is, um, the heart?" He returned to the cardiac notch and Jacklyn's mysterious nova. "Seriously, where is the heart?"

"It's not there . . ." Khloe said.

Rory's stomach heaved, and he was nearly sick. *She doesn't have a heart . . .*

Patrick shook his head, pointing at the monitor beeping steadily. "That is impossible. You can't have a heartbeat without a heart. It's a mesh around . . . a . . .uh, transplant organ?" He fell quiet after as they all stared at the image. "Rory?"

"Ya?"

"Are you two punking me?"

"Not this time, Pat," Rory said. "Have you ever seen anything like this before?"

"No," Patrick said, and they all watched the nova bloom and recede again. "It's not even blurry. These images are crystal clear." The clicks and thumps of the idling MRI filled the silence. As though stuck in a loop, Patrick started scrolling over the images again, but a flicker of black among all the white caught Rory's eye.

"Wait, wait. Go back. Uh, posteriorly. I saw something."

Patrick scrolled, and the images slid until the nova filled the screen.

"Stop! There."

In the center of the white, a smudge of black like smeared ink on a fresh page. But that wasn't quite right. It had defined edges. Rory squinted at the image. Something about it tickled his memory. Then a cold realization came over him, quickening his heart. *I've seen this before.*

Rory's hand found Khloe's shoulder. "Give me your grandma's necklace."

"My . . ." Her eyes snapped over to Patrick, who was still staring at the screen.

"Khloe, please."

She reached into her pocket and drew out the ruby necklace, handing it over. The gem gleamed, its inner light brightening at his touch, numbing his fingers. He held it up to the screen and steadied himself against the desk. The silhouettes were alike, both craggy with similar ratios. Only the shading was inverted.

"It's a mythstone," Rory said.

"Mythstone?" Patrick said, blinking at the glowing gem. "What the hell is going on?"

Rory shook his head, dazed, unfocused. "I can't tell you."

"Why not?"

"Just delete it all."

"But I—"

"Now, Pat!"

Patrick paled. "Yeah, okay."

"Shhh, both of you." Khloe held a finger up to her mouth. "Does anyone else hear that?"

Beep-beep-beep. The heart monitor beeped rapidly, and Jacklyn's once steady pulse spiked unevenly.

Rory looked into the room and saw Jacklyn's legs thrashing. "Stop the scan!"

Patrick held up his hands. "I'm not running anything!"

Rory ran to the door and heaved. The muffled whine erupted into a piercing wail. Jacklyn's back arched, and she thrashed against the machine's sides. He grimaced and covered his ears, running into the room. The magnetic field's effects were immediate, tugging at the pens in his pocket and lifting his identification badge off his chest. The lights flickered, and he caught a faint wisp of smoke in the air.

He grabbed Jacklyn's legs in both hands and pulled with all his might. She barely moved. Khloe appeared across the table and reached in. A pen slipped from her pocket and flew into the magnet, quivering against the wall next to Jacklyn's head.

"You can't have metal in there!" Patrick shouted by the door over Jacklyn's scream.

"Get her out!" Rory said to Khloe. "One, two—"

They pulled together, and Jacklyn slid out all at once. Rory caught her in his arms as they tumbled to the floor.

"Jacklyn!" he said.

She continued to scream and thrash. Both her eyes were wide open and bloodshot, and a thick froth of red-tinged drool dribbled out of her mouth. Where Jacklyn's back pressed against him, he felt the *thing* inside writhing.

"On her side!" Rory called and deflected one of Jacklyn's spasming arms. They rolled her over in case she threw up, but Rory knew there was little he could do until the seizure passed. If it ever did.

"Jacklyn!" Rory tried again.

"I'm calling a code," Patrick said, with a finger plugged into each ear.

"No!" Rory and Khloe yelled together, and Patrick froze in the doorway.

Jacklyn's shriek spiked into a banshee's wail. Rory covered his ears, praying the sound would stop. Jacklyn arched off the ground, and the cords of muscle in her neck and arms bulged. The pressure swelled inside Rory's skull, threatening to burst his head open. He clamped his eyes shut. The lights brightened in a blinding snap, and then suddenly, it all ceased at once, plunging everything into black.

As his senses returned, Rory heard himself breathing first, a hollow sound bouncing around in his own skull. He opened his eyes in the complete darkness. Not even the emergency lights came on. "Jacklyn?" *Where are the generators?*

Rory heard a moan nearby and followed the sound with his hands. He crawled forward and felt a flash of heat and pain. Rory yelped and jerked his hand back. From the void, something sizzled, and he smelled smoke.

Clack. Clack. Clack. Emergency lights came on, throwing a dim yellow glow through the room. Rory saw Jacklyn stir beside him. He rose to his knees and peered down at her.

"Hey, hey. Are you okay?"

Jacklyn looked up with hollow eyes. Her cheeks were gaunt and sunken, as though she'd been drained. When she spoke, her voice came raspy and soft. "Take me home. Hero . . ." Her head dropped back against the floor. Rory swallowed, trying to keep the cramping fear at bay. *Shit, what did we do?*

"Oh my god," Patrick said, staring at the smoking scanner. "It's completely fried."

"Patrick!" Rory snapped. "Listen carefully. The machine shorted out when you were running your last round of checks. It must have been an issue with installation, understand?" Patrick stared wide-eyed, and Rory continued. "Delete the images. They can't exist. It's for all our safety."

"Our safety?" Patrick said. "Shit, Rory, what have you gotten yourself into?"

He nearly said *I'm still not sure*, but shook his head instead. "Something big. I'm sorry I can't tell you more. I will when I can, but right now, can you help us?" He gestured to Jacklyn. "We need to get her out of here."

"Ya, sure. Consider them gone." Patrick sat and punched in his password.

Rory let out a sigh of relief. "Thank you, Pat. Really."

Patrick turned from the monitor and nodded. "Yeah, just . . . be careful. I'm here if you need anything."

Rory started toward him, but something caught his arm. It was Khloe.

"Someone's going to come check on this soon," Khloe said. "We can't be here."

Rory looked over at his old friend. *I'll make it up to you, Pat.* He turned and hooked his arms beneath Jacklyn's shoulders. "Help me get her back to the wheelchair," he said. "She needs Caroline."

Chapter 39: Keeping It Weird

Wednesday, April 25th, 20:40

Portland, Oregon

Jane leaned against the hotel balcony's railing, taking in Portland's twilight glow. The shimmer and shine of city lights gleamed off its lazy river, which split the city in half—east from west.

On the west bank, tall office buildings lined the shore and packed into the shelf of land between the hills and the river. To the east, she saw more trees than buildings—colorful homes making alleys through the woods. They were two different worlds, one brick and money, the other gardens and art. They needed each other and, in a way, she reasoned, it made the city like two halves of one brain with an eclectic collection of bridges connecting the two hemispheres. The dichotomy lent itself to the city's mantra, spray painted into a vast rainbow mural on the building across the street: *Keep Portland Weird.*

The slogan felt appropriate given how the case had gone so far, though not all of it had been a surprise. The killer's note, Maxwell's pendant, a miracle child, a one-armed woman, and a hippie? All in pursuit of the mysterious Seed. It all qualified as weird to her, though she hadn't puzzled out yet how it pieced together.

What wasn't weird, though, was the Director's reaction to Emmett's honesty. She'd warned him and, to her word, hadn't said, "I told you so." Not that she'd had the chance. Jane didn't know what was said, but she guessed by her confinement to her hotel room that the overall conversation had gone poorly. Emmett probably confessed and then was promptly steam-rolled with threats and bullying—classic tyrannical tactics.

So she waited. And waited. And waited for Emmett to knock. Until the whole day passed without a word.

The local news channel provided some distraction. She learned that Hill Hospital was playing host to a celebrity patient: a senator's child in critical condition from drowning. The journalist painted the patient, Conner, in an angelic light, and Jane tried not to imagine her nephew or niece in the same situation. Several times, the correspondents also mentioned the miracle boy, Tommy, and his remarkable recovery. A quick interview with what had to have been the Senator's spokeswoman stated that the entire team hoped for lightning to strike twice. Wishful thinking, but then again, these were weird times.

Jane was puzzling out any connections when she heard a knock. She hurried over, ready to see Emmett looking contrite, but a letter slid under the door, and she heard footfalls recede down the hall.

The envelope was blank and unsealed. She frowned, pulling out a plane ticket and a scrap of paper in Emmett's messy handwriting:

A car will be here in the morning for you. The ticket is paid for. We appreciate all your assistance but no longer need your services. —Emmett

That was it. Not a drop of emotion, of regret. A Hallmark card would have been warmer.

"Muff that," Jane mumbled. They weren't sending her home. Not after she'd gotten this far.

Based on the note, the Director had shaken Emmett's confidence, which meant she needed an equal and opposite force to counter him. The longer he sat with this, the more his response would solidify. An idea came to her quickly—an idea her therapist would approve of, but she needed Emmett in person, which he actively avoided. So, to get him to come to her, she'd need to get his attention. Tossing the letter on the bed, she scanned the room. On the bedside table, she spotted a lamp.

Jane grinned. "That'll do."

"Look out below!" Jane shouted, watching her chair plummet to the grassy, lamplit courtyard below. It hurtled toward the remains of the lamp, the painting, and the television she'd already ejected from her room. The chair landed with a *CRACK*. Pale splinters of wood shot out in all directions. She wondered if she could fit the table through the balcony doors.

"Sorry!" Jane waved down at the growing crowd of onlookers. "Can you let Emmett Torin—he's staying here—can you let him know I want to talk to him?" She ducked back inside to size up the table.

A few minutes later, as Jane tipped the table on its side, her door burst open, and a red-faced Emmett stormed in.

"You got my message!" Jane said, delighted.

Emmett looked ready to strangle her. "What the hell are you doing?!"

"Well . . . I need to talk to you," she said, dropping the table back on the floor and wiping her brow.

"This was to talk?" He ran a hand through his dark hair, looking completely overwhelmed. Stubble covered his chin and crawled up his cheeks. From somewhere beneath his disheveled suit, a stink followed him. "Dawson is downstairs talking with the manager, keeping this quiet. Goddamnit, Jane. What are you thinking?"

"You were ignoring me! This"—she picked up the envelope and tossed it on the bed—"is muffed, and you know it. If you do it, you're going to regret it."

The words didn't have their intended effect. Emmett's glare creased with confusion.

"Not in a mobster way," Jane fumbled for better words. "I'm

saying you'll regret it for yourself, like inside."

"Jane, are you high?"

"No, and I'm serious, Emmett. I'm worried about you, especially if I'm not here."

He opened his mouth, but she cut him off.

"Please, hear me out." She held up his letter. "Give me that before you send me home."

Thankfully, Emmett closed his mouth, considering before he sat on the edge of the bed, wearing his skepticism like a mask. He picked up the envelope and set it on the bedside beside him, clearly indicating that its contents were still in play.

Jane rushed to fill the tense silence, pacing as she talked. "I know where you're at because I was there once, too. On the verge of a big bust, the Director breathing down your neck. Promises of promotion. Parties. Dreams coming true, it makes the pressure so intense that you throw up every morning."

Emmett's scowl broke, and a knowing haunted his eyes. Jane hit her mark.

"You follow your orders. Most are reasonable, a couple of questionable, but you're a good worker-bee, so you make a compromise—you sell a piece of yourself—telling yourself that it's for the job or the money or you're doing good. But each compromise chips something inside of you." She tapped her chest twice as she turned and marched back.

"All those chips are adding up, and at some point soon, you'll barely hold yourself together. Because there are pieces of yourself that, once broken, can't be repaired the same." An old ache radiated inside Jane's chest, and her eyes clouded. Memories rushed back. Long after hours, sitting in the Director's plush office. He'd poured her a drink, rattled off another pearl of wisdom, and tipped his glass in silent toast. She'd loved those moments with him. And, once upon a time, she might have even loved him.

"I'm telling you all this because it happened to me, Emmett, and I'm seeing it happen to you—the same recipe, even. But maybe we can change the outcome. Make one where you live and don't hate yourself afterward. Plus, as your friend, I gotta tell you— you look like an absolute muff. When's the last time you bathed?"

A welcome smile appeared on Emmett's face, and he exhaled. "I'm not sure, honestly. Three days? And who says I'm your friend?"

Jane stopped near the window. "You did when you came up to my room instead of sending Dawson and his goons to kick me out."

Emmett nodded slowly, then patted the envelope beside him. "For the record, those are orders from the Director. It wasn't my call to send you home."

"It's in your handwriting."

"Ya." He swallowed. "It is."

"That's what it was like for me, too, at the end. I emulated him, jumping at the chance to make him happy."

"I'm not—" Jane pointed at the envelope, and Emmett frowned. "Point taken. You said the end. End of what?"

"My time at the Bureau and my muffed-up relationship with the Director."

"You two were—"

"Close. Or so I thought."

Emmett sat up straighter on the bed, his dark eyes studying her. "What happened, Jane? I've asked around, even called in favors, and I still got nothing. No one knows why you left."

"Why I left . . ." Jane blew out a long breath as she wandered over to the bed. She plopped down beside Emmett. "The short answer is because the Director is an asshole."

Emmett laughed, warming Jane's heart. "The longer answer is I went a long time without listening to my hunches. Just following orders and, because of that, getting further and further from myself. Until I shot and killed a woman who I wasn't even sure was guilty. I barely knew anything about her, actually. She was a ghost and a thief, and I hunted her for months. Honestly, I got lucky finding her in this rinky-dink cantina in New Mexico. Half starved, delirious with fever, and yet she wouldn't submit. I still remember the way she looked at me. Not anger, but pity. Like I was a lost child. I realized later that I was, and if I'd had the courage to challenge bad orders, that woman might still be alive. I wonder all the time what she could have taught me. Maybe Raven Lee doesn't exist."

"That would have made my life considerably more boring," Emmett said and grinned.

"Mine too."

"Back when I asked Raven to help me, you were going to say no until I mentioned the Seed, weren't you?"

"Ya."

"What is it? Why does the Director want it so bad?"

Jane shook her head and moved next to the window. She looked out over the cityscape, marveling at the twinkling lights dancing across the rolling river. "I don't know, but that woman I shot, after I told her I was sorry, she said to me, 'It doesn't matter now. The Seed is safe.'"

"She was protecting it."

Jane nodded. "I was hunting something I didn't know existed. The next day, I stormed into the Director's office and demanded he tell me everything."

"I assume that went poorly," Emmett said.

"A complete disaster. I was mad. I threatened to tell the newspaper. He told me I was out of line. That I was just there to, and I quote, 'follow orders.' I pushed back at that with *a lot* of cussing. He fired me. So, I set his desk on fire." She chuckled at the memory of the leaping flames. "I didn't learn until later he got the better end of the trade. It felt good then, but that began a long, downward spiral of regrettable moments. I didn't cope well."

She felt dizzy as the words gathered in her head. He had to know where her path led so that he wouldn't follow it, but there wasn't a good way to pretty up suicide. "A few months later, I tried to kill myself. I'll spare you the details, but suffice it to say, I didn't see any point in living anymore. I was blacklisted, banned from the job I was born to do, broke, and far from sober. I felt . . . abandoned. Alone. Hopeless, like there was no light to find anymore."

"Damn, Jane," Emmett said, shaking his head. "I'm so sorry."

"Thanks." She paused, watching the water flow silently by. *So peaceful.* "The doctors said I failed my suicide, which isn't the best phrasing. Feeling like a failure got me into that tub to start with. With a lot of work, a couple of good counselors, and time, I started listening to my hunches again—trusting myself. It was hard. Lots of regressions. Next was forgiving myself, and when I did, I discovered, to my shock, that I liked who I was. I could make my own light."

"That's really beautiful, Jane," Emmett said. "Inspiring."

She sighed, her anxiety bubbling in her stomach. It always did that after she was vulnerable. "Thanks."

After a moment, he said, "Why didn't the Director come after you?"

Jane shrugged, turning to face him. "He would've. But"—she paused for dramatic effect—"I had a hostage. My fugitive left me not only regret but a hard drive packed with dirty little secrets as well. She stole it from a secret research facility, and the Director badly wanted it back. I kept it."

"That's a hell of a hunch."

Jane crossed the room, grinning. "It got me here, hasn't it? And you're talking to me right now, so my hunches are on to something." Her smile didn't last long, though, as she leaned down and picked up the envelope with her ticket home. "My hunch is telling me that there is a choice coming soon. One we will both have to make, but you'll be the decider."

"And what choice is that?"

"Who gets the Seed?" She set the envelope in his hand and looked him in the eye. "No pressure."

Emmett expression twisted in confusion and then sadness before he dropped her gaze. Jane replayed her words in her head, hoping they didn't sound too corny, but they felt true. He sighed, rubbing a hand over his stubbly chin. "Shit. I was afraid of that."

Jane felt relieved that she didn't need to spell that out for him.

"I don't know what to do, Jane," Emmett said. "This is all . . . too much, you know?"

"Ya think? Fortunately"—she tapped the envelope in his hand—"you still have options."

Emmett looked down at the envelope and weighed it in his hand. Jane waited, the anticipation screwing tight in her chest, spiking when he looked up at her. He opened his mouth, but a deafening buzzing erupted from the surrounding walls. "Is that—" The light in the room swelled into a blinding glare, and a jagged run of pops followed—light bulbs burst in quick succession. Then, the buzzing stopped as fast as it had come, and the entire room plunged into darkness.

"What the muff?" Jane whispered. She listened but heard nothing—no electric hum, no soft buzz of modern life. The eerie and total silence raised goosebumps on her arms. No lights shone beneath the door, so the hall was out, too. She raced to the window. Beneath a dark blanket of clouds, not a single light shone from the city.

Behind her, the bed creaked, followed by a loud thump.

"Argh! Wall."

"What knocks out an entire city's power?" she asked the darkness.

"Air conditioners? Brownouts."

"This isn't California." Something big had happened. Excitement fluttered in her stomach. Only a force of nature was strong enough to do this. "Muff me . . . It's a clue."

"A clue?" Footfalls drew closer. "It's a blackout."

"But what *caused* the blackout?" Jane looked out over the darkened city and up the hill toward the black patch where the hospital was only minutes before. Apparently, the generators hadn't fully recovered. "Something is going on here, and I'm willing to bet the blackout came from somewhere around that hospital. Everything weird recently points in that direction."

A heavy fist slammed against the hotel door. *BAM! BAM! BAM!*

"Jane!" Dawson bellowed from the hallway, and the door swung open.

Shafts of bright light cut through the darkness. She winced back, shielding her eyes. In her periphery, she saw Emmett. He was watching her, but his expression was unreadable.

Dawson's broad silhouette filled the door frame, back-lit by flashlights. His face hid in their shadows.

Emmett straightened, picking up his mantle as he walked over to Dawson. "What's going on with the lights?"

"A surge. I'm getting more information." Dawson found Jane. "What's going on in here?"

"We're reviewing the case," Emmett lied. Jane was careful to keep her expression neutral.

"I thought she was going home," Dawson growled.

A man with a phone pressed to his ear emerged into the light. Dawson leaned down and listened. "Move to secure the area. Deploy everyone." The man slipped away, and Jane heard boots pounding the carpet down the hall.

"Electric company says it was a blown transformer," Dawson announced.

"That knocked out the entire city?" Jane said. One transformer wouldn't do that.

"Source?" Emmett asked.

"Hill Hospital."

Jane coughed and glanced at Emmett. He gave a small laugh, dumbfounded.

"I'll have my teams scour the area. Make sure it's not our fugitive creating a diversion." Dawson glared at Jane. "And her?"

"She stays," Emmett said, and Jane had to refrain from kissing him. "She's produced results already, and something tells me we're going to need all the help we can get."

Dawson snorted, folding his thick arms. Jane held her breath. Dawson was a loyal dog. "The Director—"

"Is just concerned about his prize. He won't care how we do it, as long as he gets it. Look, he told me that if we deliver the Seed, we both get our due rewards. His words. I don't know what that means for you, but I'll never worry about anything again."

Dawson shifted as the lights behind him stilled. "And if we fail?"

"If we fail"—Emmett shrugged casually—"I'll resign and take full responsibility as lead. You'll be in the clear. It was my call to keep Jane around, not yours."

Jane raised both eyebrows nearly to her pink hairline. Emmett was playing a dangerous game.

Dawson sucked his teeth. "Fine. It's your funeral. I'll report back when I've learned more." His white teeth glowed in the dark. "I'll let you two finish your . . . conversation." He shut the door, snuffing out the light.

They stood in silence, listening to the heavy footsteps recede down the hall. Outside, rain patted against the windows, picking up intensity.

"Don't read too far into this, Jane," Emmett said from the darkness near the door. "We're taking this one more step, then reevaluating, understand?"

"Works for me," she said. "So, what's next?"

"I already secured the Director's approval to access the hospital records. Too much coincidence, and he agreed. Meeting with the hospital is set for Fri—" *THUMP.* "Ow, damn it! Stupid bedpost."

"When?"

"Friday."

"Nicely done." Jane said. The blaze of excitement around the outage calmed, leaving behind a question she needed to ask. "Hey, Emmett? Why didn't you send me home? You could track the power outage without me."

"Ya." Emmett cleared his throat. "I could, but I want you around, Jane. I want you around because I think you might be the only one being honest with me."

"Is that you trusting your hunch?"

"Ya, I guess it is."

"That, my dear Emmett, is the hardest first step."

Chapter 40: A New Host

Wednesday, April 25th, 21:39

"Should be just ahead."

Rory leaned forward from the backseat of Khloe's compact car. He squinted through the rain pummeling the windshield, creating fat, wet *thumps* with each drop. The wipers snapped back and forth, but even at their limit, they couldn't hold back the deluge. He could barely make out the road. Where Portland's glow normally illuminated the horizon, there was nothing but a black fog. And as they wound down the dark, rain-soaked hill, a grim sense of responsibility set in. *Where are all the lights?*

"Please say that wasn't us," Rory said.

Khloe glanced at Rory in the rear-view mirror and gripped the steering wheel tighter. At the edge of the car's headlights, a glistening wall of brambles came into view.

"There!" he shouted over the noise, pointing over Khloe's shoulder, but the headlights didn't show the turnout. The driving rain muddled every detail into a blurry dark green and gray. "Wait, no. A little further, I think." He looked out the rear window. "Or did we miss it?"

"We probably passed it," Khloe said through clenched teeth. "We'll be lucky if I don't drive off the road in this." She shifted in the seat, guiding the car around another curve. "How is she?"

Rory looked down into his lap, where Jacklyn's head rested, her body curled into a ball, face streaked with pain. Despite the three blankets they stole on their way out, her body shivered and spasmed. Rory pressed two fingers against the hot hollow of her neck and felt for a pulse. She was burning up.

"Caro—" Jacklyn moaned and turned away from him.

"Alive," he said, relieved, though he didn't feel confident

reporting much else. Given Jacklyn's lack of a heart, he wasn't even sure how she had a pulse. Some of his patients had a pulse without a working heart, but they all had enormous machines pumping their blood. Jacklyn had a . . . well, he still wasn't quite sure what he'd seen. *A mythstone?* Whatever it was, it kept her alive.

"I feel bad leaving Patrick like that," Khloe said.

Rory's throat thickened, and he forced himself to swallow. "It'll all work out." *Be okay, Pat. Please be okay.*

"They're going to fire him."

"We don't know that."

"Rory . . ."

"Can we just focus on one crisis at a time?" Rory snapped. He had no bandwidth for Patrick right now. He felt like he'd fallen behind again, missed something crucial that would explain what the hell was really going on. Ever since Caroline showed up, the world had picked up speed and rushed by him. It was the same feeling each time he moved foster homes, disoriented, with new rules and new personalities to learn. Whatever Caroline had dragged him into, it was huge, evolving, and every time he thought he got a grasp on it, something changed, hurling him in a new direction. Rory's head throbbed.

"First, Jacklyn needs Caroline. Then . . ." He sighed. "We'll sort the next thing out."

She frowned, but Rory was thankful she didn't push him on how.

Khloe pressed closer to the windshield, squinting as she slowed down. "Up here?"

He shook his head. "I don't know. The rain . . . And I'm normally on a bike. Maybe we should—"

A cloaked figure appeared at the edge of the headlights and stopped in the middle of the road.

"Look out!"

Khloe screamed and slammed on the brakes. Rory flew forward, his nose smashing into the back of the headrest. Stars sparked in his vision as the car swerved and jerked to a stop. Jacklyn groaned.

Outside, the figure swept around the side of the car.

They found us. "Drive!"

Khloe stomped on the pedal. "The car is dead!"

Rory frantically searched the floor and grabbed a plastic ice scraper. *They can't take her!* The passenger door opened, and he brandished the scraper like a sword. "Stay away from her!"

The figure pulled back the heavy hood, and Rory saw Caroline with a tattered strip of black cloth wrapped around her eyes. Rain soaked her white hair in seconds, but she didn't seem to notice anything but Jacklyn. Caroline tenderly cupped her cheek, sighing when Jacklyn stirred.

"I was so worried," Caroline's hushed voice cracked.

Rory, realizing he was still holding the ice scraper, let it fall to the floor.

"Oh, my god . . ." Khloe said and dropped her head against the steering wheel. Both hands trembled. "Please, never do that again."

"Thank you for bringing her back," Caroline said. "I'll take her and—"

"We saw it, Caroline," Rory said, surprised by his own authority. "The mythstone inside Jacklyn."

Caroline stopped. Rain dripped off her nose as she turned to look at him. "How?"

Rory swallowed. "We . . . took a picture."

"You what?" Caroline's tone went cold, sucking the heat from the cab. "How?"

"An MRI," Khloe added.

Caroline's expression darkened as she stroked Jacklyn's forehead. "You fools. You gambled with her life."

Rory winced, knowing she was right, but it wasn't like he had much to go off of. "How were we supposed to know? You don't tell us anything!" Jacklyn moaned again, grimacing, and his next hot words cooled on his tongue, stinging his aching head. "Look, I'm sorry. We didn't mean to hurt her. But she—"

"We are so sorry," Khloe cut in, glaring into the mirror at Rory.

"What?" he said. "We needed—"

"Answers," Caroline finished for him. She leaned in, wrapping her arms beneath Jacklyn. Cold droplets sprinkled his arm, cooling his hot skin. Then she lifted Jacklyn as easily as though she was an infant. Jacklyn curled into Caroline's chest, a hint of a smile coming to both their faces, until Caroline darkened again. "And are you any closer to understanding, Rory Nash?"

"Not really," Rory said sheepishly. He saw Khloe's reflection cringe in the mirror, but remained silent.

"Only more unmoored questions?"

He nodded, not feeling this chastised since church.

Caroline drew in a deep breath and peered down the road behind them. He followed her gaze, suddenly aware of how exposed they were. He scanned the road, expecting to see—he didn't even know. More blood moths? A slobbering monster? Or maybe another mythstone-wielding sorcerer? Anything felt possible.

"That explains the blackout, at least," Caroline said, her demeanor softening. "What's done is done and can't be unmade. From now on, no more gambling without collaboration, understand? We *can't* lose."

Both Khloe and Rory nodded.

"Good, now get to the Cove. Quickly. The roads aren't safe anymore."

———

A purple and gold sunset wrapped around the horizon. Gulls glided on the warm breeze as skinny-legged sandpipers scurried back and forth with the wreck-strewn tide. Like the ribs of great wooden whales, planks jutted out of the sand, and half-buried masts flew an array of tattered flags. The foaming tide rolled in and out, carrying lengths of rope, tattered rigging, and fragments of barrels. Another ship, a strange, low, angular design Rory had never seen before, had smashed itself on the black rocks beneath the cliff. Its popping timbers echoed off the stone. Rory judged a storm had come to the Cove, and part of him wondered if that was his fault, too.

He followed Caroline toward the vast green tent tucked in the cliff's shadow—half the structure had fallen, lying in a sandy mound beneath broken posts. The whole way, she cradled Jacklyn, whispering something he couldn't make out. When the cave came into view, she called ahead in that melodic tongue, and golems, sprouting healthy turquoise mushrooms, emerged from beneath the sand and shook off the grit. Without breaking stride and no further words, Caroline disappeared inside her tattered home.

Rory wasn't sure what to do. *I guess we wait.*

Golems dragged a large cast iron cauldron from the cave and struggled to get it hanging over a non-existent fire. Rory volunteered to help, glad to have a job to distract him as he sorted through the clutter in his mind. He sent golems to gather wood. A couple brought back soaked planks, but enough returned with something dry that Rory got the fire going. Flames crackling, the golems busied themselves with preparing a white broth that smelled of onion and rubber. Rory sat, hands up to the heat, as he stared into the glowing coals. His mind went elsewhere, exploring the mountain of questions he'd been saving.

He didn't get far before a loud clatter jarred him. Frustrated clicks followed, and he looked up to find Khloe peering at two overloaded grocery carts pushed by bickering golems. Each cart contained a random assortment of blankets, books, and bright plastic toys. She caught him watching her, and he quickly poked the fire.

"When will we know about Conner?" she asked. Her voice was cold—exhausted.

"I don't know." He shrugged. "Tommy took a little while. He could already be awake."

"I hope so," Khloe said, and Rory could hear the part unsaid. *To make this worth it.*

Caroline reemerged from the tent, and Khloe dropped off. The Wyth had discarded the cloak in favor of a breezy rainbow dress speckled with what looked like blood. She immediately went over to the carts and heaved out a large duffel bag that clanked noisily as it moved. She set it down carefully next to the fire and unzipped it. Pouches, tubes, and jars filled the bag, each with labels written in fine cursive.

After selecting a few different vials, Caroline turned to Khloe. "Listen carefully. This is an ancient recipe for a regeneration tonic. This recipe has saved many Wythian lives, but it can be toxic when improperly prepared. May I show you?"

Khloe blinked, surprise written across her face at suddenly getting a lesson, but she nodded anyway and kneeled down.

Caroline upended a large leather pouch into her hand. Five tiny ice-blue mushrooms fell into her palm. "These are Iceheads. Boil these first. They take the longest. You'll find them in underground ice lakes. They like the little pools near the frosted stone. Don't worry about refrigerating them; they keep much longer than you think."

Khloe nodded, then quickly pulled her small notepad from her pocket.

"How is she?" Rory asked. He sounded more exhausted than he expected.

"That is a lazy question." Without looking up, Caroline added the Iceheads into the cauldron, turning the broth ivory white. "It demonstrates little comprehension."

Rory felt his cheeks burn. "I'm not in the mood for riddles."

Caroline drew a long wooden spoon from her bag.

Rory's temper flared. "Don't ignore me!" He stood, but didn't remember standing.

Caroline gave him one flat look. "Patience, Rory. Clarity follows patience." Her tone was tight, a perfectly manicured anger that drove Rory's from him. He remembered Caroline cutting down golems, practiced and precise. He swallowed, taking his seat.

"Sorry."

Caroline dipped her chin in something like acceptance and turned back to Khloe, whose eyes moved between the two warily. Caroline held up a vial of bright orange liquid. "This is Knave's Tears. Collect them only on paydays. You'll want them fresh and happy. Just a drop will do." She added it to the bubbling white broth, and a cloud of noxious, tarry vapor rose, stinging Rory's nostrils and eyes. He coughed, waving away the cloud.

Caroline reached for another pouch, removing a clear bag with a coarse tan powder. "This is ground Cilid carapace. Don't go looking for more. It's too dangerous. For that reason, you must never waste a grain." She withdrew a pinch and counted out ten grains into the cauldron. A puff of smoke coiled off the bubbling surface with each grain, and the broth turned a vibrant yellow. She stirred the yellow soup without a word until she lifted the spoon to her lips and sipped. "Needs another Icehead." She tipped the leather pouch, but nothing came out. "Bother," she muttered and returned the pouch, stirring the pot slowly. The sickly contents bubbled and popped.

"You saw a mythstone?" Caroline asked, a note of curiosity in her voice. "On this MRI?"

"We thought so," Khloe said. "Is it?"

"We believe so, too."

"She's a Merged then?" Rory said, the word still feeling odd in his mouth, like a new language he was still learning the grammar for.

"Yes and no."

Rory stifled a sigh. *So much for clarity.*

"You called the Merged abominations," Khloe said.

"*They* are. Those who fuse for greed will always be," Caroline said plainly. "Jacklyn did not. She did it for . . . duty. For all of us." She tapped her spoon against the cauldron's edge. *Thung-thung.* She set the spoon aside and let the broth bubble. Caroline lifted her hand, and three long fingers danced across her mythstone necklace, leaving each stone glowing blue, green, and then yellow in turn before they faded.

"I told you there are four types of mythstone, and that was only partially true. We believe there is a fifth, though no one has ever seen it. The few passages from the Shepherd's Stones we have translated refer to it as the Seed. It is a unique Aspect. And, according to those same records, very dangerous."

Khloe jotted down another note. "Jacklyn has this . . . Seed inside her?"

Caroline nodded, breaking a stick and feeding it into the fire, her expression grim.

Rory blinked. Something didn't compute. "But . . . it heals

people too, so it can't be all bad—right?"

Caroline considered him for a moment. "Rid yourself of that false dichotomy, Rory. The Seed is good in the sense that it heals, but nothing is free, so your immediate question that follows must be . . ."

"What does it cost?" Khloe said.

Caroline turned, and Rory felt the full weight of her attention from beneath her blindfold. "Once bonded, with no guarantee of success. The Seed makes room."

"Makes room?" He pictured the Seed inside of Jacklyn, its white body filling her cardiac notch. "The heart. It destroys the heart?"

"The Merged have no hearts. No souls. They have traded them for a share of the Aspects' power."

"Oh my god." Khloe stopped writing and shot a worried look at Rory. *So much for keeping things simple.*

"That . . ." Rory forgot the next word. The implications overwhelmed him with yet more questions, so many they were getting hard to keep straight. So much was still missing that he wondered if there was such a thing as wonder fatigue. He'd felt Jacklyn's inexplicable pulse himself. Yet, he felt an eagerness. Despite the gnawing fear, finally knowing energized Rory. It felt good, light. He settled for a breath, then another. *One crisis at a time.*

A log tipped over, throwing up a burst of orange embers. Caroline held her long hair back before leaning down and sniffing the purple-hued steam. "Nearly done." She glanced over at Khloe and smiled. "You can tell by the tang."

"Oh, uh, ya. Tang . . ." Khloe muttered, turned the page, and kept writing.

Rory considered a dozen different questions. Caroline seemed in a giving mood, and he wanted to capitalize while he could. But as he tried to grab just one question to ask, they all escaped him like a school of spooked fish.

Over the fire, Caroline aimed her spoon at Khloe, then at Rory. "You two are now a part of a minuscule membership of privileged knowledge. Do you both understand? There are severe consequences to endangering the Seed."

They both nodded, and Rory felt as though there was a threat veiled in her words.

"Good. Now, Khloe, pay attention. You only want the cream off the top. The rest is toxic. Take your time." Carefully, Caroline skimmed her spoon over the top, gathering the slimy layer that congealed on top. Without spilling a drop, Caroline carefully spooned the yellow goo into the first vial. She popped a stopper in before starting on the second. When she stoppered the fifth and final one, she turned to Rory. "Now that you've calmed, would you like to try your question again?"

It took Rory a second to realize what she meant. *Jacklyn.* Ignoring her patronizing tone, Rory reminded himself of an old nursing trick when dealing with uncooperative families: keep it about the patient. "Is Jacklyn going to be okay? She stopped breathing. I had to do chest compressions."

The fire crackled, and Rory suspected the worst until Caroline set down the spoon next to her vials and folded her hands. "She'll have a tough couple of days, but she'll live."

"Thank goodness," Rory said, feeling dizzy with relief.

"But," Caroline continued, "her body is broken. She only has . . . she only has a few days left." The last words barely made it out before Caroline folded over and pressed both palms into her eyes. Her body convulsed, wracked with sobs, the deep, soulful bawl that only came from realizing a long-held fear. Her visage of the consummate protector broke into something far more human. He knew the dour expression she wore, the sound of that cry. Many loved ones made it when the hospice team knocked on their door. Like them, Caroline wasn't ready to say goodbye. Few people ever were.

Jacklyn can't die . . . He didn't want it to be true, not after they'd come so far. It felt unfair.

"I'm so sorry." Khloe wrapped her arms around the taller woman, propping her up. Caroline leaned against her, burying her face in Khloe's shoulder as she cried.

Rory bowed his head as a fresh gust sent orange embers twirling through the air. "That's . . . ah, geez," he said, feeling equal parts rude and stupid. "I'm sorry. Jacklyn is . . . a hero. We shouldn't have . . ." He trailed off. It felt like way too little, way too late.

Caroline's sobs slowed, then subsided, leaving her blindfold soaked with two dark circles. "Thank you." She sniffed. "Both of you. And it's not your fault. Nor is it mine." She let out a ragged breath before straightening and soothing her expression. Within seconds, the terrified lover receded, replaced again by the warrior witch. "Ends are always, and have always, been inevitable. And hard. This one comes sooner than my liking."

What happens to the miracles? No Jacklyn meant no more healing. It would be back to the same hopeless cases he faced before he chased his wisp. He pictured the tear-soaked stairwell, that boyfriend, and the look on Octavia's gray face. His heart revolted. *I won't go back.* No, it was more than that. *I can't go back.*

Caroline's sigh drew him back to the present. Her expression was far off. "I'm going to tell you something now, something Jacklyn won't appreciate, but given our change in circumstance, I hope she'll understand. We call the one who carries the Seed within them the Host. It is the Host's primary duty to ensure that the Seed remains contained and safe. This is a burdensome assignment, one only a *qualified* candidate has any hope of accomplishing. Vetting is vital because many Hosts have faulted, but none yet have failed."

If not prepared. A distant alarm went off in Rory's thoughts, and an idea clicked into place. *A qualified candidate.* "Wait," he said. "Wait. That means . . ." He stopped to double-check. "That means you need a new Host, someone new to carry the Seed."

Khloe's eyes widened. "Oh! Of course."

Despite the severity of the topic, Caroline nodded enthusiastically. "Exactly! Very good, Rory. But who?"

Rory puffed up, and as he basked in his cleverness, a thrill shot through him, catching him off-guard. *Could . . . I be the Host?* For a fleeting moment, he pictured himself, hand extended and reviving one child after another. Everyone smiled. Just as quickly as it had come, a deep ache shattered the image. His throat tightened as images flooded him like a ghostly procession: sitting alone during chemotherapy, watching other kids play with their parents, Octavia draped in a white cloth. His failures, one by one, strangled him, and he felt nauseous again.

How could I ever carry such a burden? I'm barely holding my shit together. The ache in his chest sharpened into a white-hot needle, piercing his heart, as the idea of being Host felt more and more outrageous. *Can't be me, but the next Host will need help.* He still needed to be involved. There was no unseeing what he'd seen, nor could he walk away, even if Jacklyn was gone. *I'll think of something.*

"Rory?" Caroline's voice broke his swimming thoughts. He stared at the crackling fire, dark brown eyes wide and unblinking. His heart pounded intensely, and Rory thought it might burst from his chest. *What is going on with me?*

"What did you say?" Khloe watched him, pen at the ready. "You mumbled something."

"Uh, what?" *I did?* He chewed his cheek. *Think of something!* "There . . . must be, uh, selection criteria for a Host." He danced around the question.

Caroline considered. "That is true—unofficially, at least. I suppose resilience is chief among them. Confidence: a Host

443

must be decisive but curious enough to never settle. The Host's life is mobile. What else . . . young? But that isn't mandatory. Younger minds are more open, and it is easier for them to understand both sides of their power—as a gift and curse."

Khloe started writing again.

A gift and a curse? Rory found a smaller stick and poked at the fire, turning the paradox over in his head. The more he thought, the more the fear rose. He was a nurse and knew a terrible assignment when he heard one. *I'm glad it's not me. Maybe I can be a Counselor?* If Caroline was describing anyone here, it was—

"Sounds like Khloe should be the next Host," Rory said.

Khloe smiled quickly, but it retreated as the gravity of the compliment sank in.

"I'm afraid not," Caroline said.

"Oh, why not?" Khloe tried to cover her hurt with a laugh.

"Because, my dear Seeker, I ask of you another role. You might be the last Wyth, and our only hope of protecting the Seed is to have Wyth guardians who are proficient in casting."

"Re . . . really? So, a Counselor like you? I'll cast?"

Caroline nodded, and Khloe gave a small "hoo," jotting down a note.

"When can we start?"

Rory stifled a sigh. *Guess not.*

His thoughts drifted back to how this whole thing had started. It wasn't Khloe that healed Tommy. He'd brought Jacklyn. He took that first risk. He drank that nasty purple potion. That had to count for something. Everyone had a role. The thought lifted his spirits. *Someone has to find a candidate. No*, he mused. *Not just a candidate. The right candidate.* He ran through the list of his people in his head. Megan, Patrick, and Bell—all were great people, but he doubted they met the requirements. And why bring Rory in when they could have gone straight to them? No, Rory's shortlist wouldn't cut it. *Then whom?*

When he looked up, Caroline was watching him behind her blindfold. She tilted her head to the side as though waiting. *Am I supposed to say something?*

"We can, uh . . . stick to the plan?" Rory's confidence grew as the idea congealed in his head. He ticked off Caroline's criteria. "Resilient, curious, confident. It'll be the same as Tommy and Conner, but this time, we're looking for a permanent Host. And we can help them after, protect them . . . guide them, you know?"

"So, a patient?" Khloe asked cautiously.

Caroline's eyebrow raised, and then she sighed loudly. Rory caught Khloe's eye, and she shrugged before returning to her notes. *Did I miss something?*

Caroline rose abruptly, yellow vials in hand. "I must see to Jacklyn."

Stick to the plan. "I'm . . . I'm supposed to be off for the next couple of days. Maybe I can volunteer to pick up an extra shift or two. I'll check out the cardiac kids first and then see if—"

"That feels wrong," Khloe said, finishing a note.

Wrong? What? "How?" Rory turned. "Caroline said we can't save Jacklyn. But we can contain the Seed and save another kid at the same time."

Khloe looked at Rory as though he'd grown fangs. "Jacklyn is going to die. Doesn't that bother you?"

Rory sighed, looking to Caroline for help, but the older woman raised an eyebrow at him as though repeating the question. "Of course it does, but that's out of our hands. But Khloe, go with me here. We find a new Host, and then we help *them* help others. Don't you see? We keep this miracle train going! This is what you've been dreaming about. It's right here, and we get to be part of it."

"But we don't know enough!" Khloe said. "And what about the patient? They're a kid! Would this be what they want? Or are we condemning them—"

"Condemning?" Rory said in disbelief. "It's not . . . It's better than the alternative!" Both Khloe and Caroline stopped and stared at him, and he quickly cleared his throat and lowered his voice. "All I'm saying is we can't quit now, not when we can help so many."

"I don't want to see our patients die either, Rory, but some people would rather die than have their heart, what? Devoured?"

Caroline shrugged, so Khloe pushed on. "After that, they have to live with a massive responsibility they didn't choose!"

She doesn't get it. Rory's frustration boiled up. Didn't she hear Caroline? They didn't have time to waste. *Maybe she's not cut out to be a Counselor.*

"How about this?" Khloe pressed on. "Let me run some tests and do a little research. Maybe I can figure out a new angle before we do something rash. Gene sequencing has come a long way; it might reveal something. If I had a little of Jacklyn's blood."

Blood work? It felt too slow. "Hold on."

Caroline produced a corked glass vial filled half-full with dark red blood.

"It's fresh," she said. "I thought you might ask."

"What?" Rory asked, stunned.

Khloe accepted it. "Thank you? How did—"

"A hunch."

"Wait." They needed to discuss this. "The Broken Star attacked this place yesterday. And what if the perfect candidate sits in the unit right now? We need to be ready to go. We can't wait for

446

some tests."

"The Cove will protect us," Caroline replied calmly, peering out over the wrecked beach. "It will hold long enough."

Khloe cut in, clearly annoyed. "Three days, minimum. And I'll remind you, Rory, you aren't the only one trying to help or taking a risk. We need to be a team."

"A lot can happen in—" Rory started, but Caroline cut him off.

"Three days. Jacklyn will need that long to recover," Caroline said with a note of finality. They both looked at Rory. What choice did he really have? He was outnumbered.

"Fine, but I'm scouting until we have a better plan."

"As long as it's just *scouting*," Khloe said, scowling. She closed her notebook, obviously mad at him. While he couldn't blame her, she was also elbowing him out of the decision-making process. *Caroline just used me to get to her.*

"Agreed," Caroline said. "Now, if you'll excuse me." She disappeared into the tent.

Seeing their invitation to leave, he stood and offered his hand to Khloe, but she brushed by him and marched up the beach without a second glance back. Really? It felt like everyone had been walking away from him recently.

He shook his head and turned to the sea, letting the breeze cool his naked face. The sun split the horizon in golden light, and Rory sucked in a salty breath and held it.

This plan wouldn't work—the Broken Star was too close. Caroline was mourning, and Khloe—well, she wanted her big discovery. Both their judgments were compromised. But let her have her tests and the Counseling. Rory had another job now. *I have to find the next Host.*

When he breathed out, the tension in his neck eased. *This is why they came to me.* He savored the sunrise and followed Khloe up the beach.

It's up to me to save the world.

Chapter 41: Healing Hands

Thursday, April 26th

Rory barely remembered the silent drive home, his failed attempt at conversation, or when his head hit the pillow. It was a beautiful morning at the Cove but past midnight in the real world, which jarred Rory's sense of time worse than working the night shift. *The real world.* What was real? *Why is real so exhausting?* Rory's brain was too numb to be certain of anything except his desperate need for rest.

He woke almost twelve hours later and cursed himself for oversleeping. *Set an alarm, stupid.* Getting back on the night-shift clock meant he could expect a couple of groggy shifts as his body adjusted. *Too late now.*

He discovered nineteen missed texts waiting on his phone, most from the nurses wishing him well with suggested remedies and poop jokes. Reading Megan's messages, guilt overwhelmed his laughter.

Hope your toilet's okay. Feel better! Received at 20:45.

His lie had worked, but he hated leaving them short. Based on her next few messages, though, the night wasn't just busy but miraculous.

BTW, something weird is going on in Room 10. Received at 20:48.

The power went out! Received at 20:52.

Conner woke up!!! Can you believe this happened again?!! Received 21:07.

"Oh . . . shit . . ." Rory said and plopped down on the couch, stunned. *We did it again.* Reading Megan's text over and over, a gush of pride warmed him, though it quickly cooled when he thought of Jacklyn. *The Seed.* It needed a Host. And she was going to die no matter what he did. Their accomplishment suddenly tasted bittersweet.

He typed out an appropriately shocked response and hit send with a smile emoji.

Switching on the news, he found that Conner's recovery had leaked. A red banner read: *SENATOR'S SON WAKES UP. SECOND MIRACLE IN PORTLAND, OREGON.*

The hastily shot cell phone footage showed Conner's arms wrapped around his weeping mother and father from his hospital bed. Rory cried, too. Some of the staff around the room had hands on their heads, others over their mouths, and he wanted to bask in that moment, the moment he helped make. But then the video cut back to the anchor, and the news marched on.

"Next up, more accusations of child abuse aimed at—" *MUTE.*

Rory dropped the remote and picked up his laptop. He needed details.

Who found him? What were his vitals? How does he feel?

He tried calling Khloe, hoping to celebrate, but got her voicemail. She didn't reply to his texts, either. He consoled himself by remembering their agreement. *She's probably working late. Or doing some research.* She wasn't one to let a little thing like sleep stop her hunt for answers.

Conner's story triggered a renewed interest in Tommy. The internet had exploded with speculation about the boys' pasts and trying to find a connection between them beyond Hill Hospital. Rory enjoyed reading the more extravagant theories. Watching the news, he counted the word "unexplainable" five times in one breathless monologue, and another anchor stopped short of extraterrestrial involvement. Most, though, barely mentioned the mysterious city-wide power outage, dismissing it as a faulty transformer and an aging power grid. A coincidence, nothing more.

Good. Rory hoped that meant less heat on Patrick. If they were blaming a transformer, then they couldn't blame him, right? Rory felt the tug of guilt but pushed it aside—the Seed was everything now. If they didn't find a new Host soon, it wouldn't matter how many patients they healed because they'd all be dead—probably. No one seemed to know for sure. He shook his head, feeling himself drift. *One crisis at a time.*

For now, he only had time for a patch job. Smooth things over with Patrick until he had more time. After that, they'd talk it out, and things would go back to normal. That's what they always did. He typed out a quick text, asking Patrick when they could meet up and talk. He added another smiley face.

———

The next afternoon, Khloe messaged him back, letting him know she'd slept at the hospital after sending off a battery of tests on "you know who." She didn't go into any further detail and finished with *Let's talk in a couple days after I know more. Be patient.*

Later, while Rory read about possible super serums used on Tommy and Conner, his phone rang: *Patrick.*

He picked up. "Hey! I'm happy you called-."

A distant and muffled voice replied, and he couldn't make out the words. It sounded angry. Then another, calmer, almost sad. Ana's? It was hard to tell. Who was yelling? He hung up and sent Patrick a quick text about needing to change his password.

After another hour, he called, but after one ring, he got Patrick's voicemail.

"Hey, uh. I'm sorry about how everything went down. And . . . and . . . I wouldn't have left if it wasn't so important. I understand if you're mad, I get it, but . . . call me, yeah? I want to make it up to you. Okay. Uh, call me." Hanging up, Rory returned to his stories.

An hour later, his phone rang, jolting him. He checked the screen, hopeful, but it was Antoni. Another sick call had left the unit short-staffed, and they needed help. Ignoring his exhausted body, he said he was ready to go, lying to himself that he'd worked on fewer hours of sleep before. He agreed to come in, and Antoni thanked him.

"No big deal. See you soon."

Rory ended the call and found Sneaks watching him, eyes narrowed, with her orange tail flicking back and forth.

"Don't look at me like that," Rory said. "I'm just going."

———

Friday, April 27th, 18:55

Rory was late.

He hadn't counted on the traffic jam of network vans clogging the Hill's twisting, narrow roadways. Even on his bike, reaching the staff entrance took him twice as long. As he worked his way through the crowd, someone with a microphone must have spotted his badge, and the swarm descended.

"Any update on Conner?!"

"How's the mood on the unit?!"

"Did you see him wake up?!"

Someone bumped him with a recorder, and he blinked through the bright lights. "No comment," he said, but speaking made it worse, throwing more chum into the water. The faces and lenses pressed in tighter, stealing his air.

Then he saw Officer Kyle barging through the crowd.

". . . harassing staff!"

The reporters retreated, and Rory ducked behind the burly security guard through the doors marked Employees Only. Only after the doors slid shut was he able to breathe.

"Thanks," Rory said, feeling his heartbeat recover.

"Of course, sir." Kyle checked his watch. "Shift-change in two minutes."

18:58.

Breaking into a run, his messenger bag bouncing ridiculously, Rory shouted another thanks over his shoulder.

———

He opened the report room door slowly, breathing hard, but only two minutes late. For a moment, he thought he might slip in unnoticed, but the door creaked. Bell, from the head of the massive conference table that filled the small room, stopped mid-sentence. All the PICU nurses turned and looked at him. He gave an embarrassed wave. "Sorry."

Bell cleared her throat, looked at the big clock on the wall, and returned to her sheet. She paused. "Isn't this your night off?"

"It was," he mumbled, shifting his bag in front of him. "But I didn't want to miss all the fun."

A soft laugh made its way around the table.

"Feeling better?" Bell asked.

Rory nodded. "Just a twenty-four-hour bug."

She gestured with her sheet for him to take a seat. He spotted Megan, who patted the chair next to her. He took it, his weary legs collapsing.

"Thanks."

Megan leaned over as Bell resumed assignments. "The reporters out there are crazy, right?"

He shook his head, dabbing the sweat off his brow. "Yeah, and Conner?" he whispered. "And the power? It was all over the news."

"Did you hear what happened?"

Oh, no. Rory smoothed his expression to casual indifference. "No, what?"

"I heard from my friend in maintenance that one of the MRI techs tried running Magus's new machine before they had finished inspecting it. Took down the entire grid. Completely fried a five-million-dollar machine. Poor guy got fired."

Rory's blood froze. *Oh no.*

Megan continued. "I heard from another friend in admin that they were just going to suspend him, but Magus threw a fit. Apparently, you could hear his yelling over the speakerphone from down the hall."

Fired? "Did the tech . . . say anything?"

"I'm not sure, but it's being investigated. With that and Tommy and now Conner, dang, this place is an epicenter right now."

Rory's mind raced. He needed to do something. He needed to talk to Patrick. He needed to find a new Host. He needed . . . *One crisis at a time.* "This'll all blow over."

She shrugged. "I don't know. It's kinda fun."

Rory forced a smile. "A blast."

Bell cleared her throat and peered over the top of her glasses at them.

"Sorry," Rory and Megan said in unison.

"Megan," Bell said, "you'll be in rooms fifteen and sixteen tonight. No change on fifteen, but sixteen started dialysis today."

Megan groaned. "Ugh, sixteen." Bell raised an eyebrow, signaling Megan to continue. "No, it's fine. I took care of them during their last admission, too. It's just . . . Dad is a bit of a creep. He keeps talking about hard baseballs and referring to his bats."

"Want me to set him straight?" A ripple of knowing laughter carried over the room. Rory saw what Bell was doing. She'd just used an old trick that took him a long two years to spot. He asked her about it, and she fessed up, saying, "Every shift needs to start and end with a laugh. One from us—for us." A little self-love.

"Hold off on the hellfire for now." Megan said. "Hopefully, Mom is here tonight instead."

Bell chuckled and continued down the list.

Megan leaned in again, undeterred by Bell's warning. "Dude, fifteen is a serious FLK. Come check him out."

"An FLK?"

"How have I not said this to you?"

"I don't actually listen," Rory said.

Megan scowled at him. "You and Owen both. FLK. Funny-looking kid."

Rory laughed into the back of his hand. "That's terrible."

"Yeah, but true. Poor little guy looks like a Picasso."

"Rory," Bell said.

Rory sat up. "Yes, ma'am."

"Jenny is back. We put her in thirteen. She has another case of junky lungs and is here for more antibiotics."

Jenny? Rory wasn't sure how the Seed worked, but he guessed it kept its Host healthy. How else would Jacklyn live so long? *But what about the mind?* Rory needed a candidate who they could teach and knew the basics already. Jenny was sweet, but delayed and unpredictable. *Can the Seed mend genes?* He wasn't sure. Healing those felt bigger than brains. *A maybe, for now.*

"You'll also have four," Bell added. "Sorry for splitting you across the unit, but the family requested you."

"They can do that?" Megan asked.

"They can if they give enough money to the hospital," Bell said,

455

shrugging. "The kid came in a couple of hours ago. A hem-onc case. She spiked a fever and has an altered mental status. Clawed the paramedic on the way in. They're worried about relapse. Possible pressure on the brain. Labs are out already, and she is *not* a fan of the hospital. They had to sedate her for the ride in, but the surgeon, I bet you can guess who, is weaning her for an un-sedated neuro-exam. Keep on your toes in there."

"I will," Rory said, intrigued. He leaned over Megan's shoulder to read the bed report.

Room 4: *Oates, T.*

He read the name again.

Tracy.

He inhaled sharply. *She's perfect!*

They could use her family's connections to research how best to support her as Host. The Oates Foundation already funded half of their hospital's research. If everything went well, maybe the Wyth wouldn't have to stay in hiding anymore. With Tracy, the Seed would be safe behind considerable defenses. And they had a rapport. He would be there to help her every step of the way. *This is it!*

Khloe's voice floated into his head. *Slow down, Rory,* she'd say. *Patience.* Chewing his cheek, he rolled his eyes at the cautious specter but found . . . she was right. He might only get one shot at selling this idea, so he had to do it right.

"One more announcement." Bell snapped Rory back into the conference room, and a broad smile spread across her face. "We have the results of the Healing Hand Award. A unit-wide vote selected our nurse of the year, and it was a close one."

Rory glanced over at Megan, who gripped her thighs. He reached over and took her hand, squeezing it.

"This year's winner . . ." Bell said.

"Megan Minder," Rory whispered. She bit her lip.

"For the first time. Let's congratulate . . ."

She deserves it.

"Rory Nash for an inspiring year of patient care." Bell started clapping, waving her sheet back and forth.

Rory's stomach dropped. *But . . . it's supposed to be Megan.*

Megan's hand went slack in his as everyone else turned and applauded. She withdrew, pained. The clock chimed three times, reading 19:10. As one, the nurses rose, gathering their bags and thermoses, and filed out toward the front lines.

"Meg," Rory said. He needed to make her understand that this wasn't his fault. "I voted for you."

"Congratulations, Rory," Megan said without looking at him. "Really, you earned it!"

She hefted her tote over a shoulder and supported her belly. "I gotta go get a report."

"Wait. Meg," he said weakly, but she slid into the shuffling line of nurses heading out the door.

I voted for you.

"The banquet will be next month," Bell said, stepping up beside him. She held a shining pin—a tiny golden hand. She took his badge and punched the pin through the top-right corner. After popping the back on, she stepped back, observing her work. "Suits you. Wonderful job, Rory. I'm very proud of you. You've come a long way since that doe-eyed baby nurse."

"Thanks, Bell," he replied numbly. He looked over her shoulder to the door, where Megan watched. She turned away and shuffled down the hall.

"You don't sound happy," Bell said.

He looked down at his badge and studied the tiny award. The

small wash of pride did little to banish his aching stomach. "It should have been Megan," he said. "She's the one who . . . I can barely get to work on time. Can I give this to her?"

Bell grinned up at him and handed him a blank sheet of paper. "That's why you won, hun. Megan will understand. Sometimes, a little hurt is what we need to grow. To get better."

Rory nodded, thinking of an adage taught at every nursing school: *patient safety is number one*. It was the backbone of their profession, but there were exceptions. That was the unofficial second lesson. Sometimes, causing pain is the only way to save a life. *Maybe a little hurt is okay?*

"Don't you worry," Bell said, gathering Rory's attention. "You two are close and will be thick as thieves by midweek."

"You're sure about that?"

"Sure as I shit." Bell grinned.

"Sure as you—" A laugh rose out of Rory.

"Start and end, Rory." Bell patted him on the arm. "It keeps us going."

Chapter 42: Relapse

Friday, April 27th, 19:15

Rory slipped into Room 4 and walked to the sink to wash his hands. He paused before flipping on the hot water and turned. "Mr. Oates, I'm so sorry about Tracy."

Mr. Oates looked up from the bedside. His sharp brown eyes matched his suit and didn't carry the same brightness they had at the waterfront. His gray hair was roughly kempt, as if brushed over quickly by hands and water. He kissed Tracy's forehead. Rory noted his skin had more color than the sheets, but as poor as the old man looked, his granddaughter fared worse. Tracy was flushed red and blotchy, with a sweat-slicked and tangled mane of brown hair. Rory didn't need to be a nurse to see that she looked septic, but her vitals told him the rest of the story. With her tumor looking this bad, she had maybe a week.

"Mr. Nash, Rory," Mr. Oates said without taking his eyes off Tracy. "I'm glad we have you tonight. She would be happy you're here." He looked up and sighed. "She would have told you that your toilet paper strategy worked wonderfully—until today, at least." He wiped a sweaty strand from her face.

"We'll get her better, Mr. Oates. I'll be with you all night."

When he met his eyes, Rory saw a shine of hope beneath his bushy brows. The shine vanished, stealing his smile with it. Mr. Oates turned back to Tracy and adjusted her blanket. "May I tell you a story? One about Tracy? You've seen her . . . persistence in action. I think you'll appreciate it."

Rory pulled a paper towel and dried his hands. "Absolutely."

"Just before Tracy's cancer diagnosis, she was five, mind you. And in a puppy phase. Everything was dogs. Sheets, backpacks, pajamas, all of it. The nannies told me often she asked for one, but I refused. Well, a few weeks before her fatigue started, I

459

learned she'd talked our kitchen staff into setting food aside for a stray she snuck home." Mr. Oates smiled. "Tracy has always been a strong negotiator."

Rory chuckled. "She's a tough kid." He tossed his wet towel in the trash and went about his initial assessment.

Mr. Oates shook his head, grinning. "I found her in the greenhouse one afternoon, sneaking that skinny thing some lunchmeat. It was one sorry dog—mange, a broken tooth, and one eye. Tracy wanted to help it, but I said no and thought that was the end. But she would not give up. All day, she talked about that dog, how it brought her sticks and chased the birds. On and on, she drove me mad."

Writing her vitals into her chart, Rory laughed. "She badgered you into it."

"Badgered? Ha, that would have been civil. She plagued me with guilt. But yes, I caved by the next afternoon, but with strict conditions. She had to take care of its . . . business. I would have none of it. And she would feed it and keep it clean. Can you guess how she did?"

"Hmm." Rory stroked his chin dramatically. "She forgot?" He inspected the bags of clear IV fluid hanging beside Tracy's bed and jotted down the rates to double-check with the orders.

"That's what I would have said too, but that dog made a miraculous recovery. Tracy fed her by hand, read her stories, and swindled treats and toys from me. She brought her back to life; that mangy dog is still part of our family. Probably curled up on my slippers back home."

Sounds like Sneaks, Rory thought. He traced the infusion lines down to Tracy's arm and inspected the catheter site through a transparent dressing. *Clean, dry, and intact.*

Mr. Oates waved his hand dismissively. "My point. After she got sick, that mangy stray gave me the idea for the Oates Children's Foundation. Together, those two taught me how one more chance can make all the difference."

One more chance. "Tracy is pretty special," he said calmly, but he was bursting inside. *She's perfect!* Khloe's specter returned, preaching patience, but he dismissed it. *If Tracy could choose the Seed, she would!* Recovery and superpowers would be a dream come true.

Mr. Oates brushed Tracy's hair again and rocked back in his chair. "They're alike, the dog and her. They're both survivors, but I'm just . . . I'm so worried that Tracy has already had her second chance."

Looking down at her fragile body, Rory resisted the urge to touch his scar down the base of his neck. He understood. The threat of relapse never went away. Sometimes, as he fell asleep, Rory would wonder if he was doing enough with his second chance—he had to make it count. There were no guarantees of a third.

Mr. Oates went quiet, turning away to clear his throat. He wiped his eyes. "Sorry about that."

"Not at all, sir," Rory said. "This is scary stuff."

Mr. Oates nodded before adjusting Tracy's pillow. "I'm told operating will kill her, but I imagine the surgeons will come in shortly to tell me that's her only chance. The chaplain said to pray, and I asked him to which department." The old man cracked a sly grin. "There are so many consults and specialists, and you hope one will have a solution. Cardiology, nephrology, neurology, so many ologies have all come through, but left nothing but theories and apologies." He drew out a small black book with a gold-dipped spine. "It's time to call on the angels, I think." He straightened the rosary draped over her pillow. "I hope they hurry."

"They're coming, sir," Rory said, wanting so badly to tell him he knew where to find one. "When Tracy wakes, we'll talk about being brave."

461

"You're a good one," Mr. Oates said. "Thank you."

A knock came at the door, and Rory glanced over to see a crowd standing outside the room.

"I'll be right back with water," Rory said. "I'm guessing you haven't been eating or drinking much."

Mr. Oates nodded, exhaustion plain in his posture. "Water. Please."

"And crackers," Rory added, stepping out into the hall. He slid the glass door shut behind him, examining the semi-circle of white-coated residents surrounding Dr. Magus, each with a laptop in hand, busily typing and obscuring the small chief surgeon.

Only one resident was using a notepad and pencil. Khloe. Even annoyed with her, Rory still found her lovely. She stood up straight, making quick marks with her pencil. Her clenched jaw and dark rings under her eyes made her scowl all the deeper, and Rory wondered just how hot she'd been burning the midnight oil.

"Once the patient is normothermic and we have the swelling controlled, we must get her into the OR," Magus droned from the center of the laptops. "If she deteriorates much further, we could run out of time. With luck, this round of antibiotics and steroids will do the trick, and we can proceed this weekend. Questions?" He barely paused. "Good."

Rory checked the clock, surprised to see Magus staying late again. But it didn't take him long to remember why. *Tracy is an Oates.* Resecting a previously unresectable brain tumor meant interviews and articles. Megan once told Rory that one of Magus's assistants said he was writing a book to get on the talk show circuit. Fix Tracy, and he had his book. Fail, and he could still be the surgeon who attempted the impossible and won the hearts of the Oates family. She was a win-win for him.

He could also kill her.

Magus continued, "In either scenario, I will perform the surgery, so I'll take Mr. Oates's consent personally. The rest of you will each come up with a surgical plan and present it to me tomorrow morning. If I select yours, you can scrub in with me." He held out his white coat. "Khloe."

Khloe blinked and stepped forward with a flat expression, but he saw the disdain written all over her face. She lifted the jacket from Magus, who didn't look up. Without a word, he spun on his leather soles and shouldered past Rory into Tracy's room. The semi-circle of residents dispersed, leaving Khloe behind, white-knuckling Magus's coat in one hand. In her other, a clenched pencil strained against her thumb.

"It can't take much more," Rory said, pointing at her pencil.

"He is . . . the worst person," she muttered. The pencil creaked. She tossed Magus's coat on top of the yellow isolation cart just outside Tracy's room. "You know, for how brilliant he is, he can be so—"

"Arrogant?" Rory offered.

"I was going to say reckless." Khloe faced him. "He'll kill her if he operates, and he knows it. That's why he's hoping a resident comes up with something better by tomorrow. There is a reason they didn't operate before." Her eyes narrowed at him like a fox who spotted a chicken out of the coop. "Weren't you off tonight? Why are you here when you're supposed to be off . . . again?"

Rory stammered. "I . . . They needed . . ." *Staffing!* "Help. Short staffed."

She raised an eyebrow.

He sighed, knowing she'd caught him. He leaned closer and whispered. "And to scout a little. Magus can't save Tracy, but we can. She meets all Caroline's criteria."

"No. No. I have another day and a half, Rory," Khloe said. "I'll get my sequencing back, hopefully with some answers. Maybe

463

a better option. Caroline said we—"

"Caroline is grieving," Rory finished. He'd seen it all over her face.

Khloe opened her mouth, but stopped and frowned instead. *She saw it, too.*

"I don't know if we can trust her judgment right now." Rory pressed closer. "She's trying to hold on to Jacklyn as long as she can. Maybe too long."

"Caroline is smarter than that." She made it sound like a wish.

He shook his head. "Grief does all kinds of crazy things to us. Another parent threw a chair last week, a mild-mannered guy. Just taken over."

"That doesn't mean she will!" Khloe snapped back.

The sliding door opened. Dr. Magus emerged, glancing between Khloe and Rory. "Is there a problem, Dr. Seeker?"

"No," Khloe said with an edge in her voice. "I was just telling Nurse Nash to page me if anything changes."

Rory smiled pleasantly, hearing the veiled command.

"Mm," Magus said, turning to Rory. "Nash, was it? I left the consent form for Mr. Oates to read over. He needs time to weigh his options. If he has questions, call me, not the on-call resident. Do you understand?"

"Yes, sir," Rory said, not taking his eyes off Khloe.

Magus held out his hand. "My jacket."

Khloe turned to Magus, and for a moment, Rory thought she might stab him with the pencil. To his relief, she snatched the jacket from the cart and dropped it into Magus's waiting palm. Without waiting, she turned and strolled down the hall. Rory chuckled and followed, giving a nod to Dr. Deedee as they passed.

"Everything okay?" Deedee wore a colorful blanket wrapped around her and eyed Rory through her thick glasses.

"Yep. Fine."

Deedee bit her lips to keep from smiling, then cleared her throat. "I won't ask, but I would recommend keeping it private."

Rory felt himself blush, though he wasn't sure if it was embarrassment or frustration. Straightening up, he started toward the kitchen to gather crackers and water. Deedee put her hand up.

"Rory, one second—I'd like your thoughts. I'm nervous about neuro's insistence on examining Tracy. I think sedation is needed, but Magus is pushing."

"Seems risky to me too, but—" He shrugged. They both knew the drill. If they resisted and Magus made a stink, the hospital would have a hard time saying no to their prize surgeon. He brought in too much publicity and revenue to risk him leaving.

"Precisely. So, while we're weaning her sedatives, just in case she has another episode, I'd like a ketamine FIMI drawn up and ready."

FIMI? Rory had never heard of it. "A ketamine what? I can draw you up a dart."

Deedee sighed. "FIMI is forced intramuscular injection. We can't say dart anymore."

"Can't . . . say? Huh." He frowned, processing. "Why'd they take it away? Saying dart was the only fun part."

Deedee laughed. "A few too many families complained about staff saying their child would be 'darted.' Marketing needed to rebrand so the hospital could make their loved ones getting stabbed by strangers less terrible for everyone."

Rory shook his head. *What a world . . .* He pulled out his paper brains and wrote the order down so he could double-check it later. "You want a ketamine FIMI? Got it. One ticket to la-la land." Rory slipped his brains back into his pocket.

Deedee smiled. "Thank—"

"Help!" Mr. Oates yelled from behind him.

Rory was moving before he could think. He wrenched open the sliding door and found Mr. Oates struggling to hold Tracy's arms as she thrashed. Her green eyes were wide open and frantic, and blood streamed down her arm from where her IV once was. Blood soaked the side of her gown, and the saline bag drained into her bed, creating a puddle in the middle.

"Noooo!" Tracy thrashed and screamed, a tornado of flailing elbows and knees. She fought her grandfather with one hand and crawled her way toward the foot of the bed and the exit with the other. It was all Mr. Oates could do to hold on.

"Tracy! Sweetie!" Mr. Oates cried. "Tracy, it's me!"

She wasn't hearing him. She wasn't hearing anything. Whether from delirium or white-hot fear, Rory knew she'd gone into primal fight *and* flight.

Keep her safe.

"We need to re-sedate her," Rory yelled over his shoulder. "Now!"

He didn't wait for Deedee's response but heard her out in the hall issuing crisp orders.

Rory grabbed a pair of gloves and threw himself toward Tracy.

When she saw him coming, she let out a wild shriek. "Get away!" She kicked her feet at him, jamming his shoulder. Rory caught her heel, but she whipped her foot like a fish on a line, jerking Rory forward.

"Stop!" she screamed.

"Tracy, you're safe!" Rory reached for her bleeding arm.

466

"It's Mr. Nash!" Mr. Oates tried to soothe her, his grip slipping.

She pulled her arm free of her grandfather and, before Rory could react, raked her nails across Rory's cheek. He felt his skin open and burn. Seizing her wrist, Rory forced her arm away, but when he tried to open his right eye, it instantly blurred and stung, so he clamped it shut.

"Tracy! Please!" Mr. Oates pleaded, pouncing again.

"Let go of me!" Twisting and writhing, she nearly pulled Mr. Oates into the bed, but Rory pinned her arm down and secured the other. Her legs still flailed freely. He needed help.

Megan and Bell burst into the room, gloved and armed with padded restraints.

Tracy saw them coming and bared her teeth, snapping at Rory's forearm. He twisted, keeping free of her mouth without breaking her wrists. She lunged again, but Bell was there and pressed herself down against Tracy's chest, pinning her torso to the bed. Tracy screamed in Bell's face, a shrill and chilling wail. Bell didn't even blink. The charge nurse sang softly about soothing sunshine.

Megan grabbed Tracy's legs, and the outmatched Mr. Oates continued to cling to Tracy's still bleeding arm, repeating over and over that everything was okay. Megan got one restraint cinched around Tracy's ankle and, for a long moment, all Rory could do was hold on and try not to get bitten.

Dr. Deedee appeared at the door with a syringe in hand. "I've got the dart!" She grabbed gloves and flicked the syringe once to clear the bubbles. "Mr. Oates, we need to calm her down before she hurts herself or anyone else."

"Yes, yes. Whatever you think best," Mr. Oates said.

"Hold her still." Deedee came around the bed, keeping the naked needle high and away from thrashing limbs. "Secure the leg."

Tracy wailed, "Let go! Let go!" She arched again, providing

467

Deedee with no stationary target to inject. "NOOO!" Tracy's free leg swept across the bed and caught Megan on the side of her swollen abdomen. She grimaced, but pinned the leg down with her body. Deedee jammed the needle into the stationary thigh. Tracy screamed soundlessly as she writhed and gnashed and spit. It took all five adults to hold her down for a full minute.

Tracy's manic strength finally ebbed into a soft whimper. They untangled themselves from the melee, panting and sweating, and attached monitors to watch her breathing. Rory got pressure on her bleeding arm and staunched the flow. Soon, Tracy snored with her eyes half open in a deep ketamine-induced sleep.

Rory blew out a long breath, but the adrenaline lingered. *That could have been worse.*

"Wonderful work, everyone," Dr. Deedee said, wiping the loose strands of brown hair stuck to her face. She kneeled beside Mr. Oates, who had collapsed in the bedside chair. She talked in a low voice, and he nodded along. Rory knew the conversation: Tracy would need to be sedated from now on. She was too dangerous. Sedation had implications for both the length of treatment and speed of recovery and was rarely a step forward.

Bell straightened the blankets and untangled the monitoring cables from the IV lines as she continued to hum her sweet song. He spotted Megan in the corner with one hand on her belly.

"Is Parasite okay?" Rory asked.

Megan nodded, still winded. "Still kicking." She cupped her breast and grimaced. "Ow. I think my boob took most of it."

"You're sure?" He wanted to reach out and hug her, but held back.

"We're both fine. Relax."

She pointed at Rory's face. "She got you good, though. Broke the skin."

Rory reached up to touch his face, but Megan caught his wrist.

"Might want to take your glove off first," she said.

Rory looked down, and his stomach lurched. Blood covered his gloves.

Octavia. The Seed. Tracy.

Friday, April 27th, 13:15

News of Conner's recovery and the mysterious power outage rippled through the city. Twenty-five hours after the power came back on Friday morning, the theories poured in, each more improbable than the last. Some bemoaned an aging power grid, others cried divine intervention, and a small few whispered of government conspiracies. Jane enjoyed the sensational stories, picking through them and gleaning what she could from that strange night. The family, the hospital, and the flustered electrical engineers gave only official statements promising further investigation.

After a candlelit dinner of the hotel's stock of canned ham and beans, Emmett and Jane sat on her patio overlooking the eerily dark city. They talked of small things, and it almost felt normal again, but something had changed between them, though she wasn't sure what yet. She watched the headlights of cars loop and glide their way through the still. Those paired lights among all the black looked like two wide, bright eyes searching for answers, but Jane supposed that might be projecting.

The next morning, Emmett looked exhausted, and she wondered if he'd slept at all. The stress was getting to the rookie, and secretly defying his boss only made it worse. During breakfast, he'd turned a sickly shade of green when the Director called for an update. His complexion only partially returned, so they stopped for a third cup of coffee on their drive up the steep hill to the white hospital overlooking the city.

"I hate lawyers," Emmett mumbled into his dwindling cup.

Jane steeled herself as they parked. "What? You don't like being talked down to for an hour?"

Emmett laughed, and Jane took that as a win.

A troupe of eight unsmiling suits ushered them into a penthouse conference room. They explained they acted on behalf of the administrators and distributed themselves around a massive black table. One stood—a pale bald man with piercing blue eyes—and presented their concerns. How public would this investigation be? Did they have the proper warrants? What would they do about the media?

"We're here to help," Emmett insisted, but it became obvious that the hospital's cooperation was secondary to preserving the warm spotlight the institution garnered following the two incredible recoveries. Jane spent most of a droning monologue studying the puffy clouds drifting over the city and tapping the pipe in her pocket.

"Right. Yes. Mhm."

Even stressed and sleep-deprived, Emmett rallied and meticulously negotiated both their cooperation and media silence until the case was in hand. He presented the signed warrant and asked for access to security footage and patient records. The language he used and the points made were all by the book, a tactic Jane found droll, but around a conference table, the book worked well. That didn't prevent the hospital officials from squirming, though. They clearly knew their bosses wouldn't be happy with a federal investigation. Jane had to hide her smile. Perhaps sadistic, but she enjoyed those in a literal white tower worrying about getting their hands dirty.

As he ended, Emmett went off script. He floated a slogan, "Serving All Oregonians," painting a mental poster of a police officer and a doctor shaking hands with a crowd of smiling faces behind them. Jane expected a laugh, but the lawyers leaned forward, imagining the public relations bonanza if their cooperation led to an arrest. Jane didn't understand. Didn't they see the issue here? But a second glance around the table showed white, masculine faces smiling back. *That won't work. You see why that won't work, right?*

The imaginary poster proved to be the clincher, and within five minutes, they completed an agreement. Hill Hospital agreed to hand over patient information on Tommy, including security footage, but they couldn't release Conner's records until they declassified them. That set off a warning bell. Conner's mother, with her substantial connections, had grown interested in Hill Hospital's incredible recoveries, too. The hospital wouldn't release the files unless Emmett submitted a formal claim to the Senator's office. Emmett protested, and Jane intervened, thanking everyone. The meeting was over.

Tommy might provide all they needed.

———

Friday, 19:15

Hill Hospital, Sub-Basement 3, Room D

Six hours later, tucked in a drafty concrete room deep in the subbasement, Jane felt her brain numb. The dry medical records and staff notes tugged her eyelids down. Her half-eaten sandwich sat on a dusty desk she'd dragged out from the corner, and she glanced at her cold coffee, trying to remember how many cups she'd had. Five? Six?

The security footage was coming, or so their mousy hospital liaison kept telling them. They had a date and rough time—a couple of hours before and after Tommy's recovery—but without a who or a what to look for, they could sift endlessly through grainy videos.

Across the desk with his feet up, Emmett dropped a thick file on the desk and muttered to himself about the necessity for so many acronyms and abbreviations. Jane agreed. She couldn't understand why an abbreviation, SSRI, was being used in two peculiar ways. An SSRI can mean both a neurochemical inhibitor, important for regulating brain chemistry and mood, or a sliding scale for insulin for regulating blood sugar levels. Confusing the two would be deadly, and yet she found them both in the same paragraph. They were getting nowhere.

Emmett stood and groaned, stretching his back and grumbling when he found their coffee pot empty again. "More?"

"More," she agreed, and Emmett set off to find their liaison.

Alone, Jane set down a dry, dead-end note from Tommy's cardiology consultation and peered down at the rough timeline from the night of his recovery.

"How is he alive?" she mumbled to herself, digging through a deep box of files for more on Tommy. Using index cards and colored pens, she layered her notes and put them in their place on the timeline. Some overlapped, helping to build a picture of plausible events. Leaning back, she studied her story map, and it didn't take long for a hunch to tap her intuition. There was something here.

"What's missing?" she leaned in closer, double-checking her notes. "Who was supposed to—" There. The glaring hole in her story stared up at her from the timeline.

"Ah!" She pointed dramatically at the desk. "Who!" she shouted triumphantly at her coffee cup.

Jane scanned her notes and read with a fresh perspective. Everything she'd found spoke of *finding* Tommy awake: the respiratory therapists, the attending, even the charge nurse, Bella Rose, first on the scene. Everyone but Tommy's assigned nurse. From what she'd learned by combing through the records, a nursing note was required at the beginning and end of every shift. She found neither and assumed Tommy's nurse would have been a little distracted, but the next logical question was why. Shock? Or something else? It was too early to be sure, but all she really had.

Jane pulled up the patient assignment list from the PICU on April 16th.

"Rory Nash," Jane said, trying the name on. She felt an excited jitter in her belly. "Where were you, Mr. Nash, when your patient rose from the dead?"

The further she dug into the nurse's file, the more surreal he seemed. His records made him sound almost too good to be true, an American tragedy. He was a ward of the state through his teenage years, with no record, unremarkable other than his pursuit of a nursing career despite long odds. He was a brain cancer survivor; his parents had abandoned him, and now he had lived alone.

Jane paused, hearing a familiar tune: lonely, powerless, traumatized—all things Jane had experienced, all building blocks to make a killer.

Yet all she read about was a young do-gooder. Mr. Nash picked up shifts, volunteered to stay late, had glowing reviews from his peers and bosses, and had even just won a Healing Hands award, whatever that was. Still, something didn't sit right. No one could go through everything he did, basically alone, and be this intact, right? He must have his own demons; Jane learned long ago that everyone did. It wasn't a matter of if you had them, but what they whispered to you. *Maybe he can't recognize them yet?* Jane mused. She'd needed Grace to discover hers. Jane knew she could not have done it alone. *Who does this guy have?*

She turned the page and studied Mr. Nash's employee picture: a round, red-bearded face with bright eyes and a pair of dimples. If this was Maxwell's mysterious bearded man, he certainly didn't look like anything impressive.

"Who are you?" Jane whispered, but only her echo replied.

The subbasement door opened, derailing her train of thought, which she watched race away with a sigh. Emmett walked in carrying a fresh pot of coffee, looking pleased, followed by their liaison pushing a cart.

"We got video!" Emmett announced. "And coffee."

As soon as the door closed, Jane jumped up from her seat and ran over. "Bring up the employee entrance footage from April 17th. Tommy was healed just after midnight."

"Why are—"

"Just do it. It's a hunch. I'll explain after."

Emmett shrugged, found the video, and loaded it, which showed an empty hallway and a security station. Jane spotted the time in the corner: *00:01*. Jane leaned closer, watching a short, burly security guard playing solitaire inside the station.

"Looking for . . . what?"

Jane frowned. "There has to be something—"

The footage cut to black and white static. Emmett shook his head, rewinding to see the officer play a card, then nothing.

"Damn," Emmett said, slapping the side of the television screen. "Bad film."

Jane shook her head. "Or it's been compromised."

"By who?"

"By whom, Emmett, please."

An idea struck her, and she held up a finger. "One sec." She ducked her head out into the hall and asked their liaison who could enter through the staff entrance.

"A badge is needed. Staff or volunteers only. We record all access in the check-in logs."

Jane inhaled, frustrated that this was the first she had heard of the logs. "We will need to see the logs from April 17th, please." She closed the door before he could reply. "Ridiculous. Could have been . . ."

"You think it's this guy?" Emmett gestured to Rory's personal file as he took another gulp of coffee.

"I'm not sure yet," Jane said. "I did a little digging. He's a cancer survivor and a foster kid who got into nursing because, and I quote from his job application letter, 'to make sure others don't go through what I did alone.' I mean, that goes straight to the heartstrings, right?"

Emmett nodded. "Sounds like an upstanding guy."

"A poster boy. And it gets worse. Later on in the essay, he mentions his parents leaving him after his diagnosis."

Emmett's eyebrows lifted. "Damn."

"And the muffed-up-express doesn't stop there. He goes through nursing school, gets a job here in the PICU, and does well for a couple of years, but recently gets just a terrible run of patients. He lost eight in two months. *Eight*. All NATs."

"NAT?"

"Non-accidental trauma. Child abuse." Jane shook her head. "I don't care who you are. That's a long, dark path, and that, my dear Emmett, changes a person."

"Dark enough to kill, though?" Emmett picked up Rory's file and studied his picture. "There is motive."

Jane nodded. "And he has a direct connection to one of our victims through his patient Tommy, and, a little bonus from my chart-sifting, he was the assigned nurse for the senator's kid, too."

Emmett's eyes widened. "Get out. That's way too much coincidence to be nothing."

"My thoughts, too."

He frowned thoughtfully. "What do you think? Revenge? Justice? Sounds like a—"

"Don't say vigilante." Jane sighed, running a hand through her pink hair as she peered down at her timeline. "The more I read his record, the less I see a mummifying psychopath. He's been here about three years, and the killer has been going for at least five. And how would he kill strangers in other states while getting his nursing degree? It doesn't make sense. I don't think he is the killer, but that doesn't mean he's not involved."

"An accomplice?"

Jane nodded. "Yeah, but something is missing. Maybe I'm just tired, but I can't understand why Mr. Nash would risk . . . everything?" She drummed her fingers on the desk.

"Wouldn't you?" Emmett asked, his handsome face appraising hers.

Jane stopped and looked at the rookie. "What do you mean?"

"You read his file. If you'd gone through all this, been where he's been, and suddenly, there is an option to stop an obvious injustice, you'd take it. The guy sounds desperate."

"Someone made him an offer he couldn't refuse."

"Something like that." Emmett dropped the file back on the desk. "Who knows? Mr. Nash could be in the dark here, too. Maybe he doesn't know about the murders."

"Hm." Perhaps it was the hours-long records binge or a caffeine overdose, but Jane's head hurt. The strands of this story tangled and wound so tight that she was simultaneously confused and certain.

A knock came at their door.

Their liaison returned carrying a thick black book. Jane thanked the small man, waiting for him to leave before she thumbed through the wrinkled and stained pages. She found April 17th. There was only one entry from that night: Rory Nash and a visitor, hastily scrawled: Aunt Jackie.

From over her shoulder, Emmett said, "Who's Aunt Jackie?"

Jane nodded. "That, Emmett, is an excellent question. One we should ask Mr. Nash. We can ask about Tommy and Conner, too, but we'll need to be careful. We can't spook him—" She paused, remembering her role and the tenderness of egos. "If . . . of course, that's what you want to do with your investigation, Agent Torin."

Emmett considered Jane a moment, his eyes scanning over the timeline of index cards, pictures, and files. He blew out a breath, resigned. "Just a few questions. There is too much overlap to ignore."

"Glad to hear it." Jane closed the logbook with a satisfying *thump*. She started pacing, ticking off the information they needed.

"We need to know about any family or friends. Is he married? Dating? Where he's spending his money? What's he spending it on? Where does he travel? We need it all, Emmett." Her heart raced. The thrill of the hunt left her jittery and flushed, and she lifted her pink hair off her neck. She thought about Maxwell, the letter, and a smile stretched across her face. *Is this who our killer wanted me to find? Or was he another breadcrumb?*

Emmett pulled out his phone and typed out a quick message. "I'll need to let Dawson know we—"

Jane stopped mid-thought. "What? No. No Dawson. No Dawson ever."

"Jane, don't start," Emmett sighed.

"Dawson is the Director's puppet! There is a good chance he's already broken our agreement. If I were the Director, I'd let me stay too. We're making progress."

"I think you're being paranoid."

"I think you're being naïve," Jane said. "And take it from his former partner; Dawson is only out for Dawson. Never forget that."

Emmett's expression darkened, and his mouth pressed into a thin line.

Jane nearly brought up the killer's letter again, but bit down on her words. As other-worldly as it sounded, she hadn't ruled out the idea that the killer might be telling the truth and had sent her on a mission to find this next Host. Her brain said no, but her hunch told her to hold on. "We'll need to decide who, Emmett. Don't forget that."

When he replied, his voice was quiet. "I haven't forgotten." He gestured at the frozen static on the television screen and plopped down on the dusty desk. "I don't know. I was hoping to have more to go on—something concrete. This all feels so abstract still. Our big connection is what? A missing note, a runaway's story, and a name in a book."

"We got to this point on less," Jane said with a shrug. "Let's take it one more small step, ya? A conversation. But that is my vote. What do you think the next best move is?"

He went quiet, thinking. He turned and looked at Jane's story map. "Either way, we need to talk to the nurse. He might have seen someone visit or can provide some answers to what is going on. But Jane, I'm not moving on anyone without backup."

"Backup? But that might be our best chance too—"

Emmett raised his voice as he stood from the desk. "I'm not risking both our lives. One conversation, then regroup and reevaluate. If we have a bead on the killer, I'll call for reinforcements, *then* we move in."

Drawing in a deep breath, Jane considered her options. She could pistol whip the rookie and go it alone, but then she'd be leaving him to the mercy of the Director and becoming a wanted fugitive. She found irony in that scenario. But she knew she couldn't abandon Emmett on that path. Unfortunately, this left her with one option—to weather Emmett's steep learning curve and pray they survived.

"It's your investigation," she said with forced casualness. "For now, what are you going to tell Dawson?"

"Does it matter?"

"Probably not, but you're playing both sides now. Isn't it fun?"

Emmett shook his head as his gaze drifted over Jane's colorful cards spread out on the desk. "I'll tell him we hit a dead end but are investigating the staff. Leave it vague, but we'll have to come up with something more convincing after we talk to the nurse. If he has nothing for us, though, then it proves the killer has been messing with us, and, well . . ." He drifted off, and Jane got the message. She'd be off the case and right back at America's Best Insurance.

"Good enough," Jane said as nerves coiled in her belly. It wasn't the ringing endorsement she'd hoped for. Emmett's skepticism ran even deeper than she'd guessed, but at least he was thinking . . . somewhat. Because, unfortunately for them both, this wouldn't be Emmett's last, or scariest, choice.

Chapter 44: Under Siege

Saturday, April 28th, 13:15

A dry wind whipped down West Burnside Avenue, sending clouds of yellow pollen and dirty pink petals tumbling down the sidewalk. Delivery men in rival brown and purple uniforms dodged strollers, packs of skinny-jeaned teens, and pairs of elderly. Waiting at a stoplight on his bike, Rory breathed in the fragrant spring air mingled with exhaust, marveling at all the people who had no idea what was going on in the shadows.

Across the street, a packed coffee house overflowed onto the street. Flyers covered the windows. Colorful printouts advertising everything from family juggling classes to drag shows to a funk band promising a whole new sound in a whole new experience.

New. He was all topped up on new. *I need a break from new.* His eyes burned, and he'd woken up with a drumming, dull ache behind his eyes. His legs felt sluggish, used, like a machine that skipped repairs. *After finding a Host, maybe we can take a vacation in the Cove.*

A barista passed by the window, carrying a tray of steaming mugs, and friends laughed on the sofa cushions. A queer thought sprang to mind: what if he marched inside and announced magic was real?

Would they still laugh? Would they gasp? Would they ignore him? Just another crazy man ringing the bell with a sign that read *THE END IS NEAR!*

The wind rolled by, and Rory shivered. *How could they ever understand unless they've seen it?*

The car honked behind him, and he looked up to see a green light. Throwing an apologetic wave over his shoulder, Rory kicked up to his pedals and headed west to grab some food, then to the Cove.

———

Armed with a bag of empanadas, Rory pumped his pedals up the hill. The road curved out of sight ahead, but he knew the brambles were just a couple of turns away. He put on the speed, reciting his pitch to Caroline and Jacklyn again in his head.

Tracy was perfect . . . well, except for the uncontrollable fits of rage and fear. Rory decided not to lead with that. He'd tell Mr. Oates's dog story first. *What was it Bell said about feedback? Start and end with something positive, and wedge the criticism between.* Rory had plenty of positives to say about Tracy, and he'd proven he could help her through her terror spells—twice. And besides, Jacklyn was dying, so they didn't have time to find a perfect candidate.

Rounding the corner to his turnoff, he nearly collided with a huge ROAD CLOSED sign. He skidded and tipped over, dropping the bag of food and barely catching himself. *Why is . . .* The wind shifted, and he caught an acrid scent. Ahead, a thick black cloud rose through the trees. He heard voices—many voices—from the base of the smoke. Right outside the path to the Cove.

A dreaded name slithered up from his memory. *Broken . . . Star.* His heart leaped. *Shit. Okay. Breathe.* He looked back down the road behind him. *I should get out of here.*

Wheeling his bike around, he heard voices shouting, and he pictured Jacklyn smoking and dying on Conner's floor. *They might need help.* He stopped even though everything told him to run. *I can't leave them.* He ducked low, dropped the food, and quietly jogged his bike over to the turn in the road, using the thick wall of bramble to shield him from whoever was outside the Cove's entrance.

With a racing heart, he leaned around the bend.

Four unmarked black SUVs idled, blocking the road and path. Rory took a small step forward, hearing the commotion die down. Moans and cries of pain echoed through the still. He forced himself to take another step.

People in puffy, gray hazmat suits picked over the Cove's burned-out entrance, like rain clouds bobbing over charred earth. The bramble patch was largely gone, reduced to blackened sticks. A few of the "clouds" carried flamethrowers and burned the patches of remaining briar. Others followed behind, toting bags and long forceps. Amid everything, there was no sign of Caroline or Jacklyn.

Where are they?

Two clouds emerged from the tree line, carrying assault rifles and dragging a clump of earth between them. Rory recognized the broken body of a dead golem. His stomach dropped as they dumped the creature in a pile of a dozen other husks. A person there cut it open with a hand torch, carefully extracted the long strands of black mycelium, and laid them carefully on a tray.

Shortly after, another pair limped out of the forest. Between them hung a slumped third cloud whose pants were in tatters, with long, jagged cuts running down his blood-covered thighs. Rory cringed at the sight of the wound but reminded himself that they were the invaders. The trio picked their way toward a group huddled near the road, many with bloody bandages pressed to slashing wounds.

Rory dared another step, trying to get a better view, when he heard the crunch of gravel from up the road. He ducked back into cover as two enormous, steel-clad trucks rolled to a stop by the group of wounded. They reminded him of the trucks used to transport money, except these each had a massive gun turret and an antenna array on top. The passenger door of the nearest one flew open.

A hulking man stepped out wearing khaki fatigues and a

disgusted scowl. A braided cord of orange hair swung from his chin as his pink, bald head reflected the sunlight. The muscles of his arms and shoulders stretched his uniform tight, but Rory saw no weapon.

"Report!" the man's deep voice demanded.

A medic ran over and gestured toward the path and then over to the burning piles. The man cut him off with a sharp slashing motion. "Did you secure the Seed?"

Rory leaned forward, breathing hard. *This is the Broken Star.*

Whatever the medic said was not what the man wanted to hear. His hands curled into fists, as he surveyed the group of wounded. His body language was clear: the mission didn't go according to plan.

Rory let out a slow breath. *Maybe they don't have Jacklyn.*

POW! POW!

Rory flinched down reflexively as two gunshots echoed through the trees. A flock of birds burst into the sky.

"Hold fire!" the man bellowed.

POW!

From the surviving swath of forest, someone in a hazmat suit stumbled into view, waving a pistol in the air as a glowing golem clung to their back. The person spun, trying to throw the golem off, but the guardian sunk its long claw into their shoulder. A muffled scream followed as the person crumpled with the golem on top.

POW! The pistol barked again.

The golem flinched as a bullet punched through its chest, spraying earth into the air. For half a beat, the creature tipped its head to the side curiously before burying its claw into its victim's neck with a spray of dark blood. The invader twisted and stilled, and the golem lifted its glowing gaze for the next

484

threat.

The bald man stepped forward, and the golem squared, brandishing its long, bloody claws. They both stood, neither moving until the man sneered. "Get on with it."

The golem charged, swinging its oversized claws. The man dodged the first blow, but the second claw tore a long cut across his forearm. For a moment, it looked to Rory that the small golem would strike again, but its attack momentum carried it too far forward, and the big man swiftly snatched its head between his palms and squeezed. A wet *crack* followed as the golem's head crumbled, flattening the glowing psybelle. He lifted the limp golem into the air as its fungus dimmed.

An orange-yellow ichor flowed down the man's arm from the golem's cut. The surrounding air rippled like a sunbaked sidewalk. *That's not blood . . . it's magma.* His mind cramped. *That's . . . that's not possible.* The magma blackened as it cooled into a growing scab. From the man's chest, a red glow backlit his shirt, and Rory's jaw dropped, knowing what he was seeing. *He's a Merged.*

The man roared. Smoke rose from between his clenched fingers, mud sizzled, and then he casually tossed the husk aside. Rory felt white-hot fear rise in him. *I have to get out of here.* He backed up, tripping on his pedals as he swung his bike. The man stopped and sniffed at the air, peered toward the Cove, and then whipped around, locking his red eyes with Rory.

Oh shit! Rory aimed the front wheel back down the road. *Go-go-go-go!*

"Stop!" the man bellowed after him, but Rory was already sprinting alongside his bike. He jumped up and flailed his leg over, trying to get his feet onto the pedals as he rolled.

POW!

The air snapped beside Rory's head, and the gravel kicked up in front of him. Instinctively, he glanced over his shoulder and spotted two hazmat suits running from the SUVs with their rifles drawn. They had the perfect angle; Rory was out in the open. He felt his foot catch on the pedals and pushed down hard as he hunkered down low, swerving and praying.

"Get out of my way!" he heard behind him, but didn't look back.

No more bullets came.

The wind stung his eyes as he flew down the hill. If anyone was coming in the opposite direction, he wouldn't be able to avoid them. Since he was dead either way, Rory pumped his pedals. After rolling onto level ground, riding the wrong way, up one-way streets, and putting at least a mile behind him, he finally allowed himself to glance over his shoulder. He saw no signs of the red-eyed monster.

I'm alive! But no sooner had the thought come than another shoved it aside. *Is Jacklyn?*

With no answer and a heavy dread, Rory raced home.

Chapter 45: S.N.A.F.U.

Twenty-eighth of April, X643 AA

Dawson slowed his pursuit, watching the cyclist fly down the road. Heat rippled through his body, and he felt a hungry presence press against his mind. The Heart of Wrath, the fist-sized chunk of red-mythstone embedded in Dawson's chest, radiated thin shafts of crimson light from beneath his clothes. The cruel Aspect, its true name long forgotten, roiled at seeing its prey escape. It wanted to hunt.

The smell of cooked meat caught his nose, and he turned, spotting a greasy paper bag on the side of the road. He upended the bag, and eight small hand pies tumbled out, followed by a greasy slip of paper. A receipt.

CARDHOLDER: RORY NASH

"Hello," Dawson said. The Heart preened, ready.

Bzzz. Bzzz.

His phone vibrated in his pocket. He sighed—someone had informed the Director. He glanced down at his forearm, where the golem's rusty claw scored his flesh. The trickle of magma cooled into black rock at his wrist. He lifted the flap of skin still dangling, and a bolt of pain shot up to his temples. Sucking in a breath, he pressed the skin back into place, damming the molten flow.

Bzzz. Bzzz.

"Stitch me up," Dawson muttered.

The Heart hissed, and a biting heat rose in his chest.

"If you want to hunt," Dawson growled, "heal."

The pain receded into the background as a dull warmth, replaced by a prickly tingle, crawled down his arm.

Dawson brought the phone to his ear. "Here, sir."

"I was beginning to think you'd been ignoring me, Donald."

Dawson blinked, steeling himself. No one called him Donald anymore. He left that name in the dungeon the Director found him in. "No, sir. Just addressing a situation."

"Oh?"

"I was compromised. A pedestrian." Dawson eyed the path through the forest.

"Or perhaps Jacklyn has found her candidate," the Director said, pausing. "And you let them escape. I am disappointed."

Dawson moved to rectify the situation. "Sir, I can catch him."

The Heart quivered gleefully.

"I'm certain you believe that, Donald." The Director's voice was calm, yet he caught an edge of irritation. "But you'd make a mess of that, too. Where is the Seed?"

Dawson inhaled, and the Heart snarled, disgusted by his fear. "Jacklyn got out before we arrived, sir. They knew we were coming and caught my team in an ambush. The blood moths weren't as effective as we hoped they'd be. This Wyth is good. More than half my men—"

The Director's displeasure washed over him like a cold fog. "That is unwelcome news. I need to consider our new situation." The sound switched over to a soothing melody. Dawson was on hold.

Both he and the Heart stewed and kicked at the gravel as he waited. Behind him, boots approached, and without looking, he held up a hand, stopping the approach of several men who snapped to attention.

Cupping the phone, Dawson said over his shoulder, "Let him go."

"But sir—"

Dawson spun around, incredulous. The man who'd spoken snapped back to attention, staring straight ahead and avoiding his eye. Dawson shook his head and looked beyond them at the injured troopers, groaning and licking their wounds. He sneered, missing the old breed of soldier—men who could take a hit. Knew where to be. The cyclist never would have gotten away if they'd set a proper watch. These troopers were sloppy and unfocused—the long campaign had eroded their discipline. And there was no room for error when hunting the Seed.

The Heart simmered greedily as Dawson considered. He checked that the hold music was still playing before he pointed at the trooper who had protested. "You!"

The man stiffened. Dawson's boots crunched in the gravel as he stepped closer, raking his eyes over his disheveled appearance.

"This uniform is not regulation."

"Sir? I . . . Inspections were this morning."

Dawson raised an eyebrow and leaned back. The Heart swelled at the insolence, and heat flowed out of Dawson's body, rippling in the surrounding air. The soldier went pale and fired off a salute. "Yes, sir. I'll get it mended."

Waving his hand at the two troopers, he added, "And take these glass jaws to the medics, then ship them out."

The trooper snapped off a salute and turned, barking orders at the others.

Dawson inspected the Heart's progress of his wound, finding the flap of skin nearly sealed by a thick crust of porous black rock. He grunted his approval.

"Donald." The Director's voice returned.

"Here, sir," Dawson said.

"This situation may benefit us."

"Very good, sir. What are your orders?"

"Jacklyn's presence confirmed my prediction. She wouldn't linger unless she'd found a candidate. She's a traditionalist, adhering to her Laws, so she is vetting them. And she is weakening by the day. Soon, she must pass the Seed on or risk releasing it."

The idea of the Seed unleashed brought a chill to Dawson's hot skin. He wasn't sure what to expect exactly, but if the Director was nervous, Dawson knew he should be too.

"They will be desperate, which means they will be working fast and sloppy. That's our opening to end this once and for all. Bring them to me alive, Donald. And it begs repeating: the Seed can't be allowed free. Do you understand? That is very bad for everyone."

"Yes, sir," he replied, as the Heart pumped angrily. "I won't fail you."

"We shall see." The Director paused, then added, "I want the Wyth alive, too. She has the Shepherd's Stone, and I want them back. And bring me this Host candidate. I'm curious about who Jacklyn selected. Worthy prospects are hard to find these days. Perhaps he might be a pleasant addition to our little family. At the very least, I'm in need of some entertainment."

Dawson swallowed his nerves, choosing his words carefully. The Heart howled its displeasure. "It will be a crowded trip home, sir."

"Yes. So, I arranged a cargo plane. It waits at a private airstrip thirty miles east."

A new theater meant new variables. "Why not the Portland airport, sir? We have it scouted already."

"Too many eyes," the Director said. "We don't need the public asking questions right now."

"Yes, sir," Dawson grumbled.

The Director paused. "Speak your mind."

"This is a Wyth, sir. I have half my original strength, no ordnance, and only two heavy transports. She is skilled and knows her mythstones. Capturing her will have casualties. And then there is Jacklyn. Even nearly dead, she'll still be deadly so long as she wields the Seed."

"I'm aware," the Director said. "That's why I'm sending you something special."

"Sir?"

"The Brand of Sicra."

"The Brand?" Dawson gaped, and he felt the Heart tremble. "I thought it was a myth."

"Myth no more. We discovered it in another Vault in Guatemala."

An alarm of caution cut through Dawson's excitement. "Was there a hive?"

"No, fortunately. Just sentinels protecting the armory."

Good. A waking Cilid hive was not something they needed right now.

"I've dispatched it and two more squads to reinforce the airstrip."

"You want to set a trap?"

"I want *you* to set the trap. Use Jacklyn as bait to reel everyone in. Maybe we can draw another Wyth cell out of hiding."

Dawson nodded. The idea had merit. One last crippling blow. "I will. And thank you, sir." He paused, adding, "And if—"

The Director sniffed. "Bring me the Seed, and I will start your war."

A wave of euphoria erupted from Heart as the Aspect greedily pressed images of conquest into Dawson's mind. On a battered and blackened landscape, he stalked toward his cowering foes like a goliath of old. A smile crawled across his face. He could nearly taste the sweet, bloody freedom only battle brought. And there, in his image of ecstasy, he found another joy he eagerly awaited. Revenge.

"Sir? What of Jane? She's convinced Emmett to keep secrets."

The Director sighed. "Your insignificant revenge must wait. Until we have the Seed, let Jane play her games. Consider this Emmett's test of loyalty. If they try to do anything with the Seed besides bringing it to me, kill them both."

"Yes, sir."

"A piece of one vision," the Director said.

"A vision of one peace," Dawson replied automatically.

The line went dead, and Dawson grinned. *My war*, he thought, and the Heart sent another wave of warmth through him. A blood-spattered medic ran up and snapped up a salute, spoiling the feeling.

"Site is secure, sir. What are the Director's orders?"

Dawson scowled at the man, hating middle management.

"Get my men back into fighting condition. And"—a hunger called and he held up the grease-stained receipt—"let's find this Rory Nash and see why he was poking around."

Chapter 46: Last Meal

Saturday, April 28th, 15:10

"This is so much better than hospital food," Jane said, taking another huge bite of burrito. She hummed happily, muted by the howling winds outside their tiny rental car. A bit of charred meat landed on the napkin tucked beneath her chin, and she reached down and popped it in her mouth while inspecting her powder-blue blazer for stains. As she chewed, she checked her bright hair in the rear-view mirror, then picked something green and unseemly off her face. She didn't want to look unprofessional. Especially for, arguably, the biggest conversation of her life.

Where is this nurse?

The two-story brick apartment complex was nothing special. Parking lot, stairs, a couple of bushes—the usual crowd. She squinted at apartment 104A from behind her burrito. Jane had already braved the wind once and knocked. No answer—just a loudly meowing cat. Cute. She didn't know why the cat interested her so much, but it felt like a point in the guy's favor. Jane offered to pick the lock, but Emmett talked her out of it.

"I could have that door open in fifteen seconds."

"No," Emmett said from the driver's seat. He hadn't touched his wilting salad. *What kind of guy gets a salad from a burrito place?*

"Maybe we should check the sewers. Sneak in. His landlord talked highly of him, and you never know about landlords—"

"Not now, Jane."

She wrinkled her nose at the untouched lettuce in his lap. "I told you rabbit food wouldn't cut it." She lined up another bite. "Your brain needs fat and carbs to think, especially before a big bust. See, the glucose is the fuel?" She chomped down and hummed again. "Mental flex-i-bility." She turned to find Emmett watching her with disgust. "Wha?!" A bean fell out.

Emmett sighed and turned to face the window, and Jane sized up her pseudo-partner. He had said little since they'd parked, and after a quick inspection, he appeared a little green around the gills. Jittery.

The wind howled, and Jane shivered, glad she was inside. "You okay?"

Emmett's face twisted, and he retched.

"Not in the car!" She reached across him to pull the door open, but he waved her off.

"I'm good. Just a stomach cramp."

"You mean a stress ulcer," Jane said. "You don't casually burn holes in your stomach." She side-eyed him. "Get some food in you and then tell me what's going on."

"It's watching you eat," he tried, but sighed and poked at his salad. "I, well, I messed up with Maxwell, and now . . . This is bigger. This could be, like, it?" She recognized the look—the same fidgeting distraction her nephew had before his first swim. It turned out that a couple of inflatable ducks strapped to each of his arms were all he needed to hurl himself in. She needed to find Emmett some confidence-building floaties.

"You didn't mess up with Maxwell . . . per se."

"I tackled him."

Jane laughed. "I wouldn't say it went smoothly, either."

Emmett tossed down his fork and ran both hands through his moussed, dark hair. She needed to get ahead of this quickly.

"My sister has a plaque on the wall with this saying. Drove me nuts when I first moved in, but it grew on me, especially after my attempt. Got me to be a more present person instead of a stressed-out time-traveler. Anyway, this plaque says, 'Borrowed Trouble Doubles.' I think that applies here."

The young agent blinked once, his face confused, but then slowly, he smiled. "Are you trying to give me a pep talk?"

"Only if it's working."

After a long pause, Emmett tipped his head back and laughed. He threw up his hands, smiling, and Jane felt the tension crack enough to let in a breath. As his fit subsided into giggles, he stared at his salad, shaking his head.

"This is insane."

"Yup."

He eyed her. "Then how are you so chill?"

"Experience?" She shrugged. "I don't know. I'm nervous, sure, but way more excited. We finally get some answers."

"That will lead to more riddles." He blew out a long breath. "The case—"

"Everything else can wait. All you need to worry about is right now." She gestured to the apartment. "One interview."

He turned in his seat to face her. "How 'bout you take the lead? We can't afford to—"

"Emmett, when I'm most scared, I'm usually on the verge of doing something new. Or difficult. Or that I love. Maybe all three. But in all those times, fear only had a say in the outcome when *I let it* screw with my head."

"Huh. That was profound."

Jane waved away the comment. "I probably stole it from a fortune cookie. Focus up. You're taking the lead on Mr. Nash."

"But . . ."

"Maxwell already happened, and we got what we needed. You rocked the boardroom—those suits were eating out of your hand."

"That's different."

"Is it?" Jane couldn't decide for herself if she agreed. She shook her head, trying to stay on topic. "Look. You'll make so many mistakes in your life. You gotta get used to them." She shrugged and stuffed the burrito into her mouth. "Go'yur queshions'edy?"

"Jane—" Emmett didn't want to wear floaties.

She rolled her eyes and swallowed the massive bite, coughing. "Come on, let's game it out. What do you want to know?"

"The location, name, and weaknesses of the killer," Emmett said.

"You must really enjoy tackling witnesses," Jane deadpanned, but added an elbow jab so Emmett wouldn't sink again. "Come on, what are you going to ask first? Specifically."

He held up three fingers and ticked them off one at a time. "I'll ask him about his link to Maxwell, Tommy, and Aunt Jackie."

Jane pursed her lips and couldn't hold back. "Maybe we should just hit him with the car instead? It would be less painful to watch."

He sagged and turned back to the window. Exasperated, she grimaced and threw her hands up behind his back.

"Muff," she whispered. "Okay, sorry. Maybe warm him up first? He's gotta trust you before he'll open up—about anything."

Emmett stared blankly out the window. "I guess I can use the Reid technique. It always worked in my trial cases. Step one is confrontation. Say we have evidence that connects him to a murderer. Step two—"

"Reid?!" Jane pretended to gag on her finger. "Coercing someone into a confession isn't a good technique, and it's the opposite of building trust. If you lead with Reid, just run me over, too."

"Well, that's my idea!" Emmett said, his face flushing. "What about you? What'll you be doing while I'm asking all the questions?"

"You talk, I consult." Jane pumped a fist into the air. "Yay, teamwork."

"Ugh," Emmett groaned. "This is so stupid."

Jane set down her burrito calmly. "Okay, you want my help here? Don't overcomplicate it. Keep it simple. Interviews are just conversations, and good conversations flow. There is no blueprint. Be human. Listen first and ask specific questions second." She waited for a response. "Does that make sense?"

Emmett's shoulders relaxed a little. "Yeah, but how does that help me with this guy?"

"An interview has one big difference over a conversation. One party is trying to extract honest, often guarded information from another. In our case, Mr. Nash and any information he may or may not have about our killer. In order to do that, and here's the tricky part: we have to give up something we have *first*. Build trust. That's where Dawson gets it wrong—he's not a builder. The Reid Technique won't work here. It's got no soul. This guy's a nurse. I guarantee he's got a built-in muff detector. Seeing so much death does that, fine-tunes it, whether you realize it or—"

Jane frowned, her mind picking over what she'd just said. There was something there.

"What is it?" Emmett asked.

"I don't know. A hunch? It took me a long time to understand that about death. Years of therapy. Something tells me, Mr. Nash . . . he's young. I bet he hasn't had the time to stop and see that for himself." She shook her head, letting the thought float into her memory and churn through her deeper mind. She made a mental note to revisit it. "Where was I?"

"Interviews."

"Right, okay. We need to connect, which makes the information we give up the key to what we get back. We can't let on that we suspect he's connected to the killer. He could go into hiding or bolt like Maxwell, so I'd keep them out to start. Talk about his patients, keep our questions about Tommy, and maybe where we have warrants. But listen to his responses and ask questions that lead him in your direction—" She glimpsed a long, red truck in her side mirror. "Oh! A fire engine!"

Jane enthusiastically waved at the crew, earning her a ring of their bell. Emmett shook his head again, tossed his salad back into a paper bag, and unbuckled his seatbelt. She watched the firetruck roll around the corner, passing a clean-shaven cyclist in green tights and a please-don't-hit-me reflective yellow jacket. In the span of a block, he checked over his shoulder twice.

"Wait . . ." Jane wiped her fingers on her napkin. "I think that's him."

"Who?"

"The cyclist. The nurse, I mean."

"He doesn't have a beard."

Jane rolled her eyes. "It's called a razor."

The man hopped off his bike gracefully as it still moved, jogging alongside toward 104A. With one more look behind him, Jane saw the man's face clearly: the same bright, round face from the employee file. Mr. Nash looked startled, fidgety, and flushed as his eyes passed over their car.

They sank into their seats.

"Bingo," she whispered.

He fumbled with his keys before unlocking the door and slipping inside with his bicycle.

Jane tore the tucked napkin out of her collar. "You're on, Emmett!"

Emmett didn't look convinced. "What if . . . I lose him?"

"So you do, and we adapt." She shrugged. "At some point, you just have to do the muffing thing. Worst-case scenario? He bolts, and you tackle him. You can do that, no problem."

"Very funny."

"That's the spirit!" She opened her door and braced herself, her hair whipping in all directions. "Let the games begin!"

Chapter 47: Sanctuary

Saturday, April 28th, 15:17

No one followed?

Rory leaned his bike against the wall and checked through the peephole. Not a soul in sight.

No one followed.

He leaned his forehead against his door.

I did it.

Like he'd swallowed a stone, he realized he'd only thought this far ahead.

Now what, genius? An answer came easily. *Jacklyn. I need to find—*

A powerful grip seized his shoulder.

"AHH!" Rory shouted and flailed. *The red-eyed man!* He beat a hand feebly at the powerful grip, waiting for pain, the crush, and starry oblivion. He spun, and through the darkness, he barely made out a small frame and leather coat. Jacklyn yanked him closer. Her eyes were black and deadly focused.

"It's me!" Rory put his hands up, trying to calm her.

"Who?" Jacklyn squinted at his face. She raised her left stump. A misty vapor rose, curling into tendrils, forming the gaseous shape of a wrist, hand, and long, delicate fingers. She pressed Rory against the door.

"It's Rory. Please!"

"H . . . hero?" With a grunt, Jacklyn pulled him an inch closer but didn't release him. "What are you doing busting in here?"

"I live here!" Rory jingled his keys. He blinked again and pointed at her stump. "How can . . . your hand?"

Jacklyn released him. "Ugh, with the questions . . . it is Rory." The vapor disappeared, and the darkness lifted. Gray daylight poured in through the drawn blinds.

How does she do that?

"We don't have time," Caroline said, gliding over from the window. She wore a pink and blue sundress with a plain white blindfold over her eyes. Rory spotted the twin-bladed ivory gauntlet strapped to her arm. "They are here."

Fresh fear washed over Rory. "Someone attacked the Cove," he said, hurrying to the window. "A red-eyed bald guy and people in hazmat suits."

Peering through the slats, he noticed a well-dressed but mismatched pair crossing the street, heading straight for his apartment. The woman was short and middle-aged, with bright pink hair and a powder blue blazer, and the man was younger, clean-cut and handsome. She took twice as many steps as he and talked while he kept his head down against the wind.

As the woman's arms rose in crescendo with her point, the man nodded, fidgeting with his jacket, undoing, then redoing a button. The woman reached up and clapped him on the shoulders.

"There are two people—"

"The red-eyed man you saw was one of the Merged," Caroline interrupted.

"That's enough, Care," Jacklyn growled. She squared on Rory. "What were you doing at the Cove?"

Annoyed, Rory pointed a thumb toward the door.

"I, uh, I found a Host candidate," Rory stammered. "But—"

"Did you?" Jacklyn asked, a note of surprise in her voice. And anticipation. "Who?"

"A patient. Tracy Oates."

"Oh." Jacklyn frowned. Again, Rory felt the hot wash of frustration and grit his teeth.

What am I doing wrong?

"Does Khloe know?" Caroline asked with a hint of impatience.

"Well . . . no."

"Never mind then," Caroline said, taking Jacklyn's hand and guiding her to the couch. "The Cove is lost. Jacklyn's health deteriorates, so we dared not make a stand."

"The golems . . ." Rory said, picturing the man tearing the mycelium from the husks.

"They heroically sacrificed themselves for our escape."

"They did their duty," Jacklyn corrected, easing herself down on the couch with a series of grunts. "And I'm fine," she added, winded. "I just need to rest."

Sneaks meowed noisily and came to investigate Jacklyn's open lap.

Rory pointed back to the window. "You can't. We gotta go. We—"

Over Caroline's shoulder, Rory spotted an overflowing grocery cart and a small yellow tent filling his kitchen. A trio of small clay pots, each with a glowing psybelle cap, were tucked inside. "You moved in?!" He clamped his hands together to keep them from shaking. *This can't be happening.*

"Just a pit stop," Jacklyn sighed, reaching down to scratch Sneaks. The cat purred happily and leaned into her fingers. "We do need your help, though."

"Help." Rory's mind raced to construct an escape plan. "There are people coming. I can distract them, and you two can slip out . . . the window or something. I'll bring the cart later and—"

Caroline shook her head. "We can't run. Not this time."

"Why not? Can't you just—" Rory fluttered his fingers like the wizards in the books he grew up loving.

"That is not how it works," Caroline said flatly. "I spent my energy rallying the golems and getting Jacklyn here safely. I need rest before I fight again."

"Great." Rory exhaled. "So, what am I supposed to do?"

"Talk," Caroline said, nodding to Jacklyn.

"Time to throw down, hero." Jacklyn shook her head and picked up Sneaks.

Rory turned back to Caroline. "We are asking for your help."

He felt a spike of pride cut through his panic, anchoring him. *Me?*

Caroline inclined her head to the door. "These two are not Broken Star. The young man is quiet, nervous, with a conflicted heart, and the woman releases a loving glow as they talk. I believe they are here for something else entirely."

"Like what?"

"I can't read minds, Rory. Only emotions. You must go find out."

His panic returned. "Okay. I need to lead them away. If they don't know about the Seed, then we're good. Right?"

"And if they do?"

"Then we improvise." Rory rolled his shoulders, forced one quick breath, grabbed his bike, and opened the door.

Chapter 48: A Few Questions

Saturday, April 28th, 15:20

"Oh! Excuse me," Mr. Nash said, wheeling his bike out. He pulled his door shut behind him.

Jane caught Emmett's eye. The nurse seemed surprised, and from the look of his reflective vest and helmet, it seemed like he was heading out again.

"Mr. Nash?" Emmett took a step forward, but the wind threw his words back at him.

Jane nudged the rookie forward. Emmett cleared his throat. "Mr. Rory Nash?" he shouted.

Rory squinted at them as the wind howled. "Yes?"

Up close and shaven, he looked even younger than his employee photo, except for the deep purple bags beneath his eyes. He was a medium, normal-looking white kid of medium height and regular build. Pretty unremarkable, although she noticed three parallel pink lines running from his left eyebrow down his cheek, too wide to be cat scratches.

Old instincts took hold, and she checked his hands. One trembled, still clutching his bike's bent handlebars, while the other remained in his pocket.

"Can I help you?" Rory shouted over the wind. His eyes were wide and questioning, almost desperate, though he kept it from the rest of his face. Impressive in a sad way, there was only one way to practice that skill. *This is the guy?* She expected this next Host to be . . . well, she wasn't sure what she expected, but not this guy. This guy didn't need another job. He needed a vacation.

Emmett paused and then, as if remembering, drew out his identification. "Mr. Rory, my name is Agent Emmett Torin."

He held his badge up.

"Oh." Rory squinted. "Uh, what branch do you—"

"Classified," Emmett said curtly, and Jane had to keep from rolling her eyes—she got the feeling intimidation wouldn't work here.

"Oh," Rory said, holding eye contact. "Can I help you?"

"I hope so." Emmett tucked the badge away and gestured to Jane next. "This is my consulting partner, Jane Kim."

"Consultants are cheaper for payroll." She extended her left hand, and his came out of his pocket empty to shake hers. His palm was sweaty.

"Nice to meet you." Rory released first.

"You don't seem fazed seeing us," Jane said.

"Should I be?" Rory almost didn't swallow—almost. *Definitely nervous.*

"Most people are a little stunned when we pop up unannounced. Do you talk to agents often?"

To her surprise, he smiled. "You'd be surprised."

Jane rolled his words around in her head, attaching them to her notes, her timeline, her hunches. *Interesting.*

Rory cleared his throat. "Is there, uh, something I can help you with?"

Jane pointed to her eye, tracing the length of the scratch. "What happened there?"

He reflexively touched his cheek. "Oh, this. From a patient." He shifted his feet, rocking on his heels.

Emmett cleared his throat. "Can we talk inside a moment?"

Rory drew out his cell phone, checking the time. "I'm in a rush. Dinner before work and—" He gestured to his bike.

Emmett frowned and pulled out his phone. Jane stifled the urge to slap it out of his hand. "I didn't see you on the schedule tonight."

She winced and held her breath. He just gave away a valuable piece of information.

"I'm on call," Rory said, eyeing the phone. "On-call isn't on that schedule." The wind rolled by, cutting through Jane's jacket's seams. Rory stuffed both hands back into his pockets. That wasn't a good sign. "You must have talked with the hospital."

Emmett looked up and immediately back down as if he had a script on the screen. Rory watched him, and Jane wondered what he saw when he looked at her partner.

"How about a walk?" Jane offered, unable to take the silence anymore.

"A walk?" Emmett said.

Jane shot him an eyebrow, and he seemed to get the message.

"A walk works great. We won't take too much of your time."

Rory waited a moment, his eyes bouncing back and forth between them, and then gestured to the parking lot. "After you."

Jane turned as the wind gusted, throwing her pink hair into her mouth. She sputtered and spat, brushing the pink strands out of her mouth, and slid into the lead position, only a couple of feet in front of Emmett and Rory. Walking ahead, with the wind at her back, it would be hard to hear their conversation.

"I'm really curious about what is going on here," Rory said after a few steps. His front tire squeaked a little as it rolled.

"Mr. Nash," Emmett began again, "we are investigating a murder. An acquaintance of one of your patients. A boyfriend of your patient's mother, actually. Do you remember Tommy Windfield?"

Rory stopped, and both his eyebrows popped up. "That guy? He's dead?"

Jane judged the shock genuine and noted it. He didn't

506

know. *Interesting.*

"I . . . I . . ." Rory's mouth couldn't settle on one word. "I don't know if I can discuss that. HIPAA is pretty clear."

"We have the warrant," Emmett said. "And as you pointed out, we also have your employer's cooperation."

"Oh," Rory said. "Okay. Wow. So, sure. What's this have to do with Tommy?" His confidence was gone.

"So you remember him?" Jane asked over her shoulder, unable to stop herself.

"Of course. Tommy is a legend on the Hill now. It was unbelievable being there . . . like . . . like magic."

"That's an interesting choice of words." Jane chuckled.

"It's about as poetic of an explanation as I got."

Emmett continued, "This man, the boyfriend, was found dead in his home a few days ago. His name was Chuck. You met him, right?"

There was a long pause, and then Rory walked again; slowly, his squeaky wheel kept time.

"Yeah, I did," Rory said quietly, almost to himself.

Emmett pushed on. "We are hoping you might clue us in on anything you might have overheard while they were in your care. Any arguments? Something in passing, perhaps? Even a small recollection could be helpful."

Rory blew out a long breath, shaking his head. "I . . . I didn't know. I'll be honest: I'm not entirely sad to hear he's gone. Anyone who took care of Tommy knows what would happen if they saw the bruises. That guy was a monster." He straightened, a note of irritation in his voice. Emmett had struck the nerve. "My chart notes will be your best bet."

The non-existent notes. The thought intrigued her. *Does he know he forgot?* Part of her doubted it. This guy looked burned at both ends.

"Do nurses ever forget to chart?"

"Oh, sure. Especially on a busy night."

"Have you?"

Rory shook his head. "Never."

Jane raised an eyebrow at that. "Quick answer. Never ever?"

He frowned at that. "Well, maybe. Once? I guess I can't say for sure. Why do you ask?"

"Just curious." Jane smiled, glad Mr. Nash didn't think himself infallible—she found it the most toxic type of delusion and a common trait among those she'd once hunted. People justified all kinds of horrors when they thought themselves a piece of a perfect mission.

She caught Emmett watching her, waiting for input. She scowled, nodding toward Rory.

"We'll, uh . . . we'll look into . . . those." Flustered, Emmett scrolled down on his phone and opened and closed his mouth. Jane waited a beat and fell in beside them, putting Rory between them, and tried to keep the nurse from closing off. "It looks like you shaved. It's a good look."

Rory blinked at her. "Oh. Thank you."

"Mr. Nash," Emmett said like a broken record, "we noticed a few sizable fast-food purchases over the last couple of weeks. Several hundred dollars' worth. You're looking fit for that much fast food."

Jane sighed. This was no longer an interview; it was an interrogation.

Rory frowned. "I sleep in a lot." He stopped walking and sized both of them up. "Are you checking my credit cards? Am I in trouble here?"

"Just standard procedure," Emmett said.

"That doesn't sound standard." Rory's voice hardened.

Emmett scrolled his phone and presented it to Rory. Jane knew who it was without seeing the picture: Maxwell. While he was at it, Emmett might as well show him the etched stone necklace.

"Have you seen this person before?"

Rory peered closer, and Jane saw his mouth tighten before his expression quickly smoothed. He studied the picture for a convincing amount of time before shrugging. "Sorry, no. I'm normally good with faces. Is he a patient of mine?"

"No," Emmett said, looking shaken by the sudden shift in roles. "We are just—"

Jane jumped in. "Done with our questions, Mr. Nash."

Emmett inhaled and nodded, glancing between Rory and his phone. "Yeah . . ."

"Okay," Rory said, looking between them. "Well, have a good day." He hesitated a beat, then turned and walked his squeaky bike down the sidewalk. Emmett walked back toward their car, muttering to himself.

Jane watched Rory go, chewing on the conversation, when her eye caught something—a long silver flicker of refracted light attached to Rory's back. She jumped.

"Mr. Nash!" she yelped and trotted after him. Shielding her face from the wind, she gave her most disarming smile. "Mr. Nash, I completely blanked. There is one more thing."

Chapter 49: Sight Unseen

Twenty-eighth of April, X643 AA

Rory Nash's apartment

"I believe Jane found your hair, love," Caroline said, peering through the corner of the slats to where Jane and Rory now spoke. "That was an excellent idea."

Outside, against the gray of her vision, Caroline watched a yellow cloud of confidence swirl inside of Jane's short silhouette. Rory, too, appeared confident, but black stripes of fear cut through him now as Jane rushed toward him with spots of curious blue bubbling within her.

"About damn time," Jacklyn said from the couch, where Sneaks had curled on her lap. She stroked the cat, summoning a steady purr from the orange tabby. "What about the other guy with Jane? Is he Star?"

"I am uncertain," Caroline said as she tilted her head to the side, considering the bright star at the center of the mysterious young man's chest. "His Stain is bright and strong but swollen with nerves. And remorse." She watched the man's silhouette steam green against the dark background of her sight. "Genuine remorse is hard to manufacture, so that makes him either honest or extremely skilled. I know not which."

Jacklyn looked up. "Is he Merged?"

Caroline studied the man but saw none of the bright monochrome colors carried by a mythstone. "No, his Stain is intact." She turned from the window as she flexed her stiff fingers inside the Kiss's gauntlet. The weapon's long, icy blades tapped against her calf. Rory might have averted another disaster, a needed reprieve, but deep down, she knew it was only a matter of time before they confronted the Merged hunting them.

Caroline faced the black void of Jacklyn.

"This is too risky, my love. Jane could be compromised. Your letter—"

"Jane hates the Director as much as I do," Jacklyn said, not inviting a response.

"That's not enough. *Hate* is a poor bond."

"It'll work," Jacklyn said.

"How?" Caroline crossed over to the couch. "Rory is . . ." she trailed off, lost in thought. "He can't see straight. Most people crave power, but he rejected his out of shame. Now, he is actively trying to pass it off to others."

"He wouldn't be the first Host to do that."

"He isn't ready to speak with Jane; his Stain is still in control— he believes its stories. Forcing this now could lead to a crash, and he takes everyone with him."

"Plenty of Hosts have done that, too."

"Jacklyn," Caroline said sternly.

Jacklyn sighed from the void, and Sneak's steady purr filled the quiet. "You're nervous. I understand that. I am too, but the last step in converting is always the hardest, the most painful. If he isn't cooperating, then we need to do something more drastic. A crash can be a good thing sometimes. It finally gets us to stop. Maybe it's time we let the hero run into his wall. Get the crash over with so he can rebuild."

"That could break him."

"It could," Jacklyn said. "Or it could work. We have to trust he can handle it."

"I'm less confident than before," Caroline said.

"That's the nerves talking," Jacklyn said. "This is what faith is all about, Care. So, whatever half-baked idea Rory brings back, whatever scheme he has hatched for whomever he picked, we agree to it. We have to help him through his last wall." She paused, and a twist of dread coiled in Caroline's gut. "I see it in him now. He's in almost as bad of shape as me. He *can't* go back to how it was. Neither of us can. On some level, we both understand that will kill us. Which makes him desperate—you can see it in his face. The Seed is his hope now. It's all he thinks about. It's all I ever thought about. You see his emotions. Tell me I'm wrong."

Caroline considered, letting her memories come in a wave. She'd seen Rory's emotional hue tinted with red recently. There was an anger there, a resistance. It was never a good sign when emotions calcified around a Stain. "I've seen it." She sat slowly beside Jacklyn. "The Seed means everything to him now."

"Ya," Jacklyn said, taking her hand. "So, if his hope is threatened, taken away, if I'm in trouble, maybe that's the catalyst he needs to finally become the person we all need him to be."

"I was hoping to avoid this."

"Me too." Jacklyn inhaled but didn't speak straight away. She did that when she was being careful with her words. Caroline braced for bad news.

"We need to talk about what happens if I'm captured again."

"I won't allow it."

"Care—"

"No." Caroline pulled her hand away and crossed her arms.

"It's not my first choice, either. Ideally, Rory and I find a place to hide for the night and you meet back up in the morning, but the trap we designed for ourselves is closing, and we don't know when it will snap shut. I need you to perform the Assay of Cully and make the final preparations."

Final preparations. The words made Caroline sick.

"This is what I need, Care. We give Rory his chance. Whatever happens, he'll need you to help him finish the Assays. All of them. That means you can't be with me in case I get captured."

Caroline saw Jacklyn's point, but she didn't want to say so. She wanted her to be wrong.

"If I am captured, you're certain you can track me?"

Caroline sighed, hating the corner she'd found herself in. Deny Jacklyn her last wish or plunge ahead into a future not even her eyes could see? There was no choice, only a selection of sorrows. That raw fear of the unknown, the expanse ahead, seized Caroline's heart. Tears welled around her stone eyes and soaked into her blindfold. She finally nodded. "Always. No matter the distance, you are my beautiful black star on the horizon."

"Good, because I want to be rescued. I want to make that very clear. Don't leave me with them because one way or another, I'm passing the Seed soon, and it better be to Rory."

Caroline sniffed, tracing Jacklyn's knuckles with her lithe fingers. "How, with death so near, can you be so brave?"

Jacklyn grunted once from the void, then leaned her weight onto Caroline and buried her face into her shoulder. Even through the leather jacket, Caroline could feel the bone pressed through the skin. She'd lost too much weight.

"I'm afraid to die," Jacklyn said finally. The words cut into Caroline. "I don't want our story to end." The words hung in the apartment.

"Time and chance . . ." Caroline whispered. She curled into Jacklyn and kissed her on the head and cheek.

The Wyth swiped her thumb over the tears. Jacklyn sniffed and turned away, but Caroline held her face close to hers. "No, we will not hide from tears. We will inflict them on our enemy." A fire lit in Caroline's chest and quickly spread up and down her limbs, emboldening her. "I am with you, always."

Jacklyn pulled Caroline in with a fierce kiss, and as the lightning storm raged in her mind, Caroline lost herself in the embrace as everything else fell away.

Caroline wrapped herself around her best friend, trying to use her body to shield her from the world. "Oh, my love. I am here," she said as Jacklyn sobbed in her arms. Their foreheads met. "I will perform the Assay of Cully. I will use everything in my power to see Rory succeed. Then, if needed, I will find you, and we will watch the sunset together."

Jacklyn shuddered as she drew in a ragged breath. "Promise?"

Caroline lifted Jacklyn's face and kissed her repeatedly, pecking her cheeks, nose, and chin with her lips. Jacklyn squirmed beneath the barrage, and Caroline was relieved to hear a soft laugh emerge from the void.

"We started this together, didn't we?" Caroline said. "We will end it together, too."

Chapter 50: Teachers' Conference

Saturday, April 28th, 15:30

Stay calm.

Walk normally.

Don't crash the bike.

How do they know about Maxwell?!

Rory's thoughts raced, and it took all his will to stay calm. He measured out his breath, one every four steps, and grasped at his spinning thoughts. The man seemed distracted, or maybe just new. Rory heard it in his flustered questions. Whatever worried him had to be bigger than Rory, right?

The woman was different. She unnerved him. She had eyes like Bell—impossibly perceptive, piercing. Rory felt lucky she was more preoccupied with running damage control than focusing on him. He smiled to himself. *I did it. Tomorrow, we can—*

"Mr. Nash!" he heard behind him.

Rory nearly dropped his bike and ran, but steadied and forced a breath. *Calm down. Innocently, slowly.*

He turned as Jane approached, her hand holding her hair out of her face. "Mr. Nash, I completely blanked. There is one more thing." She stopped within arm's reach and nodded back toward her partner. "Thank you for tolerating that . . . uh, performance."

Rory shook his head, not understanding.

"My partner. He's pretty new."

"Oh. Uh, ya, he seemed pretty nervous."

"No kidding," Jane said, smiling easily. "Do you have a couple more seconds?"

No! "What do you need?"

Jane stepped up beside Rory and placed her hand between his shoulder blades. The touch was unexpected but gentle, guiding him down the uneven sidewalk. As they fell into a lazy stroll, Jane dropped her hand. "My partner just passed his exams, and this is his second interview. I was hoping to get your help with some constructive criticism, something he can build on. Part of my consulting package is feedback."

Rory glanced at Jane, who looked back at him, relaxed.

"Um, he was rigid. A little rude." Rory stopped, realizing he didn't know where he was walking, and he wanted to avoid more questions. "I really should get going."

"Of course, sorry to keep you so long. It's just that I know you're a nurse and could teach him a few things about diplomacy. We'd appreciate any feedback, no matter how honest."

Rory sighed and shrugged. "He needs to soften his questions. Be more human, you know? At the hospital, we start with questions like 'Where is home for you?' Follow up with, 'I've heard that place is nice this time of year.' It sounds cheesy, but it gets people to open up."

"Create a bond. Build that trust," Jane said, appraising him. "Smart. Any other pointers from your work? You had to have learned a bunch of them working in intensive care. Whewie, I can't imagine the conversations you have to have. Tough."

"It has its moments," Rory said flatly.

"And that Octavia case? Damn. I feel for you. Must have been terrible."

Rory felt dizzy. He looked at Jane. She seemed genuine, but this suddenly felt like another line of questioning.

Leave. Now.

He opened his mouth to excuse himself, but Jane jumped, startling him. "Hey! Weird idea to pass by you—something we were joking about. Would you mind giving us your medical

516

opinion?"

"If you ask me to look at a rash"—Rory forced a smile—"I'm walking away."

Jane gave a bright belly laugh, and he warmed to her. She wasn't the villain he'd been expecting.

"Ha! No, no. It's just something you said earlier about all this being magic." She paused, her eyes finding his. "Do you think that's what saved Tommy?"

Rory froze. He tried to say something, but nothing came out, so he just stared at her. *She knows?*

Jane waited a beat, then waved her hands in the air. "Don't worry about it. It's just this silly debate we've been having. He thinks it's a top-secret experiment of some new wonder cure, but I said that's crazy." She glanced at him again. "Right?"

Rory shook his head, still not sure if Jane was playing with him or not. *She can't know, can she?*

"I didn't think so." She clapped him on the shoulder again. "Thanks again, Mr. Nash. I'll pass along your feedback." She reached into her pocket and pulled out a small white square. "Here's Agent Torin's card. If anything comes up, call us."

He took it and nodded, unable to shake the lingering unease that Jane knew more than she let on. She seemed honest and kind, but Bell's cautious voice floated by. *Everyone holds a piece of themselves apart.*

"Don't be hard on him," Rory said, tapping the card against his palm. "We all gotta learn."

"Ah, don't worry." Jane snapped her fingers. "Ah, muff. I'm so scatterbrained today. Can I swing a name by you and see if you recognize it?"

Rory nodded, half-turned away, trying to escape.

Jane fixed her gaze on him. "How's Aunt Jackie?"

She knows.

Chapter 51: Place Your Bets

Saturday, April 28th, 15:34

Aunt Jackie. The name had the precise effect Jane was hoping for.

Rory folded his arms, giving himself away before he ever spoke a word. "Hm, I'm sorry. I don't recall that name."

Liar. Jane struggled to contain her excitement. She forced herself not to look away, not to check the trees and parked cars for the Director's little spies. *Goodbyes first.* "Nah, no worries. Another fishing line." She turned back toward Emmett, using her back to shield her growing smile. "Have a good day, Mr. Nash. Call us if you think of anything."

"I will." Rory gave a quick wave and stepped over his bike, pedaling in the opposite direction.

Jane slumped her step disappointedly as the wind raced up behind her, tousling her pink hair. Emmett stood across the street, leaning against their red rental. He looked confused or annoyed—it was hard to tell which—and his frown persisted as she hurried over.

"Well, that didn't go well." The wind muffled Emmett's voice.

"No, it went perfectly." Jane clapped. Over her shoulder, she watched Rory Nash disappear around the corner. "This nurse is a terrible fibber; he'd only have been more obvious if he'd written a confession. Makes me like him a little more, actually. Maybe his file was right . . ."

"His employee records?"

Jane nodded. "Maybe this guy actually belongs to the ranks of the good ones dealt a bad hand. Perhaps even if our fugitive isn't lying, then Mr. Nash is to be the next Host." She put a hand up, knowing Emmett's response by heart. "A leap too far still, yes. I agree. Trusting a murderer and getting killed isn't high on my list either." That seemed to mollify him as he settled back on his heels.

"But the jump got shorter today because check these out." She pulled three silver hairs from her pocket. They snapped in the wind, failing to break free of her grip. She held them up to Emmett, gleeful.

He looked from the hairs to her and back, and his eyebrows slowly rose. "More silver hairs. You're thinking it's another breadcrumb on our killer's little side quest."

"I'm saying it's interesting and shouldn't be overlooked. That's all. And I'm saying yes, it could be another breadcrumb. Because I'll bet my shoes that these are the same hairs as we found with our killer's letter. The killer wants us to pay attention to this guy. Why? Is he the next Host? Is that who they want us to help?"

He raised a questioning eyebrow. It wasn't the level of enthusiasm she'd hoped for. "Maybe Mr. Nash is the murderer, has fancy penmanship, and wears a silver wig."

"Shhh!" Jane glanced around. The sidewalk was clear. She stepped closer to him, catching a whiff of his sweet cologne. "Mr. Nash is definitely not the murderer."

"How do you know?" Emmett's eyes narrowed suspiciously. "And don't say it's a hunch."

Jane rolled her eyes; Emmett sounded like the Director again. "No. And for the record, my hunches got us this far. His and the killer's timelines don't line up. Let's get back to the car, but walk slowly. Go up to the crosswalk to buy extra time. I have a feeling we're being watched." She stole a glance back over at Rory's apartment and its drawn shades. "The killer is probably up there. Right now."

Emmett's eyes widened, and he followed Jane's gaze.

"Don't stare."

Emmett quickly picked at his fingernails and fell into a lazy step next to Jane. She barely noticed as her thoughts came tumbling out. "Mr. Nash fumbled for his lies; too inconsistent. Old lies are easy; we've told them a hundred times. New ones aren't; you're still sorting out the details. He wasn't well practiced, which means whatever had got him spooked was something new. Recent."

"He's got a stressful job."

"It can't just be his job. I bet he has that dialed in, like a mask." There was something there, but she couldn't quite grasp it. "No, this guy is a sponge . . ."

"A sponge?"

"Something I read once for a case. It was talking about paramedics, but I've found it applies to everything under the umbrella term of 'healer.' Society is messy because people are messy. Pros, to be sure, but lots of flaws. Which leads to lots of spilled blood. Society can't clean itself up, it isn't alive or autonomous, so people have to do it. The article called those people the sponges of society and warned that once a sponge soaks up enough blood, it changes them."

They reached the crosswalk and waited for a green light. A long procession of cars passed them, led by a puttering hybrid. "You had me up until the sponge metaphor," Emmett said dryly. She looked up and found him smiling. She scowled back, part of her wanting to slap *that* smirk right off his face, but the rest of her mind was elsewhere, chewing on what she just said. There was something there: a morsel. Something about Mr. Nash, but ringing true about her as well. *You must teach the next Host the secrets you learned in the dark.* It felt right there. She just couldn't put her finger on it. *Come on, Jane. Think!*

"And I think you're getting off-topic. Chuck's murder. Did you see Mr. Nash's reaction?" Emmett said, rocking on his heels.

"That seemed like genuine surprise."

Jane set her new hunch aside. It wasn't ready yet, and she felt the bite of her irritation. "And did you see his hands shake after your ill-advised question about Maxwell?"

"Hey—" he started, but Jane kept going.

"And he almost swallowed his tongue just now when I mentioned Aunt Jackie." Last in line came a yellow Volkswagen van covered in colorful stickers. The driver, an older wizard-looking man, gave Jane a wave, which she enthusiastically returned. "What a friendly city."

"What?!" Emmett's face went slack. "You asked about Aunt Jackie?" He peered down the street. "He bolted for sure." The light turned green and Jane stepped into the street with Emmett hurrying to keep up.

"I don't think so," she said, "He's still around. He's protecting something. It's the only reason an honest man is evasive. He's definitely been in contact with the killer, but I'm not sure he knows they are killing people. That'd be an interesting twist."

"That's a bold prediction based on a five-minute conversation."

"You can learn a lot about someone in five minutes, Emmett." Another gust ripped into them, and Jane quickly wrapped her arms around herself. "I thought it was spring here. Brrr." The wind howled around them, the cold biting her fingers and ears. Jane picked up her pace and held down her fluttering pink hair as they neared the rental.

Emmett stuffed his hands in his pockets, fishing for his keys. "It seems like a big leap to me," he said.

Jane frowned over the top of the car. *Why is he avoiding the evidence? It's right here.* She had an idea why. "I think Mr. Nash was right, Emmett. You are twisted up tight, too."

Emmett's face reddened as he slid his keys into the rental's lock. "You asked him about me?"

"Well, yeah." Jane scooted around the back bumper, raising her voice so she wasn't misunderstood. "If you'd witnessed the same catastrophe I did . . ." She paused, sensing the inevitable poor outcome of that conversation thread. *Stay on topic.* "Look, I was just trying to get more information, okay? I used you as a third party to get him to open up. Interview 101. Plus, you really do need to work on listening. It's the only way to flow."

Emmett jerked open his door. "You kept interrupting me! How do I *flow* with you popping in and asking about grooming and magic?"

"It's called making a connection, you robot," Jane deadpanned, pulling open her door. "It's a human thing. We call it trust. And Rory Nash. I'd bet a bundle he's in the shadows on this. Just like us."

Emmett pressed his lips into a thin line but said nothing and folded himself into the rental. Jane took it as a concession and popped open her door. She slid into her seat and shut the door, throwing the cab into silence. They both paused, dazed, their ears adjusting. The tips of Jane's ears ached from the cold.

"Regardless," Emmett said, pulling out his phone, "we have to be ready."

"Ready as in . . ."

"Backup. I'm getting a surveillance unit over here pronto. If he is in contact with the killer, this is the logical first step. You said you wanted more information."

Jane thought about throwing the phone out the window, but knew that would destroy any chance she had of convincing him. "Fine," she said, not wanting to lose him too early. "That's one idea. Counter proposal. No surveillance van, just us. Let's keep this small, like very small. We stake this place out tonight. See what we see, then take the next step. There is no need to get others involved."

"Too risky," Emmett said, a beat too quickly. He was running on reflexes. "We do it by the book. Let our team know and set up containment. We do this once, and we do it right."

Muff me. "As your consultant, I can't recommend—"

Emmett tucked his phone into his pocket. "A surveillance van is on its way. You're free to leave if you don't like the direction I'm taking this." The car roared to life, filling the quiet of the cab. His words stung, burning from the salt in his tone. He gripped the steering wheel with both hands, and his knuckles turned white. Then he mumbled something and turned off the car, and the wind outside howled. He turned to her with something like pity in his eyes. "One of these days, Jane. One of your hunches will be terribly wrong, and you're going to get another person killed."

Jane sat in silence. Specters of her long-ago fugitive came flooding back. *It doesn't matter; the Seed is safe.* Emmett was right. She'd thought the same thing before, but learned how to soothe her fear through Grace. Fear, she learned, destroys everything but itself. There wasn't room for doubt when the stakes were high, and they had always been high around the Director. But try as she might to be rid of it, the doubt never fully left. Deep down, she knew one day she'd place a big bet and lose. She was human, after all, and that terrified her when she let it. Hearing it from Emmett, though, it felt worse than she imagined.

He faced forward, his eyebrows furrowed. "Sorry. That was harsh."

"But true," Jane said softly.

He nodded and licked his lips before turning to her. "I haven't forgotten what you said. I know we have a choice to make about the Seed. It's all I've been thinking about, actually, and my first priority is not getting turned into a mummy. Dead people don't choose. So we go safe and secure until we know more." He paused, then added. "And don't leave, okay? I'm going to need your help. Please." His pity turned into a plea. "I need your advice, even if I disagree."

"Thanks," Jane said, quickly wiping her eyes. "I'm just curious: Which way are you leaning on the whole Seed thing?"

"I have no idea. Given the evidence, all the options seem to suck."

She nodded, "Ya, they do. If it comes down to it, though, and you get to pick, are you going to give it to the Director?"

Emmett took a deep breath and started the car. "If it comes to that . . . I don't know, but it's my big bet."

Jane's heart sank. She waited for more, but he didn't continue as he pulled out into the street. They rode in silence for two blocks before a disturbing thought came to her. "Once Dawson has the Seed, the Director won't need us anymore. Me especially. Your bet could get me killed."

"That's not going to happen," Emmett said.

Jane sighed, seeing Emmett's defenses up again. She clamped her mouth shut and watched the brick buildings pass by her window. She let her dark thoughts wander, dancing around her conversation with Rory Nash. Was he who the killer pointed her at? And what was she supposed to teach him that they couldn't? The more she mused, the more certainty grew in her. She needed to talk to Mr. Nash again. Alone. She couldn't say why, but she felt it calling her.

The car slowed and stopped at a red light, and Emmett cleared his throat, interrupting her thoughts. "I'll keep you safe," he said.

Jane snickered, looking at him and seeing sincerity written all over his face. He really thought he could. It made her love him a little more. "I don't know if anyone can, but if someone could, I bet it's you."

He flexed his hands idly on the wheel.

"Can I make a request?"

"Not a demand?"

"No, not this time."

"What is it?"

"I want to talk with Mr. Nash before Dawson makes him disappear. I only need a few minutes."

"Why?"

"I need to be certain about him." She shrugged, leaving it at that. She wasn't sure—it was what her hunch was telling her.

Emmett considered, then nodded. "I'll see what I can do."

The light turned green, and for the first time since Emmett walked into her cubicle, she felt the heavy set of uncertainty settle into her stomach. She sank back into her seat, watching the city pass by, trying unsuccessfully to find a scenario where the Director lost and neither of them died.

Chapter 52: Evacuation Plans

Saturday, April 28th, 15:40

Rory peeked over a row of laurels, watching the agent's car turn the corner. He counted to five and then to ten for good measure before he broke cover and rode home. As he approached, his door opened, and he ran inside, panting.

"They are gone," Caroline said, shutting the door behind him. "You did wonderfully."

"They knew about Maxwell and Aunt Jackie." Rory sucked in a deep breath and turned, staring out the peephole. He saw an empty landing and no one coming. He slowed his breathing and turned, finding both Jacklyn and Caroline surprisingly calm.

"Aunt Jackie?" Caroline cocked her head at Jacklyn, who lay on the couch, stroking Sneaks.

"You said no one reads those security logs," Jacklyn mumbled from the couch and Rory swore he heard a faint rattle. *The pneumonia.*

"I didn't think anyone did," Rory said, tossing up his arms.

"What's done is done," Caroline said sharply, closing the topic. She turned to Rory. "With the Cove lost, and this apartment watched, we're without a sanctuary."

Rory looked back at Caroline blankly, wanting badly to come up with a brilliant plan to save them. If the agents had his employee file and his bank statements, then they had everything they needed. Having the camper van would be perfect, but Patrick still hadn't answered his calls. They could steal it, but Patrick would report it missing, and he couldn't tell anyone at work and risk pulling them into his mess. They all had families. He didn't. That left only one actual option.

Rory sighed, wishing there was another. "We'll go to Khloe's."

"Agreed," Caroline said without elaboration. "I suggest packing a bag."

Rory nodded and hurried to his room.

"Who were those two working for, hero?" Jacklyn called. "FBI? CIA? KGB?"

KGB? "The Russians are after you, too?"

"Everyone is after us, hero."

Rory wanted to ask more, but shook his head. *Focus.* "They didn't say. Classified."

"You didn't ask?" Caroline said, amused.

Heat flushed Rory's face as he stuffed a pair of jeans into his duffle bag. "I was a little distracted." *Don't forget socks.*

"Classified my ass," Jacklyn said. "They're Broken Star."

"Those two?" Rory remembered the man he'd watched bleed lava. The agents he'd just spoken with seemed tame in comparison. *And underwear.*

"Guaranteed," Jacklyn huffed.

"Perhaps Rory is right, love," Caroline said. "They may not have chosen a side yet."

Rory thought that sounded ominous, but kept it to himself as he zipped his backpack shut, hoping he'd packed enough. He did not know how long he'd be gone.

Jacklyn snorted, shaking her head. "Killers with a code."

Caroline raised an eyebrow at Jacklyn. She knew something, but another thought came to mind. *Killers . . .*

"There's another thing." He came back into the living room with his backpack over his shoulder. "They said Tommy's abuser was murdered." Neither woman reacted, which made it all the stranger. "Do you know anything about that? Because I'm not sure how it connects."

Caroline sighed and looked at Jacklyn. "It's time, my love."

Rory looked wide-eyed at Jacklyn.

The Host sighed. "I'll just scare him off."

"I'm not going anywhere," Rory said angrily, tossing his bag on the floor. "Look, I'm in. The Seed, the Host, all of it—I'm here for. I saw a guy bleed *lava*. I was bitten by a carnivorous moth and stabbed twice. I've put in the time, haven't I? What do I have to do to prove to you guys that I can handle . . . whatever it is you won't tell me about?!" He felt his outrage spike, then cool, knowing it did as much good at the bedside as it did in real life. He shook his head as wariness set in. "You came to me, remember? Here I am. Now, please tell me what's going on."

Caroline smiled warmly. "Tell him, Jacklyn. He's earned it."

"Earned it . . ." Jacklyn muttered, petting Sneaks. She searched him for a long moment, then shrugged. "Okay. But you asked for this, hero." She shifted, drawing a meow from Sneaks before she began. "I told you, Care, and I had a run-in with your government?"

Rory nodded. "You were captured, but what does that have to do with the murder?"

"Because it's why we were betrayed. Your government wanted this—" She held up her stump, and the light in the room dimmed. Sneaks scampered off Jacklyn's lap as a chill followed a moment later, and Rory's breath puffed out in front of him. Smoke and ash coiled off Jacklyn's stump. Rory started back, his heart drumming in his chest, but Caroline was there beside him. She set her hand gently on his shoulder, anchoring him as he watched in awe as a swirling hand of shadow wiggled its fingers at him.

"What the actual fuck is that?"

"This is the Seed," Jacklyn said, turning her hand over. In her palm was a swirling hole, like a midnight hurricane. "And it's what everyone wants. A weapon."

"Weapon?" Rory shook his head. "But it heals . . ."

"It's a nice byproduct, isn't it?" Jacklyn said, flexing her shadow hand. "But everything costs something, hero. Miracles aren't free."

Rory's mind reeled, and as it churned, he felt like he always knew there was a catch. His thoughts landed on one heart-wrenching idea: "That's where you went when you left town . . . to kill that guy. You went to go . . . what? Recharge?"

"Something like that," Jacklyn said. The shadow hand twitched and dissipated in a cloud as the light returned and the room warmed. Rory shivered, still watching the space where the hand once hung. Caroline guided him over to the couch and pushed him into it next to Jacklyn. He plopped down, still processing, wondering what it said about him that he wasn't more outraged. When he gathered enough wits for a question, he asked, "How does it . . ."

"You don't want to know."

Rory swallowed, nodding. "Why didn't you tell me?"

"Would it have mattered?" Jacklyn said. "Would you trade that guy's life for Tommy's?"

Rory hated that his answer came fast. "No."

"Would it have scared you off?"

Rory nodded.

"That's why, hero. I didn't want to spook you." She turned to Caroline, standing beside him. "Happy? He's terrified now. Can we go?"

"We need to rest," Caroline said. "Not until nightfall. It's too risky."

"We're stuck here until then?" Sneaks crept closer and sniffed at Jacklyn's hand. Jacklyn scooped her up, and Sneaks purred, settling back into her lap. "I suppose that's not the worst thing."

Caroline settled on the floor, cross-legged in front of them. "A story then. To pass the time. The one of our escape will do." She nodded at Rory. "It's a fascinating one that I'm certain you're curious about."

"Oka . . . ay," Rory said, still dazed.

Jacklyn blew out a long breath. "Fine. But I'm telling it."

Caroline dipped her chin.

"Where to start . . . uh. Sure. October, 1962. Cuban Missile Crisis played out, and the war parades resumed the next day. Both sides flashed their doomsday weapons like a couple of mad peacocks on the world stage after coming a breath from blowing it all up. It was insanity. And the fear was everywhere, because everyone was paying attention. It was the closest we've come to wiping ourselves out."

Rory remembered watching videos of mushroom clouds when he was young. They practiced ducking beneath tiny desks. Folded in and admiring the mosaic of gum stuck underneath, he'd wondered how a bit of wood and aluminum would protect him against an atomic blast.

"In the background, making sure the parades had plenty of bombs and soldiers, was the Broken Star. The Star can't abide by peace. Peace means prosperity, and prosperous people are hard to control. They ask questions and organize and have time to dig. Everything you want to avoid while secretly consolidating power and unearthing the past."

It took Rory a moment to realize what she was talking about. "The Shepherd Stones?"

"And other relics from that time," Caroline added. "The Star seeks these treasures out, gathers them, and wields them when needed to further their ambitions."

"You know of Chernobyl? In the 80s?" Jacklyn said.

Rory nodded. "The nuclear meltdown in Russia? It was an

accident."

Jacklyn scoffed. "Accident. It was a Merged with one of the artifacts, a blade that steals souls. They killed fifty guards on their way to the core, and then they pulled the safety cord. You know the rest."

"But why?" Rory said.

"Punishment?" Jacklyn shrugged. "Or someone there asked questions they didn't like. Who knows?"

"Why doesn't someone stop them? The Wyth."

"Because the Star is everywhere, hero," Jacklyn said bitterly. "And the Wyth . . . they're hiding."

Caroline's lips pressed into a tight line a moment before she spoke. "The Wyth have long attempted to infiltrate the Star, to bring them down from within, but often those that aren't killed are recruited, so we stopped trying long before I became the Host's Counselor. That left us blind and overpowered. We were forced to remain in hiding, protecting the Host. Until October 1962 . . ." she trailed off and looked at Jacklyn.

"I was getting to it," Jacklyn said, shooting a glare at Caroline before continuing. "Vietnam raged, and the world seethed, a perfect screen for the Star to do their work, but they were caught flatfooted when a clever couple of Wyth smuggled pictures of atrocities and leaked them to the media. Hard to ignore images of pits filled with dead families."

Rory swallowed, looking down at his hands, not sure what to say. He tried to block the images, but they came anyway, and it made him sick.

"The ensuing public backlash broke the Star's grip on the narrative and almost their whole operation," Jacklyn said. "It was no longer a just war as they had been selling, and the outrage boiled into the streets. We saw a window. It was time the Host came out of hiding."

"And that didn't go well."

Jacklyn grunted and then fell into her thoughts, groaning as she lay down on the couch. Sneaks purred until she settled, then perched on her chest. Jacklyn smiled, scratching Sneaks beneath the chin.

Caroline picked up the story. "It felt like our moment had come. The youth of America, the so-called counter-culture, were energized and differed from anything preceding them. Humanists, they claimed. Save the Earth, end all wars, rebuild the law, and craft a common story. All promises of a world a Wyth could believe in. Many of my sisters emerged that year to join the fight. Jacklyn and I joined them. We just needed the right connections, since we were largely starting with nothing. We moved cautiously. The Seed's safety was still priority number one."

"We walked right into their trap," Jacklyn said. "Perfectly tailored."

Caroline nodded, smoothing out her dress. "They told us they were with the U.S. government and meant us no harm, which, at the time, I think were both true. They brought us to a secret base researching the forgotten apocalypse, specifically casting and the application of Aspects to relieve the world's numerous crises. Famine, disease, and the like. This is what we'd always wanted, and they offered resources, protection, and freedom in our work. They showed us what they had found: a warehouse full of treasures dug up from the past. Books and scales. Armor and tools. It was they who showed us the Shepherd's Stones and the scraps they'd deciphered. We translated more and, in doing so, learned fragments of our past. It was the most fun I've ever had. Bliss, really. Every day, a new discovery. We built friendships there."

"What changed?"

"New management," Caroline said. "A man we now know as the

Director took control."

"Everything changed after he got involved," Jacklyn said from behind her back. "Like a switch, out came the demands. Pushing for a demonstration. For science, they said. I explained to them that nothing is free, the same way I had to explain it to you, and their requests turned into threats after that. We decided to leave, and boom, the shackles came out. The Star had us from the beginning, stringing us along."

"*We* made a mistake," Caroline said. "It is not yours to bear alone, and we did learn a great deal."

"Painful knowledge to earn."

"Most is."

Rory paced into the kitchen and back. He ran both hands through his shaggy, red hair while his mind floundered in its attempt to layer everything Jacklyn just said with what he knew. A question arose. "Why didn't they just take the Seed, though? They had you, right?"

"They tried," Jacklyn said, pulling down the front of her shirt and revealing her sternum. Scars crossed scars, making a thick line down the center of her chest. "They cracked me open more times . . ." She drifted into silence, then whispered. "But the Director is afraid of the Seed, too. They couldn't risk me dying."

"So, they don't know what's inside, either?" Rory said, dumbfounded.

Jacklyn shook her head. "No one does, but they eventually took something. Toward the end, they extracted a piece of the Seed. Whatever it was, it took a collection of memories with it. I used to know things, things I'd never learn from places I'd never visited, but whatever they took, it took that too."

Rory's mind latched onto a glimmer. "But you're both here. You escaped them, so you've beaten the Star before, right? We can do it again."

534

Jacklyn snorted her dissent, and Caroline's lips pressed together. "Jacklyn and I have a disagreement about this. I believe we received help. Someone inside the Star."

"Don't give him dreams of angels, Care," Jacklyn said. "You want the truth, hero? The only reason we got out was because the Star got sloppy, and we got lucky."

"I don't believe in luck," Caroline said.

"Then where has our guardian angel been the last thirty years?" Jacklyn snapped.

Caroline lifted her chin but said nothing. This was an old argument. "Since our escape, the Star has hunted us. Now a Merged has taken our home, and we are here."

Rory pictured the man's red eyes again, utterly massive, with magma trickling down his arm. He swallowed a hard lump in his throat. "You can beat him. The Merged."

Caroline looked over to Jacklyn on the couch, who shook her head slowly as she stroked Sneaks. "We'd prefer to avoid a direct confrontation."

Rory's stomach dropped. The more they talked, the bleaker their situation seemed. There had to be something on their side. Caroline was a Wyth, and Jacklyn had the Seed. That had to count for something. *This fight can't already be lost.*

The air felt thin. He pointed at the heaping grocery cart. "You have something hidden, right? A 'break in case of emergency'?"

Jacklyn laughed weakly. "Hero, you're looking at what we got. There isn't a damn—"

"Let him see for himself," Caroline said. "We are not without teeth." She nodded at the cart.

Taking that for consent, Rory hurried over and unhooked a bungee. The cord snapped back, and he threw the tarp aside. Beneath the towels and wrapped in wool, his hand found something cold and slender. He drew out the tarnished-gold sword hilt he'd once held in this apartment. That felt like ages ago now.

"Yes! This. How does it work?" He held it up, gripping it with two hands and admiring the strange flowing characters etched into the cross guard. "Does it need, like, batteries?" He turned it over, looking for a panel, but found no seam in the steel. He shook it and held it up again. Nothing.

"It's, what, just a hilt?" Rory tossed it back in the cart and resumed his search.

"Ouch!" He pulled his hand back, blood welling from his finger. He pushed aside a box of old books and a lamp and carefully pulled out a long, ornate feather forged completely of iron. It was delicate but heavy. Another string of flowing symbols ran down the quill to the sharp tip.

"What's this do?" He touched the tip, and the quill left a black smudge on his finger. Rory stared at the smudge, rubbing it between his fingers as his frustration boiled. "Great. A fancy pen." He tossed it back. "These aren't weapons."

Caroline shook her head and stood, walking toward Rory. "You must learn to use them first."

"Then teach me!" Rory shouted.

"You are not ready," Caroline said evenly.

"Oh, come on!" Rory's voice rose. "Stop telling me I'm not ready! I couldn't be more ready!"

Sneaks scampered off Jacklyn and under the bed, as Rory glared at Caroline. A chilling thought cut through him. "You don't trust me."

The women exchanged long, somber looks, and Rory breathed quickly, willing himself to hold back his tears. Hadn't he proven himself? What more do they want? The bitter thoughts ate at him.

"I told you I'd scare him," Jacklyn said.

Caroline turned back to Rory and stepped closer, putting her hand on his shoulder. "Of course, we trust you. Don't be ridiculous—that's why we are here and asking you for help. Can we please set this aside for now? I assure you, everything will make sense in time."

Rory didn't like it and nearly said no, but heard the urgency in her voice. "Alright, for now."

"Thank you."

"We need a new Host," Jacklyn said. "I believe you mentioned a candidate."

Rory blinked slowly, exhausted. "I did?" He wasn't sure if he had or not.

"What's the plan, hero?"

Rory adjusted his shoulders and stood straight, readying his pitch. "The candidate is at the hospital. I'm off tonight, so we'll need to lie low until I'm scheduled tomorrow." Rory glanced at the window, hating the only option that seemed to work. "Hopefully, Khloe is home. Either that or we sleep in the woods."

"Too exposed." Caroline gestured to the cart. "A roof is preferable for Jacklyn's health."

"I'll be fine," Jacklyn groused.

"You are sick," Rory said, drawing out his phone. "But Khloe needs a heads up. She could be in danger, too."

"No!" Jacklyn said. "Calls aren't safe anymore. We go in person."

This wasn't how Rory pictured going into Khloe's apartment for the first time. He looked down at his phone and then tucked it away. "Alright, but we can't be pushing that grocery cart around. I have a couple of old backpacks, but you'll have to leave everything else here."

"Fine. Let's sort out what to keep." Jacklyn winced as she rose. Caroline stepped beside her, but Jacklyn waved her off. "I'm fine, woman."

Caroline smiled and wrapped an arm around her anyway before helping remove her jacket. The two leaned together, and Rory saw the strain on Jacklyn's face. They took small steps toward the grocery cart, with Caroline whispering encouragement. Standing in the light and without her jacket, Rory could see Jacklyn's skin was taut against the bone.

Her body is failing . . .

"Rory," Caroline said, coaxing him from the gloom.

He shook his head. "Yes. Here."

"Tell us a story while we pack—tell us about our new Host."

"Oh, yeah. Well, her name is Tracy," Rory said. "And she is very brave."

Saturday, April 28th, 22:57

Rory hesitated, then knocked gently. The sound boomed down the long, gray hallway. He peered around, expecting to see angry faces pop out and ask questions, but aside from the heavy bass thumping through a wall down the hall, there were no signs of anyone, not even light through the peepholes. The sane were asleep.

"Come on, Khloe," he whispered, picking the leaves from his hair. They kept to the bushes and alleys on their way over and hid behind a dumpster to avoid a suspicious black van. Add in Jacklyn's need for rest and food, and what would have taken Rory twenty minutes by bike took several nerve-wracking hours. "You're sure this is her place?"

"Yes," Caroline said behind him, but didn't elaborate on how she knew. She stooped down with Jacklyn's arm slung over her shoulder, but she didn't appear affected by the journey or the extra weight. Anxious jitters crawled up Rory's throat. He pictured Khloe opening the door, smiling beautifully, and ushering them to safety. There was so much to tell her. She'd be upset about him pushing his plan for Tracy, but he was sure she'd understand once she heard the whole story. The timing didn't work. After, they could rest and recover. Maybe even a hug. Or a kiss. Or . . . The thought made Rory's jitters pop like firecrackers.

He knocked again and pressed his ear against the door.

Nothing.

Shit. "She might have gotten called in." He knocked again, louder this time. He had to risk it.

When the silence followed, Caroline asked, "What's our contingency?"

Rory gestured toward Khloe's door. "This was our contingency." He pounded on the door. "Khloe!"

A pinprick of light appeared in the peephole. The deadbolt unlatched and swung open. Khloe stepped into the doorway, blearily eyed. She wore a yellow tank top and black leggings, her blonde hair perched atop her head like a sparrow's nest. She coughed, trying to whisper. "What the hell, Rory? What time is it?"

This wasn't the welcome he'd been expecting. "Late, sorry."

She blinked slowly and looked over his shoulder to Caroline and a slumped Jacklyn. She seemed to sober. "What's going on?"

"It's a long story. We need to hide out here."

"Ya, come on," Khloe said, stepping aside. She flipped on her entryway lights, and he recoiled from the sharp glare. "Is everything okay?"

"Not really," Rory said, stepping past her into the apartment. Jacklyn followed him in, but Caroline stayed in the hall.

"I must depart," she said.

"You're leaving?" Khloe and Rory said together. He wondered what could be so important that she had to leave now.

"This place is as safe as we will find, and there are tasks that must be completed tonight." She looked at Jacklyn, her meaning hidden behind her blindfold, but Rory thought she looked nervous.

"They can't wait?" Rory said.

"It can't," Caroline said, her gaze not leaving Jacklyn. "This could be our last chance."

"Thanks, Care," Jacklyn said. "Really."

Caroline smiled back, then reached into her cloak and drew out the tarnished sword hilt, handing it to Rory.

He looked down at the blade-less weapon. "It doesn't work for me."

"Not *yet*," Caroline said, tapping her chest with two fingers. "But it's here, waiting to be unlocked."

He nodded, still unsure what exactly that meant, but took the hilt. It felt heavy and cold in his hand and remained frustratingly inert.

"Keep the door shut," Caroline said. "I'll return as soon as I can." Then she swept from the room with her green cloak billowing behind her.

The three stood there, each wearing a grim expression, until Khloe shut the door.

"What's going on? Are we in danger?"

"Always," Jacklyn said and held out her hand. "Help me sit down, hero." He stepped in beside her, her arm feeling so thin between his fingers, and eased her down into a dining room chair. "We best rest. It will be a big day tomorrow."

"Big day?" Khloe looked at Rory, confused, but then her eyes narrowed. "What does that mean? It better not involve Tracy."

Tracy is the only option we have. He cleared his throat and straightened. "Things have changed, Khloe. The Star attacked the Cove, and they know where I live. It's why we are here." He paused, leveling his voice, trying to sound confident. "We're passing the Seed to Tracy tomorrow night."

"She isn't a fit candidate."

"Why not?"

She pointed to her eye. "Who scratched you?"

He shrugged—she already knew the answer. "Uh, a patient."

"Tracy." She shook her head. "That's my point. She can't accept—"

"Tracy is a good kid! And an excellent candidate. She just got scared."

"I'm not saying she isn't a good kid, Rory," Khloe said patiently. "I'm saying her chronic fear is a huge liability with that much power."

"Not around me," Rory shot back. "I mean, us. The three of us together—needle monsters, remember? We make a great team. We can help her control her fear. And the Seed."

"You don't know that. We need to understand what it is. Study it. That means tests. Diagnostics. Drawing blood. How well do you think Tracy's going to do with that?"

Rory opened his mouth to reply, but nothing came.

"Exactly."

"Well, it's our only option right now."

Khloe's fire dimmed, and she suddenly looked a little sheepish. "Well, maybe not our only one."

Rory blinked, confused. "What do you mean?"

"Where is it?" she said, flipping on lamps as she searched. As light filled the room, it revealed an entire catalog of modular tan and white furniture. The couch looked pristine, barely used, and sat alone except for an ottoman made of cloth and wood instead of cardboard. Above the couch was a small painting depicting two horses running over a grassy hill toward a distant sunset.

"Where is what?" Rory said, his nerves spiking.

"My phone," she said, tossing a pair of blue pillows off the couch.

Rory took a tentative step forward. "Khloe, tell me what you did."

"I reached out, anonymously, to see about getting some help." She lifted a cushion. "Found it!" She picked it up and scrolled. "They want to meet us."

Rory felt the words drive into his stomach and knock the wind out of him. "Who?"

"The Evergreen Society," Khloe said.

Oh, shit . . . He looked over and saw Jacklyn watching, anger plainly brewing across her face, adding to his sharpening nerves. He wished Caroline was here.

"I just sent out feelers," Khloe said without looking up. "Again, completely anonymous." Her mouth spread into a wide grin as she read. "He replied personally."

"Who is 'he'?" Rory said.

"Kenneth Connell," Khloe said, continuing to scroll.

"What?!" Jacklyn roared. The room went quiet as a storm gathered around her.

"He is interested in the sample I sent," Khloe said, her enthusiasm gone.

"What *sample*?" Jacklyn's tone sent a shiver up Rory's back.

Khloe, confused, looked up from her phone. "The one Caroline gave me. What's wrong?"

Jacklyn's face knotted up, and she hissed each word. "Kenneth Connell is a snake, a liar, and he will never come near me again."

Khloe blinked, confused. "I . . . I don't understand. How do you know him?"

"How do I know him?" Jacklyn snarled. "How could I forget him? I saw him every day for years on the other side of steel bars as he prodded me with every manner of probe. He works for the Broken Star and heads their research department."

"Wait, hold on," Khloe said. "I hear you, but . . . he's a humanitarian. A good person. He's on the shortlist for a Nobel Prize. He wouldn't torture anyone." Her voice arced up slightly, questioning.

"You want that to be true, doc. But people wear many masks," Jacklyn stared, hard and cold, at Khloe. "This is another trap."

Khloe's confidence wavered. "It can't be . . . I'm —" She looked at Rory, pleading for backup, and he found himself suddenly at the center of the storm again. He didn't know what to say. Too many people and too many priorities had confused everything. He wanted it to be simple again and fumbled with his knotted thoughts. Khloe obviously believed she was helping, but if Jacklyn was right, then this CEO couldn't be trusted. That aside, placing the Seed into the guardianship of a corporation felt ridiculous—desperate even. The Evergreen Society was an unknown variable at best. He knew Tracy.

"She's compromised," Jacklyn said without taking her eyes off Khloe. "We'll have to execute the plan without her."

"Wow," Rory said, hearing the escalation. "Perhaps we should—"

"No, hero. She put the Seed in danger. That breaks rule number one. This is exactly what I was worried about."

Khloe put up her hands. "What? Come—No, you've got it all wrong." She tripped over her words. "There is a misunderstanding."

"No mistakes here, doc," Jacklyn said. Her tone made Rory's hair stand on edge.

Khloe's eyes danced back and forth, trying to find traction. "We can find a better Host. The Society could help. We need allies. Badly. These people can offer sanctuary."

"Or prison!" Jacklyn shouted. The lights flickered.

"There is risk there, too," Rory said in a soothing tone, trying to bring the tension down. "Our plan doesn't involve trusting a torturer. Tracy—"

Khloe glared at him, jabbing a finger. "Giving that girl the Seed is wrong, and some part of you knows it. I can't, in good conscience, let you condemn that little girl."

"We're saving her!"

"No, Rory. You're not doing this for her. You're doing it for yourself."

"You don't even know me!" he spat back. His anger flooded him, dropping a wall between them. Everything he'd done was for his patients. Everything. She'd only just seen her first code. *How dare she!* Rory's fists clenched, and a dozen sharp remarks passed through his head, but through the heat of these thoughts, a hollowing premonition emerged. *She's going to tell someone. She's going to mess the whole thing up.*

As though Jacklyn heard his thoughts, she added, "We can't let you interfere, doc." She held out her hand to Rory. "Give me the Dozer."

"The what?"

She pointed at the sword hilt in his hand, but he hesitated. He met Khloe's blue eyes, her expression caught somewhere between terror and defiance.

"I'm trying to help," Khloe said, her eyes growing wide with fear.

Rory's stomach twisted as he looked down at the inert weapon in his hand. "What are you going to do?"

"Buy us time to complete the mission," Jacklyn said again, coaxing with her hand. "I won't hurt her."

"Rory, please . . ." Khloe said.

He swallowed, trying to picture a scenario where this would end well, but it seemed to him that he had made his decision. He'd picked his path. Where was Caroline when he needed her? With a wave of nausea, he handed the Dozer over.

Jacklyn took it and swiftly stepped toward Khloe. The lamps and overhead lights flickered and snapped as she passed, throwing snarling shadows across the walls.

Khloe's eyes widened, and she retreated backward. "Wait, let's talk this through . . ."

"Sorry, Doc. I wish this went differently." Blue and white light welled from the hilt's glyphs. A cloudy three-foot blade of dark blue smoke erupted from the cross guard, throwing off a slow-rolling fog that splashed against the floor.

Khloe bumped into her ottoman and then remembered the phone in her hand. She started punching something in. Jacklyn swung, barely allowing her time for a startled yelp before the blade passed through the side of her neck. Khloe's eyes fluttered back into her head, and her body went slack. Jacklyn dropped to a knee and caught her, carefully lowering her body onto the sofa. The blade dissipated, and the light of the glyphs extinguished. In three heartbeats, it was over.

Rory raced forward, kneeling and pressing his fingers against the inside of Khloe's neck. There was no blood, no wound, and he felt a slow and steady pulse against his fingertips. "What did you do?"

"She's okay," Jacklyn said. "The Dozer doesn't cut, but she'll be asleep for a day or so." She met his eyes, her cold calmness meeting his frantic second-guessing. "We had no choice, hero. She was going to ruin everything and put everyone— everything—in danger."

Rory nodded, not feeling so sure. He checked Khloe, waiting for a breath, and said a prayer of thanks when her chest rose. Jacklyn reached into her pocket and drew out her red mythstone, ran her finger over it, and then tucked it back inside Khloe's sweats.

Jacklyn sighed and rubbed her hand over her face as she rose and paced the apartment. Rory watched her, then the door, praying Caroline would walk back through. But the Wyth didn't appear, leaving him with his consequences. Khloe's chest rose and fell again, a soft moan escaping her lips from whatever dream the Dozer threw her in. He slumped back onto the floor. *We were supposed to do this together.* It wasn't until then that he realized how frail that future had been.

"Better get some rest, hero," Jacklyn said. "It's going to be a long day tomorrow."

Rory looked at Khloe and felt sick.

"Sleep," Jacklyn said. "I'll watch after her."

"I can—"

"Go." Her tone didn't leave room for negotiation. "I need to be alone."

He hesitated, watching Khloe steadily breathe, wondering what he could do to make this right. Unfortunately, his mind found nothing; they were committed now. He grabbed a tiny red throw pillow and curled up in the corner. He listened to Jacklyn's raspy breaths, wondering what Khloe would think when she woke up—if she'd talk to him so he could explain. Maybe she'd even forgive him.

Please. It's the only way.

Chapter 54: Time and Chance

Sunday, April 29th, 18:01

Rory slept badly. The floor was hard, but it was his old nightmare, returning with a new twist, that gave him fits.

Falling asleep in the PICU while on duty, this time on the floor of Room 4. A cacophony of alarms screeching. Lurching awake, heart pounding wildly. Leaping up, sprinting to the sliding door. It was jammed. Heaving against it, but it wouldn't budge. A pool of thick black water oozed from between the tiles on the floor, filling the room. Finding a bright orange bucket in the corner, scooping the black water, but the tide rose too quickly. Water tasted like blood. Panic, tossing the bucket aside, looking up to climb, standing on a gurney, and reaching for a missing ceiling tile.

But this time, something new. From out in the hall, a pack of hungry howls. Listening, breaths short and tight. Wolves? Long shadows appeared against the wall, baring long, curved teeth. Jumping toward the ceiling, but falling into the blackness. The wolves—

"Hey!" Jacklyn's voice broke in.

Rory bolted upright, his body sweating and achy. He blinked around for his bearings and found the painting of the two horses and the sunset. *Khloe's.* Just below the painting, she lay still as death, asleep. Rory's dark thoughts returned. *Wolves.*

"It's after six." Jacklyn crouched down beside him, putting her hand on his shoulder. "Showtime."

"Six?" he said, shaking his sleep off. "Shit, I gotta go."

"I thought so, too." Jacklyn's nose wrinkled. "No offense, but you stink."

Rory sniffed his shirt. A pungent scent violated his senses; he smelled like two days of running. "I'll bike up now and shower." His stomach grumbled, and he realized with everything that had happened yesterday, he'd skipped dinner. The thought of warm empanadas made his stomach growl again. "And get food." He could fit it in.

Rory rose, his body popping and stiff from the unforgiving floor. "How is Khloe?"

"Slept better than we did," Jacklyn said. "I'll meet you outside at ten. Same place as Tommy."

Rory's backpack rested by the door, and he checked its contents: scrubs, shoes, pens, paper, a stethoscope, and his badge. The gold pin felt smooth beneath his thumb, and he paused, marveling at his younger self. The person smiling up at him was a completely different person.

"Wish me luck," Rory said, tossing his backpack over a shoulder.

"Caroline would say she doesn't believe in luck," Jacklyn grunted, sitting on the couch next to Khloe's curled body. She placed a hand gently on Khloe's shoulder. She stirred, then settled, drawing a grim expression from Jacklyn. Rory wondered if it meant regret.

"How about good timing and good opportunity, then?" he offered, trying to raise their spirits. "Does that sound Wyth enough?"

"Too wordy." The corner of Jacklyn's mouth flicked. "She'd say it's all time and chance."

"That doesn't leave a lot of room for choice."

Jacklyn shook her head. "No. It doesn't." She pushed a curl of blonde hair from Khloe's face. "Good luck, hero."

"Thanks," Rory said and blew out a breath. An idea popped into his head. "Why don't you come with me? We don't know if this place is even safe. Maybe the hospital would—"

"A fine idea," Jacklyn cut in and patted her wilted thigh. "But this old body doesn't have much more in it."

"What?" Rory shook his head. "You're Aunt Jackie."

She sighed. "Not for much longer."

"Come on," Rory whispered. *I need you.* His panic rose as he dropped to his knees beside Jacklyn. "What if . . . what if we go find Caroline and buy some time? We can make a new plan."

Jacklyn reached out and took Rory's hand, surprising him. "Care and I, we've been scraping together time since we escaped the Star. And bought more besides, with blood. There's nothing left to scrape, hero. I've lived a long, full life. I've done more than I ever thought. Hell, I fell in love with a goddess, and she loves me back. What more could I want?"

The Host tapped her chest with two fingers. "But the Seed . . . the Seed is heavy. So heavy. And I'm ready. It's time for me to rest. Let someone else take a turn." She stared into space, lost in memories. Uncertain what else to do, Rory squeezed Jacklyn's hand, summoning her attention. She peered at him, and he saw the fatigue carved into the pockets surrounding her dark eyes. Rory had seen cadavers with more vitality.

"We're going to do this. You and me." Rory felt his throat tighten. "And you've done enough, more than enough. You . . . you taught me miracles are real, and I . . . I didn't . . . I think I was done after Octavia; I was done trying to help. Done with . . . everything. Until you and Caroline jumped me and showed me something I'd lost."

"What was that?"

"Hope. That I'm not alone."

Tears welled in her eyes, and she lifted his hand, tapping her dry, papery lips against the back. A pair of fat droplets ran down her cheeks. Rory's vision blurred.

"None of that, hero." She released his hand and wiped her eyes with her sleeve. "We've got jobs to do and need to stay focused. Here, take this." She drew out the Dozer and handed it over. "Just in case."

No blue smoke poured out when he touched the pommel. "Will I need it?"

Jacklyn smiled up at him. "I hope not." She shooed him toward the door. "Go on. You go get the next Host ready. I'll watch Khloe and work on not dying."

Rory laughed despite the circumstance, feeling himself settle; graveyard jokes had a way of soothing harsh reality. He held back the urge to give Jacklyn a hug, to thank her for that gift. "Ten o'clock," he said instead.

Jacklyn nodded. "I'll see you on the other side."

———

19:03

His master plan of a shower and quick dinner sputtered when the shower nozzle jammed and, combined with a clogged drain, quickly flooded the locker room with a cold, shallow pool. He spent dinner time mopping up the mess and then sprinted to report, sweating.

Standing outside the report room brought a dizzying sense of déjà vu. He was late. Again. The young nurse on his badge was never late. He'd been on time, precise, a cog in the wondrous machine, just like Bell taught him. Forcing himself to breathe, he adjusted the Dozer tucked into the waistband of his scrubs. He hoped he didn't need it, or that it would even work, but having the hunk of metal calmed his nerves. Worst case, it was heavy and would make a mean projectile.

Opening the door at three past seven, he slipped inside, nodding at the head of the table. Bell sat there, wearing her white curls up in a red scrunchie and matching scrubs with smiling black cats. She eyed the clock before nodding back, then continued scrutinizing the unit census sheet. The list looked full. Rory's thoughts raced. A full unit didn't always mean a sick unit, but also rarely meant a calm shift. *One step at a time.*

He hurried toward the open seat between Katherine and Megan—empty but for Megan's bag of magazines. He approached and waited awkwardly by the chair. They hadn't really talked since Tracy's sedation, since the award.

"Hi," Rory said tentatively.

Sitting back from the table, the census sheet resting on her belly, she glanced up. "Hey." She looked down at the chair. "Oh—yeah. Sorry." She slid her bag off the seat and waved at the census. "It's bad tonight."

Relieved, he said hello to Katherine, who gave a brief nod without looking up as she continued to scribble down notes on her sheet. The Dozer jabbed him in the side as he sat. He shifted it, trying to be discreet, and turned to Megan. "Thanks for saving me a spot."

Megan tugged her long sleeves up to her elbows. "Always do." She smiled, and just like that, they felt normal again. Almost. She eyed him. "You're late again."

"Shower malfunction," Rory said. "Had to mop it up."

Megan chuckled, shaking her head. "You have the worst luck." When she looked back up, her eyes leveled on his.

"Hey, sorry for being weird about the award."

"I get it," Rory said. "I felt cheated, too. My candidate didn't win."

She nodded. "It would have been nice. To be recognized."

Rory bit his cheek and tilted his head. *It's my award.*

"I have an idea," he said, lifting his badge and pulling off his golden pin. He presented it to Megan in his sweaty palm. "Here.

I want you to wear this."

"Rory . . ."

"You earned it. Way more than me," Rory said, holding out the pin. "You inspire me. And it's mine, so I can do whatever I want."

"You sure?"

He nodded and thrust his palm forward. "Something to show Parasite. Show'm how cool their mom is."

"I *am* a badass." She plucked the pin out of his hand and turned it over. "Thanks, Rory. Really. This means the most."

Rory beamed. It felt good to correct an injustice.

"Let's get started," Bell said from the head of the table.

The unit was busy—seventeen rooms. Two critical patients, with a third threatening to crash, two dialysis patients, and the three empty rooms all reserved for inbound Level One traumas—like Octavia—two by wing, one by wheel. By the end of the shift, they'd be full if they kept everyone alive. Around the table, Rory saw veteran faces drawn, steeling themselves.

Rory steadied his breathing. *And I have to figure out a way to get Jacklyn in.* Looking at the census sheet, his plan felt increasingly impossible.

Bell thanked the extra staff who had volunteered to come in, and Rory applauded with the rest. Reinforcements meant hope. Without them, Jacklyn would never make it to Tracy. His first bit of luck.

Bell handed out assignments to the silent group. Occasionally, a nurse spoke up to clarify a diagnosis or plan, but no one argued, and no one complained. She announced Tracy was scheduled for surgery tomorrow and assigned her to Katherine. Apparently, Dr. Magus thought he'd discovered an experimental surgical option, which meant a chlorhexidine bath and pre-op labs for Tracy, a sleepless night for Mr. Oates, and a deadline for Rory. It was tonight or never. He blinked, feeling nauseous. If he failed—he wouldn't let himself finish the thought.

One step at a time.

He was about to ask if he could switch to Tracy when Katherine's hand shot up. Holding off, he listened, hoping for good news. Katherine asked for a break at eleven—for fifteen minutes to talk to her husband, who had emerged from the fog of war. Before anyone else could speak, Rory's hand shot up, eager to volunteer. Bell checked her sheet and nodded, and Katherine thanked them both. It was the best opportunity he would get, though it would be an hour later than his plan with Jacklyn. He hoped she'd wait.

Bell kept the report brisk. When Rory's assignment came up, he heard a familiar name: Jenny. Bell paired her with the first of the new admits—an infant who had fallen out of a third-story window. The family would arrive any minute. He held his breath. Big traumas often took hours, if not days, to stabilize. He had four hours.

His optimism rebounded when Bell said Jenny had floor orders and was only admitted because she hadn't yet finished her regimen of antibiotics. A simple assignment. More good news.

"Last thing, before we get to it," Bell announced, "that little girl here last week for the dog bite is back on the ward upstairs. An infection, but they got it early, so she should be fine."

Katherine raised her hand and Bell nodded an acknowledgment, continuing, "Her lips are fine, no leeching this time, but we're collecting money to get her balloons and a toy from the gift shop. Let her know we are thinking of them down here."

Katherine lowered her hand.

Bell passed a Hill Hospital hat around, and the nurses pulled out their wallets. Everyone at the table tossed a bill into the hat as it passed by. It reminded Rory of collections at Mass—a long, long time ago. "I have a card here for everyone to sign before shift end. I know the family will appreciate you all." Her smile faded as she glanced back at the census, and she removed her glasses. For the first time in Rory's memory, Bell looked tired—small. The wrinkles of her forehead deepened, and he saw the same wariness he felt. He wanted to jump up and hug her and tell her he understood that he was there for her, but her eyes snapped up before he could move, and she straightened.

"I wouldn't take any other team than this one here tonight." She tapped the edge of her glasses on the table. "It's going to be busy, it's going to be hard, but remember now, you all know your craft. You've been here before, so let's keep it simple. Ask for help. Know what you don't. Stick to the 'Five Rights' and speak up when something feels off. If we do those, everyone makes it to morning." She stopped and donned a pristine smile, and Rory watched her gather the tension. She cut it. "After that, it's day shift's problem."

They laughed. Bell had done it again.

———

19:29

Rory hadn't finished planning his night on his paper brain when he got word his admission had arrived. Luckily, the baby had fallen two stories, not three, and landed on a hedge. They were conscious, though sluggish, when they arrived, accompanied by a pair of shaken parents. Over the next ninety minutes, Rory tracked the clock while executing his orders and answering the steady stream of questions. The infant escaped the ordeal with a few purpling bruises, a new teddy bear, and more vigilant parents.

Rory ate three packs of crackers for dinner and rinsed them down with a cup of lukewarm, industrial-strength coffee. He barely had time to swallow before he heard the second admission announced. Megan's patient: a teenager in a terrible car wreck.

A crowd of specialists, all with long strings of red letters on their white jackets, grew outside her room. Residents of different departments dashed up and down the hall, punching in orders and calling for reinforcements. The attending physician orchestrated treatments. Specialists made the plan, and the nurses carried it out. Their faces were drawn as they worked. The numbers looked bad—another tragedy.

One step at a time.

———

21:21

The third admission arrived: a sixteen-year-old male who had chugged drain cleaner. The success of their suicide attempt remained unknown, but the cleaner had disintegrated the boy's throat, and if he survived, he would eat and drink through a tube for the rest of his life. Rory's heart ached, and he took deep breaths to steady himself. *You're not alone*, he whispered.

Bell called in the cavalry. The on-call physician and two more nurses arrived shortly after nine. Dr. Deedee, with her cup of tea and blanket around her shoulders, took half the unit, and the chaos stabilized.

For five minutes, everyone breathed. But then the alarms rang— Megan's patient had crashed, and the window for Katherine to make her call felt like a pipe dream.

Breathe.

With grim determination, Rory tried to be everywhere. He primed lines, turned patients, and ran updates to terrified families in the waiting area, all in an effort to salvage even a tiny window to get Jacklyn to Tracy. After that? He'd figure it out later.

———

21:50

At ten minutes to ten, Rory threw up in the bathroom. It was mostly acid and bits of cracker, and it burned. He wiped his mouth and got back to work.

Stepping back on the unit, he watched the orchestration of men, women, and machines. An unexpected wave of gratitude overwhelmed him. He saw them as he imagined Bell did every night—in a flow. Despite the exhaustion and high stakes, the floor brimmed with energy and compassion. *"When the unit runs right, we save lives,"* Bell once said. *"We're an engine of hope."*

Someone called for towels and fresh linens, shaking Rory from his thoughts. He hurried to the linen cart, stacking rough cotton linens in his arms. As he reached for a sheet, he wavered, blinking. A sense of loss seeped into him.

After tonight, I might never be a nurse again.

The thought slammed into him. He nearly buckled.

Not now. The Seed is all that matters.

He grabbed a blanket, turned, and plunged back in.

———

22:06

At some point, Rory lost his paper brain, and his plans disappeared with it.

He overheard shouting—the frantic father of the suicide patient and Bell's calm tone mediating the conflict. The shouts boomed down the hall, demanding to know what they were doing to save his son's life. "Dr. Strong" was called over the intercoms, and security arrived, parking themselves right on the path Rory had hoped to bring Jacklyn in. Officer Kyle was with them and talked with the dejected father.

Rory rerouted his plan, but the alternatives weren't as direct. He was gaming out smuggling Jacklyn in a laundry cart when his patient's mother came running out of his room.

"His face!" she shouted.

Rory rushed back into the room and found the baby lethargic with a slight droop on his right side. A stroke or delayed bleeding from the fall. For the next fifty-four minutes, with the help of Dr. Deedee and blood thinners, the child's symptoms improved.

At eleven o'clock, Bell summoned Deedee to another room, but not before the attending listed strict instructions: low-dose vasopressor to stop further bleeds. Rory reached for his paper brains, rediscovering he'd lost them. He scribbled it down on his palm instead. Juggling dosages in his head, Rory hurried to the medication room. His window was closing.

23:01

Zero point zero five milli-units, a kilogram, a minute . . . Rory whispered to himself. Looking around, most of the nurses in the hall were also whispering reminders to themselves. It was that kind of night.

He burst into the med room, gathering tubing and supplies. He saw Room 4's medication bin and realized with a lurch that he'd forgotten to give Jenny's last dose of antibiotics an hour ago.

"Shit."

He grabbed Jenny's antibiotics, packaged in an identical IV bag as the blood thinners—500 milliliters of clear liquid and red labels with tiny font identifying the pharmaceuticals inside. He squinted at them.

From the corner of his eye, he caught a wild motion and looked up to see Katherine waving him down through the window. He tried to wave back, but a syringe slipped out of his hands and clattered against the tiles. Katherine pointed at her watch with a questioning shrug. He managed a nod before ducking back into Tracy's room. He checked the clock: 23:03.

Rory could hear Bell in his head. "Five rights, safe night." But there was no one else in the medication room, and no one was readily available outside to double-check him. *Is time speeding up?!*

"Screw it."

———

23:06

Jenny's infusion ticked away on her pump as Rory closed the sliding glass door behind him. He'd strung up the meds in record time and skipped recording the administration on the computer. *Later.*

Katherine stood outside her room, watching him anxiously. He waved at her, put up one finger, and pointed at the IV bag in his hand. She nodded and checked her watch.

"Oh, hi, Rory!" Danielle walked up wearing sweats and a black and orange sweater. By the smell of her, Rory guessed she must have finished her smoke break.

"Welcome back," Rory said. "I just hung Jenny's meds and—"

"Oh?" Danielle frowned. "I thought she was done? They canceled her last dose."

Rory's heart jumped into his throat. He hadn't checked the orders in hours. He'd been too busy. "Are you sure?"

She nodded and cocked her head, peering at the IV bag in his hand. Her frown turned into a quick smile. "Oh, you're fine, Rory. Those are her antibiotics . . ." She stopped, and her eyes widened.

Rory made a sound he'd never heard. Like air escaping from a pressure cooker. He looked down and read Jenny's name on the label just above the word *amoxicillin*—the antibiotic. Not the vasopressor.

"Let me, uh," he sputtered. "One sec."

"Rory?"

"It's nothing!" he lied. "I forgot something in the room."

He pulled the door open and rushed inside, though he knew she would follow. He could feel her eyes on his back as he slid around the bed. Jenny was fast asleep with a pair of headphones on, with the faint sound of children's bubblegum rock. Rory reached the pump and stopped the infusion before checking the IV bag. He grimaced when he didn't see Jenny's name on the bag.

"Shit," he whispered.

He'd never made a med error before; he always double-checked his medications. Bell would say the best thing to do was be upfront and honest. There would be some forms and a couple of tough conversations with management and the family. While it was careless, he thought he caught it quick enough to avoid harming Jenny. His real problem was not having time for forms or conversations. Not now. He had to go.

"What's going on, Rory?" Danielle said from the doorway. "What did you give her?"

A flash of hot frustration melted away his icy dread.

Danielle stepped toward the IV pole, and Rory plucked the bag from the tubing, stopping the pump as IV fluid splashed against the floor. He stepped back, unable to think what to say.

The machine's alarms screamed, and Danielle circled Jenny's bed. Rory retreated in the opposite direction, keeping Jenny between them. She stopped and fixed him with a dangerous glare. "Let me see the bag, Rory."

"It's nothing." Rory continued around the bed, the pump still screaming, hoping to make a break for the open doorway.

She blocked the door. "Rory, don't do this. Mistakes happen. Just tell me what it is."

Rory stopped, trying to summon up the words to make her understand.

"I—"

Bell appeared in the doorway. "You going to silence that pump?" she asked, smiling, but that vanished when she looked at Danielle. "What's going on here?"

"Rory gave Jenny the wrong medication, but he won't show me."

His heart drummed in his ears. "Bell, I can explain, but right now, I need to go relieve Katherine so she can call her husband and—"

Bell's eyes narrowed in disbelief. "Did you not hear what Danielle just said?"

"I did," Rory said, "I did. And she's right—"

"She's *right*?!" Bell said, her eyes widened behind her glasses.

Danielle gasped and covered her mouth.

"Wait, wait," Rory said, putting out his hands. "Hold on. I caught it before anything happened. This isn't a big deal."

Bell stepped forward. "Let's see the bag and talk this through."

"I . . . I can't do that, Bell. I have to go." He rose onto the balls of his feet like he was about to jump. "I'm already late."

"Have you lost your mind?" She put out her hand. "Give me the bag." She stepped around the side of the bed toward him, but he retreated. Bell stopped and fixed him with a withering gaze. "You think real hard about what you do next. Think about what I've taught you."

"I know, Bell. I just—" Rory didn't know what to say. He hadn't planned for this. He turned to Danielle. "I'm sorry, I—" His eyes flicked up to the clock: 23:05. "I'll be right back." He marched straight for the door, hoping his size and conviction would deter them from interfering further. It didn't.

Bell's finger clamped onto his arm as he slid past her. "Are you diverting?"

Diverting? "No!" Rory said indignantly. *She couldn't understand.*

Bell didn't let go, whispering, "I've heard that before. This work can break you. Rory, do you need help?"

"I'm not stealing drugs." Rory yanked his arm, but she held fast. "Let go!" He met her eye and expected to see fury but, to his surprise, found concern.

"Please, Rory," she pleaded. "Don't do this. Please, give me the bag. I'm asking as your friend."

The image of her broke his heart, but everything—Tracy, Jacklyn, the Seed—depended on him. His next words boiled out of him. "I can save her, Bell. I can save them all." He felt tears welling up. "I found a way." He searched her for any sign of understanding, but all he saw was pity. He looked down at the bag in his hand and thrust it forward. "Here."

Bell released his arm, and both women leaned together to read the label.

He dashed out of the room, his mind racing. Getting back into the hospital would be difficult now. Maybe Jacklyn could incapacitate anyone who stopped them? If that's what needed to be done, he thought, then so be it. *This will work.*

"Rory, you stop right there!" Bell's voice rang out behind him, echoing down the white-tiled hall.

Everyone's eyes turned and tracked Rory, and he felt his face flush red. He picked up his pace and spotted Officer Kyle with a phone to his ear, staring at him.

"Rory, stop!"

Kyle set down the phone and stepped toward him. "Sir, we need you to—"

Without thinking, Rory broke into a panic-fueled run and threw himself against the entry door. Shouts and footfalls followed behind. Ahead, the carpeted hall turned to the left, and he quickly calculated the quickest route outside. He needed to get to Jacklyn. He turned the corner and jerked to a halt—a short, pink-haired woman in a black suit grinned up at him.

"Hello, Mr. Nash."

The younger, handsome Agent Torin and a pair of burly armed men in Kevlar vests walked behind Jane. "We were just coming to find you."

Alarm bells rang in Rory's mind, narrowing the world. He backed up, turning toward the unit, only to find Kyle and Bell behind him. His eyes flicked back and forth. There was a way out, he was certain. He just hadn't seen it yet. Lying hadn't worked, so maybe the truth would.

Rory stepped toward Bell, but Kyle intervened, placing himself between the two. "Okay. Okay. I know it's going to sound crazy, okay, but Aunt Jackie, you both remember her? She saved Tommy that night. It was actual *magic*. There is this . . . Seed thing and—well, I'm not completely sure how—" He shook his head. He wasn't making any sense. "Aunt Jackie came back. For Conner. She saved him, too. We had to sneak her in with a resident's badge, but—"

"Sir," Kyle cut him off.

Rory blinked at him, but found no understanding.

"Sir, unauthorized use of a badge is a violation—"

"Fuck your rules, Kyle!" Rory snapped, stepping forward. "I'm saving kids' lives! What the fuck are you doing, huh?"

Kyle didn't flinch. "—of the employee handbook. I'll need you to turn over your badge and go with these people." He gestured to Jane. The woman watched him with intense scrutiny, as though memorizing his every word.

Rory felt his breath leave him.

"Mr. Nash," Agent Torin said. "You're under arrest for abetting a murderer."

Rory stopped cold. "What?" He shook his head. "No. I didn't." He pointed at Emmett and shouted, "He's lying!" He looked around for sympathetic faces among Bell and the others behind her but found only sickened concern. "Bell, believe me. You have to. I know what's going on here! Those aren't the good guys—they work for the Broken Star. They're after the Seed! They are trying to stop the miracles!"

"Come with us, Mr. Nash," Jane said, stepping closer to him. "Please don't resist."

Agent Torin nodded to the men behind him, and they swept forward in unison. The fluorescent light gleamed off their handcuffs.

They are going to torture me, just like Jacklyn.

Rory looked at Bell, pleading for her to understand. She looked heartbroken.

"Please. Don't do this."

He moved toward the door, and she stepped in front of him.

"Get out of my way."

Bell didn't budge. "I can't do that."

"Move!" His entire body tensed as he glared down at her.

Her eyes drifted to something just over Rory's right shoulder. He followed her gaze and found the Dozer, dim as always, poised to strike in his trembling fist.

Bell's chin lifted, though her eyes welled with tears. "Go on."

Rory blinked, looking between her and then the Dozer. *What happened to me?*

He dropped his arm, letting the hilt clatter to the floor. "Bell . . ." Words failed him. "I wouldn't . . . I'm . . . I'm sorry."

Officer Kyle drew a Taser from his belt and stepped forward, seizing Rory's arm. "Don't resist, sir." Then added, "Please."

No! He shoved Kyle with both hands. The surprise attack knocked him off balance, buying Rory the narrowest window. He bolted for the doors but made it only a few steps before they were on him, driving him to the ground. They wrenched his arms behind him, kneeling on his back until Rory screamed. He tasted iron, wriggling with all his might as they pressed down harder.

"Seed . . ." Rory wheezed, but found himself unable to draw a full breath. He tried to fight, but his shoulder threatened to pop from its socket.

"Last warning, sir," Kyle said above him. "Stop resisting."

Rory squirmed. "Seh—" He looked up from the floor and saw Bell, tears streaming down her face. She shook her head slowly behind her cupped hands.

The pressure on his neck and chest lifted, and he sucked in a burning breath. A heartbeat later, electric fangs sank into his thigh, crackling into his skin. His entire body cramped, and his back arched, popping the cartilage in his spine. Every nerve burned. When he screamed, only a soft moan and drool leaked from his lips. Then the fangs disappeared, and he slumped against the ground, spent. He coughed, sputtering, as his tongue flopped uselessly in his mouth.

"Beh," he wheezed.

In that moment, through the fear and pain, Rory hated himself.

Chapter 55: Asset Acquired

Twenty-ninth of April, X643 A.A

Dawson's hand swallowed the metal doorknob, and he paused, listening. Not a peep came from the other side of the door. He grinned. *Do it.* The Heart of Wrath warmed in his chest, and he looked down at the glowing fist. Orange light radiated out, outlining the bones through his skin. In his palm, the metal door handle popped and crackled. He opened his fingers, and smoldering metal pooled and sizzled on the gray hallway carpet. He shook off the last of the molten goo and nudged open the door. Behind him, his troopers slipped past and inside, the lights on their rifles sweeping the dark apartment.

The corrupted presence inside the Heart touched his mind, pressing a hungry word there. *Find.*

"Jacklyn," Dawson said, stepping into the darkness. "Let's make this easy."

The floor creaked beneath his weight, and he swept his eyes back and forth. A streetlamp cut through a partially opened curtain, throwing deep shadows into the corners of the apartment—any one of them could hide the Host. Straight ahead, he found an empty chair beside the couch where someone lay, apparently sleeping. A tension grew between his shoulders, and he felt the Heart snarl. *It couldn't be that easy.*

"There on the couch," Dawson said. Two lights snapped over and highlighted the figure with two white orbs. It was a woman, but not Jacklyn. Blonde and too young. Had to be the doctor involved, Doctor . . . something. Seeker? He took two long strides over and leaned in close to her face, his beard braid dangling, grazing her lips. He inhaled.

"Dozed," he said over his shoulder and grinned. "In her own home. Shameless."

The Heart shifted, cooing and calling. Dawson followed the scent and reached into her pajama pocket. He felt something hard, then a burst of attention and curiosity. The Heart hissed, and the presence retreated. Dawson drew a red mythstone from the doctor's pocket. "A baby Wyth." He turned the stone over, probing the small shard and feeling the small Aspect retreat. "With a baby Aspect," he snickered. "Go ahead." The Heart's presence reached down his arm, sending a ripple of pins and needles through his fingers as it pressed into the foreign stone. Dawson felt the struggle, the young darting and dashing with nowhere to run. The outcome was inevitable, and soon, the little fire Aspect's power would be theirs.

Two men hurried forward as the rest of his troopers fanned out. Their boots banged through the quiet room. Dawson glanced up at the painting above the couch: horses running into the sunset. He chuckled. "So much for fairytale endings."

Dawson waved to his troopers waiting behind him. "You two, bring her. The rest of you search the apartment." His eyes scanned the deep shadows. "The Seed is here somewhere." He felt a swell of heat in his chest as the Heart's presence returned in full. He lifted his hand, holding the doctor's dormant mythstone in his palm. There was no cloud to the stone now, no emotion radiating from it. His fist glowed again, and he squeezed until he felt the stone pop, and he let the shards trickle onto the doctor's unconscious form. "Thanks for the snack."

"ARGH!"

One of his troopers, reaching for the doctor, curled unnaturally inward with the crack of splintering bone. The man rose off the ground as the shadows slipped off Jacklyn, her misty hand gripping his chest. Dust ran down his legs and overflowed his boots as he spasmed, falling to the ground in a grisly gray mound. The second trooper tried to raise his rifle, but the Host drove her fist through the faceplate of his helmet with a wet pop. The man slumped to the floor, his blood pooling on the rug.

Dawson's skin crackled, and he and the Heart roared their challenge.

Jacklyn tossed the mummy aside and lunged at Dawson, her shadow hand extending into a vicious claw.

Predictable.

Dawson sidestepped her reach, leaving Jacklyn grasping at air and too frail to recover. He drove his smoldering fist down with everything he had, connecting with her cheek. A jolt of lightning fired up his arm, sending all his nerves singing. It was like punching a stone pillar. Jacklyn slammed into the carpet. *Crack!* Wood splintered. Lengths of jagged wood tore through the surrounding rug. Shaking out his numb hand, Dawson readied another blow, but paused as Jacklyn moaned, her eyes half open. Her shadow hand flickered and dissipated in a faint cloud. The Heart demanded more, delighting in the pain.

Dawson shuddered, tempted by the Heart's promises, but forced himself to lower his fist. The light in it faded a moment later. He was glad he didn't hit her harder. Anything more might have thrown her through the floor, which would have been difficult to cover up, or worse, kill her. The thought made Dawson's scorching skin cool and prickle, and even the Heart recoiled at the idea. Whatever the Seed contained, they both agreed it needed to stay that way.

Two troopers emerged from the bedroom. Their lights swept their dead comrades before landing on Jacklyn's still form on the floor. Dawson held up a hand.

"Get the mag-cell."

They saluted and hurried off.

The Heart throbbed with victory as Dawson kneeled, smiling at the drooping Host.

"Jacklyn," he rumbled. "This is no way to welcome an old friend."

"Come a little closer, and I'll give you a hug," Jacklyn said. She tried to rise, and for a moment, Dawson thought she might, but she sagged and dropped back down to the carpet. This was not the same Jacklyn of five years ago. The meat was gone from her bones. The rage in her eyes had faded. She was tired and weak. Part of him had hoped for a challenge; the Heart always wanted a fight.

"You know the drill. Cooperate and save yourself from the pain. Just tell me where Caroline is."

"Never heard of 'em . . ."

"Did you send her away, or did she finally wise up and leave your doomed campaign?"

"Fuck you."

A sly smile pulled his mouth into a sneer. "No. She's too loyal. Love does that. Which means she can't be far. An Assay, perhaps? You've always been the stickler for your little laws."

Jacklyn coughed, and flecks of blood landed on his pants. "Don't worry," she said, using her breath. "She'll . . . find us." Her eyes rolled back, and she slumped against the carpet.

A jolt of nerves rose from his belly. He'd hoped to neutralize the Wyth by now. Even aged, Caroline would be formidable. Her mastery of casting was still etched in Dawson's nightmares. Dawson's chest warmed as the Heart's irritation grew; it wanted the fight. It needed that fight. His nerves dissipated as he remembered the present awaiting him at the plane with his reinforcements. The Brand alone would tip the scales in his favor. What chance did this one Wyth really have?

"We'll be ready," he said to himself.

"Sir?" someone said behind him. Dawson rose, looming over the trooper. The man stiffened. "Orders, sir?"

He grinned, savoring the sharp fear wafting off of him. "Bind and load the package. Watch that left arm. And what is Emmett's status? He should have the nurse by now."

The trooper snapped off a salute and tentatively approached Jacklyn, stepping over his mummified comrade.

"Get ready, boys. The game has changed. The Wyth is hunting us now."

Chapter 56: Seizures

Sunday, April 29th, 23:26

Jane couldn't put her finger on it, but something grated against her intuition. "This feels too easy. Doesn't it?"

Beside her, Emmett made no response, turning Rory's strange sword hilt over as they followed the stocky hospital security officer through a subbasement. Emmett ran his thumb over the grip, down the smooth, looping symbols, as though friction would derive meaning from them. It wasn't steel or brass or bronze; too light, with a tinny scent that reminded her of licking batteries. The cross guard had no gap, nothing a blade could emerge from like a switch knife. Its crafter did that on purpose, though she could only guess why—a sword without steel felt impotent. Strangest was the pommel. Long, almost designed for two hands, but it balanced easily in one. And the symbols, each linked to the next and etched straight into the blue-tinged metal. Seeing them again made her feel dizzy. They looked eerily like the symbols in the killer's note with an ominous translation.

"And his name was Death," Jane whispered so that only Emmett could hear. "And power was given to them over the four parts of the earth."

He made no reply, and Jane ached for him to say something, to give her a clue where he was at, which way he was leaning. Despite so many unanswered questions, it would be time for Emmett to cast his vote soon. Not her, though. Jane had stopped kidding herself the moment Mr. Nash shouted about the Seed. She wasn't getting a vote anymore. It wasn't a question of if a crackdown was coming; it was a question of its magnitude. She hoped Emmett understood that and did nothing stupid.

Jane nodded at the guards behind them, trying again. "Guess the Director doesn't trust us after all."

Emmett tensed and glanced over his shoulders at the six armed guards behind them. Jane was relieved to see him uncomfortable—it meant he understood the status quo had changed. The extra armed guards waiting for them in the tunnel had only reinforced her hunch.

Come on, Emmett. Don't clam up on me now.

Ahead of them, the tunnel curved, and Jane felt the first whispers of a dank breeze as their footfalls ricocheted off the concrete walls. White water pipes ran the length of the long halls like dry bones. Occasionally, they passed an orange bucket, set out to catch the drips falling from color-coded pipes high overhead: red for hot, blue for cold, and green for oxygen. The dim light, combined with the wet air, felt like a different planet compared to the glaringly bright and sterile wards. They passed a gray door with a brass plaque labeled "Morgue." The hairs along Jane's neck stood on end. Far away from public eyes, there were no cameras here, and they hadn't seen another soul since they started their walk. Places like this were where things went to disappear. *Keep it together, Jane. Now it gets interesting.*

Behind them, two helmeted troopers dragged Rory Nash between them. His dirty sneakers squeaked on the linoleum, bouncing when his toe caught. He didn't even attempt a step, letting himself dangle between the two as he stared at the floor. *You're supposed to be the next Host?* He looked more like roadkill than a chosen one.

Jane listened to the rhythm of the echoes and gauged her next move. Perhaps, on a good day, she could bring all six down without getting killed, but inevitably, one of them would start shooting, and in close quarters, the risk was too high. She couldn't fight—not now, but soon. By now, Dawson should have the killer and the Seed. As far as she was concerned, fixing that was priority number one. Do-able. Hard, but doable. Her problem was she still didn't know what to say to the nurse. *You touched death*, the letter said. *You must teach the next Host the secrets you experienced in the dark.*

But what secrets? Death was death, wasn't it? The end. Given his files, he knew all that, same as her. So what else was there to say?

Jane glanced over her shoulder at the troopers. She gave a cheerful wave as they rounded another corner in the subterranean maze. She clicked her tongue and slid closer to Emmett. "So, boss, what's your plan?"

"My pl—" He drifted off, bouncing the sword hilt against his hand.

"Decision time, Agent Bait."

To her surprise, he coughed out a laugh and shook his head, but his conflict returned with his knotted brow. He swallowed, but then disappointingly remained mute. "Come on, Emmett. Give me something here. I'm floundering. Do you at least remember our deal?"

He watched her for a moment, then nodded.

"You gonna let me?"

He took a couple of steps and nodded again. It wasn't the vote of confidence she'd been hoping for, but a wave of relief came all the same. She didn't know what she was going to do yet, but at least she'd get the opportunity to make that choice.

"I have another request, then."

"You always do," he said, sounding a little more like himself. Maybe the shock was wearing off.

"I need the nurse's phone. I'm guessing that if Dawson has the killer, the Director will put the clamps down on this entire operation. My services won't be needed anymore."

"You don't know that," Emmett said, though he didn't sound convinced. He cleared his throat. "Why do you need his phone?"

"Evidence. Can you get it?"

"Evidence of what?"

"I don't want to ruin the surprise."

Emmett shook his head, a sliver of a smile creeping through. "I'll see what I can do."

"Thanks."

Their escort reached the end of the hall with two large sliding doors blocking the way. Blocky red letters spelled out *EXIT ONLY* across the fogged glass. The security guard swiped his badge against a sensor, and the door slid open. A blast of cold air swept over them, and Jane shivered. She felt it in the back of her nose and the tingling inside her bad knee—a storm.

Overhead, the clouds sat close and heavy. The troopers fanned out toward two black SUVs with twirling red, blue, and white lights parked in a jackknifed *L*. A huge, armored truck on the sidewalk loomed to their right with a dozen men with rifles in hand.

"Muff me," she said. "Kinda overkill, don't you think?"

Ten feet away, beyond a long length of yellow *CAUTION* tape, a small crowd had gathered, many with their phones and cameras raised. Jane wasn't surprised. Posting was already happening. The news was spreading. The Director wouldn't be happy.

Bzzz. Bzzz.

Emmett sucked in a breath. "It's him."

"Better answer," Jane said.

"Sir, where should we take him?" asked a trooper holding Rory.

"The truck," Emmett replied. "Oh, give me his phone first."

Bzzz. Bzzz.

The trooper patted down Rory's scrubs and pulled his phone from his pocket. The nurse didn't protest, hanging limp, utterly defeated. Jane felt for him, remembering that gloomy feeling well when your world collapsed. Unfortunately, if Jane guessed right, his night was about to get a lot worse.

Bzzz. Bzzz.

The trooper handed the phone to Emmett, who stashed it in his jacket and hurried off. "Hello, sir. No, sir, I'm here— Uh, yes, sir."

"Excuse me," a voice said behind her. She looked up at the burly security guard. His name badge announced him as Officer Kyle. "It looks like your team has it from here, ma'am."

"Thank you for your help tonight."

"All part of the job, ma'am," he said, standing still and watching her expectantly.

"Is there . . . something else?"

"There is, um—" Kyle stepped closer. "I'm not entirely sure what Mr. Nash has done, but whatever else he might be, I can vouch that he's a kind kid. He does right by others around here." He shuffled nervously. "I just thought someone should speak for him since . . . well, tonight wasn't his best." The security guard fell quiet, perhaps wanting to say more, but gave a stiff nod instead. He turned and marched back into the hospital.

"Fascinating." She watched two soldiers lift the nurse by his armpits into the back of the armored truck. People liked this guy. All his reviews from patients and peers were overwhelmingly positive, yet she wasn't so certain Rory Nash liked himself. They'd raided his apartment hours before, hoping to get lucky, but only found a cat at home. The state of the place, with its cardboard box tables and bare walls, was depressing, though the small altar of patient gifts and cards gave a glimmer of hope. Jane learned long ago, from her own derelict dwelling, that a home reflected a soul. Which meant Rory Nash was in a dark place.

Which, she supposed, was why the killer sent her on this mission. *I touched death. I know where he's gone.*

Watching Rory's life self-destruct in real time, she revisited her own implosion and the deep shame that followed Grace's arrival in her hospital room. Thick bandages covered each of her wrists, but her sister waited until she was ready to ask. Jane wanted her to leave and shouted for her to do so, but Grace sat with her anyway, holding hands, and then she said something that saved Jane's life.

"You're not alone. I'm here, and I'm not leaving."

A sudden pressure swelled in her chest and stung her eyes. The unconditional love captured in those simple words brought Jane back from oblivion. She wondered if Rory had ever heard those words said to him—and if he had, did he even believe them? Seeing him slump over as they shackled him to one of the truck's benches, she doubted it. All the fight in him was gone now, leaving an isolated, hopeless shell.

A hot flush passed through her body. She blinked, feeling the word resonate in her collection of hunches.

Hope, her hunch whispered in the wind.

"That's it!" She stared at the twirling red and blue lights, and her thoughts slammed together, crystallizing. The abstracts of magic and murder coalesced into a unified idea she could practically taste. *I survived the dark he's in. I know how to come back.* Mr. Nash didn't, and he needed the hope required to make the journey—just like Grace had given her. It was a path not traveled alone. Unfortunately, telling him all this would be the simple part. The trick, and her greatest struggle, was believing it and herself again. And for that, she needed evidence, something to remind Mr. Nash of what he was capable of. *Hope.* The killer's riddle seemed so simple now.

Renewed purpose blazed in Jane, but the fire dampened when she spotted Emmett hurrying back with a grim expression. He signaled to one soldier overseeing their prisoner, a man with a pair of red stripes on the shoulder of his black uniform. Some team leader. Jane braced herself.

"What's going on?" Jane asked.

"Change of plans," Emmett said without looking at her. His voice dropped. "You were right. The Director is bringing everyone in." He held up the sword hilt. "He wants this and says I have to arrest you, too."

Jane blew out a long breath. She'd been waiting for this since Emmett first walked into her cubicle. "The big moment is here, Emmett." She met his dark eyes and saw his regret. Had he chosen?

"Jane. I'm sorry. I didn't want this."

She nodded, disappointment pooling in the pit of her belly. "I can't say I'm surprised." Emmett's face grew grave. "None of that, Agent Bait. This isn't even close to over. Everyone, every single one of us, gets used at some point. It's what we do the second time that defines us."

Emmett nodded, and Jane hoped he understood what she was saying. One wrong step, a slight miscalculation now, and they'd both be dead.

"I'll protect you, Jane." He leaned close to her. "And I'll figure something out about the Seed, but . . ." he trailed off, looking uncomfortable. Jane got the gist of it: *But there's only so much I can do.*

It looked like he was about to say more, but the red-striped soldier arrived. "Sir?"

"I just received new orders from the Director." Emmett pulled back, and the soldier straightened. "Dawson has secured the asset. We'll meet up with him before heading to our extraction site." Emmett put out his hand. "Handcuffs, please."

The soldier unclipped his cuffs and handed them over. Emmett continued. "We're taking both Jane and Mr. Nash into custody, unharmed and secured until delivery. I want them both in the armored transport, understood?"

The soldier's eyes snapped over to Jane, and he turned his body—his hand dropping to his gun. "Yes, sir."

Emmett turned to Jane. All she could read on him was a mask of cold authority. "Please don't resist, Jane. Your wrists."

She swallowed, then slowly held out her hands. Part of her brain screamed to fight, but she was one against many. Perhaps an opportunity would come. Emmett stepped closer, blocking the view of the soldier as he clicked the handcuffs around each wrist.

"How long do I have with Rory?"

"Five minutes, maybe," Emmett replied quietly, then raised his voice. "Turn around."

She made a small show of resisting but complied, feeling Emmett's hands patting down her waist and pants. In her pocket, he pressed the smooth river stone against her side. She expected him to reach in and remove it, but he continued without hesitating. *What's he up to?*

His hand passed over her pocket again, and she felt a dull weight drop next to the keystone.

"Good luck," he whispered, then his hands were at his sides, and his voice rose. "Load her up. We move out in two."

Chapter 57: The Price of Miracles

Sunday, April 29th, 23:40

KA-CHUNG. The armored truck's door slammed shut.

A dim quiet enveloped Jane. Her short legs dangled from the cold steel bench, and the chain looped through a ring bolted to the floor pulled on her wrists. She focused on her breathing— steady, slow inhales and exhales to calm her racing heart.

"Okay. Okay, no worries. No problem. Hakuna matata," she mumbled, blinking around as her eyes adjusted to the darkness. Near the back of the cage, she spotted a hunched shadow.

Rory hadn't moved. She barely recognized the confident nurse she'd interviewed only a day before.

"Hello again," Jane said.

His eyes drifted up to her and focused, though he said nothing.

"This isn't too bad for a prison, am I right? At least we've got company."

Nothing.

Jane held up her wrists and jangled her chains. "Seems like we both made mistakes."

He stared at his chains for a moment, then his eyes squeezed shut. Pain creased his face as his chin dropped to his chest, and he went still.

"Read the room, Jane," she murmured to herself.

Their chains rattled as the truck's engine roared to life. Outside, she heard voices and the thud of boots on concrete. Inside, Rory shifted, and his face alternated between dim blue and red light. She wondered if she'd ever get to see Grace and the kids again. Closing her eyes, Jane took one more deep breath and set her fear aside, just like Grace had taught her. She had a job to do. *Hope.*

The truck lurched forward, sliding Jane and Rory down their benches. Ignoring a twist of nerves in her gut, she mentally started her timer. Five minutes.

"Look, I don't have a lot of time to hold your hand through this like I got, so I'm going to lay it out for you, okay? No tricks. Only truth—the truth you've been working very hard to avoid because, from what Jacklyn told me in a letter, it's not just our lives on the line here. It's everyone's because it's about the Seed."

Rory looked up. *Good.* If he hadn't, it wouldn't matter what she said next.

"Jacklyn sent me to find you. She wrote me a letter that she stashed near Chuck's body. She is a serial killer, Mr. Nash."

His eyes dropped, but he acted surprisingly tame from the news, which raised an interesting thought.

"You knew?"

Rory nodded. "I know she killed him to save Tommy."

"Did she tell you about the dozens of others over multiple years?"

Rory squeezed his eyes shut. "No."

"Does that bother you?"

"Of course it does!" he snapped.

Jane frowned, then thought she understood. "But it was worth the price?"

Rory pressed his lips tight, shaking his head. She'd hit the mark. "I didn't know until yesterday," he said, a defensive edge to his voice. "I didn't."

"I get it," Jane said, feeling relieved that was one less conversation they needed to have. "And, well, bad as it might sound, I can't say I disagree. Muff that guy." The truck sped up as they started down the hill. Jane spread her feet wide to keep from sliding again as the truck pitched forward. She checked her mental timer. *Stay on topic.*

"You're a thoughtful guy. Let me ask you something. What lie do you tell yourself?"

"What?"

"What's the lie? The illusion of reality you paint for yourself. You grew up rough. You must have told yourself a lie to survive all that, something that gave you strength. And as a nurse, I mean, I've read about nurses, sponges and all. Is your lie there that you can make a difference? That you can save someone? Maybe save yourself? How do you keep yourself going while you're sopping up all that blood?"

"I'm not . . ."

"It was rhetorical," Jane replied. "I think I know you, Mr. Nash. Not everything, of course, but I'm an excellent judge of character and a different kind of survivor. I read your job application—very moving. The part about not wanting others to go through what you did alone really tugged at my heartstrings, but to be honest, I knew you were a big bag full of muff. No one is that wholly selfless; we all have egos. That little show you put on upstairs is proof of that."

Rory's face twisted with guilt, and Jane felt a pang of regret. The truck bounced, throwing them up and down as she mulled over her next words, trying to strike right with so little time. "I think you've been lying to yourself, Mr. Nash, for a long, long time. It makes sense why: distance. The truth is painful. Some of it is unbearable. Why would we want to get closer to that? But you have, and you've felt it. The cracks inside. The insomnia. That burning pressure in your chest. I bet you've been late more recently after always being punctual. You've been mad where you're patient. Your mind wanders, so much so that you can't see all your relationships falling apart."

Rory fidgeted with his chain. She was on the right track.

"In the near-constant wreckage of my life, I discovered something about these types of lies. The only way to unravel them is to understand how they started."

He looked up, growing still.

"It's trauma that plants the seed," Jane said, getting to her point. "When a stranger kills your brother or the man you loved most, throws you away, and burns down your life, those are moments when the lie takes root and bends reality to make it more palatable. Your parents sound like two grade-A pieces of muff for abandoning you—leaving you with unanswerable questions that haunt you every day of your life. Why didn't they stay? Why wasn't I enough?" She paused. "Am I worthy of love?"

"Stop," he whispered. His head dropped into his hands, and he wept softly into his palms. She tried to reach out to comfort him, but her chains pulled her arm short.

"Rory . . ." Her voice came out strained, and she cleared her throat. "Look at me. We don't have time for tears yet. Those can come later. We can watch a rom-com and hug it out." A fresh sob shook him, and she hated to continue, but the only way was through.

"You gave an answer, the only answer you could to protect yourself. You told yourself no - and why wouldn't you? It is what the evidence indicated, and the alternative was letting people close again where they might hurt you. Then, you doubled down, adding a layer when you convinced yourself that it was your fault you were alone. On and on, layer after layer, until the lie is more real than the truth, and here we are, a wanna-be white knight and a has-been detective sitting in chains with no one to blame but themselves."

She sighed, not sure where she was going, but hearing the truth ring with each word. "I get it. My lies have tried to destroy me before. Nearly succeeded once, but I got help. I learned to hear the patterns in my lies, the voice inside that uses fear and shame to keep me rooted because . . . I don't know, some piece of me thinks that is the safe option. I'm sorry to say the voice never goes away, but once you know the pattern, you can quiet them by thanking them for trying to protect us from pain."

Jane's throat tightened as she pictured her twin and maybe their last hug. "That's what my sister taught me, and she saved my life."

Rory finally looked up, something like hunger in his wet eyes. *He wants that, too. He wants to be free.* The thought emboldened her.

The truck turned suddenly, and Jane leaned to keep her balance as she debated how to proceed. She needed hours, not minutes. How does one distill a lifetime's worth of learning into a few minutes? She didn't have an answer, but the killer's letter flashed through her mind: the job only she could do. It was time Rory knew—whether or not he was ready.

"After meeting you, I think I understand why Jacklyn picked you. Maxwell said she called you a hero. I think it fits. You're a good one—and I would know. I've spent most of my life working for the bad."

Rory blinked at her, his face long with worry. "Picked me for what?"

Jane swallowed, trying to think how best to say it. She worried she'd push him over the edge, but saw no other way forward.

"You're the next Host."

Rory blinked and quickly shook his head as if he'd already considered this and ruled it out. "No. Nope. It's Tracy. I told them. I'm not—"

"Good enough? Worthy? Capable?" Jane finished for him. "That's your trauma talking again."

"But they would have told me. Caroline. Jacklyn . . . they would have said something . . . sooner."

"Would they?" Jane couldn't imagine how hard this was to absorb, but as the truck pulled to a stop, a surge of adrenaline pushed her on. "There are apparently some law that-."

"Laws?" Recognition sparked in his eye.

"Laws. They forbid them from saying it directly to you, but I guess there is no restriction on third parties. I'm a loophole."

"It can't be me. I'm . . . I'm not—"

Jane raised an eyebrow. "There it is again. Hear the pattern? The rhythm. But I have something to counter it." She reached into her pocket and drew out Rory's phone, leaving Maxwell's keystone in place.

"That's mine." His eyes grew wide. "Wait, we can make a call and—"

"Was yours," Jane said, turning the screen on and glancing at the doors. "And no one we could call could help us. Now, what's your password?"

She held the phone out as far as her chains would allow. He didn't budge, his eyes flicking between the nine-point grid pattern on the phone and Jane. She sighed dramatically. They didn't have time to waste. "I can't do it without you. Please, let me in."

His expression shifted, a little color returning to his cheeks, though he still looked on the verge of being sick. "It's a cross."

"Interesting." Jane traced lines through the middle of the screen. The phone opened, and she searched through his recent photos. The truck jostled again, and the smooth ride across paved surfaces gave way to the noisy grind of gravel and dirt. They'd turned off a main road and had to be near the rendezvous with Dawson. Her fingers flew as she searched for April 17th.

Jane nearly cheered when she found the video, time-stamped just after midnight, with a frozen picture of a young, round-faced boy sitting on the lap of a dark-skinned nurse wearing cat scrubs. Around them, other nurses, all women, were smiling, crying, or both. Her hunch bailed her out again: these days, no one could witness a miracle and not record it.

The truck came to an abrupt stop, and she almost dropped the phone as she flailed for balance.

She pressed play and held the phone up for Rory. The beeps and squeaks and laughter of the hospital poured through the phone. Rory watched, his eyes brimming with tears again, as Jane heard Tommy giggle. Then the audio changed, and Jane turned the phone so she could see, too. The nurses moved about their jobs with wonder-struck smiles, but the sound of a heavy sob cut through the audio, someone nearer the camera. The footage shook for a moment, then froze on the older nurse and boy, hugging and smiling.

"You helped do that," Jane said. "Of everything you could have done with the Seed's power, you kept it quiet and saved some forgotten kid. That was an enormous risk. If they had caught you—" She shook her head. "And, as an encore, you do it again."

From outside, she heard Dawson's voice.

"Where is she?!"

Emmett replied, but she couldn't make out what he said. Whatever it was, Dawson must not have liked it. "Open this now!"

Rory hadn't taken his eyes off his phone. "I'm not a nurse anymore."

"Not an employed one, no. But it changed you, and no one can ever take away what you've accomplished."

He sank back on the bench, letting his head drop against the metal wall without taking his eyes off the screen.

"Get this damn thing open!" Dawson bellowed from outside.

Jane ignored the mounting fear in her belly and spoke quickly. "You wrote that you didn't want people to go it alone. Well, I agree. And while the chains aren't a vote of confidence, I'm here to help."

"Why?"

Finally, an obvious answer. "Because I trust myself this. And my gut is screaming at me that you are different. And we muffing need different."

KA-CHUNG. The heavy bolt lifted, and the grind of steel reverberated through the cab. Jane had seconds. Rory's gaze drifted over toward the doors, but Jane snapped her fingers. "Focus up!"

Rory locked onto her.

"I did my job. Now it's time to do yours. The Seed is yours. And don't worry about being perfect. We just need a"—she scrambled for a metaphor as her heart picked up speed— "a . . . torchbearer. Ya, that'll work. Someone to carry the load and not trip until they can pass it off to someone else. That's it. You can do that."

KA-CHUNG. They both turned as the second bolt slid, and the hinges groaned.

"Hey-hey!" Jane snapped her fingers, collecting Rory's attention before holding up three fingers. "Three choices. Fight, flight, or freeze. We're damned if we freeze and dead if we run. So we have to—"

The rear doors swung open, and an alarm of fear robbed her of words. Biting headlights filled the cab, and she winced, shielding her eyes. Dawson stood, arms crossed, and surrounded by armed soldiers. As her eyes adjusted, the glare receded, and behind them, a dark hillside rose. Through its trees, crowning the top, Jane made out the white lights of Hill Hospital.

Emmett fidgeted at Dawson's side.

"—fight." Jane realized she was still holding the phone out, and based on Dawson's expression, he saw it at the same moment she did. He glared down at Emmett.

"Bring me that phone." A beat later, two soldiers jumped into the back of the truck, rocking it.

"Don't I get a call?" Jane surrendered the device and held her hands up as far as the chains allowed. "Easy, boys."

The soldiers deposited the phone in Dawson's meaty palm, and he folded his fingers around it. He sneered and squeezed. *CRACK!* The phone splintered, and he turned his palm over, letting the bits of plastic and glass sprinkle over the ground.

"Mother—" Jane had the cold realization she'd badly underestimated him.

"Jane. I've been looking forward to this."

Time was up.

Dawson gritted his teeth, glaring at Jane. "How did she get that phone?"

Bright headlights poured over his shoulder, soaking the inside of the cab and the loose circle of troopers around him. Unmarked black SUVs, Hummers, and a second armored truck all rumbled a few steps behind, ready for his order to leave.

"I . . . I don't know," Emmett sputtered. He reeked of fear and confusion, but that didn't mean he wasn't lying.

Dawson grunted, wondering how much of Jane's inane theories had rubbed off on the Director's little protégé. The Heart of Wrath spiked, greedily demanding blood.

"Patience," Dawson whispered. He rounded on Emmett. "And why are these two together? She should speak to *no one*."

Emmett's face blanched. "The Director said to secure her. I figured chains and an armored truck were the best way."

It made logical sense, but Dawson didn't like his tone. Jane needed to be eliminated.

"What's the matter, Donald?" Jane sing-songed from inside the cab. "Have I been making too much sense?"

Dawson stepped up into the truck, its suspension shrieking with the weight of the man. Jane and the nurse both tipped slightly toward him. The Heart preened, egging Dawson on.

"Good god," Jane said. "You've gained some weight."

He could smell the fear wafting off her, sweet and sticky, like candy. He took a long stride toward Jane, showing her his fists— the skin radiating molten light. "I've gained more than you know."

Emmett gasped behind him as both Jane and the nurse scrambled backward until her chains pulled taut against the iron ring on the floor. Fear choked the cab, sending the Heart into a hungry frenzy. They both knew Jane was trapped, even as she jerked frantically against her chains.

On the other side, the nurse froze, staring at Dawson with open terror. *Candidate, indeed.* "Pathetic."

"The Director called just now," Emmett said with a shaky voice. "He wants to bring everyone in. That includes Jane, Mr. Nash, and this . . . thing." He held up the Dozer's hilt.

Dawson stopped short, his sweltering fists dimming back to flesh, and he turned, drawing another wave of groans from the stressed metal beneath his feet. "Accidents happen."

"Do you want to explain that to the Director?"

The idea made even the Heart of Wrath cool. The Director did not like bad news, and Dawson had seen other Merged have their mythstone . . . uninstalled after a few too many setbacks. Those screams still haunted him. He eyed Emmett, then the Dozer. The boy's fear smelled different, dense, and wild. It wasn't fear for self. The realization brought on a canny smile. "Smells like you've fallen in love."

Emmett's eyes lifted to Jane for the briefest moment, but a moment was all Dawson needed. "You've been compromised." He lifted his gaze to the soldiers standing just behind Emmett. He nodded, and they stepped forward, seizing Emmett's arms.

"Wait!" Emmett said, jerking his arm but unable to break their grips. "Wait." Another trooper pulled his pistol and aimed it at Emmett's chest. Dawson chuckled and pictured burning Jane's toenails off, one at a time.

"Dawson, listen," Emmett pleaded. "I'm Broken Star now. The Director wants to make me . . . like you. A . . . a Merged."

The Director had hinted as much several days ago, but it was still a surprise to hear it coming from so young a mouth. "Did he? Adams!" Dawson bellowed. A veteran trooper with sandy white hair and three red stripes on each shoulder stepped forward. Dawson knew the man well—they'd gained prestige hunting Wyth together after Dawson's ascension. Of all the soldiers under Dawson's command, Adams was the least incompetent and knew the value of both loyalty and discretion.

"Sir?" Adams said, snapping off a crisp salute. The veteran's eye shifted to Emmett for a moment, then back, and Dawson caught the sharp stench of contempt. "Send the Director an update. We have everyone but the Wyth. And confirm what Emmett's claimed. Go."

"Sir." Adams's eye lingered on Emmett before he turned and jogged into the bright lights.

The truck moaned as Dawson shifted, sniffing at the air. There was something that didn't quite line up for him yet—the boy's fresh scent. "What about Jane?"

Emmett swallowed. "What about her?"

"You love her." Dawson tapped the side of his crooked nose. "No one tricks the nose."

Emmett lifted his chin, looking directly at Jane. "Love has nothing to do with this. She tried to use me for her own ambition, but I can play that game, too. I don't want to see her die, but . . . well, death is a part of this game."

Cold. Still. "She has been with you for weeks. I have worked with her for years. I know how she corrupts your thinking. You cannot be trusted anymore."

"She can't corrupt me."

"Oh? And why is that?"

"Because I have armor. I know who she is."

Dawson stopped. *This should be good.* "Jane, listen up. This will be educational for you." He waved a hand at his troopers. If the kid fought or ran, he'd only prove Dawson's suspicions. "Let him go." They released Emmett, and Dawson rounded on the handsome, clean-cut young man, and growled, "Go on."

"The Director ordered me to get close to her. To be . . . bait. It was the only way to build trust enough to fulfill the mission. She wouldn't help me otherwise. He said once I got past her thorns, I'd understand two things: how she sees the world and thus where she is weak." He gestured to her, sitting in chains. "It worked, obviously."

The Heart preened. The kid was savage. Dawson turned to Jane, mocking sadness. "Ouch. That must have hurt." The confidence had left Jane, leaving her slack and bowed on her bench. The savory scent of fresh betrayal wafted off her. A promise, said or otherwise, had been broken. It was delicious.

"More," Dawson said, feeling his blood rise.

"I learned . . ." An uncomfortable pause followed, and Emmett's gaze dropped to his hands. The Heart salivated for the coming truth. "I learned deep down she's lonely and terrified and powerless. She blames the Director for that, and it's made her myopic. It has since she was blacklisted. Blind to everything else. So whatever vaunted hunter she once was, now she's a toothless lone wolf who compensates for her inadequacies with drugs and snarky opinions no one cares about. That's why she tried to kill herself."

Jane finally broke, slumping against the wall—right where Emmett's dagger had pinned her.

Dawson laughed, his white teeth blazing. "And that's why we don't share, Jane. It always comes back to hurt you." The Heart flared in approval.

"I will serve the Broken Star," Emmett said firmly. He paused, nerves radiating from him. "From the look of it, service has its perks. Though I'm still a little lost in what we are trying to achieve."

Dawson's eyebrows rose. The Heart radiated affection toward

the youth. He had a hunger in him and that Dawson could work with. *Perhaps not as useless as I thought.*

Adams stepped out of the bright headlights. "Sir, headquarters is aware of our situation and they pass along their congratulations."

"And the plan?"

Adams shifted, apparently disappointed by the news. "Capture the Wyth, evacuate out east, and return home. They also confirmed Emmett's story. The Director is apparently very pleased with our team's performance and is planning a celebration. I was told to convey your reward, and the next phase is already underway."

Dawson inhaled, smiling. *At last. My war.* He laughed, deep and long, a relief as much as joy. The echo boomed inside the armored truck. "HA! Yes. Yes!" He grinned at Emmett. "Well done. Keep that ruthless focus, and you'll make a fine Merged." He nodded toward Jane. "What would you do with her now?"

"Gag and bag her. Put her under guard where you can see her. She'll try to make trouble."

"I agree. Captain Adams, you heard him. Load her up in the forward vehicle. I want a pair with her at all times. If she does anything . . ." Dawson let the end hang like a question, curious about what Emmett would say.

The young man's reply came fast. "Shoot her."

Dawson nodded. *Good.*

"Sir," Adams said. "What about the doctor? She's still asleep."

"Jacklyn's transport?"

"Mag-cell is bigger than we thought, and the escort vehicles are full."

Dawson grumbled. He hated logistics. "The doctor was dozed." He considered, knowing the long sleep the runetech weapon induced. "She cannot be woken until it has worn off." The truck groaned as he stepped down to the gravel. "Put her in with the nurse. Neither can do any harm in there."

A pair of troopers thundered up to collect his prisoner. Leaving the logistics of prisoner reassignment to Adams, Dawson stepped up to Emmett and took the smaller man's shoulders in each massive hand.

"The look on Jane's face." Dawson inhaled deeply. "Scrumptious." He held out his hand. "The Dozer."

Emmett frowned, not following, then looked down at the artifact in his hand. "What is it?"

"An ancient . . . tool or a sad excuse for a weapon. It was stolen from us." He gestured with his broad hand, and Emmett handed it over. A tingle passed up his arm when he took it, like he'd fallen asleep on his arm, and the gap in the cross guard illuminated with a blue glow. A cruel smile peeled Dawson's lips as he tucked it into his waistband.

"Wait," Emmett said. "What's the next stage? I need to know if I'm going to help."

Dawson was hoping he'd ask. He wanted an excuse to talk about his reward. He felt the Heart's enthusiasm egging him on and doubted the Director, in his good graces, would care if he gave his protégé a preview. "The last war."

"War?" Emmett said, a fresh wave of fear coming off him. The Heart swelled hearing the word again.

"On the grandest theater, for all the stakes," Dawson said, remembering the first time he'd heard the Director's sales pitch. That was the day he finally found someone who understood him. "A global war that touches everything and tears down all those walls that divide us into tribes. A war where possession and wealth dissolve, and from their primal pool, humanity's next great age emerges. It will be a war of unification, Emmett, to bring collective purpose to the wayward. Think about it: our entire world—its billions of souls and all its resources—is focused and organized. In such a dream, we might all transcend this planet and its limits and take our conquest and hunger to the stars."

Emmett's mouth worked open and closed, but no words came out. A pang of irritation rose in Dawson. He'd expected more enthusiasm. Overhead, in the distance, a rumble of thunder broke the night's stillness. Dawson looked to the sky at the dark clouds passing over the moon. "Caroline is coming."

"Who?" Emmett said, reeling.

Dawson eyed him as the Heart bled impatience. He had to remind them both that the kid was waking up. "The last Wyth. She's a zealot of a dead religion but a powerful caster. We've eliminated her sisters and all their hidden villages, but Caroline evades us, sprouting new pockets of her damnable teachings as she goes. This time, though, we have the advantage. She has to hunt us because we have her lover."

"She's a caster? What?" Emmett closed his eyes, clearly overwhelmed. Dawson grinned, enjoying the helplessness seeping off the kid. He reached out and, with a bit of force, guided him toward their transport. The Heart curled and shimmered in his chest, cocooned in the warmth of a dream coming true.

"Tell me, Emmett, what do you know of magic?"

Chapter 59: Assay of Cully

Translated from:

Disc - Shepherd's Stone

Sub-ring - *Codex*

Script - *Law of Hosts*:

Assay of Cully:

Let the tribe of the candidate demonstrate their loyalty and the source of their motivation. Seek and tempt those time-bonded to the candidate into betrayal, and do so without revealing your true intent. Offer treasures for secrets, wisdom for skullduggery, and weigh their reasoning. True loyalty is never born of fear.

A candidate passes if the offer is rebuffed through love with secrets kept.

A candidate fails if the offer is taken, and secrets dealt.

A candidate fails even if the offer is rebuffed but denied out of fear.

Amendment (s):

- None -

—

Twenty-ninth of Apru. X643 AA

Arbor Lodge Park, Portland, OR

Caroline shivered, mourning the loss of her hair. A heavy mist fell from the clouds gathered overhead as gusts whistled through the branches, plucking white blossoms from the park's tall trees and tumbling them through the lamplight. It was tradition for any Wyth to shave one's head before battle. Balding one's scalp was a noble tradition meant to display humility and acceptance of an unknown fate. Still, she missed her hair's warmth, the way the sea breeze made it dance, and the feel of Jacklyn's fingers running through it as she drifted to sleep.

A fresh breeze tugged at her green cloak, and she pulled it tighter around her shoulders. Keeping her hood low, she adjusted the bulky duffle bag hanging off her shoulder, causing her satchel to jingle as she scanned the park's perimeter in one sweeping gaze. Against the expansive gray background of her vision, she saw a bright yellow-gray cloud swirling within an anxious jogger, a calm turquoise of someone sleeping in the public restroom, and not another soul in sight. It was a minor reason to celebrate, but one to be thankful for; Caroline wouldn't have to worry about an audience. Still, despite no evidence that the Broken Star was here, she couldn't shake the feeling she walked into a loaded trap.

To the east, a motion caught her eye. A blurry speck drifted across the horizon. Jacklyn was on the move, which meant the Merged had her. The thought made Caroline's heart sink. She'd pictured that last night being so different, for them to be together and whispering those things they'd never get to say again. Instead, last night, there were no kisses, no touch, no rest. Just the knee-buckling fear she may never see her Jacklyn again. She caught her thoughts before the flood of doubt could sweep her away, focusing on her breathing. *Fear has no sway here,* she told herself. *Fear has no power over me.* She repeated it, and steadily, the flood receded.

"I'll be there soon, love," she whispered to the night. There was just one more thing to do: pray Rory was who they thought he was. She turned her gaze across the street to a blue house on the corner. A red *Sold* sign still sprouted from their lawn. A yellow silhouette bobbed between the drawn curtains. *Someone at a loss of sleep.* She wondered why.

Caroline caught a flash of yellow from between two trees and tensed, reaching for her Kiss. The yellow silhouette bobbed along the park's far side, and Caroline sighed in relief. It was only the jogger, and other than them, the neighborhood slept. She steadied her weary heart by blowing out another long breath into a steaming cloud while listening to the rain drumming off the leaves overhead, re-centering herself. She savored the smell of the warm earth and cold rain. *Time is not an ally,* some piece of her whispered.

Stepping closer into the shadows of the trees, she unfastened a small leather pouch hanging off her belt and released the drawstrings. Within were rings of bone, brass, steel, and quartz, a ring of moss, and another of gut. Each marked a different Wythian Path. Each represented a lifetime of learning. Caroline took a deep breath, clutching the bag to her heart. She hoped she wasn't the last one to wear the rings and know their meaning.

She removed the silver rings from her fingers one at a time, recalling the trials to earn them. Splitting the apple, touching another's emotion for the first time. Learning to dance. Touching the essence of Silt and Skipper and even Sunder. She dropped them into the pouch one at a time until her fingers were bare. The flesh beneath each ring felt tender as she flexed her naked hands. She tightened the strings, held the bag to her lips, and kissed it.

"Farewell."

Caroline unzipped the oversized duffel bag and withdrew an oiled cloth-bound bundle. Beneath the bundle lay the Shepherd's Stones, glittering in the lamplight from the hundreds of tiny white diamonds filling the bag. None carried Aspects, yet they'd always held such high value. She unwrapped the bundle and drew out her Witch's Kiss, oiled and ready. She slipped the twin-bladed gauntlet onto her arm, cinched the straps tight around her forearm. In a smooth motion, she set the bag of rings inside, atop the Shepherd's etched rings, and zipped it closed. Checking the park again, she found no new colors and set off for Patrick's home, her bare feet padding against the wet pavement.

The Assay of Cully had begun.

———

Caroline swept up the path past the *Sold* sign, closing on the front door. She smiled at the series of stone dragons posed in the garden and reached up to touch the rainbow flag fluttering over the garage. The wind chilled her bare feet, and the ache in her toes told her of a coming storm. *Good.*

She stopped three steps from the front door and held her right hand high. With her left, she reached into the folds of her cloak and tapped the topaz hanging around her neck. The gem swelled with amber light, and Sunder groused before it noticed the storm, too. The Aspect's tone changed, and it hummed, ready to play and ride the lightning. Together, they looked skyward and reached for the clouds.

"Could you spare a little help?"

The surrounding air grew still as the wind withdrew. Slowly, the tiny hairs along her arms rose. Caroline's heart quivered in anticipation as she watched her hand. A thin tendril of blue energy leaped between her outstretched fingers. Then another. Then three and five. She marveled, grateful, as her entire hand crackled and snapped.

She closed her fist and never saw the lightning bolt, though she felt it strike. Energy slammed into her body, absorbing into every cell. Sunder danced with the enthusiasm of a child-promised candy, sending arcs of light crawling up and down her body as it played.

"That's enough," Caroline said. "We don't want to scare them if we don't need to." The arcs slowed. She felt Sunder pout.

The wind returned with a howl, protesting such rough handling. As though in retaliation, a gust rolled off the house, slamming Caroline in the face. Her hood blew off, and the stiff wind rushed over her scalp and back. She shivered again and reset her hood. She felt Sunder laugh.

"Very amusing," she deadpanned and hopped up on the wooden deck. The duffel bag thumped down, and Caroline stretched, enjoying being free to move. Smoothing her cloak to conceal the Kiss, she lifted her fist to knock, her skin prickling again. Sunder bristled against her consciousness, pressing shades of red and yellow into her thoughts. Warnings. She turned, facing the park again—eyes narrowed. Something was amiss.

"Skipper," Caroline said, tapping the sapphire around her neck. She felt the tug against her body, and the energy humming in her body dimmed. The world changed. A gray background remained, but tiny blue comets filled her vision as Skipper highlighted every fresh raindrop in blue light. The streets, trees, and homes were all coated as the rain broke and spread like cobalt syrup poured over the gray and black world. New shapes came into view: cars parked along the street, trash cans, and a tall playground. *Where are you?*

A raindrop burst mid-fall at the edge of her vision, then another, far closer. Skipper showed her where to move.

Caroline spun, bringing her weapon up. The bullet sparked against the Kiss and punched into the siding behind her.

BLAM!

She scanned the blue-gray world for any emotional hues, lowering herself into a crouch, waiting. Another raindrop burst off to her right. Sunder swelled as Caroline's eyes raked the street. The energy stored in Caroline arced through her, lashing out in a yellow-blue bolt. She heard a pop and a flash of heat as the energy redirected the bullet and punched another hole in the home.

BLAM!

From within a compact car down the street, the barest shadow of two proud purple silhouettes turned white as her gaze landed on them. In the passenger seat, she made out the dark outline of a large caliber rifle against the white. "There." Launching forward, she sprinted down the path and bounded into the street.

The sniper fired again, but Sunder slapped the bullet away, sending it skipping down the street. With three vaulting steps, Caroline closed the distance, leaped into the air, and drove her Kiss through the open window. The blades sank into the sniper's chest with gruesome ease. A wet sound choked out of the body and she pulled back, turning her gaze on the driver, now fumbling with a dispatch radio.

"Now! Go now!" he yelled.

There were more.

Caroline rolled over the hood, and the metal depressed with a *thump*. She drove the Kiss through the windshield; the glass caved around her armored gauntlet. Her second stroke proved as precise as her first, and the driver's white silhouette flared before fading to black.

A big SUV screeched around the corner, and Caroline readied. Perhaps it was exhaustion, perhaps frustration, but without thinking, she raised her Kiss and took aim at the foe. She tapped Sunder's topaz.

"Do it."

Sunder cackled, gathering the storm's gift. Caroline's jitters faded as the Kiss glowed orange, blue, then white as Sunder pumped more energy into the steel, sending it crackling between her long, forked blades. Iron filled her mouth as a crooked bolt of light erupted from her. The SUV exploded in a blossom of heat, snuffing out an orb of blue around it before the rain refilled the space with light.

Burning, the SUV lurched to the side and slammed into a cement lamppost. Caroline watched the wreckage down the length of her Kiss, not ready to exhale. She waited. Ready for anything to crawl out of the inferno, nothing stirred as the flames grew. Lowering her weapon, she sighed, relieved. The Merged, known as Dawson, wasn't here.

A spark of pain welled from her shoulder, but she felt no blood. She wondered when she'd injured it. Perhaps deflecting bullets and punching through windows was a younger Wyth's work.

Rolling her shoulder and neck, she turned back toward Patrick's home and spotted a tall silhouette filling the doorway with a bewildered, bright blue cloud. Carline sighed. It wasn't the introduction she wanted, but it's what she had. On her walk back, she found her legs shaking. Despite the storm's donated energy, the focus and energy required for such casting had drained her. Dawson had to have known this ambush wouldn't work, but forcing her to cast, to use her bodily reserves, was a shrewd plan—and if his sniper got lucky, all the better. The Wyth took a quick inventory, annoyed at her fatigue.

A startled scream broke Caroline's thoughts, and she looked down the street, where people appeared on front porches and peeked out their windows at the blaze. Complex swirls of yellow, white, and blue filled their silhouettes. Such a public display wasn't part of the plan, but it had been done now, and it had become yet another problem for someone else. In the distance, she heard the wail of police sirens. She couldn't be here when they arrived.

A smaller white silhouette appeared behind Patrick, grasping his arm and trying to pull him back into the house. As Caroline took the first step, she put on her best smile.

"Patrick Rockell?"

"You . . . killed them," Patrick said, a white fear spread.

"Yes." She took the second step.

"Stay away from us!" the woman beside him said. *That must be Ana.*

"I can't. I've come for information." The third step creaked.

"Stop right there!"

Caroline did. "I know Rory."

601

His hue deepened into blue, questioning. "Who the hell are you?"

"A friend," Caroline replied and watched Patrick's color swirl. The color of their fear was different, a brighter hue. *Fresh. Dawson must have visited here.*

Patrick's gaze stretched out to the burning vehicles but remained in mute shock.

Caroline leveled her gaze at them both, collecting their attention. "Listen, I don't want to hurt you, but I need you to tell me what you told them." She waved at the wreckage. "About what you saw the night of the blackout." She took the third step and rose above them, coming so close she could smell the toothpaste on their breath. "Tell me now."

"I . . . I . . ." Patrick then did a curious thing. He looked at Ana, and his emotions rapidly changed from shocked to scared to shy, and then bright pink love tinged with a vibrant turquoise regret. Caroline tilted her head to the side, ensuring she read the man correctly.

"You didn't tell her."

"Tell me . . . what?" Ana said, her white silhouette filling with a hot red mixed with pink. "Is this about the machine malfunctioning?"

"It did," Patrick said. "Technically."

In the distance, the sirens closed.

"What did you tell them?" Caroline hissed.

He stopped and shook his head. "Nothing."

"Tell who what?!" Ana said, her pitch rising. "Who is this, Patrick? What the hell is going on?"

"My name is Caroline." She turned back to Patrick. "Why didn't you tell them? They must have offered you money, a job perhaps? And do not lie to me." She paused, sweeping her gaze over both of them. "That is your only warning."

Patrick took a deep breath, squaring up to Caroline. "A man came."

Caroline had her suspicions. "Describe him."

"Big guy. White, shaved, but with a weird red beard. And his eyes, they were—"

"Two hot coals." She nodded. "I know this man. You told him what you saw?"

Patrick's silhouette turned yellow, then white again, and he dropped his eyes. "He said I'd never have a family if I didn't." Ana gasped. Patrick shifted his feet, and his emotions buzzed yellow and white. "But I didn't tell him anything. I promise. He said . . . a lot of terrible things, but I just couldn't."

Ana squeezed his arm, her color shifting protectively. Caroline savored the gesture of love. She hated to break it, but she had to be certain. He hadn't yet passed the Assay of Cully.

"Why couldn't you, Patrick?" she demanded, so close to the end of the Assay. "Nothing was preventing you. It was Rory who got you fired."

Ana flashed red. "What?!"

Patrick shook his head. "Yeah. But I couldn't. I made him a promise."

Caroline gestured for him to continue. "Why?"

"Why?" Patrick's cloud went hot violet, then dimmed touched. He dropped his chin. "Because... because we're family. He's been there for be through... almost everything. I wouldn't have..." A grim black edged his shiloutte. *Fascinating.*

"You're lying," Caroline said. She waited for him to melt into the white fear of a caught liar, but a ripple of red passed through, showing his frustration at her challenge. She watched another moment, letting the sirens grow closer.

Patrick lifted his chin. "Not about this." His conviction blazed pink.

Caroline took a step back. "I'm impressed, Patrick Rockell. Given the circumstances, I don't know of anyone passing with such flying colors."

Patrick sniffed and shuddered. A light blue sadness washed over him, mixed with relief. Caroline gestured to the massive duffel lying on the deck. "The contents are yours. Protect them. If you can, if he survives tonight, find Rory and make sure he gets this bag. He will need it for the war ahead."

"But—"

Caroline raised her voice. "This is your charge now. Both of yours. The Shepherd's Stones are for Rory. The rings are for Khloe—"

"Khloe?" Patrick said. "From work?"

"And the diamonds are to be used at your discretion."

Ana kneeled down, zipping open the bag. Her hand came to her mouth. "Oh, my god. She's telling the truth."

"I am," Caroline said. "Take these treasures and leave. Immediately."

"But we just bought this—"

Caroline's naked hand lashed out, catching his cheek and snapping his face to the side. She regretted it immediately, but she didn't have time to dawdle. The big man blinked at her, cupping his cheek. "They will kill you if you stay." Confusion roiled in them both, and Caroline pressed closer. She waited a moment for the fact to sink in as they surveyed the burning SUV and dead men. They shook their heads, staring at the bag, then Caroline, then at each other. The sirens wailed.

"I'm off to help Rory, but I need your help to get to him. Something fast. Do you have a car I can take?"

"Car? But you're . . . blind?" Patrick stopped, then waved his hands. "Nevermind. We only have one car, and I guess now we need it."

"You do." Caroline eyed the sports car parked in the neighbor's driveway and sighed. It was going to be *that* kind of night.

"Oh, wait! I parked the campervan just around the corner." Patrick gestured.

Caroline turned back. "Is it fueled?"

Patrick nodded.

"Functioning?"

He nodded again.

"I'll take it."

Patrick reached for the key hanging just inside the door and handed it to Caroline.

"You are rare, both of you," she said, accepting the gift. "Rory loves both of you. Be proud of what you've built with your time together." Patrick slumped, brimming with complex colors and questions.

"And Ana, take this." She reached into her satchel and drew out a vial with a bright pink liquid.

Ana took it. "What is it?"

"A fertility tonic. When you're ready for children, two spoonfuls a day and conception will follow. I'm certain you will raise a proper Wyth."

The sound of sirens grew louder and the first of the police lights danced through the buildings at the far side of the park. Caroline gave them both one last smile. "Farewell." Leaping off the porch, she hurdled the fence and slipped around the corner into the darkness.

Chapter 60: Acceptance

Rory shivered, making himself as small as possible. He hid from the wind as the chilly night air howled through the narrow-barred windows of the prison truck. After twisting and turning to get out of the city, they had rumbled along a relative straightaway for what felt like hours. Or at least long enough for his butt to fall numb against the steel bench. Muffled heavy metal music came from the cab, giving a frantic background to Rory's reeling thoughts. Eyes closed, he watched Bell's wounded expression and the white tiles passing by between his feet as they dragged him away. It was enough to shut down, but another cluster of memories kept the power flickering.

She said . . . I'm the new Host?

Perhaps it was progress that the thought didn't make him feel like throwing up anymore. Whatever else Jane Kim was, she made sense. And as Rory thought more about it, he doubted her sincerity less, even though her arrest might have been staged. He mulled over what she'd said about fear and his choices, how her face had fallen when her partner betrayed her. Like Bell's. It wasn't a good night for either of them, and, at least for him, there was no one to blame but himself. He wished he'd figured it out sooner.

Me? No, it can't be me. I'm not—

But the small voice in his head countered. It sounded like Jane. *But there is the lie again.*

He steadied himself as the weight of her words sank in. Caroline and Jacklyn had picked Rory, but they still couldn't tell him why. This meant that during all those long looks between them, those times he had felt hopelessly adrift in a sea of change, it was all by design. A hot prickle of shame crept up from his chest. *I'm such an idiot.*

Rory looked around his mobile cell, feeling the walls press in.

Shackled and caged, he felt he'd lost the fight already.

Maybe if I'd listened better.

If I'd asked a different question . . .

If I'd . . . if I . . .

If.

Rory sighed, leaning his head against the cold, vibrating wall. In all the scenarios, there was only one common denominator. *Me.*

They arrested Jane, capturing him. Jacklyn too. Caroline was somewhere out there, doing who knows what. If they were going to save the Seed and prevent disaster, then someone would have to fight that living volcano. Someone would have to end this. He looked down at his trembling hands and prayed it wouldn't have to be him, but a sneaking suspicion told him otherwise. He could take this one small step on a vast, twisting path. *A torchbearer.*

The cab lurched, tossing him up and slamming him back down. He grimaced and waited for the pain to fade before opening his eyes. Khloe lay on the steel bench across from him, chained and taking slow, deep breaths. She clutched her arms around her body and curled into a tight ball. Her yellow tank top and thin leggings were barely anything against the cold. *Maybe we wouldn't be here if I'd just listened to her. Or maybe it was a trap.* Either way, Khloe and whatever he hoped to have with her were now collateral to his ignorance.

A torchbearer . . . he reminded himself again, staving off his fear with another deep breath. *Don't drown now.* But his gut twisted. He heaved, turning in time to avoid Khloe. Vomit splattered across the grated floor. Staring down at his sick, the fear took hold and hooked its lie. "I can't do this," he said to the air. The quiet, frantic music and cold metal creak answered back.

He squinted back tears as Bell reappeared behind his eyes. He wished she was there. To shine a light on what he should do. But that was gone now. More collateral. *I'm so sorry, Bell.* The pressure behind his eyes built. *What am I going to do?*

A soothing memory overtook him. Maybe the last of Bell's pearls. "Sometimes, when it seems hopeless, all we have is saying it out loud," she'd whispered to him recently as they watched a family place a beaded necklace on their son's pillow. He remembered the feel of her hand cradling him, her words warm. "If nothing else, to hear your fear out loud. Powerful thing feeling heard, especially by yourself."

The hot sting of bile struck his nose like smelling salts. His senses jerked him back, and he found his cheeks wet and his vision blurred. *Was I crying?* He didn't remember.

Rory shifted on his bench, shaking as he tried to rub the feeling back in his legs. He wondered how long he'd been crying. He couldn't say, but Bell's words once again provided light. *I'm . . . not alone. Not anymore.* Jane. Jacklyn. Caroline. And Khloe. They were all in this together now–ready or not. If he failed now, he would let them all down, and he never wanted to feel that way again. He was tired of disappointing everyone—especially himself.

Just a torchbearer. It was a place to start.

A surprising burst of optimism radiated, and for a moment, his spirits lifted. The thought rippled through him, hollowing out a space in his heart. A decade's worth of weight and scars came into focus and decoupled, untangling him. He expanded, and a crystal-clear, daunting purpose filled the void in that newly created space.

I can do this. I can . . . He swallowed, letting the weight of his next words sit in his chest. *Be the next Host.*

The truck bounced, throwing him back into the present. He shivered, but this time felt a warmth from within. With a sniff, he wiped his eyes with his wrist. *One step at a time, Rory.*

"First, let's get out of this prison."

He looked around, eyeing the thick metal bars, leaving him alone again with the question of how. He shook his head and laughed, which welled with mirth at the audacity of his situation. Laughing felt mad, yet good—a relief as though he was setting something down he'd been carrying for a long time. Suppressing a shudder, he listened. The wind howled through the hazy, barred window, and the truck jostled again, his chains cutting into the raw-red skin of his wrists. "Maybe we can—"

A boom of thunder exploded in the silence. He leaped up with a shout, rattling his chains. The truck swayed beneath him, but he steadied his stance. Peering out the window above him, dark clouds churned in the sky, spinning slowly like a gathering hurricane. "No way . . ."

Suddenly, a furious rain pummeled the truck, and lightning flashed. The wind raged against the bars, rocking the cab as the clouds spun faster and faster. Then, the maelstrom's eye stretched down from the heavens, touching the horizon with a narrow funnel. Gunshots erupted, followed by explosions of bright lights behind the truck.

"Khloe!" he shouted. He looked over at her, still asleep.

Rory heard angry shouts coming from the cab, and the truck picked up speed. "Hey! Wake up!" He stomped his foot against the floor. "Wake up!"

A blur of heat and light flew past their window, throwing up clouds of steam as the rainwater vaporized in the fire's wake. *That came from the front of the column.*

BOOM! The truck swerved, and the tires squealed. The side of his knee slammed against the bench, and a sharp pain fired through his leg. He grimaced but didn't have time to balance before the truck lurched again. Stumbling, he kept his footing, though Khloe slid off her bench with a heavy thump.

"Khloe!" He kneeled beside her. Blood trickled over her eye, but she was breathing. "I know you're mad at me, but I need to touch you."

As he reached for her, Khloe's thin blonde hair rose, splaying out and standing on end. On his arms, the hairs stood. *Static.*

Zzzap Zzaap. Rory looked up and saw thin arcs of yellow-blue light appear inside the metal cabin.

"Oh, shit," he said and then yelled as loud as he could.

The sky outside flashed, swallowing them in light. Blinking, he was weightless. Khloe floated by, and he glanced down at his chains, dancing in the air. *This is it.*

A predator had arrived.

Stretched from all corners of the dark, swirling stormhead, the lightning converged. Bolts touched and fused, flickering occasionally until another bolt rebuilt the structure. A figure formed with great crackling wings and a long, jagged beak; an eagle with talons outstretched as it boomed its war cry. With each beat of its wings, bolts raked the roadway in the distance, renting the pavement like a plow through the earth. When its beak opened, thunder vibrated the air.

Dawson felt a chill cool his burning skin, watching the massive Aspect lock eyes on him. He'd put down several greater Aspects before, even fusing one to his Stain. It wasn't the bird whom the Heart of Wrath demanded their blood—it was the Wyth who'd been able to summon it. *Caroline.* Only a Path Master could pull off such a feat without dying for their hubris; those Wyth were indeed rare and had an irritating habit of taking too long to die.

"Speed up," he said.

"Sir?" his young driver said, shaking. The boy had just joined, filling in for the casualties inflicted by the golems. He reeked of fear.

"Faster," Dawson growled.

The driver went white, and they sped up. The farms and tree-coated hills around them turned into a green blur.

Beneath the bird, a boxy campervan raced down the highway behind them. Caroline leaned out the window with one hand on the wheel and the other holding a blazing yellow mythstone high above her naked head. Forked tongues of jagged light danced between bird and stone like a lightning rod, tethering them together. Dawson marveled at the Aspect's raw power and felt the Heart bristle. Another predator had come. Another alpha.

Seeing the thunder Aspect summoned an old loathing from deep within Dawson—a loathing not his own, like an ancient grudge rekindled. He could hear his heartbeat in his ears, and he snarled the Heart's challenge. Next to him, the driver sank into his chair with a grim expression. *Good. He understood.*

Dawson snatched the radio and bellowed, "Engage the Wyth! Keep her away from the Seed!"

"Roger," Captain Adams's voice came over the speaker. In the mirror, he saw the rear SUV detach from the convoy and drift back toward the Wyth. Black shapes leaned out every window and took aim at Caroline. Dawson waited, the Heart warming and filling him with jittery energy.

Gunshots popped from the rear of the column, and a dazzling curtain of lightning descended from the Thunderbird, shielding Caroline. The bird dimmed as it absorbed the fire. *There.* Dawson smiled. He didn't need to defeat the Wyth when he could outlast her. Energy was the currency of casting, and even a Master had a budget.

Dawson shoved his finger in the twelve-volt cigarette lighter on the dashboard. "Not too much," Dawson said as the cab lights flickered and the Heart sang, siphoning heat and wrapping it inside his chest. Merging provided a significant advantage over other casting techniques. Where a Wyth needed time to recover and rest, a Merged stole more energy. Attrition would be Dawson's ally.

He caught his driver staring at his smoking and now glowing finger. "Steady, or I'll throw you to the witch." The driver's eyes snapped forward as he white-knuckled the steering wheel. He spared a glance into the back of his SUV where Jane Kim sat bound, gagged, and hooded, with armed troopers on either side. Yet despite the security, Dawson didn't trust the little woman not to pull something. Emmett sat in the seat before her, twisting around, watching the firefight.

Dawson slapped the back of Emmett's head to get his attention.

Emmett's expression had a stupid look of disbelief. *"That's* a Wyth?!"

"Focus." Dawson pointed at Jane. "Shoot her if she so much as sneezes."

Emmett nodded once. "Where are you going?"

Dawson pointed behind them. "Dealing with *that.*" He pulled his red-hot finger from the lighter.

The Heart released the stored heat, and it flowed through his hands. He drove his boot into the door, and the hinges exploded, sending it sparking off the concrete behind them. The wind howled, the driver yelped, and Dawson hooked his right arm around the doorframe, stabilizing himself and freeing his left hand. He leaned out, the speed and wind tugging him, but his grip held. He raised his free hand, and the Heart's heat condensed into a perfect blazing sphere.

He took aim and whipped the orb at the van behind them. The fireball skimmed the armored truck, sending up a sheet of steam off its metal flank. Caroline ducked behind the mythstone, and lightning rained down from the Thunderbird. The Heart crowed a direct hit, but the triumph was brief. Caroline emerged from the inferno, slumped and smoking but damnably alive. The Thunderbird's brightness dimmed. The Wyth felt that one.

Gunfire continued to pour into her, and the Thunderbird's shield of light grew sluggish, its wings slapping away bullets. Caroline shook her head and aimed the glowing topaz at Adams's two SUVs. Silver bolts raked forward, splitting one and punching a hole through the other. Both vehicles swerved and burst into flames, their troopers flying through windows and skipping across the pavement.

"Goddamnit, Adams!" Dawson said. She was right behind the nurse's truck now.

The Thunderbird arched its back, and a moment later, another bolt exploded forward, slicing through the truck's body and punching a crater in the road in front of it. The truck pitched forward, dropping into the hole. The cab compacted on the lip, flipping the heavy transport high into the air. Dawson watched, amused. She might do him a favor and dispatch the other captives. The Director would understand collateral damage.

Then, in that blissful moment, hundreds of thousands of brightly colored feathers burst into the air. It was as though a flock of birds of paradise enfolded the truck before it slammed back to earth. The rest floated in the air like some exotic, downy curtain. For a few seconds, the wall of twirling color blocked the roadway until the damnable campervan burst through in pursuit. The Wyth gunned for the last truck, the one with the Seed.

"She's got the Quill," Dawson grumbled. Someone in Storage better have a good explanation as to why. *Irrelevant,* he thought. While its utility was undeniable, the Quill couldn't alone carry the day. What were a bunch of feathers compared to an army and the Heart?

Dawson ducked back into the cab and grabbed the radio. "Engage! All units engage!"

"She'll fry them!" Emmett protested.

Dawson grinned. "Write their family a card." He leaned back out.

The remaining two SUVs broke their escort position around the Seed and closed on Caroline. Gunfire followed, drawing more lightning.

"Break!" Dawson readied his second fireball. "Come on, witch. Break."

Caroline slashed her arm out as though scything wheat and the Thunderbird struck. A thick bolt cut through the first SUV, tore across the roadway, and buried itself into the second. Both vehicles tumbled almost silently behind them, throwing bits of steel and bodies across the highway.

Overhead, the churning clouds slowed. The Thunderbird's light dimmed, and the great Aspect's wings slackened. Caroline, one hand still driving the wobbling van, peered up at the breaking storm. The Heart barked for the kill.

The fireball felt deadly coming out of his hand—his aim, perfect. He watched, mesmerized by its beauty. Caroline threw up the gleaming topaz, but no lightning came. Fire engulfed her and receded rapidly behind him. As the light cleared, the campervan was a stopped ruin. Shards of amber glistened across the roadway, and for a moment, he thought it was done, his hope rising until he spotted the witch rise with a heavy lean. She lived, but it had cost her more than just a mythstone.

The Thunderbird spasmed, arcing its back and wings. The delicate strands of light woven together unraveled and snapped like wire under stress. A bolt came loose like a coiled spring released. Asphalt burst as bolts tore through the road. A roadside fence caught fire, and another sent up sprays of sod. The Aspect's body exploded with a booming thunderclap, leaving the air crackling with yellow light before it disappeared.

"Pathetic!" Dawson cackled. He thought it would be harder than that.

He swung himself back into the passenger seat with a satisfied nod. The Wyth was strong, but age had caught up to her. She was not the vibrant, lethal witch Dawson remembered dueling before. With the Brand, more troopers, and heavy munitions waiting for him, capturing Caroline felt easy.

Emmett cut his reveries. "Is she . . . dead?"

"Injured," Dawson said. "She'll come for us soon enough."

"How do you know?"

"Because we have the Seed."

"But she took out the truck. If the nurse survived, he's the next—

"

"He is weak, too!" Dawson shouted him down. "If he is their best candidate for Host, then the Wyth is far more desperate than I thought. That war is over." The Heart snarled against Dawson's mind, despising the thought of dwindling hunts. "On to the next one."

Emmett wilted, keeping his voice low. "What about Adams? His men? Maybe some survived."

Dawson turned in his seat, meeting Emmett's eyes before his hand latched onto his jaw.

"Hey!"

Dawson squeezed Emmett's cheeks to cut him off and let the Heart press heat into his fingertips. *Not too much, we need him a little while longer.* The Heart reluctantly obeyed as Emmett moaned in pain, grabbing at Dawson's arm to little avail.

"They did their job," Dawson said, squeezing a little harder. "So shut up. And do yours." He released him, and Emmett fell back into his seat, touching the angry, blistered skin from Dawson's touch. "Understand?"

Emmett swallowed, then nodded. Fresh fear wafted off him.

"Good."

Rory stirred as his head throbbed. He drew in a ragged breath and groaned. *Alive?* He shifted his arms, wincing at the fresh pain that thankfully faded. His chains pulled taut, and as his senses re-knit, he felt a strange softness against his face. He opened his eyes to complete blackness, shifting again and feeling fine filaments tickling his arms and legs. There was nothing solid beneath his feet . . . or was it above him? He blinked, disoriented.

Something in his memory about avalanches told him to spit—a crude way of revealing gravity. Summoning what saliva he had, Rory spit, letting the drool dribble out of his mouth. The wetness ran down his right cheek toward his ear. He wasn't sure how that helped him yet, but at least he knew which way was down.

Taking stock, Rory gathered himself. He remembered lightning, fire, and . . . Khloe!

"Khloe?" Rory said, panicked. He couldn't see anything. "Khloe!" He stretched out his arms, but his chains held, and he winced as the cuffs bit into his raw wrists.

Muffled, tinny footfalls thumped against the metal above him. Rory clamped his mouth shut and sank down, cringing when his chains rattled. The footfalls stopped and for a grueling stretch of seconds, Rory waited with his heartbeat drumming in his ears.

Metal shrieked, and Rory flinched back, letting out a yelp. Two parallel lines pierced the truck's hull not two feet from his head, casting two thin shafts of silvery moonlight onto a pool of colorful feathers. *Feathers?* Was all he thought before a bloodied hand reached through one opening, gripped the thin strip of metal between the cuts, and jerked back. The steel compacted between the fingers, and the entire strip of metal pulled back in a scream. Moonlight flooded in, and somewhere outside, the mangled steel clattered against the pavement.

Rory jerked on his chains but couldn't move. He was a sitting duck as he gaped through the gap and the edge of the moon in a calm, cloudless sky. A face eclipsed the moon, peering down at him. "Rory Nash," Caroline said, relief clear in her voice. "I'm so glad you're alive."

"Caroline!" Rory's body sagged with relief. "You're here! What . . . what happened? I saw a storm. Was that—"

"That was Sunder," she replied. "There was a skirmish, and I was not as successful as I'd hoped to be. Dawson still holds Jacklyn, and we lost Sunder."

Her words dampened Rory's relief. "Oh, no. I'm so sorry."

"Sad, to be sure, but I like to think he finally got his wish."

Rory nodded and tried to move, but the feathers absorbed him like quicksand. "Did you . . . where did all these . . ." His questions backed up again, clogging his tongue.

Caroline held up a metal feather in her other hand, the one Rory had pricked his finger on only a day before. "This Quill is a remarkable tool. We don't have time for how. I wasn't sure it would work."

"You weren't sure?" Rory said, aghast.

Caroline ignored him, lowering her head through the gash, and peered around. "Is Doctor Seeker here too?"

Khloe! "Yes! At least she was before the wreck," Rory said. "Khloe!"

A muffled whimper came from somewhere below him. He tried to reach for her.

Caroline placed a hand on either side of the gap, heaved, and the steel parted, creating an opening large enough for a body. Stunned by her strength, he watched her lean in, wearing her twin-bladed gauntlet and hanging upside down as the blade tip stretched toward him.

Rory flinched back. "What are you doing?"

The question drew a smile from Caroline. "Freeing you. Hold your wrists up and apart as high as you can toward me and stay very, very still."

Rory raised his hands up and apart. She lashed out, a single decisive slice through his chains. Green sparks burst as they split, and the tension on Rory's bloodied wrists eased. Caroline reached out a hand, beckoning him. Despite having little leverage, she lifted him from the belly of the truck and deposited him unceremoniously next to a charred wheel well, and the smell of burning gasoline and manure welcomed him into the open air. He sat on the truck's flank, high above the ground, dazed as his vision adjusted to the light. *Where are we?*

The wind rolled over him, plucking away stray feathers and tumbling them over the wreckage stretched out on the highway behind them. Between the sprawling green fields on either side of the road, the asphalt was ripped and gouged in several places, like a maniac giant took a knife to the road. Scattered across the highway were bits of jagged stone and still bodies lying at unnatural angles. He counted five corpses of wrecked vehicles. *Caroline did this? Alone?*

Rory listed and shook his head. He peered across the moonlit fields, wondering what he could do compared to such raw power.

"I'll be right back," Caroline said, jumping through the opening she'd torn.

"Wait!" His knees ached, but took his weight as he rose and picked his footing carefully. He stood at the edge of Caroline's portal and peered down at the rainbow feathers, listening.

"Moo."

Rory jumped and turned to see a pair of cows standing at a nearby fence, watching and chewing, unimpressed by the carnage.

"Stupid cow," he said, blowing out a breath to calm his racing heart.

A hand erupted from the feathers.

"Ahh!" Rory flinched back, but then recognized Khloe's long, strong fingers with a silver thumb ring. "I got you!" He grabbed the hand and pulled with all his strength. Khloe rose, spitting out feathers, as she gasped for air. He lifted her carefully over the torn metal, her unfocused eyes blinking. Caroline's hand emerged a moment later and Rory helped haul her out as well.

"What happened?" Khloe said, lying still.

"Yes, Rory," Caroline echoed her tone hard. "What happened after I left?"

Rory swallowed. "Jacklyn . . . used the hilt-thing on her. Said it made her sleep."

"And did you stop her?"

Rory shook his head as a fresh wave of shame rolled over him. He looked up to find Khloe scowling at him. "Khloe . . . I . . . ." He closed his mouth, certain he was about to say something stupid. Silence followed, and the few feet between them stretched into a thousand miles. He felt alone again and shrunk, staring at his hands.

"I see," Caroline said. "A foolish choice, but done now. I am relieved to see you both alive still. Not everyone can claim that after they encounter a Merged." She turned to Khloe. "They must have taken you while you slept. We are east of the city now. There was a fight, and we took casualties. Fortunately, we still have—" She paused, groping at her hip. She looked down with a frown. "My satchel."

"Your . . ." But Rory didn't even finish his question before Caroline vaulted off the truck and sprinted away, weaving through the debris. *Where is she going now?* Dazed, Rory's eyes lifted to the far end of the wreckage beyond the van. Several sets

620

of headlights had gathered. He made out a small group of onlookers and was sure someone had called the police. "We need to get out of here. Come on."

Rory scrambled off the back of the truck and lowered himself onto the ground. He looked up, ready to help Khloe, but found her staring down at him with blazing, fixed eyes. The colorful feathers clinging to her thin clothes quivered in the chilly wind. She shivered but held her ground.

"This is your fault," she growled, gesturing to the flipped truck. "We didn't have to be here. We had allies—"

"*Potential* allies," Rory countered, his thinned composure giving way to frustration. "It could have been a trap! And you shouldn't have snuck around and gotten others involved! We had a deal!"

"Exactly! We were supposed to be partners, Rory. Instead, you tried to be the hero—"

"I . . ." was all Rory managed before Khloe shouted over him.

"You what, Rory? What's your next excuse? You attacked me in my home!"

Her words felt like a punch. Rory opened his mouth, but nothing came out. *She's right.* He had excuses for everything recently, and now he'd run out. Jane was right—the truth was the only way forward.

"I'm sorry," he said, looking her in the eyes. "I really, really am for . . . everything. But especially for coming to your home and getting you mixed up in all of this. You deserve a lot better than that."

Khloe studied him a moment, then gingerly, she hopped down, waving off his assistance. She grimaced as she landed and favored one foot. "Thank you. Now, tell me what else happened."

"Well, I found out I'm the next Host."

621

"What?"

"Guess they are pretty desperate." *That's the lie*, Jane's voice echoed from his memory.

"Host? I thought . . . Tracy?"

"Was just part of some test Jacklyn and Caroline have been putting me through. I don't understand it or why, but they picked me for the job."

"Who told you? Jacklyn?"

"No. A person named Jane—no one, you know. She was working for the Broken Star, but I think she's trying to help us now."

"And you're sure?"

Rory nodded and shrugged. "As much as I can be anymore." He spotted Caroline stop near the smallest of the wrecks. He wondered where she got a car as she kneeled and prodded the flames with her forked blades like she was stirring embers.

Khloe followed his eyes. "Come on," she said and started toward Caroline. "Talk fast."

As they picked their way through the broken glass and mangled metal, Rory recounted the events of the last couple of hours. He spared nothing in his catastrophe at the hospital, and Khloe listened quietly as he described his final encounter with Bell. Reliving the events brought fresh stabs of shame. *What was I thinking?*

"Khloe, there is something else you need to know."

She watched him, but remained quiet.

"It's Jacklyn. She's . . . she kills people. It's how she could heal. I don't know much more than that, but I thought you should know before—" He left off, not sure what to add. He didn't know what was going to happen.

Khloe blinked twice before a frown knit her features. Turning away, Khloe watched the fires burn and, after an uncomfortable pause, finally gave a low, slow whistle.

"She had to balance the equation."

"The what?"

"The energy equation," Khloe said, then nodded to herself. "The cost of healing Tommy and Conner. Nothing is free. It's a terrible cost, but . . . so what? I wouldn't change helping Conner. Would you?"

Rory wanted badly to say he would have, that saying so would make him a better person, but he just shook his head. "I'd trade that boyfriend's life for Tommy's every time." There was the truth, and the ease with which he said it scared him. *Does that make me a monster, too?*

Ahead, Caroline had moved to the other side of the wreck, still trying to use her gauntlet to snag something in the dying fire. Beyond her, more headlights gathered, and a small group of people tentatively advanced down the road toward them. Rory's mind started working out what to say to them, but he faltered out of excuses.

"Do you want the job?" Khloe asked.

Rory's mind reeled back, and he found her scrutinizing him. "What?"

"Do you want to be the Host?"

He balked. On one hand, he could heal anyone; on the other, he didn't know if he could kill. Even if they got to Jacklyn and transferred the Seed, and it didn't kill him, then what? If he used the Seed to heal, then he'd need to replenish the energy somehow. *Balance.* It was an impossible choice, but one Jacklyn had picked him to make.

"Yes." Despite the fear, Rory was certain. *A torchbearer.*

"Good, because I think you'll do the job. And do it well," Khloe said. The sudden vote of confidence caught him off guard, and he smiled at her, unsure of what to say.

"But," she continued, "you're going to need smart people around, and you'll need to listen to them. I don't know if you noticed, but this"—she gestured to the surrounding carnage, letting her words hang in the air—"this is unsustainable."

"Agreed."

Khloe looked down at her feet, still in slippers. "And since we are in an honest mood, I guess it's my turn. I should have told you I was sending the blood sample to the Evergreen Society. I got greedy and panicked because you were acting weird and I got possessive of the Seed. It . . . I . . . ."

"I get it," Rory said. "The Seed has that effect, and we were both trying to do what we thought was right." It scared him to think that he'd been willing to force the Seed on Tracy. If they pulled this off, he realized just how careful he'd need to be—the power of the Seed could warp him. And those around him.

Khloe sighed, examining her bloody wrists. "I suppose I'd have been pretty upset too if you'd sprung that news on me, especially after seeing the Cove destroyed and having to talk to those agents. You don't deserve to shoulder all the blame alone."

Alone. The word ran through his heart. "Thank you."

Khloe jabbed a finger at him. "Doesn't mean I'm not mad at you still."

"Completely understandable."

"Good, because I am," she said. "You're an idiot."

"No objection here," Rory said. Small, downy feathers still clung to her hair and clothes. In the moonlight, her skin shone, and she looked radiant. She caught him staring a little too long and raised an eyebrow.

"Yes?"

Rory inhaled, feeling his next words drawn from his truth. "In a weird way, I'm glad you're here. I don't . . . I don't feel as alone when you're around." He felt his cheeks burn hot.

Khloe's hands were cool against his hot flesh, and she pulled his forehead down to hers. "I don't either." She held his face there, cupped in her hands, then backed away, letting her hands drop. Rory ached for her touch again, fighting hard for the words to capture what he felt—something clever and romantic—but as they stood there, her eyes searching his, he smiled at her and let his silence speak for him. She grinned back, and he knew she understood. He hoped there would be time for words later.

As Caroline tossed away a smoking bumper down the road, metal rang against the stone. She stooped down and fished a charred leather pouch from the flames, quickly batting out the flames and rummaging through it. Small glass vials glistened in the moonlight, though the shards of several broken ones did, too, as she tossed them aside.

"Let's go," Khloe said, starting toward Caroline. "Jacklyn."

"Hold on," Rory said. "Khloe, this is going to be dangerous. You should get as far from all this—from me—as possible."

Khloe met his eye. "Rory, look. I'm not asking for permission. This is my choice. If you're Host, I'm Counselor." She quieted, picking feathers from her hair. "Deep down, I think this is what I've always been searching for—answers to the questions no one asks. Mysteries and magic. So please, don't fight me. I'm already in."

Their eyes met, and Rory felt a well of gratitude overwhelm him. "Thanks."

"I have two conditions, though."

"Okay."

"One. *When* we get the job done, I get first crack and control of any research projects you're comfortable with. I want to understand the Seed. I need to figure out how it . . . implants and interfaces. Maybe, I don't know, we can figure out a way to contain it with no need for a Host."

Her dream was a deep breath of optimism. "That would be amazing."

"Two. We're partners. For real, this time. No more lying or back door plans for either of us, okay? Equals."

"Done."

"Good. Then we can work together." She smiled again, and that introduced a new thought. One that he'd never contemplated before. *Maybe this will work. Maybe . . . we can do it.* The thought touched something deep in his chest, tapping into the fragment of his potential future. A sudden ache followed but faded a moment later when a burst of warmth flooded his body, flushing him with heat despite the chilly night air. Rory rubbed his chest, uncertain of what had just happened. "That's weird."

"What?"

"My chest. I've been getting this heartburn or something recently, but this felt different." Pins and needles spread down to his hands, and he wiggled his fingers. "My hand is tingling."

"You're not allowed to have a heart attack."

Rory shook his head, looking around. "It's not that." He didn't feel any pressure. If anything, he felt relief, like something had been unstuck. "That is so weird."

Muffled shouts rose from down the road, and Rory spotted a small crowd approaching. Individuals broke off, searching for the wreckage. He felt a prickle of dread when he saw four or five people around one of Dawson's troopers stirring. Caroline hadn't gotten everyone.

"That's not good," Khloe whispered.

Rory touched her shoulder, hoping to instill some confidence, though he felt his knees weaken.

"Go help Caroline. We'll need her if things go sideways."

"What are you going to do?"

A burst of dreadful optimism welled in his chest. "To talk."

"That's Broken Star, Rory," Khloe said, shaking her head. "They just kidnapped us. He's probably armed!"

"Maybe," Rory said, fighting back his growing fear. "Go."

He turned and ran toward the group, repeating an old nursing mantra.

This is your hundredth time. This is your hundredth time.

Chapter 63: Assay of Tiff

Translated from:

Disc - Shepherd's Stone

Sub-ring - *Codex*

Script - *Law of Hosts*:

Assay of Tiff:

Let the candidate's foes, not their family, demonstrate their respect and the source of their motivation. Let the gulf of conflict reveal both ire and empathy until a balance is demonstrated.

A candidate passes if empathy prevails from common bond with no return.

A candidate fails if ire prevails from lack of bond.

A candidate fails if the candidate demands a return.

Amendment(s):

(859 AA) - Let those with common bond live. Let bond-breakers die. No foe may linger in a candidate's wake.

(4955 AA) - Let those friends of the candidate, those Oracles eager to deal judgments, deliver their sentences for the candidate to bear witness. Only then will the candidate's shade of love be shown.

—

"Excuse me!" Rory said, slowing his pace. A small group of onlookers stood a few yards back from the wounded trooper lying in the roadway, watching him with trepidation. The three red stripes on the trooper's shoulders matched the crimson pool reflected in the moonlight beneath him. *Femoral. He's losing too much blood.*

"Hello, my name is Rory Nash, and I—"

"I'm with the military." The trooper coughed, leaning hard on an open wound in his thigh. Rory spotted a pistol holstered at the man's hip. "Domestic counter-terrorism. That man is a terrorist and traitor! Seize him!"

A dozen sets of eyes landed on Rory, knocking him back a step. Murmurs broke the wind-swept silence. Everyone tensed.

Raising both hands slowly, Rory kept his voice level and calm, like the first time he talked to Sneaks. "I'm not armed. Or a terrorist. That man is losing blood. I can help him."

"Liar!" the trooper barked, wincing and grasping his thigh. "If he succeeds, we're all in danger!"

Fear rippled through the crowd. The whites of their eyes glowed in the moonlight. Rory was losing control of the situation. "I don't—"

"What happened here?" someone demanded from the crowd. "Explain yourself!"

"Ya!" another echoed, followed by a wave of similar demands.

A torchbearer. Be honest. Rory blew out a long breath, unsure how to end the next bout of silence with a hostile crowd. "There was—"

They didn't listen; they all shouted at once. He'd waited too long.

"He doesn't even know his own story!"

"He must have a bomb."

"Murderer!"

"Wait." Rory raised both hands higher and backed away. His foot slipped on broken glass, and he slid, pleading with the encroaching crowd. "Hear me out, please!"

"Grab him!" someone shouted.

"Don't let him get away," another called.

"STOP!" Caroline's voice pierced the din, and the crowd stalled. Her blood-stained Kiss gleamed menacingly in the silver light. Behind her, Khloe clutched a burnt leather satchel, looking between the crowd, Caroline and Rory.

"Leave," she demanded. "Go home to your families."

The crowd stood in stunned silence. She took a deep breath, and Rory saw a gleam of emerald light from her clenched fist. The earth bulged beside her. Gasps and cries of alarm went up, and people backed away. Caroline held her arm out, palm down, stroking the air. Stone and dirt rose, stretching up to her hand, curling back on itself and solidifying. A pair of emerald eyes opened from the mass, and then it shook itself, sending a cascade of earth and clods tumbling to the ground. A great cat emerged the size of a tiger with dark silt stripes patterning its back and legs. Arching itself, it pressed into Caroline's hand as it surveyed their audience.

Gasps turned to screams, and people broke, sprinting for their cars.

Rory turned back to the trooper and saw a man standing a few feet back—the only one left from the crowd of frightened onlookers. He was tall, barrel-chested, wearing overalls and a red hat. With a spark of recognition, he focused his wide eyes on Rory, then the elemental cat.

Caroline strolled forward with the tiger prowling by her bare feet.

"Stay away from me, witch!" the trooper spat. He tried to stand, but hissed in pain and clutched at his gushing leg.

"Captain Adams." Her hands balled into fists. "Still serving the wrong master."

"My side is winning, bitch," he spat back, his hand dropping to his pistol.

The earthen tiger's growl rumbled through Rory like the bass

630

from a subwoofer. Adams froze.

"Enough people have died," Rory said, feeling their attention on him. "Please, can we just talk?"

His words meant as much as the wind.

"Go ahead," Caroline said, never taking her eyes off the man called Adams. Rory had never heard her voice so cold. "I'll gladly usher *you* into the beyond."

Adams drew his pistol in a smooth motion.

"No!" Rory shouted.

Caroline flicked her wrist as the barrel turned, and the tiger lunged.

BANG!

Light flashed within the elemental's clamped jaws, and a ribbon of bright red blood sprayed across the ground. The tiger jerked its head away, and a sickening snap followed. Adams screamed. Rory's stomach heaved as he stared at the bright white bone protruding from a bloody red stump. Adams crumpled, eyes wide, as he clutched at his mangled arm. "My arm! Ahhh!"

"Consider yourself lucky." Caroline stepped closer. "If I had the gift of time, I would flay you."

Adams moaned, spittle flying from his mouth as he spoke. "It doesn't matter what you do to me." He smiled, baring his red-stained teeth. "We still have your girlfriend."

Silt growled, vibrating the ground and shaking Rory from his stupor. Caroline's lip curled, and her Kiss glinted as she took aim.

Adams raised his chin, his blood pooling on the roadway next to him.

"Stop!" Rory stepped into Caroline's path. "He's unarmed now."

"This isn't your ivory hospital, Rory," Caroline hissed. "You can't save everyone. Lives must be lost. A Host must embrace this." She slid to the side, trying to step around him, but he raised a gentle hand.

"Rory," she seethed, her Kiss humming. "You protect vermin. A man who has handed death to countless Wyth. He is a war criminal—a torturer. Get out of my way."

"A Host has to balance life, too. Who to save. Not everything leads to death—there are miracles, too. There must be room for mercy." His words surprised him as though recited from a book he hadn't yet read. *Do I believe that?* A warmth spread out from his chest, but he didn't know what that meant.

Caroline lifted her chin, her jaw flexing irritably as she watched him through her muddied blindfold.

What do you see? Rory thought. *I can't lie to you.*

Her eyebrow lifted, Kiss still poised. Then she nodded once to herself, lowering the Kiss. "Thank you, Silt," she said, lifting her hand from the earth tiger's back. Something like a purr tumbled out as the tiger broke and scattered into a mound of broken earth. Behind her, Khloe stepped forward, a mix of apprehension and awe as she looked at the ruined pile.

"You believe what you said, Rory Nash," Caroline said. She tapped her chest - over her heart. "The soul doesn't lie. And while you have much to learn about war, perhaps you are right. This next war will be different, so we'll need new ideas for how to fight, but I pray your optimism doesn't get us all killed."

"Me too," Rory said. A stone of responsibility settled in his gut. He turned back to Adams, who had paled into a purple-gray from anemia. "Let me see your leg, I—"

"Eat shit," Adams snarled, grimacing as he pushed himself to his good knee. "That one has just as much blood on her hands as mine."

"We don't kill the innocent!" Caroline snapped.

"By whose definition?" Adams shot back.

"Stop!" Rory said. "Adams, you can help us. You don't have to die for—"

"I'm already dead," he said. He pushed himself up and grabbed a long strip of metal from one of the wrecked vehicles. He propped himself up with the crutch, panting in shallow breaths. "You can kill me, but either way, I'm leaving on my terms." He took a labored step, wincing. Then he limped into the fields, dripping blood the whole way. Rory gave him ten minutes before he passed out.

Caroline stepped up behind him and caught the smell of smoke, sweat, and lavender. "He shouldn't be allowed to leave."

"He won't go far," Khloe said from just behind her. "He's bleeding too much."

"The good doctor is right," Caroline said. "We should end his suffering."

"That's not what I said." Khloe turned to Caroline. "We need to find Jacklyn. That's priority number one."

Caroline scanned the eastern horizon, nodding. "I see her." She pointed, tracing her finger across the moonlit pastures to the east. "They are a few miles ahead, moving slower now. They must have turned off the freeway, heading north."

"We can't follow fast enough. We need a car—and a guide," Rory mumbled, looking around.

Someone who knows the area—shortcuts.

He spun around and saw the barrel-chested man still standing there, staring back at him with the unmistakable squint of recognition. The man blinked, then said, "You hit my truck."

Rory's mouth fell open. *What was his name?* He searched his memory. Fragments of information flew by. *His sister . . . liked cheese curds? A cattle farm. What was his name? He called the girl a niece. He called her . . . Peanut. Ben? Was that it?* He took a chance. "It's Ben, right?"

The man's eyebrows shot up. He nodded.

"I was also Peanut's nurse."

Ben nodded. "I remember."

"Did she get the balloons?"

"Yeah." Ben's eyes drifted up to the wreckage. Rory didn't have time to explain anything—the magic, the bodies, the lightning. *Keep it simple.* "Look, I'm sorry to have to ask—"

"What in God's name happened out here?" Ben cut in. His brown eyes landed on Caroline, lingering on her blood-slicked Witch's Kiss.

It would only be a matter of time before Rory heard sirens. He needed to be gone before they arrived.

"Ben, I—" *Simple.* "We need your help." Rory pointed back toward Caroline and Khloe. "These are my friends. We're not terrorists."

Caroline slipped up beside him. Her hand touched his arm, and she straightened, appraising Ben. Rory felt a bubble of hope— and fear—as the big man took a step back.

"I will not hurt you," Caroline said, though that didn't seem to ease Ben's worry. He surveyed the wreckage, looking uncertain. It was too much, too different. *This has to be about him and me. Make it personal.*

"Ben, I wouldn't ask for help unless I really needed it. I'm terrible at admitting when I'm in over my head." He sighed, shaking his head. "Please. We're stranded. That other guy—the one who claimed he was with the military—his friends took mine. Abducted her, actually. We're trying to catch them before they fly away forever."

Ben stood silently, his eyes surveying the burning cars. The silence stretched on long enough that a dread crept from Rory's stomach into his throat. *What do we do if he says no?*

As the silence stretched further into discomfort, Ben's gaze landed back on Rory.

"You said fly, right?"

Rory's spirits lifted. "Yes."

"Old Man Willis sometimes rents out his south pasture as an airstrip." Ben looked in the direction Caroline had pointed. "Just yesterday, I heard a big cargo plane land there. Thought it was odd, but I figured it was a fertilizer drop."

"That has to be it!"

Ben nodded, obviously still processing. "And your friend, the people who took her, those people have powers too?"

"Some of them, but I'm not asking you to risk your life. Just one ride. For Peanut."

"Peanut . . ." Ben pulled off his hat and ran a hand through his thinning brown hair. *Come on, Ben. Take the leap.*

Beside him, he felt Caroline tense. She must have had a plan should Ben say no. He bumped her with his shoulder. "Give him a second," he whispered.

Ben sighed and replaced his hat as Rory's insides twisted with nervous anticipation.

"A one-way ticket?"

Rory nodded.

"Alright. For Peanut."

Rory and Caroline climbed into the back of the cab behind Ben and Khloe. The diesel engine roared to life, and they sped east.

"I love Waylon Jennings!" Khloe called over the engine and the loud twang of the music from the radio. Ben chuckled, glancing

635

nervously at Caroline in the rearview mirror before comparing favorites with Khloe. Their conversation felt thankfully light, given their night and where they were headed, making it seem almost normal.

Through the noise, Caroline leaned over and whispered to Rory. "Well done. You've passed."

"Passed?" He didn't need to finish the question. "Another test."

Caroline considered for a moment. "I suppose there is little harm in telling you now, so near the end. Just now, you passed your Assay of Tiff. Earlier, thanks to your friends Patrick and Anna, you passed the one of Cully."

Rory froze. "Is Patrick . . ."

Caroline held up a hand. "I gave them the Shepherd's Stone and instructions to find you after this is all done. They accepted. You should be proud of that friendship, Rory. It survived menace and time."

Rory sagged in his seat, fear of the worst feeling silly now.

"And if I'm not mistaken—" Caroline leaned forward and whispered something to Khloe, who offered her hand. Caroline then took Rory's in her other, the cold metal of the kiss brushing his knuckles. A jolt of electricity snapped through his fingers and up his arm, and he and Khloe yelped.

"Yeah, you gotta watch these potholes out here. That's why you gotta have the truck!" Ben shouted over the noise.

Caroline's face lit up into a broad smile. "Magnificent," she said. "The Assay of Mercy is done as well. I'm very proud of you both. Congratulations, you've converted your Stains—so very few are ever able."

"Our what?"

"The Stain of a soul is both a stifling chain and a well of power. You now know your chains, how they feel and sound, so it's up

636

to you if you wear them or not."

"Hold on—might get a little bumpy," Ben called out, and the truck rumbled around a corner. Rory braced as the cab bounced.

"Does that mean we can"—she pointed at Caroline's mythstones—"cast?"

"Yes, Dr. Seeker, and so much more."

The cargo plane waited, just as the Director promised. Painted in a dark gray, it would be difficult to see against the night sky. A couple dozen black and red armored soldiers swarmed around it, working in rows, passing sandbags from the hold, down the ramp, and onto a wide semi-circle around the rear of the plane. *Defenses*, Dawson thought. The Heart sniffed in contempt. If the Wyth got in close, the sandbags would mean little, but at range, they might give his troopers a chance.

The plane's nose pointed down a long strip of patchy grass stretching toward the mountain in the distance. Dense trees flanked either side—so close that Dawson wondered if the wing tips might snap a few low-hanging branches on take-off. This strip wasn't intended for big aircraft, but it managed to land one well enough. He supposed that was why the Director had selected it. Not a soul expected them out here.

Baa. Baa.

"God, grant me the serenity," Dawson growled, stepping off the ramp and into the grass. The plane groaned, relieved to be free of his weight. Beneath the dark, cloud-shrouded mountain, spread out along the grassy runway grazed a flock of puffy white sheep. Someone had forgotten the vital job of ensuring their departure. Right now, Caroline wasn't Dawson's immediate problem. Finding good help was.

Baa. Baa. The sheep's lazy bleats raked against his nerves. The Heart warmed in his chest, offering a fun solution.

"Why is there mutton all over my airstrip?!" he shouted at the nearest trooper. The man jumped and ran toward the sheep, flailing his arms and shouting profanities. The sheep cleared a path for him, but instead of running off, they wrapped the hapless man and kept eating. This flock was used to the farmer's tricks.

"The rain might drive them to the trees," Emmett said beside him. Dawson found him looking up, and he followed, finding dense gray clouds crowding around the bright moon.

"And how would you know that?"

Emmett inhaled and let out something like regret or shame, mixing with the scent of his fear: "Family."

Dawson nodded. He understood the smell now. "We can't count on rain. Not when bullets will do." The Heart's hungry presence cooed happily, then swirled and settled into his chest; he tasted the iron.

"You!" Dawson snapped, pointing at a trooper placing a sandbag. "Bring me an MG4—" He paused and did some math. "With two, no three, extra cartridges. I'll clear them out myself. And who's in charge of this pathetic fortification? Send them out with my new toy." The trooper saluted and ran up the ramp.

"Massacred sheep are going to take a while to remove," Emmett warned. "Can't be good for the wheels."

"Yes." Dawson shrugged. "But it will be an excellent exercise for the men. They are nervous, and they should be." He turned, smiling at Emmett. "You're nervous, too."

"Of course I'm fucking nervous," Emmett said, shifting on his feet. Red welts from Dawson's hand still marked his cheek. "Did you see what that woman did?"

"A witch," Dawson seethed.

"What?"

"Not a woman—a witch."

"Fine, the witch," Emmett corrected. "She is coming for us. She's . . . powerful!"

Dawson nodded. "So am I."

A pair of sheep wandered close to Dawson for a mouthful of grass. "I'm going to kill you!" he yelled, and the soldiers in earshot picked up their pace.

THUD.

He spun and spotted six troopers struggling to unload a steel coffin from the back of a truck.

"Stop!" He put his hand up as he approached. "I want to talk to our honored guest." The men groaned quietly as they set the Mag-Call down. He strolled over and kneeled, finding the two brass latches on the box's lip. He pressed and saw a series of green and red lights illuminate. A short, piercing beep followed, and a sweet-smelling gas hissed from the sides. A thin seam appeared, and when Dawson pushed gently, the lid disconnected and slid soundlessly, locking upright and open.

Inside lay Jacklyn Seed—or what was left of her. Dawson marveled at how frail the once powerful fighter had become. Time, he supposed, but the nature of the Seed is to consume and destroy, and its Host is not exempt. Jacklyn had nearly killed him in Cambodia and again in Mexico City at that damn casino, but both times he slunk away, humiliated but alive. That wouldn't happen this time. He'd spent sleepless nights imagining their final duel. The feel of that fatal blow that ends her. They were better than sex, but those dreams were against a strong, strapping Jacklyn with her billowing claw. The shell in front of him was not that, and the Heart soured in disappointment.

"Calm down," he said, tapping his chest. "We still get a fight."

His eyes drifted to the pink stump of her left arm, and he clicked his tongue. What a duel it would have been. Something for an epic. "What a waste."

"She's sedated, not dead," Emmett cautioned.

Dawson looked up at Emmett. "Nervous about this too? A Merged shouldn't fear pain." He placed his hand on his chest, smiling. "Our passengers are not always gentle with their demands."

A groan came from the cell, and Dawson peered down. The Host's dark eyes bobbed open and closed as she took slow, shallow breaths.

"Good to see you awake," Dawson said. "Wouldn't want you to miss your girlfriend's death."

Jacklyn glared at him, gritting her teeth as her left arm rose, sucking shadow and smoke from thin air as a hand condensed. Emmett jumped back, drawing his gun. Dawson leaned back, heat building in his fist in case Jacklyn's little prison was poorly advertised.

Blue track lights lit up around the edge of the metallic coffin, and a dull thumping beat rapidly. Dawson felt an invisible tug on his belt buckle and buttons. Jacklyn's back arched as she moaned, and the shadow hand dissipated. She collapsed back, panting as a bead of fresh blood trickled from her nose.

Dawson held the fire, watching, waiting for Jacklyn to rise again, but she didn't. Nodding his approval, he let the heat dissipate in a hiss and puff of steam. "So it works." He ran his fingers over the rim again. "The Director will be happy to hear that." If the mag-cell was any indication, then it could be a technological route by which to control the Seed. Such a device would be glorious, Dawson imagined, the ultimate baton to police the world with.

"That?!" Emmett said from behind his trembling pistol. "Her arm . . ."

Dawson rolled his eyes. The rookie was still playing catchup. "The Seed, Emmett. Beautiful as a red dawn. A weapon from the past and the face of the future."

"A weapon?" Emmett blinked at him, pointing at Dawson's hip. "Like that one?" More fear wafting off him, though with a hint of surprise. Or was it remorse? Dawson couldn't quite tell.

Dawson frowned, not following, and looked down to see the Dozer still tucked into his waistline. "This? No, this is a toy compared to the Seed." He pressed down on the brass triggers, and the cell lid slid back, locking with a satisfying click. He looked up to find Emmett still pointing his gun at Jacklyn. "Put that away."

Emmett hesitated, eyes darting to the closed cell, before he slipped his gun back into his holster.

"Alright," an aggravating voice broke in. "Easy boys! You know, you should get this bag cleaned. It smells like the last person's blood. Hey! Watch the neck, I'm ticklish."

Dawson growled and turned as Jane's escort shoved her toward him. "Why is she not gagged?"

"Donald, is that you?" Jane said with mock sincerity. "Donald, I've been trying to tell these nice men that you and I go way back, but they don't seem interested in my story. Tell them about the time I kicked your ass in the sparring tournament. Or the time I aced the firing range, and you shot a hole in your boot."

"She chewed through her gag, sir," one of her weary escorts sighed.

"And let me tell you," Jane continued, "it tasted as bad as this bag smells. Do you ever wash this thing? Because hygiene is—"

"Shut her up."

Without hesitating, the man on her right drove his fist into her stomach, and air burst from her lungs. Jane groaned and doubled over. The other man drove his knee up into her face, and Dawson heard a satisfying crack from inside the hood.

"That's unnecessary," Emmett shouted. "Stop!"

The two escorts paused, letting Jane fall to her knees. Beside Dawson's boot, Jane coughed wetly inside the hood. The Heart demanded more, but Dawson wanted Jane to experience her entire defeat. The Heart warmed to the idea.

"Pick her up."

The troopers jerked Jane back to her feet.

Bzzz. Bzzz.

Emmett reached into his pocket and pulled out his phone. "The Director."

"Let him know we have the Seed and are making final preparations to capture the Wyth."

Emmett nodded. "What about the ambush on the road?"

Dawson knew the Director wouldn't like their losses, but it was better to hear it from him. "Yes, that too. But make sure he knows we have the Seed secure."

Emmett stepped away but stopped and glanced at Jane warily.

"She'll be alive when you get back." Dawson scowled at Jane's escorts. The two troopers stood at attention. "Load her and the mag-cell in the plane. Make sure they're both strapped down tight."

Emmett didn't look pleased with the arrangement, but he held his phone to his ear and walked away.

From the direction of the plane, Dawson caught the tart scent of apprehension. Someone was nervous about talking to him. He turned and found a slight, bespectacled man approaching in fatigues, black body armor, and a single red stripe on his shoulder denoting the rank of lieutenant. He didn't look like a soldier like him and Adams. It seemed more like someone had pulled the man out of the accounting department, given him a title, and thrown him into the fray. Recruiting must be hard, he mused.

"The Brand, sir," the lieutenant said, holding out a long metal case. Dawson's spirits lifted.

The Heart flared curiously, sending flutters through his belly. "Let me see it."

The lieutenant set the metal case on the ground and quickly drew a key from around his neck and inserted it. A lock clicked, and he lifted the lid. The Brand of Sicra rested in black foam, stretching the length of the long case with five feet of razor-sharp steel. It glinted and shone, a neat row of four etched runes along the trench of the fuller. The presence of a double-long pommel and an extra-wide crossguard told Dawson the weapon was made for two hands. Otherwise plain, the blade was beautifully preserved. Dawson would have never guessed it carried such a ghastly past.

As he brushed the hilt, Dawson felt a chill against his skin. The blade rippled with a ghostly pink-white, and his pulse quickened when he saw a skeletal face appear in the reflection before sinking back into the blade. A faint wail, the souls of the damned—Star and Wyth alike—sealed inside the Brand. Legend was that if the blade ever gathered enough souls, it would make its bearer indestructible—a legend Dawson was excited to test.

The Heart shuddered and swelled, and heat poured down his arm. It demanded the blade. Dawson seized the leather grip and hefted the great sword with one hand. He turned and held it straight out, testing the balance. It was perfect. With a grin, he swung the weapon in a lazy arc, watching the ghostly sheen and the faces of the damned ripple behind the blade as it passed through the air. The sword's wails peaked as the blade moved, but fell quiet again when idle. It wasn't a stealthy weapon, but that suited him fine. As Dawson looked around, every trooper stared, and thick clouds of fear wafted off of them, creating a delicious fog.

The Heart, savoring the scent, pressed more energy into the sword. Dawson stabbed the blade at the moon, and translucent pink flames erupted with a chorus of spectral moans before everything fell quiet. He smiled like a wolf at the moon.

Someone cleared their throat beside him, shattering his moment.

Dawson glared at the lieutenant. "What's your name?"

The man snapped to attention and saluted. "Lieutenant Verily, sir. I've been overseeing our preparations."

Dawson swept a hand toward the plane and the dense flock beneath it. "If you're in charge, then tell me, why are there sheep on my runway?"

"I've been focused on getting our position fortified and—"

"I don't care. I want them gone. Now. Or you'll be clearing carcasses."

Verily saluted again and shouted orders at several nearby troopers. Three soldiers dropped their bags and went about shooing sheep, though their woolly nemesis paid them little heed—moving a few feet before settling down again.

Dawson massaged the bridge of his nose. "Why me?" The Heart flared, outraged, and pressed a savage thought into his mind. Dawson liked it. It was tempting, but he shook his head. "No, no. We need them for now."

"Sir?" Verily said.

"Report," Dawson said.

"Sir. Patrols set in the woods to the north, south, and west. Each has flares for the moment they encounter anything. We're finishing the fortification now."

"And the RPGs?"

"The rockets are being unpacked. Do . . ." Verily paused, shifting his weight. "Do you think we'll need them, sir? The rockets, I mean."

Dawson raised an eyebrow. He missed Adams. "Never hunted a Wyth?"

"No, sir."

Dawson nodded, and feeling the weight of the Brand in his hand, he brimmed with confidence. "Against most Wyth, I'd take care of this myself. They're poorly trained, so it's a short duel, maybe some fireworks, and it's over. Against this Wyth, at least the younger version of her, I'd order two divisions and an air strike that kept the bombs falling until I couldn't see the bottom of the crater. We don't have that, but Caroline isn't the same; she is old now. Still deadly to people like you, but she is not a match for me. Time has stolen that from her. All she has left is her tricks."

Fear drifted off the lieutenant, and Dawson rolled his eyes.

"Yes, *Captain* Verily, we'll still need the rockets and a team to watch our prisoners. No doubt she'll make a play for them."

"Captain?" Verily blinked. "Sir? Captain Adams—"

"Was killed en route." Dawson didn't elaborate, leaving now-captain Verily to produce another pungent billow of fear.

Dawson surveyed the cargo plane and the crates with DANGER-HIGH EXPLOSIVES being unloaded.

"Sir, the Director wants to speak to you." Dawson turned and found Emmett holding out his phone. Verily stood frozen in his salute.

"I'm here, sir," Dawson said.

"Donald, I'm disappointed the Wyth ambushed you. You got sloppy."

"I didn't expect her to gain transportation so—"

"I'm not here for excuses," the Director cut in. "Your heavy losses worry me. I know your history with this Wyth, and I now see it has compromised your judgment. You underestimate her."

His tone cut worse than any blade, and Dawson boiled with irritation. "Sir," Dawson said through gritted teeth. "I assure you—"

"You are to depart immediately. Bring me the Seed. Afterward, you can correct your mistake, hopefully with newfound perspective."

The Heart of Wrath flared in outrage. He'd made a promise.

"What about my war?"

"War will keep."

Dawson's eyes flashed red. *No.* "I can defeat Caroline now, sir. End it. Caroline must be the last Master. I've hunted all the other ones down. We can end the Wyth, sir!"

A long silence followed, and despite the Heart's warm satisfaction with his words, each mute second that passed made Dawson regret them even more.

"The Wyth are not our chief concern," the Director said. "They are a dying breed, Donald, bound for extinction. We aren't going to gamble the greatest prize against a certainty, understood? Bring the Seed. I will not ask again. A piece of one vision."

Dawson sucked in a breath, trying to cool the Heart's outrage blazing against his mind.

"A piece of one vision, Donald." There was a threat in his tone.

"A vision of one peace," Dawson muttered, though he had no thoughts of peace.

The line went dead, and he handed the phone to Emmett, seething.

Captain Verily turned and raised his voice to the troopers. "New orders! Wheels up in five!" The troopers paused, looking up. "Leave the bags, reload the munitions! Get these goddamn sheep out of here!"

The Heart snarled, seizing hold of Dawson and pressing a tantalizing thought into his mind. *Just capture the Wyth anyway.* She was old. He had rockets and the Brand. He took a deep, slow breath and exhaled tingling anticipation. *Control your own destiny,* the Heart hissed. When he returned with both the Seed and the Wyth, no one could deny his dominance and success. Among the Merged, he'd be the only alpha. *We will have our war.* He took in the mountains and woods, smiling. *And it will begin here.*

"Kill that order!" he bellowed. "We wait. We fight."

Verily wheeled around. "Sir, the Director gave us—"

Dawson drove the Brand of Sicra into Verily's chest. The blade glided smoothly through his flesh, burying halfway to the hilt before it stopped. Verily gasped, staring down at the steel. From all along the blade, the wails came. Spectral hands reached out, clawing at Verily's wound, grasping and pulling, leaving blackened skin in their wake. The Captain screamed a terrible sound, but his tongue and cheeks withered and shrank, strangling the noise into an eerie sob. When the sound ended, Verily's body crumbled into dust, leaving only his pierced chest plate hanging from the Brand.

Dawson jerked the blade free and tossed the armor aside. He held up the sword, turning it around as he watched Verily's tormented likeness ripple across the blade and then vanish into the steel. *Magnificent.*

He leveled the blade and regarded his troopers, all staring at Verily's remains. "There is no retreat," he said flatly, gathering their eyes. "Anyone who does ends up with Verily." The troopers scrambled over each other to get back to work.

Next to him, Emmett shook visibly. The Heart preened.

"Yes?" Dawson said.

"S-sir. Yes, sir."

"Good. Now go get Jane settled. If she gets out, I'm coming for you."

Emmett scampered off toward the plane, leaving Dawson alone among all his busy bees. With a satisfied grin, he rested the heavy blade on his shoulder and swept his gaze over the airstrip. "Where are you, witch?" The only response came from the sound of a light drizzle pattering against the plane. Dawson's skin steamed.

Chapter 65: All Aboard

"Sit."

A rough hand shoved Jane into a straight-backed chair. She groaned as she landed, and her cough tasted like blood. Taking a punch didn't hurt this much before, but she supposed it had been a while. Her ribs and nose throbbed; either were broken, but everything else felt intact. *Bet I look beautiful.*

She tried to get her bearings, but the stiff, musky bag over her head dulled the light and sound, making her disorientation all the worse. *A plane.* That's what she thought Dawson had said. *Where is the Seed? And Rory?*

Two heavy thuds plopped down on either side, and her escorts' shoulders squeezed her between them.

Between the hollow ring of boots on a ramp and the soft whine of engines, Jane pieced together she was aboard Dawson's plane. She savored the break from walking and listened as a grunting group set something heavy down in front of her.

"Bolt it down," someone commanded.

She made out dim flashing lights around a gray box through the black cloth. She wondered what it was. A trunk or chest? More thumping, followed by the sounds of rivet guns. Something clipped her foot, and a man growled, "Tuck'm or lose'm."

Jane drew her feet back and tucked her legs beneath her seat. "Pillow?" The word was slurred. They must have hit her harder than she thought.

"Shut up," someone said.

While she was walking toward the plane, she'd heard the sporadic bleating of sheep and wondered just how far out from the city they were. The Director didn't want to take any chances with the media, but it would be a miracle if he could keep the explosions Jane had heard off the news. She wished she could have seen them, though something in her gut told her that tonight's events were far from over. She shifted her weight and felt the tight bonds around her shoulders and wrists.

"Move again, and you'll be flying asleep." One of her guards growled.

Jane went still. She wasn't going anywhere without help. *Muff me.*

A voice broke through her melancholy. "Is she secure?"

Emmett! Her spirits rose, but she kept quiet, not wanting to test her guard's resolve.

"Which one?" the guard to her right replied.

"Both," Emmett said with a hint of anger.

"The cell isn't going anywhere," the left guard said, and a metallic thump followed. "And this one"—he nudged her with his shoulder—"knows what she's in for if she makes trouble."

"Good. I want you both on the ramp. The plane is our ticket out, so we can't lose it."

"Dawson said—"

"Dawson just murdered Verily. Do you think he'll think twice about killing you or me if we lose the plane?"

A silence followed, and Jane felt both men tense, though she couldn't tell out of anger, fear, or something else. Still, whatever Emmett was trying to do, he was getting a reaction. *What's his plan?*

"Look," Emmett said, "I'm just following orders, too. We need to make sure no little surprises sneak around the side while Dawson glory fights the Wyth."

"These two?"

"I'll watch them. They won't go anywhere. I'm not here to get

650

killed." Another pause, and Jane held her breath. Bets were down. Now, it was time for Emmett's moment of truth.

"If it means I don't have to smell that fucking hood anymore, then fine," the right guard said, and the pressure and heat of his body lifted away.

A sigh came from Jane's left. "Better view of the fight, anyway." They stood too, leaving Jane cold, but with space to expand.

"That goes for all of you," Emmett's voice rose. "Protect the plane, and we all go home."

There were a couple of murmurs of approval, followed by the sound of boots ringing across a grated floor. Whatever Emmett was trying to do, it seemed he was one step closer.

After a long, stifling silence, the bag slid up and off her head, catching her nose on the way out. Pain and light seared the back of her eyes, and she squeezed them shut as her pink strands fell, brushing her face. Blinking, she slowly opened her eyes and made out Emmett standing over her in the yellow dim of the cargo hold. As he came into focus, she saw panic in the whites of his eyes. It seemed Emmett had learned the fate of all bait.

Emmett tapped a finger to his lips and nodded toward the freighter's rear. A group of six armed soldiers stood halfway down the broad, hazard-striped loading ramp. At its base, under floodlights lifted on yellow tripods, a semi-circle sandbag wall protected a dozen more armed men. As her eyes adjusted, she saw more dark shadows moving among the defenses.

Dawson strolled into view and toward the apex of the arc, leaning a great sword over his shoulder. Jane might not have seen Dawson murder the newly appointed captain, but she heard his death knell. The memory of the sound made her shiver. That sword was a ticket to hell.

Dawson pointed to one of the heavy machine guns, and its crew stood rigid, saluting. He sheathed his sword across his back and hoisted the weapon off the tripod. Smiling, he loaded belts of ammunition around his neck.

"Can you fly this?" Emmett whispered.

Jane's eyebrows jumped up, and she rerouted her attention. "I'm sorry, what?"

"The plane. Can you fly a plane?"

"Does a simulator count?"

"Did you crash?"

"A couple of times, but who doesn't?"

Emmett groaned and then raised his voice, aiming it over his shoulder. "Keep your mouth shut, or the Director gets your teeth." On the ramp, she saw two of the soldiers glance up.

"Are they coming?" Emmett whispered.

One guard shook their head and said something Jane couldn't make out as they returned to their watch.

"No." Jane forced herself not to smile. "He gets my teeth?"

"I'm improving and just the question. Can you fly?"

She took in the massive aircraft with a sweeping look, triggering an alarm bell in her head. The aircraft was massive, like nothing she'd ever tried to fly before. "K'ay. Uh. I'm confident I can get us off the ground. That's pretty straightforward. It's the landing piece I'm concerned about."

Emmett didn't even blink at her response. "We'll figure out landing later. We need to get out of here, like now." He glanced over his shoulder toward the front of the plane, then added, "When I give the signal, make for the cockpit."

"What about the pilots?"

"Getting ready to fight like everyone else," Emmett gestured toward the sandbags. "All hands on deck."

It would be chaos, a good time to try to steal a plane. She spotted the metal box before her, with a glass lid and a person inside.

She'd bet her life that was Jacklyn. "What about the Seed? And Rory and—"

"Rory is dead," Emmett said. "They crashed. No one could survive it."

Oh, no . . . Jane's heart dropped. He seemed like the real deal. "You saw his body?"

"No."

A hint of suspicion crept in. "Then did you . . ."

"Jane," Emmett said, his mask cracking. "He's gone. We have to adapt. This is our play now. Survive."

A burst of laughter rolled from the ramp, followed by finger-pointing. None of them turned around.

"Hey," Emmett said. "You're dead if you stay, okay? I can't protect you. Dawson is seeing red. He murdered Verily and didn't think twice about leaving Adams behind." He pointed to his burned cheek. "I don't give myself great odds either."

Jane nodded. Dawson was out for blood, and Emmett was smart enough to get the hell away.

Emmett patted the metal coffin. "If the Director empowers people like Dawson, then he shouldn't have this. And Dawson said they're trying to make a weapon out of it. So maybe we take it and . . . I don't know, hide it? And if everything goes to shit, then at least we have a bargaining chip—just like you did before. But that's all later. We need to leave first."

Jane didn't hate the idea. Living and seeing Grace and the kids again sounded like a gift. And thumbing her nose at the Director after she claimed his prized possession would feel good. Still, it felt wrong somehow. Off. Like the hot flush after a kind lie. Not what should happen, yet it was not entirely wrong either. It was confusing and made her stomach twist. She wished Rory was here. The Seed was supposed to be his job, not hers. A torchbearer, she'd told him. Those words felt hollow now.

"Come on, Jane. Help me," Emmett said, his eyes pleading with Jane for something she didn't have. "Please."

Muff me, Jane thought, not seeing a good way out. Dead now or dead later seemed the only options, but at least dead later meant if she went down, she'd go down swinging. "Okay, let's get this thing off the ground."

Chapter 66: Caroline's Gifts

Keep the mountain in front of you. Those were Caroline's parting words. It was a simple direction that kept his mind focused and away from the unknowns. In the distance, through the swaying pines, rose Mt. Hood, draped in soggy clouds. The surrounding forest glistened, the fresh rain still clinging to leaves and roots, catching the moonlight. It was beautiful, and on any other night, he and Khloe might have stopped together to admire it, but seeing the great mountain inch closer, Rory couldn't help but feel it was actually a headstone, and he was marching toward his grave.

"Keep the mountain in front of you," he repeated and drew in a long breath. He tasted hot bile. *One step at a time.*

"Where's Caroline?" Khloe asked, her teeth chattering at the end. The wet air wrapped around them, and while Rory had a little protection from his scrubs, Khloe's tank top couldn't keep out the chill. Beside him, she hugged Caroline's burnt satchel to her chest, which gently clinked every few steps. She shivered and picked up her foot, setting it down carefully on the shadow-swept floor.

Rubbing his arms, he took his eyes off the dark ground for a moment to scan the forest for any sign. Ben hadn't even left before Caroline darted away, repeating the directions as she disappeared into the trees. Rory felt naked without her. Exposed.

"Scouting?" Rory offered. It seemed reasonable. Perhaps the Broken Star lurked in the trees, and Caroline picked them off. *Perhaps not . . .* "Are you . . ."

"A little cold," Khloe said; her lips were turning blue. Rory slid a step closer, catching her eye. "Okay?" She studied him two strides more, then stepped into him, pressing together. She was freezing and needed a warm blanket and tea, but they didn't have either. He put his arm around her instead. "Okay?"

Khloe nodded. "That's better. Thanks."

One step at a time.

Somewhere in the branches ahead came the soft hoots, and they jumped. An owl passed overhead, only a swoop and shadow in the night, sending its hoots bouncing off the trees. *Breathe.* But the air got stuck in his throat. He stifled a cough. Breathing wasn't working. *Keep calm. Keep calm. Oh my god, what am I doing?* It felt like they had been walking for hours, though if he turned around, he could still spot the edge of the tree line where they had entered. Something in his brain wouldn't let him forget which way was out. Now, *out* was nearly out of sight.

"Hey," Khloe said. "You there?"

Rory racing heart stumbled, caught between his fear and her nearness.

"Ya," he said, feeling dizzy. "It's just . . . This is mental, right? Because I'm—"

"It is." Khloe smiled. "It absolutely is." She nudged him forward, and his feet picked up their stride.

"What's next?" Khloe said, tucked beneath his arm.

"I have no idea." He pushed aside a low-hanging branch. "I'm just hoping I don't throw up again."

"I'm glad I'm not the only one," she said, ducking and separating, darkening him until her heat returned as they pressed on. A surge of gratitude rose, lifting and warming him. "Thanks for being here," Rory said as the heat touched his cheeks. "With me, I mean. I couldn't do this alone."

"Me either," she said, smiling. The fear squeezing his chest loosened ever so slightly at her touch, enough that the next breath came easier. *Keep breathing.*

Rory sighted the silver-capped mountain through the trees and stepped forward toward Khloe. Still no sign of Caroline, and

Rory wondered if they'd walk straight into a trap before she appeared. *Are we . . . bait?*

A light rain stirred the forest, filling it with sporadic pats that picked up the tempo. "Perfect," he said. "Rain."

Khloe shivered again. "Well, maybe we . . . Ahh!" She pitched forward, and Rory stumbled with her, only their nearness preventing a fall.

"What was that?" she said.

Rory squinted into the shadows, probing with his foot. He struck something solid. There, in the darkness, slumped over, he saw a body. Rory stifled a cry, stepping back. A smooth red line split the skin across the man's neck like a gruesome grin, and thankfully, bandannas and goggles covered their eyes and faces. Rory needed nothing to add to his nightmares.

"A patrol." Caroline's tired voice came from ahead. "Watch your footing. There are others."

Rory spotted four other corpses scattered around a stump where Caroline sat, hunched forward with her elbows on her knees. Branches littered the ground, with their clean-cut stumps decorating the surrounding trees. She straightened and held out a small orange flare gun. "This would have warned Dawson." Rising, she grimaced and pressed a hand to her side. In the low light, Rory saw her tie-dyed dress spattered in blood.

Rory rushed forward, his nurse mind taking control and forgetting his *out.* "Let me see that."

Caroline protested as he stooped down to get a closer look. "Rory, I assure you—"

"Quiet," he said. "Turn here toward the light." Caroline sighed and stepped to her right into a slice of dim moonlight. The cut was deep and narrow, but appeared to avoid anything fatal. *A knife wound? She'd need surgery.* "We need to pack this and keep pressure on it." He looked up at Caroline. "This has to hurt like hell."

"It does, I assure you, but I have something for it." Caroline beckoned to Khloe. "My satchel, please." Khloe clutched the bag tighter, then handed it over, shivering. Caroline surveyed Khloe, then sifted through the bag. Glass clinked together as her hands worked. "You're freezing, my dear. Both of you need to change clothes." She waved at his blood and mud-covered torn scrubs and soaked sneakers. "You're not dressed for combat."

Rory looked around at the bodies and noticed that two of them had missing shirts and boots. "You looted the bodies?!"

"What good are they to them anymore?"

Khloe sniffed and silently set to work, stripping off her damp clothes.

"I don't know, Caroline. I—"

The Wyth stopped rummaging and sighed. Slowly, she lifted her blood-speckled face to meet him. "Rory, I respect your position on preserving life's sanctity, but some will never share your optimism. Death is and should be a last resort, but there must be death for new life to emerge. Ours is not an infinite world."

Rory swallowed and watched Khloe buckle a heavy vest over a green jacket. The stolen clothes hung loose, but her hands swiftly cinched down the straps.

"How do you know how to put that on?" Rory asked, surprised.

Khloe shrugged. "My aunt and uncle ran an army surplus store back home. They made sure we knew what everything did." She bent down and pulled on a pair of boots. "Caroline's right. You'll need this." She stood and tossed him a thick black shirt and a bulletproof vest.

The idea of wearing the dead man's clothes made Rory's skin crawl, but the idea of bleeding to death, because he didn't wear them, overrode his dilemma. Rory's nose wrinkled as he peeled off his scrubs, trying to keep focused as Khloe stole several glances at him.

"What about you?" Rory said, tugging the shirt on. "Don't you need armor?"

"Pond Skipper and I have a solution. These vests are too bulky, and I'll need my mobility." Caroline drew out a canvas pouch from the satchel, pulling from inside a fistful of tiny, indigo puffballs radiating a soft light. *Psybelle spores?* She scattered them over the ground, humming a soft, sad melody.

Khloe laced up her boots, eyeing the spores. "What are you doing?"

"Seeing if Silt can find us reinforcements." Caroline dusted off her hands, releasing the last clinging puff.

"Golems?" Rory asked eagerly.

"Something like them—if we're fortunate."

"I thought you needed metal?"

Caroline faced him. "Their skeleton isn't the issue. These spores aren't as mature as the ones spread during Remembrance Day. Not enough time gestating. They will be . . . cruder."

Rory didn't ask what that meant. *If they help us, bring on creepier golems.*

The Wyth plucked the cloudy emerald off her necklace and placed it in the gauntlet of her Witch's Kiss. The gem flared to life. With her free hand, she stretched her fingers into the dirt and whispered, "Hurry, my friend."

The ground bulged and radiated outward in a muddy ripple. The dirt rolled beneath his new boots, and Rory had to brace himself against a nearby tree to keep his balance. As the terrestrial wave disappeared out of view, Caroline returned to her satchel. "Finish up. Once my preparations are done, I cannot wait for you."

Khloe finished dressing first and picked up one of the assault rifles lying on the ground. She inspected it, checked the clip, and sighted it. She slung the weapon over her shoulder and stepped around Rory to help him tighten his armored vest. With a grunt of approval, she held out a boxy, black pistol.

"Watch the kick," Khloe said. "Safety is on—it's the little switch on the side. Hold it with two hands. Point the sight from your nose."

Rory eyed the weapon and took it, feeling the cold steel weight in his hand. His stomach clenched, and he prayed he didn't need to use it.

"Quickly now—I have things for you both." Caroline waved them over. "I lost most of what I hoped to use, but not all." She drew out a square of fuzzy brown paper that reminded Rory of dried seaweed. Caroline tore the square into three even pieces. "Deadman's Moss. You'll find it in crypts on moonless nights. A small piece will remove the pain without addling the mind, but too much will freeze your breathing. A thumbprint size will do." The Wyth popped one piece in her mouth and held the other two out. "Start chewing. It's tough and takes a few minutes to work."

A pain-killer? Why do we need . . . The thought froze Rory. *Because the pain is coming. There was no avoiding it now.* Rory glanced down at the corpse by his feet. Khloe took a piece first and sniffed it, her nose wrinkling. Rory took his piece. The moss's soft appearance was misleading—it felt like steel wool.

"Chew thoroughly," Caroline added.

Rory and Khloe exchanged a brief look before they each stuffed their piece into their mouths. The taste was disgusting, like the putrid flavor of spoiled milk, but Rory forced himself to chew the dense fabric and gag it down. Khloe retched, but kept it down.

"Do you have the Dozer?" Caroline said.

"The hilt? No, Dawson took it."

Caroline's lips pressed flat and Rory felt a wash of shame, like he'd messed it all up already. "We'll make do."

From the satchel, Caroline drew out the metal quill Rory had pricked himself on before. She handed it to Khloe.

"This artifact is called the Iron Quill, and like the Dozer, it takes energy from you to use. Their brilliance, though, is that it also needs no training to control." She traced her finger down the strange symbols running the Quill's spine. "The rune here regulates that for you and tells you what it does. The Quill creates feathers."

"Feathers?" Khloe said, and then her eyes went wide. "Like at the wreck."

Caroline nodded. "Its application is wide. To do the same, you need to soothe your fear first. Fear and doubt act like a clog in a pipe, stopping your energy's flow. Keep hope close to your heart; believe the feathers will appear, and the artifacts will not fail you."

"What if we can't?" Rory said.

"Despair, and they will abandon you."

Khloe let out a long, low breath, turning the Quill over. "What happens if we run out of energy? We pass out?"

"Something to that effect," Caroline replied. "Your soul could implode, taking the body with it."

Rory's mouth fell open. *Implodes?!*

Khloe looked uneasy holding the strange device now, holding it away from her body.

"Go on," Caroline said, turning over her satchel and shaking it. When nothing fell out, she passed one hand over the numerous patches and then gently patted it on the ground. "You only need practice. Try it out."

Khloe frowned and then flicked the Quill, pretending to write with it in the air. Nothing happened. She exhaled, dug her feet deeper into the earth, and tried again. The runes along the Quill flickered, and a burst of three feathers, red, blue, and yellow, puffed out and drifted lazily to the forest floor. Her face lit up. "Did you see?!" She swayed a step, blinking. "Wow." Rory stepped to help her, but she steadied herself.

"I'm okay." She shook her head. "It just has a kick to it."

"Very good, Dr. Seeker," Caroline said. "Though you don't need to hold it so formally. What did you think about?"

Khloe blushed. "I . . . I thought of you and GamGam."

Caroline touched one hand over her heart, her expression sweet. "Thank you for that gift, Khloe. Know, with every part of you, that your grandmother is with you, as are her people. We are proud."

Khloe let out a shuddered sob and threw her arms around Caroline. The Wyth smiled, wrapping her long arms around Khloe and pressing her cheek into her matted blonde hair. For a moment, the two seemed to glow together in the moonlight. Far off, frog calls filled the silence as they held each other, and Rory felt a hot pressure build behind his eyes.

Caroline unwound and stepped back, leaving Khloe smiling with a tear-streaked face. She took the Quill from Khloe's hands and handed it to Rory. "Your turn."

Rory wiped his eyes. "What?"

"You don't want the most important moment to be your first time." She pressed the Quill into his hands. "Practice."

Rory took it, feeling the weight of it. *Okay, easy. Remove the clog. Shut up, fear.* Rory took a half-hearted swing, but nothing happened—just like the Dozer.

"Don't think too hard, Rory," Caroline said. "Remember, you are well acquainted with your fear. It is your shadow, after all;

you are a shepherd for others. What would you tell a student when trying something new?"

"Pretend like it's your hundredth time," Rory said.

"Try that. It's your hundredth time," she repeated, stepping around him. "Courage."

Control my fear. Find my silence . . . "My hundredth time."

"Feel it here, Rory." Caroline tapped her chest. "From here, fear tightens, courage expands."

Rory swallowed and held the Quill up.

"Close your eyes and tell me, what will you do? Be specific."

Rory squeezed the Quill. *Please work.* "I'm going to free Jacklyn." *Just a little feather. Anything.* "And I'm going to take the Seed—" His stomach heaved, and he tasted hot bile in the back of his throat again.

"Stay with it." Caroline's voice broke through. "And Dawson?"

Rory pictured Dawson lowering him into a vat of lava, and all sense of bravery threatened to flee his mind until a single thought cut through. *Dawson cannot win.* "I'll fight him, even if he"—he swallowed—"kills me." Maybe it was something in his tone, maybe it was that his mind didn't scream at him, or perhaps it was Caroline and Khloe's presence, but Rory believed himself. *I am a torchbearer. I'm not alone.*

Something released in his chest, and a flood of warmth passed through his body. Khloe gasped, and Rory opened his eyes. A cloud of rainbow feathers twirled in the air in front of him.

"Holy sh—" A wooze took him, knocking him off balance. Strong hands caught him.

"You did it," Caroline said.

"I feel dizzy," Rory said, letting the forest stop moving.

"That gets easier. For now, remember this feeling. You've earned this courage no matter what your Stain might tell you. Stains do not define us; we define them."

"I—" A faint tingling running past his wrist tugged at his attention. "Are my fingers supposed to be numb?" His last word came slurred, and he looked at Caroline. "What—"

"That would be the Deadman's Moss," Caroline said. "Which means our finale has arrived."

"No," Khloe said. Her slack expression said she wasn't ready either.

Caroline smiled at them. "My friends. Merely walking into these woods would test the mettle of any hero of antiquity, yet here you stand, ready anyway. For that, you have my deepest love. Regardless of tonight's outcome, I am so grateful to have known both of you."

The Wyth drew in a deep breath. "And tonight is all that matters now—Jacklyn and getting Rory to the Seed in time. I will create a diversion. Dawson is set on his duel, and I shall not deny him it."

"Can you . . . beat him?" Khloe asked.

"Much can happen in battle. Too much chaos. The outcome is never certain."

"That's not a yes."

Caroline smirked as she checked the straps of her Kiss.

"There has to be—" Rory started, but Caroline waved him off.

"I am the only way to keep Dawson's eye off the Seed long enough. He wants me. He wants to defeat me before another can claim that prize. I have a bit of a reputation among the Star." She stood tall. "And they are right to call me a witch."

Caroline pointed ahead toward the mountain. "The plane is there. As is Jacklyn." Her hand drifted off to her left. "Follow the treeline, stay out of sight, and watch for patrols. Get as close to the plane as possible and run for it when you think you have a chance. Don't hesitate. Do what you need to keep the Seed contained." She looked pointedly at Rory. "Whatever it takes, understand?"

Rory nodded, feeling the weight of the pistol in his pocket. A sickening sensation crept into his belly.

I'm going to use it . . .

"You can't go out there like this," Khloe said. "You're wounded. Let me—"

"No," Caroline said crisply, "the Seed is the priority." The Wyth then looked down and frowned, probing her wounded side, then nodded to herself. With a quick jerk, she pulled her sapphire mythstone free from her now-empty necklace. "Fortunately for us, it rained." She lifted the sapphire. "Skipper, would you mind? Nothing too fancy. We need to conserve energy." Piles of pine needles crackled around them. Beads of moisture, catching shafts of moonlight, rolled up from the ground and climbed onto Caroline's bare feet, disappearing beneath the hem of her dress. The wet patches of Rory's clothes dried, and he looked down to see the last two droplets fall from his jacket and slither across the forest floor toward Caroline.

The droplets rolled down Caroline's arms, up her neck, and condensed around her wounded abdomen. In a flash of light, they turned into a thin, clean sheet of ice covering her entire body. Caroline held out her hand, causing several cracks to appear in her glowing skin as though lit from within. The armor held its shape, clinging to her like skin. Inspecting her glittering hand, Caroline kissed the sapphire mythstone.

"Well done, Skipper," she said. "That will do. Just keep me patched up as best you can."

"That's amazing," Rory said, transfixed.

"I find it a bit gaudy, but Skipper forges fine armor," Caroline said, adjusting the straps of her ivory gauntlet once more.

665

Reverently, she ran her palm along the length of each blade, praying in a lilting language before kissing both blades. "One last time," she whispered. With a nod, she turned to Rory and held out the small orange flare gun. "If you would do the honors."

"You want Dawson to know you're coming?"

"Yes."

"Why?"

"Because I want him to know there is at least one soul in this world who does not fear him." She turned toward the plane— toward Jacklyn.

Rory felt dizzy. There wasn't a second of hesitation in her purpose. Her courage buoyed him, and he straightened. He looked at the gun and sighed, raising it to the sky. He looked over at Khloe, who nodded. "For Jacklyn."

"For everything," Khloe added.

"For love." Caroline waved the sapphire in a broad arc. A moment later, a thick blanket of fog rose through the ferns, expanding and wrapping the trees in a thick blanket of mist. A chill of anticipation ran up Rory's back, and he realized he no longer felt any pain.

He pulled the trigger.

Chapter 67: Fire and Stone

"Baa for me." Dawson slid his finger over the trigger, pointing his gun at the fat ewe. "One more time."

"Fog!" someone shouted behind him. He spun around, seeing a thick mist pour from the forest, tumbling onto the airstrip.

Pfffffff. A flickering red flare arched lazily through the sky to the west. One sheep bolted, then another, and another, until the entire flock stampeded south, away from the plane and into the woods. Dawson grinned, savoring the panic and watching the runway clear.

"She's here," he whispered, then raised his voice. "Look alive, boys! The Wyth came to play."

Troopers raced to the sandbag arc and aimed their rifles in the flare's direction. Dawson hefted the heavy machine gun in one arm and looped an ammunition belt over his shoulder to feed the weapon as he fired. A gun line of thirty-strong aimed down range and waited for something, anything, to emerge. The Heart growled, his pulse beating in his ears. They didn't wait long.

A dark silhouette strolled forward through the fog, taking smooth, confident steps. Dawson could feel the witch's gaze boring into him. The moonlight shimmered off her body as Caroline swayed, refracting in cracks covering her skin. *Armor?* he thought, and the Heart laughed at the idea. *End this.*

"Fire at will," Dawson roared and pulled his trigger. The gun line erupted, banishing the eerie silence.

Crack-crack-crack!

The gun vibrated his entire body, spitting smoking brass casings onto the ground.

The Kiss flashed, throwing up sparks as it intercepted bullet after bullet. Dawson squeezed harder, but his rifle wouldn't fire any faster. The Wyth's advance quickened as she found a rhythm hidden within the bullet-storm. Nothing seemed to touch her. The Heart demanded more.

"Ordnance!" he called.

A beat later, a rocket launched from behind his left shoulder. The witch threw up her hand, holding the emerald. A wall of rock and dirt leaped up, and the missile exploded against it. Another rocket fired, and Caroline summoned another earthen wall, picking up her speed and closing the distance.

"We'll do it your way, then." Dawson tossed the smoking gun aside and reached behind his head. The Brand's hilt sucked the heat from his fingers as he slid the weapon free. The howls of the damned trapped inside the blade called for her. Dawson wasn't sure what the Wyth was thinking. She was outnumbered and out-gunned.

A skeletal hand burst through the ground, latching onto his boot. He jumped, stomping his foot and ripping the hand from its buried body. The ground shivered, mounds of dirt rising all around him. He swept the Brand low, cleaving a skull with a large, sprouting mushroom cap emerging from the earth. The weight of the blade sliced through the bone, barely hitching where it made contact. More emerged, and he backed up toward the gun line.

The cacophony of machine gun fire sputtered, and sudden cries of pain and fear rang out. Misshapen skeletons, assembled from bone, stone, and earth, emerged everywhere, overwhelming his troopers. Some carried cloaks of crawling insects, others, dense clouds of angry flies swarming and choking the men. Dawson spun to see bony claws raking a sniper lying on the ground, pulling him under the earth, screaming.

His trap deteriorated, but this was it. No more variables. Caroline had played her last card; if this was all she had, it was still not enough. Not when he had the Brand. He stalked toward her, clearing a golem from his path and stepping over bodies. Caroline stopped and waited, not ten feet off.

"Just you and me, witch!" Dawson barked.

"Give me the Seed!" Caroline called back. Her Kiss sparked as she swatted away another bullet. "Do so, and I will grant you a swift end." She stepped toward him, lifting the Kiss, ready for his attack. Not a whiff of fear rose from her.

The Heart pulsed in his chest, filling his mind with images of victory. Heat poured from his skin, rippling the surrounding air and filling him with a boiling desire. "Kill my men. It makes no difference." He paused, nodding toward the plane. "Or hers. I never thought I'd see a Wyth stoop to necromancy."

"Who do you think invented the dance with death? Perhaps your education is lacking in such matters."

Dawson laughed. "I know everything I need."

"Perhaps." She smiled, catching him off guard. "Or perhaps the Seed isn't as safe as you think."

Dawson nearly turned to look at the plane but caught himself. It was just the type of opening the witch would exploit.

"Nice try, witch."

Driving the Brand into the ground, he drew a knife from his belt and held up his hand, slashing the skin. Thick globs of magma dripped from the wound, hissing and blackening. Dawson turned his hand over and brushed away the igneous clot. The molten rock plopped on the ground, igniting the grass.

The Heart lunged for the fire, and the pool swelled, sucking and melting the earth around it like a widening jaw. A clawed hand emerged, grasping the edge, hauling itself up like a demon climbing out of hell. It stood on two wiry legs, dripping magma from a long, snarling muzzle curled around black fangs. Two massive smoking embers, its eyes, narrowed at Caroline, and from within Dawson's chest, the Heart howled in unison with the ten-foot, bubbling wolf.

Caroline stared as the flaming wolf shook itself, flicking specks of scalding lava and starting a hundred tiny fires in the grass. The Wyth slid to the side, avoiding one of the burning flecks, and sized up the towering Aspect. Still no fear.

"Silt!" she said, flicking her emerald.

The ground trembled, and Dawson bent his knees to keep from losing his balance. The ground beside Caroline swelled, forming a pair of angular shoulder blades beneath her outstretched hand. As the stones settled, a feline face emerged with glowing emerald eyes. An immense stone cat prowled beside Caroline. Dark orange stripes of clay arced over its stone back, its long talons ripping through the dirt.

"You're wasting your energy," Dawson said, retrieving the Brand.

"And you're wasting time."

He raised the Brand of Sicra and bellowed his challenge. The Heart of Wrath roared its approval, and together, they charged.

Caroline screamed in defiance, and her stone tiger snarled like two grinding boulders. The titans of fire and stone slammed into each other, raking and biting. Dawson whipped the Brand through the air in a wailing white-pink blur, bursting in a shower of crimson sparks where the blow collided with the Kiss.

The duel had begun.

Chapter 68: Duel of Demigods

Left. Right. Left. Right.

Rory's feet found a beat. He squinted through the darkness, barely avoiding the outlines of branches and tangled roots as they appeared and faded behind him. The Deadman's Moss numbed his leg and lungs, allowing him to sprint forward, ignoring the slapping branches as adrenaline pulsed in his ears.

Jacklyn. Left. Right.

"Stop!" Khloe shouted beside him.

Rory skidded to a halt at the edge of the trees. Enormous lights flooded a long clearing up ahead. He blinked, trying to focus on the many shapes and sounds overwhelming the scene. What looked like dirty, skeletal golems swarmed over helmeted troopers, and scores of dark-armored soldiers lay motionless in mud and clods of grass. Rory did not know how to tell who was winning, but a few golems broke off and loped toward the remaining troopers near the plane, who fired on the pockets of attackers.

Something large and orange caught his eye, and Rory stopped running. He stared, unable to find his breath. What looked like an immense, flaming wolf lunged at a striped cat made of stone. He wondered if Caroline had tried to warn him of this during Remembrance Day. The wolf creature reminded him of the horror that stepped from the bonfire, except this one was twice its size. Silt was in terrible shape—a pair of long, glowing claw marks ran down the tiger's granite flank, and it danced back and forth, trying to evade the attacks and draw the wolf back. Rory wondered if Aspects felt pain.

Below the titans, Caroline and Dawson collided, sending shock waves through the trees and kicking up rings of dirt. Caroline's motions were smooth, exact, and complemented perfectly by Pond Skipper. Every time she seemed to misstep, Skipper would project a column of ice from her glittering armor, deflect a blow, and allow Caroline to slip away. Dawson swung his massive sword, grinning madly as he closed on Caroline again and again.

Rory watched, awed, as Caroline twisted her body, catching the sword between the thin blades of the Kiss. As she turned, a spike of ice erupted from her armor and pierced Dawson through the shoulder of his sword arm. He slapped the attack away, but not before a trickle of bright magma sprayed the ground, spurting from the wound. Again and again, he was pierced, and the air shimmered as heat poured from his body. A moment later, Caroline spun away while Dawson roared in frustration.

"Hey!" Khloe's voice came from further off, and she waved him over to the edge of the trees. Rory ducked low and ambled over, trying to stay hidden. They looked into each other's eyes and spoke at the same time.

"Caroline is—"

"We need—"

Khloe's eyes widened, looking past him, and he turned. Just behind them, a trio of soldiers stared at them. For a long moment, no one moved—until one trooper lifted their rifle. Khloe tried to turn, but Rory was already on the move. Wrapping his arms around her, he pulled them back into the forest and ducked behind a gnarled stump.

Sound consumed everything. He clamped both hands over his ears and shrank down as small as he could as bullets pummeled the stump, raining splinters of wood. Khloe shifted and screamed under him. His hand fumbled at his hip, groping for the solid weight of the pistol. Shaking, he pulled it out and aimed over his head.

Just point and pull.

"We gotta move!" she yelled over the shots. He lifted his head with the barest fraction and slid to the side. Khloe wiggled free and pulled her rifle across her body. She leaned out, but more bullets bit into the bark, and she winced back, covered in splinters. They weren't going anywhere.

We need Caroline. From out in the clearing, a boom followed, kicking leaves and dirt into Rory's face. He spit, blinking away the sting. *She's not coming.*

"Cover me!" Khloe said.

"Cover?"

"Now!" She popped up and squeezed off a pair of shots before rolling out of view.

"Khloe!" He switched the pistol to his left hand, reached above his head, and fired blind. Return fire came, vibrating the stump until Rory thought the wood might shake itself apart. A sudden burst of heat pierced his hand. He dropped the gun and pulled back to find a two-inch piece of wood sticking out from the base of his thumb. The moss deadened the pain, making it vibrate more than burn, but it didn't prevent Rory's heart from picking up speed as he watched blood run down his arm.

I don't want to die.

Rory yanked the splinter free and squeezed his fist to put pressure on the wound. An explosion of rifle fire sounded nearby, and he flinched, turning toward where he thought she'd gone. Khloe yelped from the darkness, and her rifle went quiet.

"No!" Rory jumped forward.

"Don't move!" A harsh voice snapped to his right. He looked over his shoulder to see a trooper rounding the mangled stump, aiming a rifle at his head. *Oh shit.* He held up his hands and sniffed at the fouling air. He was suddenly overwhelmed by the powerful stench of manure. Beside them, the ferns rustled.

"What the—" the man said. Then he screamed.

A half dozen skeletal golems burst from the bushes and clawed at the trooper. Blood arced against the silverlight. He turned his rifle and sprayed bullets, exploding a golem's head into maggoty tar. The creature collapsed at Rory's feet, but more kept coming. The man continued to fire, but the golems fell atop him, plunging their long, bony claws into his neck and face. Rory watched, chilled by the simple brutality, as the man stilled.

Then the golems all turned and looked at him with blue glowing eyes, waiting. Rory touched his neck and felt the cool weight of the riverstone press against his skin. "We're friends." The golems all cocked their heads to the side, all to Khloe, then to each other. Rory braced, not sure what they'd decide.

"Rory?" Khloe's voice broke his fear. The golems' blue eyes followed him as he ran toward the sound and found her behind a mossy log.

"Are you okay?"

"My leg."

Thigh. The word set an alarm bell off in his brain. *Tourniquet for pressure. Clean water and bandage.* Kneeling, he squinted through the shadows and found torn fabric and blood on her thigh. He breathed easier after he saw the wound. *Nothing arterial.* Despite all the blood, it wasn't deep.

"I don't think it hit anything important," Rory said.

Khloe grimaced. "Rude."

"I didn't mean—"

She swatted him and held out her hand. "Help me up."

Rory caught the joke and helped her up.

"How's your hand?" she said, testing her weight on her leg.

Rory uncurled his fist and looked at his mangled palm. Fresh, red blood seeped out of the hole in the meat of his thumb. He squeezed it shut again, blowing out a breath. "Can't feel much, luckily. I think okay."

She nodded. "I don't feel much either."

Rory found the golems still waiting, but their collective eyes aimed out across the field. There, the duel was not going well. Caroline's movements had slowed, a beat later than before. Her pristine posture now stooped; she looked spent. A section sloughed off her ice armor, leaving the exposed skin beneath red and welted. Dawson pressed the attack, relentless with his pressure. Each blow, every narrow deflection, caught Rory's breath now. One wrong step, and it would be over. Nearby, the wolf had the stone tiger on its back, and the two Aspects continued to rake each other with elemental fury. *We don't have much time.*

As though called by a soundless song, the golems turned as one and loped toward the plane.

One more step, he thought and forced his feet to follow. Khloe needed no encouragement, leaning on him as they broke cover. Flanked by golems, they limped across the battlefield toward their fate.

Chapter 69: Hijack

"Jane!"

Emmett needed to stop screaming. He was ruining the moment. Jane had always loved zombie movies as a kid, the swarms, the hiding, the jump scares, all of it, but she never thought she'd experience something like one. Maybe it was the shock or a blooming concussion, but these bony-not-zombies behaved an awful lot like zombies. *What are they?*

"Jane!"

There he goes again.

Most of Dawson's army lay dead and alone, scattered behind their fortification at the base of the plane. A trio of them held the ramp, picking off the not-zombies as they swarmed forward. But even downing a score of shamblers, more kept coming. Their bodies piled up the ramp—just like zombies would.

They aren't eating anyone, some sleeping piece of her said. It made her nose hurt.

"Damn it. Snap out of it!" Emmett again. She was vaguely aware of him pulling on her restraints.

Someone screamed, and Jane watched one of the trio break and run, only to be tackled by two not-zombies and dragged away. While bone might break against armor, it was only a matter of time before they found the gaps. Her gut churned when she saw red, jarring her musings. Something in her told her to run, which seemed reasonable, unlike what she was seeing.

SMACK!

The blow to her cheek came as a surprise, ringing her broken nose like a bell. Pain seared her senses, ricocheting inside her skull. She cupped her throbbing face.

"Owww."

"Jane?" Emmett said, panting. "Are you back?"

She peeked open an eye and saw him with another slap loaded.

"Present."

He turned and ran to the opposite side of the bay.

A surge of firelight came from outside, somewhere behind her. The plane jumped, sending Emmett tumbling. He glimpsed outside, and his eyes widened, catching a blossom of firelight. He scrambled back to his feet. Something like a howl followed from outside, like the bay of boiling rock. Jane's back prickled. *Dawson?*

"Clear the ramp!" Emmett called out from across the cargo bay. He slapped a button on the control panel, and the plane shuddered, its hydraulics lifting the ramp. One soldier turned and ran up the incline while the other shouted to keep shooting. The non-zombies swarmed into the opening, and the rear guard went down screaming and disappeared into the swarm.

Nearly closed, a creature's lumpy head appeared over the ramp's edge, but Emmett's pistol barked, and the creature disappeared in a burst of sludge. The surviving soldier took position beside Emmett, and the two dispatched one after another as the creatures clawed their way inside.

At last, the ramp pressed shut, dripping with blood and mud.

Ting. Ting. Ting. The creatures scratched at the bay door.

"What the hell are those things?!" the man cried, his voice cracking. "And where the hell is Dawson?" He started toward the side hatch. "He needs—"

BLAM!

The soldier's head snapped to the side, and blood sprayed the bulkhead. Jane recoiled as the body slumped onto the top of Jacklyn's steel cell and pooled blood on the glass. Emmett watched the body, weapon still aimed, before he tucked it back in his holster. Jane's mouth hung open, staring at the once handsome kid, ambition burning in his eyes. Something had changed, something she recognized in herself, and she wasn't sure she liked it for either of them.

He kneeled before her and produced a small key for her cuffs.

"Muff me, Emmett," Jane whispered. "What happened to you?"

"I wised up." The cuffs clicked open, and the weight dropped off.

She rolled her wrists, enjoying the freedom but uncertain about Emmett's transformation.

"The plane is ours," he said.

The chaotic scratches on the rear door changed, spreading up the walls and overhead. She eyed the ceiling.

"They can still damage the engines," Emmett said. "We have to leave. Now."

Jane followed the tinny sounds as they seemed to spread to the wings. *Transformations can wait.* "Time to fly." She swung her legs out of her seat and felt the blood tingle back into her feet as she followed Emmett to the cockpit.

Chapter 70: Hecatomb

This is magnificent. Dawson swung his sword in a high arc, drinking in every second of his masterpiece. *Now, this is a duel.* Caroline was giving him a splendid gift. It was everything he'd dreamed it might be: a duel meant for a ballad. A doomed last stand featuring him in his favorite role.

Caroline ducked his attack, throwing out her Kiss as she passed under the spectral blade. His thigh burned as she passed. He threw a fist low, trying to catch her off position, but she foiled him again. She tucked and sprang, passing over his glowing knuckles. She sidestepped his lunge, twirled beneath his guard, and blossomed, firing another streak of pain up his back. Gritting his teeth, he threw out an exploratory boot in her path. He clipped her foot, not enough to knock her off balance - not yet - but enough that they both felt it.

"I'm getting closer," Dawson said, squaring at the witch.

"So am I." Caroline flicked the cooling magma from her twin blades.

Dawson cut low, aiming to sweep the Wyth's legs, but she hopped over the sword and spun out of his reach. She finished the fluid spin and landed without a second step. Behind that blindfold, she met his gaze, lifting her chin in a defiant salute.

Perfect. Dawson couldn't ask for a better opposite. Or for a better performance. Caroline played her part as though commanding a stage, performing her last heroics with all the hope of a fool.

"If attrition is your plan, you'd better reconsider," Dawson said, rolling out his clotting shoulder. Black rock cracked and rolled down his arm, pattering on the ground and adding to the litter. He took a step, and she countered, keeping the distance between them.

"Perhaps you need to reconsider yours," Caroline said, stepping forward.

Unnerved, Dawson slid to the right and back, not wanting to repeat his misstep. His back still burned.

Caroline retreated a single bounding step and dropped to a knee before checking the bottom of her foot. Dawson shifted his grip, watching while he took stock of the other duel. The Heart was winning, but like the witch, this earth Aspect was stubborn. The great stone cat lost an emerald eye and sported scores of gashes, but hadn't wavered in ferocity. Or tricks. The lycin lunged, but the tiger's body descended into the earth like a stone dropped into a pond. The wolf stumbled forward, blazing red eyes searching for its missing quarry. Dawson felt the ripples of the Heart's frustration - it was hungry and denied. The tiger reemerged behind the Heart, onyx claws tearing and prickling Dawson's senses as they flicked fiery droplets onto the grass.

Caroline grunted, stealing his attention back. She pulled a bit of bloody black stone out of her foot and tossed it away. Then she placed her fingers on the ground. Her blue mythstone flashed, and water drops hurried up her arm, filling in the cracked sections of her sagging armor.

"Clever trick," Dawson said.

"Thank you," Caroline said, her gaze locked onto him.

"How's the foot?" Dawson said. "That looks painful."

"It's from your blood," she replied, rising and readying herself. "Bet it hurt."

Dawson laughed. *There is even banter.* "These"—he gestured to the long, igneous gashes down his forearm—"I didn't notice any of them." He bent his arm, hiding his wince as he brushed away a black scab. More sharp black stones pattered against the ground. "They sting. A little."

Caroline sniffed, shifting her Kiss into a high guard.

Dawson lifted the Brand, but the motion felt forced. Something felt off. He could feel the Heart's anger like a sultry breeze on his back, but the heat never touched his arm. It took him a second to realize why; he wasn't ready for the ending; he was having too much fun. And there was something wrong with Caroline still. Despite her tattered appearance, she still had a thick confidence wafting from her. It smelled sweet, too much like hope, and it wouldn't be a real victory, an absolute victory, unless he shattered both body *and* spirit. There could be no doubt who was supreme.

Dawson considered, then lowered the Brand cautiously, making it an offer. He half expected Caroline to pounce on his lowered guard, but she gave a single nod and slid half a step to her left, folding her feet together like a ballerina. *Not opposed to a break either.*

"What is your plan, witch? I can't figure it out."

Caroline folded her hand over the Kiss's gauntlet, pointing the blades straight at the ground. "Leave, and I'll mail you a picture."

Dawson grinned. "Your wit is still as sharp as your Kiss, witch, but we both know neither can kill me. And your little nurse is roadkill. No way he survived that crash, so that leaves, what? Just you? The trick with the psybelles was cute. Casualties will be high. I'll have to pretty that up for my debrief, but if this is your entire plan, it lacks any chance to defeat me."

"So. It. Seems." There was a chill in her voice.

"So what is it?"

Caroline nodded, considering. "You really want to know?"

"I'm intrigued."

She pointed at his waist. "First, I'm taking that back."

"What?" Dawson looked down and found the Dozer tucked into his torn, charred fatigues. In the thrill of battle, he'd completely forgotten about it. "That's going to be—" He heard a footfall, skin on earth, and threw up the Brand. A burst of crimson sparks showered the blackened grass at their feet. Caroline cartwheeled, bringing her up behind Dawson as he whirled to keep up. He was a beat too late as her Kiss flashed and carved another pair of furious lines up Dawson's flank. The blades bit deep, and he grit his teeth as the pain washed over him before it cooled. He drove her off with a haphazard slash as the Brand's ghosts wailed.

A few feet off, Caroline collected herself. In her gauntlet, she now held her two gleaming mythstones, and in her other, she brandished the Dozer. The cross guard lit up, blue mist poured from the hilt, and a three-foot blade of blue mist glowed against the night.

Dawson seethed, touching his empty waistband. "That's mine, witch."

"Was," Caroline corrected. "You got sloppy."

"You broke the rules."

"They're your rules."

Dawson growled, irritation eating away at his enjoyment. This scene was getting worse by the moment. The Kiss hurt, but the Dozer was a problem.

The Heart's ecstasy boiled against his senses. Nearby, the lycin's jaws latched onto the tiger's neck, hissing as it tore ashen gashes in its rival. The tiger clawed back, and Dawson felt those too, but the Heart had its death grip. Which meant their duel was nearly done. Just the climax remained. *Absolute victory.*

"All good things come to an end, witch," Dawson said, dropping the Brand into a low guard. "Even you. Someone should have taught you that. So, let's make the end easy for everyone."

Caroline's forehead creased, listening.

Dawson drew a line with the tip of the Brand. "Kneel here, and it'll be done. I'll make it quick. And if you do it, I'll make sure

Jacklyn doesn't suffer too much." He spread his hands and smiled. "You have my word—"

"Lies." Caroline attacked in a tie-dye blur, surging forward and inside his defenses. Spikes of ice fired off her armor, penetrating and stealing his balance. He parried the Dozer, but earned the Kiss. He deflected the second sweep of the vapor blade and felt Caroline take a slice of his calf. She pressed the tempo. Again and again, she struck at him, Dawson's eyes growing wide as he fought to keep the rhythm. Another block, another bite. An icy spike caught his elbow, slowing his backswing. Caroline pounced, plunging the Dozer into the gap. He rolled his shoulder back, and the vapor hissed against his skin as it missed, but he'd sold his balance to avoid the blow. Caroline flowed into her next attack, screaming in defiance as she drove both blades of her Kiss through his left knee. White-hot pain flooded his senses.

"Gah!" Dawson snarled and rolled his impaled knee away, tugging on the flats of her blades and bringing a fresh wave of agony from the deep wound. But the misery was worth it. Wherever the Kiss went, Caroline followed. The witch fell a step toward Dawson, robbing her of her speed.

He latched one massive hand around Caroline's gauntlet and squeezed. The metal caved, and both mythstones popped in a burst of blue and green shards. He felt every bone in her hand and wrist shatter. Caroline's mouth hung open in agony, but no sound escaped as her armor sloughed off and shattered against the blackened ground. The stone tiger let out a sad, rumbling howl, and Dawson looked up to see its emerald eye flicker. The stone Aspect crumbled, and the Heart threw up its head and howled.

"It's over."

"Aaaagh." Caroline swung the Dozer. He dropped the Brand and caught her fist. She sneered at him, sweat running down her forehead as he forced her arm back. He pried open her long fingers until the Dozer thumped on the ground. *Futile.* Her second hand shattered like the first, but Caroline screamed this time. He savored the note as it rose when he tugged on her mangled gauntlet. He bit back the pain as he jerked the blades free. Caroline dropped, shaking and crying, as azure and emerald dust trickled from her pulverized hand.

Dawson recoiled as he tried to put weight on his injured knee. The joint was crippled and wouldn't be much good until the Heart returned in full. Even then, it would take weeks to heal properly. The trade, he supposed, was worth it. It cost him mostly pain, while Caroline lost everything. *Disappointing.* "You spoiled the ending." He hefted up the Brand over his head, ready for the smell of blood. "Good riddance."

A deep whine of jet engines crescendoed from behind.

The plane! Dawson spun around. In the floodlights, he saw bodies of golems and troopers scattered around the rear of the plane as more of the creatures crawled along the fuselage, heading toward the wings. The engines whined higher, and the plane jerked forward, rolling down the runway.

"Jane!" Dawson bellowed and threw a lazy swing at Caroline, but she rolled away, clutching the Dozer to her chest. Dawson considered finishing her, but the mental image of the Director tearing the Heart of Wrath from his chest refocused his attention. *The Seed.* He called to the lycin. "Get over here! I need you to run!"

The wolf released a crackling growl at Dawson. Its amber eyes flicked over to Caroline, and then the plane before it shook itself and crumbled into ash. Dawson felt a wave of relief as the full presence of the Heart returned, smothering the pain as he turned, his maimed knee wobbling, and sprinted after the plane.

Chapter 71: Adaptation

"My moss is wearing off," Rory said.

Khloe nodded, her arm draped over his shoulder.

With each heartbeat, new and numerous pains throbbed all over his body. Rory's punctured thumb burned most of all, getting worse with each step. But bad as he felt, Khloe looked worse. Limping, she grimaced as she leaned on him with a fixed jaw— with her moss wearing off, too. The gunshot to her leg must be excruciating now. Each painful step brought the plane a little closer, and in it was Jacklyn. She needed him. *Right. Left. Right. Left.*

"Khloe," Rory said, breathing heavily.

"Ya?"

"Ready to run?"

She whimpered but nodded, eyeing the open distance.

She's counting the steps.

"If things turn sideways," he started.

"Shut up."

"No, I want to say something. I—"

"I said, shut up." Her eyes dropped to his mouth and narrowed for a moment. She reached up and seized the back of his neck, pulling his lips down to hers. He stumbled mid-step. Her kiss was intoxicating, hungry. As swiftly as it had come, she released him and pulled back. He blinked down at her as she smiled. "Me too. Okay?"

The plane's engines whined, and the aircraft lurched like someone had forgotten to take off the parking brake.

"Uh," Rory said and pointed. This wasn't part of the plan, not until they were aboard, at least.

The plane jolted again, but this time, it began rolling down the runway.

Rory's eyes widened. *Jacklyn!*

"Go!" Khloe shouted but then grabbed his arm. "Wait!"

A roar of outrage echoed over the clearing, and the towering fire wolf vanished from the corner of Rory's vision. Dawson sprinted after the plane, his massive sword in hand. Fire spread up his arms, burning holes in his fatigues and leaving a trail of thick smoke behind him. *If Dawson was moving . . .* He turned and spotted Caroline's thin form limping toward them.

What now? Rory's mind raced, but it shouted only one answer. *Run.*

He slipped from beneath Khloe's arm, wincing sympathetically as she sucked in a labored breath. "Get Caroline."

Unarmed, Rory's boots pounded down the dirt runway. Fear weighed on every muscle, willing him to stop, but a greater clarity allowed him to push on. Ahead of him, Dawson ran alongside the plane near the loading ramp just as the engines picked up speed. Rory gasped as the man punched a hole into the fuselage and tore the door from its hinges in two smooth motions. Dawson flung it aside, and it bounced to the side of the runway.

Just get to Jacklyn. Rory put his head down and opened up his stride, pushing everything he had into his weary legs.

It wasn't enough—the plane pulled away, shrinking as it hurtled toward the mountains in the distance.

No.

Jane sank into the pilot's chair as the hazy mountains closed.

"Lift," she said, pressing a button on the panel overhead, engaging the aircraft's elevators.

"Drag." She made a mental note of the landing gear controls. She dropped her hand to the massive lever between her and Emmett in the co-pilot seat and pushed it up.

"Thrust." The force pushing her back in her chair increased as the forests turned into a green blur around them. For the first time, she let herself believe—if she could avoid crashing, they might pull this off.

"We did it!" Emmett said, pumping both fists in the air. "We did it!"

Jane's heart skipped, and she imagined hugging Grace again. "We did?"

"We did it, Jane!" Emmett drummed the control panel, smiling like a maniac. "We—"

Emergency lights flashed on a panel overhead.

"What are those?" Emmett jerked both hands off the panel. "What did I do?"

"Dunno."

A screech of agonized metal echoed through the cargo bay behind them, and a moment later, the wind ripped into the cockpit. Jane squinted at Emmett and found him standing with his gun in hand, victory gone; his eyes were wide and fearful. He was a young man who realized he didn't want to die.

POW! Emmett's gun erupted, leaving a high-pitched whine in her ears.

POW! She cringed, clamping a hand on one ear as she pressed the thrust down, sinking her further back into the seat. Emmett tumbled backward.

"Come on, come on!"

It started low—a deep growl, chilling Jane's blood.

"Emmett!"

They stared at each other for a horrible moment. Dawson was aboard. She started sweating and couldn't take a breath. Heat overwhelmed the cockpit, and she turned to see a massive hand with seams of glowing magma seize Emmett by the throat. The gunfire ceased as Emmett's eyes pleaded with Jane for something she didn't have.

"No!" Jane screamed. "Emmett!" His face twisted in shocked pain. Then he was gone, jerked from view.

"Emmett!" Jane yelled. She took short, shallow breaths, hot tears rolling down her cheeks. She had done this.

"Jane!" Dawson boomed.

A shuddering fury welled in Jane. It was time to play her last move in the great game. Her hand dropped to the throttle, and in that instant, Jane thought of Grace. She wished she'd had one more day.

"I'm sorry. I love you."

Jane slammed the throttle forward. Fighting the force dragging her back, she seized the yoke and—

Thick fingers clamped onto her head, and the heat that followed was unlike anything she'd ever known. The smell of cooking flesh and burning hair filled her senses, lighting every nerve in her body on fire. She heard herself scream.

In her struggling consciousness, through the dizzying veil of pain, Jane cranked the yoke hard to the left, vaguely aware of the shift beneath her. The vise clamped around her head and lifted, ripping her from the seat. As she flew, she caught

Dawson's blazing red eyes wide with fear as the entire plane tipped around them.

Survive this, you muffing traitor.

Then she was past him—weightlessness at the apex of flight.

Rory had never seen a plane crash. He'd seen videos, mostly of bad landings and a couple of shaky takeoffs, but those recorded disasters paled in comparison to experiencing one.

The bulky cargo jet plummeted down the runway one moment, then veered to its left, shrieking like it'd been hooked. Wheels sparked and snapped. Its wing disintegrated against the thicket of the old forest. More metal screamed and trunks splintered. The cockpit compacted against a pair of massive spruces, folding and rocking the giants back on their roots. A wave of churned dirt and stumps followed as the body of the plane distorted, lurching to a stop. With a final moan, its broad tail rose in the air, like a whale's above water, and crashed back down, cracking the fuselage.

Rory slowed and stutter-stepped forward, almost tripping as the wreckage shrieked as it settled. He half expected it to explode. When it didn't, he regained speed. Jacklyn!

Debris covered the ground. Watching his feet, he jumped over logs and torn sheet metal. The strong, stinging odor of fuel stung his nose. Hurry!

The torn open hatch had folded in on itself—there was no way he'd fit through. He dashed to the plane's rear, where he saw the loading ramp had cracked open, wide enough to crawl through.

He put his ear to the opening and listened, waiting to hear any sound of life inside, but he only heard the groans of trees as the plane rocked. Swallowing down the nervous lump in his throat, Rory crawled inside.

The world within the plane was black but for the shafts of dim moonlight slanting through the cracked hull. Branches and pine needles littered the ground. The sharp smell of fuel mixed with a wet-sweet scent of freshly chopped wood. Overhead, the bits of tree that hadn't broken formed a patchy canopy against the plane's vaulted ceiling. Tilted on its left side, Rory walked carefully on the wall, disoriented.

Jacklyn? He made his way through the cargo hold toward the cockpit, squinting into the gloom. Avoiding several splintered logs, he stumbled over something pale in the shadows. Rory peered down—it was actually two somethings. His stomach coiled with revulsion when he realized what. Bodies lying together.

They lay face up, a tangle of limbs and splinters. Jane's burnt scalp rested on Emmett's stomach as though the two were relaxing in a grassy field, watching the clouds. Moonlight pooled across her face, revealing the terrible burns. Most of Jane's hair and forehead were gone, replaced with blisters and charred skin between thin streaks of bright pink hair. Her blue suit lay in tatters, stained with blood. Emmett's clean-shaven face twisted upward unnaturally, his neck blackened, a blackened fist-size hole through his chest.

Rory felt sick and squeezed his eyes shut, willing his stomach to hold and the truth to change, but neither cooperated when he opened his eyes. Jane was still dead, killed, trying to help him. He burped, and he tasted bile. For a long moment, Rory stared at the bodies. He'd never get a chance to thank her. To return the favor. He was slipping away in the back of that truck, but she wouldn't let him go. And Emmett was his age. That could have been him—still could be him. Both were once strangers. The sharp pang of sadness and an immense gratitude struck him. They'd crashed this plane and bought everyone else an opportunity.

"Thank you," he whispered, though it felt woefully inadequate. "Jane, I . . ." There was more to say, something honorable, but he choked on the words.

The plane groaned and shifted beneath his feet, and he peered into the gloom that was the front of the plane, listening.

Where is Dawson?

The plane lurched again, raising the hairs on Rory's arm. Get out!

The dead would have to wait. If he survived, he'd come back for them. He scanned the hold again, focused on sharp edges, something solid, something heavy . . . His heart leaped—spotting a steel box, pine needles covering its cracked lid. This has to be it. He jumped toward it, slipping and brushing aside debris, and peered through the cracked glass. From the flickering light, he saw Jacklyn stir. She was alive.

He felt around the coffin's edges for a release. He banged on the coffin.

"Hey! Wake up! I need you to push!"

She tilted her head to the side but didn't open her eyes.

Rory knocked hard, shouting. "Wake up!"

Her green eyes fluttered, wincing before focusing on Rory. A lopsided smile stretched across her face, and she mouthed the word "hero."

Rory grinned back. "I'm here. I'm here!"

Jacklyn nodded and mouthed, "Late."

Rory's eyes blurred as he shook, sniffing and smiling at her. Even so, near death, she chided him. He held up his hands and mimed pushing. Jacklyn nodded, and he took up position. He nodded three times and shoved the lid away with all his might. After a couple of seconds of futile struggle, the coffin's lid slid off, and Rory nearly fell into the cell on top of Jacklyn.

"Ugh, caref—" Jacklyn wheezed.

They stared at each other, and Rory waited. "Is this—" he said. "The Seed. Do I . . ."

Jacklyn shook her head. "I don't have the juice. We try now, and we're both dead. I need energy, and I need it—"

The plane jerked to the side, and Rory clung to the coffin's edge to keep from falling. CRACK! Splinters rained down. He covered his head as needles showered them. The air snapped, something whipped his cheek, and he looked down to see a jagged branch lodged in the grated floor. He touched the side of his face, stunned. That was close.

"It's him," Jacklyn said.

Who? But he knew who she meant. "That's impossible," Rory muttered, but then realized who he was and how he'd gotten here. "Never mind. What do we do now?"

Jacklyn frowned, and she stuck her hand out. "We need to leave."

"Can't you just—" He pointed at her stump. "Use it?"

"I can if I touch him," Jacklyn said.

Rory swallowed. He was afraid she might say that.

She reached for him, and he heaved, pulling her up. She was so heavy.

"Help me," he groaned. "I need you to walk." He grunted as he pulled her toward the crack in the ramp, carrying her down the first two steps until her feet flopped down as they picked up momentum. "That's it. Left. Right."

Rory helped her through the gap and followed as quickly as he could, grateful to be out of the plane. Sweating and limping, he carried her away from the crash, putting precious distance between them and the monster within the wreckage. They needed to find Caroline—she'd know what to do.

"Keep going!" Rory managed between labored breaths. "Left. Right."

"Rory!" Khloe's voice cut through the air. Ahead, Khloe and Caroline shambled toward them, leaning together. Khloe looked in terrible shape, limping on her wounded leg, mud, and blood splattered all over her mismatched fatigues and pajamas. Caroline sagged, shivering badly as she clutched two pulverized hands against her chest. The sight stole Rory's breath. The pain she must feel . . .

"Care," Jacklyn said.

"Almost there," he said. "Quick feet now."

Behind them, the plane groaned, and Rory stole a glance in time to watch the aircraft crack further, breaking trees as a wing landed. Several small fires swelled, and he thought he saw a long shadow move across the canopy.

The final ten feet between them vanished, and Rory let his spent legs relax. Both he and Jacklyn crumbled to the ground. Khloe whimpered as she did the same with Caroline.

"Are you—" Rory started but stopped to suck down the cool air to douse his burning lungs.

"It hurts." Khloe cringed, then nodded at his bloody hand. "You?"

Rory nodded, working to catch his breath. But the pain he felt faded as Jacklyn collected Caroline in her arms. The gruff Host rocked the Wyth as tears filled her eyes.

"You found me," Jacklyn said.

Caroline reached up and stroked Jacklyn's silver hair with the side of a mangled hand. "I made a promise, my love."

"I'm sorry. I didn't know—" Jacklyn's voice caught.

"Hush now," Caroline whispered. "We are together."

Jacklyn nodded, and Rory's heart ached. He reached for Khloe, who was reaching for him.

"Oh, love," Caroline said, shaking her head. "I thought of so many things to say, so many pretty ways to say I love you, but I've gone and forgotten them all." Tears soaked through her blindfold and rolled down her cheek.

"No, no, no. Shhh. Shhh." Jacklyn cupped Caroline's face, caressing her wet cheeks with a thumb. "I bet they were beautiful."

The Wyth leaned into her palm, kissing it tenderly.

Jacklyn glanced up at the moon. "We were close, Care. I really thought we'd get to see the sunrise one more time. The Cove was the best in the morning."

Caroline's gaze turned to the sky. Together, for a peaceful moment, they watched the stars.

"No sun, so we'll claim the moon instead," Caroline said.

"Consider it ours." Jacklyn smiled, though it wavered as she sagged.

"Oh," compassion thick in Caroline's voice, "you're spent."

Jacklyn nodded. "I hurt. And I'm so, so tired."

"Me too." She stared up into Jacklyn's eyes as her expression grew serious. "There is one gift left to give."

Rory looked at Khloe, but found her crying silently. What gift?

"No."

"We must."

"No!" Jacklyn coughed and buried her face in Caroline's shoulder.

The Wyth stroked her hair. "I insist."

Jacklyn shook her head defiantly.

"Jacklyn Seed. My sweet, stubborn jewel. You refuse me?"

"Yes."

"Why?"

Jacklyn swallowed. "Because . . . I'm a coward."

"You have many qualities, love," Caroline said. Her grin

695

blossomed. "Cowardice is not among them."

"It is."

"Tell me how."

"I always wanted to go first. I don't want this world without my sun."

"My poet." Caroline laughed, like the chime of a silver bell, and drew Jacklyn in for a kiss.

The realization slammed into Rory, and his stomach dropped. "No." Caroline couldn't die! There had to be a way. He leaned forward to protest, but Khloe squeezed his hand, pulling him back. He understood her message: *this wasn't our moment.*

A dull rumble came from the plane, and Rory turned in time to see it list and slide a foot to the side. Timbers cracked, and flames rose, catching the low-hanging branches, though the recent rain seemed to slow its spread. Something detached from the fire and fell to the ground in a burst of embers. Rory held his breath as he watched it for a moment. It moved.

"Uh, Khloe . . ."

Rising from the ground came a living inferno wavering on two legs. Lava dripped from hundreds of wounds as Dawson limped forward, dragging the ghostly Brand with his only hand. His left arm was gone at the shoulder. Molten rock flowed freely down his side, hissing against the moist air. A cloud of steam followed Dawson as his many wounds pulsed with angry orange light.

Rory's mouth was dry. "Ja—"

"I see him, hero."

"Jacklyn!" Dawson called out, stumbling a step. He swung the Brand in a flat arc, and the sword howled. "Jacklyn!" He scanned the airfield until his blazing gaze landed on Rory. Dawson's eyes narrowed as he staggered toward them, a deep gash in his cheek making him appear to have a jagged, horrific grin.

"It's time, love," said Caroline.

"But I'm not ready."

"Neither am I, but we'll do it together."

Rory turned back around, his stomach cramped from the sickening mix of sorrow, adrenaline, and fear.

"I'll wait as long as I can on the other side," Caroline said.

Jacklyn shook her head. "What if you aren't there? What if I can't find you?"

"You will," Caroline said. "I'll search for you, too. Always."

Jacklyn gathered Caroline in a fierce kiss. They lost themselves in each other, and Rory squeezed Khloe's hand as the pressure behind his eyes gave way. He cried for their loss and their life. For their pillar of love. He wanted someone to kiss him like that in the end. To love him that fiercely. And he wanted to love himself that much so he could love them back. Caroline taught him that.

Jacklyn's shadow hand entwined in Caroline's white hair, and Rory drew Khloe closer. The pain slackened from Caroline's face, and Rory swore he saw a smile touch the corner of her mouth. She drooped in Jacklyn's arms, her lips slipping apart as the wind rolled by. Flakes of skin swept away in patches, swirling in a lavender-scented cloud of smoke and ash.

Something inside Rory left on that cloud, too, sapping the courage he'd only just discovered. But that would have been the last thing Caroline wanted. He squeezed Khloe's hand harder and bit his cheek. For Caroline.

Jacklyn sobbed, bending over Caroline's unraveling body as dark vapor poured down her forearm. The surrounding shadows collected and deepened, blanketing the two women from view with a black shroud. It swirled there, their own personal hurricane. Then it broke, doused by an invisible bucket. The shadows splashed and soaked into the grass, leaving Jacklyn alone, staring down at her empty hands. She closed her fist and leaned her head against the ashy knuckles as her bruises faded and cuts closed. A beautiful final gift.

"I'm so sorry, Jacklyn," Rory said. What else could he say?

"I didn't know..." she croaked, between sobs, "It would be that hard."

"Caroline was an inspiration to me . . . like someone not from this world. An angel? I don't know . . ."

"A goddess."

"A goddess." Somehow, it felt true. "I like that."

"Jacklyn!" Dawson bellowed. A peal of maniac laughter followed. "Oh, Jacklyn! It's just you and me now."

"That's not true," Rory said.

Jacklyn's wet eyes opened, meeting his eyes. The pain in her dark eyes tugged at his heart.

"We're here for you. You're not alone."

Jacklyn sniffed, nodding. "Thanks, hero." Her eyes slid to Khloe. "Both of you."

"She's dead!" Dawson cackled again. "The wicked witch is dead!"

Jacklyn's expression darkened, and she aimed her rage at Dawson. As she stood, a fresh burst of smoke rose from her arm. "Hero, you better take this. Caroline wanted you to have it." She held out the Dozer. Blood covered the grip.

Rory took it, relieved and terrified to have it back.

Jacklyn rolled back her shoulders and flexed both hands. "Job's not done yet, hero," she said without taking her eyes off Dawson. "Last two Assays to go. Beat him," she tapped her chest, "And take this damn thing. Ready?"

"Is that all?" Rory looked down at the Dozer, shaking in his hands. Torchbearer. I can do this. He nodded, feeling his heart trying to break free of his chest. "I'm—" He blew out a breath. "I'm ready."

"Doc?"

Khloe nodded, clutching the Iron Quill.

Your hundredth time.

"Let's finish this." Jacklyn flexed her shadow hand. "Caroline is waiting for me."

Chapter 74: Assay of Pluck

Translated from:

Disc - Shepherd's Stone

Sub-ring - *Codex*

Script - *Law of Hosts*:

Assay of Pluck:

Let the Candidate face their foe without a harness. Death must not just be a possibility but present in the Candidate's mind. Let the Candidate show their knowledge of conflict, for each must govern well the power they would keep. Let conflict show the virtues untestable by sister-Assays.

A Candidate passes if they fight and survive

A Candidate fails if they succumb to fear

A Candidate fails if they succumb to death

Amendment (s):

(233 AA) - Duels provide fertile ground for the Assay of Pluck.

(1112 AA) - The grander the foe, the grander the Candidate's army must be.

(4197 AA) - Retreat will not be tolerated. Struggle is not to be delayed.

—-

The clouds hung low, diffusing the slivers of moonlight into shafts of wilted gray. As Rory turned, Dozer in hand, the landscape was still. Only the rising wind and Dawson's hissing footfalls cut the quiet. Watching him advance, it took everything in Rory not to turn and run, screaming.

"Please say you have a plan."

Jacklyn didn't take her eyes off Dawson. Her stained T-shirt hung from her body, and she sighed. "We win if I can touch him, but you'll have to stun him or distract him first." Her shadow fist opened and closed.

"Distract him," Khloe said, fear clear in her voice. Rory felt it too: the pressure and the lack of air. Blood and mud covered Khloe's stolen fatigues, and her wispy hair gathered in a barely contained tangle on the side of her head. But despite her wounds and exhaustion, her eyes were open and focused—present. Terrified, but present.

"Hypothetically," Jacklyn said, with no hint of optimism.

She's nervous, too. Surprisingly, that made Rory feel better. Even staring down a Merged, it was nice to know he wasn't alone—fear was so isolating. After a pause, Jacklyn added, "We have to initiate soon. The longer we wait, the more he heals. We can't win on endurance."

"It's a sprint then." *Just like a code*, he thought. *You've done this before. Kinda.*

"That's the idea." She pushed herself up straighter. "I'll make the first move. Dawson will focus on me, so find your openings when you can. Don't hesitate. It's going to be hot in there. If you miss, get out of the way, then come again—harder. If you strike, stay in close and don't let him recover. Rory, with that Dozer, you only need one clean hit."

"One clean hit," Rory repeated, as though saying it out loud might will it into existence.

Jacklyn turned to Khloe. "Keep him from cooking us before we get to him. Dawson loves whipping fire around, trying to look all-powerful. Just do what you can. And don't push it," she warned. "We don't want to lose you to an overdraw." Jacklyn looked at Rory, then the Dozer. "Goes double for you, hero."

They both nodded, and for a brief moment, Rory wondered what an overdraw would feel like. Would he realize when his soul imploded? He shook his head, pushing the fear aside. "One clean hit. Keep moving."

"Right." Khloe blew out a long breath. "Spiritus boni, right?"

"Breathing is good." Then, another thought hit him. *Why risk it?*

"Shouldn't I just take the Seed right now? You have the energy, right?"

Jacklyn stepped past Rory, eyes on Dawson. "No telling how the Assay of Hosts will go. Could kill you or knock you out for an hour—or a year. For me, I had nausea for three months and was bloated for six more. Every Host is different. Plus, you aren't the warrior, hero. I am."

"Enough scheming!" Dawson shouted. His maimed body leaked more magma with every step. Hundreds of small fires burned in his wake. He lifted the Brand, and a flash of red light welled from his chest. Rory spotted a jagged crack and a fist-sized ruby mythstone within. *His heart.*

Fire raced up Dawson's arm and consumed the blade as he leveled it at them. "It's over."

"Incoming!" Jacklyn yelled, turning and shoving Rory into Khloe before leaping aside.

They toppled over as a beam of fire shot from the sword and sped by between them. He barely had time to blink when, five feet back, the beam struck the ground and tore a narrow smoking gash in the dirt. Sitting, Rory tried to find his breath. The beam would have split him in half.

Dawson's pace quickened and fire crawled up his arm again, the Brand pointed at Rory. "Worthless."

"Khloe," Jacklyn said.

Khloe squeezed her eyes closed and thrust the Quill above her head. A comet of rainbow feathers streaked into view and erupted midair. The fluttering curtain hung for a moment before a bright light backlit them. *WHOOSH.* The downy curtain ignited, blazing outward from its center. Heat slammed into Rory, and he threw his hands in front of his face. Nothing got through.

Go! Rory's legs propelled him forward, the rest of his body trailing behind. He shielded his face with an arm and plunged through the burning curtain. On the other side, Rory spotted Dawson thirty feet ahead. Jacklyn sprinted ahead of him on the right, rounding the curtain with long ribbons of ash peeling off her shadow hand. He spotted Khloe moving to his left, Quill in hand, though she stumbled a few steps. The effects of casting catching up to her.

Dawson aimed the Brand at Jacklyn, but the re-energized Host closed too fast, seizing the blade with her shadow hand and forcing it toward the sky. A beam of white light fired into the heavens.

Dawson shifted his grip, bringing his considerable weight onto the blade.

Jacklyn gritted her teeth, holding the quivering blade as she slid backward.

Dawson grunted, pressing forward a step. "Interesting. Not reaved. I suppose you need a soul for that."

"I'll kill you for what you did to her," Jacklyn hissed, straining against him.

"Why?" Dawson brought his red eyes close to Jacklyn, and he sneered, his breath hot as hellfire. "I'm not the one who killed her."

For a moment, they were locked, then a flash, and he saw his opening. He ran forward, Dozer in hand, his own heartbeat deafening his protest. *STOP!* He forced the fear aside. *Twenty feet.* In his hand, the Dozer's runes flickered, and vapor seeped from the hilt.

Jacklyn's eye flicked to Rory—she must have seen the

opportunity, too. She wrenched the Brand and Dawson's left knee listed laterally, wobbling. A wishful thrill swept through Rory. *Ten feet.*

Jacklyn drove her free fist at the mythstone in Dawson's chest. The Merged rolled to the side, and her punch pierced the blackened skin of his mangled shoulder. He growled in pain, and Jacklyn screamed, pulling her scorched hand back. Magma bubbled from the fresh wound.

Dawson kicked, slamming Jacklyn in the chest and forcing her to the ground. Rory choked, trying to see, but eyes and throat burned in the sweltering heat.

NOW! Rory swung the Dozer with everything he had. A jolt came from within his chest, and the runes swelled. The billowing blue mist condensed in a three-foot gaseous blade hissing from the heat. *It's working!*

Dawson's head snapped around and growled. His sword wailed as he rounded, raining droplets of glowing lava.

The Brand and Dozer collided in a flash of crackling bolts. He felt the blow hum through his entire body as the runes flared brighter.

Dawson leered down at him, spectral hands from his blade reaching for Rory. "You missed."

A comet of feathers engulfed them and, an instant later, erupted into fire. Dawson roared in outrage as the heat of the swirling inferno knocked Rory back, burning his skin. Something heavy caught him in the stomach, and he flew, landing hard on his side with an agonizing crunch. The air burst from Rory's lungs, and he rolled on his back, gasping for air.

A searing pain below his armpit told him ribs were broken. He couldn't take a full breath. He pushed himself to his knees, gasping in pain as he spotted the Dozer lying in a tuft of charred grass. Rory grabbed it, pressing a hand to his side. It didn't help. Each breath sent another agonizing wave through him as he rose.

Khloe lay a few feet away, her back arched, convulsing. *Oh no.* He wanted to run to her, but forced himself to focus. Jacklyn needed him.

Rory stumbled forward, trying not to black out as he readied himself for another charge. *This is it.*

Dawson stepped toward him, towering over his hunched body, but left his back invitingly exposed. Jacklyn rose and coiled to attack. Dawson's burning eyes followed Rory's over his shoulder, and the Merged smiled.

"Jacklyn! No!" Rory tried, but it was too late.

Jacklyn leaped at Dawson, shadow hand extended for a killing blow, but he'd sprung his trap. Twisting to the ground as he fell away, he drove the point of his sword up and into Jacklyn's stomach.

"No!"

She moaned, caught mid-flight, run through. She took a feeble swipe, but Dawson held her just out of reach. He roared as he lifted the sword up and then drove the point and Jacklyn into the ground. The tip sank deep into the earth, pinning her. He stumbled back, cackling. The ghastly blade snuffed out, leaving three feet of trembling steel protruding from Jacklyn's guts. She curled around the blade, blood seeping from her mouth. Her face creased in pain and concentration as she grasped the blade with both hands and pushed, trying to free herself. The weapon slid an inch before she cried out and stopped, letting her head drop to the ground.

The Dozer's blade disappeared.

"Come on!" Rory implored, shaking the hilt.

Dawson spat out a glob of magma and leveled his burning eyes, pointing at Rory. "Pathetic. Your nurse can't even use the children's toy." He slapped the pommel of his sword, and Jacklyn spasmed, coughing blood. Dawson frowned in mock sadness and limped toward Rory, favoring one knee. Rory retreated a step, holding the idle Dozer between them.

Dawson laughed. "You think this is how it ends? That you will win? It's an illusion. After I leave you here, mangled and alone, I'll find them—your friends, your patients, Patrick and Ana." His eyes blazed. "And I'll make sure they remember it was you who failed them as they die—just like Jacklyn failed you." The ruby mythstone swirled, and Rory stared at a fiery eye peering from the cloudy mythstone.

Jacklyn stirred. "Fuck you."

"Stay still!" He slapped his sword again, vibrating the blade. Jacklyn gurgled in pain, and her shadow hand snuffed out. Her chest moved.

Rory's heart thundered in his ears, and he glanced around, hoping to find anyone, anything, to help. But there was no one now—just him. *I'm alone;* the thought stopped him.

No . . . He glanced down at Jacklyn and over at Khloe twitching in the grass. He looked up to the night sky and felt the heavy mist falling on his hot skin, cooling him. Caroline, Khloe, Jacklyn—they would always be with him, no matter what happened tonight. The realization made the clamps on his chest and gut ease, and despite his broken rib, he breathed easier. *That's a lie. They're all with me.*

"I suppose I should thank you for delivering me the Seed and helping kill the witch." He took another long step toward Rory, pushing him back. "You run? From the inevitable? Spineless. COWARD!" he shouted, and Rory stumbled back, terrified. "I'm doing you a favor. You'd be a weak Host."

No. That's not true.

Dawson laughed. "Just like your parents, actually. Weakness breeds weakness. So this"—he gestured between them—"really isn't your fault. You're just the wrong guy for the job."

706

Rory stopped, staring at the Heart. Something in Dawson's words was familiar, like the faded memories of a reccurring dream. *I used to believe that.* The thought sobered him and filled his belly with fire. *I'm a torchbearer now.*

"You're right, Dawson," Rory said, taking a small step toward him. Dawson's smile slipped away, and he cocked his head, appraising him. "I might be a terrible Host."

A tingle in Rory's chest grew and spread down his arm. From the bottom of his vision, he saw the Dozer's runes glow. "I have no idea what I'm doing." He took another step. "I'm in way over my head."

"You can't win, *nurse*." Dawson flung the last word like a slur.

Rory ignored him, and the Dozer glowed brighter. "But the Seed is mine. I'm its torchbearer. I won't let you take it."

A cloud of blue vapor erupted from the Dozer's golden cross guard, and the runes blazed. Vapor crackled as it condensed to form a glowing three-foot blade, and for the first time Rory could remember, the voice telling him to run vanished.

Dawson's molten eyes narrowed. "Jane . . ."

Behind Dawson, Jacklyn coughed again. Dark red blood bubbled from her lips. Her eyes focused first on Dawson, then Rory. She blinked at the glare coming off the Dozer, and then a lopsided grin crawled up one cheek. Rory didn't wait.

He charged; Dozer held high with a ribbon of blue vapor trailing in their wake.

In one smooth motion, Dawson ripped the sword from Jacklyn's gut and bellowed. Fire and ghostly faces climbed up his sword in a high arc and crashed down on Rory. He brought the Dozer up with both hands, throwing himself beneath it.

The blades met in another flash of light and another, but the Dozer held.

Behind Dawson, Jacklyn rolled over to her knees and pressed her hand to her stomach as blood leaked between her fingers. She looked up at the Merged, and her pale face contorted into rage. Her shadow hand sputtered and condensed.

Keep his attention.

Rory deflected another blow and slid a step toward Dawson's bad knee. The Brand missed, thumping into the ground with a hiss. Rory danced back as he had seen Caroline do, provoking Dawson to pursue. Dawson swung in an arc, aiming for Rory's head, eyes fixed on the Dozer. Ducking beneath the blow, Rory dipped further to the right, forcing Dawson to keep up or risk exposing his back. The villain's knee wobbled inward, but held.

Keep him moving.

Dawson sliced high again, and Rory brought his Dozer up just in time. His head swam this time, white spots sparking in his vision. He nearly dropped the hilt, but kept his feet moving, shaking his head as his vision cleared.

Just a little more.

He feigned an attack, drawing a wild counter. The wailing blade sailed an inch from his chest—so close he felt its chill. The heavy Brand pulled Dawson off-balance, and he shifted his feet to compensate.

"GAH!" Dawson snarled, as his knee twisted awkwardly. The joint gave, and he stumbled. In the blink of an eye, his flank opened.

Rory lunged and drove the Dozer into Dawson's chest. It passed through him clean, with little more than a puff of white vapor as it entered. There was no blood, no cry, but something kicked Rory in the chest like a mule as the runes surged. He withdrew the blade with a tingling arm and stars sparkling in his vision.

Dawson's eyes rolled back, and he dropped to his knees with a sickening crunch. His lids hung half closed as he looked up at

Rory. For a moment, they regarded each other, both dazed. *Finish this.* Rory brought the Dozer up and down through Dawson's body again. Another kick, and Rory staggered. Dawson rocked and crumpled forward, landing face-first in the dirt. Embers burst from his body like a collapsing pyre. Rory felt sick and dizzy, but in his rage, he lifted the Dozer again.

"Stop!" Jacklyn's voice was a croaked whisper. She was on her feet, doubled over with her hand pressed against her stomach. Bright red blood leaked between her fingers. "You'll overdraw." She flexed her shadow hand. The smoke and ash thickened, and with each step, her fingers and nails elongated into claws.

Rory lowered the gaseous blade, blinking and pushing out breaths to keep conscious. Jacklyn collapsed onto her knees. Rory hobbled forward and steadied her.

"There are others," Dawson slurred, lifting his head as he tried to rise. "You'll always be hunted." He laughed like a drunk.

Jacklyn seized his smiling face with her smoking claw, sinking her nails into his cracked flesh. The churning black hurricane of her palm sealed against his skin. Dawson's eyes went wide, mouth open, but his scream never came. Jacklyn leaned in with bared teeth. "Say hi to the devil for me."

The ruby in Dawson's chest flickered, and Rory saw the blazing eye within widen as cracks snaked through its surface. Seams of orange light exploded through the cracks and cuts on Dawson's body, growing brighter and brighter until the lights ceased all at once. The ruby in his chest shattered with a savage POP, and red shards cascaded from the hole where Dawson's heart should have been. A cloud of steam belched from his mouth, ears, and eye sockets, followed by a loud crackling as his rocky arms and legs cooled and contorted, curling toward his chest and freezing into a tortured statue.

Rory shook, letting the Dozer fall from his trembling hands. *We did it?*

Jacklyn drew back her claw, stumbling a step.

"Is it over?" Rory asked, still seeing stars.

"We're not— Mphm!" Jacklyn spasmed in pain, and she pitched forward, clutching her head. Rory stooped to catch her, helping lower her down. He pressed a hand into her gushing wound, feeling her hot, sticky blood flow through his fingers. Jacklyn grimaced, glancing down before she winced again.

"We can find—" Rory started.

Jacklyn shook her head. "No time." Blood dribbled out of her mouth as she held up her shadow hand. "Last Assay."

Somewhere to the west, a rapid, rhythmic thump caught Rory's ear. He turned toward the sound, recognizing it. He'd met many life-flight crews on the roof of Hill Hospital. Those were rotary blades. Helicopters were approaching. "Who's coming?" Rory wondered aloud.

Jacklyn turned her eyes skyward. "Your. Next problem," she managed. "It's been fun, hero, but—" She grimaced as her entire body spasmed. "Caroline's waiting for me."

Rory stared into the black void of her palm, flinching back. "What do I do?" he whispered.

"Take my hand. The Seed does the rest."

Rory lifted his gaze and met Jacklyn's dark brown eyes, full of tears.

"You can do this." She buoyed him. Rory nodded and brought his shaking hand up to hers, their palms hovering inches apart. He could feel the heat draining from his skin.

"Hero?"

"Yeah?"

"No more hiding."

Tears sprang free and rolled down Rory's cheeks.

"I promise," he said, shuddering as he sobbed.

Rory's heart constricted. He wasn't ready to say goodbye; he had too much to learn still. But as he felt her hot blood against his palm, he knew goodbye was all that was left. "Jacklyn, I . . . It's that—"

"Time, hero." The helicopters grew louder.

"Thanks for digging me out."

Jacklyn smiled through the pain. "What are friends for?" She closed her eyes, and for a moment, the pain left her face. "I'm ready."

Rory pressed his palm to hers, interlacing their fingers.

A bottomless cold and an enveloping warmth collided somewhere in his chest. The world spun, and the last thing he felt before his consciousness slipped away was the sickening sensation of barbed tentacles slithering down his arm and raking at his bones.

Chapter 75: Assay of Hosts

Translated from:

Disc - Shepherd's Stone

Sub-ring - *Codex*

Script - *Law of Hosts*:

Assay of Hosts:

If all other Assays are passed, then let the Candidate's integration be the final test.

A Candidate passes if the Seed lets them live.

A Candidate fails if the Seed destroys them.

Amendment (s):

- None -

—

"Mr. Nash?" a voice called from behind a bright light. "Mr. Nash, are you awake?" A pause and the smell of wet earth followed. "He's breathing! Get him moving." The voice returned louder again. "Mr. Nash, you're safe now. Can you open your eyes?"

Rory's body crashed against his senses. His head throbbed, and he squeezed his eyes tight to clot the pain. Weightless, yet heavy. Rocking, yet still. Something rough against his skin. He opened his eyes, wincing at the moonlight until the bobbing, starry sky came into focus above him.

"Where's . . . Jacklyn?" He sounded terrible—hoarse and raw.

A commanding voice replied. "He spoke! Hold on." The stars halted, and a red-haired man with angular cheeks leaned into view. He wore a crisp black suit, the kind that meant money. Rory tipped his head to the side and found they weren't alone. Blue-armored men carrying strange, sleek rifles - like something out of a sci-fi movie - surrounded them.

"Mr. Nash, I am so relieved." The red-haired man's smile beamed down. "I'm Dr. Kenneth Connell, but you can call me Ken. I came to help."

Fatigue fogged Rory's mind, and he felt hot reflux burning his throat. That name—he knew that name.

"Connell?" He remembered Khloe saying something about him. And Megan's magazine. That felt so long ago now.

Ken continued. "I'm certain you have questions, but we can't loiter. The Broken Star will—"

"Put me down," Rory croaked.

"Mr. Nash, we need—"

"Now."

Ken sighed and looked ahead, then nodded. "Of course." He gestured to Rory's handlers. "Set him down. Gently, please." The stretcher lowered and nestled on the ground as the guards all watched him from behind their black goggles.

Rory sat up and looked around, spotting the plane's wreckage behind them, with a swarm of people picking over the scattered debris using squat vacuums. Three sleek, black helicopters parked on the airstrip buzzed with activity. Small groups of hazmat suits walked around putting out fires while others, armed with long forceps, gathered rocks and placed them into individual bags. The place was being scrubbed.

"Quite a mess," Ken said and half-heartedly chuckled. "The freeway cleanup has been challenging. There are still witnesses to locate."

Rory raised an eyebrow.

Ken put up his hands. "Not like that, I assure you. We purchase their silence. A handsome sum for those who got lucky, but that's how the world works, isn't it?"

Rory blinked at the man. Ken sounded genuine and could have locked them all up while he was unconscious if he'd wanted. Rory hefted his leg over the edge of the stretcher and sat with his foot on solid ground for a moment, willing his head to stop pulsing.

"Khloe. Where is she? *HIC!*"

Rory thumped against his chest with his fist, hoping he would dislodge whatever was stuck, but another sharp hiccup followed, shooting acid up his throat.

"We found Dr. Seeker," Ken said cheerfully. "She had a nasty overdraw, but we got her an infusion, and she's stabilized. She's already aboard the helicopter and awaiting transport."

Rory felt his chest lighten as if he'd dropped a heavy stone. "What about Ja— *HIC!*" He winced again, rubbing his burning chest. *What the hell is going on?*

"Jane?" Ken's expression sobered. He pointed toward the nearest helicopter, and Rory saw several hazmats dangling IV bags and hustling alongside a crowded stretcher. Through the mass of people, Rory spotted a small, pale body on a stretcher. They'd intubated her, and now one of these strangers squeezed a mint-colored bag to force oxygen into her lungs. "Jane Kim is in a coma. They got her heart beating, but I'm afraid her brain trauma is severe. The prognosis is . . . poor."

"Jacklyn can heal her," Rory said, looking around, but didn't find another stretcher.

"Mr. Nash," Ken said, his voice tightening. "Jacklyn Seed is . . . is gone."

Gone? The fog around his mind lifted, and he inhaled. He remembered swirling images and sounds from the fight. Jacklyn pinned to the ground. Her shadow hand. She told him to stop before he overdrew. The black hole in her palm. The emotions crashed over him, welling up behind his eyes. He didn't want it to be true.

Ken nodded. "I'm very sorry."

"Her body?"

"Gone."

Rory pictured Caroline dissolving into ash, and his head lolled onto his chest.

Ken cleared his throat, obviously uncomfortable with what he wanted to say. Some part of Rory knew how he felt—bad news was always hard to deliver.

"What else?" Rory said with a heavy heart.

"I'm so sorry to tell you, but you're the Host now." He pointed at Rory's left side.

Afraid to look, Rory's eyes fell to his left arm. There it was—a neat, pink stump. He stared at his missing limb below the elbow. *A dream? This has to be a dream.* He told his left finger to flex and felt a tingle. He reached across his body and touched the stump gingerly, probing its reality, but his fingers told him the truth.

The implications flooded him: he now carried the Seed. Its power and its responsibility. It was his choice now, the choice Jacklyn and Caroline wanted him to have. Would he use it? How would he choose? How had Jacklyn chosen? He felt a rush of adrenaline telling him to get rid of it. But it was too late. They were bound now.

Rory turned his stump, examining the puckered skin around its edge. "We passed." A bubble of pride rose in him, though subdued by the cost. His hand went to his chest, and he felt his new passenger shift eerily beneath his skin. "We did it . . ."

"By all appearances, the Seed has taken well," Ken said. "I'm not sure whether to congratulate you or grieve with you, Mr. Nash, but in any case, you should be proud. Very few in our history have earned the title of Host."

Host. The word sat heavily, squeezing his lungs. *Breathe, Rory.*

"You seem to know—" Rory hiccupped again and rubbed his chest. "What's going on?"

Ken's expression frowned for a moment before his face lit up. "You're full."

Rory looked up, not following.

The clean-cut man tapped his chest. He didn't look the part of a shrewd CEO as he rocked forward on the balls of his feet, bobbing. "The hiccups, it means too full. Brimming, really. Jacklyn passed along everything she had left, and it's too much for you to hold. You'll need to discharge."

"Discharge?" Rory said, and then he pictured Jacklyn standing over Tommy. "Like, heal someone?"

Ken nodded. "Pass the energy, yes. The symptoms will only worsen until you do."

"How do you know so much about the Seed?"

"I . . . studied it for a time." He looked over at the helicopters.

A memory of Jacklyn rushed in. She was red-faced and shouting, refusing. "You experimented on her."

Ken clenched his square jaw, and Rory saw something true pass through his eyes, but he straightened, and his expression softened. "I was doing what I thought best at the time. For all of us. The Seed has the potential to redefine our world. Save billions and rewrite history. I found out too late that I was being used, and I didn't want to be a pawn. So, I bided my time and, when the moment came, helped Caroline and Jacklyn escape."

"It was you?"

Ken nodded. "Nearly got myself killed." He drew up his pant legs, revealing two metal braces from ankle to knee. "Almost lost both legs in the explosion. Half the lab collapsed. I was the only one from my team that made it." Ken shook his head, lost in memory, before whispering, "I'd do it again if it came to it."

"Why?"

"Call it my moment of awakening. Something needed to be done, and I was positioned to do it. Nothing valiant about it." Ken nodded at Rory's stump. "I'm sure you understand."

Sponges. Rory nodded, appreciating the honesty. Many times as a nurse, he'd seen parents try to fudge details about their child's admission, breezing over key facts that made them look bad or stretching or shrinking the time frame to best suit their ego. Ken's frankness felt warm. "It can be hard."

"I empathize." He turned and gestured to the helicopters. "I'm late, certainly, but I feel I'm on the right side now." He leaned in close and dipped his chin away from Rory. "Though, Mr. Nash, there will be many, even within the Society, who will not be happy to see you alive. The Star's agents are everywhere, I know, because when the Evergreen's Board voted to mobilize— and even with the evidence and stakes clear—the vote fell short. Too risky, they claimed."

Interesting. "So, your Board doesn't know."

Ken shook his head. "They will soon, but by then, I'll have proved my point. Besides, being the founder grants a degree of leeway." He checked his gold watch. "We've already stayed too long. I promise to answer all the questions I can."

"That can't be it," Rory said. "It must be personal for you." He dug his finger into his thumb. Something felt off; something was missing. Wouldn't helping him put a huge target on the Society's back? Was he helping them just because he wanted to *do the right thing*? Another memory flashed—a picture in a magazine. Megan's gossip. A pale girl and rumors from Boston. "Your daughter. She's sick."

Ken's mouth opened and caught before it pressed into a flat line. "She is."

"You want . . ." Rory took a deep breath and looked down at his new arm. "Me to help her?"

Neither spoke, appraising each other. Ken's gaze never wavered. "For Sheen, Mr. Nash. I'd do anything."

Another honest answer. "If I refuse?"

A mix of anger and sadness flashed across Ken's face, but faded in the next breath. "I will be heartbroken. The energy cost for healing is—"

"Human souls."

"—high. Yes. I learned a painful lesson when I tried to control the Seed before." Ken patted his leg to reinforce his point. "I'm a man who hates making the same mistake twice."

Rory understood—he'd tried to control the Seed too, harness its power for himself, and his faulty quest had destroyed part of him. "*HIC!*" He ground his knuckles into his sternum, trying to relieve the burn. He felt something grate against his ribs, and he recoiled. He had to move this energy, and an idea came. "Khloe will live?"

Ken gestured toward the helicopters with growing impatience. "Yes, if we—"

"Then take me to Jane." Rory pushed himself off the stretcher and down to his feet. He expected his legs to ache after his strenuous night, but he found them refreshed. Bending his knees, he admired the newfound strength in his muscles. He'd never felt so strong, so smooth in his own skin. *The Seed had its perks.*

Ken's eye twitched, and Rory watched him mask his displeasure by checking his watch.

They have a history.

"I know you want to help," Ken said, "and forgive my frankness, but do you even know what you are doing?"

"No," Rory said. "But if you're about building trust, you won't stop me from trying." He felt the Seed squirm in his chest as pins and needles rushed over his left arm and down into his missing hand. Ashy smoke curled off his pink stump.

Several men jumped back, weapons raised, but Ken held up his hand. The CEO stared at the smoke with awed wonder, as though he were watching someone rise from the dead. Rory tried to play it cool, but he felt his heart . . . or whatever it was now, quicken in his chest. *What have I become?* He looked around for Jacklyn, knowing she was gone, and felt his emptiness spread.

Ken broke the silence, still watching the shadows billowing off Rory's stump. "I'll help you." He slipped a walkie-talkie off his belt, and Rory spotted a pistol and holster hidden beneath his suit jacket. "Hold the evacuation. We're coming to you." He clipped the device back on his belt and smoothed out his jacket. "Let's go."

Ken led the way toward the helicopters, and Rory matched his stride, walking beside him. His men followed a few steps back, carrying the stretcher.

"You have a guardian angel, Mr. Nash," Ken said after a few quiet steps. "I received an unexpected tip about this airstrip, but we weren't certain whether the information was genuine or just another ambush. It wouldn't be the first time. But after seeing Dr. Seeker's genetic sample and its advanced state of decay, I knew what we had. Did you know Jacklyn was coming apart at a molecular level?" He shook his head. "I cannot even imagine her suffering."

"She is—" Rory exhaled. "Was a fighter. She never let up."

"Mr. Nash, I believe I can help you avoid a similar fate." Ken's voice lifted with enthusiasm as he continued. "The greatest coverup in human history took place ten thousand years ago. The scale is . . . boggling, frankly. We've discovered immense underground structures. Sealed without a lock. A true riddle. Why would the survivors of an apocalypse spend their precious time and resources building such structures only to bury them? We have guesses, and most of them revolve around your new passenger."

Ken's strides never broke as he held up the Dozer. Rory gasped and reached for it, though his hand stopped midair, his eyes focused on Ken. The CEO smiled. "It's yours. I was just holding onto it. I can't get it to work, anyway." He handed it back to him and turned to continue walking. Rory ran his thumb along the runes. *Thank you.* It felt like an old friend.

"This artifact is a prime example of what I mean," Ken said over his shoulder, and Rory jumped to keep up. "It is easy to create a weapon that kills, but ones that subdue? Safely? That alone speaks volumes about its creator's ingenuity. Their mercy. And it begs new questions: Did their police force all carry such items, or is this unique?" Rory heard echoes of Caroline and her campfire lessons.

Ahead of them, below a helicopter's lazy, churning blades, Rory spotted medics lowering Jane's gurney. They performed their synchronized dance as they administered care. A pang of loss echoed in his heart as he wondered if he would ever nurse again. *Later,* he told himself.

"That's quite the pitch," Rory said, shifting his thoughts back to Ken.

Ken beamed. "Thank you."

"Mr. Connell, Ken," Rory hiccupped, "I'm tempted, but . . ." Rory considered. "Jacklyn told me no more hiding."

"Jacklyn was—"

"I agree with her."

Ken frowned. "I see. You want to go public?"

Rory nodded. "Yes. With everything."

"People will believe it's fiction. A conspiracy at best."

"We'll work on the messaging then. If we're the only ones who know, then we're alone, and if we want to win this fight, we can't do it alone." His determination surprised him. It felt good to speak his truth. "Would your Board agree to help?"

Ken ran a hand through his red hair. "Most won't like it, but . . ." He considered, and a grin spread across his face. "Together, why not? We can do anything." He held out a hand, and Rory took it. It was a small gesture, but it seemed in good faith.

Rory stopped behind the medics and peered over their shoulders at Jane. He'd never seen someone so ghostly pale who wasn't dead. Her red blood shone bright in the moonlight, and she reeked of burnt skin. A breathing tube rose from the swollen mass of her face, connected to a bag a medic squeezed for each breath. Burnt into her scalp, angry black blisters rose in the valleys of her hair's pink mountains, all in the sickening outline of a massive hand.

"May I?" Rory asked tentatively.

The medics looked up, then at each other, then at Ken, who nodded. One pair rose, making way for him as another continued supplementing Jane's breaths. Rory kneeled down, watching her chest move.

"How does it work?" His eyes had been closed. He looked down at the wrinkled flesh of his fresh stump.

Rory felt the Seed twist in his chest. His mind spasmed, and he doubled over, clutching the sides of his head as a reel of alien memories tore through his mind's eye. He was in his apartment, hugging Caroline on a couch. In a rotting home, with a terrified man and a woman holding a shotgun. Sliding a sun-bleached book onto a dusty bookshelf. The memories kept coming, one after another, and he retched. He saw the hospital, ocean waves, golems, Sneaks, and—

The last memory lingered the longest. In a dark room, a boy lay intubated and still. Rory saw himself standing across the bed, eyes closed. The shadow hand appeared in his vision and lowered down toward the boy—Tommy. The hand pressed the pad of its thumb against his bare chest, and a pulse of white light exploded.

Rory sucked in a breath of wet air and felt a pair of sturdy hands bracing him. His head throbbed as he opened his eyes and found Ken kneeling beside him, holding out a handkerchief. "Your nose is bleeding."

Rory touched his nostril and came away with a bloody finger. "My head . . ."

"Memory storms," Ken said. "Your symptoms are getting worse." He gestured to Rory's left arm. "Just hold an image of your hand in your mind, and it takes shape."

Rory turned and raised an eyebrow. "Another one of Jacklyn's lessons?"

Ken cleared his throat. "Yes." He gestured to Jane. "To discharge, you place your thumb—"

"Over the heart," Rory finished, enjoying Ken's surprise. "Almost like a defibrillator."

"An excellent analogy," Ken said. "The first step, though, is to summon the hand."

He recalled an image of his left hand and held it in his mind. As Ken said, the Seed responded, and thick black smoke burst from his pink stump, condensing into a perfect replica of the image in his mind. Despite being attached to him, Rory flinched back, holding the arm away. He turned his new appendage over, marveling at the dense clouds and their tiny, spiraling hurricanes sliding up and down his arm.

"Everyone should close—" He winced as his mind quivered and cramped. Another memory storm built into a painful migraine, and Rory cried out in pain. A sudden light grew, and Rory forced himself to squint down at Jane, lowering his shadow hand, afraid he might turn her to dust. He laid his knuckles flat on her sternum, pressing his thumb into the bone.

The Seed sucked the warmth from him and fired a pulse of light from his chest. A gasp. Several shouts. The light traveled down his arm, through his thumb, and plunged into Jane with a flash. Her entire body convulsed, arching and popping unnaturally as light poured through her skin and out her open eyes and mouth. Then she collapsed back on the stretcher, limp, with his thumb still in place. Rory held his breath.

A trickle followed, wet and thick like a muddy creek.

"Magnificent," Ken said.

Rory's spirits rose as he watched Jane's skin knit closed. The boils and blisters popped and fell like withered, black balloons. Once blackened, skin pinked with life. But her hair, however, didn't regrow, giving Jane a patchy, somewhat rockstar-burn-victim look. Startled whispers rose from the medics. In moments, Jane's physical damage was undone, but as he watched the steam rise off her, he wondered if the damage to her brain might have been too severe, even for a miracle. He thought of Tommy.

"Jane?" Rory said. *Come on.* Her chest rose and fell on its own, which felt like a win, but the rest of her didn't stir. *Come on, Jane. I'm bearing the torch, like you said. Now you have to help me carry it.* Still nothing.

From the corner of his eye, Rory noticed his shadow hand still billowing smoke. Jacklyn's had always turned off, though Jacklyn was also always unconscious after healing as well. This was uncharted territory.

"How do I turn it off?"

Ken frowned. "You can't?"

The question was answered enough. "You don't know."

"It always turned off on its own before."

Rory shifted, bringing his shadow hand closer to Ken. The CEO jumped back, startled, ending up on his feet.

"Forgive me," Ken said, looking bashful and pale. "I've seen the Seed's effects firsthand. Here—" He held out a brown leather glove with a soft white lining. "Wear this. We don't want any mishaps."

Taking the glove, Rory nodded. He looked down at Jane, waiting for her to open her eyes or something, but nothing. *Maybe I was too late—*

Jane's dark eyes shot open, and she grabbed her breathing tube with both hands.

"Don't!" Ken shouted, but Jane jerked the wet tube out, retching and gulping down a lungful of air.

Blinking and dazed, Jane found Rory. Her face twisted into a perplexed frown, which morphed into a lopsided smile. "You're alive?"

"I could ask you the same thing."

Her grin grew as she looked around. "Did we win?"

Rory exhaled hard, willing the ache in his chest to ease. "It cost us friends, but yeah, we won."

"How . . . Dawson . . ." She reached up with a shaky hand and touched the bare sections of her scalp. She winced and drew her hand back. "What . . . happened?" Before Rory could answer, Jane's gaze slipped over his shoulder to Ken. Her grin twisted into a snarl. "You."

Ken frowned. "Hello, Jane."

Jane thrashed, trying to sit up, and reached for Ken. Two medics tried to grab her, but she swam beneath their grasping hands and rolled off the gurney, dipping around Rory and closing the distance. A guard stepped in front of him and caught a quick elbow to the throat. Jane snatched his rifle in one smooth motion and leveled it at Ken.

Ken held up his hands, naked disdain on his face. "Welcome back."

"Fuck off, bootlicker!" Jane snapped back.

"I thought we weren't cussing anymore," Ken deadpanned.

She jabbed the barrel at him, and Ken flinched back. "I don't know how this weapon works, but if you so much as fart, I'll start pushing buttons." Her eyes drifted around to the others aiming at her. "Tell them to put their weapons down."

"I won't do that."

Rory stepped to Ken's side. "Jane, hey. Hey! Look at me."

Her eyes moved to his.

"Please, put the gun down. He's on our side."

"Our side?" Jane hissed. "He's one of them! I saw him kissing the Director's ass every morning for years."

"I declined his offer to merge," Ken protested. "And my reports to the Director were part of maintaining my cover. I had to keep his trust."

Jane scoffed. "Yeah, the mansions and private jets were a real hardship."

"I'm not the enemy, Jane." Ken kept his voice level. "I tried to recruit you, to bring you in on resistance, but you were too afraid. You chose a cubicle."

"That's it," she barked. "I'm pushing buttons."

"Jane, you were dead!" Rory shouted.

His words had the intended effect. She stuttered and lowered the rifle.

"What?"

"I healed you. Just now."

"Oh . . . I was wondering why I smelled like bad barbecue." Her eyes dropped to Rory's shadow hand. "So, you . . ."

Rory nodded.

Jane whistled, long and low. "Aunt Jackie?"

Rory shook his head. They looked at each other for a moment, sharing a goodbye. He stepped toward her. "Ken says there is more Star in the way. Do you believe that?"

After a long inhale, she gave a tiny nod but kept her eyes fixed on Ken. Then she started laughing, slowly at first. The gleeful sound rolled out of her. "The Director is gonna be so pissed." She laughed, shaking her head. "He'll send everything he's got. Tonight, if he can."

"What do you think we should do?"

"Run, then hit him. He won't be ready for a counter."

"We can't fight," Ken said.

"Not war," Jane said. "Just shift the status quo. Destabilize so he can't recapture the narrative. That's how he does it now."

Rory watched Ken, who considered, then nodded. "A sound theory. We can discuss specifics once we're at the safe house."

Rory nodded, relieved seeing them on the same page. "Now, if everyone doesn't mind putting their guns down, please? We're all on the same team." He gestured to her rifle, and Jane rolled her eyes and handed it over to Ken. *One small step forward.*

The helicopter's engine spun to life, and the rotary blades picked up speed. Ken's jacket fluttered, but his perfectly coiffed hair didn't move. Without another word, he turned toward the second helicopter but stopped after two steps, patting his chest. "I'd nearly forgotten." He reached into his jacket, drew an envelope, and handed it to Rory.

"I mentioned I received a tip about tonight. This note was with it. I found them in my briefcase, which was locked, on my way to the airport. A masterful plant."

Rory took the envelope. Written across the front, in impeccable cursive, read: *Mr. Rory Nash.*

"What's in it?" Jane asked. "I know you looked."

"You'll have to read like everyone else, Jane." He signaled the team of guards, hazmats, and medics, and they all hurried toward the helicopters.

Rory felt the heft of the envelope, curiosity burning inside him. He looked up and found Jane studying the paper, too. "Want some answers?"

Jane nodded toward the helicopters. "For the record, I don't like this at all, but there is no way I'm letting you board without me."

"You just want to read this," Rory said.

"Of course I do." Jane grinned, then winked at Rory. "I think we're going to be good friends, Mr. Nash. Come on, open it, open it!"

Chapter 76: Letter from the Dead

First of Maia, X643 AA

My Beloved Rory,

Foremost, know that I am very proud of you. Regardless of the outcome of tomorrow, I want you to understand how rare it is to come so far in such short order. For that alone, you have earned my unending admiration.

As for the battle, my grand hope was that this letter would find you whole and unharmed at its conclusion. If so, it means I did my duty, and we made our own fortune. If it has not, or you came upon this letter another way, then my spirit grieves with you. If you are resentful or hurting, know I ache with you. If you weep, I know the anguish. Pain takes time and attention to process— that is the nature of Stains and the only way to unlock their power. When you are ready, I ask that you read the rest of this letter. If nothing else, perhaps it will give you some closure over the maelstrom you blessedly survived.

Foremost, know Jacklyn and I tried our very best to aid you in your journey. We, like all teachers, carry our own past—full of our own Stains, making their own voices. We can only do our best to know them and not pass them on. I truly wish your path to Host-hood could have been done painlessly, but that is not the Seed's way. There can be no growth without the loss of things we hold dear.

Perhaps we could have smoothed your learning had our paths crossed earlier, but I imagine you would not have been ready. Your Stain is deep, Rory, conjoined, innervating your childhood. It is layered, complex, and beautiful. And powerful. It's a major reason we chose you as our candidate. We had to help you dig down to find its roots and source. Only there can you find the key of grace to unlock your wellspring. Understand this—a Host must embrace change. They must be ready to let go and adapt, to read the tide and shift with history. There is no easy way to teach that, though some, like you, have a knack for it. As teachers, we were fortunate.

When we found you, you were ready to depart, ready for change, though you knew not what. When I first touched your hand and your soul on our way to the bus stop, I knew we had found a potent candidate. Jacklyn was reluctant, of course, always the survivalist, but even she couldn't deny your strength and conviction. She dreamed of a warrior Host, one who'd lay waste to our foes and its minions. In you, I touch a fighter, not a warrior. Courage was your sword. Our debates were fierce. In the end, we tested you—a Minor Assay with a minor injustice. A little old lady and her rings. Then, you drank the Wisp's Well I slipped into your bag and proved to all you were the right candidate.

It wasn't long before you understood the power that Jacklyn wielded, and we knew it was only a matter of time before you came back, despite our warnings. Everyone does. Of course, they do. The Seed has an allure all its own. Once you returned, we learned your Stain was more extensive than we'd expected. You readily surrendered your questions for proximity and a modicum of control over the Seed's power. We were nervous, but thank the All-Mother for Dr. Khloe Seeker.

She was not part of the initial plan. In all honesty, her arrival made this devout Wyth interrogate her mistrust in fate. She accomplished what would have taken Jacklyn and me months to do. She resurrected your curiosity, and little by little, you asked questions again. You probed your past—and your Stain. It was only a matter of time until you two discovered the Seed, and together, you set your Stains to convert at an incredible rate. That is a constant we've seen with Stains. They always convert faster with help. Always keep this in mind.

From that point on, we needed to buy you as much time as possible, but could only afford a week before you collided with

Jane. Which leads me here—running errands and dropping off deliveries while you and Jacklyn wait at Dr. Seeker's residence. Alone. Truth be told, I wish I could have had that last night with my Jacklyn, but duty, no matter how infuriating, demanded otherwise. You understand.

That is all I will say about the past. I hope it answers your questions, and I apologize for where I fall short. Tomorrow, they will take my Jacklyn. I know there is little chance I will see her again. Today held our last kiss, and for that alone, I choose to write of a sunnier future.

For the rest of this letter, I will assume that our plan was successful, that we defeated Dawson, and you survived the Seed's passing. Congratulations. There are things you need to know:

First, the Seed is still a great mystery. There is much we don't know about it and its origins, so you will need experts who can help you find out. I have recruited an expert, though he comes with a checkered past. I believe it was Dr. Kenneth Connell who freed us, and I took a risk - this letter - by recruiting him on your behalf. Even if you don't trust Kenneth Connell now, he can teach you about the inner rings of the Broken Star and the race to uncover our long-hidden past. Both he and Jane served the same master, and thus, Jane will provide a counter to Dr. Connell. Heed them both evenly as you navigate the present in order to decode the past.

Second, I leave several treasures in your care. On this letter's back, you'll find three recipes that I prepared most often for Jacklyn. A tonic for headaches, a tincture for sleep, and a balm for dry skin. I recommend using them early and often to minimize the Seed's effects. Besides the recipes, I have left precious cargo with your friend Patrick. He will look for you, too. Find each other when it's safe.

On that note, please be gentle with the Shepherd's Stones. They are fragile and thousands of years old. Treat them well, and they will tell you untold tales that span thousands of generations. Jacklyn deciphered several symbols and made guesses on several translations in her notebook, which Patrick has. Recover the discs and build on our work. When inspiration strikes, try your hand. The translation is unofficially part of the Host's duties. Also with Patrick, you'll find my Path rings mixed with those of my fallen sisters. I leave these to Dr. Seeker, Jane Kim, and anyone else who earns them.

Third, there is the matter of the Counsellorship. If both Jane and Khloe survived, you will be the first Host in known history to have two Counselors, which feels appropriate given the world's complexity. Balance their insight, but know you make the final choice on behalf of the Seed. In addition, you might find the occasional memory, not your own. Those memories should belong to Jacklyn, though she wondered if the Star's violation of the Seed might have garbled others. If her memories survived, then you, too, have our story with all its ups and downs. May it help you understand it is love that carries you through life's worst trials.

This leads me to my last request. I believe the Wyth are in danger of extinction. With so many dead or hiding, there will be no quorums until a new generation of Wyth are taught not just how to cast but also of the winding Paths to focus a caster's mind. Wythian stories, our teachings, need to be shared, or we surrender casting and its power to the Broken Star, or worse, oblivion. To rebuild the Wyth, you will need to find them. This is no simple task; we are born in the fog. Those that have survived are terrified of exposure, lest the Star learn of their whereabouts and strike. The hope of a new Host may draw some from hiding. Reach out - help them find their courage.

You will need to teach the next generation about their Stains—a task I never fully completed with you; the Laws of Host handcuffed me at formative times. Now that you have the Seed, those Laws no longer govern, so heed me well. No one casts without first processing and converting their Stain.

Acknowledging that one's Stain exists is the first and often largest hurdle. If there is one, there are often multiple. It will shut down its hosts, lashing out to protect itself. I know you are familiar with this; you've heard the inner chorus of shame. Find a Stain's patterns and be rewarded. Once the pattern of thought is recognizable, the revealed Stain is ready to convert—piece by piece, with each revelation granting more power and control. Patience and grace are the key. Remember, you have only just begun this journey, the bare minimum for the Seed's acceptance. Given time and a great deal of work, you will cast and then teach others how.

Never give up on yourself. Never give up on the others. None of us can go it alone.

Farewell, Rory Nash. Whenever you doubt yourself, read this letter and remember your accomplishments today. I hope it hastens your understanding of yourself and the World-That-Was, but most of all, I hope my meager words bring you some amount of peace.

With great love and admiration,

Caroline

Chapter 77: A Light in the Dark

Oates Children's Hospital

Rory chewed his cheek. It felt strange to sit in the report room again. Memories with Bell and Megan and all the others rolled through his mind like a lazy haze. Without this room and the people who filled it, he would never have learned how to fight, care for another, or become the Host. How does one say thank you for all that? To make amends for leaving it so badly? He picked at his fingernail. Nursing saved his life twice, and sitting, waiting, with all those memories—he hoped his choice today would be enough.

Rory reached over and idly prodded the back of his leather glove tucked into the cuff of his blue dress shirt. Instead of feeling the pressure, he felt an electric twitch in the stump of his left arm as the glove dimpled. He pulled back, and the fabric re-inflated. He bent a finger back, certain he couldn't, but he felt nothing even when pressed flat against the back of his hand. The glove slowly refilled like a balloon, and the finger straightened again. In his mind, Rory told the glove to make a fist, and it did. He told it to turn and twist and splay, and it did. He looked around and spotted a pencil.

"Stop that. It's creeping me out," Jane said, slouched in her chair across from him, her shiny dress shoes propped on the report table. She watched his gloved hand with her nose wrinkled. Her wounds had healed, though her head still looked as though a bear had torn rents in her scalp, creating valleys of red scars slicing through her pink hair. She'd restyled it to a shaved right side and a bright pink comb-over, though it couldn't hide all the damage. Rory had a new hairdo too, another side effect of the Seed. The roots of his hair and beard shone silver, just like Jacklyn's. It made him look older. Feel older. He supposed he was now.

"What is taking so long?" Jane asked, scowling at the door. Through it came the muffled sounds of many voices. She crossed her arms with a scowl. "This feels off."

Rory reached for the pencil. "How so?"

"It's too big a step. I mean, I'm all for flipping off the Director, but this . . . you're talking about changing the world overnight. That doesn't happen."

This wasn't the first time she'd voiced that concern in the past two days. Rory discovered that the former detective or man-hunter or whatever she was didn't hold back. A good attribute for a Counselor, but it would take some getting used to. Since the battle on the airstrip, Rory had learned, among many other things, about Jane's sister's nose hair, her niece's lisp, and the wild, gravity-defying pursuit of a woman who had turned out to be Wyth a long time ago.

"Which is why it needs to be done," Rory said, glancing at the clock. "The Director runs the show, right?"

"I think he owns it, actually."

"Exactly. We do this today, and we show everyone there is a different way."

"What way is that? Your way? Because that sounds like the Director."

Rory nodded, thinking. Power drew a line he'd crossed before and didn't like the person it revealed. After spending the last two nights awake thinking about an answer, he settled on something that let him sleep.

"Not mine, ours," he said. "We're going to share everything. Ken said he had located Patrick and Ana and was bringing them in so we can start studying the Shepherd's Stones soon. Caroline said those are the key to understanding . . . everything. Casting, the apocalypse, the inevitable ethical grey areas, everything. After we reveal it, we give people time to digest it. We do that, and I hope we'll see that we don't need to be stuck in this status quo."

"That's still a big ask for many comfortable people."

Rory chuckled. "Call me an optimist."

Jane raised an eyebrow. "Optimism, huh? You don't hear that much anymore." She considered while tapping a finger on her chin. "But, hm, let's consider the immediate ripple effect. The problem with changing the status quo is there are winners and losers. You'll be the miracle man. Sure, you'll even help a few folks, but there will be *billions* all over the world feeling the aftermath - whatever it is. You pull off what you're planning, and you're asking for every sick person in the world and their families to come after you. There will be threats and violence. You'll be hunted, worse than Jacklyn."

Rory had come to that conclusion, too. He'd asked himself a hundred different ways for an alternative. "It's inevitable until we change something. The alternative is doing nothing, and we stay stuck in"—he gestured to the room and the world beyond the walls—"this."

"Yeah, I guess we're screwed either way, huh?"

"So why not?"

"Optimists." Jane pinched the bridge of her nose. "Okay, less meta. Riddle me this: how are you going to recharge after your little show *today*? Draw names? Roll dice?"

I don't know. Rory's stomach clenched. Ken said there were many ethical barriers to consider and was "looking into it." For now, it was food, sleep, and Caroline's tinctures until they came up with a better solution that didn't require killing anyone. "Ken says he has some . . . contacts." He squirmed. "We'll figure it out."

"Ugh, you sound like me." Jane dropped her feet from the table, and her eyes drifted to the empty seat beside her. "So take it from me, Rory. We all have to own up to our choices, and sometimes it's a brutal price to pay."

Rory understood, flexing his left hand, and they fell into a brooding silence. He guessed where her thoughts went. *Emmett.* She'd asked about Emmett only once, in the helicopter, and he told her the truth. She had been uncharacteristically quiet for the rest of the flight and had not brought it up since, but he noticed that whenever he was mentioned, she would drift off, losing herself in thought.

He wondered what Caroline might say to Jane. She was always good at giving perspective. Something Wythian about time and chance and Stains, but those were Caroline's words, not his. Instead, he did for Jane what she'd taught him in the back of a truck.

"You did your best. We all did."

"My best," she scoffed, staring at the chair. "I was blind. I thought I could help him, but I gambled and . . ." Her voice cracked. "I killed him."

She's got a new Stain, Rory thought, making a mental note. *We all do.* He tipped his head and tried to find her eyes, remembering what Caroline said about Stains converting faster with help. "Hey. Take it from me. Try as we might, we can't save everyone. We . . . do our best. But that doesn't make it hurt less." He sighed, feeling the pang of loss. He wished he'd gotten to know Emmett more. He wished Caroline and Jacklyn were here. "You saved me, and the Seed, too. Doesn't take away the other parts, but it's important to remember that too while we're processing."

Jane nodded. "Thanks." Her eyes drifted back to the empty chair. "I just miss him. He might have started out as bait, but . . ." She shook her head. "I bet you two would have gotten along. He was sharp."

Rory smiled at that. From what he understood about Jane, that was a big compliment.

"And," Jane added, "I get what you're trying to do, and I support it, but it's just uncharted territory, you know? Makes me itchy." She held her index finger and thumb close together. "And a wee-bit excited."

"Me too." Rory rubbed his chest, and the Seed squirmed.

The report room door opened, and a cacophony of voices from the hallway broke in. Khloe slipped inside and closed the door behind her, deadening the noise. The sight of her, alive and strong, took the edge off all the recent loss. She'd needed transfusions and an entire day of rest, but the doctor had bounced back and didn't waste any time planning their future.

"We're almost ready," Khloe said, looking polished in a navy suit—a gift from Ken.

Rory straightened. "It's time?"

"Almost." Khloe jerked a thumb over her shoulder. "Dr. Connell is getting the last pieces in order, so you'll have a clear path."

"Do we really need that guy to do this?" Jane said.

"He's got the network."

"And the labs," Jane said pointedly, looking at Khloe.

"Yes, and the labs," Khloe said, beaming. Rory had overheard Ken's sales pitch for Khloe to head his new casting research division. Limitless budget, full autonomy, access, and world-class staff. As uncertain as Rory felt about Ken, seeing her so excited about the future warmed him.

"Just . . . be careful," Jane said, looking over her shoulder at the door. "Don't get hooked on his money. It's just another handcuff." She was right, further compounding his uncertainty, but it had to wait for another day. He had a world to change.

"Try to keep an open mind, Jane," Rory replied. "Trust takes time. We're not the only ones taking a risk here."

"Open mind," Jane muttered as she stood. "I'll remind you of that when you're being dissected for Doran Corp shareholders' dividends." She straightened out her suit. "Well, let's go break their game, shall we?" Turning to Khloe, she nodded at the door. "Sounds exciting out there. Anyone international show?"

"I think . . . I think they *all* did," Khloe said, and Rory's stomach flipped. "When Kenneth Connell puts out a release, if a network wants to call themselves news, they better show up."

The door opened wide, and hungry voices broke the room's stillness. Rory cringed as he saw bodyguards creating a human wall between the door and a horde of cameras, shouting faces, and glaring lights.

"Sir! Sir! How's your daughter?!"

"Dr. Connell! Does today's announcement have anything to do with the recent so-called miracles?!"

"What do you have to say about your high pharmaceutical prices?!"

Ken stood beaming, without a hair out of place, and waved to the cameras. "Thank you all for coming today. We'll be getting underway soon." He stepped into the room, and one of his bodyguards shut the door behind him. He smiled at them each, even Jane. "We've drawn quite the crowd. If you're ready—" His eyes landed on Rory. "After you."

Everyone looked at him, and he felt their expectations crash into him like a wave. *No one else can do this. No one goes it alone.* He drew in a deep breath and stood.

"Okay," he said. "Let's go."

———

Rory didn't remember the walk from the report room to the PICU taking so long, but normally, there wasn't a throng of reporters clogging the hall. Ken's security detail pressed their way through the flashing lights and cameras. Khloe snatched his hand and guided him through the crowd. Jane took up the rear and delivered sharp rebukes to any reporter who got their microphone too close. The twenty-second walk felt like twenty minutes, and by the time Rory was free of the crowd and onto the unit, he was rattled, sweating, and grateful to his friends.

Reporters, thankfully, weren't allowed on the medical unit, but that didn't stop the staff and family members from gawking. The entire floor seemed to slow and spin, watching and waiting. Each dreadful moment of quiet coiled in Rory's stomach. He spotted familiar faces whispering behind hands and strangers demanding to know what was happening.

"Back to it, all you," Bell's commanding voice broke the silence.

The unit obeyed, and everyone got back to work, though with one eye glued to the circus. Rory spotted Bell at the charge nurse station with Megan sitting beside her—Parasite was late. Rory's heart lifted, and he gave a small nod to Bell, who peered at him over her red-rimmed glasses before returning to her work. Megan gave him a questioning eyebrow, then a little wave. Rory returned her question with a shrug and a wave of his own.

"Rory," Ken said behind him. "We'll be in Room 4."

"Room 4?" Rory's mind flashed to Octavia's linen-draped body, then to Tommy's smiling face.

"Is that an issue?"

"No," Rory said. "Not anymore."

Ken frowned, not following, but Rory glanced at Bell and Megan. "Can I have a couple of minutes?"

"Can it wait?" Ken asked.

"No. It's just . . . I didn't leave this place on great terms."

"This is your Disneyland, huh?" Jane said, providing no context. Rory was about to ask when Jane patted him on the shoulder. "I feel you." She peered up and down the hall. "Room 4 is—"

Rory pointed, and Jane wandered off in that direction, stopping to ask a respiratory therapist if she could play with a ventilator.

"I'll make sure she doesn't wind up in the wrong room," Khloe said and squeezed Rory's hand. "I'll see you inside. Wait, Jane! That's room three." She hurried after, apologizing to the respiratory therapist as she passed.

Ken checked his watch. "We're on in five minutes."

"I won't be long," Rory said. "Any update on my request?"

"Legislation takes a long time to move through our system. I have my lobbying team on it." Ken considered for a moment. "I give it a 50/50 chance of passing. Maybe, 60/40 depending on the election cycle."

"Better than zero," Rory said, patting the heavy envelopes against his hand. "I'm surprised your Board didn't balk."

"They did." Ken grinned. "But I sold it as an investment in the security of our best asset."

Rory wasn't sure he enjoyed being called an asset, but finding fault in the results was hard. "Thanks."

Ken gave a curt nod and checked his watch again. "Four minutes."

Rory spun on his heel, tucked his gloved hand behind him, and crossed over to the nurse's station. When he reached Bell and Megan, he leaned over the long bar-topped desk and said, "Hey." *Smooth opener.*

"Hey yourself," Megan said, wearing maroon scrubs with long black sleeves beneath. She leaned closer, her dark eyes snapping over to Ken. "Is that—"

Rory nodded. "*The* Kenneth Connell."

Megan's mouth dropped, and she wagged her eyebrows at him, grinning.

"Megan, please," Bell said beside her. Her snowy curls perched in multiple red bands atop her head, complementing the fluffy cats on surfboards covering her scrubs. She glanced over her glasses at Rory. "We're busy here."

He understood, though it felt like a punch. He'd risked a patient's safety, violating a nursing commandment, and he'd made it even worse by lying and running. Bell had every right to be mad.

Megan clamped her mouth shut and gave Rory a sympathetic nod. Rory felt a distance he'd never experienced with either of them before. He supposed that's how it would be from now on, but it came so abruptly that he wasn't sure how to proceed. He sighed, wondering how to simultaneously say sorry, thank you, and goodbye.

"Training to be charge?" Rory said, hoping to kindle any kind of conversation. *That was almost my job.*

Megan nodded. "Yeah, Bell is showing me how to—"

Bell slapped her pencil against the desk and fixed Rory with an impatient frown. "Can we help you, sir?"

Sir. Rory's heart ached to hear the formality. Bell reserved it for misbehaving parents.

Bell continued. "I'm not sure what you've got planned here, but you need to hurry up, understand? It's distracting the staff and family, and visitor hours end soon."

Rory was at a loss for words. Bell had never taken that tone with him before. "Bell . . . I—"

She raised an eyebrow at him, waiting.

Please forgive me. "Please forgive me. I was an idiot that night and never should have lied, or run, or threatened anyone. Especially you."

Bell grunted, and her eyes returned to her clipboard.

"Wait," Rory said, reaching over the counter and putting his gloved hand on the pencil. "I have something I need to say. For me. And I'd like you to hear it."

"What happened to your hand?" Megan asked, eyeing the black glove.

"It's a long story."

Bell's mouth tightened, and she set down her clipboard and folded her arms, studying him. "Alright. Go on then."

"Do you remember Octavia?"

"Of course I do," she said flatly.

"Well, I haven't been able to stop thinking about her. About all those kids, the preventable ones, the ones we had to mop up after because we're sponges. It's not right. For us, but especially those kids. I keep asking myself, how could those happen? How are so many forgotten?"

Bell lifted her chin, and something softened in her eyes.

Rory hurried on. "I had to do something." He gestured to the unit. "What we do—what you do here—it's incredible, even miraculous. The battles won here are feats for epics. The problem is, outside of these walls, no one seems to care. Or notice. It's a cycle I didn't know I was a part of. And I'm done with it. We're going to change it—today."

Bell blinked, waiting. Her eyes flicked over to Room 4 and back to Rory. He took his opening.

"I admit, along the way, I got lost. I hurt you. And I have to live with that. But that's why I'm here—to start again and help a friend." He paused, uncertain where he was going, but feeling the words ring true.

Bell's eyes narrowed, and Rory couldn't judge her reaction, but Megan's was clear enough. Tears filled her eyes, and even pregnant, she looked about ready to hop over the counter and give him a hug.

"Mr. Nash!" Ken's voice carried over the unit, and Rory turned to see him tapping his watch.

Rory held up a finger and hurried on. "Nursing—you—gah! You both taught me so much. How to care for strangers, how to translate science into love, and how . . ." He paused, trying to find the right words. "You showed me how I want to live my life. So, thank you, is what I'm trying to say."

Bell's expression softened, and she looked down at her hands. A flash of heat touched Rory's cheeks, but the sting of embarrassment didn't come. Instead, he felt the relief of letting go. "I know it's not enough, but . . . Dr. Connell is helping me lobby for a federal holiday for healthcare workers. A day where we call out the symptoms and share our stories. I want people to know what happens here and *why* it is happening." He glanced over at Ken, who watched from Room Four's doorway. "I gotta go, though. It's showtime."

"Tracy?" Megan asked.

Rory nodded. "Ya. I think I can help her."

Megan frowned at first, but it eased into a sad smile, and she toddled around the counter, throwing her arms around Rory in a fierce hug. A moment later, she broke away, wiping her eyes. "Thank you, Rory. I can't wait to see what you do."

"You're the superhero, Meg. And . . . and I should have listened to you more."

"Damn right." Megan sniffed.

Rory laughed, and fresh tears streamed down both their faces.

Bell pressed her lips tight on the other side of the counter, and she inhaled. Something passed between them. Perhaps an understanding. Perhaps a sad goodbye. But then her hard expression cracked and she pulled off her glasses, blotting her wet eyes. "Now look at what you've made me go and do."

"Mr. Nash!" Ken called again. "It's time!"

743

"Go on, Rory Nash," Bell said, resetting her glasses. "You go do that good work."

"I will." He turned, blinking back tears. The door to Room 4 was open and waiting for him.

—

Whooshing ventilators, a beeping heart rate monitor, and the steady clicks from the tower of infusion pumps sounded like old friends. He paused and took a deep breath. The room tasted stale despite the clean sheets and a fresh green gown on Tracy. Someone had tied yellow bows in her hair, and in the low light, Rory could nearly convince himself she was only sleeping, but for the ghostly pallor of her skin.

Jane leaned against the far wall, watching Ken while Khloe sat at the head of the bed, talking with Mr. Oates.

"Mr. Nash." Mr. Oates stood, offering his hand to Rory. "I'm so happy to see you. Kenneth tells me you can help Tracy. The doctors say she . . . she doesn't have much time left."

Rory nodded. "I can." *Tell the truth.* "Or, rather, I think I can."

Mr. Oates sighed, then looked gravely at Tracy. "It's life. When isn't there risk?"

Rory closed his eyes for a moment, and Jacklyn and Caroline's faces appeared in his mind, holding each other. "For the ones we love, the risk is worth it."

"Tracy would trust you. She was very taken."

"Thank you, sir," Rory said, feeling his neck and shoulders tighten.

Mr. Oates kissed Tracy's forehead, but the little girl didn't stir as her pulse beeped across the monitor.

"We'll give you some space," Khloe said and stood. Mr. Oates leaned back, watching. Rory took a slow breath and pressed his feet firmly into the floor.

"Everyone ready?" Ken asked, checking the room.

Rory opened his mouth to speak, but nothing came out. There was nothing more to say.

The room went deathly silent but for the machines.

He blinked, staring down at Tracy, watching her chest rise and fall.

"The glove," Jane said, and Rory looked up to see her pointing at her hand.

He reached over, slid each finger out of the glove, and pulled it off. A chill took the room, and Rory's next breath puffed from his mouth. Mr. Oates gasped and muttered a quick prayer.

Rory turned his shadow hand over and stared into the black void swirling in his palm. "Spiritus boni," he whispered and felt a calm wash over him when he looked into the abyss. He turned his hand over and held up his thumb. The Seed responded, squirming against his ribs. A beat later, his entire body hummed in anticipation, and a burst of black vapor poured from his hand. The Seed was ready.

In the hush, Rory lowered his thumb to Tracy's chest, stopping an inch away.

"Don't cover your eyes," he said and pressed his thumb down.

A fierce light swelled and swallowed the room. And for the first time, Rory Nash knew no fear.

THE END

Acknowledgements

I've learned, despite some stubbornness, that books are never born in isolation. It takes many hands and brains and countless hours to make any story come to life. Especially an epic.

To my parents – thank you for making reading fun and introducing me into countless worlds of wonder.

To little yeti – thanks for co-creating so many worlds with me.

To River and Rhea – I love you both. I'm excited to share this with you someday.

To my beta readers – Carey, Katy, Marble, Rik, and Marilyn – thank you for helping me find the courage to continue when I wasn't sure what I was creating yet. Your insights and suggestions made this story far better than I could have ever made it alone. Seriously, y'all are the best.

To Rox, once again– the O.G.Wyth and co-conspirator of Aspects. Whatever comes of this story, I'm proud we got to build something wonderful together.

Made in United States
Troutdale, OR
02/01/2025

28547221R20452